WHO LEFT GOD PLAYING WITH MUD?!

WHO LEFT GOD PLAYING WITH MUD?!

ADAM

Contents

Foreword and Author's Notes 1

1. Genesis—The Jester's Song 3

2. In the Company of the King 18

3. The Writing on the Wall 40

4. The Word Merchant of Phoenicia 58

5. Tablet House 70

6. Doubles, Delusions, and Reflections 80

7. Mud Schooling 92

8. King Out of a Reed Basket 98

9. Raging Beauty and the Bull 111

10. Bazaar 117

11. Slave Meets Goddess 130

12. A Farewell to Wisdom 137

13. From Heaven to the Netherworld 146

14. Soul Searching 161

15. Slave God 166

16. A Sculpture in Love 177

17. Holy Vow 186

18. Father, Daughter, and Midwives 207

19. Mayram 216

20. Shu-dagan and the River of Dreams 223

21. Make Love and Death 241

22. When Myth Births Reality 248

23. Besieged by Love 253

24. The Sins of the Lamb 263

25. Share the Love 270

26. The God-Maker 275

27. The Silence of the Gods 290

28. Long Live the King.....309

29. Majestic Justice.....330

30. From Sunrise to Sunset An Angel is Born.....339

31. Harvest Games.....355

32. Divine Board Games.....370

33. Honor Thy Enemy.....378

34. Home, Prison, Shrine, and Grave.....382

35. Deluge of Lies.....390

36. Beating from the Heart.....395

37. The Grave Robber.....407

38. Feast in Peace.....411

39. A Wall of Eyes and Ears.....422

40. Lionized.....428

41. King Humbaba.....432

42. Any Way Out.....437

43. The Beauty in the Beast.....444

44. No Spitting!.....461

45. By the River of Babylon.....470

46. Burning River.....482

47. Predator or Prey?.....499

48. The Savage Demon of Vengeance.....505

49. Love Letters.....531

50. Reunion.....548

51. By the Gods of Babylon.....558

52. No Pain, No Game.....575

53. The Father, The Son, and the Holy Ones.....579

54. Epilogue—The Sage's Song.....605

Notes from the Dirt of History.....613

All Babblings Lead to Babel.....627

The Holy Mother of Plagiarism.....631

Foreword and Author's Notes

This is a work of fiction; or, more precisely, an organic work of fiction. "Organic," for I took pains to make it 99% free of any unnatural or supernatural ingredients—the likes of active gods, mythical monsters, witchcraft, superheroes, and super-sized super-bad-assed villains. Moreover, I avoided the use of any preservatives, like the ones added, generously, to the "Licensed Never to Die"—characters who miraculously survive against all odds, over and over and a plethora of overs again.

Don't get me wrong, I do like sci-fi and certain fantasy genres as long as they don't overdose on absurdities.

Regarding the oxymoronic "true, fictitious story" description used on the cover: it is an indisputable fact that the supposedly true stories of any faith are treated as nothing more than works of fiction by most others.

In the novel I employed some actual historic characters, locations, and events—history that survived the wrath of time on mud tablets from ancient Mesopotamia (modern-day Iraq and Syria). The tablets were deciphered and translated, thanks to the dedication and monumental efforts of archaeologists and language experts over the last two centuries.

An expert in Mesopotamian history would notice that I have altered the names of some prominent individuals of that era. The reason is when I read a novel, I find myself greatly annoyed by names that twist my tongue to the point where I have difficulty eating later (I read books containing such names only when I'm on a diet or fasting).

At the end of this novel, I have added brief notes of an historical nature. A few contain material that might spoil the reading experience by hinting at the outcome of some events.

That said, some of those historic notes that reached us on inscribed clay tablets from what is recognized as the Cradle of Civilization, and from the writings of the Greek historian Herodotus, are greatly helpful in explaining certain bizarre and unsavory practices of the ancient inhabitants of Mesopotamia. One example is the ritual in Chapter 17 (Holy Vow), which might seem farfetched for it is shockingly contrary in character to the highly conservative nature of the nation's current culture. Bear in mind that this reversal in traditions from the promiscuous to the virtuous took thousands of years that were, and still are, rife with some of the most turbulent events in human history.

Also, I asked the editors not to go out of their way in correcting the grammar in songs and dialogue. One example is where the word "dew" is used as a verb to denote shedding tears. I very much doubt that any of the characters in the novel who composed and recited poetic songs had in their possession a degree in poetry from an Ivy League institute in Mesopotamia, nor do I think they were awarded blessings for that purpose by the gods of Sumer and Babylon.

GENESIS — THE JESTER'S SONG

Gods strolled the realm of Heaven—sullen, dull, hopelessly bored.
Another routine day, nothing interesting, their yawns broad.

They accosted mighty Anu, father of all the divinity,
Creator of everything—from here to the endless infinity.
From the elusive ghostly dreams to the captured firm reality.

"Great Anu, this is unbearable. Can't live like this forever.
We need some amusement—thrills to spice life better."

Anu vowed to please the children with endless delights.
Sleepless he remained, six days and six nights.
Restless, he walked the distance from the moon to the sun.
"Toys." He snapped his fingers. "Those should bring loads of fun."

On the seventh, he gathered the immortals for a declaration.
"Thought of an amazing pursuit—I'll call it 'The Creation.'
Make two creatures—crafty, cute, and clever.
Both in our image, only mortal—can't live forever."

That day all gods assembled, eager to watch the birth
Of the two so-called humans, on a place named Earth.

Anu asked for assistance from a gullible, scorned god.
Treachery met no resistance; like a lamb he was slaughtered—dirt
gorged on his sacred blood.

The mud Anu shaped into a figure, in its mouth he breathed life.
"Man, your name is Al-dem—now you need a wife."
Another lump of mud he crafted. "Behold your woman—Lilith."
Naked, the couple mused: *These bodies—what to do with?*

The pair roamed happy and free the vast spans of paradise.
Bliss showered the lands, placid clouds sailing blue skies.

Still, Lilith always dwelled on a thing she was missing.
Al-dem's hairless, flailing tail kept her guessing and quizzing.
How it resembles a snake! I swear I hear it hissing.
Beguiled, she called to Anu: "That fountain tool of his—how it
makes me curious!"
God's voice quaked the ground: "Don't you dare touch it, or I'll be
furious!"

Yet, God in his mysterious ways, a wicked deed he pursued.
While Al-dem soundly slept, his tool Anu embellished into the
shape of a tasty fruit.

Once Lilith saw it, she hungered for a taste.
Why leave it to wither? That would be a waste.
She took it in her mouth—how strange, it got fatter.
Overwhelmed by joy, Al-dem's heart was about to shatter.
Then Lilith offered her fruit, probing as to what would happen.
But Al-dem wasn't hungry—instead, deep he thrust his weapon.
They flew to seventh heaven, immersed in clouds of pleasure—
Engulfed in fiery joy, ecstasy beyond any measure.

A loud, frenzied cry fell from the sky above:
"How dare you ignore me and taste the fruits of love.
For your disobedience, I cast you both out—
Out of My Paradise!" Anu screamed in a thunderous shout.
"Al-dem, you'll work hard—toil, sweat, and suffer.
Lilith, through childbirth, in pain you will shudder."

Their first boy, Ab-el, a shepherd he was made.
Ka-en then followed—as a farmer he was trained.
On a hot, sultry day, Ka-en was swamped by desire.
The wand between his legs rose higher and higher.

To Anu he pleaded: "O great Almighty, bless me with a girl!
Madness has gripped my rod—it won't go back to curl."

"How sad, how cruel, you split my heart in two,"
Came the reply from Anu, out of the blue.
"I gave you life, but no wife—not fair, that's true.
Surely you deserve a blessing, Ka-en ... Screw You!"

Anu and his children filled the heavens with laughter.
Impatiently, they waited for what would happen after.

Ka-en rushed to his parents, seeking some advice,
A way to control and master his prickly device.

Al-dem saw him coming, became soaked with fright—
The boy like an animal, rabid, ready to bite.
He grabbed a hefty stick, saved for this occasion,
Prepared—ready to strike, no time for hesitation.

"Father, how can I deal with this monster, dirty spitter?
Getting so big and hard—I fear it's about to splinter."

Al-dem stood tapping the stick on his palm.
The balls I must hit, with force and no qualm.

Lilith came rushing. "Is that Ka-en? I hear his voice.
Oh, how do I miss him—come in, let's rejoice."

"'Come in—let's rejoice!'" Al-dem sighed. *"Hear that bitch!"*
"Son, you'd better stop. Don't you even dare to flinch!"

Blinded by desire, Ka-en could only discern a warm, female lover.
His father's blazing threat, 'twas naught but senile blather.
He darted like an eagle folding its wings,
Knocked the old man sideways, after dodging all the swings.

His wild needs brazenly plain, Lilith begged him to refrain.
"The disgrace, O Ka-en! The lust demons you need to tame!"
The words she cried in vain; Lust hardly listens to Shame.

Luckily, Al-dem recovered—a blow he squarely landed on the boy's
head.
Ka-en spun around, face marred in pain and dread.

His vigor went sinking faster than a rock.
His sturdy rod folded—humbled in bulk.
Recouped his proper senses—but was abandoned by luck.

Now armed with a knife, sharp and gleaming,
Al-dem dashed in a dart, madly screaming.

Swinging the weapon, he leapt on the attacker.
"A sure cure for you, *pervert*—this finely honed dagger!"

The slice Al-dem aimed to rid the boy of manhood.
Ka-en wiggled his body as best as he could.
His tool slithered free—alas, chopped short of the top hood.

Gods dropped to their knees, chuckling. "This madness is total!
Laughter would've killed us, had we been mortal."

In fits laughed Anu, then words he rammed like thunder.
"This, we have to remember—this utter blunder.
And look how the tip glistens with much better vision.
It shines with such joy—brings me to a decision:
All boys will have to go through circumcision!"

Ka-en took off, fleeing—both heads bleeding.
"Father, terribly sorry. Forgive me, I'm pleading."

"For this abhorrent sin, I cast you out.
No longer you're a son!" hollered Al-dem with a dreadful shout.

Aimlessly, Ka-en walked, hurt in body and ego.
Marched on and on till he fell with vertigo.
Came back later, in the darkness of night,
Brilliant stars shining; Moon full, pearly white.

"How terrible to be lonely, no mother, no father.
But wait, how did I forget—Ab-el, my only brother!"

Ka-en jumped to his feet, hope flooding his heart,
Rushed to see his brother, who was so wise and so smart.

Ab-el listened in earnest, then ardently blared.
"This problem is serious, yet nobody cared.
Best way to get blessed, the gods we must please.
A feast of food and wine—the recipe to appease."

Ab-el started to his herd, picked out goats and sheep,
Butchered the animals till in blood he stood deep.

Wheat, fruits, and greens, Ka-en picked from his farm.
The bellies of the gods, with his cooking arts he'd charm.

Three days and three nights, they cooked, toiled, and labored.
Sanguine and hopeful—by the gods they'd be favored.

On the day after, with screams they showered the skies.
Had the gods marvel: "What's the source of those cries?"
Delicious smoke ascended, so pungent and aromatic.
All immortals descended—pushing, shoving, rowdily frantic.

"How succulent and tasty, these dishes of cooked meat.
What? Are you serious? Is this broccoli and wheat?"
The beef they devoured faster than a breeze,
Yet none touched the veggies but the birds and the bees.

With mouth diligently chewing, Anu cheerfully toasted.
"Jolly good boy, Ab-el—the goat is perfectly roasted.
Yours is a reward all men cherish and seek—
A woman of such beauty, her love will make you shriek.

"Now, as for your offering ..." God eyed Ka-en, frowning.
"Your insult, so egregious, couldn't be more astounding.
Repugnant and disgusting, that's to say the least,
Such food should not be eaten—not even by a beast.
Luckily, I feel generous—you'll still get a reward."
Wickedly, Anu smirked. "You'll live life lonely, forever bored."

Ka-en whispered, beseeching, "Brother, let's share the woman, please—
To feel and touch that arse would surely give me peace."

"Have you gone insane?" Ab-el spat the words out loud.
"Ignore Anu's will, and he'll send us the demon death squad."

That night, Ka-en listened to his brother's lustful moans.
Gods' orgies rained from heaven torrents of amorous groans.
It seemed to take forever till the noise faded,
But Ka-en had a plan—patiently he waited.

When all were exhausted, snoring in their sleep,
Ka-en alone was wakeful—in silence he did creep.
He mounted Ab-el's woman, gently, ever tender.
Tired, she resisted but soon did surrender.

"Ab-el, this is good ... you've gotten so much better.
Oh, yes, yes, like that, you're making me so much wetter.

Your thing has grown much larger, almost twice the size—
The thrust, way way harder, deserving of a prize."
They climaxed together, shaking heaven and earth.
Both roared in sheer pleasure; blown was Ka-en's stealth.

Ab-el, in a stupor, saw the wife beneath,
A hairy arse on top, shaft pulling out of her sheath.
"Bitch, I doze a little, and you act like a whore!"
She cried, "I thought it was you, coming back for more."

Ab-el charged his brother, incensed, mightily pissed.
His fists, unlike his father's, the target never missed.

Ka-en's loins he battered with the fury of an avenger.
His brother fell to the ground, helpless, in mortal danger.

In agony Ka-en moaned; cruel blows suffered his rib bones.
Crying, he desperately reached, grabbed the largest of stones.
His arm arched wide to follow with a solid blow.
Ab-el's head ruptured, blood streaming in a steady flow.

"Ka-en, I see your brother in a pool of his blood!
Again, you appall me—I, Anu, the Mighty God!"

"God, if you're so caring, why didn't you stop the fight?
YOU deviously caused it and kept watching with mighty delight!
My offer you mocked and rejected—left me desolate with lust.
Hard I tried to please you. This punishment is not just.
The universe you created, this Earth—the whole lot.
I asked for a mere woman. Too much! You can lick my BUTT!"

"Ka-en, you insolent bastard! Your death you've just written!
With hot bolts of fire, I'll have you burned and smitten!"

The gods rushed their father, straining to hold him back.
"O great mighty Anu, this man don't you thwack.

Crazy, funny, and daring, he's so capricious.
Please do forgive him—he makes us go delirious.
The others do nothing but eat, drink, and crap.
It's all so annoying—makes one want to snap."

Anu came back to reason, sat on his throne,
Went deep into thinking, all night till dawn.

"Listen, my children; I'll let this go for once.
Forgiven he will be—will get another chance.
Now wake him; the scum, this dirt of the ground.
Time for him to hear of the fate to which he's bound."

"Boy, you're lucky, you got away with murder.
How stubborn—the nerve—you're completely out of order.
Surely you don't listen—it seems you are deaf.
You failed my tests miserably—should mark you with an F.
So here is what follows, since you didn't pass.
With a hot bolt of fire, I'll carve and letter your arse."

Ka-en bounced up in agony, sprinting like a horse,
With lightning stamped and branded—God's way to endorse.

The clouds of heaven scattered, gods laughing, all hysterical.
"The boy should get an award; so humorous—how theatrical!"

Anu stood tall, smiling—jubilant,
A crowd of gods around him, all lively—ebullient.

"Sons and daughters of mine, it gives me great pleasure—
Was wise to save this fool, who turned out to be a treasure.
Throngs of women he'll get, plenty to spread his seed.
Numbered as the stars, his likes they shall breed.
The stamp on his behind will pass to his progeny.
In it there is embedded an abundance of hate, violence ... tyranny.

"Savagery, wars, and butchery fervently they will foster,
Quakes, plagues, and hunger—the carnage we will bolster.
For the future, this I promise: never a dull moment,
Watch, savor, and cherish the humans in their torment,
Yet, those fools will praise you, ask blessings every day,
Proffer votive offerings, while on their knees they pray,

"Let the heavens shine and sparkle, 'tis cause for a celebration,
Eat, sing, and dance to your heart's incantation,
Fill and raise your cups—let's toast to the health,
The greatest story of them all—Humans on Earth!"

"And that's how it all started," said Gaga, the humpbacked jester, concluding the song he recited to the king and functionaries of the court. "The story that was, is, and will continue to be."

"Your Majesty!" The priest, En-shakush, rose from one of the glazed-brick benches flanking the stairs to the throne. "This man has gone too far with his insults to the gods—far beyond the bounds of disrespect, deep into blasphemy. His version severely distorts the Epic of Creation, which was passed to us from the gods through the first men who walked on this blessed earth. We all know our father god, Anu, created the first man and woman, and they were perfect. But this, *this insolent jester*, fails to mention that many of the humans who followed—the ones rife with defects—were the works of drunk gods who toyed with reckless attempts to imitate the immaculate work of mighty Anu."

En-shakush waved a hand in Gaga's direction with a gesture of contempt. "We have a perfect example. Look at him, Your Majesty; only a senselessly drunk god could create something hideous like *that*. And then to portray the gods—may they forgive me for saying this—as a sadistic, bloodthirsty gang that delights in watching humans suffer! It is beyond the gravest of heresies ever heard."

King Sargon didn't say a thing. He calmly grabbed some pomegranate seeds from a bowl, tossed them into his mouth, and looked at Gaga, expecting an answer.

"Majesty," Gaga responded, "I don't understand! Why all this anger over an innocent song?"

"Innocent!" En-shakush went berserk. "And he dares call this …
this filth of a song, innocent!"

The jester had anticipated the attack and followed up:

"If for any reason the gods I have offended—not over these
shoulders my head would be suspended."

"Majesty!" the priest erupted. "Instead of repenting, now he
dares challenge the gods to decapitate him. He should be punished
by nothing less than death for this stubborn demeanor—his heretical
insults!"

Gaga was ready again:

"How dare you render the gods so hopelessly weak! Feeble to
exact any justice, have no powers but to peek! Why, to show their
fury, it's the mortals' help they always seek?"

"Majesty." En-shakush was shaking with anger. "This man is
beyond redemption. The gods could, on a whim, squash him like a
bug. But right now, they are testing us to see if we are faithful enough
to do their bidding. I urge you not to disappoint them. Have this man
executed forthwith!"

A wicked smile crawled on Gaga's face, and he countered:

"This reeks of betrayal—words traitors sing. The gods to test His
Majesty! 'Is he worthy to be king?'"

En-shakush blanched, realizing he had fallen into the very trap
he was weaving for the jester.

"Your Majesty, he's playing with words. I didn't mean to—"

"Enough!" Sargon roared, sending pomegranate seeds shooting
out of his mouth as he sprang off the throne. "I just sat for the first
time on the throne! My arse didn't get enough time to warm it up, the
crown is not yet on my head, and you have me listen to this nonsense!"

"Your Majesty, it was never my inten—" En-shakush tried to
pacify the king.

"I said *enough*! I don't want to hear a single word more." Sargon's
voice was clipped with fury. "I intended for this gathering to be casual

and friendly—to get to know you better while we have a modest feast and some entertainment. Come to the front and get on your knees, both of you. Now, it's time that *you* know *me* better ... Naplanam!"

"Majesty!" Came the reply from a guard, who stepped forward from behind the throne. His muscular body bore scars of battle, visible all over his bare chest, arms, and face.

"If either of these two breathes a word, I order you to chop him to pieces!" Sargon took a deep breath. "Naplanam, this place is somehow crowded. There is one head too many ... you know what to do."

Naplanam grinned wildly. "Which one, my king?"

The jester and the priest, both deprived of the freedom to speak, could only tremble in fear.

"I don't know. They had me all confused." Sargon pondered. "Maybe ... you decide. I trust your judgment; after all, you acted on your own to save my life in battle. So, snuff out one of these two miserable lives. Don't rush, take all the time you want. Only after you're done, do let us know what prompted your final decision."

"Yes, Your Majesty."

Naplanam stepped away, descended the stairs, and walked to the two trembling figures. He knelt between them and, gently, as if about to make love to them, he slipped their robes down over their shoulders to better expose their necks. Tenderly, he patted their backs as he stood.

It had been a long time since he last experienced the thrill of killing. He savored the smell of fear. Wanting the pleasure to last, he wasn't going to rush into spilling the blood. Though he kept quiet, his lips moved now and then as if asking a ghost for advice. He shook his head, seemingly dissatisfied with the answer. The whole assembly watched as his silent debate drove him to move back and forth between the two hapless men.

Sargon gobbled up another handful of pomegranate seeds and chewed calmly, pleased that Naplanam was patient with his sword. His eyes shifted to study the faces of the seated noblemen—the unwilling audience to this grisly drama. It was good to make his men nervous; let everyone present know it could just as easily be him kneeling under the sword on the whim of the new king. That should make them think twice about betraying him. He spat the hard part of the seeds out into a bowl and, with mouth closed, his tongue snaked behind his pursed lips, brushing along the front teeth to remove a wedged seed. When that attempt proved futile, he summoned the nail of a middle finger for assistance and successfully dislodged the pestering seed, which distracted him from the scene playing before him.

Naplanam kept pacing the floor, deeply immersed in thoughts, when a faint smile crossed his face while his lips recited invisible words. Slowly, he moved to stand between the two kneeling men and bowed to his king.

"I am ready, Majesty."

"Go a-*head*." Sargon gave him a nod.

The priest and the jester were both breathing heavily as though hoarding air for their journey to the next life. The onlookers on the benches, sensing death enter the court, stiffened as hard as the bricks beneath them.

All eyes were on Naplanam when he stepped swiftly to one side and, in the blink of an eye, dropped his sword. A head rolled across the stone floor and a shower of blood sprayed out of the body that collapsed behind it. The spared man collapsed too when his tensed body went totally slack at realizing he would not die today.

The bloodshed drowned all signs of life in the court until Sargon's hand scrabbled the bowl for more pomegranate seeds.

"Well done, Naplanam. A splendid, single, clean strike," Sargon commended, then shoved more of the juicy seeds into his mouth and spoke while chewing. "Peace, at last. Now, tell us—what made you slay the priest and not Gaga?"

"Yes, Your Majesty." Naplanam cleared his throat, then recited:

"Priests there are aplenty, jesters but a few.
None would miss this one. As for him, my eyes would dew."

With the last line, he held his hands out toward Gaga, who was looking up at him with a blend of relief and lingering terror.

Sargon's chewing slowed to a halt, his eyes glued to Naplanam, when abruptly he coughed out a barrage of seeds, some flying far enough to land in the blood pooled on the floor below. He chuckled briefly, then started coughing; something stubbornly lodged in his throat and his breathing became labored. His personal healer rushed up the stairs to pat him on the back, gently at first, then harder as Sargon continued to gasp for air.

Just when it seemed that Sargon was about to meet his end by the wrath of the gods—their punishment for killing a priest—a tiny seed shot out. Gradually, his color returned to normal and his breathing eased before he erupted into a fit of laughter, broken by short heaves of coughing. The anxious healer kept slapping his back until the spasms ceased, and Sargon waved him away.

A tense buzz rippled through the court, with stifled dismay among those who for brief moments had hoped they were seeing the demise of the new king.

"Naplanam—you bastard!" Sargon hollered. "After saving me from the enemy's blades, now you want to kill me laughing!"

"Never, Majesty! My loyalty to you will never waver." Naplanam sank to his knees, pulled a dagger from his belt, and placed its point against his chest. "Say the word, my king, and I will stab myself in the heart without hesitation."

"Nonsense! Stand up, Naplanam." Sargon caught the laughing fit again but managed to regain himself. "Oh, by the gods, I can't remember ever laughing so hard. Was that a poem you just recited?"

Without waiting for an answer, Sargon addressed the court. "You heard it—a poem! Naplanam ... *executed* a poem!"

Nervous chuckles issued out of the seated men, and murmurs were tossed around, all in agreement with the king.

"Yes, it's a poem."

"No doubt, a fine poem it is."

"A short one-liner, but *definitely* a poem," Sargon asserted. "A brute, a killer who would scare the demons of the underworld ... and *a poet*! Naplanam, I never imagined you having such a soft, artistic side. Where did that come from?"

A faint rosy color covered the tanned, stony cheeks of an embarrassed Naplanam. "Majesty, on those long, dull sieges of walled cities, some of us used to kill time by singing and having poetic competitions."

"So, all that time you took—it wasn't to decide who to execute. You were only composing the poem."

"Majesty, you are absolutely right."

"Gaga, what do you think of Naplanam's poem? Brilliant, right?"

The jester was back on his feet after recovering some of the strength robbed by fear, grateful that his head was still attached to the uneven mound on his back.

"Majesty, it's a line … worthy of praise. … A splendid poem."

"Gaga! I was expecting a poetic answer," Sargon mocked. "What happened, did the sword slash the poetic edge of your tongue? You have to do better than that, or I will give your job to … Naplanam."

Laughter seized Sargon once more, when a guard came rushing in, bowed, and spoke with urgency.

"Majesty, forgive my intrusion, but the princess is heading here, right now."

"Take the body away! Hurry!" Sargon ordered.

Two guards rushed to the body while Naplanam darted to pick up the head of the priest, but the shaved, blood-moistened head slipped out of his hands and went rolling on the floor, which distracted one of the guards carrying the body, and he slid on the bloodied surface, bringing down the man at the other end of the corpse. Both men went splashing down into the red pool just as the girl walked in on the macabre scene.

"Oh, by the love of Ishtar!" She turned around in revulsion. "What happened here?"

Sargon rushed down the stairs and wrapped his arms around her to shield her from the grisly scene. The guards stammered apologies as they passed him on their way out. Sargon shook his head in frustration.

"What did you do to him?" the girl demanded.

"It wasn't me," Sargon said, walking her up to the throne. "Something he said must have angered the gods, and just like that, his head fell off."

Enheduanna gave her father a skeptical glare. She was too smart to buy this story, and he knew it. He kept her facing away from the horrid spot while slaves wiped the blood off the floor.

"Everyone leave. Now!" Sargon announced. "I want to be alone with my daughter."

All were happy to oblige. No one wanted to spend a moment more in the shadow of death that stank up the court. Only Naplanam remained, standing guard at the entrance.

"Yes, my lotus flower," Sargon said while softly stroking Enheduanna's black hair, which cascaded below her shoulders. "What urgent matter brings you here?"

"I don't know what to wear for the coronation ceremony," Enheduanna complained. "Can I go to the market and pick what I need for my own clothing? Those fools you assigned don't have the slightest idea about dressing a princess."

"Absolutely not! It could be dangerous if someone recognized you. You know I have a lot of enemies who strive to hurt me and those dear to me."

"Don't worry, Father, I'll dress like a commoner. Just send a guard to watch from a distance. I'll be fine. Please, please, for the love of Ishtar."

Sargon knew it was hopeless to argue with his daughter. She had been born with a robust character, not to mention his share of spoiling her.

"Naplanam," he called. "Get the two best guards available. I have a job for them."

"Right away," Naplanam answered, using no honorifics to address the king. Sargon didn't require the adulations when only those closest to him were present.

"Oh Father, the gods will bless you to be the greatest king of all times." Enheduanna hugged him. "I will personally ask them for that in my prayers."

Shortly, Naplanam returned with two guards.

"Men," Sargon instructed. "I assign you to go with my daughter. Do what she wants, but allow no harm to come to her. Understood?"

"Yes, Your Majesty."

Enheduanna turned to leave. On the way out, she saw traces of blood within the crevices of the floor. She turned back to her father.

"Really, Father, what happened to that man?"

Sargon glanced at Naplanam and answered, grinning. "Poems sent him to his doom. A poet was his executioner."

In the Company of the King

S HE MOVED THE MIRROR SIDE TO SIDE, STUDYING HER DRESS IN the silhouette that reflected off the polished copper plate. The embroidered white flowers on the white fabric were barely visible in that sickly orange surface. Even her smile looked miserable.

"Use this mirror."

Amare turned and snatched the other mirror from her aunt's outstretched hand; this one was larger, made of smooth polished silver, handle and frame of cedarwood. The image was sharper with the new mirror. Her bright smile was fully restored upon surveying the dress again. She twisted in half circles, exploring her reflection from every angle, the lower fringe of the dress folding in and swelling out with soft rustling sounds as it raced to match her moves.

Tammara watched her silently till she ran out of patience.

"Well, does the dress meet your high expectations now? This is it, no more alterations! If you don't like it, back to storage it goes."

Amare swirled around to face her. She lowered the mirror, took a long look at the woman she considered more a mother than an aunt, then rushed at her with a hug.

"Oh, this is the most—the most beautiful dress … except for one problem."

Amare pursed her lips, then laughed when Tammara gave her a menacing frown. "All those girls who will give me the envious eye."

"Praise the gods, a miracle! Finally, she's happy." Tammara threw her arms up in the air before her expression melted to a sad smile. "My child, I wish your mother were alive to see how beautiful you've become."

"By the gods, Aunt, is this a dream? To be invited to the king's coronation banquet, and to wear this dress. Am I to keep it?"

"No!" Tammara replied in a clipped voice. "I'm lending you the dress only this once, for the ceremony, understood?"

"Yes, Aunt." Amare didn't protest, yet sadness crept to cover the smile that was almost a permanent feature on her face.

"You fool." Her aunt smiled, changing her stern demeanor. "Of course you can keep the dress. Why would an old hag like me need it? If I walked the streets in that, I'd be the laughingstock of everyone in the kingdom."

Amare hugged her again. "No, Aunt, don't talk like that. You are and always will be beautiful."

"I doubt it. And if you keep hugging me this hard, my tender bones will snap and leave only a heap of old clothes on the floor."

Amare released her. "Oh, I love you, and I love this dress. I'll never take it off—will wear it for the rest of my life."

Tears snaked down Tammara's cheeks.

"Why are you crying?" Amare was alarmed.

"Just tears of happiness—perhaps of sadness. Soon, a handsome man will take you away."

"Oh Aunt Tammara, I will never leave you. No man can make me leave you."

"I'll have to recite some prayers to keep the attention of the goddess Ishtar away from you. They say she's jealous of beautiful girls; she wants to keep all the handsome men for herself. I hope she's too busy with her lovers to notice you."

"Oh Aunt, you're too much with those superstitions."

"Superstitions! I wouldn't be surprised if the gods descended for you. There would be no room left in the court for the king, priests, nobles, or any mortal."

"Aunt, the gods would not be the least bit interested. Watching us mortals must be so boring, like watching fresh mud bricks dry in their molds under the sun."

"Amare, don't be stupid. The gods have a great appetite for beautiful girls and handsome men. Think of Ishtar—she has more lovers than hairs on your head, most of them mortals. Need I say more?"

"Don't worry, Aunt. If any god approaches me and tries something, I'll kick him in the balls." Amare giggled. "His holy balls will hurt for eternity."

"Girl! Where did you learn such blasphemy?" Tammara scolded her. "O merciful gods, please forgive this foolish, childish girl, and her mindless thoughts. … Amare, ask the gods to forgive you, or you can forget about the coronation banquet."

"Forgive me, Aunt, excitement got me carried away." Amare looked up to the ceiling, raising both arms dramatically. "O gods of heaven, do pardon my foolishness. I will always be obedient and servile to you—as long as you don't let my aunt lock me away and have me miss the ceremony."

She lowered her hands and retrieved her radiant smile, erasing anger off her aunt's face.

Tammara sighed in resignation; exhorting her niece to take the gods seriously was futile.

A knock on the door expelled the pestering gods from the scene. Amare ran to the door and flung it open, knowing who was on the other side: her friend Iltani. Amare, as always, wrapped her in a hug and tried to lift her, but Iltani was taller and heavier, and Amare gave up after a few tries.

"At last, you're here!" Feigning impatience, Amare rebuked her friend. "I almost left without you."

"Silly girl, always complaining. Look at you! You're not going with your hair like *that*."

"I don't have anything nice to dress it with. What am I supposed to do?"

Tammara frowned at her niece. "You have more ribbons than the count of your fingers and toes. One of them should do."

Amare returned a sly look. "With this dress, only a silver ribbon will match."

Tammara shook her head and walked away. She came back with a silver band resting on the palm of her hand.

"Will this silver ribbon do?"

"Oh Aunt, it's exactly what I want. I don't know what I would do without you."

"And I know exactly what your mother would've done to me if she were—" Tammara couldn't think of a proper word. "She would've killed me for spoiling you. Come, let me dress your hair."

Tammara braided her niece's dark hair deftly and stepped back to assess her work.

"Good enough. Now, I need not tell you how much I value this ribbon. Make sure you bring it back. Lose it, and I'll shave your head!"

"Don't worry, Aunt, I won't lose it, and I will polish it for you, too."

"Just go, enjoy the ceremony, and don't fool with anyone. May the gods protect you from evil spirits."

"If evil spirits show up, I'll tell them my aunt is Ishtar, and she will kick their butts," Amare quipped.

Tammara's hands pressed against her ears. "Out! get out of here before you drive me to madness and incur the gods' wrath upon us." She kissed both girls, pushed them gently out the door, and watched them stroll down the road.

Her eyelids closed for a long moment, only to open with tears streaking down her face, just like every time Amare walked away from the house. The superstitions always returned, along with the feeling she might be seeing her niece for the last time.

Superstitions had never bothered Tammara before her own daughter was born. Her husband had always mocked such beliefs, calling them a plague of the poor. But a neighboring friend fully believed in the superstitions and had frequently warned of the grim consequences to those who ignored them.

"You need to ward off the evil spirits when your child sleeps," her friend cautioned. "A necklace with a good-sized, silver amulet of Pazzuzu is the best safeguard."

She was referring to the hideous demon with a body resembling an erect, four-winged penis with a snake's head and the claws of an eagle. Pazzuzu was revered by mothers despite his malicious nature, for he was believed to be the archenemy of Lamashtu—another evil entity and leader of the spirits that crept in unnoticed and snatched the souls of vulnerable infants while they slept, dragging them to the netherworld.

Tammara had dismissed the advice of her overcautious friend.

"I would be buried in charms if I believed in the countless demons, spirits, and all their kin. I'm not opening the gates of my tranquil life to the armies of superstition."

On a beautiful day, Tammara was strolling the market while carrying her daughter, when a needy woman approached and begged her to buy a bronze charm of Pazzuzu she no longer needed. Tammara bought it only because she felt sorry for the woman. Back at home, she tossed the charm into a small box.

Her daughter was no more than four moons old when death had shown Tammara its ugliest side, stealing the life of her baby girl in her sleep.

Tammara cried for days and nights on end, beating her chest.

Had I worn that silver amulet of Pazzuzu, would my child be alive today?

She was driven to bury the bronze charm of the demon far from home after whispers started to echo in her head, which she had attributed to Pazzuzu himself, scolding her for casting him aside, rendering him useless to protect her child. Likewise, she had stopped seeing her close friend, whose eyes seemed to reflect silent accusations for not heeding her advice.

Tammara placed her daughter's body in a jar that she sealed with bitumen. Every night, she would cradle the jar as she sang a sad melody, hoping that the goddess of the netherworld, Ereshkigal, would have pity on her, and by some miracle bring her baby back.

One day, Tammara's only sister and her husband left their child, Amare, to cheer her up while they went on a short trip to visit the husband's family on the other side of the Euphrates River. They never made it back; on the return trip, the boat sank, and the river claimed their bodies. Tammara ended up with Amare in her care, but her love for her niece was touched by guilt: she always wondered if the goddess of the netherworld had responded to her prayers, giving her another daughter but taking the lives of Amare's parents in return. Because of that guilt, Tammara never allowed Amare to call her "Mother."

After being struck by those family tragedies, superstition had finally found a path to storm Tammara's heart. She hadn't wasted any time in buying a new amulet of Pazzuzu—a silver one, which she had worn ever since, even though Amare had turned fifteen a moon ago. The amulet seemed to work; no serious harm had come to the girl at any time. Amare had grown up to be full of life. She was of average beauty, but with her levity and the smile that rarely left her face she rivaled the most beautiful girls in the city.

Clutching the silver amulet of Pazzuzu, Tammara muttered a prayer to the goddess Nanshe, protector of the orphans. Her gaze followed the two girls until they turned a corner, and sadness overwhelmed her; it wouldn't be long before Amare's beauty and levity wreaked havoc on someone's heart, and there was no amulet to keep men away.

Tammara was ready for her girl to be snatched into marriage, but she would do the impossible to ward off the beasts of the netherworld.

𒁹 ◇ 𒄑 𐎗 𝍠

The cow didn't appreciate the noisy crowd; its head shook sideways, pushing away the hand holding the fodder. The young man who was trying to feed it cursed silently. He placed the hay in a wicker basket, then shoved it in the cow's face, but the stubborn cow wiggled its head off the basket, jostling the young man back in the process. His mouth twisted in anger, now muttering curses, and he spun around in frustration, when his eyes met those of a girl who was laughing, apparently at him. Embarrassed, he distanced himself from the cow and walked back to the cart behind it, searching for something manlier to do. He knelt to conceal his embarrassment, feigning to check one of the two wheels and the leather belt wrapped around it, his movements exaggerated and self-conscious.

"You shouldn't force the cow to eat."

The unexpected voice rang right above him, and briskly he turned toward the source, only to lose his balance. His arm stretched out to grip onto something, finding only air, when, in a flash, a hand darted to the rescue, gripping his. He looked up and saw Amare's bright smile. Instantly, strength surged freely into his legs. He sprang up to his feet and stared down at the hand he was now holding as if he had found a gem.

"I think this is mine," joking, Amare gently withdrew her hand.

"Oh, yes—your hand. Forgive me." Reluctantly, he released it.

"You should be gentler with the cow," Amare said. "It's nervous in the midst of this crowd. Who put you in charge of the cow?"

"Well, the chariots I work with are pulled by horses, not cows." The reply came with a hint of pride. "I wasn't supposed to be here, but my friend fell ill, and he begged me to take his place and bring the cow."

"Poor cow. I pity her for having to deal with a charioteer."

"I've never dealt with a cow before. Horses are what I know best."

"Somehow horses scare me," Amare said. "I keep a safe distance away from them."

"Oh, horses are the most docile animals. They're easier to tame than these stupid cows."

"I find that hard to believe." Her words sounded like a compliment, which gave him a dose of courage.

"My father is a horse trainer in the army. He taught me how to work with horses, even ride them. I think I learned how to ride a horse before walking." He laughed. "I'm only joking—but I do ride horses, it's no lie."

He waited for her response, but it didn't materialize, save for that disarming smile. He went on, desperate to continue the conversation.

"My father is working on a chair that can be strapped on a horse's back to make it easy for any man to ride."

Amare kept silent. She was wondering what had made her walk to this boy and why she was still listening to him.

"I can take you one day and show you my horse. Let you feed it." He stopped, barely aware that he had asked her out.

"I would love to." To her own surprise, the answer came so fast she hardly felt her lips move.

He was elated and wondered for a moment if she was the daughter of a goddess who just wanted to mingle with any mortal, rich or poor. She could not be a girl of the nobility; such girls were always busy searching for a man of wealth and influence. His type, they would never engage.

"Are you a goddess?" he couldn't help but ask. "A curious

one—come down from heaven to play with the mortals?"

She laughed, shaking her head.

"My name is Ashur. What's yours?"

"Amare."

"Amare, I can show you the royal stables, maybe teach you how to ride a horse. The guards won't mind, they know me."

"I don't think my aunt would allow me."

"You must!" he insisted. Realizing his rudeness, he rushed to make amends. "I mean … it's your destiny … written by the gods."

"The gods revealed *my* destiny to *you*? Riding horses!" Amare scoffed at the nonsense, but she was eager to hear it all the same. "Go on—tell me more about *my destiny*."

"Patience! Give me a moment to recall. It was in a dream."

"Hmm, a dream!"

"Yes, a dream I had last night—so it can't be a coincidence. It must have been a sign from the gods, trust me on that." Ashur paused briefly, and recounted:

"From far away, I saw the silhouette of a noblewoman on a horse, which moved so smoothly—as if floating. Suddenly, a rock, a large one, popped out of the ground. The horse swiftly leapt over it, but the woman lost her balance and fell off the horse. She wasn't hurt, but she looked like she had taken a mud bath."

"And you want me to learn how to ride a horse. Forget about it!"

"Let me finish the dream." Ashur spoke assertively, confidence well-saddled on his back. "Then, weird sounds rang from above— more like gods laughing. The noblewoman stood up, cursed at them, then began hurling stones at the sky when, without warning, she disappeared, leaving the horse behind. Moments later, a beautiful girl came out of nowhere. She had a lovely face, like a full moon brightening the night—just like yours. She had dark eyes that could absorb a man's soul and send it into a sweet dream … like yours. And a charming smile—"

"Like yours!" Amare interrupted.

"No, not like mine!" Ashur frowned. "Charming, like your smile. Then, the girl walked toward the horse so gracefully, like a gentle breeze that tamed the stallion even before touching it. She mounted it like a queen sitting on a throne. Then, like magic, the horse grew wings and took off to the skies."

"That's one remarkable story—more like a poem."

"I'm a charioteer." He feigned frustration. "No poet, nor a story-teller. And this is what the gods revealed to me in the dream—the destiny they chose for you. Do you want to anger the gods?"

"I wouldn't dare. But the girl in your dream could be another."

"Oh, by the gods of heaven. Someone help me convince this girl I'm telling the truth. Very well, if I'm lying, let the chariot roll over me, squash my body, and send my soul to the netherworld."

Ashur lay down before the chariot, his waist right next to the wheel. The cow mooed unhappily at this unwelcomed body placed behind it.

Amare gasped in alarm over the handsome, foolish boy who risked being crushed by the chariot. She grabbed one of his feet, trying vainly to pull him out of harm's way. Frenetically she kept pulling and her braided hair came loose when, abruptly, the sandal came off his foot. She fell onto her back, sandal still clutched in her fist. A wave of laughter swarmed the crowd before it swiftly receded, cut short by a roaring voice of authority.

"What's going on here?" a man dressed in military attire bellowed at Ashur. "In the name of the gods, boy, why are you outstretched next to the wheel?"

Immediately, Ashur sprang up. Amare was already on her feet, dusting her dress off.

"What is your name, boy, and what is your duty here?" the man demanded.

Ashur's heart skipped a beat on realizing he was being chastised by none other than an army general.

"Ashur, sir. I work in the king's stables and was told to bring this cow to the coronation ceremony, sir."

"I think you will do a better job as a king's jester. The whole crowd seems to be amused by your act."

"Forgive me, sir, but I slipped on some dirt and …" Dumbfounded, Ashur struggled to spin a convincing story before the general.

"And I guess you, too, *slipped* on some dirt." The general eyed

Amare, who was a little dazed from the fall.

Ashur rushed to defend her. "Sir, she just came to help me feed the cow, but the cow … pushed her."

Sensing that Ashur was in trouble, Amare stepped toward the general. "Sir, it was my fault. It's the first time I've come this close to a chariot, and I must have done something that disturbed the cow." She smiled, knowing how men responded to her smile.

The general squinted, peering intently at her.

That smile seems familiar. His memory raced back in search of the time and place where he had seen such prominent joy on a girl's face.

It looks like her! Why is she here? But, I could be wrong—I hope I'm wrong. The thought agitated him.

"Are you—?" he started but stopped short at seeing the high priest with his entourage approaching him.

"Are we going to start this procession?" Ishullanu, the high priest, said impatiently. "We have a hectic schedule—need to start right away. Soon, the crowd will be filling the streets and it will be complete chaos."

"May I have a word with you first?" the general said to Ishullanu. Then he turned to Amare. "You stay here. Don't go anywhere."

The general took Ishullanu by the arm and walked some distance away where they could not be heard. He appeared to be trying to reason with the high priest, while glancing at Amare now and then. Soon a heated argument ensued, until finally the general walked away with the gait of someone who had lost a major battle.

"How strange!" Ashur was puzzled. "I thought I was about to be given five lashes—at least. I've seen that general exact such punishment for incidents much less serious."

"I feel like I met him someplace before," Amare said before noticing she was still clutching Ashur's sandal. She tossed it to the ground, missing his feet by a hand.

"Your smile must have calmed him down," Ashur teased her, and slipped his foot back into the sandal. "He's probably saving the punishment for later when the ceremony is over."

"Well, you deserve it for being such a fool—lying before the wheel and risking your life."

Ashur returned a sly smile and pointed his foot, lightly kicking a wooden block wedged under the wheel. Amare gawked in disbelief for not noticing it.

"I will crush you for this." She waived her fist in a playful display of anger. "I'll tell that general to give you ten, no, twenty lash—" Abruptly, she stiffened as she patted her hair self-consciously.

"Oh, mercy of the gods!" She let out a faint scream.

"What is it? Are you hurt?"

"I lost it—the silver ribbon that bound my hair, my aunt's ribbon." Amare was frantically searching the area next to the cart.

"Don't worry. It must be somewhere around here where you fell," Ashur said calmly.

"She'll kill me. That was her husband's gift when he proposed to her. She said if I lost it, she would shave my head." Amare searched desperately. "Where could it have gone? It should be easy to spot." She turned around and saw Ashur standing with absolute indifference.

"It's all your fault, and you're just standing there, watching!" Amare snapped, resisting the urge to curse him.

"The gods just revealed to me where to find it." He couldn't hide a smirk, and at once, Amare knew he was fooling with her again.

"Maybe you should work as a messenger for the gods," she erupted. "Well, out with it. I need to join my group. No more games, please."

"The gods say first you must obey my dream and start learning how to tame horses. Do you swear to that?"

"I swear by the gods, I will do that."

"Starting when?"

"Maybe … seven mornings from now."

"The gods say they don't want to wait that long."

"Fine. Five mornings."

"Still too long."

"Three, and the gods better be happy!" she said through gritted teeth.

Ashur stretched his arm out with the silver ribbon dangling between his fingers. Her eyes opened wide at the sight of her little treasure, and she snatched it.

"If only I had seen this block under the wheel, I would've removed it and let the chariot crush you," she said with such ferocity that Ashur was unsure if she was joking.

"It couldn't crush me any worse than your charm did."

Her cheeks dressed in a rosy shade, and her irritation yielded to a conquering smile.

"So, I will see you in three mornings," Ashur said. "Forget about the stables, we'll go there later. Let's meet somewhere else."

"Where?"

"I take my horse to graze by the river, right outside the south gate of the city—by a lush, green field; you can't miss it. I'll be there in the morning when the sun is just about to mount the horizon."

"I'll see you there—three mornings from now."

"You better," he smirked, "or, next time you lose the ribbon, I won't be around to help find it."

Amare walked away, engulfed by a strange feeling of elation.

Is this just a dream? She couldn't resist a glimpse back.

"And wear that ribbon!" Ashur yelled.

She nodded, clutching at the ribbon.

No, not a dream. Dreams could never be this sweet. This must be love.

𒀭 𒀸 𒌋

"You are an embarrassment!" Iltani suppressed a scream, utterly aghast at Amare's transgression. "Have you lost your mind? The spectacle with that boy! They will throw you out—send you home. I'll kill you if I'm thrown out—miss all the excitement because of you. Do you know how lucky we are to be here in the first place?"

Amare shrugged. "They can send me home if they want to. I won't miss a thing."

"Oh, oh—fool falling in love with the first boy to flirt with her."

"Who says I'm in love? He's simply funny, smart, and ... a charioteer."

"Charioteer! Why is he tending a cow, then?"

"I don't know. I guess they don't want horses that might go running wild in the midst of this crowd."

"Amare, I hope you're not taking him seriously. You could easily have a wealthy noble and live in a lush house with servants tending to you. Don't be a fool and go after some stable-worker, *charioteer*, and end up tending to cows and horses instead."

Amare was hardly listening. Her glances kept tracing Ashur through the crowd as he guided the cow, following a priest to the back of the assembly.

Ishullanu was screaming at the priests to rush in the task of organizing the groups.

"Why are all these priests here?" Amare asked, hoping to evade the tantrum of advice from her friend.

"Every ceremony comes with prayers to thank the gods for their generosity. You wouldn't want to anger the gods by showing no appreciation for the gifts they shower on us, would you?"

"Anger the gods!" Amare replied, slyly. "I wouldn't dare."

A priestess with a grim, authoritative face came shrieking at all the girls to gather, then had them split into two lines, leading the marchers. Iltani stood right behind Amare, who turned her head to steal another glance at the chariots, all the way at the back. Her face brightened when Ashur waved to her.

"You are hopeless," Iltani remarked, shaking her head.

Ishullanu gave the signal for the march to start, and instantly the air burst with music—drums, lyres, flutes, and clapping hands, accompanied by joyous singing. Forward they marched toward the palace that loomed in the distance. Halfway down the road leading to the main gate, the priests directed them to turn, herding the procession onto a side street. They marched onward, turning onto other streets—all vacant save for a few posted guards—until they reached the mouth of a passage stretching underground, its walls lined with torches.

"Why aren't we going through the main gate of the palace?" Amare asked, unable to restrain her curiosity.

"Oh God, drown me in a deluge of patience!" Iltani sighed. "Only the king and his entourage go through the main gate."

"So how are we getting to the ceremony hall?"

"They have tunnels winding underground like a spider's web. Now, stop asking silly questions. We … are going to have a great time."

Amare looked around. All the marchers seemed jubilant, reveling in the festive mood, grateful for being invited to the king's coronation ceremony.

The passage opened into a large hall, lit by torches all along the walls. The flames danced vigorously to the arriving party as the air vibrated through the flurry of clapping hands, beating drums, music, and singing.

The high priest, Ishullanu, ascended a platform and screamed, seeking attention, but his voice shrank to a whisper amid the cacophony beneath until some of the revelers perceived that he wanted to be heard; shortly thereafter, the room was stilled to an eerie silence as if a god had ordered it.

"Men and women of the great Uruk!" Ishullanu started. "Today, we celebrate our king and ask the gods to take good care of him. May they bless him with eternal life. … Now, before we move on to the main ceremony, in the company of the king, I want everyone to go to the front tables, pick up a cup of beer—it's from the king's special brew—and go back to your place."

The priests began filling cups from large skins as the invitees filed past the tables to get the drink. With everyone holding a cup, Ishullanu raised his own cup and cheerfully shouted, "To our beloved king—may he live for eternity!"

The crowd chanted back: "May he live for eternity!"

Amare took a sip of her beer. "Praise the gods, that was a short sermon. How I wish all prayers were like that."

"I have to agree. I was dying of thirst," Iltani replied, and took a gulp. "Oh, this tastes so good. Imagine—we're drinking from the king's special brew. Only distinguished visitors to the court get to taste this."

Iltani took a second gulp, then watched as Amare raised her cup in a toasting gesture—not to her, but to the boy with the cow, now standing at a far side of the hall.

"What's so special about this boy?" Iltani asked impatiently. "It seems he holds your heart hostage."

"I told you, he's a horse trainer. He works in the king's stables."

"He trains them to pull chariots?"

"Not only that." Amare dropped her voice to a conspiratorial whisper. "He says he can mount a horse and command where it goes."

"Horse dung! No one can ride horses; they are too wild. I heard of a poor man who tried to mount one—he fell and broke his neck. This boy is nothing but a common liar."

"I believe him. I've heard of a tribe in the north that rides horses with the ease of riding asses."

"I'll believe that when I see it," Iltani retorted. "The gods made asses to ride and horses to pull chariots. This nonsense you're talking about, how come I've never heard of it?"

"Because you're too busy thinking about affluent nobles who like to keep their arses stationed on nice comfortable cushions. Anyway, what is a horse but a bigger, taller ass?"

"Big or small, tall or short—the fact remains, that boy is dying to mount only one thing, my dear foolish friend, and it's neither an ass nor a horse—it's *your arse* he wants."

"Enough of this dirty talk! He seems to be sincere. Stop spoiling my sweet dream."

"Wake up and start dreaming about marrying a rich noble, and make *that* dream come true. Forget this charioteer; they smell so bad, people will think you're married to a donkey."

Her friend's words could not dim Amare's mood; she was numb with happiness. The music started again, and she joined the crowd in the singing; then, like a floating butterfly, she was dancing.

Soon, thirst tackled Amare. She raised the cup to her mouth, but it was empty of beer. She laughed and showed Iltani, turning her cup upside down. Iltani laughed back, her cup was almost empty too, and she pointed to the tables where the priests were refilling the cups. Weaving through the crowd, they passed by the high priestess, who mysteriously was dead quiet, sadness dominating her expression— nothing like the frantic, commanding woman she was when she first arrived.

With their cups refilled, the two went back to their place, shaking their bodies in a bouncy dance.

"This is what you'll miss when you marry that cow boy," Iltani teased. "But don't worry; as a best friend, I'll come to visit in your stable—forgive me, I meant home."

"You won't find me there." Amare spun once. "I'll be on top of a horse, storming the fields, racing the sun god from sunrise to sunset and the moon god from dusk till dawn." And she went twirling in circles till she grew dizzy. She brought her feet to a halt, but the floor refused to stand still. To regain her balance, Amare grabbed hold of Iltani, who was also feeling wobbly. The floor beneath them had lost its firmness, slipping under them like mud in a strong river current.

Amare felt a hand grab her arm then ease her down onto a wicker chair. She watched as Iltani's tall body swayed sideways, tilting to the front, then springing back like a date palm tree in a storm, which sent her laughing until Iltani faded to a shadow. Amare's eyelids grew heavy and slowly they closed. Her head drifted downward as if in a solemn prayer. Gently, she succumbed to sleep.

𒀭 𒂍 𒐖

"Beautiful girl."

"Yes, she'll be the king's favorite."

"Probably will make a queen."

Amare could hear them through a window that opened into the deep recess of her sleep. She wanted to scream back:

I'm in love with a young charioteer! No king or luxury of a palace can change that!

But her tongue felt weighed down, her eyelids stubbornly lazy to open.

This must be a dream. And sleep tightened its grip on her.

"The dress, the stitching …" Nidala, the high priestess, trailed off while she observed the sleeping girl. "Must have been tailored for her by someone who adored her."

"She'll wear this dress till it blends with her ashes."

"Pity! Such a beautiful creature could've married a wealthy noble," Nidala persisted. "Or even better, she could've become a priestess and made the *high priest* very happy."

Ishullanu ignored her and called to his assistant, who came rushing.

"Is all taken care of? We're running late."

"Yes, chief. They're all out: maids, singers, dancers, cooks, sentries. All dead or dying, except for one."

"Who's refusing to die?"

"A boy tending to a cow."

"Bring him to me."

Three priests came dragging the boy, who was struggling to break free. When he saw the girl slumped in the chair, strength abandoned him and he collapsed to his knees. He searched her face, silently begging her closed eyes to open.

"You didn't drink the beer?" Ishullanu asked.

The boy was quiet, intent on the girl, desperate for signs of life.

"Maybe he's deaf," the assistant offered. Ishullanu dismissed him with a wave of a hand.

"The king's brew isn't good enough for you?" Ishullanu asked softly. "Why didn't you drink it?"

Amare's chest moved, and a breath of life crept back into Ashur.

She's still alive, it's not my imagination.

"This is not the crowning ceremony?" Ashur murmured.

"Oh, bless the gods for unleashing your tongue." Ishullanu clasped his hands. "The crowning ceremony is about to begin in a short time. But sadly, not here. ... I wonder where?" He rubbed his temple as if thinking. "Must be where they have—*a throne*. I guess you asked the wrong person for directions. Here, we're holding a different ceremony."

Ishullanu whisked off the white cloth covering the altar. "A sleeping ceremony for ... the king sleeping inside this *coffin*. All those invited should feel privileged to join him in sleep, and later wake up in the next life to keep him happy. Well, we didn't tell them about this, but I'm sure they will love the surprise."

Pleased with his humor, a grin spanned Ishullanu's face. He loved dark humor that involved the misfortune of others.

"Cheer up, boy, why the sad face? A ceremony is a ceremony, and it's better to be invited to one than to none. Now again, why didn't you drink the beer?"

"The special king's brew!" Ashur gazed at Amare. "You added the sleeping potion to it. We give that to sick animals; the wrong doses kill them. I know how it tastes; after one sip, I had my suspicions and I spat it out."

"So why didn't you warn your friend here?"

"I never expected this, wasn't sure … thought I might be wrong." Ashur raised his head and looked Ishullanu in the eyes. "I'm the son of the horse tamer in the palace—even the king knows me. Let me leave with her. I can make her throw up and save her. She won't know what happened here, and I won't utter a word about it either. I swear by the gods of heaven I will keep the secret."

"Oh, you work in the king's stables. I'm so honored." Ishullanu bowed slightly. "If I let the two of you go, then I'll have to let her friend go too … and surely your cow would also want to go along. I can trust you and the two girls not to say a thing, but the cow …" He sighed. "Alas, the gods granted me no powers over animals, and, as you know, cows are gossips."

"If I'm harmed, the king will find out, and not even the gods can spare you his wrath. Remember how your priest was beheaded?"

"Listen boy, one foolish priest is never a concern to the gods. However, harming their surrogate on Earth—well, that's akin to asking them for a most dreadful fate; even the most hardened king would fear the consequences. Now that you mention the gods, I believe it was *they* who had you delivered here to avenge the sacrifice of my priest and even the score with Sargon."

Ishullanu cherished that sense of godly might when implementing the powers at his disposal. This next victim would meet a fate no better than that of a rabbit clawed by an eagle.

"She liked you." Ishullanu pointed to Amare. "I could tell from that worried look on her while the army general gave you a scolding. Too bad, now she's on her way to join the king in the next life. Still, it's not too late. Drink the special brew, and you can snatch her before he does. … Someone get him the beer."

A priest brought a cup to Ashur.

"Drink it! Unless you prefer to be buried alive. You can scream all you want; sadly, no one will hear you. A whisper might get through to the surface, but people would assume it's the Galla demons from the underworld having a brawl, or a feast. So, which is it going to be? A slow, agonizing death or a race to join your beloved?"

Ashur looked at Amare. Their young love had been aborted upon conception, sacrificed by priests for some dead king. He didn't hesitate and took the cup.

"Drink it to the last drop," Ishullanu said. "No one will refill it for you in the netherworld."

Ashur stared at Ishullanu while he emptied the cup in one gulp, then hurled the empty vessel at him. The high priest twisted his body and the cup bounced off his shoulder.

"I'm on my way, my love. Wait for me." Ashur fixed his eyes on Amare, ready for his journey to begin.

Ishullanu sneaked behind Ashur, and with his sacrificial knife he sliced the boy's throat open.

"Why keep her waiting?"

Ashur collapsed with the last image of his love to guide his soul.

The priestess Nidala grimaced, eyeing Ishullanu with disgust.

"My departed king will love me for this," Ishullanu beamed. "And the gods—nothing pleases them better than fresh, young blood."

Nidala's face remained twisted into a disturbed contortion.

"Woman, you're getting too emotional!" Ishullanu chided. "We can't wait for him to die, and there's the crowning ceremony to attend. Now, move your lazy arse." He turned to his assistant. "Is everything done as I ordered?"

"Yes, Holiness. All the bodies are laid down in place. The grave of the king, as you can see, is surrounded by his favorite clothing, food, drink, board games, and weapons."

"One more thing." Ishullanu pointed to Amare. "Take this girl off the chair and lay her at the base of the coffin. Hurry up, we still have to close and seal the entrance."

𒀭 𒅍 𒐊

Amare had already slipped far away, unaware of her surrounds. She was walking empty city streets under a moonless night, anguished by an eerie feeling of sinister ghosts watching her. She arrived at a gate where a narrow beam of light squeezed in through the edge. The ray caught the silver ribbon she was holding and its glow stretched and swelled until it consumed the gate. Amare stepped through the breach, and her eyes opened to the dawn of a new day. Far beyond, she could see the silhouettes of the small hills outside the city walls. The sun was about to ascend the hills, and Amare searched for a charioteer with a horse, but only desolation met her eyes.

Sadness found her, and she raced away; she would not let her smile fall hostage to the brigands of sorrow. She ran and ran until she felt the soft touch of grass under her feet, and dew splashed to soft mist that washed over her eyes—tears for those who refused to cry. Then, out of nowhere, a rainbow came to the rescue and floated her to a meadow of flowers that danced to the caress of a jasmine-perfumed breeze. She joined the dance, accompanied by the sweet melodies of singing birds. Her arms stretched wide open as though readying to capture some of this wonder, this miracle of witnessing the birth of a glorious day, before it eluded her like her love had; but she wasn't fast enough.

Loud, blowing wind stormed the air, scattering the birds to the sky, stripping the flowers of petals, and sapping the fragrance from the jasmine. Swirls of dust burned Amare's face as a dark shadow started descending like a hungry predator. Yet she stood defiant and looked up to the heavens, a protest aimed at the cruel gods about to depart her lips. But before her words could launch the attack, the wind decimated them.

Amare was taken aback with awe, for the tempest was but the wake of a winged horse, flapping its giant wings as it descended. The ground shook upon its landing, and Amare shivered in excitement. The gods were forgotten, and her heart burst with joy when a hand emerged through the dust cloud, grabbing hers.

With a cheerful grin on his face, Ashur lifted her up onto the horse, seating her in front on a saddle fit for a queen.

"I was afraid you wouldn't come," Ashur hollered over the wind.

"I didn't come for you," Amare teased. "I was only curious if your dream interpretation made sense."

"So, did I disappoint you?"

"Well, I expected you to show up riding a winged cow, towing a cart."

Together, they laughed.

"I don't see your ribbon. Did you lose it again?"

"It's coiled in my pocket—don't want the wind god to steal it."

"Good, never trust a god."

Ashur tugged on the reins; the horse beat down with its hooves to release the ground's hold on them and fanned the air with its powerful wings, commanding the wind to carry them away.

"Where are we going?" Amare shouted over the roaring wind.

"To the ends of Earth, high above the heavens, where no god or mortal can hurt us."

𒀸 𒁷 𒐲

The priest lifted the girl from the chair, carried and laid her on the brick platform next to the king's coffin. As he walked away, he felt something move behind him. He glanced back and recoiled in fear, losing the reign over his feet, which raced backward, bumping him hard into Ishullanu, almost toppling the man to the ground.

The gods' proxy unleashed a litany of curses, followed by a slap to the face of his foolish assistant. All those who were not honored to accompany the king on his journey to the next life turned their heads toward the commotion that could've disturbed His Majesty's eternal sleep; then, simultaneously, all stares shifted to the girl.

Amare was still asleep, so it seemed, but she was moving. Slowly, she sat up, her eyes snapped open, and she stared at the two priests before her. Like stone pillars, they froze still.

Amare did not see the priests, for she was in a faraway place, soaring the skies. Below her, the hills looked flat and the meadows stretched so far as if they had gulped the horizon. To the east, the rising sun and the sun god, Shamash, shrank to the size of a bug. Amare mused on how beautifully everything had turned out: the singing, the dancing, this ride on the winged horse with the boy she fell in love with. They would be together forever; nothing would separate them. Oh, how she wished for Aunt Tammara to see her now. Amare couldn't wait to tell her about everything ... but there was always tomorrow.

Hurry, Tomorrow, she prayed, *don't take too long arriving.*

It had been a long day and Amare was exhausted. She reached into her pocket, gripped the silver ribbon, then leaned her head on Ashur's chest. She closed her eyes and smiled for eternity.

THE WRITING ON THE WALL

"Yes, Lord, 1 am listening."

"The humans 1 have doomed. Yours is the only family 1 will spare, but my commands you must follow."

"Lord, your commands 1 will faithfully obey."

"Build a large ship; it must be square with three decks and a roof on top. It should be of a size that would accommodate your family and a pair, male and female, of every creature roaming the earth. When the time comes, abandon everything and board the ship without delay."

"Understood, my Lord," 1 said obediently.

Isaa stopped reading and looked away from the wall.

"Father, why all this anger? Why wipe out the humans after creating them in the first place?" the inquisitive young man asked, to better understand the epic story carved on the palace wall.

The unfinished room was huge, seventy paces in each direction. It was destined to be a new library to house a vast collection of tablets in diverse subjects—art, religion, science, history, not to mention the saga that was already inscribed on the wall.

Ibrahem had chiseled much of the story himself, but now he was at work on a statue. He took his eyes off the work and paused to answer his son.

"Men's evil must have reached a level that could not be tolerated. Isaa, don't worry about the details, just work on your reading skills." Ibrahem went on with the chisel, chipping the fine features on the stone bust.

Isaa resumed reading:

The first moon I spent making the plans. The following five moons, I gathered the needed materials. On the seventh moon, I started building the ark with the help of my sons. We never took a break except to eat and sleep, whereas the townspeople never tired from mocking us. They would walk around the structure, some taking off their clothing, and pretend to be swimming, drowning, rowing a boat, or washing their garments.

In the evening, the ark became their favorite gathering place; they would drink, sing, dance, even fornicate in the vicinity. Work was the easy part compared to the pestering we had to endure from the wicked ones. Truth is, the hard work helped us ignore our tormentors. After finishing the boat, we started gathering a pair of every animal breed on Earth.

Curiosity interrupted Isaa again.

"Father, how is it possible to bring all of those animals together? Wouldn't the savage ones eat the docile ones in such a closed space? This doesn't make any sense."

"Cages; they separated them in cages. ... Son, don't distract me, I need to finish this sculpture. Just keep on reading."

Ibrahem was more than satisfied with Isaa's level of reading proficiency. His mind was roving outside the palace, over the menacing, silent storm that always brought a deluge of unrest whenever a new ruler sat on the throne.

As tiny chips flew from the king's bust, Isaa's recital of the epic story echoed again.

Once all the tasks were accomplished, I called up to the heavens, "Lord, I have the ark readied as you instructed."

And the Lord replied right away. "Tomorrow, before the first rays of dawn begin to wrestle the moon away from the skies, go inside the ark with your family. Lock and seal the entrance gate. The rest of the humans, to death I have condemned."

And sure enough, as the Lord promised, the dawn arrived with its golden rays to herald the beginning of a new day. But before I closed the entrance gate to the ark, an ominous cloud appeared out of nowhere, shrouding the horizon from end to end. It carried the darkness of a tomb awaiting the dead. Then, like a beast hungry for its quarry, the cloud raced over the ground. People started running in horror even before the first raindrops fell.

The same people who had been mocking us throughout all those long moons of labor now came rushing to board the ark. I went inside, jammed the gate closed, and sealed it. Instead of the taunts and mockery, there were pleas and cries for help as their hands pounded on the hull. The sound was deafening, like a whole market bazaar of people trying to break down the door. My heart felt a crushing sorrow at their predicament. But I knew if I opened the locks, the flood of humans would sink the ark along with the rest of my family and me. The Lord wished to annihilate them, and who was I to go against the Lord's wishes?

When the Lord saw my pain for those to whom I was denying help, he felt pity for me, and he sent thunder rumbling like legions of drummers that almost tore my ears apart, crushing the pleading noises. Yet, I knew people were still out there. I couldn't stop myself from looking through a hole in the door, and against my earnest prayers, there they were, still clambering for help.

Then, the floodgates opened. The heavens poured out their anger as if the oceans had all climbed up to the skies and taken a swift dive down. Adding to the calamity, another deluge came gushing out of the earth's entrails. Violently, the ship quivered and rolled to one side, doomed to a watery grave, were it not for the mercy of the Lord, who balanced it back to safety.

Peeking through the gate's hole, I could no longer see any trace of survivors. The sole thing visible was water, cascading down so heavily, you could barely see beyond an arm's length. I knew that everyone had washed overboard. Lucky were the ones who drowned right away; those who hung onto driftwood for dear life only made the suffering last, for life would be granted to no other but the fish.

Isaa paused when his father called for two servants to wrap a piece of heavy cloth around the bust and carry it out by the ends of the fabric with extremely cautious steps; dropping the bust of the king would doom their heads to drop under the sword.

"Finally, I'm finished with that." Ibrahem turned to his son. "Go on, Isaa, keep reading. You're almost at the end of the epic."

And so, the rain kept pouring under pitch-black skies. It was impossible to know for how long; there was no way to tell days from nights. The brutal rain sounded like dead bodies of men, women, children—hammering at my head, telling me how selfish I had been in abandoning them. I sat there, helpless, my guilt and sorrow raining down with the tears that joined the waters leaking inside. Only when the wells of my eyes had run dry did the rain suddenly stop.

I peeked outside through the hole, and my heart soared at sighting the stars; their tiny flickers of light poured streams of life deep within my soul. But fear still lingered on, for the Lord could at any moment change his mind and decide to finish off the last traces of humanity—my family and me. Yet, the scent of fresh air was so overwhelming, after all that time in the dung-saturated smell of the ship, that I was ready to sacrifice everything for one deep breath out in the open. I threw the gate wide ajar, and my whole family scurried outside. The exhilaration was immense as we looked up at the night sky that had taken off its dark robe of clouds and dressed in the shiny spangles of countless glittering stars.

But the thrill disappeared when we looked down the side of the ship. There was nothing but water strewn with the floating carcasses of humans and animals, drifting aimlessly as if in search of a gate to the netherworld where they could rest forever. Boats, wrecked and shattered to small pieces, rode the waves as they told the sad story of the ones who clung to hopes of outlasting the flood on flimsy boats. As for the few survivors who boarded the sturdiest ships, theirs was a grimmer story: with all the lands, including the tallest mountain peaks, entirely submerged under one vast ocean, those enduring ships caught the attention of the storms god, who joined forces to help in eradicating the survivors—blowing their ships toward a most dreaded fate, one that filled the hearts of the bravest sea adventurers with horror: the fall off the edges of Earth, down the precipice, into an endless dark pit where even the gods dare not venture.

Isaa stopped reading. Ibrahem was busy cleaning his tools and stowing them away in a leather bag.

"Father, why are the gods so angry—so ruthless in punishment? Aren't they the ones who created the humans lacking in obedience?"

"I should've made you read another epic before this saga of Gilgamesh," Ibrahem replied, "The Epic of Creation. It tells how some gods were so badly drunk one day that they slaughtered one of their own, mixed his blood with dirt, then carelessly, in pathetic attempts to replicate the wonderful creation of their father, Anu, delivered a group of horribly flawed humans. Yes, it's the sad truth, son; all the deranged and wretched of this world are the result of dreadful works by drunk gods."

Isaa pondered for a few moments. "But if Zuisudra was wise and obedient, and we, the humans of today, are all his descendants after that deluge, why are there those among us who still defy the gods? Wouldn't the gods send another flood to wipe out humanity? Next time, it could be for good."

"Isaa, Isaa!" Ibrahem was growing tired of the questions. "If we can't even understand why people do what they do, how are we to understand what the gods have in mind? With their grand powers, moods, vanity … it's a mystery. Don't try to make sense of it. In any case, who knows if this deluge story is true or just another creation of a storyteller—an inflated tale based on a survivor of a great flood? Isaa, I bring you here to improve your reading skills. What you see here is historic: not the story itself, but the first writing of a full story—the Epic of Gilgamesh in its entirety, carved on the wall for all to read. Well, not all—for now, only those with access to this palace. But in the future, stories will be written across walls and on clay tablets everywhere, for all to read and enjoy."

"But, Father, not many people out there can read."

"That will change. More and more people will learn how to read as we progress in teaching this skill."

"What about the storytellers? That will kill their profession."

"Son, I wouldn't worry about them. Not everyone is going to learn the skill. To learn reading, you need to think, and thinking is one of the hardest tasks you can ask of men. Most would rather carry sacks of wheat on their backs all day than make the slightest effort to learn how to write a few cuneiform symbols. In the future, there will be two classes of people: those who can read would be wealthy with decent jobs; the ones who can't—poverty and slave labor to be their destiny. As is always the case, the wealthy and powerful will make sure there is an abundance of those laborers to perform the hard and menial jobs by never allowing them an opportunity to learn and advance."

The two slaves came back, and Ibrahem snapped at them.

"You took your sweet time moving that bust; two maids could've done it faster. Now clean the floor; I don't want to see a single speck of dust."

"Sorry, Master. Yes, Master," they answered with repeated head bows.

Ibrahem turned back to his son. "Isaa, I have an audience with the king. Keep on reading aloud. Let the walls listen to your voice. The echo from these walls will carry their firmness into your heart and make you stronger. Wait here till I come back."

"Yes, Father."

Ibrahem walked away. The two servants kept busy cleaning the floor while Isaa resumed reading.

We looked with broken hearts at the floating ruins, and our hopes sank to the deepest pits of despair. My wife and children had regretted not being swept away by the flood; death they had welcomed to spare them this agony and the suffering yet to come. I dropped to my knees and prayed to the gods to show mercy and end the misery besieging us—the only survivors.

Bless the sun god Shamash, for he was the first to answer my prayers. He sent the rays of his beloved sun to greet us with hope as it climbed, ending the longest night ever witnessed by humans. And

Shamash, as if laden with guilt for confining the sun in the underground tunnels for the duration of the storm, ordered the sun to move at a pace three times slower than normal. He also talked to his half-brother, the storms god, and convinced him to calm the wind that was pushing the ark to the edge of the Earth. Then, Shamash ordered the sun to amass its rays over the highest mountain.

We stood, dazed with joy, witnessing the summit emerge. Oh, what a sweet sight it was—like watching your first child emerge from his mother's womb. We were that newborn, too; our innocent minds dismissed the past and our eyes opened to new hope. Death and destruction drifted beyond the precipice of memories. We sang and danced as the warmth of the sun flowed like a mother's caress over her newborn child.

Then, Almighty Anu sent a gentle wind, steering the ark to settle on top of Mount Nimush. I had to suppress my tears of joy, fearing they might bring the rain back. We all went down, out of the ark, and kissed the mud on the mountaintop. I begged Shamash to intercede on our behalf and asked for compassion so the gods would not abandon humanity again to such a grim fate.

Isaa paused and looked around. The two slaves were gone. There was only him and the walls telling him the story in his own voice.

Seven days later, I set a dove free. It flew away but returned at the end of the day after failing to find any tree branch to rest on. Days later, I released a crow; it, too, returned hungry and tired. I waited a few days, then released a raven. It flew off and didn't return. It must have found trees to rest on and food to eat.

Dry lands began to appear. Tiny islands at first, then steadily they expanded and joined to form large swaths of land that stretched to cover the horizon. I began releasing the animals, a few at a time, until the ark was free of all the wild ones. We gave the gods praise for the mercy they had bestowed on us, and made offerings of slaughtered livestock. We brought out skins filled with beer and wine from the hull of the ark, then infused the air with the sweet fragrance of burned cedar and myrrh. The gods came rushing down from heaven; it had been just as hard for them to live without offerings since the deluge had wiped out all the temples where they had savored those delicacies. They clustered around the offerings from this humble human, Zuisudra. Gods, great and small, cried tears of joy with the emotions of mere mortals.

When mighty Anu saw that, he felt both pain and relief. He stepped off his golden throne and thundered for all to hear, from the highest heavens to the deepest pits of the netherworld:

"I, Anu, father of all gods, creator of everything—the inert and the living, mortal and immortal—have this to say after witnessing the calamity brought on by the Great Deluge: I deeply lament this act—the senseless rage that lured me into executing this vast obliteration of my beloved creation.

"Zuisudra, your relentless struggle, bravery, and steadfast resolve have merited our admiration. I hereby bestow upon you the gift of immortality. As for your family and their descendants, I promise they will never have to fear another disastrous act of this magnitude. ... Now, let's enjoy these offerings by our hero Zuisudra, and celebrate the passing of this colossal calamity that almost sent all my mortal children to the abyss of oblivion."

Isaa stopped reading. He felt as if he were being watched, and slowly, he turned around. Paces away stood a tall man with an inquisitive look, apparently wondering what Isaa was doing in the new royal library.

"Forgive me, sir," Isaa said. "My father, Ibrahem, is the king's sculptor. He told me I could stay here to read the Epic of Gilgamesh on these walls while he is at an audience with His Majesty."

"I know you are Ibrahem's son," the man replied. "You don't remember me?"

"Forgive me, sir, but I don't." Isaa shook his head while his memory raced, successfully retrieving the man's image. Yet, he didn't retract his answer.

The man saw the truth betrayed on Isaa's face; nonetheless, he hid his disdain behind a fake smile. In the upper echelons of society, it was imperative to always maintain courtesy, even with young or low-ranking men. There was no guessing who might one day jump the ladder to a higher rank. One's chances of gaining status and keeping assassins off his back greatly improved when one mastered the art of acting.

"I'm Gudea, Nissan's father. He was in the tablet school with you. We met once."

"Oh yes, now I remember." Isaa's expression of surprise wasn't convincing, but he was still new at this game. He tried to appear as if he had all but forgotten the incident that had first brought them together, although it was as clear in his mind as if it had happened the day prior.

Three winters ago, he and Nissan had attended the same tablet school for reading and writing. The master was absent due to sickness, and the task of assessing the students' writing was temporarily assumed by the "learned brothers"—a name given to the senior students with the highest skills who had been assigned by the master as his substitutes.

One learned brother had approached Nissan and pointed out a significant mistake in his writing assignment, which required the full work to be redone on a fresh clay tablet. Nissan argued and blamed the learned brother for not checking the work when the clay was fresh and soft, which would make it easier to erase and correct the mistake. Learned Brother simply told Nissan that the extra work would improve his skills. Yet, instead of rewriting a whole new tablet, the stubborn Nissan tried a different approach; he moistened the faulty section on the hard clay tablet to soften it, then made the necessary corrections. The patched work was rejected outright by Learned Brother, who deemed it below the school's standards and insisted that Nissan redo the full work.

Feeling snubbed for a trivial error, the short-tempered Nissan cursed, shouting at the master's substitute that a camel would make a better learned brother than he. But Nissan's demeaning words fell on deaf ears, and the stern assistant calmly walked away. Madness commanded Nissan to grab his rejected clay tablet—the size of two hand palms—and smash it on the head of Learned Brother, who swayed in place, barely maintaining his balance. When the assault failed its purpose in quenching Nissan's anger, he briskly charged Learned Brother, shoved him to the floor, and rained punches on his face. The other students stood watching, reluctant to intervene, except for Isaa, who tackled Nissan, and on the floor they wrestled.

The mayhem was extensive; tables shook violently, spilling trays of fresh tablets and sending the day's work for half the class crashing to the ground, their writings ruined. A few students sprang to help Isaa, afraid their own work would be trashed as well. Only then was the crazed Nissan subdued.

Later that day, with the fathers of both boys present, the school chief delivered the punishment: Nissan was expelled from the tablet house, and Isaa was banned from school for a full moon period.

"How is Nissan?" Isaa asked the father politely while his thoughts screamed: *That bully, mad son of yours. Is he still the same pile of dung he used to be?*

Gudea's thoughts were seething with fury, too. *How is Nissan! … The son of pigs dares to ask, as if he missed him.*

"Nissan is doing fine. He's in Babylon, learning the art of making cylinder seals. He's also a learned brother in the Sacred Marduk tablet house."

"I truly regret that incident." Isaa paused, hesitant of what to say. "The quarrel with Nissan. We could've become good friends, were it not for … his temper."

"Oh, that squabble! Don't worry, it's all buried in the past," Gudea smiled, not a whiff of deceit in his voice. "You were children then. Foolishness is part of growing up—part of the learning process. How about you? By the gods, you have grown so much since I saw you last."

"Yes, that was some time ago." Isaa didn't know what more to say. He shifted his feet awkwardly and gazed down at the floor.

"Do you like the stones covering this floor?" Gudea broke the silence. "How about the ones carved with reliefs on the walls!"

"They look so unique," Isaa replied.

"These stones are from Phoenicia—trades I made on previous trips. Those lands in the west are blessed by the gods with large assortments of stones, perfect for building structures that stay tall and last forever—eternal like the gods. Here, in these lands of Sumer, you only have mud bricks to build with; I call those "mortal structures"—like humans, they quickly disintegrate; the elements and ravages of time will reduce them back to dirt."

"You must have seen plenty of those stone buildings."

"Yes, everywhere in Phoenicia, the Nile regions, and lands farther west. There is heavy work for the laborers in the cutting and moving of those stones, but once erected, no storm or flood could erase or shake them even a whisker. Once you build with stones, you don't want to use any other material.

"I've sailed beyond Phoenicia over a sea that is so vast, you have to sail for days to reach its banks at either side. It dwarfs the sea where the Tigris and Euphrates rivers meet by the city of Ur. Those lands bordering the great sea by Phoenicia have riches of rocks so magnificent that our king would be tempted to invade them, if only they weren't so distant—leagues and leagues across the sea."

Isaa heard someone approaching. He let out a subtle sigh of relief at seeing his father.

"Gudea!" Ibrahem greeted, his face chiseled into an expression of happy surprise that hid his distaste. "Bless the gods for bringing you back safely from the far lands of Phoenicia."

"And bless the gods for seeing you in good health, Ibrahem, with your son grown to be so handsome and learned. By the gods, he can read the Epic of Gilgamesh on these walls, and not a single mistake."

Ibrahem nodded his thanks. "Gudea, I greatly lament the loss of your wife."

"It's the will of the gods." Solemnly, Gudea nodded. Though sorrow was tearing him apart, he managed to conceal any emotion, which might be taken as a weakness, and right away he changed the course of the conversation. "I was telling your son about the lands beyond the sea of Phoenicia and their stone riches. I brought back loads of those on this last trip, enough to satisfy the king's appetite for expanding his lush palace. ... I can see your son here, soon to follow in the steps of his father in becoming a palace sculptor, carving the stones on the new palace wings."

"I doubt that, Gudea. Many others are more skilled than Isaa in this art." Ibrahem modestly denied the talents of his son, warding off the evil forces of envy such flattery might attract.

"Nonsense," Gudea argued. "He seems like a smart boy, a fast learner. I can tell, watching him recite the lines on the wall. At this young age, I dare say he reads better than the high priest."

"By the gods, Gudea, he's not half as good as the high priest!"

Ibrahem abhorred the high priest, Ishullanu. The man was more feared than the king himself, and most people believed that the gods responded to his prayers. One rumor alleged that if Ishullanu cursed a man, evil would befall him and all his loved ones. The only way to counter the curse was to visit the temple with generous sacrifices and gifts to supplement the prayers for forgiveness. While the king was the gods' choice to run the affairs of the land, Ishullanu and his priests were the gods' surrogates, ordained with the task of cutting down all those who dared exhibit any hint of blasphemy or disrespect toward the divine authorities of heaven. The priesthood's judgments were final, never to be disputed.

The execution of the priest En-shakush, who had been second only to Ishullanu, presented a challenge to the priests and their authority. Since nothing of consequence had happened to the executioner, Naplanam, or to King Sargon himself, there was a growing threat the people would cease to fear the priesthood.

Knowing this, Ishullanu had acted swiftly to repair the damage. He issued a tablet with a message that was heralded in the main squares of Uruk, disclosing that En-shakush was a disgrace to the priesthood for exploiting his priestly position to enrich himself. It proclaimed that he had stolen from the offerings in the temples and he had gone so far as to threaten people with unmerited curses unless they offered him gifts to spare them the gods' wrath. King Sargon was vindicated for performing the will of the gods to have En-shakush brought to justice, and it was those same gods who guided Naplanam to shed the priest's blood and spare the jester, Gaga.

"Ishullanu is a highly blessed man," Ibrahem answered Gudea, praising the very man he loathed. "Our god Anu himself endowed Ishullanu with intelligence and wisdom second only to the gods. I know of no human who can claim otherwise. Isaa could never match our high priest in any aspect."

Ibrahem spoke clearly for the walls to hear. The high priest had spies, and Gudea's words in praise of Isaa could travel far, only to echo back with the wrath of Ishullanu.

A heavy silence followed. Isaa cast a sidelong glance at his father, seeing agitation scribing its deep lines on his face.

"I think His Majesty is expecting you." Ibrahem said, hoping to tactfully make Gudea leave and end the encounter, which had turned irritating.

"Oh, our king must be impatient to know about the building materials we brought. It was one of the biggest trade voyages, if not the biggest," boasted Gudea. "An army of camels, columns of carts stretching back as far as you can see—some carts so large they needed six horses to pull. Oh, how I wished we had those giant creatures, the elephants from Nubia; we could've used their massive strength. Eight moons we spent trading for stones of all types, from different regions.

"It saddens me that the former king who commissioned me on this endeavor didn't live long enough to see all the building material he sought. But I'm sure King Sargon will be thrilled. ... Well, better not keep him waiting. Ibrahem, I leave you now. May the gods bless you and your family with health and good fortune."

"And may they heap good health and fortune on you too, Gudea."

Gudea walked a few steps, then turned around. "Ibrahem, I forgot to tell you: some stone blocks are not suitable for building but could be useful for sculptures. We marked them with black circles of bitumen. You'll find them in the storage rooms next to the stables. I'm giving those away to the sculptors I know."

"I appreciate your generosity." Ibrahem returned a faint smile.

Gudea made a slight bow and walked away. Ibrahem relaxed his jaw, the fake smile faded out of his face, and immediately he started off in the opposite direction. He needed to get out of the palace to spend more time with the person who made him feel most at ease: himself.

Nothing but the shuffling sounds of their sandals reverberated within the corridors as Ibrahem and his son chased the way out. That gave Isaa the eerie feeling of walls following on his heels. Those walls mostly carried the wisdom and the rules of the land in cuneiform inscriptions, which Isaa had read on previous visits. But he started loathing the walls after he unwittingly had them engrave his mind with details of the harsh punishments suffered by the violators of those rules.

He had witnessed an assortment of appalling savagery administered on doomed men. The most recent had been exacted on enemy captives from the eastern regions. They were forced to dig a large pit, then made to watch as soldiers desecrated and smashed statues of their divine gods. Next, the captives were forced to walk barefoot over their gods' sharp fragments on the way into the pit. Once inside, they were stoned with the same debris and buried. Fortunate were the ones who died before the burial.

Nightmares had haunted Isaa ever since. He would wake up short of breath after an arduous struggle with bodies piling over him in his dreams.

Isn't death enough of a punishment? Isaa always pondered this question when passing a section on the walls that portrayed those savage arts of gore and torture. The cuneiforms on these walls almost came alive to Isaa, silently screaming their agony. He wouldn't be in the least surprised if blood came seeping out of the cuts on the stones. Other inscriptions felt as if they would reach out to snare and nail him to the wall, then follow up with the mutilations portrayed on them.

Isaa couldn't comprehend why he was so soft-hearted. Most of his friends would not miss a single execution. They would drag him along to the event as if it were a festive outing among a lively crowd, to watch up-close the grotesque end of the condemned.

Is this normal, this lust for blood? It occurred to him that his aversion was probably a weakness, and he resolved not to expose it.

How he loathed the day when he had first read those cursed walls. Death takes time off some days, but it never stopped screaming out of those damned stones. Isaa had always wondered if his father had participated in scribing this reviled bloodbath on the walls. Fearing his hate might extend to his father, he never dared ask him.

On the way out, Ibrahem avoided the main wings of the palace, taking a narrow corridor used by the servants and commoners who worked there. At the end of the passage, a heavily fortified door opened to the outside. A sentry gave them a brief glance without saying a word.

Outside, the sun instantly screamed at their faces with an onslaught of the searing rays that Shamash, the sun god, heaped on the city. Humidity was another enemy to confront; the wind god was in a deep slumber, not bothered by the prayers of people who begged for a breeze to give them respite from the stifling mugginess.

The street leading beyond the palace was almost deserted, save for sentries who appeared and disappeared between hidden niches in the buildings. Beyond that zone, as if separated by an invisible barrier, a broad street exploded with life like an oasis on a desert's edge. Throngs of people congregated in the city's main market to satisfy their worldly needs, while others flocked to the temples with gifts and sacrifices that catered to the endless heavenly needs of the gods. In the center of it all was the ziggurat, towering like a god over the surrounding structures, which looked small and humbled as if bowing in obeisance to the mighty ziggurat.

"Master!" A voice leapt across the street and a man came zigzagging between donkey carts loaded with merchandise.

"Yes, Neti," Ibrahem answered without looking at his slave; his eyes were searching for a thought in the distance.

"I've gotten all the foods you wanted, Master," Neti said as he approached, "except for the meat portions. The butcher raised the prices. He claims the priests paid him a visit to bless the cows, and he had to pay them."

"By the gods, greed is spreading like a plague in this city." Ibrahem was furious. "Bless the cows—seriously! What nonsense is this? It's time I paid him a visit. ... Isaa, you continue to your tablet school."

"Yes, Father. See you later, Neti."

"See you later, Isa—Master Isaa,"

Isaa didn't like to be called "master" and had asked Neti not to do so unless his father was around. Sometimes, that slipped Neti's mind.

Isaa smiled at him and went on his way.

"Since when are they blessing animals?" Ibrahem grumbled. "The bastards—another ploy for robbing people. I wonder who the greater thief is, the butcher or the priests!"

"Master, according to the butcher, it's for the coming festival."

Ibrahem fumed. "Every moon we have a couple of festivals for one god or the other."

Most of the merchants had temporary stands, set up each morning and taken down at dusk, but the butcher had secured a brick structure, one of a few such shops in the market.

"Blessed be your day, Master Ibrahem." The butcher met him with an uneasy grin.

"I hope the blessings in your greeting won't cost me extra," Ibrahem snapped at him.

"Ibrahem, my friend, what am I supposed to do? They came—two priests—and said that on festivals, the gods will not accept offerings unless the animal was blessed by the priests while it was still breathing. They made me pay for the blessings."

"Words! Those bastards utter a few words, and I end up paying extra—why? Would the meat taste better after the blessings? Or am I paying for breathing the sweet scents in this shop, wafting from the *fragrant dung* of your *blessed* animals!"

"Ibrahem, I swear I had no choice but to pay for the blessings. May Anu slice me to pieces like a cow if I'm lying. Go ask all the butchers in the market. The priests went around blessing everything—sheep, pigs, goats, ducks, chickens. Men are joking of a beggar who trapped a pigeon, and the priests chased him to bless it—that's how mad it is."

"Fine, but I swear, if you're lying, I will send you the tax man first thing in the morning."

"Ibrahem, you're a good customer. I won't raise the price for you today—but only for today."

"I'm not asking for favors. I'll give you the extra payment."

"No favors," insisted the butcher. "I said it already; same price today."

Ibrahem sent Neti to take the meat home. He walked the length of Ziggurat Road, then turned to Ishtar Walk, where the main temple of the goddess stood. He was greeted by a priestess who offered love in honor of her holiness Ishtar in return for a donation. He politely declined for he had a pressing matter to attend to. He reached a tavern, went inside, and found the owner of the largest brick-making yard that supplied the city. After a little chat and a beer, Ibrahem continued his quest, following the brickmaker's directions toward a parcel of land where bricks were piled high for use in the construction of a new temple. He walked past men who were digging the foundation, studied their faces, praying to find the man he sought. He trailed laborers who carried bricks bundled in reed baskets on their backs like human donkeys, but none satisfied what he was looking for.

"That stone-headed brickyard owner must have been imagining things." Ibrahem spat out his frustration and wiped away the sweat dripping from his eyebrows. Fresh beads raced to retake the territory, clouding his vision, blocking his thoughts. The temptation to walk away empty-handed back to the cool comfort of his home grew stronger as the sun flogged with its rays, whipping more sticky sweat out of his body.

Just when he was about to abandon the search, a movement caught his attention from the foundation pit on the far side. Ibrahem dragged himself to where a man on his knees was spreading bitumen on top of a neat row of bricks. He hopped across the pit to get a better look at the man.

Aware that someone was watching him, the laborer glanced up after embedding a brick in the sticky tar.

Seeing the man's face, Ibrahem gazed in awe. The bricklayer became irritated and began talking in the language of tribes from the western regions—Aramaic. Ibrahem knew a little of the language but couldn't understand, for the man was talking too fast. Then the laborer started using hand gestures, flashing both palms five times, to convey the message that he would be busy on this job for fifty days.

Ibrahem nodded while his hand went into a side pouch and produced a silver piece that gleamed in the sunlight.

"For you to start today," Ibrahem spoke clearly and slowly in

Akkadian combined with the little Aramaic he knew. "Then one more every day. Tomorrow one. After, one more. After, one more."

The man was confused by the mix of the two languages, but, as with all men, the silver brightened his comprehension.

"One day ... one silver?" the bricklayer managed to ask in Akkadian.

"Yes." Ibrahem smiled. "Silver today, silver tomorrow, silver forever."

The laborer dropped the brick he had already picked up, climbed out of the pit, and took the silver. Ibrahem led the way and the bricklayer followed, ignoring the screams behind him from the man in charge of the job, ordering him to go back to work.

The resemblance is miraculous. Ibrahem was stupefied. *The man would've been perfect if only he spoke the language. Oh well, what mostly matters in a double is his appearance. As for speaking, a king need not utter a word if he chose not to.*

Ibrahem forgot about all his discomfort and beamed in amusement. The irony of life—to have a wretched version of king Sargon, in tattered clothes, following him just like his slave Neti!

The Word Merchant of Phoenicia

T**HE TWO WINGED BULLS STOOD HAUGHTILY IN THEIR LUSH NEW** residence, seeming to smile at the man who first sensed their hidden beauty and brought them this glory. Eons they spent as mere stones, unnoticed among giant boulders somewhere in no-man's-land. Now, expertly sculpted into grandiose figures, they dwelled in the royal palace, admired by people from the highest echelons of society.

Gudea stood staring at the winged bull statues. He was too disturbed to greet them like he normally did. That encounter with Isaa and Ibrahem in the library threw his mood into disarray. Oh, how tempting it was to bash Isaa's head against the wall to silence his barking of the Epic of Gilgamesh, then soothe the agony of the cuneiform-carved stones with the boy's blood. But Gudea had not reached the privileged social status he enjoyed by allowing his emotions to run wild.

"Son of dogs, that Isaa," Gudea murmured his rage to the winged bulls. "He must take me for a fool—to say he could've been good friends with my son."

Gudea could never forgive Isaa for the hell he had gone through after his son Nissan was expelled from the tablet house. That reckless school brawl, over a few scribed words not meeting the approval of the foolish learned brother, changed many fates. If only Isaa hadn't interfered, causing the mayhem which followed, the matter would've been treated as just another fight between two boys. Nissan would've been punished with a short suspension from school, and life would've resumed its normal course.

My boy would've been here, in Uruk, not far away in Babylon. My wife's fate and …

Gudea closed his eyes to block the daydreams of the tranquil life he had planned for—plans that destiny had chosen to throw into cruel turmoil.

Finding another good school for Nissan had not been hard. But after that bitter experience, the boy turned more violent, as if that one incident unlocked the gates to a madness that lay hidden deep within him. It didn't take long before Nissan was thrown out of the second tablet house. Gudea sent his son to the city of Larsa, hoping that a change of surroundings would help make Nissan forget the past, but within a moon a messenger was sent all the way from Larsa to inform Gudea that Nissan had smashed a tablet on the master's head, that he was given ten lashes in front of all the students, and was to be kept in detention in a small room until Gudea came personally to take him away.

The next school was one in the city of Eridu. There, it turned so bad, they had to rush Nissan out of the city after he beat a couple of boys and their parents came after him, intending to kill him.

Gudea gave up on his rebellious son, and, in his despair, he broke a most sacred vow.

He had sworn to the Sumerian gods that his former wife would never see her son again after she left him for another man who lived in Babylon. She had accused him of cheating on her during his trips—and she was right. But he was only human; he couldn't resist the temptation of tender company on those long, hard journeys. Meanwhile, she hadn't been faithful either, and once she had secured enough of his wealth in gold and silver, she left for Babylon with her lover.

Gudea married again, and his new wife treated Nissan like a son, but the reckless boy had never reciprocated her affection. After giving up all hope of reforming Nissan, Gudea broke his vow to the gods and sent his rebellious son to his mother in Babylon. He cursed the Sumerian gods the way a drunk man might curse another, not worrying the least about his vows. He blamed the gods for not helping despite the countless offerings he proffered to cure his son of the insane temper afflicting him.

Before sending the boy to Babylon, Gudea had given Nissan a firm ultimatum to correct his ways or else Gudea would disown him and leave him no inheritance—even a single cracked brick from the house would be denied him.

On the way back from his last trip to Phoenicia, Gudea passed through Babylon. The thought of visiting Nissan filled him with anguish, which seemed absurd for Gudea—a man who had traveled to far foreign lands and faced all sorts of perils. Yet this trip to the unknown—his son—felt like the most insane thing to undertake.

What sort of angry demon would I encounter? Wouldn't it be better not to know? Anxiety almost had him turn around upon approaching the house, but his fist was already knocking on the outside gate. A servant opened the gate and led him to Nissan.

The individual who received him had the looks of his son, but something seemed out of place. The young man, without wasting time on greetings, wrapped him in a warm, lengthy hug.

"Forgive me, Father," words of remorse surged, "for all the trouble and hardship I caused. I swear by the gods of Babylon to make it up to you."

This could not possibly be Nissan! Something is very wrong. Disbelief overwhelmed Gudea, then he realized that this son was burying his face in the embrace to hide the tears.

Who are you trying to fool? Where is Nissan? … Could this be a sweet dream? Well, whatever it is, no harm in making it last.

"… and I'm a learned brother in the Sacred Marduk tablet house." Nissan was talking about his achievements as they sat drinking beer in his room, which faced the open courtyard in the house his mother owned.

"Those school masters are torturing me," Nissan said with mock outrage. "They frequently have me instruct the boys while they roam the city for drinking and women. But, Father, I don't care. I like what I'm doing, and all the students respect me because I treat them fairly. … Father, there is something I can't wait to show you." And Nissan walked to a cluttered corner in his room.

Did that woman have identical twins? Doubts sent Gudea wondering about his former wife, who was probably there at the time, in one of the other rooms of her house. *And for some reason, she kept me in the dark about this one, hiding him away in Babylon!*

Nothing made sense to Gudea—this transformation of Nissan, a change no less miraculous than that of an ugly maggot turning into a butterfly. The angry boy who wove trouble all around him had emerged from the cocoon as a man with pride in the beautiful colors of his skills, knowledge, and the responsibilities assigned to him. Gudea remained apprehensive; his son might have an affliction where the madness retreated for short periods before reemerging in full force.

By the gods of Babylon! Gudea mused about the words his son had spoken earlier. *Maybe those gods have something to do with this incredible change!*

But Gudea didn't dwell on that thought; after losing faith in the Sumerian gods, he hadn't adopted any new gods. When a trade deal involved a client who was zealous about a certain god, Gudea would shower praise on that deity, only to appease the client. His faith went as far as securing the trade deal, nothing more.

Nissan came back wearing a pleasant smile; another stunning conversion from the fury that used to mask his face. He slipped a leather necklace over his father's head.

"I made this myself," Nissan said, a hint of pride in his voice.

Gudea's hand slowly reached for the attached stone pendant—an agate cylinder seal. He squinted to decipher the shapes engraved on it.

"Wait, Father." Nissan detached the pin that secured the seal to the necklace. On a table next to them he placed a fresh piece of clay; he flattened it with his palm and rolled the cylinder onto the clay, leaving the impression of the seal, then started explaining its details.

"The boy is kneeling to the gods, repentant, asking forgiveness for mistreating a tender, loving woman—here, standing behind him. She tried hard to be a mother, but he never gave her a chance. ... Father, give this gift to her on my behalf and kiss her for me on both cheeks." And Nissan kissed his father on both cheeks.

A taste of salt touched Gudea's lips—his own tears. After all those efforts to retrieve his son from the demons of insanity had resulted in abject failure, miraculously, a gentle, loving Nissan had been reborn.

The next day, Gudea visited the main temple with a sheep for an offering. Whatever trivial remnants of faith in the divinity he had, were bolstered by the closest thing to a miracle he had ever experienced.

Gudea walked to the altar, knelt, and thanked the gods of Babylon for giving him back his son.

𒌋 𒀭 𒁹

Gudea neared the main reception hall of the palace, where two sentries stood so still they only lacked the wings to give them the appearance of statues. The army general, Gungunum, greeted Gudea from the distance with a nod, but signaled for him to wait where he was.

A team of priests, headed by their chief, Ishullanu, closely studied the liver and twisted intestines of a slaughtered sheep that lay splayed on a table. Opinions and arguments were exchanged in interpreting the subtle clues embedded in the folds of those entrails—omens that foretold of future menaces and turmoil. King Sargon was pacing behind, impatiently, eager to hear their findings.

Gudea watched the new king. They had met on a few occasions when Sargon was still a general, but they had only talked briefly. Back then, Sargon seemed aloof, off in a distant world.

Many were the rumors about Sargon's mood swings. One gossip maintained that he had beaten his wife to death right after she had given birth to their daughter, Enheduanna, because he wanted a son— even though his wife had already given him a male heir, Naram-sin. Gudea heard this from a drunk noble at a royal banquet. Yet openly, people spoke of how Sargon loved his wife and showered her with all that a woman desires, and how her sudden death at childbirth was the culprit behind his volatile moods. As for his daughter, he quite often called her "Princess," as if he knew he was destined to be king.

But there was one thing about Sargon that no one contested: he was a rare general who fought alongside his soldiers and shared the scars of war with the bravest among them. No one was surprised that as soon as the former king was on his deathbed, Sargon wasted no time in marching on the palace with his loyal army to take control of the city and declare himself the future king. The noble who slandered Sargon as a wife-killer went missing a few days later. There were no rumors about what happened to him; the only gossip was about where he had moved to—the bottom of the river or farther west, under a sand dune.

While waiting, Gudea mulled over all the privileges extended to him: to walk the palace halls with all its wide spaces, lush with riches from all over the world, exchanging pleasantries with the elite nobles. Weirdly, all of that had become no more exciting to him than strolling through an open market bazaar.

No guard stopped him on his way to meet Sargon the Great, King of Sumer, the most feared king of all lands from sunrise to sunset and all that lies within the four corners of Earth … on and on the list went with title upon title heaped on His Majesty—words which elevated certain mortals closer to the gods.

"Words," Gudea whispered to himself. He had been in awe of the power of words since the day when fate had come to him dressed in the form of a mature man.

Would I be here today had fate not chosen my ears to hear those words? Gudea's thoughts carried him back to the past, to the faraway place of his birth: Phoenicia.

𒀭 𒂍 𒐲

He was a small-time merchant in the market. A man was haggling with him over the price of a wide leather belt studded with jasper stones. Gudea lost his patience when the man insisted on a price and refused to go any higher.

"I'll give you the belt at this price on one condition," Gudea finally said. "I wrap it around your neck till you stop breathing."

The man cursed him and walked away, and Gudea lashed back with curses of his own.

"Do you need help, sir?" Gudea was still fuming as he addressed another customer; one about the age of his father, who had passed away the previous winter.

"How much for that belt?" the man asked.

Gudea was stunned for a moment, then grinned in disbelief. "By the balls of Baal! Where do you people come from? Weren't you here when I was screaming at that mule-face? You must be hard of hearing, old man. One silver piece!"

"No need to shout; my hearing is fine," calmly, the man answered. "Now, I don't have any silver, but I'm willing to barter."

"I don't see anything on you to barter with."

"I have words," the man said assertively.

"Did you say *words*?" Gudea could not suppress a chuckle. "Thank you for the humor. Now keep moving, old man, I'm not in the mood."

"Yes, words. That's what I will give you for the belt."

"Old man, you want this fine belt in exchange for *words*? Not only are you hard of hearing, but you're going senile too. Save your breath and keep your words, you might live a day longer."

"The secret of success in any trade is not all in the goods you sell; a good part of it goes to *words* spoken well," the man recited, then paused briefly. "You don't have to give me the belt now. I'll be back for it in ten days."

"*That's it!* You're totally insane!" Gudea shook his head. "Some barter! I'll go broke sooner than I thought."

"I shall be back for the belt in ten days," the man repeated, and started to turn away.

"Old man—or should I say, *word merchant*—don't show me your face again—not in a day, ten days, a whole moon, or *ever*. You hear?"

"My noble merchant, I already told you, my hearing is fine," the man answered, solemnly. "I just hope that *you* heard *my* words. I shall be back, and I trust you will honor your end of the deal. Have a good day, and may the gods bless you and all your loved ones." And he walked away.

Gudea went silent. He felt deflated and ashamed of himself, as if the man had actually given him something precious and left with nothing in return.

Ten days later, shortly after dusk, merchants were stowing away their goods under whizzing bats that reveled in displaying aerial skills gained by trading grace in flight for demonic maneuvers unmatched in their frenzy by any other creature of the air.

Gudea was standing with his merchandise already stashed away in leather sacks when he caught sight of the word merchant. He slung the sacks over his shoulders and walked toward the man.

"Good day, noble sir. I believe you came for this." Gudea handed him the belt, then went into his pouch and came out with a small silver piece in the shape of a duck with its head tucked along its back. "I feel like I cheated you on the deal. This silver piece will better even the trade."

The word merchant took only the belt. "A deal is a deal, and I'm happy you honored the agreement." He wrapped the belt around his waist. "Does it look good on me?"

"It looks magnificent—wiped a dozen winters off your age. I see a handsome young man."

The word merchant laughed, then gazed at Gudea for a long moment.

"May I barter another deal with you?" he asked.

"Say it, my noble sir, and consider it done."

"You," the man said. "I want to barter for you."

Gudea was tempted to curse him; yet, to his amazement, he managed to smother the impulse.

"I'm not for barter. I am not what you think!" Gudea turned around to leave.

"You are exactly what I think," the man called out to his back. "A man to be trusted, a man of honor, and a man I can rely on to help me in my trade; those are the goods in you I wish to have."

Slowly, Gudea turned around. "I thought … you had me confused for a moment. I completely misunderstood." A smile crossed his face. "May I give you a few *words* of wisdom: The secret of success in any trade is not all in the goods you sell; a good part of it goes to *words* spoken well."

The man laughed. "And a wise *word merchant*, too. Now I'm even more determined to get you." He paused, ruminating. "I was about your age when an old man approached me just as I approached you. He offered me *words* in exchange for a wool garment, which, to no surprise, drove me mad. The rest of the story, you already know. Now here I am, doing the same. That's why I feel like I know you as I know myself.

"Do you think you're the only one I approached with words for barter? No, there were many others. All ridiculed me, some threatened to beat me. Anyway, what matters is this: when I went back, I found that many ignored my words—stubborn, not the type that want to learn. Others listened and benefited just as you did, however, when I asked for my part of the deal, they either laughed, waved me away, or gave me something worthless. Their greed surpassed their appreciation.

"Now! I have no family and my partner, my mentor, wants to retire for whatever time he has left in this world. I trade in stones, mainly for building and sculptures. I travel to faraway lands, far across the sea of Phoenicia and up north of the lands of Assyria, to get those stones. I take them to the lands of Sumer, where all the great cities are—Uruk, Eridu, Isin, Mari, Ur, Babylon, and many others. There you have the most powerful rulers on Earth, and with their power comes riches. As you might know, those lands were not blessed by the gods with stones. They build with mud bricks—clay hardened by the sun or baked in kilns. But the rich nobles covet stones. So, if you're interested in learning the trade, if you're ready to work hard and have no fear of crossing seas and deserts, you may join me. Wait for me here tomorrow morning when the sun is a full circle over the horizon."

Gudea stood silent for a moment, then sat down on the ground. The man looked at him, puzzled.

"Noble merchant," Gudea said. "I'm not moving from this spot till you return tomorrow morning."

"Then I have to impose the condition that you go home and get some rest, for the goods I'm trading for—by which I mean *you*—might get damaged if left out in the open through the night."

The man reached with his hand, helping Gudea stand up. "I leave you in the protection of the gods. Now go home."

Gudea stood unyielding.

"Go home, young man. Now!"

Reluctantly, Gudea walked away like a child following an elder's command.

Two winters later, after numerous training assignments, the day arrived when Gudea walked through the city gates of Uruk, and he found that his expectations were modest compared to the beauty and excitement displayed before him in that city. When it was time for the return journey, sadness filled his heart, though that made him all the more determined to work hard; he had stepped into a dream and resolved to grab hold of it so it would never escape his reality.

Gudea had achieved it all and was living the dream, but before long, nightmares found him and started visiting his reality uninvited. His first wife had left him for another man. Then, his second wife, whom he loved and always longed for on his trips, left him too—not for the embrace of a lover, but for the dark, murky depths of the Euphrates River. He had paid the high price fate demanded for the goods it delivered. And fate couldn't have timed the payment in an uglier way—just when he was going to surprise his wife with the decision that he was done with traveling, that he would visit the market to look for a vendor who would barter an item of value for a line of wise words from a word merchant.

𒀭 𒁉 𒐖

Waiting outside the reception hall of the palace, Gudea couldn't help but muse. *What if fate had not brought about that brief encounter with the man who became my mentor? Most likely, I would still be selling belts in Phoenicia; my grand dreams of Uruk diluted in time, forgotten with age.*

He was startled out of his reverie by the sudden waving of a hand. King Sargon was urging him to come forward. Gudea sprang in a rush, bowed his head upon approaching the king, then dropped to his knees in obeisance.

"Forgive me, Your Majesty, I wasn't aware it was me you needed. I am Gudea the Phoenician, back from the trip commissioned by the departed king—may the gods give him peace in the afterlife. I am here to serve Your Majesty in every way I possibly can."

"Stand up, Gudea," said Sargon. "You don't need this entire introduction; I remember you from previous encounters—my memory is still intact." He turned to the men clustered around the dead sheep. "Honorable priests, you may leave now. Ishullanu, I'm grateful for the premonition and will heed your advice."

"Majesty, may the gods always watch over you and protect you from all evil." Ishullanu offered a slight bow and left with the other priests.

"So, Gudea," Sargon said, smiling, "our friend from Phoenicia. Thank the gods for your safe return."

"O Great King, I am much honored that a lowly merchant like me would be remembered by Your Majesty." Gudea bowed again.

"Gudea! If you are a lowly merchant, then I am a queen of bees!" Sargon laughed and put an arm around Gudea's shoulder.

Not expecting the embrace, Gudea couldn't contain a startled look of surprise.

"Don't worry, I won't sting you. If I were to sting anyone, it would be those priests who bring nothing but bad news," Sargon quipped, then gestured to the army general, who remained in his presence. "I presume you already know Gungunum, my most trusted general."

"Yes, Sargon, I know Gudea," Gungunum interjected, "since way back before you grew a sting needle."

"Why are you studying the entrails?" Sargon asked the general.

Gungunum shook his head while squinting over the sheep's bowels. "I don't understand! Priest or no priest, it's impossible to make any sense out of this clutter. I believe this practice of predicting the future from animal guts is nothing more than the load of dung you find inside them."

"I have to take their warning seriously, just in case," Sargon replied. "So, Gudea, how did your trade mission go?"

"Praise the gods, it was very successful, though I give much credit to the soldiers who accompanied us. They must be lauded for their bravery as we faced countless perils and raids by the barbarian bandits—the dwellers of the cedar forests of Lebanon and the vast desert. Sadly, we lost a few valiant soldiers, but that is something expected in any undertaking of such a grand scale."

"Gudea, I hope you brought plenty of cedar tree logs?" Gungunum asked. "We have tunnels to build."

"Yes," Gudea answered, "the logs should arrive in a few days. We cleared large expanses of cedar forests in the mountains of Lebanon; the scent of the bleeding forest reached the heavens. The gods had been negligent for not sending another monster to protect their forest after their horrendous guard Humbaba was slaughtered by Gilgamesh. I guess by now they have corrected that mistake, only after we claimed our harvest of trees. ... But, why use cedar? This durable, heavenly scented wood is best used in furniture and plush rooms—not tunnels."

"Well, Gudea, those priests studied the entrails of the sheep," Gungunum explained. "Aside from the bad dung ... they saw some bad omens in the liver and the twists of the intestines. They say Sargon's life is in danger—in what way, they don't know. It could be poison slipped into his food; a man, a woman assassin, or perhaps a mad slave—we've had a few of those kill their masters. Or it could be a band of traitors. We need to prepare for all threats. This palace doesn't have any secret tunnels, so we're going to build one using the cedar logs for support. This talk is to be kept a secret among us. We know you're a man to be trusted. In fact, we trust you more than any Sumerian out there."

"And who is going to do the work and keep the secret?" Gudea asked.

"Who else but you, the master builder, and *His Majesty*, Sargon!" Gungunum laughed. "No, that will take forever. Well, we have some war prisoners from the last campaign. Good food and drink will give them an incentive to work. Once the job is completed, they'll be rewarded with a feast they never dreamed of in their whole miserable lives, and some exceptional wine will send them deep into a dream— its tunnels lead straight to the netherworld."

TABLET HOUSE

"CURSED BE THIS DAY!" GRUMBLED THE HEFTY ROYAL GUARD, Tiny, whose nickname jokingly contrasted with his size. "And cursed be the day when our god Anu chose to give wisdom to this Nabu god, protector of those fucking scribes. Oh, how I hate the learned with their tablets. They get all—wealth and power, simply by sitting on their arses, scribing on clay. Meanwhile, soldiers like us face enemies who want to scribe on our flesh—poke our bodies with swords, spears, and arrows. Our blood ends up mixed with the enemy's blood, turning dirt into mud—to bake under the sun. And what do you get for protecting the kingdom—an honorable burial in the sacred warrior ground! That is, if they don't abandon your shredded body for the dogs and vultures to feed on."

"Let's enjoy an easy day, Tiny, stop whining!" replied Killer, his small-built companion. "Do you think I like being here outside this knowledge house, standing guard all day? No. I would rather be in battle, hacking at flesh and bone. *But*, it's good to get a taste of peace— be nice to people sometimes."

The man was nicknamed "Killer" for a skill and savagery in battle that belied his docile appearance. Many brave and strong enemy soldiers had confronted him, slightly dropping their guard, confident he would be an easy kill, only to be cut down swiftly and fall mortally wounded with an expression of surprise dressing their death agony.

Killer searched the ground, now and then leaning down to pick up stones and pebbles of two sizes. Having gathered enough stones for his next duel, he carved a large square in the dirt with the point of his sword, then crossed it with lines, making smaller squares inside—the only drawing he excelled at.

"Tiny, forget about Nabu and his disciples, and get ready for a good board game—a rematch. There's no way you're going to win this time. Here, Tiny, yours are the large pieces."

The burly guard laughed. "Killer! In real battle, you earned your title. But in this board game, the dogs will be licking your wounds."

𒀭 𒂍 𒐊

Boys started arriving at the gate, and as they did, each gave the guards a solemn greeting. Tiny and Killer responded with an intimidating gaze that made the boys quicken their pace to a near-run. The guards laughed, savoring their powers at instilling fear in these future elites of society.

Isaa met his friend Samian at the end of the road leading to the school. Samian was the first to notice the two guards.

"Isaa, what are those two doing here?"

"Royal guards. A royal envoy might be visiting."

"Isaa, don't make any smart comments," Samian whispered, even though they were beyond earshot of the two guards. "A nod, a short greeting, and fast through the gate we go."

"Two miserable guards and you fear them like gods!" Isaa taunted, not bothering to lower his voice. "A few winters from now, they'll come asking you to write them a letter of assistance from the city for their heroic services. And not long after that, they'll be lying on the roadside, drunk and begging."

"The only one I see begging is you—for trouble. Isaa, by Anu's sacred arse, don't fool with them. Keep that big mouth of yours shut."

"Oh, the blasphemy!" Isaa quipped. "It's my duty to inform on you for this insult to his holiness, father of all gods, Anu. Where are those guards when you need them? Ah, there."

Before Samian could respond, Isaa rushed toward the guards.

"May Anu bless your day." Isaa nodded in greeting and went past the guards, then promptly stepped back to stand over the game board carved up in the dirt.

"Interesting game. Samian, come take a look," Isaa called.

Though Samian kept his distance, Isaa went on with the comments.

"Quite an intriguing game … small pieces side is in trouble, already two pieces down. Yet, there is one move that could reverse the outcome—one smart move."

"Killer, you hear that?" Tiny grinned. "This means if you lose, you're not smart enough for this kid."

Killer furiously kicked the stones off the dirt board, swiftly gripped Isaa by the top of his tunic, and pushed him hard against the wall.

"Yours must be the small pieces." Isaa swallowed, realizing that the guard's demeanor didn't match his docile looks.

"A smart boy! Surely, he is." Killer stabbed out the words with a sharp tongue. "But only in board games. As for the game of life and death, *stupid—fatally stupid!*"

"Forgive me," Isaa said nervously. "I meant no insult; I was just trying to make the game more interesting." He glanced at Samian, aware that he had made another slip of the tongue.

Samian glared back. *I told you to shut your mouth*, said the expression on his face.

"So, my game is boring you," said Killer. "Huh, you think you're special because you know how to scribe on mud! Well, mud boy, I too relish playing with mud. It really excites me, especially when I pile it to bury smart people like you, *alive!*"

Isaa knew he was in trouble. It wasn't his first time committing an act he came to regret later; something reckless in him—an impulsive drive—plunged him into situations ordinary people would avoid. Up until that moment, the outcomes had been relatively benign, but this time luck abandoned him when confronted by a royal guard who went by the name "Killer."

"Let go of him at once!" A commanding bark erupted from behind.

Instantly, Killer took his hands off Isaa before turning to the source.

"What's going on here?" demanded the chief of guards, Hukura, who had just arrived on the scene.

Tiny stepped forward to defend his partner.

"Honorable Chief, these two were playing a board game outside." He gestured at Isaa and Samian. "We told them to go inside, but they refused. So—"

"Let me guess what followed," Hukura interrupted him. "So, these two *tough, fearless* kids decided to pick a fight against my two *vulnerable* royal guards—since, of course, the odds were stacked in their favor. But *luckily*, I happened to be in the neighborhood to save your skins. What time did you two arrive here?"

"At sunrise, as ordered, sir," Tiny answered.

"The story is getting better. So, it seems … these two boys came before sunrise to play a board game *in the dirt, in the dark*. I guess they couldn't wait for the gate to open to go inside, where they must have a nicer game set." And Hukura snapped in a fury. "Have you no shame? Trying to fool me with such a fucking stupid story in front of everyone here!"

The chief composed himself and turned back to a girl in his company, flanked by two more guards. "I apologize. Do forgive my language."

He shifted his gaze down to study the game board. "One, two, three, four … six lines up. One, two, three … six lines across. You two, since you like this game so much, you will be rewarded with a board that you can carry all the time, wherever you go. It should make you smarter, so next time you'll come up with a better story when you want to fool a high-ranking commander."

Hukura turned to one of the guards flanking the girl. "When these two go back to the quarters after this assignment, tell the commander to carve a similar game board on their backs with a dagger. That's an order, and I'll personally check if the work is carried out to my satisfaction. Also, assign two different guards to take their place tomorrow."

"Yes, Chief."

Isaa was still standing in the same place, but his attention strayed from all the trouble he had caused and rested on the girl. She was dressed in a simple white tunic with a plain white shawl over her shoulders. A leather necklace with a cylinder seal of green jade hung over her upper chest. Her smooth dark hair fell below her shoulders.

She had the fair, unpunished skin of nobility; the sunrays of Shamash that scorched the commoners had had trouble finding her.

The sweet scent of jasmine floated on a wispy breeze toward Isaa, who stood some ten paces away, craving a glimpse of her face. But she stood sideways to him, fixated on the chief and his diatribe.

More students were arriving now, and Samian sneaked with a group of them through the gates while Isaa remained still, patiently hoping to catch the girl's eyes.

"What are you waiting for?" Hukura screamed in Isaa's direction. "Do you want a game board on your back too?"

Right then, the girl's attention was drawn to Isaa, giving him a brief glimpse of her face as he started to move, but the distraction had him stumble off balance on a stone. Embarrassed, he rushed to the tablet house, possessed by an urge to take another glimpse back at her. By the time he found the courage to turn his head, it was already too late; her back was to him as she walked with the guards toward another compound of rooms. He was about to move on, when some force turned his head further back to look beyond the gate.

Chills ran through him when his eyes locked on another pair of eyes—those of Killer—cold with fury.

𒀸 𒋗 𒍣 𒉿 𒌍

Nabu, father of scribes, fountain of knowledge,
We treasure your guidance—your favor for this privilege.
Give us the diligence and needed skill.
Help us finish the tasks with patience and will.
The hand with a pen, make it steady and sharp,
To leave pleasing marks like music from the harp.
Shamash, hallowed are the sunrays you shower on the tablets,
Enki, we beseech you to ward off the rain droplets.
O Nabu, bless the mud to carry your wisdom,
Forever to last throughout the kingdom.

The boys finished reciting the prayers and remained standing in wait for their master, Ur-nammu, to tell them to sit down. He seemed to be lost in thought, when abruptly he snapped, startling everyone.

"Cursed be this day!"

Having noticed the students still standing, he waved for them to sit. Grudgingly, he rose off the wool cushion that covered a brick bench. Back and forth he paced until he found a trail of words to follow.

"Boys, before we begin the class, I need your absolute attention. A new student will join us. Things will change immensely with … her arrival."

The boys exchanged glances of surprise, seeking confirmation of what they had just heard.

"Yes, you heard that right—*her*. 'Enheduanna' is her name, and if you're not familiar with the name, she's the daughter of King Sargon." Ur-nammu paused to swallow his frustration.

Confused chatter erupted among the boys. Ur-nammu didn't bother to silence them but raised his voice.

"In my whole life, I've known of no woman who has taken on the study of the reading and writing arts. Not in this land, not in the land of the Nile, or the Phoenician territories; not in any realm within the four corners of Earth. And here we are … *blessed* to have a girl joining our classes—and not just any girl, but *a princess*.

"This will bring nothing but trouble to the tablet house. I talked to our chief master, Akiya, and he told me he would *try* to convey a message to the king in hopes of convincing him to reconsider his approval of this blunder. Yet, earlier today, *our princess* was briefed about the general rules and workings of the school, before starting tomorrow."

Ur-nammu looked so miserable, as if the girl were some god's wrath, sent for the sole purpose of obliterating the tablet house along with those attending it.

"Master, permission to speak." A boy raised a hand. Ur-nammu gave him a nod.

"Did the gods approve of this?"

"Supposedly, yes. The king consulted the priests, and approval didn't take long to arrive after the king gave them a feast—and most certainly filled their pockets with gifts of precious stones. So, to no surprise, the gods *loved* the idea and blessed our tablet house with—A GIRL!" Ur-nammu couldn't contain himself, shouting like a madman in a bustling Uruk market.

The boys were bemused; they had never seen their master so worked up. He was always composed and soft-spoken. Even when administering punishment to the unruly, he never showed undue emotion. This unmitigated rage made some boys think that a demon had possessed him. No one dared ask any more questions.

Again, Ur-nammu started pacing the floor and resumed talking, though he seemed to be talking to himself.

"And our chief master … huh, I must be dreaming to think Akiya would change anything. Most likely he's sitting right now, marveling about what sort of a gift from the king would soon be stuffing his pocket.

"This is a travesty. The whor—" He managed not to finish the curse. "She, Her Highness, has bestowed upon us the favor of *modesty*. She says, 'Call me Edunna, not Enheduanna, simply Edunna. And absolutely no honorifics nor any exceptional treatment.' She wants to be treated just like the rest of the boys—a boy with a vagin—" He stopped short again. "That is, as long as she's within the confines of the tablet house. Now, outside, she reverts to—Her Highness. The two guards you see by the gate will escort her on the way from and to the palace. Do not provoke trouble with the guards. I know you all come from wealthy, reputable families, but that will not help you. … Isaa! What was that commotion about this morning?"

Isaa stood, his head down. "Nothing, Master. I just made a comment about a board game they were playing. One of them didn't like it."

"Boys, listen very carefully, all of you. You spend your time after school strolling the streets, in the market, thinking about what to feast on, which clothing to buy, or which precious stone will go better with your sandals. Now, guards like those outside have experienced the other side of life—the very ugly part; they were tossed into bloody battles, tearing enemies limb from limb, literally shredding them. They love to wear the red color of blood and relish the taste of it on their lips. The slaughter field is their favorite market bazaar; if a dead enemy soldier wears rings on his ears or nose, they take and wear them—with the man's ear or nose still attached. After a victory, they walk with enemy heads spiked on spears. They are the elite in the savage art of killing; *that* is what qualifies them to be royal guards. Now, a job like this here, standing outside all day, bores them to death; and a bored killer is a savage, thirsting for blood to spill. So, this is my advice to you: do *not* be their amusement. Understood?"

"Yes, Master," the boys answered in subdued voices.

"Good. Considering this new development, I have urgent tasks to deal with and won't be able to instruct you today. Just get busy with matters where you need improvement. Practice making clay envelopes. Remember, you must have the right consistency of mud in your envelope, so it won't crack easily. After all, a broken envelope rather defeats its purpose in securing the message on the tablet inside. ... Samian, Isaa."

"Yes, Master." They stood up.

"As learned brothers, you take care of the class while I'm away. I still have hope that the gods will intervene, and tomorrow Shamash will flush away this dark veil of a nightmare with his sun-rays and greet my eyes with good news." And Ur-nammu walked out.

Isaa was throbbing with an excitement that kept him awake the whole night. The shadowy image of Enheduanna, or Edunna, never left him alone.

𒈦 ◇ 𒀸 ᴡ 𝗜𝗜𝗜

During prayers the next morning, the boys sounded as if they had lost their voices through a collective malady. One voice dominated all the rest—that of the girl, Enheduanna.

Ur-nammu was sitting, holding a tablet, but he wasn't reading; hearing Enheduanna pray clouded his eyes with fury.

These cursed boys are not helping. Speed up the fucking prayers! His body stiffened with the effort to rein in his rage.

The boys weren't keeping their voices down because they were timid in the presence of the princess, but rather to better hear her sweet voice reciting the verses. Hers was a soft, delightful melody that stole from the praise venerating the gods. And, to savor the girl's singing longer, the boys went slow with the prayers. If they had the choice, they would've prayed to all the gods of Sumer, Babylon, the Nile, and the lands beyond.

After enduring the girl's oration, Ur-nammu cleared his throat and looked up with red eyes that had seen no sleep the prior night.

"Before we start the class … let us give a warm welcome to a new student—Edunna."

She stood up, nodding her head in acknowledgment. Ur-nammu opened his mouth to continue the introduction, when Enheduanna unexpectedly began to talk.

"It is my pleasure to be in this class; more like a dream come true. I know some of you might feel I shouldn't be here—that I am imposing—simply because my father is the king. But I swear by the gods of heaven that I am doing their will in drinking from the fountain of knowledge they have bestowed on our gracious land. Thank you."

Anger scattered the words Ur-nammu had prepared, leaving him lost, not knowing how to continue, when a voice came to the rescue.

"Permission to speak, Master."

"Go ahead, Isaa."

"Yes, Master. We made an assortment of clay envelopes yesterday. Would you like to check them?"

"Not today. Good job, boys, good. Let's start with some …" He paused to collect his thoughts. "Isaa, go over some lessons with Edunna to appraise her reading level."

"Pardon me, Master." Enheduanna stood up and spoke without asking permission. "I'm advanced in my reading skills. I have read the Epics of Creation and Gilgamesh, among other writings. It's only scribing skills that I lack, Master."

Ur-nammu was almost choking with rage. He would've loved to find out who had taught her to read and savage him to death.

"Isaa, use the writing wax trays to start with Edunna," he instructed with a strained voice.

"Master, out of curiosity," Enheduanna stood up again. "In the land of the Nile, they invented a way of writing on papyrus. It's a very light material, almost like a feather, and—"

"I'm familiar with papyrus," Ur-nammu interrupted her. "It's a material that won't endure the adverse effects of nature. Wind will blow it away and rip it to shreds. Tiny drops of water dissolve the inked words into blots of nonsense. If fire rages, papyrus will add fuel to the flames before it goes up in smoke. Papyrus writing is an invention that time will render useless."

"But, Master, many learned men say this will be the future of writing," Enheduanna replied courteously.

"Edunna, it won't be the future here, or anywhere. The day we use it for writing will be the day we use papyrus instead of clay bricks to build palaces."

The boys laughed, giving Ur-nammu the courage to wage an attack on a different front.

"If you really believe in this papyrus thing, then by all means, go to the land of the pharaohs. I'm sure our Great King Sargon can arrange for a *papyrus* school there. ... Never forget, writing started here; this very land of ours was the first to be blessed by the gods with the gift of writing—on mud tablets, not papyrus. And that is how it will continue—on mud tablets." He turned to the boys. "Very well, class, I have to attend to some important matters. Keep yourselves busy with the works I assigned you."

Ur-nammu knew he hadn't assigned any tasks to his students, but he had reached the limits of patience and was desperate to rush out—to make sure he had the last word. If Enheduanna were to utter a word more, it would drive him to curse the whole royal family. And one thing he was certain of: Sargon would not appreciate that.

Doubles, Delusions, and Reflections

"**I**'M STARTING TO FEEL LIKE A STATUE MYSELF—SITTING LIKE A statue."

Sargon complained and shifted on his throne in discomfort. "How much longer will this take?"

"Have patience, Your Majesty. I'm almost done," Ibrahem answered while chipping away at a bust of the king.

"Maybe I should put my double to some use and have him sit for the sculpture."

"Majesty, then it will be a fake sculpture. Like lead layered with gold, it won't possess your inner strength, your bold and majestic ferocity."

"Fine, Ibrahem, just speed it up," Sargon said, then laughed. "My double, he surely looks like me. Imagine me as a bricklayer!"

Ibrahem smiled. He was tempted to tell Sargon that it had been the first thought to grip his mind upon seeing the man.

"Your Highness, he's nothing like you in character. He's but a wretched fool with the smarts of a donkey."

"By the gods, Ibrahem! I keep telling you I'm tired of hearing honorifics—Majesty, Your Highness, King of Earth from sunrise till *dung*-set. I get enough of this in the formal receptions. I enjoyed it in the beginning, but now it's so annoying—makes me want to abandon the throne. My arse is getting sore with everyone around keen on kissing it. I can imagine the day when they show up and say, 'Majesty, we have this gift—a dagger—let us help you wear it, Your Highness.' In the back they stab me and say, 'Hmm, O Great Sargon, maybe it will look better in the stomach.' Another stab. 'Magnificence, let's try the four corners of your body.' Stab, stab, stab, stab—thus the stabbing will go on, sunrise till sunset.

"I pity the gods for having to endure listening to all those glorifications by the countless people of the land. It must be driving them insane. So in return, they strike us with disasters—plagues, floods, droughts. Maybe I should issue a decree to ban praying—give the gods some rest—like, once every seven days."

"Your—" Seeing the look of disapproval from Sargon, Ibrahem trapped "Majesty" before it escaped the tip of his tongue. "You have a good thought there, but I'm sure the priests would not approve."

"The priests … what am I supposed to do with those devious priests? They have the backing of the people through the fear of the gods. That bastard Ishullanu, he dared retaliate for the execution of that foolish priest of his by burying the son of my horse trainer. He says the boy must've ended down there, in the burial chamber, by accident. That boy, Ashur, was a marvel—rode on the back of the horse like a falcon riding the wind. We could've learned a few things from him. Imagine our soldiers riding those horses and charging the enemy! We would be unstoppable; all city-states would kneel to our armies.

"Ibrahem, my men say good things about you, which confirms my trust in you. People outside don't know you are my personal sculptor, and those who know don't think of you as any more than just another sculptor. I want you to blend in with the commoners, be my eyes and ears in the streets of Uruk, so during these long sculpting sessions we can talk about whatever happenings might prove to be crucial— specifically, the sway those priests have on the common man. Those 'wrath of the gods' sermons they preach could turn the people against me. If there is a plot to topple me, the priests would be the ones weaving it. They cause me a lot of anxiety, and now, after killing one of their own, I must have become their main adversary."

"You shouldn't fear them," Ibrahem said in a sure voice. "You have been chosen by God to lead our people."

"What god chose me?" Sargon was intrigued.

"None other than Anu, the father of all gods."

"You're not a priest, Ibrahem. How would you know the will of the gods?"

"A dream I had days ago." Ibrahem dropped the tools and approached the king. "A very strange dream. So clear, I swear it appeared sharper than I can see you from this short distance. I struggled to make sense of it, and was afraid to talk about it, for you might take me as a man who had lost his mind. But now that you reveal your trust in me and your anguish about the priesthood, I can say with all conviction that my dream relates the will of the gods: that *you*, not the priests, should represent them in this world."

"A dream … a prophetic dream!" Sargon mused. "Once, I had a dream like that. I too, am cautious not to tell anyone about it; people might think I'm going insane."

"I have total faith in whatever you reveal to me."

"Yes, Ibrahem. It goes all the way back to when I was the chief commander on the siege of Mari."

"That was one bloody siege."

"Yes, one that changed my destiny and convinced me that I should be king," Sargon reflected. "We camped outside the city of Mari for two moons, trying everything to break through its walls. We used battering rams on the gates, built long ladders to climb the walls. They fought back, hurling bricks, stones, even their own dead soldiers. They toppled the ladders and poured boiling oil onto us from above. I ordered our troops to build a high tower—higher than their fortifications. We dragged and pushed the tower to the wall. They showered us with arrows tipped with burning naphtha.

"My officers urged me to pull back, arguing that we were running out of water to put out the fires, with no time to replenish the stores from the river. The tower suffered only minor sporadic fires—easy to snuff out, nothing out of control—yet my officers panicked. They said our soldiers were being roasted alive in a wooden kiln, that many of our warriors were demoralized by the thought of meeting such a horrible end. They feared a mutiny against those in command that would ultimately lead to my assassination.

"I didn't listen to those spineless cowards. Instead, I climbed to the top of the tower, faced the enemy, and, with my arrows, I dropped many of the defenders. When my soldiers saw me, their chief, fighting alongside them, they got a boost of courage. Before long, our moving tower hit the wall. Ibrahem, that thud on the wall filled me with euphoria. I felt like the gods were there, watching and bestowing on me powers a mere human should not possess. I drew my sword and was the first to jump over the wall, cutting down the first enemy before my feet touched the ground."

Sargon spoke like a poet reciting the bravery of men at war.

Ibrahem was surprised by the jump-over-the-wall part. According to witnesses, Sargon was on the ground when the tower hit the wall, whipping the slaves who pulled the tower and promising them an agonizing death if they stopped. The same accounts related that he did climb up the tower, afterwards, but was cut by two arrows as he charged the wall. His bodyguards brought him down, back to his tent, and that was it. Yet, Ibrahem didn't display any hints of doubting the king's version of the story; he knew that history was the fabrication of the powerful and the winners.

"Then my troops followed," Sargon continued, "but not enough of them to take the ramparts and proceed to open the gates below, all because of the hesitation of my officers. I was cutting the enemy down till my blade went dull. Then, out of nowhere came this giant soldier with a hideous face—no human could've conceived such a creature. Many a brave soldier would've fled at the mere sight of him. I almost did, too, but I knew the gods had sent him to test my courage. I stood my ground, ready to defy death." Sargon's arm rose as though wielding a sword.

"Your bravery is so great," Ibrahem lauded, feigning awe, "as to inspire the gods to meddle in the affairs of mortal beings, a thing they rarely do."

"Ibrahem, the sight of that monster took me aback, giving him a split of a moment's advantage to swing his sword and slash my upper arm, missing my neck by a finger. My guards were about to drop him with their arrows, but I knew the gods would be angered if I cowered in fear of that challenge, so I ordered them not to aim their arrows at him. I fought the monster, bleeding and weakening all the while. I knew brute force would not make me the victor; cunning was the way to defeat him.

"Just when I was losing hope, a ray of light flickered against the monster's helmet. Bless the god Shamash, for he sent me the message that he would help me. My sword had become dull with a thick cover of blood, so I flung it at the monster and rushed him like a gazelle—a move which took him by surprise. Still, he swung his sword, but I was faster than the death riding on his blade, though I suffered a cut to my thigh as I raced past the brute. Lying before me was the sword of an enemy soldier I had killed earlier. That blade was shiny and spotless, for its bearer had sliced nothing but air before I tore life out of him. I snatched up the sword as the monster turned around to finish me, but the sun was behind him, and Shamash sent his rays to the sword I wielded, reflecting intense light into the brute's eyes, temporarily blinding him, giving me just enough time to plant my sword into his heart with the last bit of strength I could muster. He collapsed, kissing the earth farewell with his huge lips. The last thing I remember was thanking Shamash for his help before I collapsed next to the savage, who stared at me with red eyes, furious even in death."

Ibrahem could only speculate as to what had actually happened: as Sargon fell, injured by the arrows, the last thing he saw must have been his soldiers jumping over the wall, being cut down before they landed on the other side. That last image had somehow been embedded in his mind and given him the illusion that it was *he* who went over the wall, killing a defender before landing. A giant, ugly soldier must have evoked the image of a monster. All those details must have become muddled together in Sargon's mind when he collapsed, congealing in his memory as he hallucinated, and while recovering from his injuries.

There was no denying his bravery. The men talked about how he had taken off his armor because of the heat of the battle and before the climb to the top of the tower, how he charged with his men, and how the arrows sliced through his upper arm and his thigh. He fell before making it to the wall and was carried by Naplanam and other soldiers down to the safety of his tent. The movable tower didn't stand much longer; it burned until it collapsed, ending the battle with a humiliating defeat.

Sargon resumed. "I woke up where torchlights flickered in the darkness of a cave. A shadow appeared on the wall; out of it walked a beautiful woman who said she was Ereshkigal, goddess of the netherworld. I couldn't believe it, for they say she's so ugly that the gods of heaven asked Anu to assign her to Earth's deepest pits, to spare them the horrible sight of her. She told me it had been a plot by Ishtar, her jealous sister, who convinced their father Anu to throw her younger sibling out of heaven.

"After asking Ereshkigal if I was dead, she replied. 'No. Your injuries had rendered you unconscious. I'm yet to decide your fate— whether your eyes would open to the bright light of Shamash or have you join the armies of the dead in my dark realm. … Sargon, you have shown bravery on the savage battlefield, but can you prove your prowess in the battlefield of love? I will restore you to the world of the living on one condition: my lust you must satisfy.'

"So, I deployed my exceptional love arts—I don't know for how long, I couldn't tell day from night. Her desires flamed till only ashes were left. By the end, she was begging me to stop."

Ibrahem greatly doubted the king's story, yet he masked his face with a convincing veneer of admiration; the story matched that of Enkido—another character from the Epic of Gilgamesh—who made love to the priestess Shamhat, nonstop for seven days and nights.

"Before sending me back, Ereshkigal gave me some advice: 'Sargon, think of me, and victory will be yours.' And in a flash, after days out of awareness, I woke up in my tent, surrounded by my miserable officers. They pleaded with me to abandon the siege, telling me that morale among the soldiers was running low after the ill-fated tower attack, and mutiny was imminent. But those last words of Ereshkigal, that victory would be mine if I thought of her, kept ringing in my ears. I tried, but failed to make sense of what she meant.

"*Spineless cowards*, I thought when my men pressed me to retreat, *I should have you all executed and sent to the netherworld, a gift to my sweet Ereshkigal.* And amazingly, like a revelation, I figured out what our goddess of the netherworld meant by 'think of me'—send the army underground.

"I gathered my commanders and explained the plan to dig a tunnel under the fortification. Again, they showed fear, asserting the plan was bound to fail: 'The tunnel would be hard to build and easily detected, which would result in another devastating defeat.

Anger would build up and the troops would tear the whole command apart.' ... Ibrahem, again they planted doubt within me.

"That night, I went to bed convinced that the tunnel idea lacked any chance of success. I planned to lift the siege and withdraw in the morning. I prayed to Ereshkigal, asking forgiveness for not heeding her words. While asleep, Ibrahem, terror invaded me in a dream like nothing I've ever experienced in real life; Ereshkigal came to my tent—furious, eyes blazing with fire that would melt stone. With her was a beast, his growl louder than the god of thunder, his face would send demons fleeing in horror. She screamed, 'How dare you fail to trust me?' Then she let the beast loose.

"My only thought was to run away as fast as the wind, though I knew the beast would catch me in the blink of an eye. The beast charged and leapt. I felt it coming like a sandstorm that strips the flesh, leaving nothing in its wake save bare white bones. High the beast sprang, and I felt its shadow passing through me before it landed on something right ahead. I stopped and watched as the beast tore savagely into its prey, which screamed and begged for mercy with a human voice.

"I could see the victim, and to my surprise, it was a man dressed in the enemy's uniform. The beast drove its sharp teeth into the man's neck, ripping it apart. But strangely, the man's screams never stopped. Cautiously, I turned to run away; the beast noticed and shifted attention to me. It crouched down, and again it leapt. Stiffened with fear I stood, only to spring out of bed, hardly breathing, soaked in sweat as if I had just emerged from a river. It took me a while to calm down and clear my head of the echoing soldier's shrieks, which somehow escaped the dream. ... Ibrahem, this time I was sure that the nightmare was an ultimatum from Ereshkigal to proceed with the plan—her promise that I would be victorious ... or be torn apart by my enemies if I ran away like a coward.

"The next morning, when my officers came to my tent expecting me to abandon the siege, I gave the orders to start digging a tunnel. They strongly protested, and one of them argued that it was a foolish idea. I wasted no time, drew my dagger, and stabbed him once in the neck. The others froze in place. I told the guards to grab the dying man and drag him out around the camp for all to see the punishment for disrespecting my orders. I summoned my priest to make sacrifices to the gods. The best of sacrifices I offered to Ereshkigal and her beast.

"The tunnel had to be dug beneath a neglected, unguarded section of the wall where an attack was unexpected, for the slope and terrain barred scaling the wall with ladders."

"Sargon, you had the gods enthralled by your bravery and talent," Ibrahem lauded him again. "I'm sure the gods halted whatever heavenly duties that busied them to watch your plan unfold."

Sargon smiled at the compliment. "I ordered lions to be brought from Uruk in secret and instructed that their daily rations be cut to half-portions. In the meantime, the men were digging the tunnel under the shadows of night. It was narrow—only one man could walk through it. The tunnel was ready by the time the beasts arrived at a hidden location some distance from our camps. I took the commanders on an excursion to clarify my plan. I could tell they still doubted our chances of victory, so I brought a captured enemy scout and threw him to the lions. The commanders watched in horror as the man was ripped apart. I said to them: 'My brave commanders, this is the best meal offered to these lions since they left Uruk. As you can see, it's hardly enough to satisfy their hunger. Out there, behind the walls, there is plenty of meat to fill them to satiety. My plan will succeed—only if you cast your doubts aside, and we work together. If not, then you, my brave men, who have grown so fat, sitting around, complaining and pushing me to accept defeat—*you* will be the ones to satisfy my hungry pets.'"

Sargon roared with laughter. "Oh, Ibrahem, I can't tell you how nervous I was—I was expecting to be assassinated right there, even though my loyal men would've defended me to the death. But bless the gods, those cowards dared not attack me; they saw better odds of survival in following my plan."

"Oh yes, Sargon. No enemy is of greater peril to a general than those from among his own army who doubt and plot against him."

"Indeed Ibrahem. Yet, there is another danger not to be over-looked: doubting yourself. But I did not—not anymore; Ereshkigal had severed my doubts, using her ferocious beast. Likewise, with the beasts I brought, all wavering from those around me was eradicated.

"So, days later, under a cloudy night, we started campfires in plain view, in an area far from the tunnel. Our soldiers were loudly singing happy songs about going home to their families, and the enemy sang back from atop the walls, cheering them on and wishing them a happy journey home. The whole city rejoiced, thinking the siege was finally over.

"With all that distraction of noise and campfires, we moved the hungry lions, after drugging them, to a space by the entrance to the tunnel. When the lions started recovering, we lit the torches that drove those beasts into a frenzy, forcing them to the only escape available—the tunnel that opened inside the fortification. Now imagine, Ibrahem, those enemy soldiers—elated by the arrival of the long-awaited peace, when, out of nowhere, starving lions come roaring to their faces. Imagine you are a soldier, opening your eyes to see the man next to you trying to scream, but in vain, for the dagger-sharp teeth of a beast are clamped on his neck. You would think it was a nightmare—time to wake up, only to find that reality was ensnared by the dream.

"Panic shattered all the discipline within the city. Then, adding to the chaos, I had slaves run with ladders to a spot far from the gate, making the enemy think we were attacking the wall, tricking them into pulling a large number of their guards away from the gates to defend the assailed sector. Meanwhile, I had archers who sneaked in after the lions, and with their arrows they picked off the few soldiers left at the gates, leaving little resistance. Shortly, my men had the gates open, where I waited on my chariot, ready to lead the troops."

"Certainly that demoralized your enemy," Ibrahem lauded, "to see you, the high commander, leading the attack against them."

Ibrahem showered more praise on his king, despite having heard from others that Sargon had never ventured too far from the comfort of his tent that night, since his injuries were far from healed. Sargon must have felt that he was entitled to this lie.

"With the gates open, we charged into the city and the blood of the enemy poured forth. A ruthless massacre went on, even after I commanded the soldiers to stop, which left me with no choice but to severely punish the disobedient men. As for the lions, they feasted on the enemy's flesh till they had to lie down; on full stomachs they napped while my soldiers ambled next to them. Ereshkigal must have been happy with all the young, brave men I sent to her realm.

"The two enemy chief commanders, who never showed their faces in combat, knew what awaited them and drank poison. As for the one who declared himself king, he wasn't brave enough to follow their example—or should I say, he was a fool to expect clemency. I had him skinned alive and left his head and those of his generals hanging from a pomegranate tree in his palace garden with their eyes open, watching me as I drank sweet pomegranate juice with my commanders, served by slaves whom I made wear the skins of their king and his generals. I surely felt like a god being served by a king."

He does have godly aspirations—just as I assumed, Ibrahem thought to himself. Sargon wasn't the first man whose vanity started to itch for a godly status upon reaching the epitome of power.

Ibrahem saw the opportunity to endear himself to the king by stroking his hubris. That would help shield him from the priesthood he so deeply abhorred. But to achieve that, a king needed to attain absolute power, and Sargon was worth the gamble.

"O Sargon—your legend, I daresay, has surpassed that of Gilgamesh, who foolishly wasted the two greatest rewards that can be offered to a man: immortality and everlasting youth. On your own, you defeated all obstacles and adversities that conspired to conquer your resolve. All of this is more proof that the gods have assigned you a destiny—one of the very few reserved uniquely for great heroes. Your feats should be carved on stone for all to see, in the present and far-distant future. I would be honored if you commissioned me to this grand task."

"Sure, Ibrahem, in due time. Now, tell me about the prophecy that visited you in a dream."

"I am more convinced now that a dream it was not; rather, a message from the gods. It started with our god Anu walking alone, talking as though other gods were listening. He complained about the humans and their disobedience. When he reached a vast lake, the fresh-water god ordered the waves to stop rippling and the fish to stop swimming, while the storms god calmed the wind so not a single strand of hair on his father would stir and disturb his thoughts.

"Anu looked to the far end of the lake. His complaints sped to the far reaches of Earth in search of an answer. But the horizon scattered Anu's dilemma with not a trace of a response. Anu, with a heavy heart, concluded that it was hopeless with the humans. He regretted saving Zuisudra and his family, who repopulated the world after the Great Deluge. And Anu resolved to correct that mistake by sending an even greater deluge—doom humanity in its entirety.

"'Let them all drown and take their problems and annoyances to the bottom of the seas,' roared Anu in rage. 'I know I promised not to repeat that calamity; however, I am the supreme god and I answer to no one. Those reckless fools must disappear, once and for all.'

"So Anu walked to the edge of the lake and leaned down to tell the water to ready all its forces—lakes, rivers, oceans, the rain clouds, underground streams, and mountain snows—then await his orders in serving the humans a final devastating deluge. But before uttering a single word, Anu saw something move under the surface of the lake. A closer look brought him face-to-face with his own reflection. It stared back at him, changing expression from grim consternation to horror, and Anu saw himself quivering under the water—drowning. The face seemed to scream a warning, a bad omen that would come to fruition if Anu proceeded with annihilating humanity. The message was as clear as the water itself.

"Anu was swamped by fear, despite knowing that he was the most powerful of all gods. Though no entity is capable of harming him, he realized that *he* could bring destruction to his own self. Right away he talked to his image, assuring it that there would be no extermination of the humans by another deluge. But the trembling reflection kept staring back, as though desperate to tell him something. The reflection raised its hand, and Anu spontaneously reached with his hand to the water's surface. As soon as he touched the water, the reflection grabbed firmly onto the hand of Anu, who understood what his image wanted to convey. And I watched our father god pull his own reflection out of the lake."

"God saw himself drowning like a human," Sargon remarked, "and spared us the wrath of another deluge! Interesting ... but what does this have to do with me—being chosen by the gods?"

"My king, before I answer, you need to know one thing: I make statues of gods, and many ask, how could it be possible for stones carved with human hands to turn into gods? Well, statues of the gods are never complete till the gods descend and leave a token of their presence inside the finished work. The gods work in mysterious ways, and they only work with a chosen few who are gifted. Many sculptors are frauds; they sell statues that the gods find unworthy to be blessed with their presence. Likewise, those priests created the belief that they are the gods' surrogates when, in reality, many are the self-serving priests of little or no faith, like that En-shakush you had executed."

"By the gods, Ibrahem, can you reveal where I fit into all of this?" Sargon was getting impatient.

"Forgive me, Holiness. I was just trying to explain why the gods chose me instead of the priests to deliver their message."

"Holiness!" Sargon laughed. "Just what I need, another honorific."

"Yes, Holiness. Throughout the dream, I could not see the great Anu clearly, for he was surrounded by a bright glow. After pulling his reflection from the water, Anu proclaimed, 'You will be the one to represent me and enforce my will over the humans. *You* are the chosen one.'

"God's reflection stood tall, and I saw its face. It wasn't the shadowy face of a dream, but one as clear as I can see you now, *just* as I see you now. Yes, it was you standing next to our god Anu. O Great Sargon, *you* are the incarnation of Anu's reflection. *You* are the true representative of the gods, sent to rule over the unruly humans."

Sargon was stunned by the revelation. Dreamily, he ambled back to his throne, collapsed on it, and waved at Ibrahem to leave.

God's messenger bowed and retreated, stealing glances at the man he had declared to be God's reflection.

As if suddenly stricken by nostalgia, Sargon sat with a gaze that traversed the high ceiling. From there, his mind soared to the realm of the immortals, to roam the vast firmament in search of his divine origin where God had birthed him out of the celestial waters of heaven.

Mud Schooling

"**A**LL WORKS START OVER THERE—THE MUD TUB."

Isaa led Enheduanna to a large chest under a roof of palm leaves, some thirty paces outside the classroom.

"The mud to make our tablets!" He flipped the lid open. "As you can see, the tub is quite large; three men could lie down in it, side by side—four deep, lying atop each other," he joked with her for the first time.

He had spent the day before instructing Enheduanna on the basics of writing, using wax boards. He was courtly and avoided any humor, cautious not to offend the princess.

Enheduanna peeked into the box, grasped its edge, and raised one leg as if to climb inside. Her kilt fell back to expose her silky thigh. A stumped Isaa stared briefly at her leg while it rested on the rim of the box before he regained himself. Lightly, he touched her shoulder.

"Forgive me, Highness, what are you doing?"

"Edunna, not Highness," she corrected him.

"Forgive me, but—are you trying to climb inside the box?"

"I want to figure out how many *women* would fit, lying side by side and on top of each other." She giggled and brought her leg down.

Isaa laughed discreetly. "Well, Your Hi—Edunna."

"Yes, Your—Isaa," she interrupted, and both laughed.

Her playful teasing set him a little more at ease. He looked into her eyes—those obsidian eyes that had robbed him of sleep the night before.

"Now, we call this box a tub for a reason." He continued in a serious tone. "It is where we also take mud baths—to be one with the mud. Apart from it being a ritual, it helps your work a lot. So, we go in the tub with clothes off—fully undressed, three at the time, just like the reed stylus leaves a three-sided, cuneiform shape on the mud."

"Do I have to do that too?" Enheduanna said anxiously.

"Most of us do it from time to time, but it is customary for all to do it before their first work. You … don't want to be an exception to the rest of the boys—true!"

Enheduanna cupped a hand to her mouth, holding back a protest. Hesitantly, one word escaped the blockade: "True."

"Good. We need one more boy to make three. I'll go fetch someone." Isaa headed back to the classroom.

Mortified, Enheduanna paced back and forth next to the box, throwing fretful glances at the classroom door. Shortly, Isaa appeared with another boy, and behind them the whole class poured forward through the doorway to witness the ritual. Enheduanna turned her back to them, her face so flushed, like it might start oozing blood.

"Whenever you're ready, Edunna," Isaa's voice announced from behind.

She froze, unable to move a muscle.

"Edunna," Isaa's voice came again. "We're now stripped and ready. Is there a problem?"

Her mind went blank. Only her maids had seen her naked, and there she was—two naked boys behind her and an army of boys watching, waiting for her to become one with the mud. She was desperate for a way out; to fail her first task in the tablet house wasn't her idea of a good start.

"Can I go in with my clothes on? I'll take them off in the tub," she said, praying for an affirmative answer.

"No," came the firm answer. "No clothes are allowed inside the tub."

She stared nervously at the mud tub, one hand clutching the top of her tunic as if it were a butterfly that might flutter away at any moment with the tiniest breeze, leaving her as nothing more than a nude image, scribed forever in the boys' minds.

That fool, chief master Akiya. Silently, she raged. *Why didn't he warn me about this mud ritual? My father will have him as a guest in the torture chamber for this.*

Long, tense moments passed, made worse by a plague of stillness that afflicted her with deadly shame. Then her heightened senses detected a trace of air shaking behind her—muffled laughter. She turned and saw Isaa and the other boy, fully clothed, holding their stomachs. The rest of the boys began laughing out loud.

Letting out a long sigh, she happily walked away from the tub toward Isaa and released her embarrassment with a slap to his shoulder.

"You're a bad learned brother!" she yelled.

"Forgive me," he said jovially. "We do this to all the new students. I wasn't sure about doing it to you—being a princess. But when you tried to climb inside the box, you had it coming."

She smiled.

"Back to your work, boys," Isaa announced, and the boys retreated in a rare show of compliance—not to Isaa's order, but out of respect for the princess.

"You know, this mud bath, it's not a bad idea after all," said Enheduanna.

"You think so? Then suggest it to Master Ur-nammu."

"Maybe I will," she replied, and waited for Isaa to say something, but he seemed lost, staring into her eyes.

"Well, Isaa, anything else to teach me after this *refreshing* mud bath?"

"Sure." Isaa snapped out of his reverie. "Workers take care of the tub; they bring fresh mud when it runs low or replace it if it's not good enough to work with. It is said that ours is the best clay in the land for writing tablets. Former students come to the school to do their projects. Even artists commissioned by the palace prefer to use our mud. I'm sure you have seen some of their pieces on the palace walls."

"Yes, plenty."

"Now, how to prepare the mud? You do that a day before starting your work. You knead it into the shape you want and leave it to dry to the right consistency. The drying time depends on how hot or muggy the day is. Through experience, you will learn how to tell when it's ready. The mark your reed pen leaves on the clay should be a well-defined, readable cuneiform shape."

He walked her behind the tub. "Here we have trays of different sizes and forms to mold the tablets. Some tasks need larger tablets, but that won't happen anytime soon for you; we will start you on small tablets."

"I might surprise you and advance to big tasks in a short time," she said, brimming with confidence. "Does anyone check the finished work?"

"Absolutely. That's my job as learned brother. And if I don't like someone's work, it's his face that will be pressed in the mud."

She smiled. "Just make sure my father is not around when you press my face."

"In your case, I'll make an exception. A learned brother needs a head upon his shoulders to perform his duties."

"No, no, no. As I said, I want to be treated like the rest, and I made it clear to my father. Don't worry, if there is any problem, you can be sure I will come to your defense."

"That's good to know, it's a load of worries off my back. ... Now, when the work has been checked, we place it outside to dry under the sun."

"What if it rains?"

"If the skies are filled with angry clouds, then we take the work to that shaded area with the roof. If it rains heavily, you can only pray—the gods might save your work."

"Do they?"

"Normally, they don't. It's a sign that our god Nabu is not happy for being presented work of poor quality, so he tells the rain and storm gods to destroy the whole batch."

"I'll double my prayers to them."

"Well, maybe they will listen to you. You are a princess, after all."

"You keep bringing up the princess thing." She scowled.

"Forgive me, I ... I don't mean to."

Fool! Stick to the training subject. Isaa rebuked himself. "Now—if you have any special work, something artistic or unique, for that we have kilns to glaze the work and make it last … forever, maybe.”

“That's one reason I've come to the school,” Enheduanna commented.

“What do you mean?”

“The gods reserved immortality for themselves, whereas the humans, they're fated to death. Writings that last are one way of cheating death by leaving something of ourselves behind.”

“I thought children served that purpose.” Isaa's palm twisted as if ruffling a child's hair.

“True. Still, writing could keep one's memory alive for many generations.”

Isaa gazed into the darkness of her eyes as though to better understand her words.

“Is there something wrong with my eyes?” She became irritated.

“No, not at all.” He had to stop himself from delving too deep into those hypnotic eyes. “Any more questions, Edunna?”

“Only one, Isaa. Are you the only learned brother in the class?”

“No.” He hesitated. “There is Samian too.”

“Which one is he?”

“The boy with the shaved head and bushy brows. He wears an oversized, red jasper cylinder seal on his necklace.”

“Was he the one closest to you by the gate, during your rough encounter with the guards?”

“Yes … he's the one.”

“It was a rather intriguing situation. Two boys: the first, was he foolish or daring … perhaps both! The other, was he smart or scared? Then again, perhaps both.”

Isaa felt uneasy; he needed to forget that incident. “Both of us will work with you, but one will be your principal learned brother.”

“Do I get to choose which one?”

Her question surprised him. He had thought the position was securely his. Before thinking of a cordial reply, words came rushing out of his mouth.

“You're the princess—you decide!” He shrugged as if he couldn't care less. “Pick and choose as you wish.”

Her eyes narrowed in anger, and Isaa's heart throbbed like a criminal about to hear his sentence. His vision delved deeper into her eyes; beyond the beauty that captured his heart, he saw fire blazing in their dark night.

"Forgive my rudeness." He looked down to evade her fury.

Brief silence was her response, followed by some lines from a song:

"Whom should I choose? Which do I desire?
The brave—wild dancer on the edge of a quagmire,
Or the wise who rhymes sweet words to my soul when it tires?"

She turned around and walked back to the classroom. Isaa watched her and sang in a suppressed voice she would not hear:

"Lucky for you who can choose—can have all to acquire.
Thief, you stole my heart—tossed it to flame amidst the love pyres."

King Out of a Reed Basket

"**D**ID YOU SOMEHOW SLANDER THE GODS?"

"No, never!" mumbled Sargon while the priest's hands stretched his jaw wide open. "I do utter words like … 'by the spiny balls of Anu,' or, 'by Ishtar's flooded love canal' … talk of that sort. That's not badmouthing the gods. … Is it? I know those are not prayers, but they're not curses either—aaah, you're splitting my mouth apart!"

Despite the king's groans of pain, the healer priest, Bilalama, kept his focus on the task at hand, inside the royal mouth.

"Well,"—Bilalama released Sargon's jaw—"you had better refrain from using bad language when mentioning the gods. It could be the reason for the toothache; if the gods don't like what they hear, they curse the mouth that uttered the words. I suspect they cursed you with the tooth worm, and it's getting fat, eating at the tooth and the flesh around it. I can recite a few prayers to ask the gods to flush it out, but they rarely bother to remove the worm after going through the trouble of inserting it. At best, they might calm it down to give you some relief."

"By the perfumed arse of Ishta—" Sargon cut the name short when the priest displayed a warning frown. "Ibrahem, come here and check this yourself. I need a second opinion."

Ibrahem stepped over to examine the mouth cavity of God's reflection.

"I'm afraid Bilalama is right; it is the tooth worm, and I think it's too late to remove it. Most likely it's already dead. These worms keep eating till they burst, and no amount of praying would help. Its body will rot along with all the flesh around it. This tooth has to be removed."

"I agree, that's the best option." Bilalama nodded. "I'll fetch a blacksmith I know—the best one for this task. He has invented a tool that fits in the mouth; with it, he taps the tooth from both sides to loosen it before pulling it out with the least pain possible."

"Go get him—I can't bear this anymore. I don't know how a stinking worm can cause me, *the king*, such pain!"

"Very well." Bilalama stepped away from the ailing king. "But it's a trip to reach the blacksmith; I won't be back till late evening. In the meantime, I suggest you drink a lot of wine to lessen the pain."

"Hurry then, go! And if he's as good as you say, I'll keep him as a royal blacksmith and tooth-puller."

On his way out, Bilalama stopped by Naplanam, who stood guard in the king's bedroom.

"Naplanam, any tooth worms you need removed?"

"No, sir!" Naplanam was surprised by the question. "I remove my teeth by myself or have a fellow soldier help me. Once, in a battle, two of my teeth were removed by the enemy; I returned the favor— removed his head." He grinned, showing two missing front teeth.

Bilalama grinned back and left.

"Damn this Bilalama." Sargon walked to a table and poured some of his favorite wine from a jar into a cup. "Curse those priests; theirs are always bad news."

"Of all the priests, he's the one I would trust most," Ibrahem said.

"You have something to tell me … right?" Sargon eyed Ibrahem as he gulped the wine.

"I know you are in great pain, but I have to relay something that has become a burden on my mind. I would never forgive myself for not bringing it to your attention immediately."

"Talk, Ibrahem. What is this urgent matter that can't wait?" Sargon was already pouring his second cup of wine.

"Rumors and gossip are spreading like a plague. They aim first to maim your name; later, like the worm in your tooth, they might grow into a treacherous beast with the sole purpose of removing you from the throne—end your rule and your life."

"Then speak. Don't fret, you're under my protection—the king,

God's reflection. What is this threat that could bring on my downfall?"

"Though you are the incarnation of God's reflection, that will not protect you on Earth. Here you are just like any other human; you bleed, become infirm, grow old … even get toothaches. The gods' intervention takes only the form of warnings that you should heed."

"Reveal to me those gossips—why should I worry?"

"I will reveal all, my king, and I swear upon my life and honor that everything I tell you is true. I fear not those men who weave the conspiracy. I have but one thing to ask of you first, and that is … to control yourself and not rush into punishing me, for the vile details I'm about to recount will greatly rouse your anger."

"If it is that serious, then you had better start," Sargon said impatiently.

"May God give me the courage. … It is no secret that the priesthood enjoys vast powers that could easily rival yours if used cunningly. I have reasons to believe that a devious conspiracy is already set in motion … with Ishullanu heading this treachery."

"Ishullanu! He might have ambitions, yet he would not dare plot against me. I know you have problems with him, for he won't compensate you fairly for your work in his temples. But you're forgetting, it was *he* who alerted me about a threat to my life after studying the sheep's entrails. He could've said everything was fine, that I had nothing to worry about, to keep my guard down when he strikes. These are serious accusations. You had better convince me, or *yours* will be the head to roll."

"This loyal subject will give his head gladly to serve you. But spare me the anger of the gods for not fulfilling the duty I strongly feel they have entrusted to me as a messenger to save you from a sinister scheme."

"Give me details!" Sargon shouted. "Enough of this empty talk. My patience is running out and Naplanam's sword is thirsty for blood."

Naplanam became alert at the mention of his name and watched the king, praying for the order to execute. He deplored the day Sargon had assigned him to be his personal guard. All the privileges that came with this job paled against the thrill of the battlefield. Naplanam was born to kill, and standing guard in the palace was killing him slowly. Now, his instinct to shed blood awakened and his grip on the sword tightened in anticipation. He would strike swiftly, and the sculptor's head would be sliced off like a watermelon—cleanly, not a jagged edge visible.

"O Great Sargon,"—Ibrahem dropped to his knees—"I offer my neck here for your guard to strike, but you need to hear the reprehensible lies your enemies are spreading among the populace. It is vile talk my tongue hates to utter, though I am not its treacherous author. When I am done, may the gods guide your judgment—either to end the life of this miserable servant kneeling at your feet or to employ him as a weapon against the conspirators."

Sargon uttered no words, but anger was written all over his face.

The weight of the total silence had Ibrahem bow so low, he wondered if his head was still riding his shoulders. He couldn't help but glance at Naplanam, who stood a handful of paces away to the side, clutching his sword impatiently, ready to dull its shine with warm blood.

"My king, let me start with the entrails of the animal. You recall that I was there after they split the animal's belly. Well, I managed to take a good look while the priests were deliberating, and there was nothing out of the ordinary in those entrails. Ishullanu was the one who said the liver was deformed and that there were strange twists in the intestines, and as always, his word is the last word. The other priests simply concurred with him—none of them would dare dispute his opinion."

"And how did you become so adept at reading entrails?" asked Sargon.

"To be a good sculptor, a man needs to possess sharp perception of the finer details—details that even priests fail to detect. When I visit the butcher, I spend time examining the slaughtered animals; the inner body parts hidden under the skin have always roused my interest. I've learned from some priests about what to look for as omens of danger. I can assure you there was no reason for alarm; the entrails of that animal had no marks whatsoever of an attempt on your life."

"If Ishullanu is conspiring, why would he put me on alert?" Sargon demanded. "Again, wouldn't it be better to surprise me with a sneak attack? So far, the only evidence you mentioned is the entrails, which you say were normal, and it's far too late to reexamine them. By now, those entrails, and the whole animal they belonged to, have left the entrails of the people and animals that consumed them."

"There is more to it," Ibrahem persisted. "A great king like you, strong and brave, with the greatest army on Earth loyal and ready to die for your glory—any scheme against you would have to be planned with cunning and patience. And I greatly suspect your look-alike is another element of the plot."

"My double! His sole purpose is to take the stabs for me when plotters strike."

"Or, the double will sit on your throne after you are assassinated," Ibrahem retorted. "They will fool your loyal subjects into believing that *he* is you, and dictate to him their wishes—rule the kingdom as they please until they decide to get rid of him."

"But he can't even speak our language. He will be exposed right away."

"They could say he lost his voice due to a malady. The generals probably would not be fooled, but they wouldn't dare do a thing; none of them have the guts to oppose the priests, for that would only bring division and chaos since most people believe that the priest-hood is the gods' proxy on Earth. When you are gone, your generals will accept this substitute, despite knowing very well he's a double.

"O Great Sargon, many kings have used doubles before, so I didn't give it much thought at the time when you ordered me to seek this man who resembles you. But when I think back to that day when they studied the entrails, it was Ishullanu who suggested and persisted with the idea that you get a double. Another reason to rouse my suspicions, which sent me searching into Ishullanu's past, was the language spoken by your double—Aramaic; Ishullanu is practiced in this tongue. I seriously believe that Ishullanu was the one who found this double and inserted him as a bricklayer in the construction of the new temple so, eventually, word about his resemblance would reach you through your master builders. I fear that our high priest wants to use this look-alike for a treacherous deed."

"Ishullanu will scheme all of this just to retaliate for one foolish priest I had killed?"

"The killing of his priest, power ambitions, greed for wealth—all of those shrink to a pittance next to a greater motive."

"That serious! Explain."

"Vengeance! Murderous hate that can be sated only by your death. I found out that Ishullanu was a temple priest who came from the city of Mari—the city you defeated. And another fact ... the most alarming: Ishullanu's father was the high priest of that city, and he was killed when your troops stormed in.

"Aside from Aramaic, Ishullanu is proficient in other tongues. He worked his way to the priesthood here, in Uruk, as a translator. His talent gained him influence and connections with many nobles, and it didn't take him long to become the favorite assistant to the former high priest, who, before long, died suddenly. Rumors blamed his death on a private, *highly passionate* mating ceremony with a priestess of the goddess Ishtar. I question that account; the man was strong, blessed by the gods with good health, free from any ailment whatsoever. I believe he was poisoned by Ishullanu, who concocted the absurd story that Ishtar witnessed the immense joy of a priestess while bedding the high priest; hence, the envious Ishtar decided to take him for herself, only to poison him later so no other woman could enjoy him.

"O Sargon, as you know, Ishullanu pretended to be so stricken with grief that he sat next to the man's body for a full day, praying to the healing goddess, begging her to reunite the man's soul back with his body. ... I have no proof of foul play, my king, but can't you sense the brazen lie—since when does Ishtar lust for old priests? We all know her lovers are young and handsome—or those who show exceptional bravery in battle, like you, for example."

"Or gods," Sargon said as he sat in an armchair, ruminating on the day when he would be promoted from a mere reflection of Anu to a proper god. The wine was doing its work on him.

"Yes, gods too, without any doubt," Ibrahem concurred. "But the one thing we can be sure of—Ishtar would never desire an old high priest no matter how healthy he might be."

"Ibrahem! So far, you've said that Ishullanu is seeking vengeance and he lusts for power, yet you haven't offered any solid proof. All that you detailed could amount to nothing more than rumors."

"My Lord, who would you fear more—the sword waved by a hardened warrior facing you, or the poison slipped into your drink by a feeble slave? Is it the roaring army with hordes of soldiers, chariots, weapons that chop and shred, or the invisible, silent plague that slowly devours the people all over the city? ... Gossip, lies, smears carried by invisible words—those veiled weapons of treachery have more lethal reach than swords, spears, and arrows. The priests are spreading the word that the gods are angry because you are cutting funds to the temples. This is their excuse for assessing the extra payments made for blessings on the livestock to make up for the shortfall. There is an uproar among the people; cities from Ur to Babylon to Assyria are on the verge of rebellion."

"I am aware of minor, sporadic disturbances," Sargon said dismissively. "It's nothing new. Those regions have always been sources of unrest, but nothing close to a rebellion."

"I pray that Your Majesty is right in this thought. But with Ishullanu pushing the priesthood to slander you among the people, it will only get worse."

"Pushing them! Slander me! In what way?"

"O Sargon, how I wish I had the bravery to tell about all the vile—depraved rumors circulated by those who don't appreciate your generosity and all you have done for the kingdom."

"Speak, man. I've heard it all from the mouths of soldiers who scream the most sordid of blasphemies at their gods."

"Only the bravest of the brave would be able to hear what I am about to utter and still forgive the messenger," Ibrahem said, hoping this exaltation would work in his favor. "They say ... they say that you were born to a prostitute, and by that, they don't even mean a priestess who gave her love to honor the goddess Ishtar ... forgive me, Great Sargon, but they do mean a common prostitute." Ibrahem bowed, his forehead just short of touching the floor.

Sargon bristled in his seat. "Go on, what else?" Wine dribbled down his chin as he spoke.

"They say she was destitute, couldn't afford to feed you. So she put you in a reed basket and sent you drifting downstream on the Euphrates River. The basket was caught in the reeds next to the royal palace where a maid found it and delivered the infant to the queen, who was barren. And so, the queen raised you secretly, making you the cupbearer for her husband, the king at that time."

"I … I drifted down the river in a reed basket and survived! You hear that, Naplanam?" Sargon began laughing, and the guard returned a grin. "Not only am I a brave fighter on land, but also a great navigator of the waters—cruised the Euphrates while still an infant, *in a reed basket*. Go on, Ibrahem, tell us more about the talents I was never aware to possess."

Hearing the king laugh gave Ibrahem a much-needed dose of courage just when prudence almost had him consider ending his shocking revelations. He took a deep breath and resumed.

"The lies tell that the queen felt abandoned by the king, who had had countless concubines to satisfy his carnal desires. So, she had him killed by getting him drunk and slipping poison into his cup—given by you, the cupbearer. She declared that the man died from excessive drinking of wine. The queen ruled the kingdom, helping you in ascending the army ranks, till that bastard son of the late king, a concubine's son, gained enough power to remove her. The story goes on to say the deposed queen asked you from her deathbed to avenge her. Thus, the smears deepen with another blatant lie … that while the new king was showing good signs of recovery from a mild illness, he unexpectedly perished. Now the rumor is spreading that you poisoned him too, only to cover for your treachery by declaring that the ailing king choked to death on hot soup."

"Sons of dogs! They dare say that!" Sargon slapped the arms of his seat with both hands. "I'll have their vile tongues sliced out, then forced back, *down their throats*! If I wanted to kill the king, I would've never used the ways of cowards!"

"Without any doubt. Poison is what *they* use in their schemes, like when Ishullanu killed the high priest before him. Now they are using the poison of gossip and slander to kill your heroic achievements." And Ibrahem went silent.

"You still have more to tell! I sense there is more."

"Sadly yes, but I beg you, Majesty, to forgo the rest."

"Speak! Just now you mentioned that my mother was a prostitute, and there you are—unharmed, still alive. Have no fear, speak."

"The gossips say … neither your son nor your daughter … is yours. They say their seed was from another man, that you are … incapable of having children. My king, they dare question your virility. And … forgive me …" Ibrahem hesitated.

"My mother, *a prostitute*, and now my children are *bastards*. Meaning, my wife was just another … *whore!*" Sargon jumped to his feet and flung his cup, which showered Ibrahem with red wine before it shattered on the floor. "*And!* Still there is more. And WHAT?"

"O Great King, it will be easier for me to accept death at the hands of your guard than say it."

"I will have Naplanam carve your belly so those priests can study your entrails while you watch. Speak!" Sargon roared.

"They say,"—Ibrahem's voice came out trembling—"they say … a beast from the netherworld was your father, and … just as a horse mating with an ass results in a mule … incapable of having any off-spring … they say it is the same case with Your Majesty, except …"

"Except what? Speak! Except what?" Rage had Sargon shaking.

Ibrahem struggled to find the words.

"NAPLANAM!" Sargon shrieked. "Get your knife ready to untie this thing's tongue from his throat!"

"Ready at your order, my king," Naplanam replied instantly.

"Majesty …" Ibrahem inhaled deeply to expel the burden. "May the gods loathe this mouth for uttering these heinous words. They say that … unlike a mule, your rod is fragile, incapable of raising its head in glory … that your seed don't shoot out like a gushing mountain spring, but rather trickle like … drops of morning dew … dribbling down a blade of grass."

Sargon was stunned as if hit by lightning. He didn't notice Naplanam, who came running as if the king were in imminent danger.

"O Great Sargon." The guard sank to his knees. "Forgive my moving without your permission, but I couldn't stand there and pretend not to have heard this vile snake spitting this venom on Your

Highness. Give me the order to cut off its head, end its life, and send it to the deepest pits of hell."

Sargon didn't answer. He was gazing at Ibrahem, considering how to make the man suffer the longest.

"Your Majesty," Ibrahem cried, "now that my mission to convey the gods' warning is fulfilled, I submit to your will and gladly welcome death. I am not worthy of breathing the same blessed air that travels through Your Holiness. But if you will allow me a few last words—"

"My king," Naplanam urged, "Let me silence this slithering serpent once and for all and end the stabs it inflicts on Your Highness with the blade of its poisonous tongue."

"O bravest of all the brave," Ibrahem wailed, "he is right. I did bring the poison to you, but along with it, my king, I am bringing the cure. For the sickness to be treated, it is best to know the disease. May the gods curse my soul for eternity if my intentions were to bring insult to Your Highness."

"Those are the vilest insults that can be heaped upon a man, not to mention *a king!*" Sargon's right hand darted out, trembling with rage. "Naplanam, hand me your sword."

Still bowing, Naplanam drew his sword from its leather sheath and held it out with both hands.

"Great Sargon," Naplanam pleaded, "I beg you, permit me to do it. Some of the sewage running within this filth might splatter and stain you."

"There are certain things a man has to do by himself." Sargon snatched the sword.

"Your Majesty, I know my words merit death." Ibrahem urgently breathed the words that could save him from impending doom. "But I plead that you spare this worthless life of mine—you need me to defeat the cowards plotting against you."

"By the gods!" screamed Naplanam. "I and all the royal guards, who have sworn to defend Your Majesty to the death, are more than capable of crushing all traitors and priests who have any malicious intentions toward you. This *bug* is of no use to you with his skill of chipping stones. Let me shut his mouth forever, chop him into pieces, and feed his stinking flesh and bones to the pigs."

Naplanam knelt at Sargon's feet, his heart throbbing in a state of euphoria he only experienced in heated battles.

Sargon didn't answer. Slowly, the sword arched up, both hands gripping it firmly. He stood motionless for long moments, then, like a flash of lightning, his fury brought the sword down.

A fountain of blood showered the head on its short roll to rest, leaving Sargon bemused while meditating on the death-smeared face. Then, his gaze turned to the sword, studying the blade from tip to hilt.

"By the savage goddess of war!" he marveled, elatedly. "Naplanam, this is one ferocious sword—a most wicked blade. Amazing, how it cut through the bone! Even in my vigorous days, I've never held a sword that sliced so—so cleanly. Could it be that my old age is retreating to youth?"

Naplanam's eyes stared in silence, unblinking, as if paying full attention to the king's next command.

Calmly, Sargon paced around the headless body. All the harsh insults were forgotten like a fleeting bad dream while he scrutinized the sword in admiration.

"The handle, how nicely studded … jade, lapis lazuli. The hilt, and its horned head of a dragon … dazzlingly detailed! Oh, and these ruby stones for eyes, furiously red—an atrocious beauty, a brutal piece of art."

The slippery floor shifted his attention to the pool of gore. He traced its origin to where the first gushing spray dotted the marble floor, and started wondering.

Could the pattern of the splatter be a message from the gods? It greatly resembles a constellation of stars. Should I bring my astrologers to examine it? And that slender trail—how it resembles a river born from those stars, flowing smoothly to settle in a lake.

Sargon's focus skimmed to the end of the red lake, to where the round edge skirted around islands that looked like … *fingers … hands!* He scowled over the kneeling man who dared disturb the smooth flow of his bloody artwork.

"Foul words were uttered here," Sargon spoke coldly. "Yours is the only other mouth that needs to be silenced. Tell me of a reason to spare your life!"

"Your Majesty," came the timid reply, "not even the smallest ant, if it walked this room, should be kept alive. But I trust in our Father god Anu. Only he can guide your sword to the punishment best fit for this loyal servant of yours."

The king raised the sword again and paused for much longer this time until the duel between fury and reason came to a conclusion. An angry scream tore out of his throat, and he sliced down with the blade before it abruptly stopped, only grazing the back of the neck below him. A thin strip of blood oozed out of the fissure. Sargon trudged back to his armchair and sat, leaning on the sword's handle.

"The gods … they made me do it," he whimpered between sniffles. "They forced the sword down to his neck. In no way was I capable of doing it myself. Naplanam saved my life during that siege of Mari; he carried me on his back, down from the burning tower all the way to the tent.

"I owe nothing to anyone, except … to him, I owe my life. No sums of payments and no favors could settle that debt, and I must confess, it often disturbed me. … I, the king, God's reflection, shouldn't owe anything to anyone! Foolish of me to have made him my personal guard—constantly reminded of him saving my life! Assigning him another post outside the palace occurred to me, but then I worried about who would replace such a loyal man."

Sargon's eyes dimmed in sorrow. "Oh Naplanam, my most trusted man! Oh God, why did you push him to kneel? Why did you guide the sword to fall on him? I was powerless—I had no part in ending his life."

"Your Highness." The subdued voice of Ibrahem came back as he knelt in the guard's blood. "The gods saw your dilemma. They helped rid you of this heavy debt so you could pay more attention to the threats endangering your kingdom."

"Perhaps you are right." Sargon wiped away the tears. "Stand up, Ibrahem, I will not harm you. Bravery is not a thing shown only on the battlefield. Naplanam was one of the bravest men out there—but you showed odd bravery in speaking those daring words. You put your life and the fate of your whole family in danger. This is not any less courageous than the valiant act of a soldier who puts his life on the line to defend his king."

Ibrahem staggered to his feet, hardly believing his legs would ever support his body again. He wobbled a little before regaining balance.

"Naplanam," Sargon addressed the man's head, "your family will be generously compensated for their loss."

"Majesty, if you will permit me to make a suggestion?"

"Speak."

"No one should know about Naplanam's death here in the palace. Ishullanu will spread the rumor that this was god's punishment for the killing of the priest En-shakush, which will make the people fear the priesthood even more."

"You're right, Ibrahem." Sargon paused in thought. "I want you to take off his clothes, then wrap his head and body with bed sheets. Change your stained robe—get one of my own from the shelves. I'll go out first and take the guards to walk the grounds. I'll send you some servants—mute servants—yes, better if they're mute, we have a few of them. Have them clean the room and discreetly carry Naplanam to the graveyard. … His family will be told that he was sent to crush a rebellion … where he will sadly go missing in battle."

After changing into a fresh robe, Sargon cast a long look at his guard. "Farewell, dear friend. Forgive me, but the gods willed you to be sacrificed. To Ereshkigal I will pray and make offerings so she favors you in the netherworld.

"Ibrahem, after burying him, get some rest. Tomorrow, we'll discuss how to deal with the vile rumors and their authors."

"Yes, my king."

Waves of blissful relief swept over Ibrahem after Sargon stepped out. But once his gaze fell on the decapitated body, fear struck back. He had always feared Naplanam—had sensed that the guard harbored some ill will toward him. Now he wondered if that hatred stemmed from the guard's premonition that Ibrahem would be the cause of his untimely demise.

Hesitantly, Ibrahem studied Naplanam's glassy eyes; in them, he detected something that made him shiver: the promise of vengeance.

Raging Beauty and the Bull

THE STUDENTS REMAINED STANDING. SILENTLY, THEY WATCHED the spectacle.

Ur-nammu was struggling to retain his balance, holding onto a table for support. The two clay tablets that rested over the trembling table slid away, shattering to pieces on the floor. Finally, when his swaying came to an end, Ur-nammu sank into his seat.

His face was as grim as it had been the day before, only now the gloomy lines ran deeper. He must have gone through the whole gamut of miserable facial expressions since the arrival of Enheduanna, a moon cycle ago.

His oldest students, who had known him for ages, could never have imagined such a vast transformation in Ur-nammu, from the methodical, attentive master into this disoriented, aloof stranger. The dedicated man, who had enjoyed teaching more than anything life had to offer, now busied himself—as one boy joked—between staring at his own closed eyelids and counting the stars in broad daylight, just to distract himself until the end of the school day.

Ur-nammu sat, oblivious to his surroundings, eyes fixed on the shattered tablets. He was drunk; it wasn't a secret anymore.

"Permission to start the prayers, Master," Samian requested.

Not a reply nor a hand wave issued out of Ur-nammu. His stillness replicated that of the statue of Nabu, to whom the students prayed.

With the master dwelling in a separate world, his permission was rendered inessential, and the class went ahead with the prayers. Everyone joined in the recitations except for Isaa, who whispered his own prayers—or rather, curses on Samian, whom he'd started to despise for being chosen by Enheduanna as her assigned learned brother.

Isaa had asked her why she hadn't chosen him, to which she briefly answered:

"Do I have to give you an explanation? Does there have to be a reason?"

Since then, the frost between them had thickened and become increasingly harder to crack. As a learned brother, Isaa could've approached her at any time to discuss the work she submitted, but he rarely used this privilege; overwhelmed as he was by anger, he resolved to stop thinking about her.

After the prayers concluded, Samian, who had worn an air of superiority ever since the princess had chosen him, took it upon himself to approach Ur-nammu, who had not shifted his behind since it had touched the seat.

"Master."

There was no reply.

"Master, we are done with the prayers!" Samian raised his voice.

Ur-nammu turned his head slowly, tempted to curse out the one who dared fill his empty head with noise, but his eyes wandered, and all he could see was the girl: *the whore who desecrated my school with her vagina.*

All the attempts he had made to keep her out had died on arrival to the school's chief, Akiya. Ur-nammu had even suggested assigning her a personal mentor, framing it as an efficient method more fit for a princess, but she had vehemently refused. His faith in Nabu, the god of scribes, was shaken after all his prayers and offerings went unanswered. Utterly defeated by one immature girl, he fantasized about humiliating her; he'd kick and slap this female interloper, then turn to the boys and say: *Now, boys, what you've just seen is your assignment for the day. She wants to be one of the boys, so let's grant her this wish. Pummel her, smack the bitch around! Beat her senseless, my boys. Make me proud.*

His thoughts were interrupted when he became aware she was staring back at him. He abruptly turned his face away as if slapped.

"Master, what is the assignment for today?" Samian's voice finally reached him.

"Assignment!" Ur-nammu was surprised, as if the boy were deaf for not hearing his thoughts.

"Assignment!" Ur-nammu repeated, and to his own amazement, a laughing streak seized him and sent him to wonder if he was joining the gods in a hilarious frenzy after they had witnessed the wild fantasies of a pathetic man who couldn't keep a girl out of his class. Or were the gods laughing at the miserable fool who never saw it coming; that lifelong, sincere work he dedicated to the tablet house, only to have his requests entirely ignored?

Ur-nammu was cut loose; the ties to the order that dominated his world were severed. He held his stomach as he fully indulged in the hysterics that tore through the wise man in his soul.

The students looked on in disbelief, watching their master join the ranks of the insane. Samian felt embarrassed, standing next to a madman, wondering if he was the subject of the amusement.

After a long stretch of laughter, Ur-nammu settled back into a somber state. He stood up and suddenly reverted to himself, a master once again. The students waited, expecting him to share the story that had triggered his manic attack.

"Gilgamesh ... we are going to write a new version based on this epic." Ur-nammu spoke as if his behavior were nothing out of the ordinary—nothing that necessitated any explanation.

"As you know, many versions of this epic have been written before. So, your assignment is to write your own version. I will assign a chapter to each of you who have reached an advanced level. Those who do an exemplary job will be rewarded; their work will be displayed in the new library."

Ur-nammu started assigning the tasks. "Isaa: the Priestess Shamhat Seducing Enkido. ... Karam: the Slaying of the Monster Humbaba. ... Tattanu, you get the Death of Enkido. ... Samian, yours is the Great Deluge story. ... Gandu, you'll do Gilgamesh Losing the Fruit of Eternal Youth. ..."

Chapter after chapter, Ur-nammu gave the assignments until, finally, he came to a brief pause.

"That's all, boys, work on these tasks. As for today, I need to attend to an urgent matter. Samian, you and Isaa work with those who are newer in school. Assist them with the tasks they need to improve on." He turned to leave when a voice stopped him.

"Permission to speak, Master."

"Yes … Edunna." It took an effort for Ur-nammu to say her nickname, and he avoided turning to face her, fronting the exit door.

"Master, you didn't assign me a chapter." Her voice was oddly high.

"You're a recent arrival. You lack the necessary skills for such a project," he answered calmly, suppressing the excitement in belittling her.

"Master, when I came here I was already well versed in reading. I have read the Epic of Gilgamesh five times. As for writing, I have advanced at a fast pace to a good level, which I believe is matching, if not surpassing, that of many of my fellow students who received assignments."

"Who's the learned brother assigned to you?" Ur-nammu asked.

Anxiety almost had Samian jump out of his seat.

"Samian. He can attest to my skills," Enheduanna replied serenely, despite an itch to scream: *You wouldn't need ask had you not been too busy getting drunk.*

"Samian!" Ur-nammu looked the boy straight in the eyes. "What do you think? Is she ready?"

For the first time, Samian wished that Enheduanna had not chosen him as her assigned learned brother. Knowing what the master wanted to hear, he felt cornered. Ur-nammu knew her work was undeniably advanced, though he had never acknowledged it. With head bowed, Samian stuttered:

"Well … I think the work she has presented so far, … she … she's right … I believe she is capable."

Scorn brushed Ur-nammu's face in a yearning to smash a dozen dry tablets on the head of the coward for fearing the princess more than the master.

"Very well, Edunna, yours is the Bull of Heaven chapter," Ur-nammu said coldly, and headed to the door.

"Master, may I speak again?"

And may your vagina cluster with vermin. … Oh my poor tongue, again I'm forced to bind you. Anger gave Ur-nammu sufficient courage to turn and face her.

"Yes, Edunna, what is the problem now?"

"Master, you're probably not aware that I'm a devout follower of our goddess Ishtar. The Bull of Heaven is the only chapter where great insults are hurled at my goddess. With all due respect, I request a change of assignment."

Her stare seemed to spark with fire. Ur-nammu diverted his attention to the wall behind her.

I need to get away from this royal whore before I lose my temper—and my head. … "The Priestess Shamhat Seducing Enkido. Does this part of the epic suit you?"

"Yes, Master, that will be fine."

Sure it's fine; the whore priestess part for the whore princess. Ur-nammu turned to the class. "To whom did I assign that part?"

Isaa stood up. "Master, it is my assignment."

"*Was!* Now your project is the Bull of Heaven." Ur-nammu didn't wait for any more arguments and he walked out.

Isaa was fuming, even though he preferred the Bull of Heaven chapter—with two men venting their anger on the goddess, instead of the female-dominated story of Shamhat Seducing Enkido. What Isaa couldn't stomach was watching a whining princess tell the master how to run the tasks. He waited until Enheduanna walked out on her own to get some clay from the outside box, then approached her.

"Am I in the presence of Edunna," he started, "one of the boys in this tablet house, or Enheduanna, the royal princess?"

"Would a royal princess muddy her hands in the proximity of her subjects?"

"Someone who tries to be one of the boys and claims modesty shouldn't go around telling the master what to do, crying about their assignment."

"Now you have a mouth to speak!" she answered while filling the molding tray with clay. "Yet, when I was left out of an assignment, you kept quiet, even though you knew very well I am better than many of the boys. If you, *Learned Brother Isaa*, had spoken in my favor, you would've gained my respect. Instead, you chase me here, *crying* about being robbed of *your* assigned chapter as if you owned it." Her tray was too full now and, inattentively, she began scooping mud back into the box. "You should be happy with your chapter—the foolish, rash Enkido cursing and hurling the bull's limb at the love goddess. He seems more your type of character."

"You seem to forget," Isaa replied, angrily, "Samian, the learned brother *you chose*, cowered down and remained silent till he was forced to come to your aid. And one more thing, regarding Master Ur-nammu—I've known that man for ages, and you should treat him with respect. The way you talk and stare at him shows a total lack of it."

"That man," she fired back, "has cried to heaven and Earth, trying to throw me out of school! I guess *that* is the kind of behavior you respect. Is it your opinion too, that I don't belong here?"

The reply stumped Isaa. He looked into her eyes and it was all he could do to stop from shouting that he was madly in love with her, and if it were up to him, he would remove the god Nabu and have her take his place—the goddess to be worshipped in all tablet houses.

Fuming, Enheduanna walked back to the class, unaware her mud tray was empty; she had scooped all the mud she had come to collect back into the box.

BAZAAR

"**N**ETI, GET MY STREET CLOTHES."

Ibrahem needed another leisurely walk through the streets of Uruk to shake off the horror he had experienced three days ago when his neck was miraculously spared the sharp edge of Naplanam's sword.

Those walks also helped him forget about the palace and the deceptions that dwelled within its walls. The smiles, the praise and best wishes exchanged among the functionaries and visitors were mostly false expressions on faces that often harbored ill will. All were actors on a quest for one common goal: to expand their wealth and power through gaining favor with those of higher authority. Ibrahem wasn't an exception, but his greed was not as insatiable as that of many others. A high profile he did not seek, following the wise proverb, "The tallest and shiniest rods are the first to be struck by lightning."

Going to the king with all those rumors he linked to the priesthood—some true, some exaggerated, and some entirely made up—had him wonder as to how he had gotten the courage to risk it all by undertaking a feat of such madness. Was it the will of the gods—perhaps he truly was their messenger! Or was he driven by his absolute hatred of Ishullanu, whom he loathed more than death? Deep within, he could perceive a great potential in King Sargon for stripping the priests of the immense powers they exercised on the people.

The last few nights he had had nightmares. One detail wedged itself in his memory: Naplanam's severed head had come to whisper in his ears: *Did you see my body? Can you help me find it?*

Ibrahem spent most of the dream looking for the guard's body—in the palace, in his home, and among the animal carcasses at the butcher's shop. Finally, Naplanam announced that he had found it. Ibrahem turned to see Naplanam's head sitting on a body—not the firm, muscular body of a soldier, but one he could easily identify. Ibrahem had looked down, and to his horror, his own body was gone.

Now, drained but euphoric over cheating death, Ibrahem would change into his street clothes and walk through the bazaar, inhaling the putrid stench that inundated the streets from the open sewage channels. The odors of living animals and the stink from the discarded parts of the slaughtered ones—all of that was easier to breathe than the jasmine-perfumed air in the palace halls.

Walking among the commoners reminded him of his good fortune; seeing what the wretched went through every day in their struggle to feed their families was the best remedy for greed. He knew that countless were the people out there who went to sleep starving, wondering whether they would wake up the next morning—or maybe, hoping not to wake up at all.

"Tell my wife I will not be home to eat," he told Neti while straightening his garb. Ibrahem was in no mood to talk to her, for she would only start arguments about where he was going on his rest day and whether he preferred the taste of some girl's body over her food. Her biting comments wouldn't bother him anymore; she had no idea of how close he had come to losing his head. Breadwinner and excellent provider that he was, he would do as he pleased. If she thought he was cheating on her—which wasn't true, not since that concubine ages ago—he might as well go ahead and cheat. The idea prompted a sudden vigor in his loins.

He walked out of his house, which was built on a high mound of earth in a wealthy section of the city—though not as extravagant as the neighborhoods farther up by Ishtar Walk and Anu View; those had roads paved with hardened brick and were broad enough to accommodate six twin-horse chariots. He took the narrower streets to avoid meeting nobles on the way; the less he saw of them, the better.

Everything seemed different about the city today. It felt livelier, as if everyone were rejoicing at seeing him alive after facing the specter of death. Even the beggars seemed to be happy, as though in the hope that a similar miracle to the one that saved him could visit them and turn their miserable lives around.

A spirited Ibrahem meandered through the bustling market square like a child exploring a world new to him. Crowds dawdled between stands walled with merchandise—fruits, vegetables, fish, meat, cages of poultry, beer and wine jars stacked high. Other merchants hoarded pottery, cutlery, tools and utensils, oils and herbs, wood and dried dung for making fire—all the cooking essentials.

Soon, Ibrahem felt weak and his pace slowed to a crawl. Since the day he was soaked in Naplanam's blood, his appetite for food had abandoned him. The sight of meat refreshed the sickening memory of the guard's body draining of life. But unexpectedly, the pungent aroma of grilled meat now hit his nose and he was starving. Overwhelmed by a revived appetite, he let his feet race toward the source of that delicious smell, when another irresistible aroma tackled his nose, carried by the breeze from the baker's hearth. He stopped there first and ordered a loaf of bread, then charged to the grilled meat stand.

"Here, fill this with meat," he said to the vendor, handing him the bread. "Add some lettuce, onion, garlic … whatever you have, stuff it all in the loaf." Ibrahem grabbed a bead of lapis lazuli from his leather pouch to pay the vendor.

The vendor mused. *How strange? To stuff food in a loaf instead of breaking chunks of bread to eat with the food!* But the pay was generous, so he proceeded to do as he was told.

Ibrahem walked to the steps of a nearby temple and sat to eat.

"How peculiar?" A girl in a priestess's attire approached him. "What an odd manner of eating—food wrapped inside a loaf! You must be from a faraway place."

"No, I'm only a very hungry man." Ibrahem smiled at the fledgling priestess. His hatred of the priesthood was mainly reserved for the higher-ranked, arrogant priests.

"Take a bite." He held the loaf out to her. "Go on, it won't hurt."

The priestess opened her mouth and wrapped it around the food. Instead of biting, she gave him a playful look.

"Go on," Ibrahem urged her.

She took a bite and chewed. "Delicious. Not a bad idea—meat wrapped inside the bread … then you wrap the mouth around it," she said, suggestively.

"Take another bite."

"Thank you, noble sir, one bite is enough. But I would like to offer you some love in honor of our love goddess Ishtar, in return for a donation."

Ibrahem didn't think twice about it. The gods had saved his life, and here was an opportunity to show his appreciation through this modest priestess. He reached into his pouch, took out two silver pieces and placed them in the girl's lap.

"Oh noble sir," she said excitedly, "so generous of you. By the love goddess, I swear to delight you with all the joys of the love art." She clutched his elbow.

"Not now, charming priestess, I have things to do. How late do you work?"

"Till sunset, noble sir. But I can await your return at a later time."

"I should be done before sunset."

"Good. I too need to get a few things for the temple. After that, you'll find me around here, waiting for you. Noble sir, I leave you now in the gods' care."

"Till I see you later, go with the gods' care."

She walked away down the steps. Ibrahem's gaze followed her until she blended with the crowd. His desire was building up, but he held it at bay; time would pass quickly as he walked the bazaar, and before the day was about to close, he would spend some well-deserved, pleasurable time with the priestess and rejoice in being alive, away from the company of the conceited characters infesting the palace. The bazaar provided everything to satisfy a man's needs, material and sensual.

He devoured the meal so fast, he felt the vendor had cheated him on the amount of meat he had stuffed in it. With mouth dried up by the food, he walked into the nearest tavern for a cup of beer. Though it was of average quality, it still bested the finest beer offered in the palace, for it was sure to lack any ingredients a foe might add with intent to poison. He ordered another cup, took his time drinking it, and licked his lips—a thing he would never do in the company of nobles. The owner was friendly, and after a short conversation he agreed to rent Ibrahem a room in the back for the night, to be paid for in advance.

Ibrahem left the watering hole feeling rejuvenated. It was a beautiful day, not stifling with heat and humidity—another gift from the gods, who had lately seemed inclined toward favoring him.

He passed a barber's stand. Instinctively, his hand brushed his hair, and he walked back, sat in the wicker chair, and asked the barber for a regular hair and beard trim—no locks or braids that might attract attention. Once that was done to his satisfaction, he resumed his joyful stroll, heading toward the section where leather hides, wool, and fabrics were sold. But clothing he totally ignored then; he was so engrossed in happy thoughts that he could've walked naked, feeling fortunate to have his own skin still covering him. However, when his eyes fell on a bracelet of jasper worry beads, the temptation was too much. He haggled with the merchant, only for the sake of haggling, and walked away with the bracelet, slipping one stone bead after the next with his thumb, counting his blessings while he dawdled through an area of the market where wooden furniture and intricate wicker-work made of reed and palm leaves crowded the busy thoroughfares.

The Marriage market loomed within his sights. "Marriage" was an ornate name for what was essentially a slave market of young boys and girls who were stripped of their value as humans, destined by fate to a brutal life that reduced them to be traded as objects of pleasure and to slave for the wealthy. The idea of getting a young servant girl had often crossed Ibrahem's mind, but his wife would watch her movements like a hawk, and probably work her to death. It would be much wiser to keep any love affair away from home, in a rented room, and save himself the headache of dealing with his nagging wife; it wasn't the appropriate time for adding domestic problems to the official ones. Ibrahem had to force his legs away from the road leading to the Marriage market, for there could be a beauty offered for sale who might cloud his reasoning.

A large crowd on the Healing Path dictated his next direction.

There were six men and three women, lying on reed mats, their pain and illnesses on display to all who passed by. People had gathered over, questioning the patients about their symptoms.

"What's hurting you?"

"Is the pain on and off, or steady?"

"Anyone else in the family suffering the same symptoms?"

"What foods and drinks did you have lately?"

"How was the color of your waste? Was it liquidy or too solid?"

Thus the questioning went as passersby took an interest in the patients' conditions, stopping to give suggestions for a cure based on past experiences of their own or someone they knew. When worldly advice fell short of providing reasonable remedies, then a passing priest might volunteer a diagnosis and a cure using the spiritual healing arts.

"Did you make offerings to the gods?" was the first question a priest would ask.

"How often?"

"Have you uttered blasphemous words?"

"Did you sleep with your neighbor's wife or commit incest?"

"Steal … cheat in a trade?"

"Had you murdered someone?"

The questions went on, covering a whole inventory of immoral deeds that merit the gods' wrath.

A boy in his teens was lying on a mat with eyes fluttering. According to his mother, he suffered from recurring violent convulsions.

"My son is a good boy," the mother cried and begged for help. "He never harmed anyone—never said or did anything that would enrage the gods."

"How about the father? Did he commit a wicked act?" asked a young priest standing alongside an older one.

The woman's expression changed from grief to guilt.

"Woman, better tell the truth if you want us to help your child," the young priest demanded.

"His father … killed a noble during a robbery," she answered reluctantly, "and was executed."

The young priest went into deep thought while his companion

looked indifferent; evidently, he was a master administering a field test to an apprentice.

The disciple sank to his knees and placed both hands on the boy's head. The youth's body went into shivers that shortly extended to his head, shaking it violently until ultimately it shot up with force.

"He's possessed!" shouted the priest, retreating.

The crowd backed up, farther extending the buffer from the mad entity inside the boy. The neophyte priest stepped back toward the boy, placed one hand firmly on his forehead, raised the other hand up high with palm opened as if leaning on the heavens to counter the force of the demon, and he prayed.

"O spirit of the slain noble, this boy had no part in the vile deed his father committed against you. The father paid for his crime with his life. I command you: stop torturing this body and leave it at once!"

The boy's shaking only grew worse, and another sharp jerk sent the priest falling back. The crowd looked on with disappointment, doubting the priest's healing abilities. But the session wasn't over; the priest hadn't conceded defeat. He took up the same stance over the boy and resumed praying.

"O goddess Ereshkigal—mother of demons, guardian of the dead, keeper of all souls! I beseech your help on behalf of this innocent boy whose body has been raided by an escaped spirit that is wreaking havoc on him in a wrestling match of no end. O Ereshkigal, have mercy on this boy! He's guiltless, yet suffering for an evil committed by his father, who was punished and sent long ago to your realm. Command the stray, vengeful spirit to retreat, back into the depths of your netherworld! Let it seek the guilty soul that wronged it in the first place."

The boy's shaking grew increasingly violent, but this time the priest prevailed and stood his ground until the shakes subsided. The boy sat up in a dazed state, unburdened by stray spirits. His mother sprang to hug him, her tears mixing with his sweat. The crowd was enthralled, showering the priest with praise, many handing him donations for the holy deed that saved the boy from a life of misery.

One man wasn't impressed: Ibrahem.

Many were the sham acts he had witnessed. The first was, when, out of curiosity, he'd followed a supposedly healed man who was freed from his ailment. Ibrahem wondered if the cure was permanent, speculating that the man's spasms might come back. What he saw next shook his faith in the priesthood. The "healed" man, who was accompanied by his wife, stopped in a deserted side street. They were approached by a priest who handed the man something. Ibrahem had no doubt it was a payment of some sort. They spoke briefly, laughed, and went their separate ways. Having witnessed this, Ibrahem noticed that the priests were in the habit of deliberately selecting their patients—most certainly, the ones who worked for them. Every so often, real patients were accosted by priests who truly believed that they were endowed with healing powers. When their litanies yielded no results, the patients were always accused of being liars in not disclosing the true reasons that brought about the gods' wrath, thus rendering the prayers futile.

The next patient Ibrahem observed was a man with a toothache. Most of the ones giving advice agreed on the worm-in-the-tooth diagnosis and recommended pulling the tooth out. Several men offered to do it for free right there and then, using a brick and a wooden stick.

Ibrahem moved on to where a woman had just arrived. She sat on the mat, rocking back and forth, complaining of terrible headaches that made her cry in pain, often enough to drive her husband mad. He would beat her senseless to quiet her down. Bruises colored her face in dark hues, and everyone felt sorry for her. Some called on the priests to come to her aid, but they walked away, claiming they had urgent matters to attend to.

A middle-aged man knelt to her side. Emulating the priests, he used hand gestures and prayers for the goddess Ereshkigal to free the woman from whatever demons possessed her. After a few failed attempts, an older man came and pushed him aside.

"There is no demon inside her," he announced. "Any more prayers and this poor woman will run for the river to drown herself along with her pain. I know how to cure her."

The sure words, coming from a mature, seemingly wise man, planted a trace smile of hope on the woman's face. She watched the man unravel the cloth wrapped around his bald head, revealing a thumb-sized dip above his forehead. A layer of scarred skin gave it the appearance of a third eye with the lid closed. The crowd moved closer; many were the mouths gaping in amazement.

"The sponge within the head," the man explained, "which cushions and stops the skull from collapsing inward, has grown too tight. This sponge is squeezing hard outward. The only cure is to cut a piece of the skull to relieve the pressure. Priests and incantations will not help; what you need is a man skilled in the use of fine, sharp chisels. As you can see, I'm lucky enough to know such a practiced healer. Of course, prayers and offerings to our healing goddess are required before and after the operation."

The woman started sobbing at such a grim prospect for a cure, but the crowd was amused by it. Many ignored the woman, only to hover around the man with the crater in his head.

After having enough of the nonsense, Ibrahem moved away from the infirm and ambled to the next area of the bazaar, where merchants hawked precious wares of gold, silver, and coveted stones to those blessed with riches. It was an ironic show of life's disparities—abundance neighboring deprivation—where the privileged happily strolled and appraised the precious exhibits their wealth could buy, while only a short distance away the cursed lay down, exhibiting their ailments and desperation.

Ibrahem resumed his stroll to the zone where the seal makers had their stands. A seal was one thing a free Sumerian had to carry to enter into any sort of written legal agreement. Cylinder stones would be rolled onto the fresh clay to seal the terms engraved on it. Ibrahem would've liked to change his ivory seal to one of gold, but a cautious inner voice warned about the unwanted attention it might bring. Nonetheless, he studied the displays, keeping in memory the designs he coveted most for the future seal he would choose when his status as a man favored by Sargon was no longer a secret.

He moved to the next area, where the cylinder seals served their purpose. Naturally, it was occupied by the learned men who took on the tasks of reading and writing clay tablets for correspondence and trade agreements.

The scribes didn't limit their services to matters concerning worldly affairs. When prayers and offerings resulted in no response, some people asked the scribes for specific tablets, addressed directly to the heavens and left at the altars of the temples; it was believed that the gods gave priority to reading those tablets, and the devotees' pleas were promptly answered. Other tablets reached all the way in the opposing direction—to the netherworld; buried with the dead, those tablets had vicious curses inscribed on them, imploring the demons to inflict the direst misfortune and harm possible on one's enemies.

Ibrahem had no interest in that section of the bazaar; he scribed his own tablets. He was moving through at a fast pace when shouts erupted. All heads turned toward the source: a scribe, yelling at a drunk man.

"I said stop pissing next to my stand!"

"I piss wherever I feel like pissing," the drunk shouted back.

"Not while I'm around!"

"What would you do about it?" The drunk kept pissing while waving his penis in contempt, prompting the scribe to tackle and throw him to the ground. As the drunk staggered back to his knees, the scribe began kicking him from behind.

"Only donkeys piss wherever they like. You want to be a donkey? Then walk like one—on all fours!" The scribe kept kicking until a few men took pity on the drunk and stepped between the two.

"I pray to the storms god," the drunk shouted while shuffling away, "to blow away the roof of your house and flood it with his piss! And … may wild dogs bite off your shaft and balls … and chew on them!"

The scribe didn't bother to answer. Back to his stand he walked, shaking his head.

With the brief commotion over, the crowd returned to their errands.

Ibrahem arrived at Anu Court, the last segment of the bazaar before his destination. That zone was assigned to the largest assembly of gods on Earth. For the right price, those gods generously consented to take residence with the believers who preferred to recite their prayers from the comfort of their homes. The icons came in a broad array of sizes and craftsmanship to suit the devoted from most layers of society, rich and poor.

Standing outside his destination, the ziggurat, Ibrahem recited a short prayer. As much as he loathed the priests, he had to go there to get paid for a statue of Anu he had worked on for over five moons.

At the main entrance on the base level, he was greeted by a priest and ushered to the workshop, where the god stood a forearm taller than the tallest man ever seen. Ibrahem stood admiring his own work, wondering if the god Anu had left a token of himself inside it yet.

"Ibrahem, what a pleasant surprise," greeted the unmistakable voice of Ishullanu from behind. "I've been longing to see you."

A wave of unease and disgust welled within Ibrahem. He had come to get paid his dues and leave, hoping to avoid the high priest, but it seemed he had been too optimistic. He turned around, a feigned smile scoring his face.

"O Holiness, to be in your presence is the most joyful of surprises."

"We are blessed by the gods"—Ishullanu smiled back and started pacing slowly around the statue—"to have a man of such skill, to portray them in all their glory; none other than the king's personal sculptor. Which reminds me—mentioning the king—I learned that some servants in the palace were seen carrying away what looked like a body wrapped in … blood-soaked covers. It seems someone was decapitated! Also, I heard … you were present. Then strangely, Naplanam was gone—vanished." Ishullanu looked intently at Ibrahem.

"A eunuch," Ibrahem was prepared, but he looked down to give his eyes shelter from the prying priest. "A eunuch spilled wine all over the king. His Majesty ordered him executed right away, then rushed out to bathe, leaving me to take charge of the cleaning."

"I heard the body was heavy to carry—a big man."

"He was a hefty eunuch, recently assigned to serve the king. Unlucky poor man: to lose one's manhood first and later—lose his head." Ibrahem made a show of sadness to conceal any hint of a lie on his face.

"So, what happened to Naplanam?" Ishullanu persisted.

"Naplanam is a brave soldier, and the dull life of the palace never suited him. He requested joining the campaign to control the

Assyrian tribes in the north. Our king granted him his wish."

"Yes, he was—I mean, he is a brave soldier." Ishullanu feigned misspeaking. "May the gods shield him from harm."

He gave Ibrahem a cold, scolding look for daring to tell what was surely a blatant lie. Then came a pause that felt to Ibrahem like it would last longer than the statue of the god he had built.

"Holiness, forgive me," Ibrahem said at last. "I have to tend to an urgent matter. I'm glad you liked the finished work of our god Anu, and I ask if it is possible to pay me the remainder of the amount we agreed on."

"By the gods, of course we have to pay you … yet, there seems to be a little problem." Ishullanu heaved a sigh. "I'm very pleased with the work—excellent in every detail—but as you remember, I asked you to build the statue to be taller than any living person. Well, the other day one of my priests arrived here, greatly disturbed; he swore to have seen a man taller than our god here. The tall man was standing in a boat, and my priest couldn't chase him. So, since there is doubt regarding the satisfaction of this part of the agreement, I'm afraid paying you now might anger our father god Anu.

"But you have my word that my men are out, looking for that tall person. Once we find him and somehow make him … permanently stand shorter, so he won't measure up to our god here, then we will gladly pay your dues, fully, not a bronze granule less. Now, I wish I could spend more time with you, but I must tend to an urgent matter. I leave you with the blessings of the gods."

Ishullanu walked away, leaving Ibrahem motionless, staring at the god's statue until a priest came to usher him out.

𒑊 ◇ 𒌑 𝗐 𒌋𒌋𒌋

The market swarmed with people feasting their eyes on all that brings joy to life. Ibrahem trudged along, rage fueling his thoughts with one image to feast his mind on: a high priest, profusely oozing sticky, red fluids out of his perforated body.

"O great Anu, grant me this wish," he muttered under his breath. "Ishullanu, I'll have you pay. One way or the other, I'll have you pay."

Aimlessly he wandered until he found himself going up some stairs. He raised his head and remembered—the temple, the young priestess. He searched the crowd, desperate to find her. His fantasy of stabbing the high priest now morphed into the more attainable carnal urge of penetrating the priestess. He waited and waited, but only seething insanity arrived, leaving him in the company of a violated ego. Unconsciously, his throat bellowed a scream up to the heavens.

"Where is that whore?"

The shrill sound brought the crowd to an abrupt stop. The madman gathered moments of curious attention, which soon dissipated when it became apparent there would be no more madness to follow. And the human bazaar resumed its normal flow of noise and chaos.

Slave Meets Goddess

T HE BUG WRIGGLED, ITS TINY LEGS FRANTICALLY STIRRING the air in search of solid ground where it could dash for safety.

Neti watched the helpless cockroach, pinned through its stomach by a sharpened splinter of wood he had used for a toothpick.

This must be how it feels to be a master—to decide the fate of lesser creatures, Neti marveled while standing under a ceiling-corner of his room, where a spider had woven its intricate web.

Gently, Neti pushed the impaled bug off the toothpick onto the web. It went into a frenzy at the touch of the fine thread. It must have watched the horror suffered by its kin as they lay snared in identical traps, where a bug could only hope for the spider to get hungry and hasten a slow, inevitable death. The roach struggled, only to sink deeper into the delicate web, to the excitement of a hairy spider that rushed to accept the gift wrapped in its own genius design of woven art.

"Enjoy the meal." Neti addressed the spider—one of the many that built similar webs around the house, undisturbed, for Ibrahem appreciated their help in hunting down other annoying, uninvited pests.

Neti left the room to perform his chores. In Ibrahem's absence, and as the head servant, he walked around the house as if he owned it.

Saura never burdened him with heavy work nor treated him like a servant. She enjoyed his company for he was a good listener and kept her entertained with details of all the happenings he observed in the city, where she sent him for goods and foods.

With Ibrahem avoiding her and Isaa spending most of the day in the tablet house, Neti became like family, and Saura genuinely gave him that sense of belonging. The man carried out his duties and more without being told, purely out of devotion to his masters; they were the closest thing he had to a family.

Most slaves dreamed of freedom, but not Neti. He had resolved that if a day arrived when Ibrahem decided to set him free, Neti would beg to be retained as a slave. He wouldn't know what to do with freedom; insecurity and loneliness would become his new masters.

Arguments between Ibrahem and his wife were happening more often. Today, Saura had rushed to visit her cousin after learning from Neti that Ibrahem had already left without bothering to speak to her. Suspecting that Ibrahem had a concubine, she needed to vent her anger, and talking to Neti wasn't enough. On her way out, Neti calmed her down, allaying her suspicions; his master was simply stressed and needed some time alone.

Neti cleaned up around the house and helped the other two servants with their duties, then headed to the workshop, where much cleaning had to be done. Ibrahem didn't allow the other two servants there, fearing they might damage his work.

Holding a wicker basket and a broom of palm leaves tied to a wooden stick, Neti moved between three unfinished statues, sweeping the stone chips, breadcrumbs, and date seeds. He mulled over how to approach his master and tell him not to leave behind a trail of food crumbs that invited cockroaches, only to complain later about the bugs.

His thoughts came to a halt when he caught sight of a bug creeping along the top of a cabinet. The bug stopped too, as if sensing the looming danger, and instinct called for evasive action. A cluster of leaves collapsed, about to crush the roach flat, but it reacted with a speed that would make a slug out of the fastest human, scampering to safety through a gap above the cabinet's door. Neti lifted the broom to inspect the kill, only to find nothing but dust. He eyed the cabinet and wondered if it housed a breeding haven for those intruders.

Ibrahem had told him not to worry about cleaning inside that cabinet, where he kept the finest of his finished statues. Neti pondered: if cockroaches could roam freely in there, why not him? He would open the cabinet, slaughter a whole colony of pests, clean whatever filth they had created, then close the cabinet. His master could only be pleased if he noticed the difference.

The cabinet stood about his height. Its door was secured by two bronze rods that slid through holes into the frame's edge. Neti slid out the rods, opened the cabinet door, and came face-to-face with two standing statues, about waist high.

Are these gods or kings? He wondered, but that didn't stop him from wrapping his arms around one, cautiously taking it down to the floor, alongside the wall. He did the same with the other statue, then followed with two more standing in the next row. One last statue remained, all the way back inside the cabinet.

Through the glow from the oil lamps that managed to seep in, Neti could see the statue's silhouette shivering at the touch of the faint light as if it were hiding a secret that should not be revealed. Neti reached in and pulled on the statue, sliding it closer to the edge of the cabinet. He took a step back, then froze at what he saw.

The awestruck Neti almost went down on his knees, but another force made him stand erect. Staring at him was the statue of a nude woman, carved out of white marble with faint veins of pink, lending the statue a hint of life. Seamless curves from head to toe accentuated her sensuality. Her perfectly rounded breasts promised to make an infant of any man, begging to suck on them. She had both arms up, hands joined behind her head, offering a seductive invitation to those she chose to be her love slaves. Her legs were twined together in a most wicked tease, playfully denying entry to the realm of pleasures between them. Her eyes were the most striking thing; unlike the large, bulging eyes of other gods that symbolized a mighty sight capable of reaching the far edges of earth, this goddess had eyes of normal size. Yet some mystical power seemed to sparkle out of their precious stones: pupils of black obsidian, dark as the caverns of the netherworld where Ereshkigal ruled, surrounded by turquoise with its deep blue color of heaven where her sister Ishtar reigned. Embedded in those eyes, Neti saw his image: a human desired by two goddesses, and a life delicately suspended between eternity and death.

At no point in his life had Neti ever felt the need for a woman. His lucky stars he always thanked for being endowed with the basic needs of food and shelter, provided by Ibrahem's family. As a slave, his chances of meeting women were limited; Saura hadn't allowed any female servants in the house since Ibrahem had made a concubine of the one who birthed Isma-el—his first son before Isaa.

Alone with a goddess who tempted the strongest of men, Neti stared at the eyes as if mesmerized by a magic spell. Although he was castrated, miraculously, he felt an intense desire resurrecting deep within his core. Temptation overwhelmed him, and his right hand moved to gently brush the breasts of the goddess. She didn't seem to mind him touching her, which roused more of his passion, luring his hand to feel her whole body and reach the godly pleasures he had always thought a eunuch was unequipped to explore. Conquered by her divine sensuality, Neti was ejected to a distant world—too far to hear the room's door open.

"Mercy of the gods! Mercy!" Ibrahem's voice stormed in, breaking with revulsion. "How dare you stare the goddess in the eyes. Get your filthy hands off her, you heretic bastard!"

Neti froze in place, his hand glued to the statue. Nervously, he turned around just when his master's heavy palm swiped his face.

"Kneel! Down on your knees, *now*! Ask the gods for mercy for this blasphemy, this insult to our goddess!"

Immediately, Neti fell to his knees. Ibrahem pressed one foot onto his servant's back until he lay flat on his stomach.

"Insolent, dirty pig! A slave, a lowlife—desecrating the goddess!" Ibrahem was bristling with anger when the sound of running feet reached him; the two other servants, who were working close by, came rushing when they heard the angry screams. Ibrahem stepped out to meet them.

"Go back to your room, now, and stay there!"

"Yes, Master."

Ibrahem closed the door and went back to Neti, who was trembling like a bare twig in a sandstorm.

"O Master, I didn't mean any insult to the goddess. Her beauty struck me numb with admiration. I beg forgiveness, Master."

"Silence, you filthy pig! The gods don't give a dung about your admiration or that of any miserable soul like you."

Ibrahem knelt in front of a statue on the floor and began reciting some verses in Sumerian, which Neti didn't understand. Neti kept stammering apologies and pleas to be forgiven.

Once finished with his prayers, Ibrahem turned to the heretic servant and announced God's judgment.

"Our god Anu wants your eyes sealed with molten bitumen for defiling his beloved Ishtar and eyeing her with lust."

"O Master!" Neti was sobbing. "I did commit an awful act, but it … it was not intentional. Lash me, double my work—but please, don't take away my sight. Plead to the gods on my behalf, Master. I'll be their most loyal servant, I beg you."

Ibrahem cast a contemptuous look at his servant and turned back to Anu's statue, recited more prayers, then went silent. After moments torturous to Neti, Ibrahem made a few nods of his head as if in acknowledgment of Anu's commands, and returned to Neti.

"I interceded on your behalf, praised your work and obedience. … Spared will be your sight, Neti; however, Anu insists that you be punished, though less severely."

Ibrahem rose to his feet. "Like a thoughtless animal you behaved, and, like an animal, you should never utter any intelligible sound again. … Anu wants your tongue sliced and burned as an offering to the goddess. Only this can smoke away the traces of your heresy."

Neti crawled to his master, planting eager kisses on his feet. "May the gods bless you, Master. Let these be the last words my tongue speaks. Forever I will be your faithful servant to repay you this favor. To the gods, I'm forever grateful for their leniency and will never again raise my head in their presence."

Ibrahem grabbed a jar from a nearby table and handed it to Neti.

"Drink this beer to help ease the pain. I'll be back." Ibrahem left the room.

Neti chugged the beer until Ibrahem returned with a basket containing wood chips and short sticks of reed. He placed a pedestal he used for his work before the cabinet where the goddess stood, then laid a flat stone block on it to serve as a makeshift altar. With an oil lamp, he lit a reed stick, placed it on the stone, then added the wood chips and more reed sticks to start a small fire.

Neti was still kneeling on the floor when Ibrahem touched him on the shoulder.

"It must be done now. You will be forgiven and spared god's wrath."

Neti could only nod. Any last words were too bitter to speak.

Ibrahem took the jar from him and poured some beer to soak a piece of cloth he was holding.

"You can straighten your back. ... Now, place this cloth under your tongue and slide it far out."

The always-obedient servant complied. His jaw quivered when Ibrahem held the tongue tight with one hand and a knife with the other, then Ibrahem started praying.

"O merciful God, this repentant slave offers this sacrifice in penance for his sacrilege. He begs to be granted forgiveness with this offering."

Neti calmed some of his distress with the thought of his eyesight being salvaged. He didn't offer the slightest resistance and closed his eyes.

𒀭 𒅗 𒐼

Isaa was in his room scribing on a tablet when he heard his father yelling, which was a normal thing when Ibrahem scolded the servants for a job poorly done. Later, Isaa was alarmed at hearing a cry that seemed to arise out of an animal in severe agony. He walked out to investigate, and a frail eerie moaning led him to the workroom. Cautiously, he pushed the door open.

A furious Ibrahem swung around to see who dared interrupt the purification ritual.

"Father, what is all this shrieking? What is going—?" Isaa froze at the sight of a man kneeling over a bloodstained floor.

"Neti! What are you doing to Neti?" Isaa screamed.

"Stay out of it, Isaa. This worthless slave insulted the goddess in the vilest manner. He touched her—lusted for her. Anu ordered he should be punished."

Ibrahem turned back to Neti and whispered in his ear. "The gods prefer that you make the offering yourself."

Neti cupped his shaking hands for Ibrahem to place the bloodied offering.

Isaa, stunned and sickened, could only watch as Neti crawled toward the little fire smoldering before the most sensual statue of a goddess he had ever seen.

This seductive statue, and its mesmerizing eyes, must have been behind whatever led Neti to suffer this brutality.

Neti reached the altar, his tears soaking the sacrificial offering before he reluctantly dropped it in the fire. Smoke floated like a departing soul, and crackling sounds seemed to cry its torment. Neti backed away from the flames that consumed his tongue, when mysteriously he felt searing heat inside his mouth as if his burning tongue were relaying its agony to him from the altar. Violent tremors shuddered his body with the pain he could no longer express in words. He collapsed, finding refuge in the dark confines of an unconscious mind.

Isaa rushed to Neti's side. The man's blood-soaked mouth made him cringe and turn to the altar where he could only stare at the smoldering sacrifice in disbelief.

"All that crying," a triumphant Ibrahem sighed. "I wonder if the goddess likes her meat lightly salted."

Ibrahem felt like a master again—no longer the fool who was deceived by Ishullanu and the temple priestess; the bleeding creature on the floor was proof of it.

The flames radiated against Ishtar's statue. She looked alive, ready for a hot meal. Her sparkling eyes gazed at the three men in the room, who joined the statues in their stillness. Yet, she failed to notice a fourth creature: a bug by her feet.

The cockroach tasted the scent of blood in the air and patiently waited. It was hungry; the gods had finally answered its prayers for food.

A Farewell to Wisdom

ABANDONED BY THE GOD NABU, WHO APPRECIATED NONE OF his prayers and offerings, Ur-nammu delved into the mystical experiences attained through the habit of drinking daily. Gradually he spiraled into the dismal funnel of drinking all day.

The chief of the tablet house, Akiya, begged him to stop drinking. He didn't want to lose Ur-nammu; no other master was half as good.

At the early age of seven, Ur-nammu was enrolled in the tablet house, where he had shown pronounced talent to become the youngest learned brother. He kept progressing at a fast pace and eventually, he became the most valued school master in Uruk. The man had never married nor had any interest in women. As for having kids, he considered each of the boys in the tablet house as a son.

He was offered the position of chief master at the tablet house but had flatly refused it, passing it to Akiya. Teaching was his joy—a routine he had chiseled into a life where order reigned just as the mornings awaken to the warming sun and the nights are greeted by the smiling moon. Of course, there were the rare eclipses now and then, but like all eclipses they had always passed with no harm done.

However, the arrival of Enheduanna uprooted the tranquil sanctity of his house of knowledge. Every time he stepped into the class, he felt her sharp gazes dissecting him, and the classroom became a torture chamber he would only dare enter in a drunk state. He fantasized for long nights about beating and violating her, but in the reality of day he could hardly look her in the eyes; the beast of the night would magically convert to prey under the daylight.

Akiya never understood why Ur-nammu was so vehemently

opposed to the girl's presence. In sharp contrast, the boys had begun to like her after the initial trepidations of being in the presence of a princess. Enheduanna deflated any air of royalty around her with her levity, and within a few days most of the boys were conversing with her. As for the timid ones, she was the one to close the distance and initiate talking and joking with them.

Akiya had hoped the master would eventually get used to Enheduanna, that things would go back to normal. But the only thing that became normal was Ur-nammu's drinking habit.

All of Akiya's attempts to help Ur-nammu came to failure. It was no surprise when concerned fathers began to visit Akiya and complain, having heard from their sons about the travesty. They demanded to know why they were paying for their children to sit and stare at a snoring drunkard in the classroom. It was only a matter of time before Akiya decided that enough was enough. He gave Ur-nammu an ultimatum:

"Tomorrow, you come back sober, or else don't bother to come back—ever."

⨎ ◇ ⫫ ⩊ ⫫

Enheduanna arrived at the tablet house with her two guards, whom she herself had selected after the commotion of the first day. She made them swear to be gentle and never intimidate her fellow students.

Oddly enough, Ur-nammu was standing outside the gate with his back to the wall, and he greeted her.

"Princess, may the great Anu brighten your day and may Nabu bless your writing clay."

"And may the gods of heaven bless your day, Master Ur-nammu," she answered with a surprised smile. It was the first kind gesture ever from the master. As she passed him to go through the gate, he erupted, shouting with his body flailing side to side.

"And may the love goddess bless the shafts while on your arse they feast and fill your vagina with the milks of man and beast!"

Ur-nammu doubled over into a laughing frenzy. Isaa and many of the other boys who were just arriving stopped and stared in confusion.

The frantic laugher of the master was abruptly cut short when one of the guards approached and delivered a powerful punch to his stomach, knocking him to the ground. The other guard moved over Ur-nammu and pulled him up to his feet so his partner could exact more punishment, when Enheduanna stepped in between them.

"Let him go!" she shouted.

"Your Highness, this man insults you. He should be punished."

"I said let him go!" Though she was furious at Ur-nammu, Enheduanna's temper shifted to the guards. "That's an order!"

The guard holding Ur-nammu shoved him to the side, where he fell face down onto the dirt.

"We will obey your order, Highness," the other guard said, "but this has to be reported to the king. If we don't, we will be punished severely. The king will find out eventually, with all the witnesses here."

Enheduanna looked at the boys, who kept watching from a distance. "One of you help him away from here."

No one moved at first, then Isaa trudged forward hesitantly. The memory of his ugly encounter with the guards was still fresh. A tacit look of appreciation from Enheduanna boosted his confidence.

Isaa helped his master up to his feet, but after one step, Ur-nammu hunched down and began to vomit the putrid, beer-soaked contents of his stomach. The students watched, grimacing in revulsion at what Ur-nammu had become. In contrast, they held Enheduanna in admiration; for despite the abhorrent insult, she stood firm to forbid her guards from pummeling the master.

Once Ur-nammu gained some control over his rebelling stomach, Isaa helped him to walk away. It was a chilling scene for the boys to watch: their mentor, plagued by an insanity that consumed his wisdom, rendering him oblivious to his own teachings on how to tackle life's problems and walk the straight path to success. Their gazes of sympathy followed every step he took, with Isaa struggling to keep him up and walking. The two disappeared around the corner, and all wondered if they would ever get the chance to bid farewell to the great master.

"No more—enough!" grumbled the innkeeper, Shaku-shmakku.

"My friend, is this how you treat your best customer? One more drink, for the love of our fucking, wise-arse god, Nabu."

"Ur-nammu, I appreciate your patronage, but it's time to close. Look around, everyone has gone home."

"Just one more drink," Ur-nammu persisted, "so I can tell you my story without any bastards snooping. I need to get it off my chest. You're like the brother I never had. I beg you, one more drink."

Shaku-shmakku had to pay the price for his success. Nicknamed "The Quicksand in the Oasis," his watering hole attracted men who came not only to get drunk but also to confide their dark tales to him. Countless were the sorrows and anguishes buried by disturbed souls who cast their burdens into Shaku-shmaku's "Quicksand," and they all walked out with a sense of being cleansed of guilt, confident that their secrets would never resurface.

"Fine, one more." Shaku-shmakku sighed in frustration and poured the wine into the cup. "Drink it, then go home. I have a family to go to."

"Family! Huh, family!" Ur-nammu muttered.

"Yes, family—my wife and two boys."

"Boys, boys—how I miss my boys!" Ur-nammu sipped on his wine.

"I didn't know you have children," Shaku-shmakku said. "Are you married?"

"Me—married! Do I look like such a fool?"

Shaku-shmakku scowled, "Oh, do forgive my tongue for uttering this *foolish question*! After all, I'm simply a fool—*a married man!*"

"Don't get angry, my friend. Forgive me, I meant no insult. I'm hopelessly drunk and I'm … let me tell you a secret."

Ur-nammu moved closer to whisper in the man's ear as if there were others spying. "Don't tell anyone. I've … I have never slept with a woman."

He leaned back to see Shaku-shmakku's reaction, but the innkeeper didn't show much surprise. Probably, he had guessed it already, or heard others confess to a similar deed—or in this case, a non-deed.

"I don't know why," Ur-nammu continued in a calmer voice,

now that his initial confession had been treated as nothing out of the norm. "It's not that I like men. No, not me, never. It's this thing about women … they scare me. You see, my father was a wealthy merchant who traded with the Phoenicians. That's how he met my mother, who was truly a Phoenician beauty. She was pregnant with me when he went on a trip with a trading party that was attacked by some marauding brigands. Among all the traders, my father was the only one killed, and he was buried in the desert. My *loving* mother somehow blamed *me*."

Ur-nammu took a gulp of wine, and resumed bitterly. "According to her, she learned about his death on the same day she became aware of me … inside her belly. She would beat me every day—morning, noon, night—and scream, 'You're but a shelter for an escaped evil spirit from the underworld, and my husband had to pay the price and die to replace that demonic spirit down there!'

"She filled the house with statues of Phoenician gods and goddesses as if to protect her from the supposed demon I harbored. I don't know why she didn't kill me when I was an infant. Most probably she dreaded my demon would be released and invade her own body.

"No, it wasn't that she missed my father—she changed lovers like hair combs, but that never calmed her down. The beating never stopped; it became an obsession. I hated her—cursed her with every breath I took. She almost destroyed me with fear and guilt, yet I must thank her for one thing: she sent me to the tablet house. I don't know why—maybe she needed some rest between the beatings. So, I found refuge in that house of wisdom, every day till the evening, when she impatiently waited for me to come home, to knock me around. Only one thing helped me endure the abuse—knowing I would have school the next day. The tablet house became my love, my home, and my life."

"*She* must have been the one crazed by a demon," Shaku-shmakku consoled him.

Ur-nammu sipped some wine. "With age, I grew bigger and stronger—and she, frailer—yet the beating continued. One fateful day, I gathered enough courage to slap her back. To my amazement, she fell on the floor—she never saw it coming. For the first time, I saw fear in her eyes, no matter how hard she tried to hide it. She stood up to punish me, but then my fears were replaced by the anger of the demon she believed me to be. I slapped her again and again—felt so powerful, I didn't want to stop, and she kept trying in vain to hit me back.

"Soon, I tired of the slapping, I closed my fist and *punched* her in the face. She flew back into a tall standing-statue of some Phoenician *whoring* goddess, banged her head and fell. As though the statue took offense at being smacked, it wobbled on its base and dove, squarely bashing my mother's head with a ruthless blow." Ur-nammu paused to gulp more wine.

"Was that how your mother died? Killed by her own goddess!"

"Yes … it was an accident. It wasn't my intention to … kill her."

Ur-nammu lied. There was one more detail he couldn't bring himself to reveal: when he found his mother was still breathing, he sat on top of her and smothered her to death with his gown.

"I don't want to lie to you, my friend; I was so relieved—felt alive, like … like a slave set free. People are born when their mothers give birth to them; I was born when I gave death to my mother. But she left me with a curse—this fear of young women—an eerie feeling that my mother's spirit has escaped the netherworld and possessed the body of a girl to exact vengeance on me." Ur-nammu gulped the last of his wine.

"Yours must have been a truly harsh childhood." Shaku-shmakku expressed sympathy. "Don't feel guilty, your mother was asking for it. I wouldn't worry about her spirit coming back. You're a good man and only good things happen to good men. Forget the past, enjoy your life. As for your secret, I assure you it will go with me to the netherworld—where your *demon* came from." They both laughed. "Time to go home. Will you be fine?"

"Now that this heavy burden is off my chest, I feel—free." Ur-nammu ambled to the door, tottering. "Shaku-shmakku, bless you for listening. Tomorrow I will celebrate—will go to Ishtar's temple, pick me a beautiful virgin and … set both of us free from our virgin burden. Yes, I'll get a virgin every now and then … make their love goddess happy."

"Sure, my friend. I'll see you tomorrow." Shaku-shmakku closed the door without waiting for a reply.

"And ... the gods be with you." Ur-nammu turned around, zigzagged a handful of steps, then fell to his knees in the middle of the alley. He sat there, gazing at the night sky.

"Will you stop dashing around!" He shouted up to the stars, which for some reason were restless, circling above him. "I want to count you."

"Out of the way, you drunk fool!" a voice rang in his ears. He spun his head, and the shaky image of a donkey came to view.

"A talking donkey!" He began laughing.

"Talking donkey, huh?" a man with an ugly grin barked to his face. "I'll have my talking donkey and the cart behind it run you over and make *you* bray like a donkey. Out of the way, fool!" The man grabbed hold of Ur-nammu when another voice rang out.

"Calm down, no need to quarrel. Let me help him."

A benevolent stranger approached, helped Ur-nammu to his feet, and walked him off the road. The cart owner thanked the stranger and moved on with his donkey.

"May fleas bounce off the donkey, to nest on your bushy balls!" hollered Ur-nammu while clinging to the stranger for support. "And may bats camp under your ceiling, shit in your mouth while you snore, and—*choke you!*"

Only a bray from the donkey answered him as the cart rolled away.

"Old man, are you all right?" asked the stranger.

"I'm not an old man," Ur-nammu protested, and he shrugged himself free of the stranger, walked to the side of the alley, and pulled his robe up.

"Don't be shy now, out with you." Looking down, he held on to his rod, letting a long stream shoot out. "No sir, I'm not an old man. Tomorrow, my little partner here and I are going to fuck a young virgin."

Once he finished, his legs wobbled and he collapsed to his knees, landing in his urine puddle.

"A virgin! Lucky you." The stranger came to help him up again.

"Then you'd better go home and get some rest. Those virgins are hard to satisfy."

"True, my friend, true. … May I ask you a favor? I'd greatly appreciate it if you would help me get home. I'll treat you to a virgin tomorrow. The fertility festivals are upon us, and the temples are flooded with virgins taking their vows."

"Now you have my full attention. Which way is home?"

"The way home?" Ur-nammu laughed. "My friend, you see that jittery moon, just follow it. Where it calms down and stops bouncing—there is my home."

"I see." The man laughed. "But that moon is bouncing too fast for us to catch up to it. I have a better idea. Come with me; be my guest at my place, and tomorrow we go straight for the virgins."

"Splendid idea!" Ur-nammu brightened. "Virgins of Uruk! Ready yourselves for rupture … and a long, rapturous night!"

"That's the spirit. Now let's go, you need the rest. You will love it at my place."

"May the gods bless you." And Ur-nammu began to cry. "It's rare to find someone who cares. You know who I am? … I'm the master of the tablet house—the best they had or will *ever* have—served there all my life. Then, just like a dog—*a dog*—they tossed me out for some, some *bitch*!" He wiped his tears away. "Bless you again. I don't want to bore you with my troubles. We're going to have the best of times. I feel like this is the beginning of a friendship that will last a lifetime."

"Absolutely!" the man asserted. "You stole the words out of my mouth. Nothing less than a lifetime."

𒀭 𒂍 𒑱

And the stranger was true to his word. It was a friendship that lasted a lifetime; alas, till that very same night.

Under the vibrant stars, the new friend extended to Ur-nammu one vigorous farewell by the river's edge before he sent the great master floating on his own, drifting aimlessly at the whim of the Euphrates.

Two ravens dotted the blue skies when something caught their attention. Through the air they glided, down to the riverbank where gentle tides whirled about a sprawled body that had been abandoned by the life it once hosted. It was merely one more of the countless tragic scenes that evoked a futile search for answers to the greatest mystery beyond. This one could only divulge a few details about the end journey of Uruk's wisest schoolmaster—his very last word, scribed on the mud by his own savaged body.

FROM HEAVEN TO THE NETHERWORLD

THE NOISY CROWD THAT GATHERED AT THE BASE OF THE ziggurat came to complete silence as they watched in reverence the winged figure that suddenly appeared, towering at the seventh level—the very top of that most sacred of temples.

God had just arrived from the heavens to bring blessings and fertility to the land. And God raised both arms up high in a grandiose gesture and was hailed by the crowd in acknowledgment of his might.

With his vanity satisfied, God proceeded to descend the stairs. The long, white feather wings sticking out of the back of his white tunic seemed to flutter in harmony with the torch flames that lit the staircases.

God also donned a headdress embellished with short feathers of assorted colors. While descending from the third level, a breeze rustled the feathers, and an orange one separated from the headdress; lazily it floated before God. The distraction made God miss a step, and he clumsily skipped it, jumping with both feet to the one below, speeding down the next four steps, nearly losing his balance before he stabilized at the landing area.

"Damn these fucking stairs—almost broke my neck!" Ishullanu murmured to himself. He thanked the gods for preventing an accidental fall, then resumed the descent at a slower pace. He hated this part of the ritual: coming down from the very top of the ziggurat. And to his frustration, the torches along the stairs seemed to flicker and dance way more vigorously than normal, making the steps appear to shake under his feet.

Upon reaching the first level, a sigh of relief departed him. He stepped into a pair of wooden sandals, which gave him the extra height he needed to look more godlike. But the extra finger of altitude made him a little dizzy. He swayed momentarily before recovering to a firm posture. Cautiously, he ascended the four steps to a raised wooden platform that was set up at the first level to give the audience below a better view, unobstructed by the brick barrier at the edge.

Ishullanu moved to the front, beaming with head raised high, brightly lit by torches on poles of varying lengths arranged to create an illusion of being submerged in flames, happily dancing around him. He was the star of this greatest of festivals: the arrival of the spring equinox, marking the start of the new year.

The priests earned their wages in the meticulous planning for those festive days. Gaining the approval of the gods was a vital undertaking to secure a healthy harvest and overall prosperity. Rituals, prayers, and offerings ran their course for seven days, nonstop. The priest who played the role of the supreme god, Anu, would be the most visible person in the festivals. Ishullanu's assistant had volunteered to play that role, ostensibly out of concern for the high priest's health during those grueling festive days, but Ishullanu would not hear of it.

The first day of festivities began with the high priest leading a procession, starting at the grand temple of Anu and ending at the heart of all the celebrations—the ziggurat. He was followed by men selected from the public for the honor of carrying a statue of Anu, erected on a wooden platform, to the top level of the ziggurat. Ishullanu had to stop the procession on each of the seven levels to catch his breath.

Similar processions ensued the following days with statues of Anu's offspring, gods and goddesses, carried from their temples. Those statues were placed on the first level, which didn't present a major challenge to Ishullanu.

Today was the seventh and final day. The day most awaited, when it would be revealed to the mortals whether they were worthy of receiving more of God's blessings or deserving of his mighty wrath.

To assume the role of the descending God in this final act, Ishullanu had to endure the strenuous climb to the top of the ziggurat, again. However, this time the task was made easier; after a banquet in the palace that preceded the celebrations of this special night, Sargon was courteous enough to offer the high priest a few guards to carry him, seated on a chair, to the sixth level. That left Ishullanu with only the last staircase to tackle before his imposing godly appearance at the ziggurat's top level.

Safely back on the first level, with the hardest of the tasks already achieved, a smiling Ishullanu brimmed with pride on proving his prowess. The time had arrived for the part of the ceremony that had made him endure all the grueling work and resist passing the task to his younger assistant.

Ishullanu turned to a man sitting in the dark corner all the way at the back and waved for him to approach.

Obediently, Sargon rose out of his modest wicker chair and proceeded with head bowed in reverence to God. Ishullanu, with a condescending stare, grabbed a wooden replica of the royal scepter from the king's hand and tossed it over the wall. He did the same with all the replicated items Sargon wore and carried: crown, jewelry, king's seal, and even the wide belt around his waist; one by one, God tossed them out of the ziggurat.

The king stood like a plain commoner before Ishullanu with only an austere tunic covering him when, suddenly, a slap swiped his face.

"Kneel," came the order from God, loudly enough for the crowd to hear. In submission, the lowly king went down on his knees, his back straight, head bowed.

"Have you ruled the people with justice, as I commanded?" asked God.

"Mighty God, justice was applied equally to all subjects, not a soul was denied a fair trial," came the king's humble answer. Still, it wasn't enough to spare him another godly slap.

"Have you ordered the death of anyone not deserving to die?"

"No, Mighty God. No one was executed but the guilty."

Another slap.

"Have you abused your powers or cheated your subjects to enrich yourself?"

"Never, O Mighty One. I have always followed the rule of law. I have never laid a finger on anyone's property, nor forsaken their rights."

The slaps and the questions continued. Sargon's eyes were tearing while Ishullanu felt his hands growing heavy and his body getting fatigued.

"Have you ever questioned the authority of the priesthood?" Ishullanu blared the tenth and last question.

Sargon raised his head a notch. A spiteful smile floated clearly over the tears on the red canvass of his face.

"No, Holiness, I would never dare challenge the authority of the priesthood."

Seeing the grin, Ishullanu was incensed. Instead of showing humility, the king displayed blunt arrogance. Ishullanu raised his hand to deliver the last punishing slap.

Swiftly and unexpectedly, Sargon bowed down and Ishullanu slapped nothing but air. The momentum carried him sideways and he felt as if the ground below him had shifted. The crowd saw their high priest about to lose his balance, barely avoiding a fall for the second time that night.

Faint sounds echoed from below—many of surprise, but to his shock, Ishullanu could detect mockery in others. He had a strong urge to go for another attempt at the final slap but quickly refrained, for to miss a second time would spell disaster. He swallowed his pride and looked to one side of the platform, where the high priestess, Nidala, stood waiting to commence her part of the ritual. Sargon walked back to his shaky, wicker seat in the back corner—the abode of the mortals.

With a nod from Ishullanu, Nidala walked to the front and began reciting prayers in the traditional Sumerian language. Though most people didn't understand that tongue, it was of little significance, for the main interest was in the event to follow.

"And the earth shivered." Nidala's voice shifted to blare in Akkadian, clearly heard and understood by the people. "Then the earth cried to the heavens, pleading, 'O Mighty God, bless me with your goodness and nourish me with your richness.'"

Nidala turned to the side to face a simple wooden couch, waist high, where a beautiful woman lay on her back. She was a celibate priestess selected from a few others who volunteered for the ritual.

Her dress was a modest brown garb—the color of earth.

Nidala raised both palms up and resumed the prayers.

"O great Anu. Take out your mighty plow and plow deep inside my hunger. Fill me with the seed of life. Nourish my thirst with your vigor and I promise to give the fruits of your sweetness to those who strive to worship and serve you."

Nidala stepped back to clear the path for God, who would bless the pleading Earth, but to her surprise, the man playing the Almighty role stood still, sweat beading on his forehead while he stared at the floor. She knew right away that something was wrong—very wrong; Ishullanu never had a problem with any ritual before. Tonight, he was acting strange, losing his balance on the stairs, then again with the slap that missed the king's face.

"And God took out his mighty plow!" She shouted the line at the top of her voice to revive Ishullanu for his coming act.

Ishullanu snapped out of whatever had immobilized him and began moving, trying with visible effort to walk straight. Upon reaching the woman, he stood still, confusion written all over his face.

"And he plunged his mighty plow … into the virgin earth!" Nidala yelled again.

As if reminded of his role, Ishullanu awkwardly raised his robe halfway, grabbed the woman's legs for support, and began pumping his waist slowly against hers, when a voice soared up from the multitude.

"He's supposed to show his plow! Why is God veiling his plow?"

So sharp and powerful was the voice, it pumped courage into other spectators, and soon, erratic shouts from all sides found their way together in a massive outburst.

"Show the plow! Show the plow!" The crowd persisted, but their request was fully ignored by God, who timidly reneged on his duty in exhibiting the core of his virility.

"You hear the people!" Sargon yelled from his seat. "Show the plow. You should not skip this part of the ritual!"

Ishullanu was distraught, his breathing labored. He stopped pumping against the woman's body and folded over her.

"Are you done already? So fast!" Sargon taunted.

Ishullanu didn't respond nor move.

"Guards!" Sargon called, and rushed to the platform. Two huge, uniformed men materialized in the back and hurriedly followed to the front.

"Move him aside," the king ordered. "Priestess! Go check for blood and seed on the woman. See if she lost her virginity."

Nidala moved with trepidation, passing by Ishullanu, who gave her a pitiful look that begged for help, as if she were a goddess with his fate hanging on her answer. She approached the woman, certain of what she would find, cursing the misfortune that placed her in this situation. The tormenting dilemma was whether to tell a lie and lighten the shame of the man she had once loved—the one who deflowered her and made her high priestess—or tell the truth and abandon him to certain disgrace.

She parted the woman's legs in search of blood, then delicately felt inside her with a finger. She returned to the king and whispered something.

"The people need to hear your finding!" Sargon yelled.

Slowly, Nidala walked to face the crowd.

"The priestess … is still a virgin," she announced flatly, with not a trace of the majesty her prayers had carried before. It was a plot; she could sense it. Lying would not help the high priest, it would only send her to the same doom.

"We are cursed!" a voice screamed out. "The gods will be angry! Our land will dry up and we will starve!"

Other voices joined; frantic wails filled the air.

"Calm down! The fertility act will be fulfilled, it's not too late," Sargon shouted. He then accosted the high priest, who was already forced down to his knees by nausea.

"Get up! Show your plow and resume the act. The crowd is getting restless."

"You … poisoned me. The banquet … the drink." Ishullanu spoke with his vision orbiting Sargon's shadow, which seemed to be dancing on the floor.

"Poison!" Sargon frowned. "What fool would dare poison the high priest and incur the gods' wrath upon himself? It saddens me to hear such an accusation. The whole court drank the same drink you had—many of my close family did, too. It would be utter madness to poison them all. The drink was a special brew prepared by Ibrahem; you know the man—he sculpted some gods for your temples—always complaining you don't pay him his dues.

"Unfortunately, it seems the brew is causing mild sickness in the ones who drank it. But my healer says it's nothing serious—just a mild nausea and some fatigue. Tomorrow you will all wake up like horses eager to race. Don't worry, it won't kill you. I'm sure the gods have already cured you—*you*, being their proxy. Now come, show some vigor; a fresh vagina is impatient to be pummeled." Sargon turned to face the crowd.

"People of Uruk! Our high priest is feeling better; cheer him on to finish his task!"

"Show the plow! Show the plow!" The cheers shook the ziggurat but couldn't shake Ishullanu to rise and stand erect for the task.

"By the mighty gods, stand up!" Sargon roared as if urging soldiers to attack. But the priest remained planted with his knees on the floor.

"Pick him up." Sargon ordered the two soldiers.

Together, they grabbed Ishullanu under the arms and lifted him up.

"Raise his robe for the crowd to see his mighty plow."

The display evoked a roar of laughter from below, followed by the biting comments.

"What are you going to plow with that—air?"

"May I lend him my plow? It's hard and overflowing with seed."

"Guards! Help him stand his plow over his balls!"

"Let them plow his arse—that might get his plow to work!"

The mockery continued until a powerful voice roared.

"People of Uruk, this is no laughing matter! Our livelihood, our land, is in peril. The gods are watching this disgrace right now, and their fury will unfold soon if we don't find a worthy replacement for this impostor."

Silence prevailed, then the voice resumed. "O Great Sargon, King of all Kings, you are our only hope. You are the reflection of the great god Anu. It must be the gods' wishes that you become their proxy on

Earth. We plead to you: deliver us from the imminent calamity that is about to descend after this reprehensible act. O Great King, we urge you: save us, for the gods' patience is fleeting and their wrath is grand."

Again, the crowd echoed with similar pleas. The king stood pensive, fingers kneading his beard to help expedite a wise decision.

"High Priestess." Sargon faced Nidala, thundering. "Am I worthy of the task? Am I God's reflection—the true proxy to take charge of enforcing his will, to perform the sacred act, and to bring blessings to this precious land of ours?"

Seeing Ishullanu swamped in disgrace, Nidala's fears of the intimidating high priest were shattered. It also unleashed a rage over the ways he had exploited her and the scores of other priestesses for his own pleasure and designs. No longer hounded by doubts, Nidala heralded her answer, hammering the words to crush the kneeling priest.

"The gods work in mysterious ways! They willed this to happen; it is their way of changing things. O Great Sargon, you are the reflection of the great father god. Your will is mighty Anu's will, and no one on this Earth is more deserving than you to take on this sacred act." And Nidala knelt. "Release your plow, sow your mighty seed, and bring blessings to our lands."

Sargon waved for the guards to approach and spoke briefly to them. They dragged Ishullanu to the back wall. One guard stood over him while the other went back to help the king peel off the only garment covering him. Totally naked, Sargon faced the shadows gathered below. All eyes were transfixed on his throbbing rod, which glistened in the light of torches as it twitched in search of the pleasure it had been denied for six days.

"We are saved!" shouted the voice that was becoming familiar. "Behold the sacred plow of the mighty king—he who will bring blessings and preserve the fertility of our hungry land!"

Hails to the plow penetrated the heavens till Sargon moved toward the woman, and all went quiet.

A bout of nervousness tackled the virgin upon seeing the naked king approach. What was she supposed to do; how to bow to the king while lying on her back? Not to mention the anticipation of the joy and pain that were bound to invade her body. Her breathing quickened and her eyelids betrayed confusion, fluttering in concert with the vibrant flames of the torches. She closed her eyes to shut away the eyes of the people whom she could not see, yet she could feel their gazes surging through the darkness below, penetrating her. Above her, the stars spied; infinite pairs of eyes, countless gods, all watching this mortal body of hers. She could hear nothing around her; her heart was beating fiercely to drown out whatever noise tried to infiltrate her ears. She was alone, yet aware of the whole universe, watching and listening to her.

She jolted when she felt flesh slither between her thighs. Hands reached up under her robe, massaging her breasts and helping her relax as waves of pleasure began flowing through her, compelling the jitters to ebb and wash away. She felt the king's hardness go into her slowly. Pain and pleasure joined forces. Spasms of ecstasy rose inside her, then teased as they withdrew, only to rise again; even the pain felt pleasurable. She managed to keep quiet, but not for long. Soon her moans of lust ruptured the silence that enveloped the temple compound. Then her robe began to slide off her body, and she joined the king in nudity. To her surprise, her timidity was gone, as if it had been stripped away with the garment.

Gripping her thighs, Sargon lifted her slender body off the bench. Instinctively, she reached out to wrap her hands around the king's neck, wanting him to give her more of this godly joy with her body gliding up and down, matching the king's rhythm. Now she was searching the darkness below for those hungry eyes, wanting to show them the joy she was feasting on while letting loose ecstatic screams that seemingly became the lone sound within the four corners of Earth, singing to a universe that had gone silent so as not to miss a single rhyme of her lust. She felt like the only one alive among all—mortals and immortals.

Sargon moved with her cleaved to him, all along the front perimeter to give the whole crowd a better view, now and then throwing glances at Ishullanu, who sat still, staring at shadows on the floor.

Though Ishullanu wasn't looking, the woman's moans screamed to him the joy that should've been his—now seized by Sargon. Those moans sadistically emasculated him, making him feel less significant than the moths that flitted around the torchlights and occasionally landed next to him.

A sudden loud cry shook the temple when the woman's passion reached its peak. Involuntarily, Ishullanu's head snapped up—forced into watching the deflowered woman convulse in rapture.

Sargon took her back to the couch. Gently, he laid her down and eased himself on top, giving her more of the regal treat. Soon, his pace sped up, making her heart race to catch up with the pleasure. Tears slid down her cheeks when her moaning thirsted for aid to express the overwhelming joy as Sargon swelled inside her and let loose the stream of his vigor in spasms that shook them both to the core.

The reign of silence prevailed as Sargon withdrew, giving way for Nidala to approach and probe the woman's love path. Within moments, the high priestess walked back to face the crowd. She raised both hands and with a strident voice she announced:

"The virgin land is nourished, the seed is plentiful. The gods will grant their blessings and our harvest will be mightily fruitful!"

Jubilation thundered to heaven, praising the gods for their mercy after the event had come so close to the verge of doom. Nidala walked to the woman and helped her put on the brown robe, then together they walked to the statue of Ishtar and knelt for a short prayer.

The king stood with his tunic back on, greeting the subjects who showered exaltations on him.

"Long live the Great Sargon, our savior!"

"May the gods grant Sargon immortality!"

"Reflection of god! Born to be a god!"

Sargon glanced back and waved for Nidala to join him.

"You have proven your worth and wisdom as a priestess, Nidala. You will be greatly rewarded."

"Majesty, I was merely following the will of the gods."

Sargon smiled, nodding his approval, then turned to address the crowd.

"People of Uruk, it is time to do your part. Go and celebrate the holy fertility festivals. Spread the seeds of love, and the gods will reward you. Our land will prosper, our harvest will be plentiful."

"O Great King!" The potent, charismatic voice soared again, silencing the crowd. "How can we celebrate when the holy ziggurat has been defiled and the criminal is still breathing on its sacred ground? He should be punished, and death is the only punishment fit for such an appalling desecration."

"But he is your high priest!" Sargon expressed gloom and sorrow as if hurt by this demand.

The instigating voice persisted. "How could he be the high priest when he is on his knees, his plow lame, weighed down by shame? The only thing high about him is his disgrace that stank all the way up to high heaven."

Wild laughter erupted from below.

"Then let the gods deal with him," Sargon reasoned.

"O Great King, this impostor also dared to slap you in the name of the gods. He insulted all that is revered by the people—gods and king. Plunge the dagger of justice into his worthless body. Wash this shame away with his own blood!"

Like a wind fanning the flame, those words drove the people into mass hysteria. The lust for flesh morphed into thirst for blood.

"Stab him!"

"Butcher him!"

"A stab for every slap!"

Sargon pleaded, "People of Uruk, let's forgive him."

Yet the shouts grew louder, all craving for blood to be spilled.

"He must die!"

"We're not leaving before you plow him!"

"Chop him to pieces! Sacrifice him!"

"Plow Ishu now! Plow Ishu now!" The joined screams echoed against the ziggurat walls.

Sargon shook his head in resignation, walked back, and stood over Ishullanu.

"It is out of my hands. Pray to the gods; they're the only ones who can help you."

"I curse you, Sargon. … The gods will avenge me. May they—"

"May they what?" Sargon snapped and leaned down so that only Ishullanu could hear him. "The gods abandoned you. When you tripped coming down the stairs, I thanked the gods who kept you from falling and breaking a limb; that would've spared you this disgrace. Also, remember when I advised you to send a younger priest for the ritual? You could've been resting in bed like the others who drank the brew, and tomorrow would've been just like any other day—eating, drinking, praying … fucking a priestess. But you were so obsessed with showing your vigor to the public—fucking a virgin. Or was it the act of slapping me that brought you the greater joy and satisfied your lust for power? But don't blame me—this was all Ibrahem's design. If only you hadn't cheated him out of his wages."

"Why? What did I do … to anger you?"

"It's a long story, Ishullanu; no time for telling. Surely you know parts of it, like one detail of … beads of morning dew, slowly sliding down a blade of grass."

Sargon grinned while he joyfully studied the man's bewildered face.

"No, Ishullanu, I'm not the type who waits for the enemy to strike first. The priesthood must be stripped of its excessive powers. Alas, we have to start with the most ambitious one—*you*. High Priest, it's high time *you* got fucked. … Guards, drag him to the front!"

Sargon turned to Nidala. "You don't have to watch this. Take your priestess and leave."

Towering over the darkness that enveloped the human mass below, Sargon raised his arms and hollered to the heavens:

"O gods of Sumer, the people demand the blood of this man, the high priest. If you clear him of fault and find him innocent of the crime of desecrating your holy temple, send a clear sign, and his blood will be spared."

Silence reigned under the stars as people held their breath to behold any heavenly sign.

No thunder swamped the chirping of the crickets or the smooth rustling of young tree leaves. The skies glimmered with the same stars, no heavenly ball of fire shot down, and no lightning dared anger the darkness.

"Slide his robe down to the waist," Sargon ordered.

The guards obeyed and stripped Ishullanu, tying the sleeves below the stomach so his robe would not fall all the way down. The pelican feather wings sewn to the garment dragged on the floor.

"Hold him up high."

In a snap, Ishullanu found himself levitating. The pair of high wooden sandals fell off his feet and the colorful feather crown slid over his face, then dove to precariously hang from his left big toe. Below him, he could only discern a mob of ghosts. His lips quivered to shout something in his defense, but the words came out silent, like those of another ghost. Abandoned by the gods, horror tightly embraced him, whispering in his head that death was about to pay him a visit.

"Your dagger." Sargon extended a hand, and at once a guard's sharp weapon was in his possession. He pointed it to the skies, shredding the silence.

"O mighty gods of Sumer! We offer the blood of this criminal to wash away the disgrace he brought to your holiest of temples. We humbly ask you to accept this sacrifice and pray that you grant us your forgiveness."

Sargon took a few steps back and stood to the left of the doomed priest.

A loud scream tore out of Ishullanu when the dagger plunged rapidly, though not deeply, in and out of his stomach. A wild frenzy erupted from below, drowning the high priest's shriek of agony.

"One! Nine more plows! Nine more plows!"

Sargon moved to the right, careful not to block the view of the spectators, raised the dagger again, and delivered a similar shallow stab to Ishullanu's upper right chest.

Ishullanu barked another cry of pain, not as penetrating as the first, but the crowd made up for it with a louder cheer.

"Eight more plows! Eight more plows!"

The king happily indulged the orders of his loyal subjects with a teasing act by slowly changing sides to stretch the time between stabs.

After the ninth stab, Ishullanu could only emit a short grunt; his voice had drained along with the blood lost from the shallow wounds.

Silence hung over the crowd in anticipation of the final thrust. Sargon raised the dagger high as if it were a holy relic to be blessed by the gods. He knelt in front of Ishullanu and told the guards to lower the priest so his fluttering eyes could better appreciate the coming farewell embrace of the dagger.

"Give my greetings to Ereshkigal," Sargon said, clutching the dagger with both hands and sinking it into Ishullanu's chest, a safe distance from the heart, not wanting the man dead yet. He left the dagger in place and told the guards to move the dying man around to offer all onlookers a better view. Ripples of euphoria shook the grounds in celebration of the grisly downfall of the once greatly feared high priest.

"Send him down!" The undisputed voice from below shouted. "He shouldn't spend a moment more on sacred ground."

"Send him down! Send him down!"

Ishullanu, with head hanging limp over his chest, could hear the crowd urging Sargon on. Shortly, the edge of the wall came to his fading view when, just like the king's fake regalia he had tossed over the wall earlier, he himself was tossed. The two wings by his buttocks rippled as if flapping, darkness rose to greet him, and after a brief flight, he landed on his back. Though blinded with pain, he managed to open his eyes and see the stars, but not for long; a hooded figure hunched over him, blocking his view of the heavens. Ishullanu stared at the deformed face that resembled a monster from the underworld. He knew him: Sargon's hideous messenger—the herald who must have been behind the voice that riled the mob.

The disfigured instigator ripped the dagger out of Ishullanu's chest and studied the blade, curiously wondering if the dripping priestly blood was in any way unique.

Ishullanu longed to get a last glimpse of heaven, yet heaven didn't bother to extend a farewell to the disgraced proxy, who disappeared under a tomb of humans that gathered up-close to watch him die. He could clearly distinguish two figures among them: a young man, his neck slashed open, and a girl with a charming smile.

Sargon waived a hand in a final salute to the crowd, then he descended the ziggurat to where his gold-plated chariot awaited. He rode away, accompanied by an escort of chariots, leaving behind a chaotic scene with men clambering over each other to get a glimpse of the sacrificed high priest.

It was late in the night. The grounds next to the ziggurat were calmer, save a few groups of men chatting around the body of Ishullanu. None of the priests dared remove the body of their vilified superior.

A gang of wild dogs soon appeared and stopped to study the scene. Their huge leader, who looked more like a wolf, took confident steps toward the humans, baring his sharp teeth and letting out long, threatening growls, making everyone retreat to a safe distance. The pack leader walked calmly to the body, sniffed and licked it, then started biting and ripping. His partners, feeling secure, rushed to join him.

Ishullanu, the gods' rabid proxy, who instilled fear into the commoners and fated so many to a horrible end, became the center of attention for one last time in a banquet celebrated at the base of the same ziggurat where he preached. He was being revered by a pack of wild dogs, gathered to voraciously indulge in the carnal pleasures of his highly priestly flesh.

Soul Searching

FRETFUL LOOKS ABOUNDED AMONG THE STUDENTS AT THE tablet house. News spread faster when fear was attached to it.

Angry souls that refused to descend to the netherworld, or had somehow found a way out of it, were always a great source of anxiety. Ur-nammu's was one such soul.

It was a common belief that if a departed soul could not identify the body which had contained it in life, then it would keep roaming in search of that body, haunting those among the living it could recognize.

Nothing in the corpse of the wise master that settled on the muddy riverbank would've made it possible for his soul to identify its body. The face was disfigured—bruised and swollen by what seemed like ruthless pummeling. Then there was the pecking inflicted by the birds until a fisherman spotted him. Ur-nammu would've never been identified had it not been for the cylinder seal on his necklace. On it was depicted a man holding a tablet, kneeling in obeisance to the god of writing and wisdom, Nabu. Ur-nammu's name was inscribed on the seal. Too bad the master didn't teach his soul how to read.

No one dared say he was murdered. The innkeeper, Shaku-shmakku, verified that the man had been very drunk when he left. So the story was circulated that he had staggered away from the inn, then stumbled into the river where he drowned. There was no ceremony for his funeral as there should've been for a man who had enlightened so many nobles and would-be nobles in the fine arts of writing and the wisdoms of past generations. People only gossiped about his last drunken tirade at the princess. The way he had died was enough of a warning to anyone foolish enough to honor his memory. His body went underground without a coffin. The only attendants were the gravediggers, who assumed he was just another beggar. They tossed his body into a hole shared with an executed man *and* a beggar, filled the hole, and left, leaving no mark on the grave to memorialize the great master.

To wipe the memory of Ur-nammu away for good, Sargon ordered the man's property and possessions be divided among his two servants. Thus, the rumors of the savage death of the master were replaced with praises to Sargon's benevolence to the poor.

The chief of the tablet house, Akiya, took over the teaching responsibilities—or rather, took over assigning those tasks to the learned brothers. He showed up for short periods to appraise the general progress of the classes and listen to any major issues, then disappeared on the pretext he was searching for a new master worthy of the position. This wasn't an easy task, for all those who qualified for the job saw in the princess a high risk that could lead to a fate similar to Ur-nammu's.

Thus, Samian and Isaa were assigned to keep the students busy. This arrangement also benefited Akiya, for he kept the wages allotted to the class master for himself. Any parent who came to complain about the lack of a master received the same reply from him:

"I'm searching for a master of high repute. Of course, you are free to take your kid out of the school, anytime." Then, Akiya would follow with the warning. "There were a few occasions when parents did take their boys to other *so-called* schools—only to regret their decision moons later. They all came back, asking me to readmit their children. Sadly, I couldn't. You need to know our school has limited space, and many parents are eagerly waiting to have their kids fill any vacated seats."

That answer was enough to keep the parents off his back.

Ur-Nammu's name became taboo. Any hint about him was uttered in a whisper, for it was rumored that his angry soul was roaming to look for his body in the place he cherished most: the tablet house. Amulets to keep spirits at bay were worn by all students—everyone except for Isaa.

Isaa's defiance was an affront none of his peers could tolerate for long. A day came when Isaa entered the class and found the boys gathered around Samian, talking in low voices. They stopped upon noticing Isaa and stared at him.

"Is there a problem?" Isaa asked, ire evident in his voice.

"Nothing that can't be resolved,"—Samian approached him—"if you wear an amulet like the rest of us. … Aren't you worried about evil spirits?"

"No. I'm not aware of any such spirit. Whose spirit are you talking about?"

"Stop pretending!" Samian tried to show firmness before the boys. "You know what I'm talking about."

"I do know of some nonsense—fools' gossip. Now, assuming such a spirit is meandering over us right now, I can assure you it's harmless. Trust me, Ur-nammu's spirit wouldn't be an evil one."

The boys recoiled in alarm as though the angry ghost of Ur-nammu would descend upon them at the mention of his name.

"Watch what you're saying!" Samian chided, and the other boys voiced resentment too.

The only person who kept out of the confrontation was En-heduanna, who sat at a bench, pressing on a tablet with a reed pen.

"Ur-nammu!" Isaa shrieked, snapping his attention to the far end of the room. "Watch out behind you!"

Alarmed, the boys twisted briskly, expecting a hideous ghost lunging at them.

"Shame on you." Isaa grinned. "You call yourselves learned. *You,* leaders and nobles of the future—believe in this mad spirit dung?" He glanced at Enheduanna. "How strange, the only one who isn't showing any fear is Edunna. She has more courage than any of you, *so-called men.*"

Enheduanna dropped the reed pen and stood. Angrily, she pulled on the chain around her neck; a shiny charm surfaced out of her tunic.

"I guess courage is a trait only reserved for you." She moved to within a few steps from Isaa, holding the medal that complemented her furious eyes out to his face.

Dazed that his intended compliment had turned out to be an

insult, Isaa stuttered in search of the right words to exit the trap he had built around himself.

"I didn't mean to offend … I'm sure you're wearing this … as an adornment, not as …"

"Wrong! It is an amulet—silver." She blocked his escape attempt. "Ideal for protection against *mad spirit dung*."

"Forgive me; it was foolish of me," Isaa replied in a sincere attempt to end the argument.

"You need not apologize!" she burst out. "For we, and all those in the city who wear charms, are nothing but a horde of *imbeciles* who believe in idiotic stories. *O brave, wise Isaa,* I bet you're dying to go home and laugh yourself to tears at *feebleminded* people like us."

Isaa's temper flared; not only did she not appreciate his apology, but now she grabbed the lead from Samian in the assault on him.

"Your Highness." Anger overwhelmed his prudence. "I advise you to wear two, three, or seven—yes, seven charms, because if I were Ur-nammu's spirit, the first and last person I would want to harm would be you."

"How dare you!" Samian jumped on Isaa, delivering a punch to his stomach, then shoved him back. Isaa didn't fight back, although he was more than capable of fighting Samian. He stood like a wall, resisting the urge to hunch over in pain, staring his aggressor in the eyes.

"I'm not going to fight you, Samian. I would rather save my strength to fight the angry spirit of *Ur-nammu*."

Samian moved, his fist readied for another punch. Isaa stood his ground.

"Stop!" Enheduanna shouted. "What are you doing? Are you going to kill him because of me, like they killed Ur-nammu?"

All eyes turned to her in shock, not because she had uttered the taboo name of Ur-nammu but because of her pronouncing what happened to their master, of which she seemed to have no doubt.

She studied their faces; they were full of angst, but to her they seemed to hold accusations of murder. Guilt coupled with confusion told her to leave, and she rushed out to the main gate where her guards waited.

The boys watched silently. No longer would she be one of them; she was the princess, and they had better behave in her presence to avoid being promptly transferred to another tablet house—one in the netherworld, where they would rejoin their late master, Ur-nammu.

SLAVE GOD

"**R**EBELLION! HOW DARE THEY REBEL?" SARGON FUMED. "I'LL show them. I'll send them my army, crush their city to rubble, and have the balls of that fucking general of theirs for breakfast. … I'll have Naram-sin lead the troops."

"Naram-sin!" Gungunum, the army high general, couldn't believe his ears. "Sargon, calm down, those few moons you've spent sitting on the throne seem to have clouded your reason. You're aware that Ur has strong fortifications, second only to Uruk. You need me to lead the troops. Naram-sin is just a boy, has no battle experience at all."

"Boy! His boyhood is over. Didn't he learn from the best—you and all those masters? He is going! Where is he?"

"Do I look like his father?" Gungunum snorted, turning a frustrated face to the side where Ibrahem was chipping away at a new statue of Sargon, commemorating his ascension as the gods' highest proxy.

"Need I ask! Our *useless* prince must be busy racing his chariot. Or, bedding some women, what else! … Hukura!"

The chief of guards approached, not bothering the king with honorifics. He was also the personal trainer for both king and prince in the disciplines of fighting and use of weapons. Princess Enheduanna, too, enjoyed watching his training sessions and often participated in them.

"Hukura, find my good-for-nothing son. Drag him here by the balls if you must."

"Right away. I know where to find him." Hukura nodded and rushed out.

"Fine, Sargon, give the command to Naram-sin," Gungunum

relented, "but send me as second-in-command."

"No, I will show all the cities that I don't need an experienced commander to crush them. Ur is going to be an example for all those who rebel."

"All of this could've been avoided had you reduced the blessings tax on livestock," Gungunum reproved.

"I already cut it in half."

"That's not enough. You do recall this tax was first introduced by the priests."

"I must confess, it's a good idea. Gungunum, if I lower it any more, people will think I'm weak and will cave under the slightest pressure. I'm the gods' surrogate; my orders should be carried out without discord—right, Ibrahem?"

"Without the slightest doubt." Ibrahem took his eyes off the statue. "Yet, I must agree with General Gungunum—the taxes should've been lowered more. But now it's too late, you should stand firm in your decision. In any case, the people should be grateful to the king who abolished the oppressive powers of the priesthood."

"Bless you, Ibrahem; no one understands me like you do. ... How is your work going?" Sargon needed to change the subject and walked down to inspect the progress on his statue. He started reading the exaltations to his name, engraved at the base of the statue, then resumed, pointing out other details to Gungunum, who couldn't help but yawn.

"Yes, Father?" a voice interrupted the one-sided artistic exchange.

"His Highness has finally arrived." Sargon bowed, sarcastically. "I hope I didn't interrupt any of your *vital affairs*."

"No, Father, I was sleeping."

"Sure, I believe you. The question is, with how many? ... Hukura!"

"I saw only one." Hukura smirked.

"I guess you didn't see the other girl busy under the covers," Naram-sin said, grinning.

"Oh, and I guess I should be proud of my son for bedding two women at the same time!" Sargon flew into a rage. "Any beggar out there in the city, if given your princely position, would outdo those *brave* exploits of yours, you useless son of a—"

He dashed forward, furiously pointing the scepter to his son's face.

"You listen to me now and listen carefully. There is a place out there called Ur, a city just as grand as Uruk—only to remind you, just in case your *hardworking* shaft made you forget. The rulers there declared a rebellion. *You* are going there to crush that rebellion. Prepare to leave as soon as the troops are ready. You will have all that is necessary of supplies, except for one thing—easy to manage without. Guess what it is? Yes, women. Any woman who infiltrates the troops will be summarily executed. I want to make sure *you* are in charge, not your *commander-in-chief*. It's time for you to learn that there is more to life than the luxury of the palace."

"Sargon, let me go with him."

"No, Gungunum, I need you here. Don't worry, he'll have enough advisers to assist him. Hukura … double, triple his training sessions. Work on him so he acts like a true warrior. I want to hear that my son can use a sword, a spear, a bow in battle. That's the real measure of a man, not the stick and balls between his legs."

"Without that stick and balls, there wouldn't be men to start with," joked Naram-sin.

"How humorous! Alas, I already have Gaga for a jester." Sargon grinned, then blasted out, "You had better not disappoint me, or I swear by the gods I will throw you someplace where the only things you can fuck are pigs and goats."

"Father, I never let women distract me."

"*Enough!* You can leave now. And don't worry about your women; I'll personally make them happy for you."

"But—"

"No buts!" Sargon snapped. "Now leave, all of you. I need to be alone—have to consult the gods."

𒐊 ◇ 𒀸 〰 𒐲

Walking back home, Ibrahem mulled over what had transpired.

Consult the gods … was he serious? Sargon must be adding madness to his mood swings. Wearing the crown quite often gives a king aspirations of joining the gods—an insanity that spurs kings to commit vicious deeds, more like demons surfacing from the netherworld. I need to be careful; even family and friends could incur his wrath and be cursed to a fate no better than that of a sworn enemy.

No ... I need not worry; I'm but a sculptor who doesn't hold any rank within the ruling elite. Moreover, Sargon favors me greatly. The mightiest king on Earth, who considers himself sort of a god, values my advice. By the gods, he spared my life and butchered Naplanam, his most loyal guard, only to cry like an infant over the man's corpse while I watched.

Ibrahem arrived home, immersed in pleasant thoughts and beaming with an energy that eluded his tired body. Life had gifted him great blessings. Apart from the disturbing news of the rebellion in Ur, his birth city, everything else was looking bright: he was esteemed by the king, the priesthood was out of power, health and wealth were heaped upon him. *Life is good.*

He entered his house, ready to spend a peaceful evening alone. But on nearing the workroom, he noticed a faint light weaving around the door edges, evoking a presence in the room. His heart started throbbing for he had not entered that room since the dark day when he had caught Neti desecrating the goddess. He didn't believe much in ghosts, but superstition—the disease that could never be fully cured—plagued him with the thought of encountering Neti's disembodied tongue, hovering in the room, lashing curses out at him. Reluctantly, Ibrahem pushed on the door to steal a glance that would put his mind at ease. With the door opening, he gaped in disbelief.

The room was lit by two oil lamps that carved ghosts in the air, playing a scene that took a stunned Ibrahem back to the past.

Neti lay motionless on a bloodstained floor. Next to him stood Isaa, gazing at the goddess with all her sensual splendors displayed in the open cabinet.

The ghost of his son did not turn to acknowledge his presence. Fear gripped Ibrahem briefly, before it was obliterated by anger. He rushed in, slamming the door behind him.

"How dare you!" His voice rang out thin and echoey as if it had come from his own ghost in the past, the one that had surprised Neti while he groped the divine statue. "Kneel and ask forgiveness of the goddess."

"And if I don't,"—Isaa's ghost regained its body—"you will slice my tongue! Offer it to her!" His words were directed at the statue, which appeared to have acquired an imposing grin, having been given a first sacrifice and now anticipating a second.

"Insolent bastard, you will bring the wrath of the gods on our house."

"Don't worry, Father, they have enough of Neti's blood to keep them happy for a while." Isaa turned around. "Neti ... stabbed himself. He must have decided to end it all; all the suffering and guilt you piled on his poor soul. He offered himself to this thing—this goddess. She's drunk with his blood."

"Stop the blasphemous talk!" Ibrahem yelled, and he cast an indifferent stare at the inert body on the floor. "Bless him for sparing us the sight of his miserable face."

"Shall I prepare an altar—bring wood to light a fire, Father? The aroma of his burning flesh should bring more *blessings* to this house."

"You're trying my patience, talking heresy because of a servant—a slave you buy at the market like you buy an ass."

"He was a man, a gentle human. But if you insist, this ass was there for me more than my father. He played with me, comforted me in bad times, told me stories, jokes, taught me tricks. You forgot who saved my life from that rabid dog: not the gods, not you—he did!"

"All of that—the playing, the stories, everything—was part of his duties. As for saving you, that's because he knew he would be dead if any harm came to you."

"No, you couldn't be more wrong. He loved me like a son, the son he could never have. Yes, he told me how you had him castrated. And how *generous* of you not to seal his eyes with molten bitumen. Huh, this innocent fool was so grateful for your intervention—how you *pleaded to Anu* on his behalf to prevent that grimmer punishment. *That* he told me, despite his sliced tongue, with words woven by his hands. Somehow, I'm relieved he's gone, freed from your abuse, butchering him alive one piece at a time."

"So I'm not your father! ... It was *I* who sent you to the tablet house. You mastered the scribe arts, the ways of the learned and the wise, yet this is how you thank me! The death of a nobody, a slave, drives you to rebel against me! What evil spirit has possessed you—taken control of your reason?"

"And what evil spirit drove you to do what you did to Neti, Father? You won't fool me with this 'daring to stare at the goddess' thing."

"He fondled her in a most obscene way! He more than deserved the punishment."

"Weren't you the one who told me the gods are capable of dispensing their own punishment if they so desire, whether in this life or after death? What is it, really? Were you worried Neti would spread the word about this splendid goddess in your possession? Why not show it to the king, instead of hiding it here? What is that sinister secret behind this statue?"

"The utter nonsense you're asking, *sinister secret!*" Ibrahem let out a brief chuckle to disguise his unease. "Sargon is only interested in statues of himself."

"This one would surely interest him. Any man would love to possess it. I must confess, its beauty has power: the body, the eyes. I don't blame Neti for touching it." Isaa defiantly cupped a hand over her face.

"Take your hand off the goddess! Where did you learn such heresy?"

"Huh, heresy! I'm done with worshipping stone gods—absolutely powerless gods, except in the fears and superstitions they plague the faithful with. You have piles of statues outside that fell short of becoming gods. There they are, broken and discarded, soon to join the dirt we step on. What makes this goddess different from those wrecked stones?"

"This goddess will crush you and whoever be your god!"

"Sure, crushing me with a stone won't be such a hard task. But I will leave to a better place—to where Neti is now, with a god who is merciful to his creation, to a place where you are judged by your deeds, and where the good-hearted will live forever."

"Forever—what a load of dung! Only the gods get to live forever. Death is the fate allotted to all mortals."

"That's the difference between your gods and my one god, who is mightier than all the other gods put together. He will crush them all, along with their armies. He's invisible, yet he—"

"Invisible, One god! You follow that loner god? Have you gone mad! O mighty Anu, deluge me with patience."

"Better than worshipping stones that can't hear, can't talk, can't do anything."

"And how do you know your *loner god* can hear you? Has he ever spoken to you? Have you seen him do anything? This invisible god of yours is the creation of beggars who can't afford to buy the cheapest of gods, so they conceived this 'everywhere, anytime' god. My gods can also be invisible; I pray to them anytime and anywhere too, with or without a statue present."

Ibrahem inhaled deeply. "Son, you're going through the rebellious phase of your life. I understand, I went through that madness myself. Nothing made sense to me, but it passed. Isaa, come to your senses. Our ancestors, back to the first man Anu created, worshipped these same gods. How could they all be wrong? True, I do make the gods from stone, but after I finish the work, the gods visit and—"

"You told me that already: they leave a token of themselves in the statue."

"I'll make you any god you like." Ibrahem regained some calm. "Any Sumerian god. Or if you prefer, Babylonian, Phoenician, Egyptian—they are all related; Anu, Ishtar, Marduk, Baal, Horus, Isis. Just don't get involved with this *invisible loner*, this greedy god who wants to be the only god around—no other gods but him. You're stepping into wicked, heretic territory."

Isaa pondered briefly. "Will you give me this goddess here?"

Trepidation showed on Ibrahem's face, and reluctantly he answered.

"For you … yes. But like you said, she is unique and shouldn't be shown to anyone. She's yours if you ask forgiveness for all the offensive talk you uttered. The gods will forgive you—they understand the folly of youth."

Isaa stole a glance at Neti's body as he knelt before the goddess. Hesitantly, he pleaded.

"Do forgive me for neglecting you … for my failure in … I should've shown better appreciation for the good things you gifted me … how you helped me throughout my life."

Ibrahem drew a long breath, relieved to have lured his son away from whatever mad group he had foolishly joined. But before he exhaled the vile air, it bottled inside his throat, choking him while he watched Isaa stand up, grab the statue, and franticly send it flying off the cabinet.

"Neti, do forgive me," howled Isaa, "and accept this offering, this sacrifice, for all the pain it caused you. Rest in peace, my faithful friend."

The goddess shattered to pieces at Neti's feet, and its head rolled, still intact except for a few chips.

A fit of madness engulfed Ibrahem at witnessing the mutilation of the love goddess. Like a leopard, he lunged at his son, murder in his eyes.

Isaa didn't offer much resistance; he accepted whatever fate his father chose for him, even if that meant joining Neti in his journey. He fell to the floor, his father on top of him. First came the angry slaps, followed by punches.

"Heretic bastard dog!" Ibrahem raged. He couldn't feel his hands while they fell upon his boy.

Instinctively, Isaa raised both arms to protect his face. He tasted blood on his lips and endured the pain; Neti's lifeless body, an arm stretch away, told of greater suffering.

Ibrahem was absorbed in a quest of washing his house clean of Isaa's act of sheer blasphemy. He didn't hear the door open, nor was he aware of persons rushing in until hands grabbed him from behind while someone sneaked in between, creating a buffer to protect Isaa.

"Hold him back! He lost his mind!"

The wail came from his wife Saura. Her own back received the blows, shielding her son until the two servants managed to drag Ibrahem away.

"Let go of me!" shrieked Ibrahem. "The bastard! I'll get those evil spirits out of you even if it means cutting you to pieces."

Madly, he jostled the two servants, who started to wonder if their master was the one possessed, considering the great effort they had to exert to constrain a man of his age.

"Calm down, Master. Beg your forgiveness, Master." They muttered apologies while grappling to control him so Saura could help Isaa to his feet.

"Filthy heretic!" Ibrahem seethed. "Abandoned our ancestral gods for a fake god! You dare honor this stinking slave, Neti, as a father—I'll have you join him!"

"He's your son! Have you gone mad?" Saura cried as she led Isaa away, her small figure guiding him like a flimsy sail steering a ship away from perilous rocks. "You want to kill my boy, my only child!"

"I very much doubt *this thing* is my son!" Ibrahem hollered. "Take this son you conceived with the devil back to that den in hell where his true father lives. Out of my house, out with the demon! I don't want to see his evil face in this house ever again!"

By the time Ibrahem had finished spitting those words, Saura was out the door with Isaa. Ibrahem's fury shifted to the two servants still holding him.

"Let go of me, or I'll sell your meat to the butcher for a bushel of wheat!"

"Beg your forgiveness. Have mercy, Master." They let him loose and sank to their knees. "We didn't want to see anyone get hurt."

"Out of this room—*now*—before you end up like him!" Ibrahem pointed to their dead colleague.

They ran out, stammering apologies.

Alone and in a state of shock, Ibrahem tried to convince himself this was nothing but a nightmare, yet the body of Neti would not vanish. With rage flaring again, he stepped to the corpse, which lay face down, and ferociously he kicked on it till the body flipped over.

"Dog dung, seed of evil. It must be you who introduced Isaa to the *loner god drivel.* To hell you go, where monsters to be your masters!"

Ibrahem's legs soon tired from kicking, but his rage was not consummated; instead, it intensified when his attention was drawn to the head of the goddess on the floor. He picked it up and went to straddle Neti's corpse. With arms stretched high, he lifted the stone head and prayed:

"O heavenly gods, creators of all that was, is, and will be. Punish this heretic and bury his soul in the darkest confines of the netherworld, where you keep the most hideous of demons!" And Ibrahem brought the goddess's head crashing down on Neti's inert face. He closed his eyes, raised the stone, and once more slammed it down. Again and again, Ishtar's stone head smashed against Neti's flesh-and-bone face.

Ibrahem wasn't himself anymore; he had become a pounding tool in the hands of blind rage. Blood and the gray cushion that stuffed the head cavity oozed through the torn flesh. The wet splatter failed to dissolve his anger until a sudden jolt of pain ran through his hand, and he let go of the stone head, opening his eyes to see that the round stone had cracked and split into two pieces, a sharp edge cutting his hand before both halves settled side by side in the shallow crater he'd sculpted on Neti's face. Blood poured from Ibrahem's hand, some of it sliding down to seep inside the remains of Neti's mouth, which had twisted into an ugly smirk as if he were mocking his tormentor and savoring the taste of his blood.

"Yes, Neti, you can smile," came Ibrahem's answer to the smirk. "With this new face, you're going to feel more at home with all the hideous beasts—your neighbors in the netherworld. You deserved your misery in this world, and more is awaiting you in the next."

Ibrahem remained on top of Neti, recovering his breath when curiosity struck.

Could a sign be hidden under these two stones? Perhaps a message from the gods! I do feel something through the stones.

He reached and slowly raised the lower piece. In the pit it had left on Neti's face, he could hardly distinguish the nose or the eyes for they had meshed into a pulp of flesh, blood, bone, and the gray matter that packed the head; all mangled in a chaotic arrangement that had no resemblance to anything he had seen in animal entrails. He put the stone aside, gently, as if to spare the goddess any further harm.

Still hopeful of uncovering a heavenly message, Ibrahem took hold of the other piece of stone, which rested on the bashed forehead. Cautiously, he lifted it so as not to disturb the delicate message engraved below.

A scream echoed out of Ibrahem at sighting the "message." He jolted back, dropping the stone to the floor, and he clawed with his hands and pushed with his feet in a scramble to distance himself from Neti's corpse.

Though both eyes were crushed beyond detection, Neti kept that hideous smirk with an added arrogant, unwavering stare aimed at Ibrahem through a newly acquired third eye, embedded in the forehead; an eye with a pupil of obsidian black, surrounded by a heavenly blue turquoise—an eye that had once belonged to the goddess.

A Sculpture in Love

THE OUTCAST WANDERED AIMLESSLY THROUGH THE STREETS of Uruk to escape the harsh realities of life that sought to crush him. Frigid darkness shrouded his soul. Even the moon denied him the warmth of its brightness, revealing only a razor-thin slice of its splendor.

Isaa drifted in the night, dwelling on the madness that had flung his life into a path of misery.

Funny how mere moments can turn everything around: the son, cherished and loved, becomes a rabid dog, chased away. I've become like one of those statues destined to become a god, only to fall just short of meeting the expectations of its maker; now discarded, so worthless that no one would waste a glance on its shattered fragments.

With a bruised face and a slumped walk, even the night villains left Isaa alone, deeming him unworthy of the effort to rob. Only emptiness dared tackle him, rendering him oblivious to his surroundings until hisses snaked through his ears, breaking his reverie and hurling him back to the realm of the living.

Isaa looked up and realized that his legs had led him to the outside wall of the tablet house. The god Shamash had already pulled out the sun over the horizon. The whispers came from the boys who walked past him to the gate. Their eerie stares at him revived the horrible memory of the morning when Master Ur-nammu, drunk and drained of the capacity for rational thinking, had made his profane greeting to the princess. Only then, through his own misery, did Isaa perceive what had motivated Master Ur-nammu to abandon all reason and allow insanity to take hold of him. A fit of laughter stormed Isaa, just like it had Ur-nammu in that same spot.

⸜ ⸝ 〣

Enheduanna was talking with a younger boy in the class—a second cousin who had recently started attending the tablet house—when Isaa approached her.

"We need to discuss your work," Isaa said, not bothering to address her by name. "Some consistent flaws need to be corrected."

"Flaws! Like what?" she replied, resisting the urge to ask about the reason behind his bruised face.

"Princess, is there a problem?" Samian came meddling in. The mutual aversion between him and Isaa was palpable in the air after their little skirmish over the wearing of ghost-repelling charms.

"We'll talk after school." Having delivered the terse message, Isaa walked away.

Enheduanna had to refrain herself from hollering: *You bastard! How dare you walk away before getting a reply from me?*

"Princess!" Samian's voice reached her.

"What?" She had heard him make a comment, but her anger dulled his words.

"Forgive me, Princess, … it's nothing. Well, maybe today I can show you how to glaze the tablets in the kiln."

Princess! Princess! She almost snapped. Samian had started addressing her with honorifics again. It was one extreme or the other; there was the insolent Isaa, who wouldn't even call her by name, whereas Samian and the other boys seemed to weigh every breath they took, worrying they might disturb her mood.

"Yes, Samian, I'm looking forward to learning how to operate the kiln, but not today." She needed to be left alone. "I … have to get some mud."

"I'll get it for you, Princess," Samian offered.

"No! No, that's fine. I'll do it myself." Depleted of patience, she raced out to the mud box before hearing another "Princess" reply.

⸜ ⸝ 〣

School was over for the day, and everybody was leaving except for Isaa. Enheduanna cast him a look that tacitly said she remembered he wanted to talk to her. She walked to the gate, letting her guards know she would be staying longer after the classes.

The idea to fully ignore Isaa and leave occurred to her. But no, she would not run away; it was a good opportunity to confront this arrogant nobody when none of the other boys was around, for she didn't want them to fear her any more than they already did.

Her efforts to be "one of the boys" were failing; she could sense the veiled unease in their conduct around her. Ur-nammu's soul must be celebrating this small victory through using Isaa as an instrument to shatter her earlier success in being treated equally. Isaa was pushing her to the limits of patience. Undoubtedly, he was planning to humiliate her, but she would be ready to answer his insolence by reminding him that she was a princess, while he—but a lowly subject.

Maybe I should have him bow to me, too!

When she returned to the classroom, Isaa was alone, carrying a wooden tray with some fresh tablets.

"What are those flaws you wanted to show me?" she asked, her face hardened into a frown.

"I'll be with you in a moment," he said, passing her and leaving the room to place the tablets outside to dry.

Clearly he's scheming something, but I'm prepared.

Just as her impatience neared its peak in waiting for him, he came back.

"What I noticed with your tablets—" he started.

"*Your Highness*," she interrupted. "That is how you—and I mean *specifically you*—should address me from now on."

"Why?" He returned a puzzled look. "Didn't you say you didn't want honorifics?"

"True, but it seems you forgot my name. Maybe it will be easier for you to remember 'Your Highness.'"

"Sure ... Your Highness. Whatever Your Highness wishes," Isaa said, lightly nodding. "Well, Your Highness, this is your work from two days ago. Honestly speaking, it's a sloppy job. Your clay mixture was too soft. Look how the characters have lost their sharpness, here … here, and here; all unrecognizable."

"Samian didn't have a problem with it. He liked the work."

"Your Highness, Samian is a master at fawning … an expert in licking arse, *specifically* when it comes to royalty."

"How dare you talk to me like that!" She banged the table with her palms.

"Pardon me, Your Highness, I beg your forgiveness." He bowed. "May I show you a few errors in the work you submitted today?"

Enheduanna eyed him for a long moment. His apology seemed sincere. "Go ahead, make it quick."

He went to a shelf, picked a tray containing a square tablet with sides the length of a forearm, and brought it to the table.

"Your Highness, feel the texture of the clay."

She touched a corner. "Seems to be fine."

"It's acceptable, Your Highness."

She shrugged and looked at him to explain the problem.

"It's acceptable *now*, Highness, after all this time drying. But *not* when you started working on it."

"Samian checked it then, and he said it was fine," she protested.

"Samian … again, Your Highness."

"Yes, Samian! What—are you jealous of him? I see what is happening. This whole sermon is nothing but a load of dung from someone consumed with envy."

"I'm afraid you are wrong, Your Highness," Isaa replied, looking at the tablet. "Envy has nothing to do with it. Here we learn writing as an art form that embraces beauty in addition to the message."

"How poetic!" she scoffed. "Explain to me where my work is lacking in art! The only problem I see here is an envious fool who thinks he's a master in the *art of writing*, sent by the god Nabu himself. Huh, flaws! Go look at your face in the mirror and you'll see more flaws than the count of your fingers and toes."

"Your Highness, if you will allow me?" Isaa reacted as if he hadn't heard a word. He walked back to the shelf and brought to the table another tray containing a tablet similar in size. "This is your last work of the day, still fresh. Take a closer look at this section." He pointed to the middle of the tablet. "As you can see, Highness, the characters lack depth and sharpness; the edges are rounded; a pain to read."

"Where? I don't see it." She leaned down to intently examine that section.

"Right there," Isaa said, then swiftly, his hand went on top of her head, pressing down on it while his other hand grabbed a cup of water he had previously brought to the table, pouring its contents to soften the clay.

Before she became aware of what was happening, Enheduanna was kissing the soaked mud.

"Can you see it now, Your Highness?"

Instinctively, she raised her head clear of the tablet, only for Isaa to force her face into the mud once more.

"Take another look, Your Highness!" he shouted while her face made its imprint in the mud. "You call this writing! Bird tracks in the mud make more sense than this!"

He let go of her, and she jolted up, wiping bits of mud off her closed eyelids and spitting more out of her mouth.

"You see what I mean?" Isaa said, calmly. "One way you can tell the clay is too soft is when it sticks to your face, Your Highness, Princess—or should I call you *Your Majesty*, venerated future queen?" He pointed to the tablet. "I can't accept this work—too sloppy."

"You wretched, mad son of a bitch!" She wanted to spit more curses but was short of breath.

"Yes, I'm mad. Madly in love. I thought maybe with your face covered in mud I would be healed from this madness, but that didn't help. You're still the most beautiful thing that has ever happened to me."

"Tell this hard head of yours to say farewell to your shoulders!"

"I would only be grateful, Your Highness; that would surely cure me."

Enheduanna stormed out the room, toward the gate.

Isaa felt oddly at peace, numbed to the fear of death. Nothing mattered anymore; his father had disowned him and the girl he loved was sending her guards to butcher him.

The guards! What if they decide to have some amusement with me first?

The grisly, sadistic practices inscribed on the palace walls raced to haunt him. *Am I to become a guest in their torture dungeons? Would people walking the street above hear my screams of agony? … Fool! People are completely oblivious to the horrors committed underground. Torture is the most intimate of affairs.*

Fear started to seep within Isaa, adding to the burden on his legs, which had carried his body all night while sleep evaded him. He collapsed on a seat next to the table and waited, scanning the room, resentful that no one was there to lend him comfort in his last moments of life.

His eyes settled on the tray with the fresh tablet. He reached and pulled it closer. Though it contained nothing but muddled clay, still, it was his last memory of her. He ran his hands over the ridges and valleys, careful not to disturb any point of the abstract shape her beautiful face had left behind. It gave him some comfort he desperately needed before eternal sleep embraced him.

The sound of footsteps came creeping from outside. Paralyzed with fear, his eyelids closed tightly in anticipation of the mortal blow. The merciless wait was interrupted by the shaking of the tray on the table. He sneaked a glance and saw his hand trembling, which prompted the clay to quiver as if trying to enunciate a message:

The royal guards—don't be their amusement.

Isaa recalled the warning by Ur-nammu regarding the vicious sentries, which added to his distress. Moments later, he sensed someone standing behind, and he wondered if this was to be the beginning of a long night of torture or the swift end to his brief journey through life.

Something warm began flowing down over Isaa's head. He couldn't fathom what it was until it touched his lips: the unmistakable taste of clay, watered down to give it enough fluidity. Slowly, the mud cascaded to envelop his head with the help of a hand working it. He raised his head a little, squinted briefly, and saw a wicker basket almost cupping his head, mud lazily sliding from its rim. He panicked; the guards were notorious for the savage games they played on the condemned.

The sudden sound of the basket skittering across the floor shook him. A dreaded image flashed through his mind: his body floating downriver, ending up on a muddy bank; a fate similar to Ur-nammu's.

Darkness began to choke him, so he opened his eyes to breathe in the light one last time. Through his mud-caked eyelids, he saw the face of Enheduanna, and he thought he was dreaming.

"Close your eyes! Don't you even flinch," she yelled, "or I'll have the guards chop you into enough pieces to make an offering in each of Uruk's temples—big and small. Guards! Next time he opens his eyes, strike him."

Resigned to his fate, his eyelids he buried in the mud again.

Her hands resumed working around his head, smoothing the clay over his features.

Eye for an eye, mud for mud. He wondered if she was retaliating with a humiliation that would build up to some horridly violent end. Would she hand him over to the guards after having her way with him? Was she smiling now as she retaliated? Should he open his eyes to see that smile one last time, though it was a wicked one?

Finally, Enheduanna pulled her hands away and shook them with snaps of her wrists, sending tiny bits of clay splattering on his face, and with a hint of anger in her voice, she chanted:

"God gave the gift of life—shaping dirt soaked in blood,
Yet many are the fools out there—yearning to go back to mud."

Isaa stiffened, thinking this was the signal for the guards to strike. But the sharp edge of death didn't respond; instead, it was his reasoning that struck, opening a gap in the muds of his fears and confusion. There was no hint of the guards—no laughter, no whispers, not a trace of their movement; she was his sole tormentor. He felt life creeping back inside him and shifted his body to shake some fear away.

"Don't move." Her voice was depleted of anger. "I'm not done yet."

Isaa felt her hands feathering the mud for a smoother finish.

"Perfect! Outstanding—it almost looks alive," she said, admiring her work. "That fool, Learned Brother Isaa, should have nothing to complain about now. He wants art—I give him art at its finest."

Isaa kept silent. He had no clue what her next move would be, but as long as the guards were outside he didn't have to worry. Then he felt something touch his muddied lips.

Slowly, his eyelids peeled up. In his confused state, he could only believe he was indulging in a dream; Enheduanna's lips closed on his. Never had mud tasted so sweet. A deluge of life rushed in, flooding his body as if a goddess were breathing a new soul into his mouth—or were they more like two mud statues, a god and a goddess, breathing life into each other?

With thoughts of death hovering all around him only moments ago, this was a miraculous turn of fate. Isaa felt immortal with that kiss and pressed his lips to hers, hoping to get a deeper sense of this eternity, when Enheduanna backed up, spitting bits of clay. She looked at him and started laughing. He could only return a warm smile after the vast array of emotions he had gone through.

"Oh, by the love goddess!" She pointed to his mouth. "The mud on the statue's lips is ruined. Do you think that stone head, *Learned Brother Isaa*, would complain about a sloppy job and *mud too soggy?*"

"No, no. I think he's getting a little smarter." Isaa waved a hand.

"Are you sure? Maybe I should call the guards to help me smash this sculpture. I can always start a new piece."

"It's perfect, believe me. He's a true mule if he rejects it."

Quietly, they stared at each other till she broke the silence, quoting a song:

"My soul says, 'Forget him, he'll only bring you sorrows.'
But without him, my heart feels like spring devoid of sparrows."

Elation stormed Isaa. His arms felt like wings ready to soar the heavens, but it was an earthly bliss he favored, and he wrapped his arms around her, pressing his lips against hers. Again, she had to pull back, spitting bits of mud.

"I've kept the guards waiting too long. I need to wash my face." She grabbed a jar of water, handing it to Isaa. "Pour the water for me. I must hurry."

Once she finished washing, she looked at him. "You want to wash?"

"Absolutely not. If this is what it takes to win your love, then I'd rather stay muddied forever."

"You do look better this way," she joked. "Too bad it's too cloudy, or I would've put you outside to dry in the sun."

"That won't be necessary. I'm already entirely baked in the kiln of your hot kiss."

"All those daydreams." She shook her head, feigning frustration. "The fantasies I had of a handsome man and a heartwarming, memorable first kiss … and this is what I end up with—kissing fresh clay on a … breathing statue."

"How foolish, but it couldn't get any more memorable." He grinned, and she playfully slapped his shoulder.

"I have to go now. By God, how am I going to explain this?" She pointed to the mud splotches on her tunic.

"Just say a mud tray fell on you by accident."

"I can't lie to my guards. I have to tell them the truth—Learned Brother didn't like my work, and he *shoved my face* into the clay." She laughed and opened the door to leave, then stopped, walked back to Isaa, and planted a light kiss on his lips. "A little more heat for the kiln. Now, my sculpture looks perfect. By the way, I saw a certain *learned brother* foolishly leave some tablets outside; with the rain starting, that's a lot of sloppy work to deal with tomorrow."

She giggled and ran out the door. Isaa, too, raced out to bring the trays inside, his gaze following her. Halfway to the gate, she slipped on the slick mud and fell on her back. His heart skipped a beat but recovered when she stood up. He almost ran to make sure she wasn't hurt but reconsidered when the two guards rushed in her direction. She looked at him, laughing, pointing at her dress as if saying: *Now this is one muddy dress.*

Isaa stood still, the rain working his face into a new sculpture. He tried to laugh, but only a faint smile surfaced over his muddy face; he was too much in love to laugh.

Holy Vow

"**I** NEED TO TALK TO YOU," ENHEDUANNA WHISPERED TO ISAA. "Don't leave at the end of the day."

"Leave? I live here," he quipped. "Is something wrong?"

"You live here?" she asked vaguely. "We'll talk later."

Isaa watched her walk away. She seemed anxious, not herself at all.

Since that day when both had revealed their love behind masks of mud, they hadn't shied away from showing a strong friendship in the tablet house. Their days became short and the nights long. In school, they would talk, joke, even steal kisses while being careful not to be caught in the act; the consequences might prove very painful if king Sargon learned of such conduct.

Seeing their friendship flourish drove Samian into silent rage with an overwhelming sense of being betrayed, even though Enheduanna kept him as her assigned learned brother. When Enheduanna laughed with Isaa, Samian had to fight the urge to cry.

Today, Enheduanna seemed so irritable, everyone left her alone. She kept to herself, casting stares that drifted beyond the horizon. Isaa agonized all day in guessing what might have gone wrong.

The boys were on the way out at the end of the school day. Enheduanna walked to her guards and told them to wait longer for she had to finish some work.

Impatiently, Isaa waited for her. Once she entered the classroom, she ran and fell into his arms.

"He wants me to marry the pharaoh," she cried.

"What?" Isaa held her in a tight embrace as if they might take her away from him right then.

"I'm to be traded like some object … like cattle. I'm the price my father must be paying the pharaoh for some deal," she said, choking on her tears.

"When?" Stunned, Isaa could only come up with one-word replies.

"I'm to leave to the Nile lands within a moon cycle. I can't bear to think of it; to be so far away from here, sitting with the pharaoh's other wives and concubines who don't speak our language. And that's not the worst of it."

"No?"

"They say he's sick and won't last long. And over there, they bury the wives with the pharaoh. Isaa, I will be *buried alive* next to the pharaoh's corpse, to provide fornication services for him in the next life. I swear by the goddess Ishtar, I will kill myself before letting that happen. I'm not sleeping with him, not in this life nor the next."

"Don't despair, my love, there has to be a solution." Isaa's tongue found its loose end. "We can run away to another city. With our reading and writing skills, we can make a good living."

"What madness are you uttering?" She backed away. "No, I can't live like that. There's an easy way out, but we must act fast."

"What way? The only alternative I can think of is to depose your father in a revolt."

"With talk like that, it's your head that will be deposed; I'm surprised you're still breathing. Now listen, I thought about it all night and came up with a solution. You see … anything you gift to the pharaoh should be in immaculate condition. For a woman to wed him, she too must be … immaculate."

"You mean …" Isaa frowned in disbelief.

"Yes, it's precisely what I mean—lose my virginity. I don't care about what follows. Whatever my father does to punish me is better than waiting to be buried alive in a foreign land, next to a dead pharaoh. This way, I will be totally unfit to marry him. My father would not risk passing me off as a virgin—that could cause tensions between our nations, even a war."

Isaa didn't waste any time. He embraced her and began kissing her passionately.

"Not here." She pushed him away.

"Why not? Let's ruin this marriage plan, here and now."

"Think! Do I need to tell you?" she answered sternly. "I'm devoted to the love goddess Ishtar, and I'm only giving my virginity away through a ritual in her honor. So listen carefully: Tomorrow, late in the day, I'll sneak out of the palace dressed as a commoner. Wait for me here before sunset, outside the gate. Don't talk to me; just follow me to the temple on Ishtar Walk. I will go inside alone to pray and take my vows, then I'll step outside. Again, follow me closely. Do you know how it is done?"

"Of course. What else do you think boys my age talk about?" he grinned.

"I'm not talking about that, silly fool," she burst out. "The silver piece and your vow!"

"Oh, I know about that part of the ritual, though … not all the details."

"It's easy. I sit in the designated area outside the temple and would be obligated to leave with the first man who drops a silver piece in my lap and recites the sacred verse. My body and love I shall offer to him in honoring our love goddess. … I know what you're thinking—that I am cheating by arranging for you to be the one."

"No, that thought never crossed my mind," he lied, but the whole ritual nonsense didn't matter to him.

"It's not cheating. The gods can always stop you one way or the other if they so desire, and I must follow the first man who reaches for me, unless he's evidently infirm. If I'm cheating, may the gods' wrath upon me be severe. Now, do you know the verse to recite after you drop the silver piece?"

"Well … not exactly. But I know where to find it, scribed on tablets in the back room."

"Good. Memorize it, and make sure you come with a silver piece. I will not sit next to the temple, where you find the beautiful and wealthy girls. The nobles are always strolling in that area; one of them might recognize me, and most likely many know by now I am to wed the pharaoh. So, my face I'll have partially covered, and after I come outside the temple, I'll cross to the opposite side, where you find the common girls."

"You're mad. You want to walk and sit where the derelicts and criminals roam? *You,* the king's daughter?"

"Only for short moments. As soon as I sit, you drop the silver piece and recite the verse, then we're gone—and I'm yours for the night." She smiled for the first time that day.

"And where will we ... do it?" He grinned.

"Where? I don't care; by the river, a date palm grove, a stable, or even here. Did you say you live here?"

"It's a long story," Isaa said dismissively. The details of his father disowning him for smashing a statue of Ishtar would be totally unwise to recount to an ardent devotee of the goddess.

"Fine, I don't have time for long stories, must go." She kissed him. "Tomorrow, my love, we will be one, blessed by the goddess of love herself."

Before reaching the door, she turned and hesitantly asked, "Have you ... done it before?"

He didn't expect this question and was overcome with embarrassment.

"Well, I ... thought about it, then ... I met you."

"You're a virgin?"

"You will be my first ... and my last."

"Oh, by holy Ishtar, two virgins, that's even better." She giggled. "Remember, tomorrow: to the temple, a silver piece, the verse, and most important of all ... have your tool ready!"

↗ ◇ 𐤃 ⩊ Ⓜ

It was the season of fertility. A shy spring moon peeked from the clouds on markets bustling with people. By the temple of Ishtar, there was a bigger influx of men and women who came to trade love in honor of the goddess Ishtar.

Most girls chose the springtime when making their vows to the goddess; men were more generous in the euphoria of the celebrations.

Unsavory thieves, and prostitutes who feigned devotion to the goddess, also found a wealth of opportunities to employ their skills in this season of abundance.

By the periphery of the temple, stretched a row of colorful brick benches, emblazoned with reliefs depicting the goddess sitting large on a throne with girls kneeling before her and men bowing in reverence. That zone was allotted for girls of high stature or beauty. Guards were assigned there, ostensibly to keep the order and stop any undesirables from nearing the area. The girls were supposed to go with the first man who threw a silver piece or something of more value in their laps. But one had to get through the guards' barrier first. With the right bribe, a path would magically open.

Many protested and argued that the posting of guards was in violation of the ritual, and that all men should have an equal opportunity and easy access to drop a silver piece to any woman in any of the designated areas. The priesthood had deliberated upon this dispute and arrived at a conclusion, which stated: Obstacles of any type—be they physical, social, natural, or supernatural—that might hinder a man from gaining access to a girl, are the work of the gods and do not have any bearing on the ritual."

Like most of the vague rules laid out by the gods' proxies, the interpretations were numerous.

Squabbles rarely broke out at that guarded section. They mostly involved two men after their silver pieces settled on a girl's lap right after she sat down. Then the guards would barge in to resolve the conflict, favoring the one who offered the best bribe to win the coveted girl.

Once a girl had fulfilled her vow—this once-in-a-lifetime, indiscriminate offer of her body for love, the girl could simply leave, or, if given the choice by the man, she could elect to become his concubine, or even his wife.

On the opposite side of the temple, the ritual was followed more faithfully. There were no guards there to interfere with the process. This side was crowded with girls who were not so blessed with beauty or riches. Some of them brought reed mats, for they might sit all day on a crumbling bench of bricks or on the dirt, only to return home with their vows unfulfilled. But there was always hope for another day when their prayers and offerings would deliver them a man to satisfy their vows.

Isaa stood waiting, looking at the opposite side of the temple. He grimaced when he saw the large crowd and the chaos. It didn't take long before a scuffle erupted, and within moments a man ended down on his back while his attacker rained punches on his face until passing men jumped to separate them.

Oh, the madness Enheduanna is about to join! Isaa winced. *To sit with the wretched of the land, only to fulfill a vow to some stone statue devoid of any powers. And she dares call me a fool!*

Yet, what about love? Only fools fall in love. And here I am ... just another fool, in love with a fool.

It was no wonder that Ishtar had been elevated to the highest ranking among the gods, aided by the droves of lovers she enslaved through her formidable powers of love and passion. To argue with Enheduanna about her staunch beliefs would only bring about the demise of their affair. Isaa couldn't comprehend why smart people would worship stone gods. But he knew better than to dwell on this question; never would he forget the lesson learned the hard way after he had shattered that bewitching goddess in his father's workroom. Instead of abandoning the stone gods, Ibrahem chose to disown his son.

Yet, Isaa felt confident that one day he would convince Enheduanna of the absurdity of such beliefs. As for tonight, he would be alone with her, touching her smooth, naked body ... bond with her. The thought got him aroused just as she stepped out of the temple. Casually, she glanced at him before walking down the stairs.

"You need to cover your face better," he whispered as she walked past him.

Quickly, she brought the head cover she was wearing down over her forehead. She stopped and took a deep breath before crossing to the opposite side of the temple, pacing fast among the crowd like someone who had walked that part of the city all her life. Isaa trailed closely, bumping into people while his sights were fixated on Enheduanna out of worry that some madman might attack her. He would never forgive himself if any harm came to her.

Enheduanna arrived at the unguarded area for the devotees and stopped next to a dilapidated bench, its bricks anything between loose and missing. Though dressed in clothes that made her pass as a commoner, she still looked a few notches above the neighboring girls.

Isaa was walking toward her, to be right next to her as soon as she settled on the bench. She sat down and spread her kilt, ready to receive the silver piece. Keeping her head down so that no one would notice her beauty, she waited, but nothing fell in her lap.

Fool, what are you waiting for? Worried, she was tempted to scream.

After moments that felt eternal, the piece came flying into her lap, followed by the verse:

"Love goddess, please bear witness, to you I pray and bow.
My oath to love your servant—to assist fulfill her vow."

At hearing the verse, Enheduanna felt a chill.

What happened to his voice? She wondered if the surrounding noises had confused her hearing. Slowly, she raised her head, praying to be proven wrong, and she froze.

A man the age of her father stood smiling, with hand extended to help her off the bench. He was well dressed but didn't have the air of nobility. Isaa was standing to the side, pale like a ghost, dazed and lost, with the palms of his hands exposed and empty—a beggar begging her forgiveness.

Grudgingly, Enheduanna picked the silver piece up from her lap, took the man's hand, and rose to her feet. The love goddess must have disapproved of this tampering with the ritual and interfered to foil their plan. Enheduanna could've refused the man, which would mean breaking her vows. But no, she would never dare anger her goddess again.

Isaa stood helpless. Feeling like a fool, he watched his love go, lost right under his nose, on her way to gift her body to a total stranger.

Enheduanna moved without looking back. Like a docile lamb, she walked away from the shepherd, led by a man from the slaughterhouse.

𒀭 ◊ 𒌋 𒀸 𒌋𒌋𒌋

The room was typical of an Ishtar Room—the name given to a bedroom where the 'devout' men served the girls with love as decreed by the sacred ritual. The furnishings were modest: A wooden bed, topped by two slender mats, two pillows, and a wool blanket. A wicker bench adjoined one side of the bed, and a statue of Ishtar stood against the opposite wall. There were cups and jars on a table by a side wall. A few oil lamps rested on the floor, though only the one by the entrance was lit.

Like in any typical brick house, the rooms were built around an open court to allow for better air circulation on hot days. The Ishtar Room was conveniently placed next to the house entrance, a good distance from the other rooms to provide more privacy for the sacred affair.

Many were the wives who railed against this ritual, accusing their husbands of using it as an excuse to cheat on them. No wonder Ishtar had become the goddess of love and war—that act of love often led to war within the family.

Enheduanna took off her head cover and turned to face the stranger destined to fulfill her vow. His anticipation of the pleasure to come already had him breathing heavily in harsh sounds. Even with him fully clothed, her stomach began to churn in revolt at the thought of him 'loving' and penetrating her.

O Goddess, she prayed, *I must have really angered you. I accept and will endure this punishment. Goddess, I beg your forgiveness.*

"By the love of Ishtar, you are beautiful!" the man said while circling her. "Could it be that my eyes are deceiving me? So blessed in body and charm, even a god would love to have you."

He began fondling her when suddenly he stopped and withdrew, an alarmed look on his face.

"How strange! A girl like you could've easily joined the guarded area with all the beautiful girls. Those guards would've stopped anyone with less than three silver pieces from approaching you. Something is wrong! Why did you cross to the other side?"

"Nothing is wrong," Enheduanna said nervously, worried the man might identify her. "I just had no idea where to go."

"I watched you leave the temple, and I followed. You walked fast, no hesitation whatsoever, sure of your direction. So tell me, what is it that I'm missing?"

"Nothing! I'm simply a virgin, seeking to fulfill a sacred vow." Enheduanna was getting impatient and lashed back at him with a hint of authority. "Now do your part of the vow. The sooner, the better."

Calmly, the man walked to her. She was about to remove her top when suddenly a hand smacked her face. She lost her balance and fell to the floor in complete shock; never in her life had she imagined anyone would dare slap her.

Towering over her, the man blurted scornfully:

"Huh. A beauty cursed with a long tongue. Cure: very simple— have her bite the dung!"

Enheduanna staggered to get up, and just as she steadied on her feet, the man clutched her jaw with one hand and violently pushed her back against the wall. One of the jars on the table fell and shattered on the floor, spilling its contents. Shortly, a voice came yelling from outside.

"Master, I heard a loud noise. Is there a problem?"

"All is fine. I'm with one of those Ishtar bitches," the man shouted. "Go back to your room. Don't let me catch you peeking. I won't need you for the rest of the night."

"Yes, Master. Good night."

"Please pardon the interruption, *honorable lady.*" The man was still holding Enheduanna by the jaw. "It seems you didn't understand the question—you lying, arrogant whore! So, I'll ask you a simpler one. What is wrong with you? What disease are you gifting me, *dear virgin*? I bet you're nothing but a dirty whore. A beautiful face and body, yet down inside, a nest of vermin is blossoming—a tunnel of horrors. I fuck you today, and tomorrow I'll wake up with some killer plague, whereupon even the demons will deny me entry to the netherworld."

He threw her to the floor and shouted, "What is your sickness?"

Enheduanna cushioned her face with an arm, letting out a cry of pain upon landing on some shards of the broken jar.

"I am a virgin—nothing is wrong with me!" she retorted, maintaining her proud tone. "I must remind you that I'm not the only one with a vow to fulfill. You're straying from your own promise to the goddess. You will be severely punished if you don't comply."

The man laughed. "Oh, I'm so scared of Ishtar—oh, the horror of her descending from heaven to punish me! ... Let her come down, *please*. Once I showed her my rod, she would lie back and beg me to fuck the divine joy out of her, right in front of you."

"O Goddess, I plead to you," Enheduanna prayed in her desperation, "punish this evil heretic. Not only has he reneged on his pledge, but he dares speak this heinous blasphemy against Your Holiness."

"O Ishtar, do punish me," the man mocked, and came to kneel on the floor, facing her. "Yes, punish me for my blasphemy, like *this*." He slapped her again. "And like *this* ... and like *this*."

After slapping her repeatedly, he stood up and kicked her in the stomach. Her shriek of pain stopped him just long enough for a grin to span his face. He had savored the flavor of his sadism and hungered for more.

He raised a leg in the air, about to stomp on her, when a blur leapt out of the shadows and tackled him to the ground in a poorly lit corner of the room. The shadow delivered numerous punches to his face.

Enheduanna picked herself up, squinting to see this savior who must have been sent by Ishtar in response to her prayers. The light was dim; all she could tell was that this gallant man was now holding a knife to the heretic's neck.

"Scream, and I will slice you!" the savior warned.

"Isaa!" Enheduanna sighed in relief upon recognizing the voice.

"I beg you, don't kill me." The man was terrified, thinking he had been set up for a robbery. "Take anything you want ... I have two pieces of silver in my pocket."

"Did he hurt you?" Isaa whispered.

Enheduanna began sobbing. Not only was her body aching but her vows had gone unfulfilled.

"No doubt he did. Forgive me for asking." Isaa answered his own question, delivering a wicked punch to the man's loins.

A scream of agony erupted out of the man as he bounced up to meet the stubby knife in Isaa's grip. Feeling a trickle of blood run down his neck struck him with dread.

"Spare me, I beg you," he cried.

Just then, the servant's voice rang through the door, again.

"Master! Are you all right in there?"

Isaa pressed the knife firmer against the man's neck, warning him with a shaking head not to say anything foolish, when suddenly, Enheduanna shredded the silence.

"Yes, yes! Bless you! O God, what joy! Don't stop, don't you dare stop!"

"Do forgive me, Master," pleaded the servant. "I won't disturb you again. Have a delightful night." Then came the faint sound of sandals darting away.

Inadvertently, Isaa's knife had carved deeper into the man's throat, and terror took a firmer grip on him as he envisioned his life slowly sinking into the netherworld.

"I beg you," he started sobbing, "I'm sorry. By the gods, have mercy. … Take all you want, everything, my clothes too. This tunic I'm wearing is one made of the finest cloth. The silver is in the pocket. Just spare me."

Enheduanna stepped closer. "Isaa, don't kill him."

"I've never killed anybody and don't intend to start now," he whispered in protest. "I just want to make sure he won't raise the alarm and have the whole neighborhood chase us."

"I don't believe you, Isaa, you seem very angry," she pressed him. "Hand me the knife before you do something foolish."

"Oh God, don't!" The man panicked. "Don't give her the knife! She's the one craving to kill me."

Isaa glanced at her face in the dim light. "Without a doubt. I wouldn't blame her if she chopped you to pieces after what you did." He pulled the man up to his feet. "Now listen to me carefully. We're not interested in your silver, valuables, or your stinky robes. We're not thieves. *We* are going to leave quietly, and *you* will stay in this room for the rest of the night. Don't get any ideas of stepping outside to raise the alarm and chase us, for we might decide to spend the night outside, in your *delightful yard*. Now outside, *she* will have the knife, and I assure you, she would like nothing better than to see your blood mix with dirt … understood?" Isaa pushed the man against the wall to stress the point.

"I swear by the gods of heaven, I will not take a single step out of this room. I will spend the night here, and tomorrow, I'll forget about the whole thing like it was a bad dream." The man spoke in high spirits for being spared a grim fate.

"Good." Isaa backed away, keeping the knife pointed at the man.

"Let's go." He glanced at Enheduanna, but she didn't move.

"Let's go!" he repeated.

"Not yet. I still owe him answers to his questions."

"Answers! Forget it, we're leaving," Isaa urged, but she wasn't listening. She nudged Isaa to the side and stood facing her abuser.

"I told you the truth; I am a virgin, free of any disease. *You*, right at this moment, would've been deflowering a virgin—one unique virgin miserable men like you could only dream of. Look at you now—so pathetic, so repulsive!"

"By God, let's move!" Isaa grabbed her arm, but she fiercely shrugged him off.

"I am from a noble family who promised to wed me to a prominent man. So naturally, I had to be a virgin. Since I don't like this arrangement, in which I have no say, the only way out is to lose my virginity. As a devout servant of Ishtar, I went to her temple and took my vows. As for why I went to the wretched side across the temple, the answer is easy, you might have guessed it by now. Some nobles would've known me, not to mention a few of the guards who frequent the palace."

Enheduanna stepped within an arm's length from the man. "Yes, *the palace.* Now, the question that must be itching this *rotten pig skin of yours* is, who am I?"

"You're not going to tell him!" Isaa grabbed her again, but she jostled him away furiously.

"I am Princess Enheduanna, daughter of King Sargon, and I've been promised to wed the pharaoh."

Stunned by this revelation, the man pressed his back against the wall.

"I can't believe this—why?" Isaa threw his arms up. "What's the purpose of telling him?"

"Don't worry, Isaa, he won't breathe a word to anyone."

Before Isaa could make sense of what she had said, she struck. In that dim room, her hands moved faster than the beating wings of a bat, repeatedly plunging something into the man's neck. Only a brief groan could depart him before the gushing blood drowned his voice. By the time Isaa moved to push her away, it was already too late.

The man slid down the wall with his eyes glued on Enheduanna, casting a stare of profound shock.

"Go rot in the pits of the netherworld,"—her raging words tore further at him—"where they store all the vermin and plagues of Earth!"

Isaa was in a state of disbelief at witnessing another bloodbath perpetrated by someone he loved—none other than the girl he dreamed of sharing his life with. He felt the chills when she started reciting a prayer over the dying man.

"O Ishtar, holy goddess of love, please accept this beast as a sacrifice from this faithful servant of yours. Death he merited for the blasphemy his cursed tongue uttered, and for all the hurt he caused when he should've been showering love."

Enheduanna tossed something down, which landed between the man's legs. Isaa looked intently: it was a fragment from a broken jar. She must have grabbed the sharp piece while Isaa was wrestling the stranger down.

After wiping her bloodstained hand on the man's clothes, Enheduanna walked to the statue of Ishtar, knelt, and resumed praying.

"O goddess, I am forever in debt to your compassion in answering my prayers and sending a savior to rid me of an evil monster. And I firmly believe this is the man you blessed to serve me with love, hence my vow won't go unfulfilled."

She stood up, walked back to Isaa, and threw herself into his arms.

"Oh beloved, I know now more than ever that the gods sent you to me. This is turning out so much better than I expected. Are you ready to help fulfill my vow?"

"What are you saying?" Isaa stepped back, taking pains to keep his voice down. "You just … killed a man. Now you want to make love over his dead body! I need to wake up from this nightmare." He grabbed her hand. "We are leaving now. The vows can wait."

She withdrew her hand forcefully. "No, Isaa, no! This is it—tonight, now, right here! If my father finds out I sneaked out of the palace—and there is a good chance he will—then I'll be surrounded by more guards than those guarding the city walls till I'm delivered to the pharaoh. It is either now or you will never see me again; I'll be far away in the Nile lands, buried under a pyramid."

Isaa kept silent. He yearned for a barren desert, away from the madness besieging him.

"If only you had dropped the silver piece before this pig did!" she snapped at him. "None of this would've happened."

"I lost the pouch." He sighed. "Pickpockets … did a job on me."

"Isaa, I'm not blaming you." She tenderly placed both hands on his chest. "This whole thing must be the gods' work. Think of all that led to this: the tablet house, my father promising me to the pharaoh, the pickpockets foiling our plan, this bastard here, then you coming to the rescue. The gods are testing our will to be together. … Why did you follow me?"

"I just followed—don't ask me why. I couldn't bear the thought … you, sleeping with a stranger. I was fuming, seeing you take his hand and walk away. I followed—ended up climbing over the house wall without thinking."

"Isaa, I was going to give myself to him. If he were loving and sincere, I would've fought on his side against you, and there would've been nothing you could do about it. But he turned into a beast. You saw how he beat me, how he mocked my goddess. He was about to kill me. How many girls had this bastard abused—or even killed? Dig that yard outside, and I bet you will find dead girls buried under. The gods sent us to rid the land of him and save the innocent. The gods must be watching, commending us for sacrificing this monster. We passed all their tests and obstacles. Don't ruin it now, Isaa, don't go against the gods' wishes." She kissed him lightly on the lips. "Do you love me?"

"More than life itself."

"Then make love to me." She held his hand, walked him to the statue, and knelt, gently pulling him down to kneel next to her. She reached into her dress and came out with the same silver piece the man had given her.

"O love goddess. This same piece of silver was used for committing me to my vow. Your Holiness has witnessed what a heretic the man was, defiling all that is sacred, and for that he was sacrificed. I have great faith … my savior, Isaa, is the one you chose for the task of honoring the vow. If you don't approve of him, I pray you stop him, and I will accept my fate as a future wife of the pharaoh."

Enheduanna pressed the silver piece into Isaa's hand, sat on the floor with her kilt spread across her lap, and waited with head bowed.

To her frustration, no silver piece settled in her lap. Her patience was rapidly depleting.

He's right here with a silver piece, what is he waiting for? Could it be that Ishtar sent a demon pickpocket to ruin our plan—first outside the temple, and now in this very room?

She resolved to silently recite a short prayer, and if he failed to act by the end of it she would forget this whole affair and submit to her father's wishes.

The prayer finished. Overwhelmed with dismay and defeat, Enheduanna resigned to her chosen destiny—the Nile kingdom. She pressed her hands on the floor to stand up, when a spark of silver shot down like a tiny bolt of lightning, hitting her lap, pinning her to the floor.

Isaa's voice descended, almost in a whisper, but it felt like thunder, making her shiver with joy.

"Love goddess, please bear witness, to you I pray and bow,
My oath to love your servant—to assist fulfill her vow."

Enheduanna snatched the silver so fast, it seemed to disappear by a magician's sleight of hand. She jumped on Isaa and they fell to the floor together. She showered him with kisses, her body feverishly gliding all over his body. One of her hands slid under his garment, brushing his intimate zone, but no changes resulted—not what she had anticipated. She kept trying, but all her attempts went in vain. She stood up while he remained on the floor, his whole body limp, just like the dead body he was staring at.

"*I* should've been the one to throw the silver in your lap, *virgin boy.*" Enheduanna kicked his side. He growled in pain, and she went down again, kissing him.

"Forgive me, my love, just wanted to make sure you were alive." She caressed him, then stood and helped him to his feet, leading the way to the bed where she had him sit facing away from the corpse. Her eyes explored the room, and a reed mat on the floor ended the search. She picked it up and walked to the dead man, who was slumped with his back against the wall. She tucked one edge of the mat behind his back and let the rest roll over his head all the way down, just short of covering the feet. Enheduanna walked back, sat on the bed, and looked straight at Isaa as if to absorb his vision of death into the darkness of her eyes.

"Oh Isaa," she sighed, "I have to treat you not only as the virgin that you are but also like a man of the wild. Like Enkido in the Gilgamesh epic—no idea what joy a woman is."

Slowly, she started to undress. Soon, the faint shadow of her naked body was dancing on the wall behind her. Isaa felt a little stirring inside as she helped him out of his own garment.

"You're all set now, like Enkido, free from clothing."

"I'm trying." His voice was fraught with gloom. "But this is hardly a situation to put me in the mood."

"Don't worry, my love, we have all night, and I came prepared," she said, smirking. "One of my maids is quite experienced, and she tells me all the intricate details of love; the ins and outs."

"Ins and outs!" A sliver of a smile adorned Isaa.

"Yes, I even made a poem about it."

"A poem!"

"You remember that school assignment where I got the part of 'Shamhat seducing Enkido'?" Her hands floated, smoothly caressing his face. "The part I stole from you—and made you angry."

"Sure, I remember—first time someone robbed me. Well, the

second time—after you stole my heart."

"Well, soon you'll thank me for stealing that assignment."

"Why? I remember you read it in the class; it wasn't much different from the original version." Isaa was talking more, recovering more of himself.

"I had to cut it short. Otherwise, all of you boys would've been running home to amuse yourselves." She laughed then took one of his hands and pressed it against her breast, closed her eyes and said through her arousal, "Now, only for you, I will recite the whole poem, and we will act on it."

"I don't understand."

"We perform what the verses say, one line at a time, no rush. *You are Enkido. I*—the priestess Shamhat."

Isaa was intrigued. He knew the story, but how different could her version be?

She began to recite:

Enkido ran the forests and plains of the wild.
Vigorous with energy, careless like a child.

All of the animals he came to befriend.
In times of danger, he would rush to defend.

Hunters at his sight, in terror they would cower.
Stricken with fear, would scurry to Uruk's tower.

Gilgamesh gave the orders. "The beast we have to tame.
And who but Shamhat was best in that game?"

The priestess, all willing, prepared for the mission.
"Majesty, the beast I shall compel into abject submission."

Readily, Shamhat departed, armed with her love arts,
Where men fell witless, stripped of all their smarts.

Came to see Enkido, kneeling by the mountain,

Drinking in the wild, out of a spring fountain.

"Blessed mother Ishtar, behold his thing.
So big and ripe—Oh, the joy 'twill bring!"

Slow steps Shamhat walked, breath heavy and deep.
Like a virgin on her wedding, silent, ready to weep.

Enkido stood unmoving, the priestess on her knees.
Her weapons at the ready, poised fully to please.

"I tell you of a secret, hidden inside thy rod.
The pleasure—tremendous—most lavish gift from God."

Jovially, Shamhat reached and brushed the giant's fruit.
Not at all fearful, patiently handled the brute.

Gently with her mouth, the kissing and teasing followed.
His wand she treated like an object hallowed.

Enkido was confounded when a deed made him wonder,
"You're so mistaken, 'tis not a cucumber."

But Shamhat persisted, determined not to falter.
Came this far—soon she would conquer.

Then all of a sudden, his member came to grow.
He cried and started pleading, "Don't ever dare let go!"

"Enkido, you silly, that's only half the joy.
I'll teach you how to play, here's another toy."

Her breasts she uncovered, pulling up the dress.
Exposed her wet vagina: "For you to caress."
The legs she parted slowly, her thighs went high.
"Taste from this honey, don't you be shy."

In pleasure she moaned, wearing a devil's grin.
"O lover, I think you're ready for the original sin.
Now take your shiny blade, sink it deep inside.
Way down to the hilt, fully to hide.
O lover, stab and stab me, hard with your tool—
Bliss showers, they drown me. Oh savage joy, how cruel!"

The pleasure was too much for Enheduanna to contain. She had to moan to vent the ecstasy flooding her, with Isaa giving her no respite. His deep kisses had her struggle to breathe through the rushing stream of joy—this bliss gifted by the gods in a rare act of generosity to the humans.

The two bodies glided over each other. Two virgins tasting the delights of first intimate love, rushing to see how far this pleasure could take them. Enheduanna cried the rapture out loud, not worrying about being heard; she was the king's daughter; her joy should be heralded to the whole city. Let Ishtar hear loud and clear that she had fulfilled her vows.

They were quiet, recovering from the intense experience in the new world they had just explored. Enheduanna rested her head on Isaa's chest, a tired smile on her face.

"Sorry to interrupt your poem," he whispered.

"I was dying for you to interrupt it." She planted a kiss on his cheek.

"Let me hear the rest of the poem."

"I forgot which line I stopped at."

"The *stab and stab* line. That's all I can remember." His words had him glance at the mat concealing the man she had stabbed.

"Oh yes." She took a deep breath, then whispered in his ear:

Love goddess, I pray and beg forgiveness.
I doubt that even you had savored such awesome sweetness.

Isaa grinned. "Was I that good?"

"Shush!" She put a finger to his mouth and whispered again. "You don't want Ishtar to hear. She's a very jealous goddess. She'll grab you, use you, then throw you out like a dog. … Well, what about me? What do you think?"

"I'll let you know after I bed another girl."

A punch to his chest and a menacing frown was her response. He kissed her passionately to calm her down.

"Oh, you … you're a goddess, you gave me a taste of heaven." He pointed in the dead man's direction without looking. "I wish that bastard would come back to life so I could slay him myself for touching you, the son of a—" He paused, troubled by what he had just said, and was overcome by an impulse to leave. "Let's go, we're done here."

"I'm tired. Let's get some sleep." Enheduanna sank deeper into the bed.

"No, let's sneak out now while everyone is sleeping," Isaa urged.

"The night is still young, Isaa. Just a little nap, I'm a light sleeper. Don't worry, even if they find us with this dead filth, what could they do? I'm Sargon's daughter; he will butcher all who live in this house once he finds out what that bastard did to me."

"And for what *I* did to you! What should *I* expect from him?"

"Relax, my love. I'll tell him I can't live without you. He'll make you a prince. You too need rest after the *hard, exhausting* task you have accomplished."

"I think it's better to—"

"This is a royal order." She feigned a commanding gesture. "Go to sleep, or I will have you castrated. We have a shortage of eunuchs in the palace."

"How cruel!" Isaa countered. "After having me taste the fruits, out she pulls the plant by the roots."

She laughed, kissed him, and fell back onto the pillow.

𒀭 𒅔 𒐉

Isaa sprang off the pillow, alarmed he might have slept for too long. Anxiously, he searched his surrounds. The man's body retained its same pose, judging by the feet that only managed to move their shadows when helped by the flailing dim light from the oil lamp.

Enheduanna was out of the bed, and he was about to tell her it was time to leave, but he reconsidered and leaned back on the pillow.

She was kneeling in prayer to the statue of her goddess. Her naked body seemed like an erotic dream: ghostly, dancing to the waving flickers of the oil lamp, and Isaa burned with desire. Watching her lips whisper prayers drove him to envy: *Why is a goddess like you worshipping a stone? Those lips should be caressing my lips instead of praising that bitch.*

To stop this carnal craving, he shifted his stare to where the lifeless body lay under the reed mat. Strangely, it no longer affected his arousal. He wondered about this force that sent men into a mad quest to satisfy this need. Looking back at Enheduanna, he hungered even more for her body, as if the act of love, this vital generator of life, felt more urgent in the presence of death.

He crept out of bed and went to kneel beside her.

"I think you missed a few lines in your poem," he said, polite in the presence of her goddess.

She returned a skeptical look. "I'm sure I didn't."

"I swear you did," he insisted.

"Can this wait till I finish my prayers?"

"Better to let me do the prayers, and you follow my lead."

She was puzzled, but more than that, she was curious. "Fine, go ahead."

Isaa solemnly bowed to the goddess and started:

"Love Goddess, 1 pray and beg forgiveness.
The urge, so strong; her beauty, her sweetness.

"O Goddess, it's she 1 worship." Her lips he ardently kissed.
Her legs he gently parted, craving more of her passion thrills.

She said, "Wait! Stop! Last line you lost the rhyme."
Fast he slipped inside her, wasted no time.

FATHER, DAUGHTER, AND MIDWIVES

"**W**HAT? *SAY THAT AGAIN!*"

"I can't … marry the pharaoh," Enheduanna declared timidly. "I'm … no longer a virgin."

"What do you mean?" Sargon bristled. "Since when? How did this happen?"

"A few days ago … I went to Ishtar's temple and took the vows to honor my goddess. Gave myself, my virginity … to the man who tossed silver in my lap."

"Gave yourself! Took vows!" Sargon tried to interpret those words in a way that made sense, but to no avail, and his legs rushed him in her direction.

Enheduanna was looking down when the heavy hand fell on her face, sending her to the floor. She began crying for this slap didn't come from a low-life stranger, but from the man who had never touched her in any way except to show his love as a father.

"Vows to honor your goddess! How about my promise to the pharaoh?" Sargon paced the room back and forth, furiously searching his way to the right course of action.

"Guards!" he hollered.

The door opened and two guards stepped in. "Yes, Your Majesty."

"Find the sculptor Ibrahem and bring him here at once!"

Enheduanna staggered to her feet. She had anticipated her father's anger and was ready for more punishment. Nothing could be worse than all those stressful days, worrying sick about how to break the news to him.

"This is absurd, unreal … *No, no, no!*" Sargon fumed. "No one—no father within the four corners of Earth—has given his daughter more than I gave you. And this is how you reward me—bedding a stranger! I gave the pharaoh my word of honor! What am I supposed to tell him now? 'Forgive me, Pharaoh, someone already enjoyed her; she's used merchandise now.'"

"Is this how you think of me? Merchandise!" she retorted. "Grooming and polishing me all this time for the pharaoh! How did he pay you, with camels and sheep?"

Sargon darted toward her. She stood firm, turning her head in an invitation for another slap, but he stopped and turned away.

"*Merchandise!* I was wedding you to the pharaoh ... *the pharaoh himself!* You would've become the Queen of the Nile."

"Only if he favored me above the others. And why would any girl want to be that queen? You know he's ailing—dying—and soon will be buried, accompanied by his wives. ... Ooh for the joy of being buried alive next to pharaoh, wearing a queen's crown," she mocked bitterly, just as the two guards stepped in with Ibrahem.

"Guards, you can leave," Sargon said before anyone uttered a greeting. After a few silent moments, he let out a deep sigh. "Ibrahem, how many midwives work in this palace?"

"I know of four," Ibrahem answered, after giving the question some thought. "But I'm not sure if they are all at hand right now."

"Ibrahem, I know I can trust you. There's a matter of utmost secrecy I will share with you."

Ibrahem nodded. "Whatever you confide will go with me alone to my grave."

"As you know, Ibrahem, I promised the pharaoh *this woman* to be his wife—"

"And I gave my vows to my goddess," Enheduanna interrupted, tears rolling down her cheeks.

"Fuck your goddess!" Sargon snapped. "Or should I say: *fuck not your goddess*—given that being fucked sends her to highest heaven."

"Don't insult my goddess."

"Sargon, please calm down." Ibrahem stepped forward. "About the midwives, why do you need them?" Ibrahem feigned ignorance, though he had enough clues to answer his question.

"You heard her. She took the vows, the *fornication vows*. She joined the fools in that *sacred whoring* ritual to Ishtar. One day I'm going to banish this practice."

"You will bring the gods' wrath upon us," cried Enheduanna.

"I only fear one god—Anu, god of all gods. And I know he's happy with me. The rest of them are nothing but spoiled children who should be slapped around—like you. And your Ishtar is just like her mother, a whore sleeping with gods and mortals alike."

Enheduanna winced as her father spat out the sinister words instigated by the endless disputes over Ishtar's birth father: Was it Anu, or the Babylonian god, Marduk?

"Princess, is it true what you are saying?" Ibrahem asked in a hushed voice.

Go ask your son Isaa if you don't believe me, she was tempted to say. "Yes, it is true."

"Ibrahem, I need to make sure she's not lying," Sargon growled. "Bring me all the midwives you can find, now."

Ibrahem walked to Sargon and whispered, "It would be better to keep this secret unknown to them, too. Dress her like a maid, veil her face and take her to another room, where the midwives will examine her without knowing she's the princess. If they ask why she needs the test, I'll tell them the king wants a virgin for the night and needs to know if this one qualifies."

"Excellent idea, Ibrahem. She shall go unrecognized. Let me hear what the midwives say once they're done. Meanwhile, I need some fresh air to restore some of my sanity."

𒐊 𒀸 𒅎 𒉿 𒐗

"Your Majesty," the eldest of the midwives said, "this girl is not a virgin. All three of us checked her, and beyond any doubt, her hymen is torn. Majesty, do you need us to check another girl?"

"How about sewing that hymen back?" A murmur escaped Sargon's incoherent thoughts.

The midwives eyed each other in confusion at what he meant.

"You can leave," Ibrahem answered for him. "His Majesty

specifically wanted that girl. He will spend the night with his favorite concubines."

The midwives bowed and walked out.

"Where is she, Ibrahem? Why didn't you bring her here, so I can slap the nonsense out of her?"

"Sargon, you need to meet this problem calmly. Her presence will only upset you more. I understand how you feel, but perhaps this folly she committed will lead to a better outcome."

"A better outcome!" Sargon scowled. "What about the fucking pharaoh? I gave him my word. This marriage would've brought our nations closer to an alliance. Then I could concentrate on the rebel cities—unite my kingdom."

"Sargon, to tell you the truth, I have a feeling that the gods intervened to correct a wrong decision. With all due respect, the marriage might not make us allies with the pharaoh's kingdom after all. As a matter of fact, it could bring conflict, especially if the princess is not happy with the arrangement. Who could blame her? The pharaoh's days are numbered. She's right to worry; there is a good chance she would be buried alive with him. Then what? You would have to retaliate."

"The pharaoh promised not to do that. He wouldn't dare. I would drive my armies to the Nile and wipe out his entire family."

"Sargon, do you think he cares? This pharaoh had already killed many of his own family whom he deemed to be a threat. His insecurity had him slay every single one of his father's offspring, and many more on the mere suspicion of it. In all honesty, since you decided on this wedding, I've spent many a sleepless night pondering what the future might hold in store. As you know, this pharaoh is nothing like his father, who was vigorous, bedding women till the day he died. Well, this one is just the opposite, so sick, he's in a frenzied race with death to finish his pyramid tomb. He has no offspring. I heard rumors that his love tool never stretched higher than his butthole."

Sargon chuckled. "Oh, Ibrahem ... I can't believe I'm laughing after our princess stunned me with that *sacred vow* dung. But, if the pharaoh lacks the vigor for the task, can we not still marry Enheduanna to him? He would never detect her ... little defect!"

"Forgive me, but that won't work. She would have to be tested by the midwives there before the marriage could proceed."

"True, Ibrahem. I forgot about that."

"What bothers me is, why would a man in his sickly condition want to get married? Only one reason I can think of: he believes that in the next life, the gods will bestow upon him a phallus that would be the envy of all men. So, he wants to surround himself with women blessed with beauty and charm, like the princess, and have them depart with him to the next life where he can indulge in the pleasures denied him in this life. Here, we build ziggurats for the living to worship and celebrate the divine gods. Over there, they build pyramids to entomb the pharaohs, accompanied by their worldly luxuries and the people to serve and pleasure them in the next life."

"We do that too." Sargon shrugged.

"Not on such a grand scale. This pharaoh is spending enormous time and wealth, not to mention the countless men who are worked to death on his tomb. He's dedicating his whole life to prepare for death. Enheduanna knows of the virgins who disappeared after the burial of our last king. She's terrified of meeting the same fate if she marries the pharaoh."

"Ibrahem, the pharaoh did assure me in his letters that no harm shall come to her."

"What if he reneged on his promise, and had her buried with him? How would you retaliate? You plan on chasing a dead man into the next life? And if you decide on punishing his people, I'm sure you're aware of their strong army, and let's not forget the hardship of marching the long distance, crossing the vast desert; all of that will take a toll on our soldiers. However, for those same reasons, he would not dare attack us. He would not waste time, effort, and expenses that could be better spent on his colossal tomb. You shouldn't worry about breaking your promise to him."

"I still need to give him a good reason to cancel the wedding."

"Tell him the truth—the princess lost her virginity. But tell him it happened due to an accident. Say the chariot she was riding went over a large stone, making her stumble over the edge in a way that ruptured her hymen. Tell him that even though she has not known any man, you still won't allow yourself to wed her to him in her condition. Send him a few gifts of gold—maybe some artistic glazed bricks to decorate his tomb."

"An excellent idea, Ibrahem. ... But, this matter of her going against my wishes greatly disturbs me. And this Ishtar nonsense—virgin, *holy whoring* ritual—I don't recall that girls needed to be virgins for the ritual."

"Well, many are the interpretations. The extremely devoted say only the pure should perform the ritual, that if a non-virgin does go ahead with the ritual, she's actually insulting the goddess, just like someone who puts leftovers on the altar instead of a freshly prepared meal. I've seen women get into ugly fights over this matter."

"Where did this ritual originate from?"

"I believe it started in Babylon."

"Babylon!" Sargon punched fist into palm. "I should raze that city to rubble."

"This won't change anything. Ishtar is revered everywhere, both here and in faraway lands, where she is given different names. And, in these turbulent times, waging an attack on any city, or rival, without a compelling reason, is too great of a risk. It would only invite mistrust and send other cities to join Ur in rebellion."

"True, Ibrahem, very true; my hands are tied. It just drives me mad—my daughter falling into the trap of a fanatical cult. I thought she was smarter than that. By Anu, what if she's with child now?"

"Somehow, our princess made a rash mistake, but she's smart. I asked her about her moon cycle. She waited till her moon went down."

"Good ... though, it's not a sure thing. Last thing I need to add to her disgrace is a bastard child. From now on, she is to remain in the palace with restricted movement outside. And, no more of that scribe school."

"That won't restore her hymen." Ibrahem scratched his temple. "I think she should continue with the learning. That will help her rise to become a high priestess. She would make a great ally within the priesthood—a great asset to your rule."

Sargon paced the room and shook his head in resignation.

"You're right. With her hymen ruptured, what is there to lose? But she will remain confined to her quarters for six days as a punishment. I've spoiled her; it's time to show her some cruelty."

"Yes, she needs to be disciplined. Though, today she was awfully humiliated by those midwives. After finding she wasn't a virgin, they scolded her with the foulest language for trying to pass as a virgin to bed the king. Good thing they knew I was waiting outside within earshot, or they would've beaten her too. She could only cry without uttering a word, for I warned her that the midwives might be familiar with her voice. Believe me, she would've gladly welcomed your slaps all day instead of those midwives holding her down and probing inside her."

"Don't worry." Sargon slapped the air. "More of those are going to land on her face if she utters such nonsense again. Our virgins are fornicating with strangers, who must feel more than *honored* to help in this Ishtar-holy-vow dung! More bastards will be born; true bastards, with not the slightest idea of their father's identity. Society will be thrown into chaos. Whatever happened to the times when girls reached marriage with their virtue intact?"

Virtue! True bastards! Ibrahem mused to himself. *How about your offspring from those concubines, whom you* virtuously *deflowered? Are they* untrue *bastards?*

"Well, Sargon, it wasn't always the case. In some regions, the ruling lord still demands to sleep with the bride before the husband. Gilgamesh was one example."

"A very wise rule. Maybe I should decree it as a tradition in Uruk."

"I would advise against that." Ibrahem grinned. "Only your enemies will encourage it. Numerous weddings, though pleasurable, would weaken, even kill you from exhaustion."

"If Gilgamesh was capable of it, I should be too." Sargon put on a serious face but couldn't hold it for long. "I know, I know; it's only a mythical story."

"Yet, Sargon, you would be surprised how many believe that the Gilgamesh epic is based on facts. They claim the Great Deluge really happened, and Zuisudra was real, that he did build a huge ark, carrying a pair of each animal. They assert we are all the descendants of his family, the only one to survive the great flood."

"Fools and nothing but fools. Ibrahem, this story would make some sense if it were the gods who delivered that enormous boat, fully built with all animals already crammed in it." Sargon snickered as he poured some wine into two cups, giving one to Ibrahem. "What nonsense ... to gather a pair of every animal breed in the world! Those fools have no idea how hard it is to hunt a lion, not to mention getting the beast alive *and* unharmed. What's more, I don't believe they had chariots back then. Zuisudra and his whole family, chasing a pair of lions, would've looked like roosters running after wolves; exhaustion and becoming lion food would've killed them long before the peoples doomed by the deluge. Now, suppose he did gather the animals, each pair in a separate cage so they wouldn't eat each other—next, he would have a problem with two ends. He would need to stack heaps upon heaps of food, so the animals wouldn't starve to death. Then comes the hard part from the other end: who's going to clean up all that dung? In a few days, you would have one giant ship of shit. Zuisudra and all his family would dive overboard to drown in water rather than drown in shit."

Sargon went wild with laughter, joined by Ibrahem.

"Yet many do believe in the story. Have you ever heard of those who believe in some solitary, one god?"

"I do recall a rumor"—Sargon sipped some wine through a golden straw—"about one stubbornly invisible, late arrival to the godhood."

"Well, his ardent followers created their own version of the Great Deluge story, with a few minor alterations to it. They claim it was their solitary god who condemned the humans. As for Zuisudra, his name they changed to something like 'Nooh.' So convinced they are of this tale being a real story, that a few of them voyaged all the way up north to the mountains where the Tigris and Euphrates rivers are born, in search of the ark, believing it settled atop the highest mountain—the first land to resurface after the deluge."

"I bet you, Ibrahem, they'll be greeted by a family of fat lions. Such fools should be given twenty lashes to bring them back to their senses. To believe in this ark-deluge fable is truly a thing more absurd, and in so many ways, than those virgins whoring their bodies to strangers in their zeal to honor Ishtar."

"All this talk about virgins reminds me: a man of modest wealth was found slaughtered in his home recently."

"How did that happen?" Sargon asked.

"His slave found him in the morning, stabbed multiple times in the neck. He said his master brought girls home from time to time. There were a few noises that night—sounds of a quarrel, things breaking, moans of lovemaking. The slave asserts it was the girl who killed his master, then stole a pouch where he carried some silver."

"This madness has to stop; now we have murder involved. Things are getting out of control. I need to make a deterring example—find a girl who whored in this ritual, stick the murder on her, and have her publicly executed."

"But Sargon, it could be the slave who killed him, stole the silver, then fabricated a story about a quarrel between his master and the girl, only to have her doomed for his crime. Some slaves hate their masters to the point where they would not waste an opportunity for a lethal payback."

"What are you suggesting, Ibrahem? Let the crime go unpunished!"

"Sure, someone should be punished, but not a girl. Countless are the motives for murder: slaves rebel, wives get jealous, trade partners cheating on profits; those are the prime suspects. As for this Love ritual, I think it is to your benefit not to interfere with it."

"Ibrahem, you've lost me. What are you proposing?"

Ibrahem approached the king and spoke in a faint voice so the walls could not hear. Sargon gaped with amusement at what he heard, then he roared.

"Brilliant, Ibrahem, brilliant! I will have the guards arrest the head servant, make him confess to the crime one way or the other, and have him executed. And you, go ahead and search for the right girl."

Mayram

"**M**AY THE GODS BLESS YOU, NOBLE SIR."

The girl slipped her clothes on, readying herself to leave. She had a firm slim body, built within an aura of confidence that fortified her beauty to swiftly conquer the strongest of men.

"Forgive me, I forgot your name," Ibrahem lied to start a conversation.

"Mayram." She spoke without looking at him; a gesture of respect.

He couldn't take his eyes off her. She appeared even more beautiful now than the virgin she had been when he had brought her to the tavern's rented room. Well-mannered and tactful, she didn't seem to possess what was required for his plans. Still, he considered keeping her as a concubine whether his wife Saura liked it or not, but promptly, prudence had him dismiss the thought; the last thing he needed was more domestic headaches.

Since Isaa was cast out, rage never abandoned Saura. She had threatened Ibrahem the next day:

"If you ever dare bring a girl for that whoring Ishtar vow, there will be blood—pools of it, not just the trickles from her fucking lost virginity!"

Yet, Mayram's beauty wreaked havoc on Ibrahem's resolve. The morning would have him crave more of the joys her body offered.

"So, Mayram, what are your plans for the future? A girl of your beauty merits a husband of considerable wealth."

"My lord, marriage is not of such importance to me. I will be a priestess and will dedicate my life to the service of my goddess Ishtar."

She smiled as if that thought were a sweet dream. It was the first display of emotion Ibrahem had seen on her calm, innocent face.

"I will leave now, my lord, and bless you again."

"You have the accent of people north of here." Ibrahem betrayed his sensible reasoning for the joy of her company.

"True, my lord. I'm from Babylon, a city of modest grandeur compared to Uruk."

"Babylon—that city is growing fast. I spent a few days there. First city on Earth the goddess Ishtar set foot on."

"Oh, bless you." She brightened. "Very few people know that. Isn't she the most loving and splendid of all gods?"

"Goddess Ishtar is one of the most sacred to me," Ibrahem said with a straight face.

"I am honored to have a man like you fulfill my vows. I was worried when I stepped out of the temple, for I've heard many stories of girls beaten by men who only have their own pleasure in mind—not the sacred task they're entrusted with."

"True, and that really disturbs me too." Ibrahem put on a sad face. "It only makes the gods angry, which brings their wrath upon all, the guilty and the innocent. Recently, a man was stabbed to death in his home. A servant recounted how his master abused the girls he brought, made them scream in pain. Most likely, he was killed by a girl after having her suffer a whole night of torment."

"Oh, how awful." Mayram grimaced.

"You mean ... awful that she killed the man!"

"No sir, I wouldn't blame her. Sadists like him deserve to be butchered. I would've done the same thing. To tell you the truth, I'm always prepared for encounters with deviant men."

"Prepared ... how?"

"My lord, I don't want you to be alarmed." She stepped closer to the bed. "You were very loving and complied with your part of the oath. As I said, I thank the goddess for sending me an honorable man like you. But if it were someone who just wanted me for pleasure and abuse ..." Mayram reached to her side and dug something out from a fold in her dress.

Ibrahem shrank back in alarm, though she had already allayed his fears. In her hand, she held a menacing dagger with a grip of an animal's bone—a thing that portrayed the horrid specter of death, which contrasted entirely with her innocent beauty.

"I would've offered the bastard's blood as a sacrifice to my goddess." Her face morphed, taking on the fierce, combative features of someone ready to kill.

"Did you ever … use that?" Ibrahem squinted, not yet recovered from the surprise.

"Countless times." She grinned and put the dagger back into the hidden pocket. "Don't worry—not on people. I slaughtered sheep and goats—sacrificial offerings to the gods. My parents are poor, so to help them I worked next to the main temple of Ishtar in Babylon, making sacrifices for those who didn't want to get their hands bloodied."

Ibrahem stared at her, failing to visualize a girl who looked as innocent as a lamb yet wouldn't cringe from butchering lambs to make a living. Hers was a beauty impossible to pair off with slaughter.

"You must have slayed the other butchers—robbed them of most customers."

"Not really. I tire fast and take breaks more often. As a matter of fact, they all liked me and helped when I needed something."

"Who wouldn't!" Ibrahem couldn't take his eyes off her. "You must be godsent."

She smiled, though the comment made no sense to her.

"Well, noble sir, I guess I've taken too much of your time. Farewell, may the gods bless you." She turned to leave.

"Wait!" Ibrahem sprang out of bed. "Mayram, do you want to serve your goddess in ways surpassing anything you can do as a priestess?"

"Sure. Whatever pleases my goddess, I will strive to do it."

"Mayram, I work in the palace, I'm the sculptor for the king. There is a matter that would greatly interest you as a devoted servant of Ishtar. Right now, I'm tired and in need of sleep. I ask you to spend the night here with me. Tomorrow morning, we will talk about it. I'll pay you for taking the time to listen to what I propose." He reached for his robe, dug out two silver pieces from the pocket, and showed them to her.

"You mean, becoming a concubine," she replied sternly. "*A harlot for the wealthy*! I detest that!"

"No, no, no. It's not that; it's purely for serving Ishtar. Trust me, I swear by the mighty gods."

Mayram hesitated, then without any further questioning, she quietly took off her clothes and walked to the bed.

Ibrahem lifted the cover for her to slide in next to him.

ᛁ ◇ ᗡ ᭩ Ⲙ

Mayram remained wide awake, haunted by trepidations as he snored beside her. He had gone to sleep happily exhausted, knowing her young, silky body would be there in the morning to release more of his lust.

She closed her eyes for a better view of her memories, of Babylon. There, outside the main temple, the sheep and goats would tremble, sensing death when approaching her. Mayram couldn't fool them with her beauty, unlike the man sleeping next to her.

Cautiously, she reached down beside the bed, where she had dropped her raiment on the floor, and pulled the dagger out.

She stared at the soundly dozing man and imagined a beast masked with a human face—one who exploits the sacred ritual only to satisfy his lust. How many helpless, innocent girls had been abused by him? So far, he had been gentle, but undoubtedly, once he was done with her in the morning, his true, demonic nature would take over.

Mayram sat upright in bed, holding the dagger to her chest while her lips moved in silent prayers. Her heart was thudding so hard she feared it would alert the man—her first human sacrifice.

No, Mayram—he's definitely not human. Thoughts crowded her mind to dispel any doubts. *He's a beastly thing, even more deserving of slaughter than those harmless sheep and goats. His type—sadists who desecrate the holy vows—only have value when their blood is spilled. Nothing pleases the gods more than having heretics sacrificed. Don't keep the love goddess waiting. You can do it, Mayram. Do it. DO IT!*

He was lying with his back to her. Carefully, she leaned over him and held the dagger next to his throat. Thinking of the first sheep she had slaughtered, she took a deep breath and gripped the dagger tightly.

Only the bone grip could stop the blade from sinking any deeper after she plunged it into the man's neck. Through the grip, she felt the shock waves of savage pain bursting out of his butchered throat. Involuntarily, the man rolled onto his back, mercilessly dragged out of a sweet dream only to be thrust into a nightmare that wouldn't abandon him as he opened his eyes to the horror of the last vision visiting them: the girl he had made love to was over him now, still naked, staring at him as though his dying eyes were about to reveal the mysteries of life and death while they intertwined in those last moments.

Mayram yanked the dagger out, and once more that night her body was stained. This time, it was the man's lifeblood, not the essence of his lust, that sputtered, spraying her body in his climactic death.

She remained on top of him, breasts heaving in triumphant euphoria. When her breathing normalized, she sank into the bed.

This bastard will never desecrate the vows of any girl again. More men like him will meet the same fate.

She was already eager for the next one.

It must be the will of the gods that brought me to Uruk; this task they entrusted to me.

Her thoughts were disrupted by the congealing blood that glued her hand to the dagger's bone grip, and she was lost in a state of confusion as to how she had ended up lying next to a butchered man, only two days after her encounter with Ibrahem.

𒀭 𒂆 𒐈

The lure of the great Uruk and its better opportunities attracted many young people. Mayram was obsessed with a feeling that a more prominent calling in life awaited her in that most powerful of cities.

Emboldened by a staunch belief in Ishtar as her protector, she had left Babylon to pursue her quest, despite the concerns of her mother. However, her father saw much in her that was a reflection of himself—brave, determined, and adventure seeking. So instead of shedding tears at her departure, he gave Mayram his blessings.

Mayram had offered her virginity outside the main temple of Ishtar in Uruk, where Ibrahem had become one of those who frequented the temple. He had bribed the guards handsomely to get her. When he asked her to stay until the morning to discuss a matter of serving the love goddess, it roused her curiosity as to whether her desire to come to Uruk had been a design of the gods. That suspicion was strengthened when Ibrahem told her about many recent incidents of girls who were beaten by heretic men, in violation of the sacred task entrusted to them regarding the love vows.

"The worst abusers are well known," Ibrahem had explained that morning. "Most are wealthy nobles. But the law can't do much to punish them, since the only witnesses are servants who fear testifying against their masters. The only justice for the victims could come from one who is devoted to the goddess, who is brave enough to believe in herself and the task at hand."

Mayram knew of the problem and was more than happy to help exact punishment on those who insulted the goddess by committing heinous acts against her mortal daughters. She felt honored to be chosen and would've accepted the offer even if there were no wages involved, though the assignments promised substantial payments in gold, silver, among other incentives, including a room in the city. She made passionate love to Ibrahem that morning to show her appreciation.

That same evening, Ibrahem visited her and asked if she was ready to start the next day. She was nervous but didn't want to cower away from serving her goddess.

By the next morning, Mayram had her mind readied for the task. Ibrahem arrived carrying a small cage with a pigeon inside. She asked him about the bird.

"You will need some blood for your virgin act." He pointed to the bird. "There—it has more than you need. Place its blood well inside you ahead of time. Also, fake the unease and pain of a girl's first intimate experience that the abuser is looking for."

He told her where to meet a guard who would escort her, un-noticed, to the temple. She had to veil her face so she would not be identified in the future. When someone from the list of abusers showed up, the guard would lure him with an offer of a uniquely charming virgin, then ready them both for the oath encounter. Ibrahem warned that because of her exceptional beauty, those abusive nobles might appear to be extremely gentle, exhibiting no signs of their true vile nature. But he assured her that all the nobles listed had severely abused girls on more than one occasion.

Ibrahem also advised that she had to complete each mission when her moon was down to avoid getting pregnant. That also served to allow a period of one moon cycle between the slayings; enough time for people to forget.

A sudden chill snapped Mayram out of her reverie. Her naked back was getting damp from the blood-soaked bed. She pushed the noble's body over the side, to the floor, and felt around the bed for a dry area.

It was a stressful day, yet very fulfilling. Placidly exhausted, Mayram closed her eyes for a brief, well-deserved rest.

Shu-dagan and the River of Dreams

"So, the gods rewarded me with the gift of eternal life for saving them the trouble of having to start from nothing in the arduous task of creating life to roam this earth again."

Gilgamesh listened in awe to the hero who had attained immortality, then asked: "O valiant Zuisudra, it was a mighty endeavor you undertook; building one enormous ark and securing a pair of each animal kind. You saved humanity and all the wildlife that walked this earth from certain annihilation by the Great Deluge."

And Gilgamesh proceeded to ask the question that had driven him on a quest to seek immortality.

"Surely there are other daunting tasks out there that beget the reward of eternal life. I plead to you, O noble Zuisudra, to intervene on my behalf and convince the gods to assign me such a task. I'm prepared to tackle any mission, no matter how formidable, to the end of sparing me the ugly specter of death."

"My dear Gilgamesh," replied Zuisudra, "the gods took vows not to cause a calamity of such a magnitude that could entirely wipe out the mortals. However, they frequently take turns in bringing misery to peoples who fall short in their prayers and offerings. Plagues, famine, quakes, and local floods are but a few ways in which the gods display their wrath."

"Enough of this nonsense. Such an absurd story!" Arbella interrupted her husband. "The girl needs rest after her long trip. You too need some rest after working like a donkey all day."

"And it's the last day I work for that son of a dog. Now, can I continue with the story!"

"Yes, Mother, let him continue."

"Fine, but only because you so desire, my sweet flower," Arbella relented. "Continue, *dear husband*, with your *thrilling tale*—but make it fast!"

"Let him tell the story at his own pace," Mayram scolded her mother, smiling. "Go ahead, Father, she won't interrupt again."

"At last, someone appreciates my storytelling skills." Shu-dagan shot his wife a nasty smirk.

After consulting the gods, Zuisudra advised Gilgamesh: "Noble king, 1 bring good news from the gods, so listen carefully. You do know about the night sleep spirits—the ones that hang heavy on the eyelids and send all mortals to the land of dreams that floats right above the netherworld. If you succeed in deterring those spirits from dragging you to sleep, by staying awake for seven days and seven nights, starting today, only then will you be spared the eternal sleep that drags men to the netherworld. Now be warned, spying gods will be on the lookout for you in the realm of dreams."

Gilgamesh was so happy, he sang and danced all day long. When the night descended, he grew hungry. Zuisudra told his wife to bring food and pomegranate juice for him.

"*Pomegranate juice!* Are you serious?" Gilgamesh chuckled. "Honorable Zuisudra, bring the beer and wine. Let's celebrate, for 1'm going to be immortal and will keep you company for eternity."

"Gilgamesh, dear friend," Zuisudra cautioned, "1 strongly advise you to refrain from drinking wine and beer; that will attract more of the sleep spirits."

"Zuisudra, Zuisudra! You make me laugh. 1'm Gilgamesh, king of Uruk, the greatest city on Earth from sunrise to sunset, where every day is a festival. 1 used to sing and dance, guzzle beer and wine for a whole moon at a time without blinking an eye."

After some argument, Zuisudra gave up, and his wife brought food, beer, and wine to the table. With a lion's appetite, Gilgamesh went on an eating frenzy. He chugged down the drinks while

Zuisudra sat shaking his head in disapproval.

"Eternal man," Gilgamesh cheered. "Don't worry, I'll be fine. Together, you and I will be the happiest among the immortals for we were once destined to die and will appreciate the glories of perpetual life better than any god. Raise your cup, my noble Zuis." He laughed. "Can I call you Zuis? Raise your cup. A toast to immortality!"

"To immortality." Zuisudra grinned and raised his cup.

Shu-dagan began laughing like a madman; his wife and girl joined in, though they had not a clue as to what amused him.

"Go on, Father, what happened afterward?" Mayram pressed. "Did Gilgamesh become immortal?"

Shu-dagan blurted the words out between chuckles.

"They both emptied their cups … in one gulp. Zuisudra dropped his cup first. Gilgamesh followed … he dropped his cup, then in the blink of an eye, his head followed the cup to the table … and Gilgamesh began snoring."

They all went into fits of laughter till their stomachs ached.

"So Gilgamesh didn't become immortal?" Mayram asked eagerly.

"Patience now. There is more to the story."

"Mayram, is this your father?" Arbella scowled. "What happened to the gloomy, silent man? The gods must have unraveled the knots on his tongue. Now that the floodgates have opened, cursed we will be under a deluge of silly stories."

Shu-dagan sighed and returned to the story:

After seven nights and days of nonstop sleep, Zuisudra woke the man up and told him that the gods who watched over the realm of dreams had seen him there the entire period. The gods were laughing so hard, violently shaking the space around Gilgamesh; and despite that, the sleep spirits never abandoned him.

"You failed the test, dear Gilgamesh," Zuisudra told him. "The gods won't listen to any more of your pleas. Go back to your kingdom and enjoy life to the fullest. Don't waste precious time in search of immortality."

Gilgamesh wailed like a child, cursing his destiny and offering his kingdom for another chance at immortality. But Zuisudra had no powers to help him. The gods, after their laughter faded, were angry over the time they had wasted on such a pathetic mortal.

With tears preceding him, Gilgamesh walked to the boat that would carry him back to Uruk. His misery gained him the sympathy of Zuisudra's wife.

"You can't send a king back empty-handed," she rebuked Zuisudra. "After going through all the hardships just to get here, he surely deserves another chance for a reward."

"Immortality is out of the question; only the gods can grant that," replied Zuisudra. "The next thing to immortality is the plant that restores youth, but the way to find it is fraught with peril."

Gilgamesh overheard Zuisudra and sprang up in excitement. "O noble Zuisudra, I beg you, tell me where to find this plant; I need to show the people of Uruk that my quest wasn't in vain. Spare me becoming the subject of their mockery."

"Very well, Gilgamesh, but you've been warned—it's a deadly quest. The boatman will take you to that part of the sea where rocks and waves have been clashing since the beginning of time with a ferocity a mere mortal cannot fathom. If you manage to survive their fury, there, at the bottom of the sea, you will find the plant that restores youth."

Replete with hope, Gilgamesh darted to board the boat, determined to triumph in this quest—to reclaim his youth from the oldest of thieves: Time.

The boatman, Urshunabi, was instructed by Zuisudra as to the destination. And Urshunabi rowed and rowed, long days and nights, until suddenly, he stopped.

"Is this the spot?" asked Gilgamesh.

"Far from it." Urshunabi pointed out. "See that massive cluster of boulders out there—the plant is somewhere at the sea floor, around the base. To take the boat any farther means certain death; the merciless waves will slam it on the rocks and shatter it to tiny splinters. I'll remain here, awaiting your return. ... Honorable Lord, in truth, my master told me to wait till your lifeless body floats back, then take it to Uruk, where your people would honor you with a burial fit for a great king.

"O brave Gilgamesh, no mortal would dare dispute your heroic deeds. I beseech you; come back to your senses, forget this madness, and let me take you straight to Uruk."

"Urshunabi, Urshunabi!" Gilgamesh laughed. "You wait here. I'll be back with the plant of eternal youth in my possession. I will be a youth in his prime when *I* give *you* an honorable burial."

And Gilgamesh dove into the water, and he swam and swam. Mad waves slammed him against the brutal rocks, yet he prevailed. Then, down he descended, deeper than any fish had ever ventured.

The seafloor was a desolate, watery desert of sand, littered with the bones of fools who had dared search for eternal youth, only to find death greeting them.

Gilgamesh cried tears of desperation that became one with the seawater; all his struggles were about to end in an empty seascape devoid of any trace of life.

He was about to give up and resurface for air before death found him, when sharp pain spiked the sole of his foot. He looked down, and there it was, buried in the sand: the plant with its spiny needles, promising agony to anyone who dared touch it. But this defense wasn't enough to protect it from a king who laughed in the face of monsters and lived a life of adventure that would make many a brave man cower.

Gilgamesh, with a joy that numbed the pain, reached down with hands that happily bled while he wrenched out the plant. He rushed up through the water, resurfaced gasping for air, and swam back to the boat.

Urshunabi, upon seeing him, collapsed to his knees in awe, hailing him. "O Great King, the benevolent gods must have watched over you, for many have attempted this feat, and it had cost them all their precious lives. I beg your forgiveness for doubting your strength and resolve."

"Boatman," Gilgamesh laughed, "not only do I forgive you, but as I promised, I will give you a burial worthy of a king. Now, take me to the shores nearest to my kingdom."

"Praise the gods. At last, a story with a happy ending." Mayram clapped cheerfully.

"It's not over yet." Shu-dagan shook his head.

"This is definitely not your father," Arbella joked. "He must be possessed by the spirit of a storyteller."

Shu-dagan went on:

Gilgamesh arrived at the shore where the Tigris and the Euphrates rivers joined forces to pierce the great sea. He caught sight of a beautiful woman, bathing nude in the water. Gilgamesh hopped off the boat, casting an envious look at the water that joyously caressed the woman's body.

"O brave Gilgamesh,"—Urshunabi detected the lust in the king's eyes—"it was an honor to have you on my humble boat, but may I offer one piece of advice before I bid you farewell. Your subjects in Uruk are patiently awaiting the return of their valiant king, eager to hear of the exploits and adventures he went through, and to applaud the fruits of his triumph. Don't let the woman distract you and rob you of strength. Start your journey back without delay."

Gilgamesh turned his palm up and revealed the plant of eternal youth, now harmless after he'd stripped it of the sharp spikes. "Boatman, remember when you said I would not survive the waves that tried to crush me on the rocks. Well, what worse peril can hinder my triumphant return, now that I carry this armor against old age? But I thank you for the advice. Upon your return, tell your master Zuisudra I was successful, that Time could no longer push me over the precipice of old age, which plummets to the nether-world."

"O Great King," said Urshunabi with his oar slapping the waters, "you have gone through so much pain and turmoil. I only fear that any more strain on your body would render you weak and vulnerable to losing the plant of everlasting youth."

"Urshunabi, Urshunabi!" Gilgamesh roared. "You make me laugh. I'm the king of Uruk, the greatest city on Earth from sunrise to sunset, where every day is a festival and lovers celebrate by taking the oath of marriage. It is my duty as king to visit every newlywed bride and rupture the burden of her hymen, to open and ease the entry path for the husband."

"Where was he when we got married?" Arbella couldn't keep quiet. "I feel cheated. Is that why you married me in secret?"

"Is that true, Father?" Mayram was laughing. "You were married in secret?"

"Don't listen to your mother. She's so lucky, yet always complaining. All the women were envious of her marrying the most handsome man in Babylon. As for the wedding, it was one memorable, lavish party."

"Lavish! He dares say lavish!" Arbella heckled him. "No wonder Gilgamesh never showed up. It would've been hopeless to convince him that such a lackluster event was actually a wedding party."

"Let me remind you why *our hero Gilgamesh* never showed up," Shu-dagan scoffed back. "Because this is Babylon, not Uruk. And even if he were still alive *and* in this city, not he nor any other son of a bitch, king or noble, would've dared touch anything that is mine, for I would've personally served him a most unique meal—his wand and balls, cooked in the juices of his very last seed."

"Listen to him," Arbella retorted. "This overconfidence of his brought us nothing but trouble."

"Just be quiet. Stop interrupting." Shu-dagan resumed with the tale.

Gilgamesh watched the boatman rowing away till he looked like an ant fighting the sea in the distance. Urshunabi's advice rang in his head as clear as the rushing of the waves under his feet. But it had been some time since he had delighted in a woman's body—long before he had begun his journey to find Zuisudra. Oh, how he longed for the touch and warmth of a woman—and there, only paces away, was an all-nude beauty who stirred his passions. But the boatman was right; he needed to save his vigor for the trip back. Once in Uruk, he would visit the new brides and bless their virginity with his royal rod. He proceeded to start the journey home when he heard the river calling him.

"O noble sir, could you help me with a favor?"

Gilgamesh turned and saw the woman waving to him, her supple breasts now floating above the water. The sight of her nipples aroused him; they seemed to stare him in the eyes—an invitation.

"Yes, young lady, what favor do you wish to ask of me?"

"O noble sir, I need help cleaning my back; I can't reach most of it. I need a good, thorough cleaning, for today I am to wed, and I want to look my best for my beloved."

Gilgamesh looked out over the sea, far off to the horizon. There remained no trace of the boatman, and his advice had disappeared along with him.

"You're in luck, young lady." Gilgamesh began to strip off his clothes, then went wading into the river. "Not only will I help you with your back, but I will also help remove the veil that blocks the pleasures inside you, so your husband can more readily enjoy the delights you offer. For I am Gilgamesh, the greatest king of all lands from sunrise to sunset."

"O Your Majesty! Blessed be the gods for sending you back to us. I feel so unworthy of this honor. O love goddess, I'm in your debt till my dying day." And the girl gave herself to the king.

Thus our hero spent the whole day. Before sunset, the girl went on her way to get ready for her wedding. Gilgamesh sat on the shore, his body spent, too weary to move on. The night arrived, and as sleep came to haunt him, a snake slithered by on the sand and watched him struggle to stay awake.

It asked Gilgamesh, "Why not get some sleep?"

Gilgamesh recounted his story to the snake: how his quest for immortality had ended in utter failure, and how he had endured all obstacles and risked his life to find the plant of everlasting youth, which he would not risk losing to the thieves of night.

"Why don't you eat some of the plant?" the snake suggested. "Restore yourself back to those young, robust days when the sleep spirits failed to overwhelm you."

"Snake, I need to test it first—make sure it's harmless. I'll give a tiny piece to an old man, wait and see if the man regains some youth. Then I'll keep the rest for myself."

"Go to sleep, Gilgamesh." The snake put him at ease, its penetrating eyes injecting an extra dose of sleep-urge. "I will coil my body around the plant. Anyone who dares come close will get a taste of my poison."

So, our brave hero fell prey, yet again, to the invincible monster of sleep. As he dozed, the snake wrapped its mouth around the plant and swallowed it whole. Right away its old skin stretched and loosened over a fresh, tight new skin. The snake happily slithered out of its old age, and to this day all of its offspring restore their youth by shedding their old dress for a new one.

"And Gilgamesh!" Mayram asked. "What of him?"

"What else? He went back to Uruk, humbled by his failures but much wiser after that intense adventure. He became a just king, never touched a newlywed bride again, and the people loved him so much that when death snatched him away, they sang and wrote his story on tablets so his name would become immortal."

"End of the story. Finally!" Arbella beamed. "Come on, my flower, time to sleep."

"It's not fair." Sad was Mayram's voice. "Gilgamesh deserved to be immortal."

"It's just a story, silly girl," Arbella mocked, then lashed out at her husband. "See what you did, foolish *wise man*. You should keep your stories to yourself."

"It's a good story, and that's how it ended. The man didn't get any more immortal than"—Shu-dagan shrugged—"than the neighbor's ass, tied outside."

He tried not to laugh but couldn't stop himself, despite Mayram's gloomy look. After he got a grip on himself, he went to hug her.

"Oh, sweet rose, don't frown like that. Shed the sadness off your face, wear a smile, and this youthful beauty of yours will be immortal."

"It's about time you say something nice to her." Arbella went to cheer her girl up. "Forget the story, my flower, and tell us about this rich noble you've trapped in the web of your glamour. Is he good-looking?"

"He's just a friend, a sculptor. He gained me work in the service of the king."

"Mayram, I hope you're not being treated as a concubine. Your charm can attract wealthy nobles. You must insist on marriage."

"Mother!" Mayram scowled.

"Woman, leave the girl alone." Shu-dagan snubbed his wife. "She's grown up and knows what she's doing."

"I don't want my daughter to make the same mistake I did."

"Mistake! How about me!" Shu-dagan pounced on Arbella and pinched her behind. "Got fooled by this nicely curved—"

"Dirty old man." Arbella pushed him away, laughing.

"I'm off to sleep," Mayram said, grinning. "I'll leave you two fools to fight it out."

"I'm off to sleep too," Arbella said.

"The night is still young!" Shu-dagan griped. "Woman, go get the best wine we have. Let's celebrate."

"You mean the cheap wine that will make your entrails eject food like a flash flood! Better that you sleep, too."

"You haven't been paying attention to the story," he grumbled. "Gilgamesh lost all because of sleep."

"What nonsense! Has someone promised you eternal life? You are to become a boatman for the gods!"

"Always mocking me, but I still love you—only because you gave me the most precious and beautiful thing in the world. I will forever be thankful to the gods for blessing me with such a wonderful child." He embraced his daughter. "If this were a dream, I would never dare open my eyes."

"Let's go, Mayram, before he starts reciting his dreams that will take an eternity to come true."

Mayram hugged her father. "Among all men and fathers, you're the greatest."

"Ah, for your innocence, Mayram," Arbella taunted. "He fooled you too."

They all laughed.

Arbella and her daughter retired to the side room for the night; it was a small room, but large enough to sleep the three of them comfortably. Its ceiling was low, with less than a forearm of clearance over their heads. The room was lit by a tiny flame of sesame seed oil from a small lamp of clay placed in a dip of earth at a corner, away from any flammable reeds.

Mayram removed her dagger and placed it to her side.

"I hope you didn't have to use that." Arbella's voice flowed softly in the dim light.

"No, Mother, I didn't have to use it." ... *I chose to use it.*

"Good." Arbella kissed her on the temple. "Never part with it. It works better than any amulet to keep evil away."

And to strip the life away from evil men. Mayram closed her eyes. "Sweet dreams, Mother."

𒀭 𒁉 𒐈

Shu-dagan took another sip of wine while he dreamily stared at ghosts sent by the faint moonlight and somehow managed to sneak inside his shack under the darkness of night.

Arbella was right about the wine—so awful, it would send any unseasoned stomach on a protest and a fast dash to fertilize the nearest field. After drinking half the cup, he walked outside and tossed the rest of the drink onto the dirt.

"One has to be drunk to swallow this vomit," he whispered to the moon that started to shy away behind the clouds.

"O Moon, hang on there and keep a lonely man company. I wonder why your tiny star companions abandoned the night sky. Must be to avoid the coming rain."

But the moon ignored his plea and opted to join the stars in their rain shelter, forsaking Shu-dagan to the solitude of a hazy night after he in turn ignored the moon's advice in joining the inhabitants of Babylon on their voyage to the dreamland—the one floating right above the netherworld.

Shu-dagan had no need to visit that land of dreams. Teased by modest dreams that were on the way to his real world, he remained awake. Soon, he would get his own ferryboat, and with diligent planning his other dream of building a brick house to live in could come true.

The thought unexpectedly filled him with sadness; he could already envision himself sitting in the new brick home and yearning for this humble reed shack he would abandon, even though mostly sad memories resided in it.

The shack was dear to him; everything that had gone into it was the product of his hard labor. It was modestly built like any other shack for the poor: deep holes were dug in the earth to mark the shack's boundary. Tall reeds, bunched together, were embedded in those holes. Each bundle of reeds was bent and tied at the top to another bundle on the opposite side, creating an arch. A series of arches formed the standing frame of the shack. More bundled reeds were used to cross-connect the arches all the way from top to bottom, completing the shack's skeleton. Next to assemble was a thatched roof of straw and palm fronds, then the walls were built by filling the gaps with straw-reinforced clay. Inside, reed mats were layered upon one another to cover the beaten ground.

Every day started with a prayer to the goddess of reeds, in gratitude for her generosity in giving shelter. And every full moon, Shu-dagan made offerings to gain her favor for extra protection against fire and floods.

"Don't worry, little shack, I won't abandon you," Shu-dagan soothed his humble shelter. "Much of my soul resides here. But you will have to share me with the brick house."

Alone with the night, his future dreams gave way to past memories; to a treacherous event from the days when he had been the proud owner of a boat.

Blessed with the hardened body of a warrior, he used to be full of life; a gentle smile rarely left his face. Crossing the river on his boat was a joy, crammed with stories and laughter. That was how he had met Arbella, who was a real beauty, envied by other women for snatching him. Everything was going right for them, and it appeared it would continue like that, until one fateful day.

It was the fertility festivals, the busiest season for ferryboats, with people coming in droves from nearby towns to cross the river, and boats crowded to full capacity. Shu-dagan used to take four people, along with a hired man to help in the rowing.

On the last day of the festivals, as if by a gods' conspiracy, everything went against him. His worker felt weak with sickness but didn't mention it, and the river flowed faster than normal. He had four passengers—three men, and a pregnant woman who would only cross the river on his boat. Just as he was about to push the boat free from the bank, a drunk, heavyset man appeared and begged to be taken aboard. The other boats were fully loaded and the closest one approaching was a long distance for the man to wait. A generous offer of a polished stone of blood jasper swayed Shu-dagan into taking the man on board.

Midway across, the man became nauseous. He tried to move to the side to empty his gut's contents into the river, when a wave rocked the boat sideways. The man managed to steady himself but couldn't hold back the messy brew churning inside him. Instantly, the other passengers came under the assault of his putrid jet of vomit. All chaos broke loose, just when a bigger wave hit and sent the unbalanced boat rolling to one side, flipping it over.

The toppled boat didn't sink but kept drifting downstream. None of those on board knew how to swim except for Shu-dagan and his hired man. Shu-dagan grabbed the pregnant woman and struck out with her toward the riverbank, saving her. The hired man saved his own skin. The other four men drowned.

A stunned Shu-dagan walked in a trance downstream along the bank until sunset, looking for his boat. Was it still drifting? Did it sink? Or did someone take possession of it after it settled on the riverbank? Those questions were never answered; the boat left no traces. On the way back, he was arrested for his poor judgment of the conditions that contributed to the death of his passengers.

What saved Shu-dagan from the executioner's sword was the compelling testimony of the woman he rescued and his good reputation among the people who came to his defense before the judge. But that didn't save him from the punishment of destitution—doomed to slave away as a hired hand on a boat, hardly sustaining his family.

Yet, life had another destiny in store for him when Mayram arrived from Uruk on a short visit.

Exhausted by the trip, she went straight to sleep. Shu-dagan left early for work the next morning, and when he returned that evening, a surprise awaited him: Mayram presented him with a leather pouch. Once he poured its contents, the intense sparkles of precious stones assaulted his sight.

"That is genuine silver and gold, Father," Mayram said with a vibrant smile. "You can buy and work with your own boat."

Shu-Dagan went numb. She had done it again—taken it upon herself to be the provider. It hurt his pride; never in his entire life had he handled anything even remotely close in value. Overwhelmed with shame, he looked down, turning his face away from the sparkling stones, when a smooth hand brushed across the scars on his chin and brought him around.

"Father," Mayram pleaded, "take this, buy the boat, and—pay me back later."

"I wouldn't trust him," Arbella said in her mocking way. "He'll disappear into the taverns, enrich their owners, get drunk, get into fights, till all is wasted. Only then will you see him walking back— two steps to the left, three to the right, before he takes a step forward."

A long moment of silence hung in the air; then, like lightning, Shu-dagan's hand fell onto the table with a bang.

"You will get all of this back with one in ten extra," he announced. "And when I get that boat, consider yourselves the luckiest people in Babylon, for when the next deluge floods the earth, you will be the sole survivors under the aegis of the greatest boatman to navigate the seas from sunrise to sunset. However, if either one of you gives me a hard time, *off the boat you go!*"

He grabbed the two of them with his strong arms and whirled around until he grew dizzy, and all three fell on the reed mats amid wild laughter. Rays of joy filled the dim room with the promise of a bright future.

The gods work in mysterious ways. Just when Shu-dagan thought that the gods had abandoned him to a harsh, miserable existence, they had sent Mayram to let him know his days of suffering were over. With hope revived, Shu-dagan hailed the heavens:

"O divine gods, I greatly appreciate your generosity in giving me a second chance. I will strive to make the best out of this gift and prove to be worthy of it. Unlike that fool of a king, Gilgamesh; despite all the storied heroics about him, he must've been a pathetic, spoiled weakling for having ruined his chance at becoming immortal … all for sleep! Then, not long after that, our *wise king* followed with another *shrewd* feat, where he was tricked into losing the fruit of eternal youth to a slithering snake … again, for sleep!

"Swelling waves! Bone crushing rocks!" Shu-dagan began mocking the legendary king to the clouds. "The real Gilgamesh probably couldn't swim halfway across the Euphrates; I bet that fool couldn't swim at all. … Huh, slaughtered the monster Humbaba *single-handedly*! What a joke! Those royal gluttons won't take a step out of their palace with less than two dozen guards surrounding them. I can only imagine *His Majesty* sipping wine while ordering his troops to attack Humbaba and die for him. … I'm surprised they forgot the mention of *His Majesty's* hairy butt, smelling like jasmine."

Something moved nearby, distracting Shu-dagan from his chat with the night. It was the neighbor's ass, agitated by the unruly madman who had nothing better to do than talk to himself, interrupting the dreams of others.

"On his own," Shu-dagan addressed the ass, "our hero, *His Majesty, King Gilgamesh*, would've failed miserably in slaying even you—my dear ass, tied up outside."

The donkey started to bray as if in appreciation of the joke, sending Shu-dagan into an insane fit of laughter that folded him over his aching stomach. It took him a while to recover, and he sat down ruminating. Not since he and Arbella were young, in the spring of their love, had he laughed this hard.

"Oh, ass-tied-outside," he resumed talking to the donkey, "bless you for grasping my humor. Oh, I feel so alive; it must be that awful wine. Ass-tied-outside, call me a fool for not drinking all of it."

But Shu-dagan knew it wasn't the wine. It was Mayram who had brought back that distant memory when she, his flower, his plant of youth, stepped into the hut the night before and showered him and Arbella with kisses, giving them this fresh taste of youth, after cruel fate cheated them out of their fair share of it.

𒀸 𒅆 𒐊

The sleep spirits that invaded the night and hang heavy on the eyelids were going frantic looking for Shu-dagan. He evaded them with the shiny dreams that mirrored in his eyes and kept him awake—dreams so lucid, he could feel the water spray as he rowed his dream boat on the river. But the rocking of that boat alarmed the spirits, and they caught up to him where he sat with his back against a tree. They clung to his eyelids, opening them into the dreamworld where Shu-dagan found himself on a giant boat the size of a ziggurat. The boat drifted to the end of Earth and slowly tipped off the edge. But instead of plummeting into endless darkness, it flew high through white clouds to where the gods stood waiting for him to row them across from one side of heaven to the other.

𒀸 𒅆 𒐊

Darkness lazily brightened to gray when the sun left the confines of night, only to find clouds blocking its way. Shamash, the sun god, aimed the daggers of his rays to tear through the clouds, but the clouds were too adamant that day, determined to win the fray.

Soothing, warm mist caressed Shu-dagan's face and washed the dream spirits off his eyelids. Frantically, he jumped to his feet, dreading that his surrender to sleep had ruined his plans, just like Gilgamesh. Timidly, he reached down and felt the pouch's contents. Up and down he bounced, rivers of joy rocking him. Unlike that foolish Gilgamesh, sleep had failed to rob him out of his future dreams. On a whim, an excited Shu-dagan started a brisk walk toward the river.

"O beloved river god, send me your blessings," he prayed.

The god of fresh water answered the prayer with a sneeze, and the mist matured to drizzle that reached the roots of Shu-dagan's memory, reviving the thrill of a past event which sent his legs into a brisk sprint that his age dared not slow down.

He was a boy again, hugging a watermelon he had snatched from a field. Under weeping clouds, the farmer gave chase, screaming:

"Son of thieves! By Alala, god of harvest, once I lay my hands on you, I will harvest your balls faster than you can slice that watermelon."

Shu-dagan laughed now as he ran, remembering his fear and how close he had come to losing his manhood. He had no idea how long he ran; the past left his awareness of time lagging far behind. Out of breath, he stopped and turned. The phantom of the mad farmer was no longer on his trail.

"The sweetest watermelon I've ever tasted." And laughter arrested him again.

From the distance, he spotted the moored boat, dancing over the waves, seemingly thrilled at his arrival. Shu-dagan rushed to join the boat in the dance.

Like the rest of the city, the man selling the boat was surely asleep. The only things pulsing with life on that desolate riverbank were the rippling river, a dancing boat, and a man impatient for a dream to come true.

Plans crowded Shu-dagan's mind: *Once I purchase the boat, I'll pay a visit to Ishtar's temple. Mayram is truly passionate about the goddess; I'll sacrifice a goat for an offering.*

He envisioned how Arbella would react, and mimicked to the river the way she would scold him:

"A chicken would've been more than enough. Ishtar curses people who gift larger offerings; getting her fat only makes lovers abandon her."

Shu-dagan didn't care; that was Ishtar's problem.

"A goat it would be for the boat."

At the temple, he would buy the ceremonial leather pouch containing the breath of the storms god, which would keep the boat balanced when the river became angry. Around the boat, he would attach inflatable goat skins to protect it from sinking. As for passengers, he would take five to seven, depending on their size. He would hire two men he knew, both good swimmers and rowers. Also, the boat could be used to move merchandise between the two banks.

By the god Marduk, there would be plenty of work, and within twenty moons I would save enough to pay Mayram back ... maybe buy a bigger boat!

His future aspirations raced south—to where the Tigris and Euphrates rivers joined before surging into the great sea. How he fantasized about sailing on those giant boats that could travel to the ends of Earth, to lands inhabited by strange peoples—lands blessed with precious stones and pungent spices that had fallen from the tables of the feasting gods in heaven, grown roots in the soil, and blossomed.

Shu-dagan dismissed those large dreams and focused on attainable, modest fortunes. Eagerly, he related his future designs to the river.

"First: the boat ... two helpers. Also, a cart to move goods inland. Now ... how to pull the cart?" The latter question jumped into the mix.

It didn't take him long to find the answer. He burst out laughing and shouted. "What else? The neighbor's ... Ass-Tied-Outside!"

Make Love and Death

IT HAPPENED A FEW DAYS AFTER HER RETURN FROM BABYLON.

Mayram visited the temple to shower thanks on her goddess for the triumphant mission against another heretic who exploited and violated the sacred vows.

She left the temple, mulling over the previous night. It was different from the first three; she gave the man a fighting chance.

The noble was heavy and sluggish. While he was engrossed in taking off his clothes, Mayram had slipped the dagger under the bed mat.

Her love act went smoothly until the right moment to strike arrived with her on top, straddling him. She quickened the pace, sending his moans to pummel the air.

Upon nearing the supreme bliss, his eyes bulged out as if they craved penetrating her beautiful face, and his hands clamped firmly on her hips, when suddenly, Mayram's arm went up with the dagger. Stricken with panic, he could only watch the blade plunge down into his chest. A chaotic shriek echoed out of him—an orgy of sounds where joy and pain fused together, while love and death coupled in a tight embrace. Mayram reached the peaks of ecstasy with the swell of his lust inside her and the burst of his lifeblood over her skin. Passionately, she closed her mouth on his, sucking out the last of his pleasure moans and silencing the groans of his death throes.

Her reverie was broken after she descended the steps of the temple, when a voice from behind came reciting a poem:

In the desert of loneliness, an ailing heart fought to endure.
It searched the vast emptiness for love—the only cure,
When it stumbled upon a fountain of beauty, so sweet, so pure.

Mayram kept walking. She was used to all sorts of comments, polite and vulgar. All of them she ignored, except on one occasion about a moon ago.

She had been by a stand in the market bazaar, examining a bracelet of lapis lazuli beads around her wrist when an unexpected voice spoke to her.

"Such a lucky bracelet, to be around a beauty like you."

She turned to her admirer: a middle-aged woman, nicely dressed, probably related to a noble.

"It would be a pleasure if you allowed me to buy it for you," the woman added.

Mayram felt a strange attraction to her, an impulse to try a carnal experience with a female. But she couldn't trust herself not to harm the woman, which might bring on the wrath of the love goddess. She returned a warm smile, shaking her head.

"I'm grateful for your kindness, my lady, but I'm afraid I can't accept your offer."

"I understand. May the gods bless you beyond your beauty," the woman said with a sad smile, and walked away.

Mayram paid for the bracelet, and after a short stroll, a sudden urge stirred inside her. She wondered if it was simply a woman's tenderness that she yearned for, or was it the lust for blood—the thought of a woman bleeding to death beneath her—that aroused her?

Trying to curb her desire failed outright. Be it for love or be it for blood, she wanted that woman.

Mayram turned around and feverishly searched the bazaar. But like a mirage, no trace was left of her admirer.

"O goddess Ishtar," Mayram whispered a prayer, "you must have sensed my weakness. Bless you for sending the source of temptation out of my reach."

Whatever urge had swamped Mayram had just as suddenly disappeared, but it was replaced by a sense of loneliness and a powerful longing for home. It was the reason she had made the trip to Babylon.

Visiting her parents, the only people who showed her unconditional love, had provided a much-needed relief from her troubling, murderous thoughts. She was content with the happiness she'd brought to them; Shu-dagan became the proud owner of a boat with her help. Arbella could foresee a bright future for her daughter as the wife of a wealthy noble. Mayram had left them with a promise she would visit again within three moons.

Now, back from Babylon, she walked the streets of Uruk, brimming with confidence, feeling refreshed and in control of her urges, when the same poetic voice from outside the temple hounded her again:

O splendid goddess of beauty, do my eyes behold your daughter?
Mercy, for with her charm, this man she could lead to slaughter.

Goddess! Lead to slaughter! The words made Mayram stop. Surely this was a sign from the goddess. At once, her desire for blood was fully revived.

"A poet!" she said amiably, turning around.

"Yes, and for the first time in my life, I see the most beautiful poem come alive right before my very eyes."

"Why chase someone who 'could lead you to slaughter'?" she asked, smiling.

"Bewitched by your beauty, I'm no more than a sheep following my shepherd to whatever fate she desires." And the man opened his palm to show two pieces of silver.

"How intriguing; the sheep offering silver to be led to slaughter!" Mayram was enjoying this dialogue.

"Not only the silver—the sheep will gladly offer its flesh to become one with the shepherd."

Mayram giggled and took the silver.

Forget your meat, my poetic stud. All I'm hungry for is your warm blood.

"Poet, sing me more poems." She hooked her arm into his, and they strolled together down broad Ishtar Walk.

As soon as they entered the room, the poet walked her to bed and helped strip her clothing off. Starved for carnal pleasure, he started kissing her naked body passionately while he hastened to disrobe himself, when the door slammed open, violently.

"Going to visit your sick mother, huh, you son of dogs!" a crazed woman stormed in. "Your mother—*sick*! Look at her—younger and far healthier than our own daughter. ... O dearest mother of my *cherished husband*, why are you all naked? Must be to have your fill of that *fountain of youth*—his HARD ROD!"

The wife leapt on Mayram, repeatedly slapping her in a jealous rage.

"Oh how worried I was about you being sick, *Mother*—daughter of the *whoring demons*! Shame on *your beloved son* for denying me the pleasure of your warm company—*Ishtar whore!*"

After inflicting some pain on Mayram's cheeks, the seething wife shifted her anger to the poet. She grabbed a jar off a small table and smashed it over his head.

Fury exacerbated Mayram's hunger for blood. She reached for her clothes—not to put them on, but to get her dagger and stab both, man and wife. Just as she gripped the handle, two servants rushed into the room to save the poet, who was on the floor, barely conscious, getting pummeled by the vicious wife. Within short moments, an older woman helped by a walking stick came in shrieking.

"Leave my son alone, you bitch—monster of a wife!"

The mayhem left Mayram no choice but to abandon the battle arena of a *happy* family love nest. She pulled her clothing on and fled.

Once outside, Mayram took off down the road, running to vent her anger. The urge to kill was overpowering now; justified or not justified was not a concern. That night she couldn't sleep. Her anger scared the sleep spirits and kept them at bay. She begged them to hang on to her eyelids, but they wouldn't trust her.

Around sunset the next day, after a long night of seething and a day of aimlessly wandering the bazaar, she headed out toward the fields and spotted her chosen victim: a young shepherd letting his sheep graze in a meadow.

Smiling, she walked past him. He smiled back but didn't say anything. A short distance away, she sat down on the grass with her raiment halfway up her thighs. Glancing out of the corner of her eye, she caught the shepherd stealing peeks at her. She shifted to face him and teasingly pulled her kilt up, just short of her sex, giving him an inviting smirk. But the boy coyly looked the other way, out across the field.

A shy one, must be a virgin. Virgin blood! Perfect.

She waited, but it became evident the boy was not going to initiate the move. Slowly, she walked over to him. He remained still, waiting for her to take the lead and show him what to do.

A virgin, no doubt about it. Without saying a word, she reached out and lightly brushed the hardness that pleaded to be released from its confines under his garment. His breathing became heavy, yet not a word issued out of him. *Must be a mute.*

She had him lie down on his back, raised his robe, and sat astride his waist, wickedly brushing her sex against his stiffness. His eyes closed with the intensity of the pleasure that only the gracious gods could have bestowed on him.

Without taking her clothes off, Mayram guided him inside her. He moaned in pain; his virgin foreskin felt as if it were tearing apart. She slowed down to allow it to stretch. When the pain eased, he closed his eyes to live the dream come true.

Mayram became wild like a lioness on top of her prey, ready to go for the jugular.

All those sheep I had sacrificed before! It's time to sacrifice the shepherd.

She wanted him to be hard, penetrating her as the sharp dagger penetrated him. Slaying him she decided to rush, before his rod went limp once his passion was spent.

His eyes were still closed when she removed the dagger from the pocket of her vestment; that move disrupted her rhythm.

Fearing this gift from the gods was abandoning him, the shepherd opened his eyes, only to see a dagger flashing the redness of the setting sun on its blade—his blood about to be written over it in a darker veil. Impulsively, his hands shot up to ward off the mortal blow. The dagger sliced one hand while the other managed to hold back the murderous grip. Only a mute's squeal escaped his lips.

Mayram had lost the element of surprise but ferociously pressed down on the dagger until its point nicked the boy's skin. Desperate to survive, he mustered all his strength and pushed back until the dagger cleared his neck, giving him a much needed boost in confidence to overcome her advantage. The thrill of dodging death reinvigorated his rod, which his assailant kept inside her.

Mayram's strength was dwindling, and eventually, the shepherd shook the dagger from her hand. Just when she thought the battle was lost, she felt his hardness thrust inside her with a tremendous force; it felt unnatural, like nothing she had ever experienced. His back arched and stiffened for a moment while his whole body started shaking uncontrollably and his grip on her went loose. Mayram sprang away from him and crawled back to safety while the convulsions arrested his body. She watched, recovering her breath, thanking the gods for their intervention.

She picked her dagger up but was nervous and hesitant about finishing what she had come for. She prayed for a signal from the gods while circling the helpless, trembling shepherd on the ground.

A streak of blood oozed out of the boy's mouth, where his teeth had clamped mercilessly on his tongue. It was the answer to her prayers; his blood was for the gods to spill, not for her.

Pity—a thing her cruel life had never allowed her the time to feel for others—now overwhelmed her for this poor creature. She wondered if he was birthed mute or if he had bitten the speech out of his tongue. One thing was beyond doubt: this spasm was her doing.

Released from the grip of her murderous lust, she tucked the dagger in her pocket and rushed to ease his suffering. She tore a piece of her kilt, knelt to his side, and forced his mouth open to free his tongue from the clenching jaw, then she shoved the cloth between his teeth.

Mayram remained holding the boy, and when the spasms ceased she tried to hug him, but he recoiled from her touch. To earn his trust, she took a few steps back, pulled out the dagger and flung it away.

She ripped another piece of her skirt and approached him with the torn cloth dangling between her fingers, asking for the hand that was bleeding. Reluctantly, the shepherd allowed her to bandage the wound.

With guilt refusing to subside, she asked his forgiveness, and told him of another shepherd who had assaulted her at a younger age. She expressed gratitude, for through him the gods had opened her eyes and cured her from the blind hate she had harbored toward all shepherds, which almost led her to slay him—an innocent victim. When at last she regained his trust, she swept him in her arms and made tender love to him.

↗ ◇ ⊐ ∨∨ Ⲙ

The moon crawled into the dimming sky. Lonely, it waited for its tiny companions, the stars, to show up and do their share of lighting the night. Then the moon watched the figure of a girl walking, also alone, on the Earth down below. It felt sad for such a fragile creature, on her own in a world where all the light of the universe would fail to remove the darkness of the evil that lurked everywhere. The moon gathered all its splendor, sending the warmest greetings to this girl while lighting the path to whatever destiny she sought. It wasn't long before the girl raised her head and hailed the moon.

"O compassionate moon god. This humble servant thanks you for the generosity of your light and the company you offer. I pray that you deliver this message to my love goddess, who I dare not disturb in her sleep. I ask her to forgive my foolishness, and I thank her for stopping me from carrying out the beastly deeds I was about to commit. May she make me stronger in the face of temptation. I renew my vows to serve her and all gods of heaven to the last breath of my insignificant life."

Beyond the guiding moonlight, Mayram saw her mission more lucidly than ever. The gods had entrusted her with a sacred duty, had given her the powers and resolve. Yet irrationally, dark impulses almost had her sacrifice innocent people. She should only place her full trust in the messenger assigned by the gods to accomplish this holy quest: Ibrahem.

When Myth Births Reality

"**H**ONORABLE PEOPLE OF URUK!"

All the heads in the crowded bazaar spun toward the loud voice, expecting to see some herald on a chariot announcing a new decree or a forthcoming execution. To their surprise, it was a man in haggard clothes standing on a pile of bricks that used to be a merchant's stall. He seemed to be afflicted with madness; his weary eyes darted in all directions as if scanning for demons on his trail.

"Listen to what I say, for the wrath of the gods is upon us!"

The crowd was captivated. His merchandise of lunacy, offered for free, promised to be the most fascinating thing the bazaar had to offer.

"Many nights ago, the master I served arrived with a girl of such astounding beauty, I thought only the gods should have the privilege of her company, and never a mortal like my aging lord.

"She was sent by angry gods; a demon robed in a most desirable body of a girl, pretending to offer her virginity to satisfy the love ritual vows. I was cleaning a room when suddenly, I heard a scream—nothing like any joyful sound of lovemaking—it made my blood curdle. I walked into the room, only to witness the naked demon girl, rubbing her body atop my master. His throat … she had slashed ear to ear. Her mouth was dripping with blood she sucked out of him. On seeing me, she flew out of the bed, thirsty for more blood—my blood. In horror, I ran and ran till I was about to faint from exhaustion.

"Believe what I say: She, the demon, slayed my master! Yet, as is always the case, it was us, the servants, who were condemned for his murder. I watched from the distance as my fellow servant was forced on the chopping block—another victim of the demon. Don't be fooled by that evil beauty; your blood is her wine! I … I've been hiding and haven't eaten for long days. I'm afraid to die … but can't hide anymore. Please, I beseech your—"

Abruptly, he was swept off his feet, and his bony frame collapsed on the loose bricks, ending his address with a shriek of pain.

"Finally, got you!" A guard beamed, and his two companions restrained the slave. The guard stepped over the brick pile and began heralding to a crowd that swelled by the spectacle like fall leaves dragged into a dust devil.

"Do not listen to him. *He* killed his master! The other servant confessed; they planned to rob the house and escape. When their master caught them in the act, they killed him. This slave is a murderer *and* a desperate liar, claiming innocence through fantasies of some charming, bloodsucking demon." The guard cupped a hand over his groin while looking down at the servant. "You can suck on this."

The crowd roared with laughter.

"I believe him!" a man hollered. "This is only the beginning; a greater wrath is yet to descend upon us. I've heard that Ishtar is begging her sister, Ereshkigal, to open the gates of the netherworld and release all the virgins who died before fulfilling their vows. Those dead girls will walk the earth and suck the blood off the living!"

"Nonsense!" the guard shouted back.

"It is true," another voice joined in. "Many of the dead girls are sending demons to possess our virgins to exact vengeance on those noble bastards who abuse and kill girls. Now, commoners like most of us need not worry; it's only the blood of the filthy, wealthy pigs they seek. I say to these possessed girls: Go ahead! Suck the nobles dry!"

"Yes! Suck the nobles dry! Suck the nobles dry!" cheered the crowd.

The guard was yelling to calm the riot, but his voice was a whisper amid the thunderous horde. He moved to leave with his partners, dragging the prisoner along, but the mob surrounded them, chanting: "Let him go! Let him go!"

Men began pulling the slave away from the guards, who grasped the common sense in not resisting the mob. They released the servant and watched him dissolve into the multitude.

The market went abuzz with arguments about what was fantasy and what was fact. Many clustered in groups, dueling in heated exchanges.

Ibrahem, who was out for his daily walk in the bazaar, stood to the side, observing two opposing teams engrossed in arguments, aiming to win this battle between myth and reality.

"That slave is a liar," claimed a skeptical one. "For someone as miserable as him, any naked girl would be *an astounding beauty*. This is what happened: he was listening outside the door while the two were fornicating, his hard rod took control of him and he went in, killed his master, and raped the girl. The girl didn't stick around for fear of being blamed, and blaming her is exactly what he was trying to do. Huh, demons and bloodsucking virgins! How absurd! He won't fool me with that story."

"Your story has no merit, either," a man challenged the skeptic. "That slave is a eunuch. You can tell by his voice—it rang like a woman's. He's not equipped to fornicate."

"Eunuchs *can* get it hard. And when they do, they lose all control," another one proposed.

"True, but only if he was possessed by a demon of a very specific nature," commented one woman.

"You mean the demon that takes residence in a man's rod, driving it to stiffen with madness!" another joked, and those around laughed.

"Fools! You can laugh all you want," screamed an incensed advocate of the myths. "But your ridicule is only making the gods angrier. Repent, or soon heaven will rain demons upon you!"

Superstition leapt into the scene. Many eyes checked the skies in dread of hails of demons. The believer gained a boost of confidence, having successfully planted the seeds of fear in their hearts.

"Have you forgotten the king who was possessed by wild spirits and turned into a wolf, roaming the desert in the dead of night? How about the father of Gilgamesh? His diabolic soul that resembles a snake still slithers around, raping virgins, using two sharp teeth at the end of a long tongue to dig inside and suck their blood. Go ask all those girls who woke up to find they had lost their virginity without being touched by a man."

One by one, the skeptics started to withdraw, knowing that their weapons of reason were powerless in penetrating the mighty shield of ignorance. It was not the demons they feared, but the superstitions that could turn the gullible into demons.

"I'm not relating fables," the myth's advocate resumed, now unchallenged. "Those are facts written on tablets by our ancestors who cared to warn us. Heed their advice! Most of you must have heard of Lilith, the first woman Anu created; with her insatiable taste for children, she would transform into smoke and let the night breeze carry her to the sleeping infants, only to change back into a woman and sniff out their innocent souls. Countless are the mothers who lost their healthy children for no apparent reason. They wake up in the morning, and the infant lies as if sleeping peacefully. But sleeping the child remains—forever."

Many in the crowd nodded in agreement, recalling a day when they were awakened by the cries of a mother who lost her child that way.

"Do not mock the evil spirits, for they will notice and target you," the zealous speaker resumed. "Protect your families with consecrated amulets to ward off malicious spirits. For the infants—a good Pazzuzu charm would bar Lilith, her daughter Lamashtu, and their vile companions from snuffing out your child's soul. Do not delay; evil is lurking everywhere, looking for easy prey. When the gods are not around to protect you, a holy charm will. You've been warned! You have only yourselves to blame when harm touches you or your loved ones. ... I leave you now. May the gods bless you with the wisdom to heed my advice."

The spectators cleared a path for the man to walk through while lauding his generous effort to save them from evil.

To one side, Ibrahem stood laughing, for he might have given some thought to that sermon had he not been aware of what started the spectacle.

"That's one shrewd, well-spoken man. Must be the owner of an amulet trade," Ibrahem muttered to himself, and wondered about what he had just witnessed.

Mayram—a demon, clothed with the body of a desirable girl! She had revived all those myths—bloodsuckers, soul snatchers, wolf men, the walking dead! ... How could such nonsense gain true believers? People must be really desperate for myths to believe in.

Then, it dawned on Ibrahem: quite by accident, he had sculpted the blurry fantasy of a myth into the firm stone of reality. Mayram was merely the tool, but *he* was the craftsman—the creator.

He started to walk, musing over other beliefs.

Beyond doubt, through endless interpretations, other mere myths must have similarly evolved into unchallenged truths, to be exploited by a few into manipulating masses steeped in ignorance.

A disturbing thought stopped Ibrahem in his tracks.

How about the gods? They can't all be real. Just like the myths, gods can also be invented. Start them small, then let the fools nourish and keep them growing till they become colossal entities. To the willing believers, a nothing could be made mightier than any formidable power out there—even mightier than ...

Ibrahem resumed walking, consciously silencing his thoughts—Anu could be listening.

Besieged by Love

ITHIN THE WALLS OF UR, THE REBEL CITY NOW BESIEGED BY Sargon's army, a man sought to find the gates of the netherworld to escape the illness besieging him. Sadly, only beads of sweat managed to escape the sweltering fever inside him.

She kissed him lightly on the forehead. "Oh, dear husband, my Elam, what curse has befallen you? Oh, love of my life, joy of my soul, do not worry; I'll stay by your side, and before long, you will regain your vigor like a youth in his prime."

"Ah, Kebboba." Elam spoke with an effort. "How can I thank you … the sweet words you shower on me. O beloved wife, I only ask you one favor … that poison you've been feeding me slowly, give it to me in a large cup. End my suffering—whore!"

"By the gods, Elam! How cruel of you?" Kebboba feigned shock. "To think I'm capable of such evil! You are my one and only man; I have known no other. This serum I give you is a miracle brew, made by the best healers in the land. It is said that the same gods drink this very brew daily. But it takes time to work, and when it does, you will jump out of bed like a horse. Your rod will stand firm like a sword, just like that first night when you tore through the shroud to my love and occupied me, body and soul. Remember, when I was so young, and you—older than my father. Yet, you flooded me with such unfathomable, heavenly pleasure. Soon we will be back to those days. This drink, recipe of the gods, will harden you, and your juices will fill me to the brim."

"Kebboba … you're always filled to the brim … thanks to his help, among others." Elam's eyes rolled toward the man standing by the front edge of the bed.

"May the gods strike me with lightning!" Shulgi, the high general of Ur's army, protested. "Our friendship is most sacred to me. I would never touch a thing that is yours. Curse this fever for making you imagine such an unspeakable thing!"

"Yes, the fever it is. Fever of lust that sends you both … moaning in joy next room … ever since I've become bedridden."

"You heard wrong, dear husband." Kebboba wore a smile she didn't bother to hide. "Those were discussions on how to best deal with the enemy sieging our city."

"Of course … the siege. That is why you want me dead … because I went against your doomed rebellion idea. … Huh, taxes too high. Taxes, my stinking arse! You two want to be crowned king and queen … while I rule over the maggots in my grave."

"Oh beloved, we're doing it for you. Once we triumph, you will be standing tall and crowned king."

"She's right, my dearest friend Elam," added Shulgi. "After I decorate our walls with the spiked heads of Sargon and his son, Naram-sin, your title will change from Ruler of Ur to King of all Kings, from sunrise to sunset. This fool of a king, *the Great Sargon*, thinks he could subdue our mighty city by sending his hopeless fool of a son. For so many moons now, they've tried everything: ramming the gates, climbing the walls again and again. We crushed them like ants and burned their butts with boiling oil and flaming bitumen. You could smell the burning flesh from the far side of the city. They couldn't retrieve their dead. Some of our men were tempted to get the bodies to feed on them."

"And feed on them they did," asserted Kebboba. "The bastards want to starve us to death, so by Ereshkigal, goddess of the deep earth infernos, I allowed our men to bring the freshly dead inside the city to give away for meat. And people had no qualms, eating the enemy."

Elam had an empty look of apathy. To him, it didn't matter who lived, died, or got eaten. He felt as if he were being cooked slowly by the fever and wondered if his wife would sell his meat to the starving.

"All is going according to the plan," Shulgi stated. "But we must be patient. Most cities would rejoice at having Sargon dethroned, and many will join our rebellion. Uruk's tax revenues will shrink, and Sargon will have to raise the taxes on its people. Uruk itself will rise in rebellion, and Sargon will have no choice but to bring his useless siege army back to regain control of his own city. Our *charming prince*, Naram-sin, will retreat with nothing to show for talent as chief commander except his sun-toasted skin and the horse dung between his toes. After his failure, our Sargon, greatest king within the four corners of Earth, will be lucky to have four corners wide enough to fit his butt in."

Shulgi paused when snoring started.

"Elam, my friend, don't tell me you're sleeping while I'm talking to you!"

"He's completely out," Kebboba replied for her husband. "Won't wake up till sunrise tomorrow."

Shulgi hovered over Elam, scrutinizing his face, and went on.

"Yes, trust me, Lord Elam, after we have Sargon quartered to pieces, you will be addressed as: Your Majesty, king of all within the four corners—of your crypt!"

Chuckling, Shulgi bowed to the sleeping man.

"Look, Kebboba, this semblance of grandeur on your husband's face. I bet he's being crowned as supreme ruler in the realm of his dream right now."

"Good! That will make me feel less guilty—*my beloved* dying in dreams of glory."

A wicked grin spanned Shulgi's face. "What makes me feel guilty is this … vast kingdom of his." He pointed to the bed. "What a waste; all this empty space should be put to some good use."

"Pervert! No, not next to him!"

Kebboba turned to walk away, when Shulgi wrapped her from behind with his arms. She resisted, shaking her shoulders. But Shulgi knew how to arouse her and slipped a hand under her knee-length tunic. His fingers crawled up her thighs as he drew her to the bed. She resisted half-heartedly, driven by this new experience where thrill twined with guilt: cheating on her husband right next to him.

Shulgi's hand besieged her in the most vulnerable part of her defenses; guilt was losing the fight against pleasure. He laid her on the bed, rendering her vulnerable to his attack with no one nearby to come to her defense, save her husband right next to her; but the man was too busy, ruling his dreamland.

Shulgi deployed his fingers at the gates of her lust walls, slowly and tenderly battering at them. The walls began opening under the relentless pleasure. The conqueror kept the onslaught that was about to culminate with deep and total penetration, when urgent banging on the bedroom's door halted the advance.

"General!" a voice yelled. "Your presence is needed at the main gate right away."

"This had better be important," Shulgi roared, angrily, "or I'll have your head spiked over the gate!"

"General, it is the siege leader, Prince Naram-sin. He's right outside the main gate, saying he comes in peace to talk and reach a resolution to the conflict."

"Let him wait!" Shulgi shouted, but it was too late to resume the plan at hand; the distraction had given Kebboba the time to gather control of herself and slide from under him. She left the room to ready herself for the encounter.

With his carnal strategy culminating in failure, Shulgi found himself alone in bed with Elam, who was still sleeping despite all the commotion. Shulgi could only vent his anger with words squeezing past his teeth.

"Naram-sin, I'll make you suffer before gifting you a most grisly death. That I swear by all the savage gods of this cursed world."

𐤛 ◇ 𐤄 Ⱳ 𒐕

The two-horse chariot went through the main gate, which closed right after the wheels cleared it. Naram-sin, in the full regalia of an army commander, somehow managed to keep a neutral expression on his normally arrogant face. Two soldiers approached the horses and brought them to a halt. Naram-sin fought the urge to scream at them for daring to stop him. He wanted to move closer to the acting ruler, Kebboba, but resolved to be tactful; better to leave ego aside while in the midst of his enemies.

He looked at Kebboba. She was just as beautiful as when he had seen her at a friendlier event hosted by his father. He had had many women who surpassed her in beauty, but Kebboba had a formidable asset—one that moved her far ahead in the game of temptation.

She was the daughter of a winemaker who grew his own grapes and supplied his fine wines to the nobility. By her thirteenth spring, her father had opened a tavern and she helped in serving the clients, which advanced her social skills and enhanced her grasp of men's interests and how to please them using wit rather than mere physical beauty. Many of the learned clients who frequented the tavern were more than glad to share their knowledge just to have the pleasure of her company. Thus, she had become conversant in the sciences of the earth and the stars.

Despite her protests, her father gave her away in marriage to the much older Elam—a man of vast riches, who had bribed his way to become the ruler of Ur.

Kebboba had never forgiven her father for this betrayal, driven purely by greed for more wealth. To her, all men had become a species of traitors to be justifiably exploited.

Elam was married to three other women. Kebboba, at the age of fifteen, was the youngest and most beautiful by far, which invited wrath and abuse from the other wives. But she was a fighter, determined to gain respect at any cost, and infidelity paved her way to gain favors from other powerful nobles. Cheating on Elam never bothered her for he was nothing more than a thief who had stolen her youth. Her strong personality combined with his old age made her the actual power in Elam's house at age twenty. Soon, her authority extended to the rule of the city. Where her powers of verbal persuasion failed, her body succeeded. At the age of twenty-two, she had become an intimate friend of General Shulgi, whose control over the army helped her stand unopposed as actual ruler, relegating Elam to nothing more than a figurehead.

Eyeing Kebboba, who was dressed like a love goddess, Naram-sin could not recall the last time he had desired a woman so desperately. Since he had left Uruk with the army, only one girl had been snuck into his tent by a faithful guard. Despite spending most of the night releasing his suppressed lust, he became insistent about keeping the girl. But the guard begged him, for someone might notice, and word could reach king Sargon. With a promise to sneak in more women in the future, the guard left with the girl while it was still dark under a moonless night.

The next morning, soldiers in the camp were greeted by one grisly sight: a girl and the prince's guard, both naked, entwined in a love embrace; their chests were breached straight through by a spear that had its ends resting on dirt mounds to support the victims in an upright posture, coupled in death. Only then did Naram-sin know how serious his father was about keeping women away.

Standing on her own chariot with reins in hand, Kebboba greeted the royal adversary.

"Prince Naram-sin, by the gods of heaven, I welcome you in peace, if peace is what you come seeking, and if you harbor no evil intent through this visit."

A trace of a smile crossed her lips for barely a moment, but Naram-sin caught it and returned one of his own.

Shulgi stood behind Kebboba, casting a grim look at the prince, who apparently had come prepared—not for battle, but to charm: his army outfit was adorned with precious stones, a tiger pelt draped over his shoulders, and a shiny copper helmet atop his head.

Naram-sin stepped off his chariot, which was adorned to match his outfit, and he bowed slightly. "Honorable Kebboba, and people of this great city of Ur. It is peace that I seek. The wise gods have revealed to us that this bloodshed and suffering must come to an end for the good of all. It pains me that this advice did not come earlier, for many souls on both sides have been lost. But the gods work in mysterious ways, and heeding their advice for peace is the wisest course to end our conflict."

Kebboba responded with a modest bow of her own. "Prince Naram-sin, the people of Ur appreciate this step you took toward peace, and I will be honored to receive you in our palace, where our ruler, my husband Elam, also awaits to receive you. Tonight, you may retire as a guest to recover your strength, and tomorrow we can start the talks as our god Shamash orders the sun to rise. Your horses will be well cared for during your stay."

"Your generosity is greatly appreciated." Naram-sin moved closer to Kebboba. "I'm confident that by tomorrow our differences will be resolved and the wisdom of the gods will prevail to bring peace to our lands."

"Forgive me, my noble lady," Shulgi interjected. "May I suggest starting the talks right away. Why prolong the suffering of the people of Ur and the troops outside? If peace is what the gods have ordered, then let us hear these proposals the prince is talking about without delay."

"Noble prince," Kebboba said, "I would like to introduce you to General Shulgi. I'm not sure if you know him."

"Honored to meet you, General. I have heard of your many exploits."

Shulgi simply nodded. Tense moments of silence followed.

Kebboba ended the standoff. "It is far better to wait till the morning. A new day always holds a better promise for new hope and goodwill. The sun is about to enter the tunnel of darkness and the evil spirits would surface with their allies of thieves, murderers—all those bent on committing vile deeds. So, tomorrow morning it is," she said with a firmness that would not be disputed. "General, let the guards escort the honorable prince to the palace so he can bathe and rest before meeting my husband."

Shulgi could only refrain from arguing. Skeptical of Naram-sin's intentions, he wondered about what scheme this enemy might be weaving. Surely, the prince had not come to be friends. No—he had come to be more than friends.

⟨ ◇ ⫐ ∿ ⫼⫼⫼

The room was quiet except for the snoring of Elam. Kebboba walked to her husband and whispered in his ear.

"Elam, wake up to greet Prince Naram-sin. He came to work out a peace agreement. ... Beloved husband, do you hear me?"

The snoring went on.

"He's afflicted with a strange ailment." Kebboba sighed. "And he drifts into prolonged sleep. But there is no rush; he might wake up soon. Make yourself comfortable, noble prince."

"My noble lady, I appreciate your hospitality." Naram-sin sat down in an armed chair, cushioned all around with embroidered pillows stuffed with fine feathers.

Kebboba went to a table, picked up a jar, and poured some of the contents into two cups. She handed one to Naram-sin.

"For peace." She raised her cup.

"For peace." Naram-sin raised his cup, but did not drink until she took a gulp of her wine.

They sipped in silence until she reached out for his hand.

"I can tell this seat is not comfortable. Come," she said, walking him to the bed. "Here it's much better. So much space on this soft bed, it's a waste not to use it. My husband won't object in the least."

Naram-sin sat on the edge of the bed. Kebboba came to sit by his side and folded her right knee up onto the bed, drawing back her skirt to bare her thigh, then a little more, partially exposing her erotic charms. Watching Naram-sin, she could easily detect his lustful hunger.

Though fully aroused, Naram-sin didn't say a word nor make any move; only his chest heaved with the agony of lust. Somehow, he was hesitant to reach for what he so desperately desired.

Seeing his torment, the torturer sadistically reached with her hand for the single string holding her top in place. Playfully, she ran a finger over it then shrugged it off her shoulder. The top slid down to her waist, exposing shapely breasts.

Naram-sin stared at what she bared, but not for long; Kebboba reached out and raised his chin up to meet her eyes.

Something about Kebboba robbed him of his imposing character. Any other woman by now would've been satiating his sexual whims—but not Kebboba. She had him under the spell of her dominance; he wouldn't dare initiate any move despite his long deprivation of a female's company. Kebboba was introducing him to the thrill of a pleasure that was new to him, just when he thought he had mastered all aspects of carnal ecstasy.

"You seem tense," she said. "You need to loosen up. Tomorrow is a decisive day for our cities. You should come to the talks with your mind at ease."

She brushed the bulge between his legs. "See what I mean—this here is rock-hard and needs to be softened; a good place to start. Take off your clothes, honorable prince; release some of your burden."

Like an obedient servant, Naram-sin stood and complied instantly. Breathing heavily, he waited for the next order.

"Lie down next to my beloved husband."

Gladly, he submitted to her command and watched as she took off her top, leaving the skirt on. She found his hand and teasingly slid it up between her legs to where her thighs met, then she channeled his fingers into a gentle massage while dictating their rhythm to heighten her arousal. Her other hand softly worked his erection. He kept his moans to a whisper, being anxious that Elam might wake up.

"Poor prince, I can tell you're starving for some … warmth."

She rose, straddled him, and gently guided his hardness inside her until he was fully inserted, then she stopped moving. Promptly, he reacted, thrusting up with his waist, and just as quickly, her hand swiped his cheek with a hard slap.

"Don't move!" she commanded.

Naram-sin was stunned. Had she been any other woman, he would've brutalized her, probably to death. But this was Kebboba, who stared at him with a wicked smile, daring him to move as she sat with her sex sieging his, restraining it from any movement. He dissented, thrusting his waist up again. She thrust down once, then pinned his shoulders to the bed, bringing her face right above his.

"Do that again, and I'll have you thrown out of the city."

She was serious; he could see it in her ferocious gaze.

"Just like your father; obsessed with power and control." She slid up and down his erection once in an angry move that sent his eyes rolling back in their sockets. "It drives me mad when I recall how your father ordered me around, telling me what to do in my own city."

Her stare challenged him to answer, but it was her husband who responded.

Elam started to babble incoherently with his eyelids closed.

Kebboba's attention was drawn to him, not in alarm, but rather in an expression of utter contempt, as though hoping he would wake up to watch her bedding another man. But to her chagrin, her husband went back to snoring after that brief spell of speaking in tongues.

Naram-sin remained still the whole while, bewildered by this woman who was a blend of pleasure, mystery, fury, and power—all in one beautiful body. To his amazement, he began enjoying this act, for even though they both lay still like a coupling pair of praying mantids, subtle changes were happening within the love arena; her walls were squeezing while his rod fought back, pushing out as it throbbed. He looked up, silently begging her to abandon that mantis coupling act, but part of him was savoring this new experience. Both moaned in whispers as if fearing the sound might shatter the blissful stillness.

"Now … who has the power and control here?" she asked, pressing as hard as she could to claim all the territory on his manhood.

"You, my lady," he said, almost breathless. "You are the supreme ruler and commander of Ur."

Her anger gave way to a devious smile of victory; then, to his dismay, she slid out of him and sat on folded legs.

"Get up," she said, grabbing his hands to pull him off the pillow. She took some time before speaking again, like a commander considering the next move in a battle.

"Soldier, your training is over. Now, I have a mission for you: Attack the gates, force yourself in … and ravage the insides of my body with merciless pleasure."

THE SINS OF THE LAMB

God revisited the vast empty meadows, lush with weeds and grass.
"Let there be livestock," he ordered. "By names: cow, lamb, and ass."
"Eat all you want," he offered, "that don't crawl, walk or fly.
'Tis a covenant for you to follow, one all must abide by."

The animals roamed their paradise, indulged in a plethora to eat.
Chewed and gorged on everything: weed, carrot, lettuce, and beet.

Suddenly, the Omnipotent thundered in a strident shout.
"Cease your feeding frenzy! You've lost your minds, no doubt.
The mantis' prayers reached Me, its grief spiked with terror.
Telling of hideous bloodshed that shook Me to utter horror.

"Behold the caterpillars, ground to tiny pieces.
Slugs, worms, and bugs, all reduced down to feces.
Who gave you permission to eat the cricket in the thicket?
You all will have to pay for the crimes you committed!"

Wail did the ass: "Compassionate, forgive me, your command I
failed to obey.
Do have mercy, I'll offer labor for penance, give thanks each time I bray."

The others shook their heads, strongly contested.
"The bugs—too slight to spot," to Almighty they protested.
"Should've given us sharper vision, so we could better see.
Or made the bugs amply alert, so faster they could flee."

Mooed the cow in a whisper, "I sniff the vile workings of a wicked trap.
Its smell stinks to high heaven—worse than my husband's bull crap."

Laugh did the lamb, "Beetles, bugs, and bees ... blah blah blah,
For such nonsense we have a perfect saying ... bah bah bah."

The earth trembled in anger, fear drummed on their feet.
God's rage went flaring, wrath boiling with hell's heat.

"First you disregard Me—defy My sacred law.
Then you dare mock Me, you lowest of the low.
For such sheer blasphemy, the punishment is most severe.
I leave you in the hands of humans, the savages most to fear.

"Paraded you will be, to a grim fate outside My temple.
Where your blood will be spilled, make of you an example.
Your bodies will be quartered, again and again, and again.
The ground right below you will be painted a deep red stain.

"Grilled on fire, boiled in water, will suffer your meat.
Only then your journey ends ... tasty, succulent food, humans love
to eat."

A sad smile adorned Mayram after she sang the "Butcher's Song" in a hushed, sorrowful voice. It was a song often recited by other butchers outside the main temple in Babylon. Mayram thought of it as a foolish song that must have been the creation of a foolish butcher.

She had hated everything about the butcher work, but she wanted to help her parents and improve their living conditions in any way possible, even if it meant soaking her hands in the blood of lambs. Many were the times when she would return home and watch her hands tremble in disgust at the blood she had spilled outside the temple. No wonder people gave her that strange look, questioning how a young beauty had ended up in a job of savaging animals. When mornings arrived, the earliest light would force her eyelids to open, and her legs would assume the command and drag her to the temple.

But as the day progressed, she found herself slicing the throats of sacrificial animals with the same ease of plucking roses.

Now, far away from Babylon and alone, whenever she felt homesick she would hold the dagger to her chest and softly sing the "Butcher's Song" as if it were a lullaby. Quite often, a few tears would fall on the dagger, and she would spread those tears with her finger to tenderly polish the blade as if it were an infant, easy to scar.

There were times when her yearning to go back to Babylon was so powerful that she would've packed her meager possessions immediately to leave and forget all about her blood-spilling past. She had already accumulated a decent wealth in gold and silver—enough to start a small trade. Not to mention, her father now had his own boat. He must have some good ideas on how to best employ the little fortune the goddess had blessed her with.

What kept her in Uruk was a firm belief that it was her life's destiny—a destiny written in blood, chosen for her in the service of the goddess Ishtar. How she became a butcher in the first place was enough proof that the strong bond with her faithful friend—the dagger—was meant to be, and never a coincidence.

The dagger, her prized possession, she treated with the same reverence given to a god. The day when her mother had gotten the dagger would forever remain fresh in Mayram's memory.

𒀭 𒁉 𒁹

She was eleven, walking with her mother, Arbella, in the market. They were so poor they could only afford to buy fruits and vegetables that were almost spoiled. At that age, she couldn't remember having ever tasted meat. Wherever there was a vendor grilling meat, she would go and stand close enough to feast on the delicious smells until her mother came to drag her away.

That day, she had chased her nose a bit too far, to an irresistible grilling stand right outside a butcher's shop where two men were talking. One of them noticed her. He smiled at her, picked up a well-cooked piece of meat and walked inside the shop, enticing her to join him. She followed to the entrance, placed a foot inside, when a heavy hand grabbed and dragged her out, almost ripping her shoulder. It was her mother.

"I'm hungry," Mayram protested. "That good man wanted to give me some meat. I want to taste meat."

Her mother slapped her. "*Stupid girl!* He wants to trap you inside. That piece of meat came from another stupid girl like you. He's a butcher of girls—he'll cut you up, eat some of you, then sell the rest to other men."

Arbella thought it better to scare the girl than to explain the perversions of some men.

Mayram cried as her mother dragged her through the streets of Babylon. Arbella was becoming aware of men eyeing Mayram's young innocence with sinister looks.

Back at their reed-and-mud hut, Mayram watched her mother dig out a dark blue stone from the dirt in a corner. Then back to the market she dragged Mayram again.

Mayram was starving. When she saw a half-rotten apple on the side of the road, she wrenched her hand free from Arbella's grip and ran for the apple. Before her mother caught up to her, the good part of the apple was in her mouth, almost choking her. They resumed walking until they reached a vendor. Mayram was eager to see what foods he was selling, but there were only utensils for preparing food and cutting meat. Her mother offered the blue stone to the man, who pointed to three daggers on display. Mayram almost screamed at her mother for wasting the valuable stone on a dagger. Arbella picked one bone-handle dagger, and they started back to the hut without stopping to get any food.

"Mother, I'm really hungry. Is Father going to bring something to eat tonight?"

"No. He'll be sleeping by the river during these festivity days to honor the gods. More people will be crossing the river back and forth, and the boat owner wants your father to be rowing for longer periods."

"Why are we so poor, Mother?"

Arbella kept quiet. Mayram was only four springs old when fate had struck their placid life, dooming them to poverty after the boat that Shu-dagan owned tipped over and was lost down the river, with his passengers drowning. To survive the new reality, Arbella had to expel all of life's warm memories; misery shows no mercy to those who yearn for bygone blissful days.

Back in the hut, Arbella sat facing her daughter with a long, mean stare.

"Mayram, you need to stop complaining and be strong. … You're not a woman yet, but in the eyes of men you've become one. Mayram, you … you are cursed with beauty. Yes, cursed! Beautiful, but poor—a prized, yet easy prey. I see the demons in men's souls hovering around you."

Arbella produced the dagger. "This is yours. I cannot be with you all the time, but this dagger can. Always carry it and treat it like a dear friend who will come to your aid when evil stalks you. You understand?"

"Yes, Mother." Mayram almost asked for food again, but knew there wasn't any.

She drank from a jar where rain had collected the previous night and went to lie on the reed mat on the floor, putting the dagger to the side. She was tired, but her stomach pestered her, nudging her now and then, pushing sleep away. She wished to complain, but there was no one close by except for her new friend, the dagger. Mayram clutched it; strangely, that instantly relaxed her. She lay embracing the dagger that softly caressed and soothed her starving stomach. Shortly, sleep overtook her.

𐤀 𐤁 𐤌

Two summers passed by, and Mayram was in a grove picking fruits from the ground. The dates had worms in them, but she didn't mind; the worms tasted fine. The basket was almost full, and the sun had already descended below the date palms. She had walked a long distance from the hut and would arrive home by sunset.

On the way she saw a shepherd who looked a few springs older than she was. He shouted at her to stop, but she ignored him, following her mother's advice to avoid strangers. The boy raced over, only to block her path.

"What do you have in the basket?" he demanded.

"Some … bad dates, overripe apricots I picked from the ground," Mayram answered innocently.

"You picked them from there?" He pointed to the grove.

"Yes."

"Is that your land?" The boy sounded belligerent.

"No." She was getting nervous. "Is it yours?"

"It's my uncle's. You're stealing—thief! I'll take you to the guards, unless …" He raised his kilt to show her his stiff rod. "You know where to put this?"

Aware of what would follow, she turned and started running, but the basket slowed her down. The boy gave chase, caught up to her, and threw her to the ground. The basket slipped out of her hand, fruits scattering all over. She fought the boy while he raised her skirt and tried to part her legs, when she successfully delivered a knee blow squarely to his balls—the best point to disable a man, as her mother had taught her.

The boy cried in pain. She broke free and ran, his shriek pursuing her.

"That's the best you can do, little whore! Get ready—today I'll be the first in your fucking life!"

She ran, screaming for help, but her calls fell short from reaching a single soul.

Some sheep grazing on one side of the pasture caught her attention, and she changed her escape route. The boy grinned, for then she was heading across, not away from him, easing the path to catch up to her. Mayram slowed down so as not to scare the herd, then walked cautiously in their midst.

"Smart thinking, filthy whore, the sheep will protect you! Truly, a *very smart girl.*" The boy ridiculed Mayram, but shortly, he froze in place upon noticing something shiny in her hand.

Mayram cast a wrathful glance at him before she pounced on a sheep like a wild beast, firmly grabbing it under the jaw. Without the slightest hesitation, she savagely plunged and dragged her knife into its neck. The sheep thrashed and kicked against its impending death while Mayram maintained her cruel grip, only releasing the sheep to let it wriggle on the grass in spasms of death.

"You monster!" the boy squealed, then took a few hesitant steps, not so sure of how to tackle the girl with the bloodstained dagger.

The flock of sheep scattered away from the slaughter scene. One young lamb didn't stray far; it did sense the aura of fear that enveloped the flock, but it was looking for its mother and soon found her. It walked to the bleeding sheep and started nudging it to stand up. While prodding its dying mother, Mayram grabbed it and put the knife to its throat.

Near to tears, the shepherd fell to his knees, pleading, "I beg you, don't! My uncle will kill me. Please, don't!"

"I will let this one go," Mayram shouted. "But first, put all the fruits I picked back in the basket."

The boy rushed to do as told. When he was done collecting the scattered fruits, he put the basket down and backed away a good distance.

Mayram started toward him, dagger in hand, and stood over the basket. Her stare dared the shepherd to make a move. And the boy did move—farther back.

Without saying a word, she tossed the sheep's severed head into the basket and picked it up.

Mayram walked away, a smile adorning her face; she couldn't wait to surprise her mother and father.

Tonight, we shall eat meat.

SHARE THE LOVE

"**F**UCK UR AND URUK! FUCK THE SIEGE! FUCK YOU, O BELOVED *whoring* wife, and this prince of peace you brought! And fuck all the gods who are sitting on their divine arses, watching me die slowly of poisoning!"

Elam ceased railing, but only briefly, to replenish his lungs with air.

"Oh, I beg forgiveness, Your Highness, Prince Naram-*shit*. I nearly forgot the most revered one: your father. *Fuck Sargon!* May flying winged bulls target his royal head with their massive dung, and make his stink reach all four corners of Earth, from sunrise to fucking sunset!"

Kebboba and Naram-sin stood over his bed, dazed by this barrage of insults and the sudden outburst of energy from an ailing man. They wondered if he was about to expire, which would give credence to the saying: "When death roams the vicinity, life displays striking ferocity."

It was totally unexpected. After entering the room, Kebboba introduced Naram-sin to her husband. Elam, who was sitting up in his bed, wasted no time in welcoming the prince with that heap of curses.

Shortly after, the door burst open and General Shulgi rushed in to take his place next to the bed.

"Did you start the talks without me?" he said furiously, skipping any greetings.

"Yes," Kebboba nodded, "and you missed the best part. Let me quote: 'Fuck Ur and Uruk. Fuck the siege …'" She looked over at her husband, a smile playing across her face while narrating his tirade.

Elam released a fragile chuckle that discharged more like a cough after his taxing rant.

"And since you're here, *best friend Shulgi*—fuck you too!" Elam's chest heaved, pumping in more air to help expel the words. "Ooh, and do I have knowledge of something that will greatly delight you, *dear friend*! ... Yesterday, after you—*son of dogs*—failed to fuck my *honorable wife*, next to me, on this bed, ... she brought our charming prince here, and she ... eagerly spread her legs wide open for him!" Elam chuckled through his pain. "She's already whoring behind your back."

Shulgi stared at Kebboba with accusing eyes.

"He's in the grips of fever, babbling nonsense," she said calmly, showing no guilt. Whether the general believed her or not wasn't a major concern to her either.

"Oh Shulgi ... *faithful friend*," Elam resumed, "I'll give you a good piece of advice. Have a jar of oil next to you at all times—to ready yourself for the long pole this whore *will shove up your arse* before she impales you up high."

Elam attempted to catapult a gob of spittle to follow his words, but his dry mouth failed to collect anything larger than a tiny raindrop, which fell short of reaching its destination, his longtime friend Shulgi. However, it was enough to deliver the last insult needed for a furious Shulgi to pull out his dagger. Elam was overcome by fear laced with relief that his ordeal would soon be over. His stare he kept on Kebboba as the blade dragged across his throat.

The prince stood motionless in a state of disbelief, giving Shulgi enough time to turn around and tackle him.

"Guards! Guards!" Shulgi shouted at the top of his lungs.

Two strong-built soldiers rushed in to see their general wrestling the royal guest on the floor next to a bloodstained dagger, while Elam bled from the neck. They leapt on Naram-sin and restrained him.

"This assassin slit the governor's throat!" cried Shulgi.

"What are you doing?" Kebboba tried to scream at Shulgi, but the shock of the sudden, grisly turn of events stifled her voice.

"Your general is lying!" Naram-sin jostled against his captors. "*He* killed the governor! Let me go! I'm Prince Naram-sin, my father will have your heads on spikes!"

Shulgi countered in contempt, "Before that, the rats will feast on your head during your stay in the hospitality of our dungeon. Guards, take him away!"

Naram-sin fought to break loose till one guard punched him in the face, knocking him out before they dragged him away.

Elam was coughing blood when Shulgi calmly picked the dagger up and approached the bed.

"Forgive me, my friend, for not cutting you deep enough," Shulgi said, staring at the dying man. "I guess the blade needs sharpening. But look at those gobs, so much larger—rich, red color, too! Now, *that* is how a governor should spit."

Shulgi wiped his dagger clean on Elam's robe while the man choked on his own blood till he went still with death.

"Oh, the tragedy!" Shulgi declared mockingly. "Now, with Elam butchered by the *prince of peace*, the prospect of peace is bleaker than ever."

"You son of a bitch!" Kebboba regained her voice. "I should've never listened to you. The prince was an opportunity—our way out of the calamity you created—and you ruined it!"

"You liked the idea when I proposed it to you—to be a queen. Then our charming prince shows up, and you change your mind, seeking a way out. And what better way to do that than *fucking the prince.*" Shulgi pointed a finger to her face. "How brilliant! I bow to your shrewdness; leaving me behind as the sole traitor, while you fuck your way out … MAKING OF YOUR VAGINA AN ESCAPE TUNNEL!"

"You said the siege wouldn't last long! The people are starving—eating slain soldiers!"

"Lady, to triumph sacrifices need to be made. It's not as if their soldiers are feasting out there in the open terrain. Sargon will not last; he has dozens of enemies. Ur is the greatest rival to Uruk. Eventually, we will crush them and become the greatest of all kings and queens. Peace or no peace, it's too late now; Sargon wants our heads spiked. Trust me, soon rebellion will erupt in many other cities, and this army outside will disintegrate. We've gone this far—don't let this arrogant *prince of dung* fool you into some peace talks. Him coming to us shows their desperation. Holding him as our hostage will give us something extra to bargain with."

"You think Sargon would change his plans to save his son?" Kebboba said, cupping the top of her head with both hands. "He must have dozens of sons from concubines. Locking the prince away in the dungeon will only infuriate him. Listen … let me go to Naram-sin and apologize—tell him we're sorry, that short tempers prevailed, and you didn't mean to hurt him. I can convince him; that's what I'm good at. It's still possible to achieve peace. The siege will be over—all back to normal. You will be the new governor, and this whole conflict will be nothing more than a few tablets buried in the mud of history."

Shulgi released a wild chuckle. "Ah, Kebboba, Kebboba. That's why I'm so madly in love with you. Even the most outlandish things you speak come out like words of wisdom in a sweet song." He sighed. "Tomorrow, my dear Kebboba, governor of the great city of Ur, we are going to bury your beloved husband and my dear departed friend, Elam, whose life was cut short by the cowardly hands of a treacherous prince in trying to weaken our resolve in our just cause. May the gods of the netherworld receive the noble Elam with favor, for he served them and our city with honor."

Shulgi raised his hands as if addressing a crowd. "Honorable citizens of Ur! I, Shulgi, your general, vow to resume the resistance. With our formidable, brave soldiers, and your relentless support, we will be victorious. The gods are on our side and with their blessings we shall abide to make this city of ours, Ur, the greatest city on the face of Earth."

He looked at Kebboba, grinning. "What do you think? Great speech, right!"

Kebboba stared silently, scorn written all over her face.

"There's one thing left to do for my dear Elam before we lay him to rest." Shulgi grasped Kebboba's hand and forcibly drew her over to the bed. "I'm truly disappointed. How shameful of you to sleep with a stranger right next to your husband while he's bedridden with sickness—right after you denied me that pleasure? *I*, who came up with the idea! *I*, your husband's best friend! You hurt my feelings, but … the gods have given me an even better idea."

Kebboba tried to break free of his grip. He pushed her hard, and she fell back on the bed. Her head hit Elam's chest, slick with the blood from his throat, and Shulgi went on top of her. Furiously she tried to fight him off, punching and slapping, but that only got him more excited. He kept her struggling until she was drained of strength.

"Dear best friend, Elam," Shulgi invoked, looking up to the ceiling. "While your body is still warm, while your soul still hangs around the room—grant me your blessings as I honor our long friendship by offering my passionate, deepest condolences to your beloved wife."

He forced himself on her to finish the task he had started the day before.

THE GOD-MAKER

HE TEMPLE SHOULD'VE HAD ITS DOORS CLOSED FOR THE DAY, but the priestess was in no rush. Normally, she would've ordered the visitors to leave, but that one girl was an exception, and the priestess waited for her to finish the prayers. It wasn't only the girl's striking beauty that was fascinating, but also her devotion to the goddess and her generous offerings. The priestess fancied this girl as a blessing from the gods. If only she didn't have the habit of going down to her knees when praying, the priestess would've probably thought that a goddess was honoring her modest temple with those visits.

Mayram whispered her prayers; she had so much to thank the goddess for. After the tender emotions she had experienced during her encounter with the mute shepherd, it became evident it was the intervention of her goddess that had stopped her from shedding the boy's innocent blood and that of the poet before him. She felt a blissful peace within. The days passed and, to her delight, the blood-lust she had been cursed with didn't show any signs of a comeback. However, one thing remained unchanged: her devotion to serve the goddess through the assignments given her by Ibrahem.

In her recent sacred mission, she delivered death with unfettered conviction. On deciding it was time for the sacrifice, she reached for the dagger in her clothes while straddling the noble.

"What are you looking for?" he asked.

"This," came her brief answer with the dagger in full view. Imbued on her face was a neutral look, free of any menacing intentions, as though the man under her were no more than a lamb, helpless in avoiding his fate. He looked at her, puzzled, with hands still gripping her waist. His defensive noble's instincts proved inadequate, only driving him to slow his thrusts inside her while staring at a dagger that took a leap up into the air before plunging into his chest.

Unlike the former victims, no rapturous thrill accompanied this sacrifice. Mayram found herself watching intently, searching his face for a confession of guilt.

There was only pain and shock clouding his eyes, with a plea for an answer to a brief question: *why?* But death was in no mood to wait for a reply.

Right after accomplishing her task, Mayram rushed to the temple and conveyed her appreciation to the goddess for the miraculous transformations she was experiencing, and for giving her the firm confidence to expedite the sacrifice. Once her prayers concluded, she took out the same three silver pieces, thrown earlier to her lap by the sacrificed noble, and placed them at the feet of the goddess. On the way out, the priestess neared her, praising.

"May the goddess heap blessings on you, my child. You're an angel."

"Thank you, Honorable Priestess." Mayram returned a cordial smile. "But I doubt that our holy goddess could bless me any more than she already has."

He opened the door to his place and limped inside.

Mayram followed this next one on Ibrahem's list to be sacrificed. Eyeing his uneven walk, she wondered if his limping was the result of a struggle with a girl victim, which gave her the urge to finish the job right away without wasting time going to bed with him. But something in his quarters stopped her.

The room was cozy with a bed standing on four wooden legs, each carved in the shape of a lion sitting on its haunches. The pillows and covers on the bed had creative designs unfamiliar to Mayram. However, that wasn't what attracted her attention.

She tried to act passively but was overcome by awe. One hand covered her mouth to conceal her admiration as she strolled around the room, which was lit by oil lamps next to each corner.

All along the four walls were statues of gods and heroes of legend, beautifully made of smoothly polished stone in a variety of colors alien to her. She forgot about the young man standing behind her, the one to satisfy her "sacred vows."

"Which one do you like most?" he asked.

"You sleep here?" Her bewilderment muted his question.

"Yes, with gods all around me." He smiled and waited for her to smile back. She wanted to, but resisted; the man was just another abuser of girls—another sacrifice.

"Can I look around … just a little?" she asked awkwardly.

"Sure. Take your time."

Mayram walked cautiously so as not to disturb the gods. It felt as if she were in heaven, granted an audience with them. A statue, half-life-sized, captivated her. She stepped to the pedestal carrying it, and moved her palm around the statue as if feeling its aura.

"Is this the love goddess?"

"Yes. You can touch her," the man invited.

"That would be sacrilegious," she protested.

"Without touching … how did I manage to make her? How would I move her?"

"You made her?" Mayram cupped a palm over her mouth again.

"All of them. And there are more in the next room, my workroom," he said modestly.

Mayram ran her hand very lightly over the statue's feet, not daring to go any higher. "This is very smooth, smoother than my skin."

"I appreciate the compliment." His hand brushed over her bare shoulder. "But you can't fool me; no sculptor can be this good."

"Ishtar must have blessed your hands. I've never seen my goddess in such splendor in any temple," she said, then pondered in anguished thought. *Ishtar must have blessed your hands! … But he's on Ibrahem's list of abusers. Could they have made a mistake?*

"I stopped working in temples," he said. "Priests are the most devious people to deal with. I would be begging in the streets if I wasted more time in their service. They're always complaining: 'See this hair crack; look, a tiny chip there; somehow the goddess looks masculine—are you a lover of men?'"

Mayram didn't perceive his trivial attempts at humor. She was overawed by the gods around her, which bred doubts about spilling this man's blood.

Giving up on any comments from her, the sculptor went on. "The few works I made for temples, those priests hardly covered the cost of the stone ... nothing for my labor and craft. Huh, they tell me: 'The gods will compensate you tenfold.' ... Oh for their *generosity*, I'm forever indebted!"

Mayram stepped to another statue without hearing a word he was saying. Something was very wrong, she could feel it. She dropped to her knees and her lips moved, uttering mute words.

"Are you praying?" he asked, raising his voice to get her attention.

"Forgive me ... I didn't mean to keep you waiting." She rose to her feet and, distractedly, slipped off the shoulder strap of her top.

"No, no, that's not what I had in mind. Put your top back on," he said, though he couldn't resist staring at her bare breasts.

"You don't want to go to bed, my lord?"

"That can wait. If you want to pray, go on, I won't interrupt. And call me Lubalanda; "lord" makes me feel too old. Besides, I'm not a noble, I only make sculptures for them. Would you like some food, wine? You said Mayram is your name?"

"Yes, Mayram. ... A little wine will do. Thank you."

"Beautiful name. I'll get the wine. My servant is out with a fever."

Coming back with a jar, he found her kneeling again before another statue of Ishtar. She seemed distressed, praying as if seeking answers to an urgent predicament. Lubalanda went to a table and poured wine into two cups. Mayram finished her prayers and came to sit in a chair next to him.

He noticed her hands tremble slightly as she reached for the cup.

"Nervous! I too was nervous my first time."

"A little. ... I'm grateful—for allowing me to pray." She took a sip of the drink. "Your work is extraordinary, next to divine."

Stop praising him! Thoughts scolded her. *He should've been sacrificed by now.*

Quietly, he returned a thankful nod while studying her.

Despite sipping more wine to calm herself, she couldn't help but grimace, feeling violated by the way he eyed her.

"What are you staring at?"

"I'm looking at the next goddess I will work on." He reached out with one hand and gently touched her cheek. "She will be the envy of all the goddesses you see here."

"Don't say that," she objected. "No woman can compare in the slightest to the beauty of Ishtar."

"Well, till I see Ishtar, you're the most beautiful thing I've ever seen."

He slipped her shoulder strap, letting her top slide down. She felt relieved when his stare floated to her breasts.

"Yes, without the slightest doubt, the most beautiful."

Sure! The most beautiful fuck! she ached to scream. *Your gentle manners almost fooled me. Show your true self. To you, I'm nothing but a good-looking whore made for a quick fuck! Vows and honoring my goddess don't mean dung to you. Time for this one to join the other filthy pigs in the netherworld.*

She placed her cup on the table, stood, and turned toward the bed.

"What are you doing?" Lubalanda reached and held her hand.

"Going to bed … the vows!"

"Don't worry; the vows can wait. Sit down, Mayram, let's chat—finish our drinks."

She sat down, and he helped her put the shoulder strap back on to cover her breasts.

Very strange. If he wants my body, why is he taking his time? … He must be drunk. That should make my task easier.

"There is something about you," he said, lightly brushing one of her hands. "A mystery. May I ask that you share it with me?"

"I'm but an ordinary girl … I hide no mysteries."

Concerned he might be suspecting her, she took another gulp of wine to cover her lying face and quickly sought to divert his queries away from her.

"You walk with a limp. Was that from birth?"

"I suppose … you could say I was born with it." Lubalanda laughed. "Like they say, 'When the gods birth you favored and blessed, with hurt and curses people will have you dressed.' You probably know what I mean."

You are cursed with beauty. Her mother's words rang in her ears. "I heard something similar."

"I entered this room one evening," Lubalanda explained, "and found my servant on the floor, bound in rope. Two robbers were rummaging through the room. They jumped on me and threw me to the floor, which hurt my knee. They bound me, too, and resumed their thievery, taking whatever small things of value in the room. Then, to my surprise, they grabbed the best goddess I had—one I had spent seven moons working on. It had no equal; nothing in this room came even close to its beauty. I begged those thugs not to take it. I told them they would not be able to sell it without raising suspicion that it was stolen. They simply laughed and left with her."

"Do you have enemies?" Mayram asked, sensing that uneasy feeling again.

"I don't get involved with matters of government, or the rulers who fashion them. I'm busy with my stonework and selling it to the nobles. First man I suspected was the previous high priest; he might have sent those two thugs to punish me after I refused to do work for the temples. Well, he's dead now—met a horrible end he truly deserved. The only other person I can think of …" Lubalanda paused, staring at a thought that seemed to float on his wine.

Mayram gulped more drink from her cup. It was the best wine she had ever tasted, and it was taking effect, relaxing her. She advised herself to be firm and not allow doubts to hamper her sacred mission.

"There is this other man," Lubalanda continued, "one who works for the king … his sculptor."

Upon hearing that, Mayram choked on the wine and was seized by hard coughing. Lubalanda sprang off his chair and went slapping her back until she recovered.

"Don't die before I fulfill your vows," he quipped. "Better now?"

She nodded.

"This wine is smooth once you get used to it."

"I'm fine now," she said hoarsely. "You can continue."

"Continue with what?"

"About the sculptor ... who worked for the king," she said, sounding casual and smiling.

"Oh, him. ... Well, he heard about my work and asked me to show him my sculptures, to see if I was good enough to work in the palace. He came, looked around, and saw the goddess—the same one the thieves stole later. After he left, I never heard from him again. But I had the feeling he was envious of my work. Possibly, he feared that the king might replace him and award me his prestigious position. ... It's just a thought; I could be wrong. And so, just like refusing to work for the temples, I made up my mind to stay away from the palace. All the deceit and backstabbing that runs rampant within its walls—that's not for me; I'm doing well on my own.

"Anyway, that's the story of my walk with the limp. Nothing heroic; no fighting formidable enemies in a raging battle, nor slaying some winged, fire-spitting monster that roasts men before dining on them. Thankfully, my leg is healing, albeit at a slug's pace. But I seek your help, your beauty, to make a goddess shaped like you; she'll be more glamorous than the one stolen. Now, you tell me your story. How did you manage to steal the beauty of the goddess?"

Lubalanda sipped some wine as he awaited a reply from her. But the only thing she offered was silence, hardened by unflinching eyes gazing at him. It was his turn to feel uneasy.

"What are you staring at?" he asked, looking serious for a short moment, then he smiled. "You look like a statue—like a different girl than when you came in. I think you've had enough to drink."

He took the cup from her and walked her to the bed, gently pulled off her top, then began to kiss her neck while his hand caressed her breasts. She came back to life, letting out a soft moan, passionately pressing her lips on his, and her skirt she dropped to the floor. His hands sensually glided down to her thighs before he let go of her to disrobe himself. She went to lie on the bed, and Lubalanda walked around to the other side.

"Forgive me," he said. "You have to go on top. I hurt my back while I was carrying a large piece of stone for my work. My bad knee buckled, and I fell. Be gentle with me."

Mayram didn't say a word. She turned over to him and closed her lips against his inviting lips. She straddled him, making sure not to let go of his kisses, then smoothly slipped his hardness inside her, lowering herself tenderly, freeing a moan of pleasure out of him.

"Is that gentle enough?" Her lips separated just enough to give way for the words to exit. She was breathing heavily, overwhelmed by a lust that felt oddly pure, while she delved into a wave of sincere passion reflecting from his eyes.

"This must be heaven," he said with her settled over him. "Mayram, I'm not complaining, but … you're not a virgin."

She froze, not because he had found out, but for her own foolishness that exposed her. No virgin could've mounted a man with such ease and fluidity. Moments of silence passed before she slipped off him and sprang out of the bed.

"Don't leave, I'm fine with that," he called to her.

Still, she grabbed her clothing, dug into the pocket, then turned back to him.

"Forgive me. You're right; I'm not a virgin." She opened her palm, revealing three pieces of silver. "Here is your silver."

"Mayram, this doesn't change a thing." The sculptor didn't reach for the silver. "I can tell you're not the devious type."

She was silent; her palm remained open.

"Not all girls have to be virgins to satisfy their vows. Many are the girls who were abused and violated. I'm sure you have your own reason. I won't ask of it—you probably want to forget."

Mayram didn't respond. She felt like a pathetic thief caught in the act. Still naked, she moved closer to hand him the loot, avoiding his eyes.

"I've heard of girls taking vows in the name of virgins who died too young. So why don't you do that for one of those girls? I knew one who vanished during the day of the crowning ceremony; Amare was her name," Lubalanda said, wistfully. "Wasn't that sad—to depart to the netherworld at a young age?"

"It is sad, my lord." Finally, she found her tongue at the mention of a tragedy that belittled her unease.

"Come back to bed."

"No, my lord. I deceived you."

"Stop calling me 'lord.' And deceive me, you did not!"

"I'm not worthy of a man blessed by the goddess. I should've told you I'm not a virgin and—" She went silent. *Spilling your blood is what I'm here for.* Her gaze darted around the floor in search of an exit out of her confusion.

"Mayram, I know what you're thinking—that I'm interested only in the pleasures your body has to offer, virgin or no virgin."

She shook her head vaguely.

"Mayram, I must confess … I carry my own share of deceit. I'm … I pick the girls mostly so they pose for me, for my work, not so much for the vow ritual. But when I saw how you knelt and sincerely prayed, I knew you were different from all the others. Look at the gods around you; most people see stones—cold, hard, silent stones. They don't feel the soul, the power embedded within them, like I do. When I work on the stones, they tell me what shape they want to have, how to turn them into gods. Essentially, it's the same gods who helped carve what you see here."

Mayram lifted her head a notch and glanced at the gods around her. She felt more shame under their gazes.

"Mayram, you say I'm blessed by the goddess. However, you are far more blessed—beyond your striking beauty. I saw how you felt the gods within these stones—their warmth and softness. You talked to them and knew they listened upon hearing your prayers. These gods brought you here so they can revel in the splendor they created. Never has this place felt so alive. It had to be their will that we crossed paths. If I'm wrong, tell me I'm talking nonsense, that I'm a fool, and you can leave. I will not stop you."

One of the silver pieces fell out of her outstretched hand, and the other two followed, yet she didn't notice. Racked by humiliation and confusion, she yearned to scream:

Yes Lubalanda, you are a fool! You have no idea how deep you are in the deceit, envy, and backstabbing of the palace, though you tried to avoid it. This even greater fool was about to sink you all the way down to the netherworld, had it not been for the grace of the gods surrounding you here.

Move! Her legs she urged to walk her out, but they were slow to respond; Lubalanda had already crawled to the side of the bed, taken her hand, and brought her to sit next to him. She felt helpless to resist.

Lightly, his hand moved to her left breast, covering it. "I sense the beating of your heart." He touched a finger to her lips. "The wind of your soul." Softly, he ran both hands along her arms. "The warmth of your blood. They are all calling to me. How can I be wrong about what you feel?"

Why are you doing this to me? She was in silent turmoil. *Show mercy! Go ahead, use me and throw me away like a whore. I am strong, I will forget you.*

An eerie sense of alarm filled her. This man who walked with a limp was stripping her of all powers with his words, peeling away at her fortitude, layer after layer, leaving her completely naked, and exposing a deeply buried weakness within she was never aware of—a vulnerability to a vicious venom: Love. It would flow through her veins—paralyze and slay the savage beast in her heart.

Mayram didn't know she was crying until his voice came back.

"Tears, the words of the soul, they never lie." He kissed her wet cheeks, chasing the tears to her lips.

He's a demon. A thought flashed through her mind. *Sent by Ereshkigal, jealous of her sister Ishtar, to weaken my unshaken devotion to my goddess. … But Ereshkigal, goddess of death and darkness, would never use love as a weapon.*

Still, she tried to resist him, but the salty taste of her tears lacing his kisses excited her, and she pressed harder on his lips.

The sculptor of gods chiseled on her outer shell and cracked the hard stone of blind loyalty to those gods. The fissures spread longer and wider until the shell split open. She felt him reach the depths of her soul, retrieve something out, and tenderly offer it to her:

Here, this is the real you.

Like a mother who had found a long-missing child, she was sobbing.

His warm kisses had her floating in a calm lake of love, when a breeze of passion stormed in, rousing that serenity. She couldn't remember how she had ended up on top of him, and the waves of her body caressed the warmth of his shore, then retreated in a gentle rhythm. Their soft moans reverberated through the air as their peaceful lake became a river of pleasure that soon poured into a raging sea of lust.

Immersed in wave after wave of relentless bliss, Mayram became alert that they were trespassing into the ocean of ecstasy—a domain reserved exclusively to the divine ones. She tried to retreat, but the forces she experienced were mightier than her fear of the gods. Her love streams were crashing around the hard rock inside her. Feverishly, she pounded on it, sending Lubalanda to groan in a pleasure that numbed his back pain. He strived to prolong the blissful assault she waged on him, but his attempts were short-lived, and their storm of passion climaxed in a joined, thunderous cry of joy.

Lying on her side, Mayram embraced the warmth of the man who had broken her shell with the mighty chisel of love. She felt complete—a free human being. Though still devoted to her gods, she was no longer a chained slave under their absolute control.

But that warmth was interrupted when she noticed the quivering flames of the lamps hurling subtle shadows from the statues against the walls. Mayram watched them convulse in a frenzy, and shivers invaded her body. She felt them—gods, staring, their eyes flaring with envious fury.

𐎍 ◇ 𐎛 𐎗 𐎏

"You couldn't do it!"

Rage and disbelief had Ibrahem shaking his head and sent his legs pacing the floor of the rented tavern room.

"I had no choice. His wife barged into the room like a mad bull." Mayram used the chaotic encounter with the poet and his crazed wife to fit her lie in failing to slay Lubalanda.

"His wife! I don't recall him being married." Ibrahem frowned.

"I'm just guessing!" She had forgotten to change this detail. "Wife, lover ... some woman, a very jealous one. She lashed out at me first, then attacked him—shattered a jar on his head. Moments later, the servant rushed in to pull them apart. The only wise thing I could do was put my clothes on and disappear."

Ibrahem stopped pacing. "You have to do another task."

"No, no more! I'm done with this … here." She held out a pouch. "I'm returning the wages you gave me to kill the sculptor." She paused, hoping Ibrahem didn't notice that she had used the word "kill" instead of "sacrifice."

"How did you know he's a sculptor?"

"It's obvious." She shrugged. "Gods crowded his room. He told me he had made them."

Ibrahem was silent, his angry gaze searched for more answers.

"I'm not doing any more … sacrifices. Forgive me, but it's getting too risky. Rumors are spreading about a demon girl slaying nobles."

"Rumors!" Ibrahem snapped. "Rumors of demon girls have been around since the time of Lilith, the first woman God created. This is nothing new. Demons of all shapes and sizes, ugly and comely, roamed the earth long before the humans. And with the creation of our kind, those demons developed a voracious appetite to wreak havoc on us. Now, the wages for this failed mission, keep them for the next one."

"Again, forgive me. I've made up my mind: no more!"

"Mayram, you're a soldier, commissioned in the service of the king to rid us of the filthy villains who infest the kingdom from within. Now, I'm being generous, giving you another chance to make up for your failure in the last mission. Get yourself ready in … about ten days."

"I am not a soldier!" she countered fiercely. "I'm just like any other girl in her early spring of life."

"*Like any other girl!*" Ibrahem shook his head, grinning. "Mayram, Mayram, dear Mayram, … while still in the early spring of your life, you've already *killed* more men than many a fearless soldier would kill in a lifetime."

"But in ten days, it will be far past my downed moon. I might get pregnant." She was running out of excuses.

"That's not my concern." Ibrahem was adamant. "Don't allow the man to spill his seed inside you. Be ready in about ten days. I'll be checking on you now and then. Don't think of disappearing, and don't assume you will find refuge in Babylon either. We will locate you simply by asking about a beautiful girl called Mayram, who worked next to the main temple of Ishtar, sacrificing lambs. And if we can't find you, I'm sure your parents would be more than happy to help."

Mayram got the chills at the mention of her parents. She had the urge to pull the dagger and sink it deep into the bastard's heart. But she knew that of all the men on Earth, he was the one most prepared for her.

"My lord, I ask you in the name of the gods," she pleaded. "I … I can't do this anymore. Find another girl."

"Just one more task. This one must be done by you." Ibrahem walked over to her and gently brushed her cheek with the back of his hand. "Then you're free to go. You won't see me again and no one will ever bother you; that I swear by the gods of Sumer and Babylon."

She nodded once.

"Now let's go to bed," he said softly.

Grudgingly, Mayram started stripping off her clothes, while Ibrahem watched her every move like a hawk.

𒌋 𒍦 𒀭 𒈨 𒐐

The gods grew tired of watching the anguished mortal pacing the room like a caged animal.

"Cursed be the day when she stepped into my life," Lubalanda muttered, but then felt pangs of guilt, as if it were words of blasphemy he uttered.

Mayram had left his home with a promise that she would come back. Lubalanda dared not step out of his place, fearing he would miss her when she showed up. Those were the longest days and nights of his life. Work on his statues came to a halt as though Mayram had stolen the main tools that expressed his skill: love and passion. As for the gods in the room, he must have recited a deluge of prayers that would've prompted them to drag her to his place to avoid drowning in his nagging pleas.

A knock on the door made his jittery heart jump. His body twisted violently toward the entrance, which sent a wave of pain radiating up his back. But the pain vanished when the door opened to reveal the jubilant face of his servant.

"She's here." The servant looked more like a god answering a mortal's prayers with a miracle. Behind him was the long-awaited flesh-and-blood goddess.

All the chains of anguish that Lubalanda was dragging shattered, and he rushed forward to hug her, but Mayram shunned him.

"What happened? Is something wrong?"

"Ibrahem," she started in a voice bereft of any emotion, "was he the king's sculptor who came to see your work?"

Lubalanda returned a baffled look. "Yes. ... I don't recall telling you his name! You know ... Ibrahem?"

Mayram didn't answer but reached inside her robe, pulled out the dagger, and held it in her open palm.

Lubalanda could only stare at the dreadful bone handle of the dagger.

"I ... I was supposed to stab you—end your life with this very dagger. ... Your life is in danger. Ibrahem might send another assassin. You must leave this place."

"*You* ... an assassin!"

She looked down, resting her answer on the dagger.

"I will leave only if you leave with me," he said, firmly.

"I was supposed to kill you, you fool, not be your lover," she snapped at him.

He parted the top of his robe, took hold of the dagger, and placed its tip against his bare chest, startling Mayram.

"If you're truly an assassin, then press on this dagger ... and I will leave ... to the netherworld—the only destiny for me without you."

"You're a total fool." Her hand reached to get the dagger away from him. He resisted, cutting himself slightly with the tip. A thin strip of blood lined his chest.

"Don't! In the name of the gods, stop!" Mayram cried.

"No, you stop! You know I meant everything I told you the other night. Why are you here—to save me? Well, I'm hopelessly wounded already by the dagger of your love. Now finish the job—stab me and set my heart free. If you can't, then do me a favor: let Ibrahem send the next assassin. Be merciful and make it fast."

Mayram was overwhelmed again by the sweet emotion that streamed warm tears down her cheeks. She had come to him determined to affirm to herself that he hadn't changed her—that she was still the same strong girl who would forget him and go on with her own life, serving and loving her goddess without wasting any of that love on a mortal. But she stood there, once more stripped of her will, waiting for him to touch her with those same hands that shaped stones and brought them the awesome beauty and power of her goddess.

Then she realized why she had really come back: not only to warn him but also to beg him to bring back that docile girl she had met the other night. She didn't wait long; he could feel and read her, body and soul, like he could feel the gods' presence in the stones. His warm lips softly brushed hers and his arms enveloped her, pressing their bodies together. They became one again: two hearts in one body, beating together to the rhythm of a love that felt eternal.

THE SILENCE OF THE GODS

THE GENERAL GROANED LOUDLY WHILE HE RAIDED HER BODY. As if stabbing an enemy, he showed no mercy. With the two of them lying on their sides, penetrating her from behind seemed to be his most favored position.

Mayram submitted to his desires and prayed for her ordeal to be over. The idea of slaying this one right away, to spare her the love act, had played in her mind. Unfortunately, the general, Alamu, never took his sharp gaze off her. He watched, salivating in excitement as she removed her clothes, depriving her of any element of surprise to help in slaying a man of his size and strength. He didn't waste time going inside her. She, in turn, moaned in a convincing act.

Aware that giving her body to this stranger played no part in any sacred task, Mayram was agonized by shame. She didn't want to be touched by anyone, except for Lubalanda, who had freed her from the frigid confines of faith and restored in her the warmth of being a human of flesh and blood, capable of giving and taking love for its own sake, not out of loyalty to some cause, master, or god.

After this night, a new life would be dawning on her. She would forget about those past blood-soaked moons. The nobles she had sacrificed didn't cause her much remorse. She was confident they were guilty of abhorrent deeds; otherwise, the goddess would've stopped her, just as she had with the poet, the mute shepherd, and Lubalanda. Without a doubt, the goddess would stop her with this last one if necessary.

Yet one thing bothered Mayram: Ibrahem. That demon had fooled and used her in the name of the goddess for his own schemes. Oh, how she wished for an opportunity to pounce on him and cut him to pieces. But it became obvious he didn't trust her anymore; he no longer slept the nights by her side in the rented room. Instead, he ran like a thief, right after stealing the joys of her body.

Allamu throbbed hard inside her and his groans went louder, much like a general nearing the end of a battle, screaming orders with the excitement of an impending victory.

Mayram was revolted by this violation of her body, of being handled like a toy of flesh. Each thrust from the general intensified her anger, yet she endured, hoping that rage would help her put aside any qualms about killing this one.

She knew he was a general when the guard at the temple had addressed him as such. Her father, Shu-dagan, hated those generals, and she had inherited this hate through the stories he related about them—how they sent their soldiers to certain death as if they were nothing more than a herd of sheep to be sacrificed.

She found sanctuary in thoughts of a happy future; Lubalanda had asked her to marry him. She couldn't restrain herself from crying in joy despite knowing she wasn't yet free from the clutches of Ibrahem, who had disgustedly declared her nothing more than a puny soldier in the service of the king.

The general's barking grew louder upon reaching the peaks of pleasure. She tried to slip out of his final penetrating thrusts, but his solid grip barred her attempt, and his fluids went gushing inside her. The bastard reneged on his promise to spill his seed outside to avoid getting her pregnant.

"Don't worry," Allamu said when he saw her discontent, "my seed is never fruitful, it never gave me a child. You have my word of honor; you will not have a child."

And my word of honor, valiant general: once I leave, your body will be like a parched tree with bugs eating at its roots, producing maggots instead of seed.

"Bless you, my lord, for helping with my vows." Saying those words had become a habit.

"Just doing my sacred duty to the goddess."

His words sounded to her like a prayer all men were obliged to recite at the conclusion of the ritual.

"My lord … may I sleep the night here? I don't feel safe leaving this late."

"I can have my servant escort you."

"Mornings promise ample safety, my lord. However, if it is inconvenient—"

"No, by all means, stay all you want … but on one condition," he grinned. "We offer some more love to the goddess in the morning."

"That should please my goddess even more." She forced a smile.

"Splendid! Now, we deserve some good rest after this grueling battle. I'm glad you're not a foe; I wouldn't last long against such a formidable enemy."

"In the morning, you will be victorious again, my lord. … Before we go to sleep, may I ask another favor? I don't mean to be too demanding, but can we switch sides? I'm used to the other side when I sleep next to my mother back home."

"Sure. I'll sleep on the floor if that would make you more comfortable."

She was disgusted at his facetious show of manners. "No, no, my lord, you embarrass me with your generosity. I only need to be on the other side."

"Anything for a beauty like you."

She switched places to where her clothes lay within reach on a side table.

"Thank you, my lord. May the gods fill your dreams with pleasure."

"And yours with joy." Allamu turned to sleep, facing away from her.

Mayram lay back, thinking about all the madness she was caught up in. But her turmoil would soon be over; only happiness awaited her outside this house, with the hope that Ibrahem would keep his promise.

She snapped out of her thoughts, jarred by the general's snoring.

It's time to end this man's life.

But something strange was happening; her hands were shaking. Whatever happened to the confidence and ease she had felt upon stabbing the last noble? It couldn't be qualms about killing this man. As a general, he must have sent legions of soldiers to their deaths, besides the countless innocent people to whom his armies had brought death and misery. She was the executioner, chosen to exact the ultimate justice on him in the name of all the fallen.

Still, this eerie feeling kept hindering the assassin in her. Lubalanda had chiseled her ferocious beast into a docile lamb. Images of herself, slaughtering sheep and men, had come to haunt her dreams lately with vivid clarity. The thought of spilling more blood had become abhorrent.

But that sick coward, Ibrahem, would not leave her alone, and would do anything to have his way. Even worse, he could hurt her parents, the only two people who had kept any trace of humanity in her until Lubalanda stepped into her life.

Anger soaked her thoughts; Ibrahem fooling her, using her body, driving her to kill all those nobles. But nothing tortured her mind more than all the innocent servants who were falsely accused and executed for the murders of their masters. At first, she had convinced herself that they were just as guilty of the severe punishment for covering the abuse of the girls by their masters. Now, being aware that Ibrahem had been telling her nothing but lies, relentless guilt assailed her.

She had hated the general from the moment he had touched her, and with each of his penetrating thrusts, she had the urge to tear him to pieces. But killing him would certainly doom his servants. Hounded by doubts, she prayed silently.

O goddess, please help me like you did before. If this man is not deserving of death, I pray you send me a signal to avoid shedding his blood. If not, then send that murderous beast to possess me again, to help end this torment.

The man's snoring suddenly soared to a higher tone, inciting anger to flare up within Mayram, wrestling the shivers to a stop, steadying her hands. That was enough of a signal to go ahead with sacrificing the general. The fate of his servants would be the gods' verdict. After this, a tranquil life awaited, surrounded by her mother, father, and a future family with Lubalanda.

She grabbed her raiment from the side table, rummaged nervously through the folds, and carefully slipped the dagger out. The grip felt different; she could've sworn it wasn't the same grip for she knew it just like she knew her own hands.

Wood! The bone handle, it feels like wood! … Now calm down—must be because my hand is sweating and shaking again.

Her heart started pounding fiercely when she raised the dagger; it felt heavier. Also, aside from its odd feel and weight, the dagger had lost all its brilliance. Was she so nervous that her eyes had gone blurry?

She squinted for a better look in the room's dim light, and her head recoiled with the shock of what she saw.

The sharp, bronze blade had turned into a rough, black shaft of dry bitumen. Through her surprise, she almost screamed in joy. Still in disbelief, she ran her finger over the edge and pressed hard. Her skin didn't split—not a tiny drop of blood squeezed out.

O compassionate holy goddess, my prayers reached you.

Ishtar had intervened to stop her once more; this time with a miracle by changing the deadly weapon into a child's toy. Again, Mayram pressed a finger against the blade, just to be sure, and went ecstatic; in her own hand she held something that had been touched and reshaped by the divine power of her goddess.

The torment was over, and a sense of elation erased the anguish. All she had to do now was go ahead with an idea that she balked in pursuing. Together with Lubalanda, she would go to Babylon and have her parents move to another city—start a new life, far from the reaches of Ibrahem. She had the blessings of the goddess, no doubt about it in her mind. The first step was to sneak out of this place.

But before making the slightest move, she froze in place, and the first step seemed out of reach.

During all that overwhelming excitement, she failed to notice that something had gone missing; the general's snoring—it had ceased.

Her heart thudded in panic. She could feel the jet of air from the general's nostrils over her shoulder as he breathed heavy in his own excitement.

"What happened? Did you have a bad dream?"

The guile was obvious in the sickening voice behind her. The bitumen dagger quivered in her grip.

"What is this you're holding?" He reached for the toy dagger.

Stunned, she let go of it, offering no resistance.

"Oh, not again! This Ellili and his trickery." Allamu yelled, "Ellili, come here at once! Ellili—now!"

The room brightened when the door opened, and in came a servant carrying an oil lamp.

"Ellili, I keep telling you to stop playing tricks on the girls." Allamu turned to the dazed Mayram. "Do forgive him, he's harmless, but he has a bad habit of sneaking in while I'm busy performing the vow duties. He replaces the girls' possessions with worthless things, like this toy dagger. … Ellili, show me what you took from her?"

Obediently, Ellili passed Mayram's dagger to the general.

"By the gods, I can detect a stinking whiff from the netherworld on this blade! This thing is one wicked dagger. I would hate to be in its travel path."

Mayram's arm flexed out to snatch her dagger back, but Allamu had anticipated that. The dagger remained safely in his hand; a smirk on his face ridiculed her effort.

"Girl, how many nobles did you send on a journey to the netherworld with this?"

Mayram was in a trance, staring at her dagger.

"I know of at least five nobles who met a violent end at the hands of—*their servants*. That was the story we were told." Allamu smiled at his servant. "Ellili, I almost became *your victim*. You know what that means; your head and body would've gone their separate ways."

Mayram kept silent. Her thoughts were so muddled that nothing made sense. Life and death had switched sides; she felt like a ghost in the presence of the man she had come to slay and his servant who would've been executed.

"You owe me one, Ellili." Allamu beamed. "The big one—your life."

"Yes, Master," Ellili answered with a slight bow.

Slowly, Mayram raised her head, expecting a servant casting an odious look at the assassin who would've caused his head to roll off the chopping block. But to her surprise, she saw a sad face with what seemed like a pained look of grief for her. Something in his eyes attracted her attention: the deep sorrow of someone who had been conquered—a dull look of hope lost and abandoned, similar to what she used to see in her father's eyes every time he came back from work. How many poor servants like this one had she condemned to death? A ferocious sense of guilt struck her on becoming fully aware that their graves were the foundation over which she was planning to build her future happiness.

"Forgive me, I'm terribly sorry," she said to the servant, and tears rolled down her cheeks. It was all she could do to express her heartfelt remorse.

Ellili nodded back as though accepting her apology. Was he forgiving her on behalf of all the other slaves who weren't as lucky?

Allamu was out of bed, putting on his robe. "I'm sorry too," he said, thinking she was apologizing to him. "A girl like you could've had a great life to match your great beauty. What a waste! How long did you think you could keep killing without being exposed?" He turned to his servant. "Ellili, did you notice anyone outside acting suspicious, spying?"

"No, Master."

"Great! Now, get me the rope, and call your wife to come here."

Allamu walked back to Mayram and forced her to lie face down on the bed. Mayram, not yet recovered from the reversal of her plans, and confronted with a brute almost twice her size, did not fight back.

Ellili returned with the rope and a woman who appeared like his perfect match in misery.

"Warda, you're about her build," Allamu told the woman while binding Mayram's hands behind her back. "See these clothes of hers? Put them on, cover your head with a shawl, and walk out to make believe that she left—just in case someone is watching. Don't come back till you're sure no one is following, and don't get caught. Run if you must—understood?"

"Yes, Master." And Warda started changing into Mayram's clothes.

"Now, Ellili, like I told you earlier, go out the back door and hurry to Hadras' house; he should be there. Tell him to come right away. Walk with him through the back door too. Oh, tell him not to put on any fancy clothes that might attract attention."

Allamu went over a few more details with his servant, then turned to Warda, who was done dressing.

"What are you waiting for? Move, there is no time to waste!"

Ellili and Warda went their separate ways.

Allamu paced the floor, his mind roaming somewhere distant, outside the walls.

While tears dried on her face, Mayram managed to slide under the bedcover to shroud her nudity. Silently, she prayed.

O goddess of love, I accept whatever fate you have in store for me. I repent any of my deeds that might have angered you; it was never my intention. I beg of you to spare the life of this humble servant of yours who has just found the beauty of true love, the true reflection of your splendor ... but if my departure from this life is what you desire, then please hurry death, for time is painfully cruel.

☩ ◇ ⊐ ∨ Ⅲ

The shrill voice stormed the quiet room once the door opened.

"Allamu! You better have a good reason to interrupt my sweet dreams, or your Ellili will lose his balls for dragging me here."

Wasting no time on greetings, Allamu walked to the bed, plucked its cover off and flung it to the floor.

Hadras' puffy face brightened upon seeing the naked girl lying on her side with hands tied up behind her back.

"Oh, Allamu, by the gods of sacred fuck! Is this a surprise or simply my good luck? Bless you, my friend, now I understand why the urgency. She's a real beauty—but why is she roped? ... Ooh, you bastard, you knew how I yearned for those days when we conquered cities and tied up their women. Oh, what savage orgies!"

"She's the assassin, the one I told you about," Allamu said.

"Are you serious? Her body and beauty are made for great fucking. Assassin, you say—no way!"

"Don't be fooled by her beauty; she's lethal. I don't know how many nobles she had killed already, but I do know why, and it is not because she's part of some new Ishtar cult of assassins who offer men's blood for sacrifice."

Allamu pulled out her dagger. "See this? It was in her clothes. I had her face away in bed while we were busy, and my groans were filling the room so my man, Ellili, could sneak in unnoticed and replace her assassin's dagger with a toy one. As I feigned sleep, she pulled the toy out, thinking it was her dagger. What do you think she needs a sharp dagger for?"

"For you, what else? For being such a miserable lover." Hadras laughed. "No one can blame her for that."

Allamu sat on the bed and forced Mayram to her back. Her lips were subtly moving in prayer.

"Take a look at this." Allamu grabbed the cylinder seal dangling from her necklace.

Hadras approached, held the seal, and took a careful look after his eyes wandered over the naked beauty of its owner.

"Looks like a praying mantis … so what?"

"Fool! What more proof do you need?" Allamu rebuked him.

"Proof!" Hadras barked back. "What proof is the fucking praying bug?"

"Praying mantis females, while mating, turn and bite off the male's head."

"You mean … their males fuck only once in a lifetime?" Hadras laughed. "Ooh, that's why they're praying: they're asking the gods to stop the females from biting their heads off, so they can live for another fuck."

Allamu ignored his friend's humor. "Love, death, and a prayer—all in one act. What better symbol for an assassin girl devoted to the goddess of love and war than the sacred praying mantis? Now, do you believe me? We have to go ahead with our plan, right away."

"Let me think about it," Hadras answered vaguely; lust for Mayram was clogging his thoughts.

"No!" Allamu snapped. "You told me you would have the troops ready to move at your orders. There is no time; by tomorrow, they'll know this assassin is missing. With no proof of my death, they'll figure out that their scheme has been exposed and will hasten to finish everyone on their "To Die" list, no matter what unrests that might bring. And *you*, dear Hadras, according to my sources, are next on that "To Die" list."

"Your sources!" Hadras grumbled. "This is high treason you're asking me to commit. If the plan fails, then what? I want to die with my head resting on a pillow, not a fucking chopping block!"

"Then wake up, open your eyes, or it will be too late to die on a pillow," Allamu shouted, then dropped his voice close to a whisper. "Fine, go home, and wait for them to visit—to chop you into pieces *over your pillow!*"

Hadras was getting nervous. His rise to the rank of general had had more to do with social connections than merit. His skills were unlike those of Allamu, who for a long period had been his second-in-command and the strategist behind all the battle plans and victories that garnered Hadras all the praise. Also, unlike Allamu, who showed bravery and took part in actual combat, Hadras always stayed behind until victory was secured; only then would he ride among the troops on his chariot and join in the pillaging of the defeated cities.

Eventually, Allamu's bravado and leadership skills carried him up the ranks to general. But after the rebellion of Ur, those achievements no longer counted; Sargon had relieved Allamu of duty because of one wrongful deed he was guilty of: being the half-brother of Kebboba, the acting governor of the rebel city, Ur.

Allamu had denounced the rebellion and his half-sister. Nevertheless, Sargon had stripped him of his title, stating that he was acting on the advice of other generals, and that it was only a temporary thing until the rebellion at Ur was over. The king had assured Allamu that no harm would come to him or his relatives in Uruk. Yet no assurances could have allayed Allamu's suspicions that sooner or later he would be targeted by Sargon's assassins. His only hope for turning fate around hung on his friend Hadras.

Silence was Allamu's next weapon. He saw through his former commander's indecision and waited patiently, knowing that he had planted the seeds of fear in the heart of the "heroic" general.

Hadras found himself alone, deprived of any advice on how to shield himself against a possible treacherous plot by King Sargon. He turned to Mayram and shouted:

"Whore, who sent you?"

She ignored him with her prayers. Her faith had never wavered, even after that "miraculous" act of the dagger turning into a toy was cruelly shredded by Allamu.

"Answer me, who sent you?" Hadras slapped her.

"Sargon, who else!" Allamu answered after torturing Hadras with added moments of silence. "Does it matter who sent her? What matters is by this time tomorrow, you will be long dead, unless you act right away—*now.*"

He approached Hadras and laid an assuring hand on his shoulder. "Why are you so worried? Didn't we discuss all this? Now is the perfect time to strike; Gungunum and his troops were sent to Ur after Sargon's fool of a son was taken hostage. That leaves you in command of most of the troops here in the city; this will be the surprise they never expected. Trust me, did I ever fail you? This is the greatest battle of your life and it is *for your life.* You only have two choices: either pounce at the opportunity to be king, or—with the stench of death soon you'll start to stink. ... Listen! You hear that? Maggots preparing for a feast. Now guess who's the lucky host? Yes, my friend, *it's you.*"

Hadras reeked of anxiety and pondered any other options available. The only one to present itself was scratching his head to remove the burden of uncertainty.

"Fine, I guess there is not much to think about." Hadras relented in joining the gambit planned by his longtime adviser.

"What about her?" He pointed to Mayram.

"What about her?" Allamu shrugged. "It's her time to die."

"I can keep her as a concubine!"

"*No,* she's an assassin—was sent to shred me with her awful dagger."

"Well, I need to calm down,"—Hadras spoke resolutely—"and this beauty is not going to the netherworld before I taste her joys. In case your plans go awry, one last fuck for this mantis before he loses his head."

"Fine, if that would put you at ease, but make it fast. I'll go wash and change." Allamu tossed the dagger on the bed. "Here, use her dagger once you're done. Don't get yours stained with her blood."

"Before you kill me, can I ask a favor?" Resigned to her fate,

Mayram broke her silence.

"You're not in a position to ask for favors," Allamu scoffed at her.

"The man who schemed the assassinations—I'll reveal his name if you promise to make him suffer."

"Well, that's one demand I would be happy to satisfy. Who is he?" Allamu demanded.

"I only ask you to tie my hands in front. They are hurting and I'm going numb at my back."

"She's planning something." Hadras became alarmed. "What difference does it make? Soon, your whole body will go numb with death."

"What sort of army general are you?" Allamu hopped on the bed to satisfy her request. "Worrying about a girl bound in rope! We don't have the luxury of wasting time."

Once Allamu finished knotting Mayram's wrists in front, he asked, "So, who is this fortunate one to receive the rewards of our gratitude?"

"Ibrahem, the king's sculptor. He tricked me into committing those murders."

"Ibrahem!" Hadras cried out in surprise. "That sly son of a bitch! I had him make some gods for me. … Allamu, now that she has confessed, forgive me for doubting you."

"So hurry up—unload your stiff tool. I'll be getting ready."

Allamu had just walked through a reed partition into an adjacent room when a loud growl of pain from Hadras made him rush back.

"The whore," Hadras screamed as he cruelly punched the girl. "She almost crushed my balls with her knee."

Mayram was trying to fight him off, but there wasn't much a bound girl could do against a man on top of her. His punches rained on her body, yet she hardly made a sound. She welcomed pain to numb her senses to the ugliness about to invade her.

"Ellili!" Allamu shouted to his servant, who was waiting outside the room in case he was needed.

"Ellili, stay with him." Allamu thought it prudent not to risk the slim chance of Mayram overpowering the general.

Hadras prepared to get what could be his last taste of a woman.

"What are you doing?" Something seemed to trouble Allamu.

"What does it look like?" Hadras said mockingly. "Man on top of a girl!"

"You forget—you're to stab her after you're done. I don't want blood soaking my bed. … Ellili, put some worn-out mats on the floor for him."

Allamu walked back to the adjacent room. Soon after, the only sounds that could be heard were the moans of Hadras.

Paces away from the revolting scene, Ellili stood silently. His eyes locked on the girl for brief moments. Looking back at him, Mayram didn't see lust or anger in the servant's eyes; she saw tears that Ellili could only hide by turning his side to her. She closed her eyes to evade her own torment.

Seeing a girl being raped roused livid rage within Ellili. But he was the master over rage and kept it imprisoned inside, just as his master Allamu had him imprisoned in slavery. Since his youth, all he had learned was how to be an obedient slave, suppress the pain of oppression, and quietly submit to abuse. He couldn't even worship a god without permission; the master was his god, and gods must be obeyed, no questions asked.

In Mayram, Ellili saw his wife, Warda. Shame and helplessness rushed back to blaze his memory with the anguish of the depraved details of one cursed night that kept haunting him.

That night, Allamu and Hadras had returned to the house after a bout of heavy drinking, leaning on each other for support. Ellili asked if they wanted to go to sleep and offered to prepare a bed for Hadras. They laughed like madmen.

"Sleep, and miss all the bliss!" Hadras quipped. "Allamu, what's wrong with your man? … Ellili, you should know by now that the last thing on a drunken man's mind is sleep."

"Ellili, how could you embarrass me like this?" Allamu chuckled. "Go tell your wife to prepare some food and bring it to the guest room. Oh, and bring some wine, we need to get more drunk." And they walked away laughing.

Ellili and his wife brought the food and wine to the guest room. They turned to leave when Hadras stopped them.

"Don't go, stay, I need some company." He pointed to Allamu.

"This man is boring when he's too drunk. His words get drunk too, and they can't find the way out of his mouth. Join us, Ellili, have some wine."

"Forgive me, my lord, I'm but a lowly servant who shouldn't receive such an honorable invitation."

"Sit down, Ellili … Warda, you too," Hadras insisted. "We're so drunk that even *you* look like nobles."

"Sit down, Ellili, and pour yourselves a drink," Alamo muttered, laughing in agreement with his friend.

Ellili and his wife obeyed and drank in modest sips as they listened to the drunk Hadras, who talked nonstop about his military heroics.

Allamu kept himself busy, eating and drinking to help digest the fictitious exploits of his friend.

"Ellili … are you aware of how fortunate you are for a servant?"

Though surprised by Hadras' sudden change of subject, Ellili answered, "Yes, my lord, I am blessed to have a great master."

"Precisely … one very generous master. Not many like him out there. Not only did he keep your balls hanging intact under your rod; moreover, he allowed you to have a wife."

"Yes, my lord. I am most thankful for his kindness." Ellili bowed, humbly.

Hadras turned to Warda, taking a long stare at her. "You have a strong, nicely shaped body, Warda."

"Thank you, my lord," she said, embarrassed.

"My lord." Sensing trouble, Ellili addressed his master Allamu, who was struggling to keep awake. "I think we have overstayed your kind invitation. It's time we retreat to our duties."

"Not yet!" Hadras stopped Ellili before he could stand up. "Tell me, Warda, did you make the vows to honor our goddess Ishtar? You know … sleep with a man other than your husband."

"No, my lord," she answered nervously. "Master Allamu allows us to worship the father of all gods, Anu. I don't follow in the traditions of the goddess Ishtar."

"Nonsense! If you worship Anu, you should worship his children too—follow their traditions."

A nightmare stormed out of the dream world, and Ellili saw it rushing in Warda's direction. Instinctively, he grasped her hand and sprang to his feet, pulling her up with him.

"Forgive me, Master," Ellili pleaded to Allamu, "but, may we leave? There is plenty of housework to be done."

Allamu kept quiet, his gaze shifting between his friend and his servant, waiting in amusement to see how Hadras would respond to this brazen act.

"How dare you?" As expected, Hadras was incensed. "How insolent! You see me talking to the woman and you want to walk away with her. Sit, both of you, and be quiet! You're not going anywhere unless *I* give you permission."

Gently, Ellili helped Warda to sit before submitting to the order himself.

"This woman must fulfill her duties to the goddess, and you're fortunate I am prepared to help. Now ... we don't have to follow all the prayers, rules, and temple rituals—all that drivel is a waste of time. What matters is the act of love itself."

Hadras reached into his pocket and threw a silver piece into Warda's lap. She froze and stared down at it while Hadras recited the verse:

Love goddess, please bear witness, to you I pray and bow,
My oath to love your servant—to assist fulfill her vow.

"Now we're ready. Allow me to undress you." Hadras accosted a distraught Warda, who could only look down, bent by the shame riding heavy on her shoulders.

Ruthlessly stunned, Ellili searched for a way to get his wife, and himself, out of this abhorrent degradation, but things were happening too fast; Hadras had already removed Warda's top.

Allamu was out of his stupor with a look of apathy regarding the debauchery about to be inflicted on his servant.

Ellili, the obedient servant, could only find one way out. He stood up and started to walk away, to escape his wife's shame and his own disgrace for not daring to stop Hadras.

"And where are you going?" Hadras called after him.

Slow and subdued was Ellili's response: "To give you privacy for the ritual, my lord."

"Did I ask for privacy? Did I give you permission?" Hadras said coldly as he removed the last piece of Warda's clothing and began to disrobe. "Allamu! You need to teach your slave some manners."

Allamu didn't answer. His eyes were wide open, seeing Warda naked for the first time. He seemed too impatient for the next act to start.

"Sit down, Ellili, sit." Hadras spoke like a mentor advising a disciple. "You need to watch and learn. I'll show you new methods to pleasure your lovely wife. Believe me, you will thank me."

Ellili looked on, fighting back the tears. He had heard of slaves who, somehow, found the courage to slay their masters. But all he had ever learned since he was young was to obey the masters. Any signs of courage were promptly obliterated by excruciating means. Soldiers were trained to obey orders and be brave. Slaves were trained to obey orders and be afraid.

He envisioned rebelling slaves as being possessed by some demon who took control of their actions. Ellili prayed for such a demon to possess him; a small demon would have sufficed, for both his master and Hadras were drunk; butchering them would have presented no harder a task than chopping meat for the daily meals. He had prayed and prayed for the gods to send him any demon that would give him the little nudge to thrust his rage into spilling the putrid blood of his masters. But the gods did not find him worthy of their demons.

Coward! Ellili loathed himself as the girl who was lying a glance away, and Warda in his memory, were being ravaged by Hadras.

When Mayram had apologized to him earlier, he wanted to sink to his knees and ask her forgiveness for squandering an opportunity to get vengeance; one he repeatedly dreamed of since that night when Allamu sat watching his friend violate Warda.

Coward! Ellili recalled standing with Mayram's dagger in his hand after he'd sneaked in and replaced it with the toy knife while his master was facing away, totally engrossed in the "love" ritual. The bastard's neck, back—his fully naked body—offered a most generous invitation to be stabbed, time and time again. Yet the slave in Ellili triumphed and had him slither outside to await his master's next command.

It wasn't death Ellili feared; death he contemplated as an exit out of his misery, but it had to walk to him voluntarily. Ellili wasn't one of the select brave slaves who, after being driven past a certain point of desperation, would act on their own, killing their masters and making a run for a slim chance of gaining freedom. As for Ellili, to kill master Allamu, he would have to ask his permission first.

How he envied Mayram's courage; such a young, beautiful girl could've had a wonderful life, yet she chose a life of battling beasts in their dens.

With all the guilt adding its torment to the chains of his slavery, Ellili desperately prayed for the gods to grant him some courage to save this girl from Hadras. But just like when Warda needed his courage, the gods never answered his pleas. They were too busy to stoop down and extend any help to the likes of him. It became clear to Ellili that when it came to helping the needy mortals, the gods were always frugal; as for inflicting pain and suffering, they granted those with great enthusiasm.

Mayram kept her eyes closed to her own ugly ordeal. She drifted back in time and space to a previous night at Lubalanda's place. His soothing voice came back to her.

"A beautiful flower like you should find shelter from the storms of life. Promise me one thing."

"What?" She'd kept the reply short for her lips were busy planting light kisses on his.

"Stay out of harm's way."

Tears welled in her eyes to hear such advice from the man she'd been sent to butcher.

Now, her tears streamed for she was leaving him forever. She needed to tell him not to mourn, that she was happy to have tasted the sweetness of life and the beauty of true love, and it only happened through him.

Thoughts of her lover were cut short by a horrid groan that seemed to erupt out of a pig. The filth on top of her stiffened in his climax, then collapsed like a dead lump of meat. Mayram kept her eyes tightly closed to spare herself the hideous sight besieging her, but tears still managed to squeeze through her sealed eyelids as she quietly prayed to her goddess. She prayed, not out of fear, but out of desperate longing, and guilt over a duty she was failing to complete.

O goddess of love, I beseech you to grant me a few moments with my beloved. I have so much to tell him ... to tell him not to wait for me, to let him know I justly deserved this fate. I want to wish him happiness and ask him not to grieve, for my heart will keep beating through his heart. I beg you, goddess, to keep death away for a mere short night. I must see ... bid him farewell. Dearest goddess, I never asked you for any personal favors before. Could you ... just this once—

Sharp pain through her chest severed her prayers.

Allamu was done washing and putting his clothes on in the next room when he heard his friend's euphoric groan of joy. Shortly, an abrupt moan from the girl followed, which sent Allamu musing.

That last sound, was it ecstasy or agony? How ironic: the groan when the joys of the flesh plant the seed of life, and the cry of pain when life is ripped out of the body—how similar the sounds.

Despite the rope binding her wrists and the brutal pain from the imbedded blade in her chest, Mayram gripped the bone handle of the dagger, mustering all her strength to wrest it away from Hadras. He let go of the grip after a brief effort, not wanting her blood to splash over him, and off the floor he bounced, an alarmed look on his face.

"Get the dagger from her!" Hadras told Ellili, and backed away to fetch his own dagger from his clothes, to be ready in case Mayram found the strength to seek vengeance.

Hadras' order went unheeded by the slave, who was stunned motionless on witnessing the savage, cold-blooded termination of a beautiful life.

She's an assassin. Ellili tried to fend off the guilt of his inaction—his repulsive weakness.

Guilt replied, mocking him: *And what about those you serve? Are they not assassins?* And the vicious guilt lunged and plunged its dagger, mercilessly, deep into Ellili's soul until his eyes bled with tears.

Mayram ended her prayers; the gods were not to be disturbed anymore. She held on to the dagger that sank close to her heart. It was back in her possession, and that was what mattered most to her in those last moments of her life. She felt the warmth of her mother's hand after she had handed her the dagger for the first time. She sensed the power of her father's grip as he'd surrendered it back to her once after a fit of madness. This best friend brought them to her side in that lonely room.

Tenderly, Mayram pulled her friend out of her chest and placed it over her heart as gushing blood joined them together in one body.

Death sniffed the sweet smell of young blood filling the air. Mayram felt it coming and closed her eyes, when, out of nowhere, the image of her lover materialized. She kissed him, drew the last of breaths, and whispered:

"Bless you, beloved, for finding me, for making me live. Forgive me, but I must leave. May our goddess dress you in her blessings … may she guard you against the evil of men."

Long Live the King

"**B**Y ORDER OF THE KING, YOU MUST LET US PASS!"
A commanding Hadras displayed the tablet to the sentry outside the main gate guarding the palace. The sentry glanced at the seal; it did resemble the royal seal, but he didn't know how to read.

"Sir, forgive me, but my superior has to see this."

"Then bring him here!" Hadras snapped. "This is a matter of utmost urgency!"

"Right away, sir." The sentry bolted to a nearby shack.

Within moments, a disheveled man came rushing out and saluted Hadras, who handed him the tablet. Upon reading its contents, his face became a jumble of alarm and confusion.

"The king inside … is an impostor?" asked the head sentry.

"A double—the king's look-alike," Hadras clarified. "Our king, Sargon, left in secret to meet the commanders of the siege army at Ur after his son was taken hostage. Now this double is being manipulated by a group of traitors, killing nobles and conspiring against the kingdom. Tell your men inside to throw the gate open, right away."

"Sir, I wasn't informed about a king's double."

Allamu stepped up next to Hadras and spat the words out:

"The whole idea is to keep it a secret, not go around telling everyone."

Dressed in military attire with a bronze helmet, which concealed most of his face, Allamu spoke in a tone that would not tolerate a reply. Hadras was not offended by this intrusion of his former second-in-command; on the contrary, he was relieved by it.

The guards atop the gate's wall watched intently, alarmed by the troops amassed outside.

"In your hands you have orders stamped with the royal seal," Allamu shouted. "Obey the orders, or you will be condemned to die for insubordination and high treason. Your men on both sides of the gate present no major obstacle to stop us from climbing over."

The threat shoved the head sentry into a speedy pace to the gate. He knocked on it, slid open a square hatch, and spoke to a face on the other side.

"Open the gate—royal order."

The gate opened with no further questions. Hadras and Allamu rushed in with the troops right behind. Before reaching the palace, eleven men of the elite royal guards confronted them.

"Step aside!" Hadras yelled as one of his soldiers approached the guards, raising the tablet for all to view. "This tablet carries the royal seal with orders to arrest the fake king—his double—and those who defend him. He has overstepped his bounds and is a danger to king and kingdom."

The lead guard shouted back, "I have known the king and served under him since he was a general. This piece of clay you bring, its orders and seal, is the only fake thing within these walls."

"Lay down your weapons; you are hopelessly outnumbered," Allamu hollered, retaking the lead from Hadras, who, upon sensing a perilous situation, started walking back between the files of his men with the pretense of heartening them for the looming clash.

"You will die for this disobedience!" Allamu threatened.

"And by the great Anu, we have vowed to protect our king till death," the lead guard yelled back.

"Then prepare to meet Ereshkigal in the netherworld," Allamu screamed hoarsely. "Kill them all!"

The royal guards knew they didn't have long to live; still, they charged with swords drawn, ready to fight to the bitter end as if they had lived all their lives for this glorious moment. Many were taken out by the archers; two struggled back to their feet and fought despite having arrows rooted in their bodies, only to meet the same swift death suffered by the ones who made it to the foe unscathed. Allamu was taking no prisoners.

Though the screams of agony from the mortally wounded were short, they were more than enough to send every living soul in the palace in search of safety. During the chaos, many unarmed men were slain by Hadras' zealous troops.

After Hadras had gained full control of the palace, two soldiers approached him, dragging a man.

"Sir, this man's features resemble the king's," said one soldier, "but he speaks in a strange tongue."

"Son of dogs! Is that you, Sargon?" Hadras studied the face that was partially obscured by a thick beard and a mustache.

The man stammered, pleading. No one spoke his language, but he managed to insert some words in Akkadian.

"No, no. Me no Sargon … other. No kill."

"Do you think he's putting on an act with this foolish tongue?" Hadras asked.

"Only one way to be sure," Allamu replied. "Strip him of his clothes."

The soldiers stripped the man naked.

"He's a double; it's not Sargon," Allamu said, smiling at the man. "My friend, did you enjoy being king? I hope you did. But you know, all good things come to an end sooner or later. We were planning to keep you as king, but plans change. I'm afraid you won't like the new plan."

Seeing the smile on Allamu's face, the double calmed down a little. "Anu … bless they," he said in his broken Akkadian.

"Are you sure he's not Sargon playing the fool?" Hadras asked again.

"The real Sargon has scars from battle wounds on his leg and upper arm," Allamu asserted.

Without warning, Hadras lunged forward and drove his sword into the double's chest.

"Now this will give him a nice, big scar." He laughed at the man's excruciating agony. "Don't worry, O esteemed double, the king will follow you soon to the netherworld, where you can resume your *double* duty."

The man's eyes fluttered as death stormed them, and through groans of pain, he uttered a jumble of words in his own language.

"Does anyone here understand what this miserable wretch is saying?" asked Hadras.

"Must be praying for the gods to curse you, my friend," Allamu answered, grinning.

"Listen, you double, whore of a king," Hadras dug the sword deeper into the man's chest while racing the words to reach him before he expired. "The gods don't speak your language. But don't despair; I'm sure some demons down below speak it."

Whatever curses the double was about to add stretched into a scream that stopped abruptly when Hadras pulled the blade out, giving death an easier entry path.

"The fewer the doubles, the easier to find the real bastard." Hadras turned to the soldiers. "Take this filth out of here."

A thorough search of the palace yielded no trace of Sargon or the man behind the mantis assassin—the sculptor Ibrahem. It was no surprise to Allamu; he knew they must have escaped through a secret tunnel. Orders were issued to arrest them or, if necessary, kill them.

Word about what had happened within the palace walls created a wave of turmoil that swept the calm of night. Hadras declared himself king, and Allamu was announced as chief general of the army. Messengers were dispatched to all the high-ranking officials in the city to attend an urgent meeting at the palace. Most complied, but some disappeared into the night, for they had no idea who was in control and were not going to risk angering Sargon if he staged a comeback.

𒁹 ◇ 𒁔 𐤅 𒐲

Hadras was all smiles as he ambled around, engaging in pleasant conversation with those who had rushed to the "invitation" celebrated at the palace court. Most seemed, or pretended, to be happy with the overthrow of Sargon. But anxiety always managed to twist the faces back to gloom when the question of Sargon's whereabouts went unanswered.

Obliged to give the invitees some assurance, Hadras climbed the stairs toward the throne, pulled a piece of cloth from his pocket, and began slapping the throne's seat with it. The crowd murmured among themselves in wonder: was that a gesture to imply slapping Sargon and striking him out of the throne, or was Hadras castigating the seat for giving comfort to the tyrant?

Once done with whatever symbolic punishment or show of power he had in mind, Hadras occupied the throne. The court fell silent with many faces wearing relieved smiles at the thought that Sargon was truly gone.

Whispers resumed circulating when the new army general, Allamu, ascended the stairs. Facing the assembly, he started his address.

"Honorable men of the great Uruk! The days of fear are over. Sargon is on the run, but he won't get too far. Be assured of one thing: his reign of terror has come to an end.

"All of you know of the nobles who were savagely killed during the past six moons. The crimes were all blamed on some *silent rebellion* by slaves who dared to kill their masters. Those servants were swiftly executed. Now, how many such crimes have you known of in your lifetime? No more than the fingers on one hand, if you ask me. The day I believe in this *slave rebellion* bull-dung is the day I will *eat* bull-dung."

The assembly broke into laughter.

"Many of you knew the story was a lie, but you were afraid to speak out. Fear no more, for the tyrant is no more. Sargon had an extensive list of men to be butchered by this so-called *slave rebellion*. Those of you who think they weren't on that list, think again—you would've probably made it onto the next list. There is no predicting Sargon. Remaining faithful to that tyrant would've granted you no favors from him. The man is elevating himself to a divine status; to him, everyone here was nothing but a mortal whom he could strike down on a whim.

"Who wants to live a life consumed with fear, not knowing when fate is going to place him right next to the savage when his thirst for blood is at its peak? The moment has arrived to unite and put our faith in a just king who treats the nobles with the respect they merit, and not a barbarian who viciously slaughters them in their sleep. Today we celebrate this change where each one of you will be rewarded for your devotion in the service of our city. Today we have a new leader; a man of courage and resolve, wisdom and foresight. *He*, who will take our great Uruk and the kingdom to the pinnacles of peace and prosperity. *He,* the one destined to be the mightiest of all rulers on Earth from sunrise to sunset—the Great King Hadras!"

"Long live King Hadras!" one noble shouted, and a wave of praises rippled through the court.

"May King Hadras live forever!"

"Hadras—reflection of God, born to be a god!"

A jovial smile crossed Hadras' face as he stepped off the throne and walked to the front, waving a hand in humble appreciation. He could envision himself in a chariot, moving through the streets of Uruk, people on both sides shouting his name, poets singing about his bravery in battle and his legacy in peacetime.

"Noblemen of Uruk," Hadras commenced, "we have to unite in the service of this great city and our kingdom on which the gods have bestowed their greatest blessings. Sargon was not only a threat to your life … he was about to bring the wrath of the gods down upon every living soul by committing one heresy after the next. Remember Ishullanu—the revered high priest and the true proxy assigned by the gods—how he was publicly humiliated and executed; a victim of a dirty, vile design by one heretic king. Sargon followed that with the most abhorrent exploitation of a sacred ritual to the love goddess. He inserted a murderous, filthy whore among the women who took their love vows in the sacred temple. More of a beast than a girl, she was Sargon's secret weapon to end the lives of *dozens* of good men who strived to serve him with the utmost loyalty. This assassin butchered her victims in a most horrific, savage way.

"But that terror is a thing of the past now. Last night, with these hands of mine, I sent her to the deepest pits of the netherworld, where demons dispense a most grim punishment for such an evil soul."

"The gods protected you, O Brave King Hadras!" a shout interrupted him.

"Yes, I have the gods to thank. The assassin was about to mortally strike me in my sleep, when the merciful gods sent a buzzing fly to alert me, a mere moment before her dagger was on its way down, poised to open a path for my soul to depart my body. One moment was all I needed to dodge death and trap her. She confessed to her crimes and her role in Sargon's vicious plot: through her young, innocent beauty, she lured the unsuspecting victims only to savagely slaughter them. Knowing the grim and just punishment awaiting her, she grabbed my hand, which held her dagger, and drove it into her own heart."

Allamu was getting restless, listening to a story that gave him no credit whatsoever. *Buzzing fly! That had to be me.* It was no surprise, though; he knew how Hadras always changed, added, and omitted details in all his stories to create a formidable character of himself. But enough was enough for Allamu; he accosted Hadras and buzzed in his ear. Hadras cleared his throat and continued.

"We have assembled a search party to look for the coward, Sargon. His son, as you know, is prisoner of Lady Kebboba, governor of Ur and half-sister of General Allamu. We have already sent a messenger with orders for the army to end the siege of Ur. With the armies of Ur and Uruk united under one leadership—instead of massacring each other, we will become the most formidable power on Earth. Prosperity awaits all the good people of the kingdom. God bless Uruk!"

A barrage of exhilaration followed.

"God bless Uruk!"

"Glory to the Fearless King Hadras!"

"Hadras! Forever King!"

Hadras was savoring the nobles' chaotic exaltations as if they were soothing harp music, when Allamu's voice assaulted his ears with another buzz. Hadras cleared his throat again to announce his first royal order.

"Now, as a token of your unwavering loyalty, I would like each one of you to stamp your seal on those fresh clay tablets at the front. This will denote your pledge of allegiance to the new rule."

The nobles became quiet. Many were tempted to sneak out of the court, but the guards at the doors didn't look friendly.

"Honorable, valiant nobles." Allamu broke the silence and stepped by Hadras' side. "I understand your fears; Sargon was brutal. But believe me—and the gods are my witnesses—right now he's running scared like a rat looking for a hole to hide in. He's the last man to fear on this Earth from sunrise to sunset. With your seals on the tablets, you are sealing away your fears and freeing yourselves from the ugly ghost of Sargon."

With those words of encouragement, the first noble dragged his feet forward. He freed the seal from the pin securing it to his necklace and rolled it over one of the fresh clay tablets placed on a table. It was the crack to help shatter the trepidations of other men, who began trickling slowly to stand in line, their seals ready to roll over the soft tablets, thus cementing their loyalty to the new king.

Many men remained seated, unwilling to volunteer their seals, thinking that their enthusiastic hails were enough proof of loyalty. Their hesitation didn't bother Allamu; he knew those were the timid ones who saw the shadow of Sargon still lingering over the throne. But with every seal leaving its mark on a tablet, that shadow would swiftly retreat until it joined its hiding owner.

The line moved smoothly until echoes of men arguing outside the entrance reached the court.

"Who dares disrupt the court? Guards!" shouted Allamu.

A sentry paced briskly toward him and whispered, "Sir, there is a soldier at the door—says he's the messenger you sent to the siege army at Ur."

"Then what is he doing here?" Allamu scowled.

"Sir, he says he has a message for you."

Allamu stared into the air in search of answers. *The fool had probably lost the tablet with the message to end the siege. His meat I'll feed to the pigs!*

"Send him in." Allamu's steely voice strained to avoid showing any irritation that might alarm those in the court.

The messenger walked in, and the noble next in line to roll his seal took one glance at the man and instinctively withdrew his seal without leaving its mark on the clay.

The messenger looked as if death were riding over his message, ready to shred him once he finished letting loose its contents. He walked to Allamu, bowed once, and delivered the first message—a silent prayer to the gods that they calm his commander.

Allamu took him aside, away from the inquisitive stares of the nobles.

"Why are you here? You should've been on your way to the siege army in Ur." A furious Allamu had to resist the urge to punch him.

"Yes, sir … but … they are here already." The messenger's voice quaked with stress.

"What do you mean? Who's here?"

"General Gungunum and his army, sir. They are outside the palace compound. He sent his own messenger with me … he's waiting outside, in the hall."

Color abandoned Allamu's face. Hadras, who was observing intently, caught that and turned ashen himself. Allamu had to dash outside before the temptation to slice his messenger's neck became irresistible. As soon as he saw the envoy sent by Gungunum, the temptation to kill became too great to ignore. He pulled out his sword and put it to the neck of the man, who needed no introduction: Sargon's personal messenger, Humbaba.

No one who had served with Humbaba could recall his real name. But everyone who saw him once would have their memory chiseled for the rest of their lives with the face of a monster, the ugliest man they would ever see.

It wasn't long before a soldier who had a problem pronouncing the man's name simply called him "Humbaba," and within short days, this new name annihilated the real one. The name suited the man, for it finally gave a face to the mythical Humbaba—the horrid creature from the Epic of Gilgamesh, guardian of the cedar forests of Lebanon, assigned by the gods to frighten the intruders away, thus keeping the forests for the sole enjoyment of the gods.

Humbaba, the man, had been cursed from birth with a head mutilated by folds crisscrossing at jagged lines in a demonic arrangement. The sight of it made people recoil in horror. Mothers would drag their children and run as if to escape a demon. Humbaba frequently heard echoes from the past detailing his ugliness. One was that of a child screaming frantically: "Look, Mother, look! A dead man, walking!" The woman had fainted, thinking death had come to take her and her son away. Some joked that Humbaba was the one man assured to send all girls in front of the temple scurrying away from their vows to the love goddess, and hence his presence should be added to the few exceptional cases where a girl would be absolved for abandoning the sacred duty.

Humbaba himself had always wondered if his head was that of the actual forest monster, attached by the gods to the body of a human, then tossed back to Earth.

When he was a boy, Humbaba used to cover his head and face with a shawl to avoid the taunts of other kids who had overcome their fear after getting used to him. Then to his surprise, those same kids started competing to befriend him for the sole purpose of having a sidesplitting laugh when they had Humbaba suddenly expose his face to terrify the unsuspecting passersby. Those acts were the earliest in his memory to bring along the vibrant taste of laughter. Grasping whatever friendships he could glean with those "horror-humor" stunts, he began to accept his appearance and the name given him later.

Humbaba's father was a scribe in the army. He taught his son how to read and write without sending him to a tablet house. The son followed in his father's footsteps, finding the army more tolerant of his deformity than the people in the city, who treated him with the disgust normally reserved for a decaying corpse. His skills with sword, spear, and shooting arrows were far below average, but he showed a true talent in writing and orating. So, his time in the army was spent at a safe distance from the raging slaughters of the combat zone. His was one of the most envied jobs in the military; reading and scribing tablet messages whenever needed by the commanders. However, fate had a plan that would throw him out of this secure position, making him the first man to be tossed in the face of the enemy, unarmed and on his own.

At the age of twenty-one, he was assigned to a general named

Sargon, who was ordered by the ruling king at the time to bring a band of brigands to justice. The criminals had been attacking the merchant convoys that traded with the northern regions and Phoenicia until, foolishly or unknowingly, they dared attack a convoy commissioned by the king himself.

Sargon, who at the time had only recently risen the ranks to general, hated Humbaba at first sight; the man's deformed face filled him with superstition. Before departing, Sargon asked that Humbaba be replaced with another scribe but was told that none were available. A furious Sargon set out, convinced he was being led to the netherworld by a demon—the scribe Humbaba.

The night they came close to the encampment of the tribe that was believed to shelter the bandits, Sargon called Humbaba to scribe a message to the tribe's chief. The next morning, Sargon called him back.

"The tablet I told you to scribe, is it ready to deliver?" Sargon said, while directing his gaze away from the ghastly face in his presence.

"Almost, sir. The clay should dry by early afternoon."

"I have a problem." Sargon sighed. "One of the two messengers they sent with me was kicked by a mule—badly injured his arm. So, I want you to take a chariot, head to the tribe, and read the message to the leaders."

Humbaba almost fainted; the message was full of language and ultimatums that practically begged for the killing of the messenger.

"Sir, what about the other messenger?" he couldn't help but ask.

Sargon raised his head slowly, to preclude the sudden shock of seeing Humbaba's face, and with anger feeding into his voice, he erupted.

"I need to keep this one messenger ready for any urgent matter that might arise! None of my soldiers is skilled in reading, nor do I expect anyone in that tribe to know this skill! And ... next time you're given an order, don't ask foolish questions. Next time, I might do you a favor and rid you of this fucked-up head sitting atop your shoulders! Now go, get yourself ready!"

"I beg forgiveness, sir." All shaken, Humbaba left the room to get ready—to meet death.

Like the skin folds marring his head, the sights, sounds, and smells of that loathed day were deeply etched into Humbaba's memory.

Time mercilessly dragged, prolonging the torment that preceded his suicidal task. The tablet with the scribed message wasn't fully dry, yet Humbaba made up his mind to carry the assignment right away. It was time to stop fooling himself and correct the mistake his parents committed in not snuffing the life out of their newborn, no matter how obvious it was that he didn't belong in this existence. He would walk to death instead of enduring the impossible wait for it. Stress morphed into a rage that had him accost Sargon well before noon—well before time.

"Sir, I am departing to deliver the message," he said, a hint of contempt in his voice seemingly saying: *I know you wish me death—you lump of dog turd—but more than you, I wish death upon my own self.*

Sargon sensed the change in the scribe's voice. It was no longer a voice constrained under the yoke of fear, but rather a voice that stirred fear. He looked up and saw Humbaba's beastly face blazing with monstrous ferocity.

"May the gods protect you and bring you back safely," Sargon replied with all sincerity and a hint of guilt in his words.

The camp came to a standstill as everyone watched Humbaba hop onto the chariot. It was no secret where he was heading, and no one envied him his new duty. The madness of being on your own, surrounded by the enemy while serving them with threats and ultimatums; it was akin to someone delivering the sentence to their own execution. Only a few saw the pure valor in the messenger's task that topped any act of bravery in the battlefield. Many soldiers felt sorry for Humbaba, yet most had hopes it would be the last time they saw his cursed face.

A rush of courage and pride overwhelmed Humbaba as he raced to carry the message that would deliver him to the netherworld. For the first time, he felt free from the bonds to a life that had treated him with the ugliness of death.

He reached the tribe's encampment and all the heads turned

toward him in shock. Voices rose, cursing this messenger from the demons, but no one dared touch him. They took him to their chief.

Though he knew the message by heart, Humbaba held the tablet and loudly read its contents. It first demanded the delivery of forty-four men to Sargon's army for immediate execution, in retribution for the massacre perpetrated on the king's convoy. The forty-four men were to be doomed for the forty-four deaths of thirteen merchants, seven camels, and twenty-four goats that were thieved and presumably consumed. The second demand was the return of all the stolen merchandise, or payment for its market value. The third demanded that the tribesmen desist from any future attacks or harboring criminals involved in such raids. The terms were nonnegotiable, and if by daybreak the demands were not met, then the wrath of the army would fall on the tribe: Every man, woman and child would be slaughtered, and their bodies would be left for the ravens to feed on and camel spiders to nest in.

Though he concluded stating the tablet's contents, Humbaba pretended that there was more to read.

"Finally, we expect the safe return of the messenger. If he is killed or injured, that would be considered a blatant rejection of our demands, and immediate retribution would follow."

While Humbaba was resigned to his fate, he was still shaken by the fear of death, which dwelled at the core of every living being. It prompted him to add that last detail, which Sargon should've dictated in the first place but had chosen to leave out in the hope of getting rid of the man with the cursed face.

Humbaba extended his arm, offering the tablet to the tribal chief, who approached him, gripping a short sword. Humbaba stood firm, his stare reaching beyond the chief's body, when the sword fell, cutting the edge of the tablet just short of Humbaba's fingers, then the blade scraped up, slowly, along his throat.

While death stroked his neck, Humbaba aimed his sights on the blue skies and prayed to have this torment over with. Two ravens circling lazily, crossed his view.

Once I'm dead, would those ravens feast on me, or would they find my meat too revolting to swallow.

He felt blood sliding down his neck as the sword took a little bite of the skin. One raven appeared to descend; soon its partner followed as though they noticed the juices of life seeping off their next meal. An eerie elation overtook Humbaba; his foreboding face would not stop ravens from consuming him. Parts of his body would be flying up in the wide-open skies instead of plunging to the netherworld. He envisaged the beauty and freedom of being part of such a wonderful creature that dared invade the privacy of the gods in their heavens.

"After you slay me,"—Humbaba found the courage to make a final request—"could you kindly leave my body for the ravens to feed on?"

Instantly, the chief, who was hesitant in deciding the fate of this messenger, stopped scraping any deeper with the sword. Ravens and their cousins were sacred to the tribe, for they shared the heavens with the gods. This messenger's wish to be consumed by ravens showed a deep respect for those noble creatures. The chief saw in that a message from the gods to spare Humbaba.

"Tie him up," the chief said. "He will spend the night outside. His fate and ours are in the hands of the gods. If he dies, we will have no choice but to fight. If he lives, then forty-four men will have to accept their fate for the good of the tribe."

Just like the day before it, that night was the most protracted and painful Humbaba had ever had to endure. Tied beneath the bright stars, he curled up and shivered in the cold, cursing the chief for sparing his life. Death assumed different roles: the lucky people got the swift killer who would strike and release the soul with barely an instant of pain. The death assigned to him was a petty, lazy thief— never in a hurry, stealing life in tiny bits, pausing for long breaks in between to savor the misery of its victim.

Humbaba's eyes roamed the night sky, looking for the ravens. They were gone, lost among the stars, and lost was the hope of becoming part of them. And the stars became so bright, he had to close his eyes and seek refuge in the darkness that would lead him to the netherworld faster. The cold numbed his body, and awareness began to abandon him.

The netherworld detected his anguish and felt pity for him. Its darkness tunneled the earth beneath, extending its reach to end

Humbaba's torment. His fading senses told him he was being lifted by what must have been demons, carrying him to the underworld, where goddess Ereshkigal ruled. His last fragments of consciousness brought a weird sensation of comfort as if death had him wrapped in a blanket after taking possession of his corpse, placing it on what felt like wood slats of a cart that would traverse the deep tunnels leading to the netherworld. The gentle rocking sent him into a deep sleep until cries of anguish crashed on his ears and the scent of fear stabbed at his nose, hinting at his arrival at that most dreaded abode where death resides.

Slowly, Humbaba opened his eyes, only to be stunned by the totally unexpected. Instead of the grim darkness, a bright sun roared, not far from its zenith in the blue sky.

By the gods! He looked in wonder. *What are those dark things circling overhead? ... Ravens! A gaggle of ravens!*

Only then did Humbaba realize that he had awakened from dreams of death to the nightmare of life.

Lying on a mat of reeds, in the shade of the same chariot that had carried him to the tribe, he instantly found the source of the morbid noise.

A man crying in despair was being dragged by two soldiers, then forced to kneel next to a block of wood with his head sticking out over its edge. Swiftly, an executioner axed the neck, cleanly felling the head to join a pile of other heads. The body was dragged away to make room for the next life to be chopped short.

Feeling awful thirst after his ordeal, Humbaba picked up a jar of water close by and drank savagely. After quenching the thirst, his gaze strayed to the executioner's ax just when it was on the way down again, only this time it badly missed the target, sending the doomed man into harrowing shrieks once the ax battered his shoulder blade, cutting flesh and shattering bone. The soldiers holding him down struggled to restrain his violently thrashing body and to properly reposition him on the block; the executioner, they scolded for a job horribly botched.

Undaunted by their complaints, the executioner deliberately botched the second strike, axing the same shoulder blade—sadistically prolonging the man's moments of imminent death only to taunt the two grumbling companions, who grudgingly refrained from making further protests and focused on pressing the tortured man over the block for the next strike, which neatly severed the head.

The scene struck Humbaba deeply with its gore. This time, the blood gushing out of the man's neck bore a resemblance to water spilling out of a jar. A wave of sickness rolled over Humbaba, and he threw up all of the water he had just consumed. He started to walk away, diverting his view from a long row of men awaiting their turn to enrich the bloodbath, when a voice startled him.

"Well done, Humbaba!"

He turned, and was greeted by a pleasant smile on a face where it shouldn't belong—Sargon's face.

"Yes, well done! One brave warrior who achieved one great victory on his own—The Battle of Humbaba. Many of our soldiers owe you their lives. You've become their hero! Still, it saddens me to tell you," Sargon's features reverted to their serious expression. "Humbaba … yours remains the most fucked-up, the ugliest face this Earth has ever conceived since its creation." And Sargon burst out laughing as he gave Humbaba some hard, friendly taps on the shoulder.

Humbaba was at a loss for words. But Sargon wasn't waiting for a reply and he ambled to the execution zone, still chuckling.

Another head was axed and Humbaba saw it rolling while his gaze followed Sargon. He was about to throw up again, but his empty stomach protested for it had no provisions for the task. He envisioned what would've happened if the tribal chief had continued digging into his neck with the sword. Humbaba's hand brushed over the dry blood adorning the wound when a thought stroked his mind:

Death had touched me … then scurried away.

His sights reached high to the ravens circling the skies, and he blared:

"Death feared me, whereas those forty-four men it hunted down. … *I* delivered death to the bandits. … *I* prevented a bloody battle and spared many a soldier a grisly end. That whole tribe, *I* saved from annihilation. Like a god, *I* changed the destiny of so many."

A sense of overwhelming power wrinkled Humbaba's face into a hideous smile. Life never felt so good. He picked up the water jar and gulped the water that tasted so sweet, taking breaks to watch the rest of the executions.

ℓ ◇ 刅 ᴡ Ⲓ

Dressed in royal guard attire, Humbaba stood tall, looking straight forward, while Allamu's blade pressed against the scars left on his neck by the blades of other angry men to whom he had delivered ultimatums.

"Out with your message, Humbaba, before I spill out your blood."

"Forgive me," Humbaba said, not acknowledging Allamu by name nor rank, "but this message is not addressed to you alone. I was told to deliver it to all those present in the court."

The incensed Allamu pressed the sword harder into Humbaba's throat.

"Tell me, Humbaba, why should I bother with your message and not slay you right here? I can hear Ishullanu's voice crying for your blood. Can you blame him, after the truly impressive role you played in Sargon's plot to rid Uruk of him and strip the priesthood of power? Smart of Sargon to have you imbedded among the wild crowd, camouflaged in a hooded gown. I was but a few steps away and watched how you riled the people with the strong arguments you hollered, using your shrill voice to stir the mob into a frenzy, which, huh, *forced a heartbroken Sargon to unwillingly sacrifice the high priest.* I watched you barking up for Sargon to have Ishullanu flung over the ziggurat's wall. Funny how everyone distanced themselves from the spot where he landed; all feared the gods' anger over the killing of their proxy—except for you, Humbaba. I watched how you accosted Ishullanu and plucked the dagger out of his chest. It must have felt breathtaking, being the one to seal the fate of the ruthless high priest. Poor Ishullanu, he must be eagerly waiting to have you join him in the netherworld, and it would give me tremendous pleasure to satisfy his wish."

With a boldness sharper than the blade pressed against his neck, and a gaze piercing empty space, Humbaba countered:

"I'm not only the messenger but also a soldier ready to die in serving my king. Yes, you can kill me, but need I remind you of the dire consequences of killing the king's messenger. All your relatives, up to the second cousin, would face a grim fate. The king had many of them detained already. Their families would have no one but you to blame."

Allamu could only return a look of contempt. Resentfully, he lowered the sword.

"Guards, escort this man behind me," he ordered two soldiers, and dashed back to the court.

Anguish marred all faces once Allamu walked in, trailed by the ghoulish figure of the one many called the Messenger of Doom.

Hadras was stunned by this development. Then, to his chagrin, he watched Humbaba go up the steps, uninvited. And His new Highness started shifting on the throne as if the seat had suddenly become infested with ants nipping at his butt.

Short of any introduction, Humbaba started his address.

"A message from His Majesty—the revered, intrepid Sargon, King of all Kings from sunrise to sunset; may he live forever." Humbaba paused, as if to give time for the king himself to step forward and deliver the message.

"First: The messenger should not be harmed in any way and should be given free passage after finishing his duty. If this condition is not met, my wrath will be unleashed on all those present, and horrible misfortune shall befall their families.

"Second: I, King Sargon, jointly with Chief General Gungunum and our brave troops, have surrounded the palace compound. The only reason we have not attacked is to spare the innocents. The troops who were involved in this treachery have surrendered peacefully and they are all fully pardoned, for they were only following orders given by those in high command. If you think you can defeat the army outside, then pray for help from God, who so far have shown unwavering support to me as His proxy on this Earth.

"Third: All those in this court are to surrender peacefully—and I, Sargon, give my solemn word that they will be judged with all fairness. Punishment will only be exacted according to the degree of their involvement in the conspiracy. And whatever their punishment may be, their families will not be harmed in any way. Also, those families will be given free passage out to any place of their choice, where they don't have to fear the reprisals from citizens who might harbor ill will against them as a result of their relatives' treachery.

"The choice is yours: either accept your fair judgment, or face annihilation along with your loved ones. May the gods bless Uruk and bring peace to its people."

Humbaba paused again as if waiting for Sargon to sit on his throne.

"This concludes the message. I will wait outside for you to deliberate and decide on an answer to send back to His Majesty."

Humbaba started heading to the exit when a knife-wielding noble dashed toward him, screaming:

"Take this answer to your fucking king!"

Humbaba stood ready to defend himself, but he didn't have to move a finger. Three nobles tackled the crazed man, dropped him to the floor, and disarmed him. One of the men suffered cuts to his arm, and he furiously lashed out at the attacker, kicking him and shouting:

"Easy for you to say, pervert young-boys-lover, for you have not much of a family to care about."

Chaos ensued, and the nobles who had lined up to put down their seals sneaked away.

"Destroy the tablets!" someone shouted, and a group of nobles rushed toward the table.

Blind rage seized Allamu, and without a warning he drew his sword and delivered a fatal slice to the neck of the first one to approach the table.

"You have to pass me first." He raised the bloodstained sword.

The nobles eyed each other, their looks clearly stating: *You go first, I will follow.*

"It's a ruse!" a furious Allamu bellowed. "This messenger, Humbaba, is lying! They're trying to scare you. There is no army outside—probably nothing more than a handful of troops. Our soldiers will go out and massacre them." He walked to his own messenger. "Tell them about the troop numbers out there."

"Sir, do forgive me. I was caught by a group of scouts not far from the city and was brought to General Gungunum. All I could see of the troops in the darkness of night were the ghosts of men, covering the stars at the horizon."

Itching for more blood to soothe his fury, Allamu waved the sword. However, the messenger had his anticipations on full alert, and he bolted away in a brisk run, not wanting his blood to stain the polished floor.

"Kill him!" Allamu barked.

The guards at the door just stood there weighing their options. As the messenger dashed through, they ran—not after, but with him. Seeing the guards gone, the exit streamed with scurrying nobles.

"You have just sworn loyalty to the new king!" Allamu hollered.

"What new king?" a noble yelled back. "Look at him—pale like a ghost, stiff like a corpse."

Hadras was sitting still on the throne, staring at his sandals that glittered with precious stones as if asking them to walk him out of this predicament. He was lost in a trance, which crisscrossed between a dream where he was wearing the crown on his head and a nightmare in which he still wore the crown but it was resting around a neck that carried no head. A mad scream snapped him out of his reverie.

"You crowd of cowards!" Allamu shrieked. "Sargon will butcher all of you, and before he does he'll butcher your families before your very eyes."

No one heeded those words, and the exodus resumed. Though the nobles had no hope of escaping the compound, they just wanted to avoid being caught in the same room with the "new king."

One noble chose a sure way to escape, by stabbing himself in the heart with his own dagger. His spasms of death had not yet ceased when the dagger was ripped out of his chest by the man who had tried to attack Humbaba earlier. The dagger quivered in the hand of its new owner, who trudged toward the throne. Casting a contemptuous look up at the abandoned new king, he screeched:

"You utter fool, whore of a king! Get your stinking arse off the throne!"

Hadras sprang off the throne and pulled his dagger out, expecting an attack. But the noble sliced his own neck instead and folded to the floor, his life draining away slowly, for the slash lacked the depth of a strong resolve.

Watching the man's blood pour, Hadras saw what fate had in store for him. His eyes blinked repeatedly in hopes of waking up from a bad dream, but the grisly scene would not vanish.

"It was a trap, and you fell into it like a fat rat." Hadras staggered down the stairs toward his longtime friend. Then without warning, he darted, flashing his dagger.

Allamu had a gut feeling that kept him alert to such treachery. Swiftly, he dodged the attack and delivered a hard blow to the back of the new king, dropping him to the floor.

Sluggishly, Hadras brought himself up to his knees.

"I was sleeping with not a worry in the world," he whined between sobs, "A soft pillow cuddling my head. You walked me into this mad plot, you son of a bitch. Cursed by that praying mantis whore, now I'm going to lose my head. ... Oh, what sorts of torture await me?"

"At least try to appreciate that girl I gifted you," Allamu answered, standing over him. "You had her sacrificed instead of *her* having you sacrificed. Ungrateful bastard! You dare point a dagger at me ... try to stab me! Without me you're nothing; you'd have had none of the glory given to your *heroics* in battle—coward! One thing I must thank the gods for: *I* don't have to listen to your *fucking fabricated, full-of-bull-dung stories anymore*! As for what awaits you—oh, my friend, your death will be a horrible one. By the gods, I hope they keep me alive long enough to witness it."

With that, Allamu decided to surrender and started walking away.

"I curse you, Allamu, I curse you!" Hadras squealed after him. "May your death be even more horrible than mine!"

MAJESTIC JUSTICE

T HE COURT WAS CROWDED LIKE A MARKET BAZAAR, BUT FOR A few exceptions: the only things on display were haggard faces of men who could only trade looks of anguish while awaiting the arrival of the one grim client: Death, who loved attending this sort of market where an assortment of souls stood poised for grabbing. Another distinguishing feature of this bazaar was silence replacing noise, as though sound had been declared merchandise to be paid for only with excruciating agony.

The place was standing room only, fully packed except for narrow paths at the perimeters and a wider one cutting through the middle, leading to the throne. The men stood at an elbow's distance from each other. Those who had been caught inside the palace compound occupied the front rows.

After the surrender of Allamu, General Gungunum led the troops inside the palace, allowing no one to leave. Soldiers were dispatched to pick up other nobles and officials at their residences. Heralds went through the main streets of the city announcing orders from Sargon for the elites to attend an urgent meeting. Those who could not show up for any reason were advised to disappear from the face of Earth.

All those present were made to suffer a long wait, which added to the pain of standing still in the crowded court—a sort of torture to men accustomed to the best luxuries life could offer.

Fear descended when Humbaba, the Messenger of Doom, walked in, went straight to the front, and shouted: "All stand up."

Since everyone was standing, all they could do was stiffen their postures. Humbaba resumed with the presentation.

"The most revered, valiant, magnanimous ruler of all within the four corners of Earth, from sunrise to sunset—His Majesty, King Sargon!"

Dressed in royal regalia, crown on head and scepter in hand, Sargon made his entrance with four bodyguards trailing behind. Two guards stayed at the bottom of the stairs while the other two followed the king up to take positions behind the throne. Sargon stopped at the top of the stairs and faced his subjects, taking some time before speaking in a tired but relaxed voice.

"Forgive me for having kept you waiting, noble men of Uruk, but I had a little indigestion. I'll try to keep this as brief as possible, for I know you came here on short notice, at an inconvenient time. Some of you"—he glanced at the men in the front—"spent an ample stretch of time here, in the palace, and never had the chance to go back to your families."

He paused and trained sharp stares about the court, as though checking for absentees.

"All of you should be aware by now of the deplorable act committed this last night—the treason—when some plotters dreamed up a plan to dethrone me. What's even more disturbing ... some of you have been fooled and misled into supporting the plot, into believing the pitiful excuse for this treachery. *You*, men whom I trusted to help run the kingdom; *You*, who were supposed to possess the sound mind—the wisdom—demanded for serving the good people of our land. The story claims that *I, the king*, was employing a young, beautiful female assassin to act as a virgin seeking the fulfillment of her vows, only to kill the nobles who were lured into her trap; nobles who were supposedly on a list I made—*a Death List!*"

Sargon waved to the guards at the rear of the court. "Bring the girl."

Three soldiers walked in, carrying what looked like a body wrapped in a bloodstained cloth, an arm dangling out to one side. They climbed the stairs, bowed, and placed the body before the king, then proceeded to unwrap the cloth.

A wave of shock swept the hall at the sight of the girl who had fallen into the grips of death that stole her life but failed to rob her of beauty. Had she not been naked, with dry blood staining her body, one would have thought she was lying sound asleep.

"Is this the girl?" Sargon screamed, looking at Hadras. "The *whore* whom you claimed had killed dozens of nobles. The *assassin* who was about to stab you before the gods intervened and sent the *buzzing fly* to alarm you?"

Hadras nodded.

"Is that a yes? Speak up like a man, not like a bug, so men can hear."

"Yes, that was her, Your Majesty."

"So, this is the ferocious killer who savagely butchered *dozens* of men. Perhaps I should use girls in our armies. ... Guards!"

The guards stood at attention.

"Tomorrow, you will all be dismissed and be replaced with beautiful girls. The kingdom should be safer with them."

The guards let out a collective chuckle before Sargon continued the ridicule. "Likewise, this girl outsmarted *dozens* of wise, learned nobles in whom I had put my trust to run the affairs of the kingdom. This leaves me no choice but to replace everyone standing here with girls."

Again, it was the guards who laughed while the nobles maintained glum expressions.

Sargon resumed, rage fueling his words. "It's a shame for anyone who believed in such a petty excuse for a revolt; an insult, not only to me but to everyone holding a high position. Look at this girl ... the innocence lost to achieve this dirty plot. A beauty—an ardent devotee to our goddess of love; how could such a fragile creature, who has no powers other than to exude love and joy, be rendered as a vile killer—a frantic assassin who spread fear among the powerful nobles of Uruk?" Sargon paused for another round of scrutinizing the audience.

"Bring in the midwives."

Two guards escorting three women walked the middle path to the bottom of the stairs. The women went down on their knees in obeisance to the king.

"Come up the steps," Sargon said softly.

With heads bowed, they went halfway up, when the one at the lead stopped and awkwardly knelt again on the steps. The other two followed suit, kneeling just the same.

"All the way up, honorable ladies. Don't fear."

Upon reaching the top, they were about to kneel next to Mayram's body.

"Don't kneel. You can remain standing."

"Your Majesty, we are not worthy of such generous grace," said the eldest one.

"Nonsense, your faithful service is never fully appreciated. Now, I will ask you some questions, and you will answer in all truth, loud enough so all men can hear. ... Is this the girl you examined a short while ago?"

"Yes, Your Majesty," they answered, almost in unison.

"And what was your finding? Was she a harlot or a virgin?"

"Neither, Your Majesty," the eldest replied.

"Could you explain?"

"Yes, Your Majesty. ... Without a doubt, a harlot she was not. Her virginity she had just lost last night, as can be seen by the distinct virgin blood smears around her vagina. Also, the tightness of her love passage, which the three of us probed, confirms that."

The other midwives concurred with head gestures.

Hadras and Allamu almost screamed in protest, but they knew that would not change anything. Their lips subtly shaped words of disbelief.

"Does anyone in the court have a question for the midwives?"

Only shakes of heads answered Sargon.

"God bless you, honorable ladies. You may leave now." Sargon waved, smiling.

The women bowed and descended the stairs. The shuffling of their footsteps was the only sound to kill a deadly silence made worse by the penetrating gaze of Sargon that blazed the men with anguish.

"Bring the tablets," came the next order from Sargon.

Soldiers walked in with trays of tablets, recently baked dry in the kiln. A wave of fear sent many into a struggle to remain standing on trembling limbs. Beads of cold sweat percolated across the foreheads, keeping cuffs busy at wiping them away.

"My faithful messenger, Humbaba, is going to read the names of those who put their seals on the tablets—men who swore allegiance to the traitor, choosing to go against my rule and against the wishes of the gods who appointed me to be their proxy. These men will be punished for high treason. As for their families, like I promised, they will be left unharmed; nevertheless, they're advised to leave for a faraway place to avoid any reprisals they might incur from the good citizens of Uruk, who are extremely angered by this treachery."

The sound of worry beads clicking against each other echoed throughout the court. Sargon was about to scream to whoever used them to put the beads away, but he reconsidered, for the blending of their sound felt pleasant to his ears.

"If your name is announced, walk to the back and a guard will escort you from there. If for any reason you find it hard to walk, raise your hand and guards will come to assist you out. ... Humbaba, start calling the names from up here."

Humbaba waved for soldiers carrying the incriminating evidence to follow him up the stairs. They stacked the tablets on a small table. Humbaba picked one and started announcing.

"Irra Gazualum,"

The first man to put down his seal in support of Hadras, a cousin of his, walked to the guards; his sentence came as no surprise to him.

"Aha-ab Namtar,"

No one moved or raised his hand.

"Aha-ab Namtar," Humbaba shouted louder. There was only hissing among some men until one volunteered to talk.

"Aha-ab has collapsed to the floor—he must have fainted."

Two guards shouldered their way through the crowd, picked the man up, and dragged him out.

"Ibranum Watrum."

Another noble walked forward slowly, as if trying to prolong the last stroll of his life a few more moments before being squashed like a bug at the hands of beasts. Staring at the floor, he ended up at the bottom of the stairs to the throne.

"Ibranum." Sargon called on him gently. "You're on the wrong path ... again."

Silently, Ibranum turned around to the right path—the way to exit the living world.

By the time the last name on the tablets had been read, two more men had fainted and a few more had to be helped on the way out.

Humbaba turned and bowed to his king.

"Those were all the seals on the tablets, Your Majesty."

With the specter of death departing the court, the men left inside breathed deep sighs of relief. Though their seals were not on the tablets, still, they equally lived the horror suffered by their doomed friends.

The removal of the convicted left the court with a spacious, empty area at the front, while the back remained tightly packed with a large crowd; no one dared move to a zone haunted by the cursed aura of the condemned.

Hadras and Allamu became the only ones standing at the front. As the leaders of the plot, they knew that theirs would be a distinctly gruesome sentence.

"So, do we have all the men who supported the conspiracy?" Sargon asked.

"Your Majesty," Humbaba replied with some reluctance. "I'm afraid there were more."

"Explain. What do you mean by more?"

"Your Majesty, when I entered to deliver the message, there was a line of men who awaited their turn to put their seals on the tablets."

"That makes them just as guilty as those who *did* put down the seal. Humbaba, I know you have a great memory gifted by the gods, not only for remembering messages but also other details—faces among them. Who were those men?"

The room became quiet; even the sound of breathing stopped as death rushed back into the court for the unfinished task.

"First on the line was ... Sargon of Larsa."

"Your Majesty, he is mistaken!" The wail came from the back. "I swear by the gods, I was at a friend's house. Many people in this court saw me there."

"Are you saying Humbaba is a liar?" Sargon hollered, "because he doesn't make mistakes. He has a memory to outlast carvings in stone. I trust this man more than any other. He risked his life in my service, strode into the midst of ferocious enemies all alone, carrying my messages. Walk to the back and face the punishment for your treachery with dignity."

"Your Majesty, Humbaba must be confusing me with another." The man was sobbing while Humbaba shook his head in rebuttal of that claim. "My friends here will testify. I wasn't anywhere close to the palace when—"

"Anyone wants to testify," Sargon interrupted in a menacing voice, "to the truth of what Sargon of Larsa is saying? Speak up!"

No one dared to look up. Be it the truth or a lie, the man's fate was already sealed.

"Not only were you willing to support the conspirators," the king raged, "but now you're trying to spread doubt in my justice! For the last time, if you value the welfare of your family, walk to the back with not a single word more uttered. And I'm warning the rest of you—when you hear your name, walk out silently. No one here—no one—is going to make me doubt the words of my most trusted man. … Humbaba, who else was in that line of traitors?"

When, finally, Humbaba's memory ran out of names, the court stank like an open sewage drain.

"Your Majesty, this concludes all the conspirators."

Now that the shadow of death had vanished, one of the nobles went into a state of euphoria, chanting:

"Long live the magnanimous, the bravest of the brave, our Great King Sargon. May the gods reserve a place for him in heaven among them. O king of this vast Earth from sunrise to sunset, may you live forever and ever."

That opened the gates for a flood of praise by all those whose names did not surface and betray them to a morbid fate. As for the two plot leaders at the front, they could only cast fleeting glances at each other. They wondered not whether their lives were nearing the end, but how horrible the path would be to that end.

Sargon smiled at the mortals who seemed willing to carry him on the throne and place him next to the gods. He waved his hands in a humble gesture to be allowed to speak, but the hails resumed. Nothing he cherished more than being fully ignored while hails glorified his grandeur.

When the throats got tired, he spoke; a serene expression replaced the fury.

"Honorable men of Uruk. Even as I give thanks to the gods who helped foil this plot, I feel deep sorrow that one of the bravest men I know, who led our troops to so many victories, General Allamu, was one of the plot leaders." Sargon looked at him and continued in a sad voice. "You came to me after the city of Ur rebelled to pledge your loyalty, and you volunteered to lead the troops to quell the revolt. You defended your half-sister, Kebboba, as being forced into the rebellion by General Shulgi, asserting that if this was not the case, then you would slay her with your own hands. I appreciated those words of loyalty, yet I was advised to relieve you of your command as general until the rebellion was over. I gave you my solemn assurance that if you chose to stay in Uruk, you were never at risk of retaliation because of your half-sister's actions." Sargon pointed to Hadras. "I believe that this man, this *general* next to you, somehow forced you into this foolish act. ... Allamu, I forgive you of the treason charges, but you cannot be fully pardoned; many of my loyal people were killed. Your punishment will be decided later."

Sargon's face made an abrupt transformation with an angry stare planted on Hadras. "As for you, *dear Hadras*—the general I entrusted with my troops to keep the city secure in these perilous times. Instead of thanking me for this honor, you jumped at the first opportunity to satisfy your greed for powers you couldn't handle. And to use an innocent virgin to justify your dirty scheme ..." Sargon glanced at the inert body of Mayram, whom many in the room envied for her peaceful appearance amidst all the turmoil.

"Her virginity wasn't enough for you; you had to spill the life blood of her pure heart. This beauty was in the spring of her life. Instead of walking and brightening the day of the people around her, now she's dwelling in the darkness of the netherworld. Your treachery pales against your blasphemy. It is the wrath of the goddess Ishtar, whom the girl was serving, that we should fear most. Therefore, your fate was decided by the high priestess of our goddess Ishtar. We pray that your punishment is satisfying enough for the love goddess to forgive our failure in protecting this faithful daughter of hers."

Sargon cast a sad look at Mayram's body. "Tomorrow, the city of Uruk will honor the sacrifice of this precious daughter of ours in a great funeral procession, the kind reserved only for the most honored. May the gods give her soul a favored treatment worthy of her sacrifice. Guards, cover her and carry her gently, as you do the bravest of our soldiers."

The guards draped Mayram in the bloodstained cloth and carried her away with the utmost care.

Sargon reverted to Hadras and spoke with a calm tone that rammed fear harder than his shouting.

"Hadras, I heard of all your exploits and victories in battle. But I'm not one of those who are easily fooled by fake tales made real through wealth—wealth that simply buys the loud mouths that holler and spin lies into facts. I was a general too and know better than the past king of your *brave exploits*. I know how you led your troops … all the way from the very, very rear."

A smirk adorned Sargon's face at nearing the end of the assembly.

"Hadras, tomorrow you will be *honored* by leading the funeral procession … all the way from the very, very rear."

From Sunrise to Sunset
An Angel is Born

THE MULE BRAYED, SHOOK ITS HEAD AND BACKED UP AFTER being driven, yet again, into a rebellious mood. It cursed its destiny to be submissive to the rule of those vertical creatures who exercised absolute control over others much larger in size.

Ellili calmed the mule, offering it hay to chew on. Keeping its mouth busy with food never failed in ending its protests. That allowed him the opportunity to strap the mule with a leather harness, which linked up to a two-wheeled cart behind.

His wife, Warda, came up smiling and planted a fast kiss on his lips.

"Here, beloved, for your trip." Warda handed him a loaf of freshly baked bread and a small jar of beer.

"Trip! It's only a short stroll around the city." He hugged her. "Oh, Warda, this will be one memorable day."

"May the gods make the day short," she said, "for I lack the patience to wait for you."

"And may the gods make the night long, my Warda, for I can never have enough of your love."

Many destinies had taken a swift turn, following the cold-blooded murder witnessed by Ellili.

Once death had snatched Mayram's life, Allamu told Ellili to wrap her body, then left in a hurry with Hadras through the back entrance.

Ellili brought a large sheet of cloth and was about to cover

Mayram when his eyes froze on the dagger she had embraced.

Get the dagger from her. The sickening voice of Hadras after he had stabbed the girl rang back in Ellili's mind, and he recalled not complying with the order. Only then did Ellili come to realize that for the first time in his life he had totally ignored a lord's order. As for Hadras, he must have sensed a murderous rage in Ellili; deferring the punishment of the disobedient slave was the wise thing to do then.

Before wrapping the girl's body, Ellili retrieved the dagger from her congealing blood. Pangs of guilt made his hand tremble for this thievery, and his tears raced down, mixing with the streaks of blood that ran off the mat, and he felt as if it were his own blood that was drained off.

He staggered out to his room. Warda was already back there, lying in bed. Though they slept next to each other, their souls were leagues apart, shrouded in shame after the sanctity of their marriage—the only thing they possessed—had been desecrated by Hadras.

Warda didn't ask Ellili about the girl's fate. She didn't want to know, but she knew something terrible had happened from the sniffling sounds of her husband, who vainly fought off the tears. Sleep did not visit them that night; the brutal events they witnessed had shredded their sleep spirits apart.

Later that same night, the streets stirred with a commotion that seemed too impatient for the dawn's arrival. Heralds screamed messages and soldiers knocked on doors. Yet no one came to Allamu's house. Then, an equally frantic madness recurred in the afternoon, but this time soldiers stormed into the house. They interrogated Ellili about the slain girl. It became obvious to him that Allamu and Hadras had fallen into a deadly trap, with soldiers referring to them as traitors. He felt elation that fate had brought him vengeance when he least expected it. Even though there was the great chance he might be executed as an accomplice, still, he would've knelt at the chopping block wearing a smile, knowing that Allamu and Hadras would face the same fate, if not worse.

When asked about the dagger, Ellili didn't mention anything that would portray the girl as an assassin and thus might help justify his master's actions. He spun a story:

"She handed the dagger over voluntarily to my master, Allamu, upon arriving here. She said it was for scaring derelicts. Later, master Allamu handed the dagger over to Hadras, who used it to stab the girl after he was done violating her."

For the first time in his life, Ellili tasted freedom with his tongue by faking the story. And he didn't stop there but continued, telling the investigator how Hadras violated other women, including his wife, Warda. The bonds of silence that shackled Ellili to the heavy burden of shame were broken.

The soldiers carried away the girl's body and, to Ellili's relief, their chief followed with no intentions of arresting him. Before the man stepped outside, Ellili asked him about the fate awaiting the two traitors.

"They'll wish they never came out of their mothers' wombs alive." The chief laughed on the way out to where a crowd gathered around a body wrapped in bloodstained cloth, on a cart drawn by a donkey.

Watching the cart move away, Ellili had an eerie thought, more like a request from the girl's departed soul, and he was more than happy to oblige. He ran after the cart, went to the chief, and bowed in respect.

"Noble sir, may I ask a favor of you?" To his own amazement, Ellili was asking someone of a high rank to do something for him—for a slave. The words came out of his mouth, making him smile with their sweet taste of freedom. Unconsciously, he carried that smile back to the house—to Warda, who stood by the door. Ellili wrapped his arms around Warda; embraced they remained for a while—two lost souls having found each other.

When the night arrived, Warda dragged her husband up the stairs to the flat roof of the house. Up there, Allamu had a bed he used to sleep in when the nights promised to be cozy with a cool breeze—a luxury enjoyed by those who owned sturdy brick houses. There, in Allamu's bed, Warda and Ellili made love. Their life as man and wife had been miraculously resurrected with blessings from a smiling moon and the vibrant stars of heaven.

The next morning, Warda woke up all excited about this sweeping change in their lives. Allamu and his friend Hadras were soon to meet justice and pay the ultimate price. Warda kept talking about what offerings to make to thank the gods for giving them back the love she had thought was forever lost. Unlike her, Ellili was silently heaving blasphemies on the gods for their cruelty—for denying him the courage to rebel and save the girl from being raped, stabbed, and left to bleed to death. But Ellili could see how thrilled Warda was and her conviction that the gods had a hand in this reversal of their fortunes. So Ellili retreated to his slave self and kept his mouth shut so as not to spoil those moments of happiness, the first his wife had experienced since a time beyond his memories.

They were holding hands when a soldier approached.

"We're about to start. Are you all set here?"

"Yes sir," Ellili answered. "The mule is harnessed and secured to the cart."

"Good." And the soldier shouted to the back, "Men, let's hook him up."

Ellili and his wife turned to watch two guards pushing and pulling on a man who was fully naked, except for a harness made of ropes snaked around his upper thighs, up across the chest, and ending with a loop behind his head. His wrists were tied in front of him. It wasn't an attire fit for an army general or a king, but it seemed like the perfect fit for Hadras.

Upon seeing Ellili and Warda, Hadras jostled the guards, turning around to escape his shame. A soldier ran a thick rope from the rear end of the cart and approached the naked Hadras, who began screaming obscenities that alternated with pleas for mercy, unwittingly luring more of the bystanders, making of himself the main attraction of the funeral procession. Swelling crowds silently watched his desperate whines. The only consolation came from the mule, which grew restless by the commotion and started braying as if in solidarity with the protests of the other harnessed creature—the human who thrashed about until a guard shoved him violently—and Hadras fell face down. The soldiers tied the rope from the cart to the loop behind his head, then turned him face up. Hadras opened his eyes just as a glop of spit landed on his face.

"Ellili!" Hadras screamed.

"Yes, *my lord*, Ellili at your service. I've been given the honor of guiding your cart. Pardon me, but I was sure you would love my idea for a joyous stroll around the city. Well, King Sargon himself gave it his blessing. Then there was this other idea that occurred to me of having you handsomely dressed up. You look majestic in ropes, *my lord*."

"Ellili, you worthless slave, son of—" Hadras shrieked, but a kick to his belly left the heavy curses with no air to carry them out.

"Shut your mouth!" an enraged Ellili roared. "Do not speak unless you're given permission!"

A guard held Ellili back, ushering him to return to his place.

Hadras was still recovering his breath when an eerie silence, followed by hushed whispers, took over the crowd. A man who would be the first to be recognized in the busiest Uruk market approached, adding more thrill to the spectacle without doing or saying a thing.

"Humbaba!" Hadras squealed. "Son of pigs! Of all the hideous faces on Earth, it is yours I have to behold on my way to the netherworld!"

"Oh how mistaken you are, *honorable King Hadras*," Humbaba mocked, leaning down over him. "The 'son of pigs' label is rightfully yours today."

Humbaba stepped over a knee-high block of a tree trunk, encircled by an audience clambering like ants over each other. Guards pushed back to maintain some clearance around the roped man who had occupied the king's throne for a fleeting fragment of a day.

"Honorable citizens of Uruk," the greatest of the heralds started.

The crowd came to silence like they always did when hearing such an articulate and powerful voice coming from an abhorrently disfigured face.

"Today we—"

"Fuck you, Humbaba!" yelled Hadras, expelling all the air in his lungs. "Ugly son of a whoring, demon bitch!"

The crowd broke into laughter, and Humbaba joined them. He was immune to such insults, having heard them his whole life; some with sharp blades carving at his neck.

"We are here for the funeral of a beautiful flower—Mayram. Her life was brutally cut short when she innocently fell into the clutches of this monster, Hadras, while trying to fulfill her sacred vows. This traitor attempted to use her to justify a treacherous plot to overthrow our Great King Sargon—the most generous gift from the gods bestowed upon this kingdom. Vile ploys like this, that defy the will of the gods, are doomed to one final destiny: utter failure.

"This plot greatly enraged the gods. A dire calamity they will deliver to our city if we fail to severely punish this criminal and all his accomplices for their cowardly scheme to gain power, and for the heinous act committed against Mayram, the devoted daughter of our love goddess."

Hadras was struggling with the ropes as if there was still hope of an escape, when Humbaba turned to him and hollered:

"Criminal and heretic, Hadras! For the death of our innocent daughter Mayram, and for high treason against the kingdom, our Great King Sargon, and our gods—you are hereby sentenced to be dragged by the mule to the rear of this funeral. You will follow the procession to our daughter's resting place, then shall continue to be dragged through the streets of the city you betrayed till your bones scatter free and leave your soul searching for your strewn body parts for eternity."

Humbaba waved and shouted, "Start the procession!"

ᛁ ♢ ᛤ ᭦ ᛁᛁᛁ

The marchers assembled outside the grand temple of Ishtar. They were led by a larger-than-life statue of the goddess, standing atop a platform carried by fourteen royal guards. Right behind came Princess Enheduanna, dressed in white to represent the royal family, followed by seven rows of virgins in pairs, dressed in blue, the color to symbolize the purity of the skies no human could touch. Then came the coffin on another platform carried by twelve soldiers. The box was made of the finest cedar wood, rumored to have been taken from storage in Hadras' residence.

People arrived in throngs as the morning progressed, and before long, the flowers they brought wreathed the coffin, making its cedar wood blossom with a fury of nature's colors that took flight with the slightest breeze, sending delicate petals to adorn the soldiers below.

Trailing the coffin platform came a group of priestesses, uttering prayers in whispers. Those were followed by the professional mourners, whose skills in wailing and imparting praise for the dead were highly sought in any funeral. To their rear came singers and musicians carrying harps, lyres, flutes, and drums, singing to the rhythm of sad melodies.

The front of the procession, with all its color, attracted the most spectators until word circulated about the convict getting roped at the far end, and a human wave sped in that direction, leaving mostly the old and lethargic spectators at the front.

𒀝 ◇ 𒁲 𑀯 𒐕

Outside the temple, Lubalanda stood watching. He seemed out of place, lost in memories of the events that had thoroughly changed his life once his heart was snared by a love that wouldn't relax its clutches on him even after Mayram had confessed to being an assassin. In fact, sparing his life made him love her even more.

Poignantly, he recalled the heavy tears she'd cried while revealing how he had unknowingly freed her from the murderous demon that possessed her, replacing it with a passion for life in all its beauty. Then she'd begged him to leave Uruk out of fear for his life. But he allayed her fears:

"Ibrahem could've sent me killers instead of the thieves who stole the goddess I crafted. Yet, he must be aware of cases where killers developed the bad habit of returning to extort—even kill—the ones who hired them. ... Eventually, I'll leave the city, but I don't perceive the urgent need for it."

"You are a fool!" Mayram lashed out at him as though he were a reckless, disobedient child. "Do you think my failure is the end of it?

Ibrahem has far better reasons to kill you now than because of that goddess he certainly stole. And unlike before, he is greatly favored by the king now; he would not fear an extorting assassin. Probably he has already hired one to strike you."

And like a scolded child forced into reason, the next day Lubalanda went into hiding in the house of a trusted friend, who helped him expedite the selling of the statues and all his possessions for whatever price they fetched.

Lubalanda came back from that sweet memory when a surge of excitement swept the crowd as the soldiers carrying the coffin platform started marching in short strides.

"Pardon me, lady," he asked a middle-aged woman next to him. "What is this procession for?"

"It's the funeral for the innocent girl killed by the leader of the plot to overthrow King Sargon. You do know about the plot!"

"Of course I know." Lubalanda nodded. "Not the details, though. I'm moving out of Uruk and have been very busy for the last few days selling my possessions. A new life awaits me with my soon-to-be wife."

"How wonderful." The woman smiled. "May the gods bless you with many children."

"Thank you," he replied joyfully.

Two days ago, Mayram had left him to spend some time with certain relatives before leaving Uruk. She was supposed to meet him by the temple at sunrise. Her lateness agitated him.

She must be somewhere around, distracted by the festive scene. Probably joined the crowd that for some reason rushed all the way to the rear. She should be here at any moment.

Searching for her, he surveyed the surrounds till his sight settled on the pile of flowers covering the coffin.

"This is one lavish funeral," he said to the same woman. "The girl—was she a close relative of the king?"

"No. She was no relation to the king, just a poor girl from some-where up north. I think they said ... Babylon. I'm not sure." The woman turned to a man standing behind. "The girl in the box, wasn't she from Babylon?"

Lubalanda felt the ground under him tremble.

"Yes, she was a beauty from Babylon," replied the man. "Her name was something like … Mariam or Maryan. That bastard—the one roped to the donkey at the back, he ravaged then killed her. He claims she was an assassin who killed many nobles and tried to kill him too."

Lubalanda grew dizzy. The ground under him was spinning fast, and he sank to his knees.

The woman rushed to his side. "What happened? Are you sick?"

Two men came to help. "Must be the sun. Let's take him to a shaded area."

𒀸 𒅛 𒐈

"Can you help a hungry man, sir, and I will pray for the gods to shower blessings and happiness on you."

Lubalanda had no idea how he had ended up sitting under a tree outside Ishtar's temple, next to a beggar. But that wasn't his main concern.

"She's on her way … she'll be here, soon," he answered the beggar, while his blank stare followed soldiers carrying a platform of flowers.

𒌋 𒍝 𒐊 𒊏 𒐈

The mule began braying again, sensing the workday was about to start.

"Someone will take my place before sunset," Ellili said, hugging Warda.

"The sunset I will worship today." She kissed him on the cheek.

Ellili yanked on the reins. The mule resisted first, then relented, pulling on the cart. Behind the cart, Hadras was on his feet when the attached rope tugged on the loop. He followed to keep some slack. His strength was already depleted by the shame and the awareness of his insufferable path to the netherworld. After a handful of steps, he twisted his ankle on a stone, lost his balance, and fell on his back with no hope of standing unassisted. The cart pulled slowly on the loop, which had been run so as not to choke him while dragging him backward. He watched the standing crowd pass by, sniggering at him and chanting:

"Hadras, Hadras—horned demons await to gore you—'n hell's fire they'll roast your arse."

Hadras closed his eyes, wishing he could shut his ears too, when a blast of sharp pain erupted in his groin. Through the surge of tears in his eyes, he recognized the woman who had anchored herself with both feet on his midsection: Warda. Twice more, the ex-slave jumped and trampled on his manhood before stepping off. His screams dissipated amid the cheering crowd, who urged Warda to bounce on him again. She refrained, though, fearing he might black out and escape his misery. She followed at his side, staring at him with a rage that the flow of time never extinguished, when a guard approached and asked her to join the crowd.

The pain in Hadras' groin faded, only to be replaced by a burning sensation with the skin peeling off his back. He was crying, occasionally throwing curses whenever he could squeeze a few words between the waves of torture rippling through him. Eventually, his desperation had him pray to the gods for a swifter end. As if the gods responded with a demand to be satisfied, he frantically started to search the faces surrounding him until he found her.

He looked at Warda intently with tears begging forgiveness; it was the last task he was asking of her. And like the obedient servant she was, Warda complied. Tears washed the flares of anger off her eyes, replacing them with pity. Then she turned and walked away from the scene—without asking Hadras for his permission.

𒌋 ◇ 𒀸 ∿ 𒐗

Peace and quiet crawled along the vicinity of the temple, capturing the territory from the noise that retreated with the procession crowd.

"That can't be Mayram," Lubalanda said to the dozing beggar, who had gone to sleep after giving up on getting anything from the madman next to him. "There must be dozens upon dozens of Mayrams in the city, visiting from Babylon."

He sat watching from a distance as the flowers became a jumbled patch of colors, when a figure parted from the crowd and walked down the road—a girl. Her dress was coated with roses, and with her lithe walk she painted the air around her in rainbow colors.

O merciful goddess, is that my beloved? … It is her!

Lubalanda sprang to his feet and tried to run, but his legs betrayed him, so he limped as fast as he could.

Mayram looked cheerful, but she was shaking her head, somehow dismayed. He was laughing when he reached her, and as he hugged her he began to cry.

"Why are you crying?" she asked.

He told her about the silly thought he had had—that she was gone.

"Oh, my love, you're such a fool," she whispered, stroking his hair. "And what is truly silly is *you*, sitting there, forlorn, surrounded by beggars while a glorious procession is taking place down the road. Come, my love, let's go join the merry crowd."

Lubalanda held her hand tightly to make sure not to lose her. He was so excited to tell her about their future together once they left Uruk; the house he would build for her and her parents, whom she held so dear to her heart. But that could wait—he would tell her later, after the end of the procession.

⚲ ◇ ⛿ ⩹ Ⅲ

The wailing and chest-beating by the professional mourners didn't sit well with the crowd on that beautiful spring day, with its sun veiled behind a thin haze of clouds and a gentle breeze forcing cheeks into a smile. Soon, some young people began a happy song, bringing frowns from some but cheers from others. Before long, the victor in this duel between the two contending squads was decided when a larger group erupted into a joyful chorus, changing the grim funeral ambiance to one of a jovial grand wedding. Dancing and clapping of hands drowned the wails of the professional mourners, who were shouted at to shut up and leave as though they were some unwelcome intruders.

The actors of grief fell to silence, but only briefly, till one of them joined the happy throng in song. Within moments, the rest of his troupe did the same, and the contagious festive celebration caught up to the whole procession, exploding in a loud, joyous parade, from the very front with its soldiers and virgins all the way back to Ellili.

Even Hadras, with eyes half-open looking at shadows of heaven, started having visions of gods happily singing to welcome him among them. His numb body drifted in and out of consciousness as it rocked over the ground. Soon, all sensations fully abandoned him, and he closed his eyes, never to wake up again.

𒑐 ◇ ⊐ ᨓ 𒐆

The throbs of the crowd's enchantment reached Lubalanda, who was gaining distance as he limped and looked around for his love. She had disappeared again. How had she escaped with him holding so tightly to her hand?

There was so much to talk about: he would teach her how to read, write, and help him in his trade. He would take her on the trip he always dreamed of, to Phoenicia and the ocean beyond, which extended to the far ends of Earth, spanning lands blessed with an abundance of stones of all sorts and colors. He would pick his own stones instead of having to work with whatever those traders brought. … But, where had she gone?

Worry deterred him from walking, and he sat on the ground, despair chasing his dreams away, when a figure separated from the crowd. His heart leapt and picked him up. It was her, dancing and singing when she approached him.

He limped again toward her, laughing, and as he reached to hug her he began to cry.

"Why are you crying?" she asked.

He told her about the silly thought he had had—that she was gone.

"Oh, my love, you're such a fool," she whispered, stroking his hair. "And what is truly silly is *you*, hunkering down, alone and gloomy, when there is all that singing and dancing. You're missing one boisterous celebration of life while brooding about death. Come, my love, let's go join the merry crowd."

He squeezed her hand to make sure she would not leave him again.

𒀭 ◊ 𒑰 ⩜ 𒐗

The numbers of people doubled and tripled until at some point it looked as if the whole city had been ordered by royal decree to join the celebration. Then the word went out that the celebrated girl was not going to descend to the netherworld; Ishtar had intervened and given her sanctuary in the heavens with an assigned task as Guardian of the Virgins. The crowd's jubilation went into such a frenzy with this revelation that when they approached the cemetery, a protest flared up. People were shouting that her soul was dancing over the procession, out of joy with her divine assignment, and she didn't want the celebrations to end that early. A large crowd blocked the entrance to the burial ground, and insisted on extending the procession. Everyone roared in support, forcing the heavily outnumbered guards to heed the demand. And the jubilant marchers streamed down another path, away from the abode of the dead toward the life of the city.

𒀭 ◊ 𒑰 ⩜ 𒐗

Lubalanda limped along till they caught up to the tail of the procession, and they mingled with the partying crowd. He was telling Mayram about the bright times awaiting them and how they would be the happiest family on Earth, blessed by the goddess with many children. But it was so loud, she couldn't hear a word. He led her away from the noisy lot, but just as he turned she was gone. He walked back, searching for her among the jubilant faces, but to no avail. In desperation, he started screaming out her name at the top of his voice. Everyone looked at him as if he had lost his mind, keeping a good distance away from him. Then, right in that small territory allotted to the madman, she appeared.

Though he was angry, joy had Lubalanda laugh after seeing her smile. He staggered toward her, embraced her tightly, and began to cry.

"Why are you crying?" she asked.

He told her about the silly thought he had had—that she was gone.

"Oh, my love, you're such a fool," she whispered, stroking his hair. "And what is truly silly is *you*, getting mad and grim amid all the happy faces surrounding you. Come, my love, let's sing, dance, and enjoy this day as if it were the last of our lives."

$\mathbf{\chi\ \diamondsuit\ \boxminus\ \vee\hspace{-2pt}\vee\ |||}$

A warm breeze of soothing mist, bringing with it nostalgic memories of the departed, haunted the air when the coffin finally came to rest on the flowers bedding the grave. The hired mourners found themselves obsolete again; now there was real wailing and real tears shed by everyone who had endured that long, wandering walk to the burial ground as they gave their last respects to a girl none of them knew, one who had become close to the gods and yet chose to spend the whole day celebrating with them. They would smile whenever their memory carried them back to that heartwarming day when an angel was born in their city.

$\mathbf{\chi\ \diamondsuit\ \boxminus\ \vee\hspace{-2pt}\vee\ |||}$

The sun slipped below the thin clouds to lean on the horizon, shooting the last of its rays through the ether in a futile attempt to cling to the heavens and save the day from drowning in the quick sands of night.

The only sound to be heard at the burial grounds was the whisper of ghosts, carried by the breeze, welcoming the new dweller. Soon, that peaceful setting was disrupted when, out of the shadows of the invading darkness, a harsh sound of uneven footsteps brought an eerie, uninvited noise. A lone figure, a living form with flesh and blood still warm, walked cautiously as if trying to spy on the secrets of the dead.

Lubalanda fell to his knees and went still like a headstone over the pile of flowers that covered the loose earth beneath. He felt pity for all those flowers; their brief lives cut even shorter, their beauty and color soon to be a thing of the past, hardly enjoyed, slowly withering away no matter how hard they tried to ward off death with their sweet fragrance.

His hands brushed over the tender petals, feeling their young lives drift away. He wanted to console them—give them a reason why their lives had come to such an abrupt end. Mayram would've known better than him, but she wasn't there. Why had she left him again?

She must be exhausted after all that walking and dancing … that's why she left. Or perhaps she's playing a game; hide under this pile of flowers, then spring up to surprise me.

Gently, he began to sweep the flowers away, layer by layer, one section at the time, expecting the roses to fly in his face as Mayram leapt on him … and he would laugh, then cry at the silly thought that she was …

At one point, his hands touched the dirt. Strangely, and just like he could feel the gods' presence through the stones, he felt faint throbs through the ground.

It's the pulse of a beating heart! She's in the box, alive! They buried her alive! … All those fools, walking next to her all day—how could they not tell she's still alive?

Frantically, with bare hands, he went digging at the dirt.

"Yes my love, it's me, Lubalanda; I'll get you out. Soon you will be safe in my arms. I will never let go of you again. Never!"

Lubalanda dug and dug until his strength was spent without much to show for it. He sat back on his knees, legs folded under him, head bowed in a trance of despair.

Under the moonlight that danced between the hazy clouds, a flower petal started trembling, and Lubalanda caught sight of it. He stopped breathing.

There she is, readying herself to pounce on me.

He waited, but nothing ensued save the delicate shifting of the petals. He leaned down for a closer look.

"A worm … nothing but a worm," he moaned, and raised his head to the heavens. "Nothing but a slender, slithering worm. Oh, you— you witty, devious gods." And he burst into a fit of laughter, then collapsed on his face, hugging the flowers, watering them with the surge of his sorrows.

Why are you crying? the roses asked.

He couldn't offer more than tears for an answer.

The warm tears alerted the earth about the inert being on its surface—a man who could feel the gods' presence in his stonework. Then the earth sensed the beats of his heart that longed for a lost love. Feeling pity for the man, the earth relayed his despair to the angel who sought sanctuary in its embrace for a short respite before she commenced her journey to the heavens. A subtle reply reverberated to the earth's surface, stirring the air above into a sad wind that gently stroked Lubalanda's hair as it mournfully whispered in his ears.

"Oh, my love, you're such a fool. All alone in this graveyard, long after the sun has set; even the ghosts are mocking you. … Oh, beloved, stop searching, stop looking for this other fool … she's forever gone."

Harvest Games

T HE PALM TREES STOOD TALL, PROUDLY CARRYING CLUSTERS OF young green dates that started to acquire a hint of yellow. The sunrays from the god Shamash would slowly cook them to ripen from their smooth, polished-skin texture to one that was dull brown and wrinkled with age, to be readily savored by the people for their sweet-as-honey taste. One ancient fable related that if it weren't for the dates, humans would've never settled there to start a civilization.

Harvest season was more than a moon away—too far to give the palm trees much attention, yet large clusters of humans gathered in the grove. It wasn't the shade under the long fronds they sought but the contest that was about to start. They amassed outside a roped area comprising the tallest group of trees and watched the competing teams of soldiers clothed in loose garb, tightly folded over around the waist, thus leaving their legs free to climb the trees.

The crowd buzzed in anticipation. Some were singing praise for the harvest god, while many loudmouths argued about the nature of the games. Days earlier, heralds had announced the time and place of an exhilarating, yet unspecified event, leaving the people going wild with the guessing game.

The commotion quieted down with the arrival of a lavish chariot, tailed by a line of other chariots carrying archers, swordsmen, and spearmen. All the soldiers who were to compete stood at attention and saluted the arriving company.

King Sargon stepped off his chariot and ascended the platform that had been erected for the best viewing. After taking his seat, his chief of guards, Hukura, proceeded to address the spectators from the same platform.

"Honorable citizens of Uruk. The Great King Sargon"—he followed with an extensive list of honorifics—"welcomes you to this thrilling new event. Before we start the games, His Majesty would like to say a few words."

Sargon stood and waved to the loud hails of the multitude, who repeated and expanded on the honorifics cited by Hukura in glorifying the king.

"Great people of Sumer," Sargon blared, and a surge of praise reverberated back to him. "I know it is too early for the harvest games, yet this harvest is so unique, it cannot wait. But first, I have a short poem to share with you, and it will be followed by the games. I hope you will enjoy both."

The place went silent, giving the birds a brief opportunity where they could whistle to the music of the breeze. Sargon cleared his throat and sang out loud:

"Sumerians: the gods blessed us with might, wealth, and pride.
But beware those amongst us who breed infighting—strive to divide.
Cowardly, they ensnare the vulnerable into their treachery whilst
they hide.

"I, Sargon, ruler of the lands from sunrise to sunset,
With eagle eyes can track them—who spread dissent and unrest.
Stained by evil their heads, hard to conceal, ripe and ready for harvest."

Sargon surveyed the crowd, as though in search of prey like the eagle in his poem, then bellowed, "Let the games begin!"

The people cheered when soldiers rushed behind the platform and went into a frenzy, removing palm fronds that covered long sticks of tree trunks spanning over a large pit in the ground. Packed at the bottom were the nobles convicted of treason, scantily dressed in rags covering their genitals, with ropes binding their arms to their sides.

Soldiers walked down a ramp into the pit, grabbed the first two prisoners, and brought them up.

Two teams of three soldiers each stood ready, circling their designated trees. On the floor around each tree were three large rings of heavy rope with a thick cushion of cloth stitched to each one, forming a modest seat harness that would tether each man to the tree on his climb.

Sargon raised his hand up and kept it there, teasing the impatient crowd. Then a burst of excited cries thundered simultaneously as he dropped his hand to officially start the games. In a flash, the first soldier of each of the opposing teams slipped inside his rope, adjusted the cushion seat on his behind, and hurried into a fast climb. His two teammates followed in pursuit, one after the other ascending the tree trunk where the fronds were stripped off. Each soldier pushed with his feet on the rounded ribs, slackening the belt, then climbing a step as he slid the belt up before leaning back on the cushion, all in one rapidly executed move. That was repeated all the way up to where all three men on the team had passed a designated height above a cloth marker wrapped around the tree. Then, all three men joined forces to tug on a rope that one of them had hauled along on the climb up.

Down below, the end of the rope was already wrapped and knotted tightly by a ground crew to the joined feet of a prisoner, who suddenly felt a strong jerk on the rope before starting to rise feetfirst into the air. The screams of terror from the two prisoners joined those of a frantic crowd that hollered and urged the teams to pull harder.

The doomed were yanked up until each one came to a point near the lowest soldier, the only one in his team equipped with a sword. While his companions held on to the rope, the swordsman mercilessly delivered chopping blows to the prisoner's neck, severing the head. Then the rope was let go and the body plummeted to the ground after the head. The three soldiers then raced down the tree. The team that landed first qualified for the next round of savagery.

The bodies of the two slain men were dumped back into the pit, where the rest of the condemned looked on in shock. The heads were taken to a clearing for the crows to peck at.

Two other teams, from a total of twenty-four, took their positions around the same trees. Two more of the condemned, close to faint after witnessing what was to be their fate, were brought up and prepared for their part in the game. Meanwhile, some spectators started their own game—wagering bets on a team to win.

Twelve teams passed to the second round, which proceeded without any major incidents, aside from the occasional slips on the bloodstained trees. The worst of those happened when a soldier lost his footing on the way up and dropped onto his lower partner. The two kept sliding down until their belts caught a rough rib on the tree trunk. To everyone's admiration, they managed to climb back to the top and finish the task despite losing the game.

The third round began with six teams left. This round went at a slower pace, and the crowd grew less enthusiastic after getting accustomed to the routine of heads rolling and bodies crashing.

One of the teams was ahead of the other when the swordsman pulled his weapon. But just as he swung his sword, the prisoner, driven by a sudden instinct to escape certain death, twisted his body violently. The soldier in the middle lost his grip on the rope, which put the full weight on the man above, forcing him to let go of the burden. The doomed man began falling just as the sword caught his neck. The swordsman lost his balance and released the sword while slipping awkwardly down the tree with the belt slowing his fall. He landed next to the prisoner, who was in the throes of death with a sword embedded in his neck. Despite the multiple cuts and bruises, the swordsman was glad to walk away, even though his team was out of the contest. The crowd applauded them all the same, for they had brought the thrill back to the game.

The blunders continued with the next team climbing that same tree, as if that tree were protesting having more than its share of spilled blood. With a prisoner high enough for the slaughter, the swordsman let go of the rope to reach for his weapon, taking short moments to catch his breath. But those moments proved too long for the top man, whose strength had reached its limits, and the rope began to slip, searing his hands, which led the man in the middle to suffer the same ordeal. Soon, one of them released the rope and the other followed instantly. The prisoner found himself rescued from the sharp blade, but he did not thank his lucky stars; he shrieked in panic, free-falling from a height that would break his bones. He was crying in agony after hitting the ground, while the three soldiers above cursed and blamed each other for their elimination from the competition. Their entertaining exchange carried on until the three were ordered to come down the tree by the chief of guards, Hukura. The prisoner was screaming out his unbearable pain when Hukura approached Sargon.

"What to do with this one?"

"Hmm, I feel kind of merciful. He can keep his head," Sargon said after a sip of wine.

Hukura grabbed a spear from a soldier on the way to the prisoner. He stabbed him in the heart, twisting the spear.

Noise enjoyed a well-deserved respite, but with those mishaps spicing up the event, the audience roared back to life.

Three teams qualified for the final fourth round. They were assigned three fresh trees, unstained with blood. With six doomed traitors left, each team would have to pull two of them consecutively.

Exhaustion was apparent on the faces of the nine soldiers. Slowly they climbed, taking breaks to catch their breath. Though no blood coated the trees, their footing was unsure, and they slipped more often. Upon reaching their positions above the marker, they took more time to rest, leaning back on the belts. The crowd was losing patience, exhorting the teams to press on, with the occasional scourging remarks by a few.

It was a while before one of the teams began to pull their captive up at an excruciatingly slow pace, which prompted the other two teams to do the same. It was torture at both ends of the rope; the soldiers were praying for the game to end, to go down and lie on solid ground. As for the condemned, it was a crawl of terror to meet the sharp edge of a sword under the flailing blades of the palm trees. Eventually, those first three of the six remaining prisoners were relieved from that terror, with their heads resting on the ground and bodies sprawled close by.

The last three of the condemned trembled violently as they watched the headless bodies being freed from the same rope that would hoist them up in an ascent leading to the netherworld. Their cries for mercy found no sympathy from a horde of fellow humans frenzied by the spectacle of death.

In this decisive round, the prize for each soldier of the winning team would be the home of his choice that had once belonged to an executed conspirator. However, this great incentive couldn't work its magic on the fatigued competitors. Unmoved by the urging of the crowd, they leaned back on their belts, their only motivation to resume the task hinged on one of the rivals to initiate the pulling.

After a long repose, one team bellowed a battle cry and started tugging. Their opponents followed, grappling with whatever leftover energy they had, hollering a battle roar of their own.

The crowds cheered at this sudden explosion of effort after the long lull, and fresh bets were wagered as the doomed felt the yanking at their feet that started the race up the trees. But the cheering didn't last too long, for no sooner had the prisoners' heads cleared the ground than the pulling slowed to a slug's crawl, gradually coming to a complete halt, and the drained soldiers looped the rope ends around the trees.

Muscles now all cramped up and bodies protesting against their fighting will, the soldiers found themselves leaning back again on their belts. They were tempted to quit, but going down without finishing the job in this final round would be a disgrace. They envied the ones who had lost in the earlier rounds and left with their dignity intact instead of looking like squirrels sitting idle atop a palm tree.

None of them had thought it would turn out to be this hard. They were the best fighters, strong and fit, but all of this climbing and rope pulling was never a part of their everyday training; skills in swinging swords and throwing spears were of no use in this battle.

"Loop the rope around your necks and jump," a scornful voice shouted from below, which spurred a hail of jeers and biting comments.

"Are you waiting for the dates to ripen up for harvest?" mocked another.

"Just think of the noble as a naked virgin, then let your hard shaft do the pulling!" And a roaring swell of laughter ensued.

Sargon was at a loss, trying to keep his calm. The whole thing had turned from a show of brutal force into a hilarious mockery. Many of the competitors he knew personally from among his royal guards, and he didn't have the heart to punish them to save face.

Hukura was aware of the king's dilemma and he took the initiative, ordering the archers to stand ready with arrows aimed at the competitors. He walked to the trees and hollered:

"If you want to be called soldiers, then act like soldiers! Finish your mission before you come down, or it is the arrows that will bring you down for this disgrace!"

The specter of looming death, successfully added to the incentive of the house prize, and infused some strength into the men's muscles. All three teams resumed pulling, their moans of pain reaching the heavens.

The condemned rose painfully slow, with the uppermost only an arm's length higher than a standing man, when a shriek of agony erupted out of a swordsman. His partner at the top reacted instantly and tossed the loose end of the rope, winding it around the tree just before the swordsman blacked out briefly and went plunging downward. The belt broke his fall as it slid erratically around the ribs of the tree trunk until soldier and belt tangled with the prisoner hanging below. Though badly hurt, the swordsman struggled to break free of his belt, and he managed to slide out toward the comforting ground. With excruciating pain, he limped away, leaving behind the hanging man he was supposed to butcher. The convict remained in a state of absolute terror; now that the treetop was out of reach, he agonized over the subsequent barbaric method they would elect to slaughter him.

The injured soldier's two companions started descending the tree, thinking they were disqualified, when a bellowing voice stopped them like a hammer nailing their belts into place.

"Real soldiers don't run from battle when a fellow soldier is injured," Hukura barked up, angrily. "Your mission is not complete!"

The other two teams, finding an excuse in the misfortune afflicting their competitors, had already stopped pulling, their rope ends also wrapped around the trees, but that wait had robbed their bodies of the last will to fight. They leaned on their belts and enviously watched the long palm leaves above, fluttering free, breezing with life.

"This is your last chance," Hukura raged, "or I swear by the gods, after we drop you, you will be sharing that same burial pit with the criminal traitors."

The shamed warriors could only cast blank stares at the headless corpses piled in the pit below, while arrows laced with death stared at them; an end they never anticipated. They entered the competition, driven by the house award and their egos, yet, humiliation was all they harvested at the top of the trees.

A short lull followed before an answer descended.

"Sir, we tried our best, but we admit defeat. And like defeated soldiers, we accept death for we failed His Majesty and the people of the city. Do send the arrows our way and get our humiliating disgrace over with."

Hukura flew into a rage, shouting, "Your Majesty. Awaiting your order to shoot down those who have failed you!"

Eyes shifted between the archers and the trees. No one had seen this coming: executioners, about to be executed.

A look of deep concern shadowed Sargon's face as he listened to the advice of the chirping crickets, the only creatures who dared speak to him in those tense moments. Stoically, out of the chair he rose and stood firm.

"Lower your arrows!" he commanded.

Hukura almost protested but kept it to himself.

"People of Sumer," Sargon went on, "those men are some of the bravest I have ever known. They have served this kingdom with honor, and they would never hesitate to lay down their lives for its glory. If fate brought this disgrace upon them today, I shall not allow it to rob them of the glory they have brought to our kingdom. And by the gods, I will not have faithful men slain like some traitors. The disgrace is upon those who forget someone's entire intrepid past, only to condemn him for one slight mishap."

Sargon sat back on his chair. Hukura didn't need any more instructions, and he hollered up the trees.

"You can come down."

"Shall we let loose the ropes, sir?" one soldier asked.

"Leave them hanging for now." Hukura chose to leave that decision to Sargon.

Once the soldiers touched solid ground, the prisoner hanging highest began to scream, pleading.

"O Greatest of all Kings from sunrise to sunset. May the gods bless you with eternal life, and may you listen to what they have to say. This is a sign from them to forgive. In the name of the Almighty Anu and all his children, I beg you to heed their wish, and you will be rewarded generously in this life and the afterlife."

Sargon remained seated, massaging his braided beard as he mulled over how to save face after the disastrous end to the event. He knew killing his soldiers would not have made things better; on the contrary, it would have angered other soldiers. While deliberating with himself, Hukura approached him.

"The soldiers you just pardoned want to talk to you."

The men were already on their knees before the platform.

"O Great King," the eldest spoke loud enough for most to hear. "How can we express our gratitude for not having us executed like criminals? Your grace and generosity are immeasurable. Yet, chief Hukura is right: our disgrace is unforgivable. This failure will stain our honor for the rest of our lives and follow us to the grave. It will haunt our families for generations to come. All of us here beseech you to give us the chance to wash this shame away with our own blood. Give us swords; let us fight right here to the death and depart this life like soldiers, with your blessings and the gods' blessings."

After a bout of meditation on their mad request, Sargon rose up and spoke.

"Stand up! Bold warriors like you should never go on their knees while others stand. Yes, stand up with pride. ... You speak of disgrace where I can only see gleaming bravery, loyalty—honor. I know many of you, and I know of no other fighters in this world who could've shown more valor. So, how dare you talk to me of disgrace? Your request is denied."

"Your Majesty," the eldest cried out, "I was always obedient when I served under you. Now, I beg you to reconsider and not deny our request." He pulled the sword they had used on the prisoners and put it to his own throat. "Our shame will have to die here with us. We are not carrying it out of here—out to our families. I hate to disobey you, but when it comes to honor, Your Majesty leaves me no choice."

A man from the other team followed with the same threat with his sword. The other six, who had no weapons, closed around their mates, staunchly showing their resolve in picking up the swords once they became available.

The whole crowd was dazed; just when they thought it was about time to leave, the intense event continued to reshape itself.

Sargon himself was speechless. The killing of Naplanam was giving him bad dreams, and the last thing he wanted was to have some of his best men die under his nose. He was wrestling with his dilemma when all eyes shifted to a man who limped toward the platform while supporting his weight on a sword. It was the soldier who had fallen down the tree in the last effort to pull.

"O Majesty," the injured man blared, "I humbly ask not to be denied the honor of dying with my brothers, for I contributed more than my own share to this failure."

Sargon gripped the railing of the platform and shook his head in genuine disbelief. Silence prevailed, except for the gentle rustling of palm fronds.

Slowly, Sargon raised his arms high and thundered, "O gods of heaven, was this your doing? Did you cause these men to fail in a cruel test of their valor?" He reverted to the soldiers. "O mighty warriors who seek and invite death: you honor your families, the whole city, and the vast kingdom for having brave men like you. No king nor god has the right to deny you this celebration, this privilege of a glorious death. O fearless heroes, as I bid you farewell, I swear by the gods that you will be forever remembered for your courage, for the life you gift to the greatness of mighty Uruk and the kingdom. … Let them fight until only one is left standing. Give these valiant men the swords that will glisten in pride with their glorious blood."

With swords in their possession, the eight soldiers paired off for the fight. The injured one found himself on his own.

"Sir, I challenge you to a fight," he shouted to the chief of guards.

Hukura frowned in surprise, but only briefly. It was obvious what the man wanted.

"And I accept your challenge, brother. It's a great honor to fight a brave warrior like you."

Everyone, including the other fighters, had their eyes locked on the aching soldier, who stood with the aid of his sword planted in the ground.

"Brother," he said, facing the fearsome chief of guards, "it's a great honor to die by your sword."

He took a deep breath, gathered all his strength, and launched himself at the chief, managing to swing his sword once.

Hukura knew the man was going down, with a slim chance of standing up again on his own. He swung swiftly, slashing the soldier's neck with a mortal wound. The fallen man's gushing blood became the signal for the other fighters to clash.

Spared the shame of death in cold blood and burial in a pit with the disgraced, their battered bodies found new energy. Their fate had reversed course for the second time; now they would have the thrill of dying honorably, in a fight under the watchful eyes of the king and the admiration of the crowd. They fought with the same ferocity given to an enemy and the respect in granting their opponent a glorious death.

"See you soon in the netherworld, brother." Those words were repeated by the victors when their opponents fell. Then they would stand to the side and wait for another victor, giving him a chance to recover his breath before they clashed. Their ordeal on the trees had not stripped away their prowess with the sword. They endured multiple slashes, refusing to go down until being struck by a mortal blow.

The crowd watched solemnly, their mocking replaced with absolute awe for these men who fed the earth with their blood.

Sargon kept standing in reverence to his men as they met their heroic ends; yet, he was relieved at the turn of events. He had evaded the embarrassment that would've made him the laughingstock of the kingdom, just as cities were getting bolder against his rule. Now, his soldiers' fighting spirit and valiant sacrifice was going to be the talk of all cities, up and down the two great rivers, to the far expanses of the realm.

The last fighter standing pulled the sword out of his brother-in-arms' chest, dragged himself to the platform and fell to his knees.

"O Mighty King," he said through a mouth streaming blood. "On behalf of all my fallen brothers, I thank you for the generosity and honor you have bestowed on us on this glorious day. May the gods give Your Majesty eternal life!" And he collapsed on his back.

Hukura rushed to the soldier and held his hand, which shivered around the grip of the sword, sending jitters through it until they joined in a peaceful calm.

"Majesty," Hukura announced, "this brave is dead. He suffered deep slashes all over his body."

Sargon turned to the people with his challenging stare, checking the faces. Even a hint of a smile would've brought doom to its owner. Once satisfied that sorrow prevailed, he spoke stridently.

"People of Uruk! What you have just witnessed is something only soldiers in raging battles experience. As you go out every day and do your work chores, complain about the wages, hard labor, and taxes, … braves like these men, who fought and died just now, ward off the enemies who come with intentions to pillage, rape—kill you and your families. Our soldiers march to battle, ready to give away their lives, nourish the earth with their precious blood, and still say, 'Thank you for the honor.' They don't cry that the sword is too heavy or the wages too small. Unlike those pigs,"—he pointed to the pit where the executed had been thrown—"they, who were blinded by greed, who had everything, and yet had nothing better to do than to conspire for the sake of amassing more wealth and power.

"To the families of these fallen heroes: be proud, for you carry their memories and share the same noble blood they gallantly gifted here. The whole city grieves with you for this great loss. We will lay them to rest with the highest honors.

"Citizens of Uruk, go home knowing you are guarded by fearless warriors and watched over by the mightiest of all gods."

The crowd burst into wild screaming, powered by a massive release of confined emotions after the brutal silence that dominated while the soldiers had themselves sacrificed.

"May the Great Sargon be granted eternal life!"

"Sargon, mirror image of God, will rise to be a god!"

The king put on a subtle, sad smile, with his hand flailing to the wave of hails. Shortly, Hukura accosted him again.

"Sargon, what are we to do with the three remaining traitors?"

"Release two, but not the loud one. Those two are to be taken unharmed to the gates of Ur and set free so they tell the people of that city what they witnessed here. The loud one, leave him to me."

Sargon walked over and climbed onto his chariot. He tugged on the reins, directing the horses to the trees, and stopped where he came face-to-face with the noble hanging upside down.

Another surge of praise to the king erupted. This time it came from the other two convicts upon getting word of his pardon. This gave the third a large dose of hope.

"O Majesty, compassionate King," the man was sobbing, "like I said, I had nothing to do with the plot. I was far from the palace. The merciful gods have intervened; they are telling you this is a mistake. Please heed their wishes and spare this loyal subject of yours—I beg of you, Mighty Sargon." Tears slithered down to the man's forehead, moistening strands of his scruffy hair before diving into the dirt.

"Sargon of Larsa," the king said calmly, "you fail to understand that it is not about who was or wasn't involved in the plot. Do you know why you're here? In part, because of this big mouth of yours; you talk too much. You comment on everything, even if you don't know dung about the subject. Remember when I was a new general, sent to subdue the city of Mari, and you assigned yourself to plan the strategy—a most pathetic one. *You*, who have never seen a battle in your whole life. *You*, who couldn't even use a knife to peel an apple, telling *me*—the general—how best to run the operation.

"But you're not unique in this. I'll have no one by my side if I kill men for nagging. Truth is, you weren't on my mind at all when I was with Humbaba, chiseling his memory with names of the undesirables who were to be announced as traitors later. Then, unlucky for you, Humbaba gave me a certain odd look, which made me recall the first time my eyes were enchanted by his *pleasant* face. And that reminded me of the man whom I should thank for assigning Humbaba to me ... *You!* Remember—when I asked you for a replacement scribe?"

"Forgive me, Majesty, but he was the only one available. I swear."

"Exactly, it was what you told me then. Also, I recall that wicked grin on your face."

"No, Majesty, no. I never—"

"Don't get me wrong, Humbaba is a gift from the gods I would not replace for all the messengers on Earth. Amazing how at first, all I could think of was getting rid of him; though his duty then was scribing tablets, still, I sent him as a messenger—a mission he was never prepared for—expecting the enemy would chop him to pieces. Yet miraculously, he returned, with the enemy assenting to all of my demands. Only then did I become aware of the asset in my possession when it came to putting fear into the ultimatums I sent to the enemies. In a way, I'm grateful to you—assigning me Humbaba. However, when I recalled that spiteful grin of yours, it spoke your name—and in Humbaba's memory, your name I chiseled. Do forgive me, but there was no way for me to pass on the opportunity of seeing your reaction once you were announced as a traitor by the same Humbaba you gifted me.

"Now, with you mentioning the gods. *I*, the King—Reflection of God—I hear the gods when they speak, louder than the cheers of this crowd. I don't need you to tell me what the gods want. And that's where you went wrong again—*deadly* wrong. We have the same name, but we are exact opposites. For instance, I'm standing now on a chariot, and *you* ... dangling upside down from a tree. And that begs the question: Is there a need for another Sargon in the court?"

The audience in the background watched intently in silence, trying to grasp anything from the remote exchange between the two Sargons. But the fate of the hanging Sargon became obvious when the one standing drew his sword.

"Sargon of Larsa, take a look." The king brought the blade at an angle to the man's face. "What reflection do you see on this blade?"

Overwhelmed by fear, the man from Larsa couldn't speak.

"If only you had kept your mouth shut like this before, I would've let you go free with the other two. But no—you had to tell me what the gods want because, like always, *you* think you know everything.

"What reflection do you see in the blade?" Sargon repeated, shouting.

Seeing his fate, the man shaped his answer in a ball of spit. Sargon was expecting this desperate insult and was fast to block the bulk of it with the sword.

"Indeed, my friend. Your neck is the reflection, and the sword wants to speak to it."

The blade whispered, and Sargon of Larsa uttered his last unintelligible words through blood surging out of his throat.

DIVINE BOARD GAMES

THE CELL SMELLED PUTRID AND DAMP; IT HAD HELD THE SAME air prisoner for too long. It would have been pitch dark in that hole if it weren't for the solitary oil lamp in the outside corridor that hurled shadows of light through the edges of the solid door.

Cockroaches scurried across the walls and floor; some kept still, except for their twitching antennas. To a starving prisoner, those brown-reddish pests looked like ripe dates that had grown legs. To the one who had lost his mind, they probably tasted as sweet as dates.

The roaches strolled around freely, not worried in the least about the uninvited guest—the once great general who had led ferocious armies that made the earth tremble on their advance, sending all creatures—be they men, beasts, or critters—to flee.

Ghosts of those grand memories ruthlessly invaded Allamu's grim reality as he sat in the cell, stripped of dignity, one leg chained to a bronze bar spiked through the floor.

The mockery of the gods; he couldn't even intimidate those pesky pests. Some cockroaches in their boldness acted as though conveying the message that he had overstayed his welcome in their home.

Watching the movements of the bugs, Allamu busied himself in search of an omen that might foretell his fate. But the flickers of light and darkness blurred their crawls, throwing the premonitions into disarray.

The subtle noise of the roaches was interrupted by whispers coming from the guards' quarters. Soon, the unmistakable human voices reached his ears, bringing a whiff of joy to him.

Silence, "the progeny of death," as Allamu thought of it, was a most hated enemy. Throughout his time in the army, Allamu had seen many a man suffer a grisly end, and he himself had come close to a horrid demise quite a few times. But death wasn't so intimidating in the cacophony of battle, where the screams and clashing of swords helped to numb the senses. He had witnessed soldiers fatally wounded, yet somehow, they didn't seem much aware of death cuddling them.

A hardened warrior, Allamu used to feel like a beast in the battlefield, running wild, unsure of which life to snatch next. Nothing was more thrilling to him than the scream of an enemy as the sword cut through him. But now, feeling helpless, caged and chained, Allamu pondered for the first time, placing himself in the boots of a falling warrior: What thoughts would those final moments bring, and what words would he shriek to the face of the one ending his life? Normally, they would be curses and wishes for the victor to meet a more violent end. But in that lonely cell, with the anguish of death roaming around him in silence, he would welcome the chance to die in battle as a blessing; he would probably give the man killing him a grateful, farewell hug. If he were to choose a way to die, he wouldn't think twice.

Faint sounds of approaching footsteps snared his attention.

Who would visit this place at this time of night? Then again, it could be daytime.

In that solitary pest house, nothing offered a hint of time. Being denied this most basic of rights—the awareness of the sun's whereabouts—added to Allamu's misery.

The corridor brightened and the steps grew louder. Were they coming to execute him? Would they grant him a final wish to select a method of death, or at least kill him outside these walls with the chirping of the crickets to distract him, instead of the dreadful creeping of roaches? Nonetheless, he delighted in the approaching luxury of light and sound, no matter what ugly fate came along with them.

The door was thrown open. A guard stepped in and eyed Allamu, grinning.

"General, forgive my interrupting your meeting with the bugs. You have a visitor." He placed the oil lamp on the floor and left.

"Good evening … General," greeted the visitor.

So, it is evening. Allamu shut his eyes briefly to savor this glimpse of time. "Why it's Ibrahem! I'm so honored. How generous of you to visit, knowing your busy schedule; making gods and … delivering beautiful assassins to the nobles."

"Well, General, one can always squeeze in some time to see men who are in a squeeze of a situation."

"Oh, for the sense of humor!" Allamu feigned a laugh. "I can't breathe, the chuckles are killing me. So that's why I was kept alive; because *you*—the executioner—were too busy composing the killer humor that would squeeze the life out of me?"

"No sir, no. I'm here to make a statue of our great army general— or should I say, just your head—once it's squeezed free from the rest of you by the sword. And don't worry about paying me for this job. Which reminds me, you still owe me for previous work. Well, seeing you here puts me in a generous mood, so I'll forgive you that too."

"Oh, I beg your forgiveness." Allamu snubbed him. "They kept me alive to make me hear you cry like a whore who didn't get paid. *You whore of Sargon!*"

"Maybe I am. But this whore still has the head attached to the shoulders, unlike many of your friends—unlike Hadras! Oh, forgive me, *His Majesty Hadras*. Last I heard about him, he was still going strong, riding behind a chariot pulled by a mule; still hanging on to his head, but barely. What a great king, this Hadras; personally visiting every neighborhood in Uruk to check on all his subjects. You should ask the guards to take you up when he passes by this neighborhood, so you can have a little chat with him. Oh, I forgot—they say he's so tired, he's always sleeping. But you can always talk to the ass."

"I would rather talk to an ass than lick royal arse."

"Do I have a choice?" Ibrahem smirked. "It's a required skill in the pyramid of power. When you raise your head, the first thing you see is the arse of the man on top of you. Give it comfort, and he will leave you alone; bite that arse, and its owner will bounce on your head, choke you with some stinking air, and bury you with his turd.

That's why you ended up in this hole—your new residence—sleeping next to your own turd for lacking the decorum to treat the king's arse nicely."

"Ibrahem, not everyone is blessed by the gods with a long tongue to lick Sargon's arse from your place at the bottom of the pyramid. If only Sargon had been toppled, the whole pyramid would've collapsed. And you, along with your stinking tongue, would've been buried under."

"It mystifies me how you didn't end up like Hadras!" Scornfully, Ibrahem answered Allamu's demeaning remarks. "One guess: your half-sister Kebboba, holding Sargon's son hostage; that would make a reasonable exchange. Foolish of Hadras to join your plot without having secured a hostage to trade for his life. As for you, General, you knew that gave you a chance, no matter how slim, to go free, unscathed. It's a gamble though, knowing how impulsive Sargon is, and whether he really values his son's life. ... Truly, I admire your courage, Allamu, and you had me baffled—why didn't you leave for a safer place when Sargon relieved you from command as a general?"

Allamu didn't answer.

"Of course, that's none of my concern; who am I but the king's sculptor! But allow me another guess. You knew that nothing could've stopped Sargon from killing anyone he disliked in Uruk, *except* for one major problem: doing so without a good reason would've been a very foolish thing to do. It would only have alarmed the rulers of all cities in the kingdom, prompting them to join Ur in the revolt, and that would've sealed Sargon's fate. The plot to overthrow Sargon was on your mind all the time, and you needed to be close to your good friend Hadras, here in the city. The girl assassin was just what you needed to get him moving."

Ibrahem paced the cell's tight space.

"You surely didn't waste time reaching the palace doors with Hadras' troops, using that tablet with the fake royal seal. It was a real surprise, I must confess. We could hear the fighting from within the palace, which sent us running—the king himself—scampering to the secret escape tunnel. It was helpful that we knew your attack was inevitable. ... Mentioning the fake royal seal, Hadras had no idea where it came from. I guess you don't know either, General! ... Perhaps some god delivered it to you ... in a mysterious way!"

Allamu remained silent.

"There is a board game from a faraway land, close to where the sun comes out of the night tunnels. Traders brought this game to the king, and I crafted a similar one of my own. The pieces resemble two warring kingdoms with kings, priests, chariots, defensive towers, and warriors. It's a game that makes one wonder if we, the humans, are merely expendable pieces on a board game enjoyed by the gods.

"This is no game of chance; one needs wit to win. You must think of what your opponent might be thinking to foil his plans. Like a battle strategy, you explore all possibilities of attack and defense. That's the beauty of this game: the more moves ahead you envision, the more advantage you get to force your opponent into a deadly trap."

"You don't need to tell me," Allamu interrupted. "The girl was the trap."

"More than the trap," Ibrahem responded with a sad smile. "Mayram ... she was the heart of the game, the beauty of the game, and the endgame. How did you know she was sent to kill you?"

"I had my sources."

"Yet, you didn't question whether those sources gained their tips from the one behind the trap!"

"You!" Allamu showed no surprise.

Slyly grinning, Ibrahem nodded. "Beautiful Mayram. What a girl! Too bad you killed her when you didn't have to. I could've arranged for her to keep you company. Savage beauty! She could've butchered all the men of Uruk. That praying mantis seal on her necklace, it was a gift from me. I've always wondered if a male mantid is aware that he might lose his head to the female while mating. That girl was the closest thing to a vicious praying mantis. I'm sure there must be more than a few men out there who would not mind losing their heads just to sleep once with a girl of her charm. ... Sadly, she turned soft and ... decided to stop killing. I couldn't let her walk away—she knew too much—so I forced her into one last job.

"Only then did your sources receive the secret messages about the praying mantis assassin who sought specific individuals—you and Hadras among them. You were spied on when you visited Hadras. We guessed that you were trying to convince him to ready his troops to dethrone the king. With Gungunum far away at the gates of Ur, that was your opportunity. Knowing how Hadras loved to be glorified, there was no doubt he had ambitions to be king, but he would not have moved on his own; he's the type who needs a push, a persuading from an assertive, trusted friend. We guessed you were getting ready when *you*, the prey, acted to become the predator. We watched you frequent the temple of Ishtar, looking for your prey: a girl assassin, wearing a praying mantis seal."

"How about the troops?" Allamu asked, looking past Ibrahem at the cockroaches. "How long were they waiting outside the city?"

"The timing!" Ibrahem replied. "That had to be planned carefully. The siege of Ur wasn't going anywhere. Soldiers were sitting outside, idle and bored to death. Many were in desperate need of an excursion. A trip to Uruk seemed like a great idea for those men, especially with the likelihood they might be needed to repel *an incursion*. So, on the same day we decided to give your sources the information about the praying mantis assassin, messengers were sent in secret to Gungunum to take a large number of troops and march them under the cover of night. Days later, they dug in at an obscure location, a reasonable distance from the city, with guards running patrols to make sure no one would spot them. Only then did we send Mayram to wait for you by Ishtar's temple with strict instructions to the guard that she was to go only with you.

"Once you and Hadras made your move on the palace, messengers were sent to Gungunum to march on the city. Royal guards were stationed to open the city gates in case you planned to secure them, which you did not; you didn't expect an army to be waiting outside. We had to sacrifice some guards and palace workers so you wouldn't be alarmed about a trap if you found the place was deserted. As for the rest, you know what followed.

"Sargon was so happy; he was expecting to trap only a few disloyal men, not a hall full of them. It's like when you aim at a few dates on a palm tree, and a whole cluster plunges down. And that gave me the idea—yes, the harvest games—except, it was nobles' heads that were harvested. Too bad you weren't invited."

"Then it was a ruse," Allamu said bitterly. "the size of the army that waited outside was inflated."

"Well, it was still too large a group for your troops to handle. Your men were wise to abandon you; their blood would've been spilled needlessly. Don't lose sleep over that."

"So the Babylonian girl was your main piece in the game, and you had to sacrifice her to win. Even when dead, you used her."

"Mayram wasn't a piece!" Ibrahem answered resentfully. "She was the goddess over the board. Allow me the pleasure of telling you she's to become a demigoddess—an angel. A shrine, dedicated to her, is to be built on the same spot where she was cowardly murdered by you and Hadras. Her body will be moved there."

"You amaze me, Ibrahem. Now you talk like you had nothing to do with her death, while you praise yourself with all the credit for your *triumph*. I've had my share of triumphs in this life—real victories I'm proud of, where I fought real men who aimed their weapons with the intention of butchering me. I always knew there would come a time when I would lose, and I'm prepared for that. All this *strategy* and *board game* nonsense is talked up by idle, dull people to keep themselves busy on their long, boring days. You, and spineless men like you, congratulate yourselves for *victories achieved* while sitting on your arses the whole time. What an utterly disgusting coward you are for using a girl to win your battle! Why are you here, Ibrahem? To savor your *victory* with the spice of my loss?"

The truth in those words rendered Ibrahem speechless. He couldn't tell Allamu how he'd loved Mayram to the point where he was going to stop using her for killing. The idea of leaving his wife Saura and moving to a new house with Mayram had filled him with the joy and vigor of a youth in his prime. He had an abundance of power and wealth; love was the only thing missing.

But all those plans had shattered when she failed to kill Lubalanda. He didn't believe her story of why she failed. The lie had been clearly evident with the change in her; that look of a girl in love was not easy to hide. Not to mention her sudden, eager desire to abandon the assignments—and him. Jealousy had torn him apart; watching Mayram leave for another man was inconceivable. To have fallen in love with Lubalanda was the gravest of sins—it merited death.

Now, no matter how much he tried to fool himself that it was her rightly deserved fate, guilt always came back to overwhelm him. He would shed tears in the night over his longing for her. It was anger that had brought him to Allamu—fury at the man who had chosen to end her life, even though he himself had been the one to deliver Mayram to Allamu.

"Yes, I am enjoying my victory." Ibrahem finally answered the man he had come to torment. "I can't deny it. As for courage in the face of death, it doesn't only happen in the chaos of the battlefield. I too have had the sword over my neck in the serenity of the palace."

"Why are you telling me all this, Ibrahem? Do you want me to laud you as a hero? I served this kingdom all my life, then was forced into rebellion, and here I am being treated like a traitor. I'm not interested in your *heroic* stories. Go tell them to the cockroaches; maybe they'll be entertained, but don't do it here. Take a few home."

Allamu crushed two bugs with his foot. They were still alive, wriggling their feet, when he picked them up and threw them at Ibrahem.

"Here, Ibrahem, you can keep these. Have them salute you for winning the game. *Hail Ibrahem the hero!* ... Now leave. I thank the gods I'm not on their game board anymore. But one thing I ask you: are you ready for the day when the gods knock you off the board?"

Ibrahem couldn't hide his emotions anymore. He angrily stomped on the flame of the oil lamp, bringing back the subtle shadows from the faint light outside.

"I will be ready when my time comes, Allamu. I just came to make sure *you* are ready for your impending trip to the netherworld."

HONOR THY ENEMY

THE PALACE GARDENS BOASTED A LARGE VARIETY OF TREES. Adorning many of those trees were fruits in their infancy, shy in their green color, camouflaged among the leaves. They waited for time to paint them in delicious colors that qualified them to be picked for the exclusive enjoyment of the king and his guests. Visiting dignitaries were welcome to stroll in the palace gardens but forbidden to touch the fruits. It was joked that the offenders who ignored the warning would have to pay the king back by nourishing the trees with portions of their bodies buried next to the roots.

Bordering the trees stretched rows and rows of blossoming flowers that surpassed the trees in their variety. Each group competed with its neighbors to be the most enchanting in that vast display of color, created by man's art and nature's delight. Unlike with the fruits in his gardens, the king showed generosity in not restricting access to the sweet fragrance given by the blooms. The invited men didn't waste this opportunity, and they ambled amid the flowers, deeply inhaling the perfumed aromas that must have been carried down by some celestial breeze from heaven.

Sargon emerged from a palace gate that opened to a terrace overlooking the gardens. He descended the stairs to a wide-open arena, trimmed of grass, stretching to the field of flowers. He strolled around, joking with everyone. The guests had to be very attentive so as not to miss the point when they were supposed to laugh, no matter how bad his jokes were, for that would be considered a lack of appreciation of the precious labor the king put into the humor. It could, in turn, cause one to spend time in a dungeon cell and be made to listen to the guards' humor—humor that promised excruciating pain.

Everyone welcomed the meeting's change of location to the open garden on such a beautiful day. It was a relief to be anywhere in the palace other than the court where the ghosts of fear had dwelled since that infamous judgment day, somehow giving it a distinct foul smell. The garden was a long walk from the court with the added luxury of the vibrant flowers, in contrast to the grim bricks and stones of the court's asphyxiating, morbid chamber.

A noble wearing a pleasant grin approached the king.

"Great Sargon, may I borrow your head gardener for one day? His work is amazing—a marvel."

"Tiriqan!" Sargon eyed the man with a frown of surprise. "This must be a mistake!"

"What mistake, Majesty?" Tiriqan was baffled.

"Where is Humbaba?" Sargon's head turned side to side in search of his messenger.

"What happened, Your Majesty?" The noble's color started abandoning him.

"You should've been on the list," Sargon said, anger twisting his face.

"Yes … I was invited." Tiriqan's voice quivered out of an ashy face.

"No, not that list. I'm talking about the list of men who collaborated to overthrow me. Where is Humbaba? Why didn't he read your name?"

All eyes turned to Tiriqan. The whole place went silent when fear pounced from the court all the way to the gardens.

Sweating profusely, Tiriqan struggled to balance himself over legs that felt like two pillars of wet mud ready to collapse under him.

"I'm just fooling with you … calm down." Sargon exploded in laughter and waved to a servant carrying a jar. "Give my friend here some wine to help him regain his color."

The invitees laughed too, feigning appreciation of the king's wit. As for Tiriqan, he was helped by a friend to the nearest bench. Slowly, he sipped on the wine to wash the fright away.

Chuckles fading to a broad smile, Sargon climbed the stairs up to the terrace. He raised a hand that held a large seal. Everyone looked up, intently, not wanting to run the risk of being caught ignoring his speech.

"In my hand, I'm holding what is, or *was*, the genuine royal seal." Sargon addressed the subject matter short of any introduction. "The traitors used a tablet stamped by a fake seal to storm the palace. Theirs was a good fake. No one we interrogated could lead us to the forged seal or its maker. Hadras is probably the only one who knows. So, let's ask him again about that fake seal?"

The nobles were at a loss, for they knew Hadras was being reduced to scattered bones all over the city.

Sargon waved to a soldier standing by the nearest pomegranate tree. The man removed a cloth covering a large branch. The invited men shrunk away from the horrid sight of a head, stripped of skin to the muscles; upside down it hung from a hook clawed through its jaw.

"Your Majesty, King Hadras!" Sargon shouted, mockingly. "Do grant us the favor of clarifying how you came to possess your own royal seal?"

Grinning, Sargon waited for short moments, then shook his head in disappointment.

"I guess *His Majesty* doesn't want to be disturbed. Leave him resting, he looks awfully exhausted. ... Anyway, as you know, I have sent messages to warn every official that *this* royal seal is no longer in use. This is a serious matter, and I probed to see if everyone complied by rejecting the orders on any tablet carrying this seal. All complied— except for two fools. I was merciful; their deaths were swift.

"I have men working nonstop on a new seal, and when it's finished, you will receive a sample for comparison that should be locked in a secure place. Until then, *you*, and all who work for you, need to be vigilant and pursue any hint that might lead to the fake seal. In the meantime, if for any reason you need my permission for some matter, you should personally seek approval from me, here in the palace. Anyone who breaks these rules is going to participate in *certain games*, which the people have come to love passionately. That will be followed by hanging in the joyful company of *King Hadras*, on that same tree. ... Any questions while we're all here?"

A noble moved to the front and spoke with head slightly bowed.

"Your Majesty. Regarding the ongoing rebellion in Ur, what is to be done to end it?"

Sargon pondered the question. "As you all know, the army that came back to deal with the *little disturbance* we had here has already returned to the siege of Ur. You also know that my son Naram-sin was taken hostage after he rushed, unwisely, without consulting me, to arrange a peace agreement with the leaders of Ur. I had to think calmly and refrain from taking any swift action. My son's fate is *not* going to be a factor in any decision regarding the rebellion; the welfare of the kingdom comes before any personal concern. After consulting with my generals, I have decided to deploy a highly specialized force led by none other than Allamu. He deserved a pardon based on his past triumphs in the service of the kingdom, and I had him restored to the rank of general."

Murmurs took off to the air until a noble dared to ask.

"Allamu! Your Majesty ... despite his treachery?"

"Yes, Allamu. Contrary to what you may think, he knows he made a mistake and I trust that he deeply regrets it. He's the only one capable of reaching out to his half-sister and bringing her back to her senses, so together we can end the bloodshed. Their people and our soldiers have suffered enough already."

"Majesty, what are those special forces you mentioned? I was never aware of their existence."

"Tiriqan, you're back to life! Yet, with such a silly question, your mind must be missing." Sargon let out a chuckle and was joined by everyone—Tiriqan too, who was sweating now with laughter.

"Oh, my friend, you must've had too much to drink. Everyone in the city has seen those special forces. They're everywhere, living among the people, all over the city. I can't explain it any better ... I'm too hungry. Let's go inside, where my cooks have prepared a unique treat for you; special dishes of lamb, pork, chicken—all prepared to celebrate a special occasion. Rejoice my faithful men, for soon peace will be dawning over the kingdom."

Home, Prison, Shrine, and Grave

THE WHITE CLOUD FLOATED IN THE AIR AS IF IT HAD BEEN COUGHED out of Earth's depths by a demon. Shadows walked through the dusty swirl, resembling evil spirits escaping the netherworld.

When the thick dust settled, the malicious phantoms transformed into wretched mortals in shabby clothes who emerged from the demolition zone to face a storm of screams from the master builder in charge. Bringing the sturdy walls down was giving him a rough time; his frustration he purged on the laborers, hollering orders coupled with a sweeping range of profanities—the other skill he'd mastered.

They were razing the entire east section of a house to construct a temple in its place. The lodgings on the west side and the garden that spanned the entire length along the middle were to be left untouched. Those two sections became the property of the new owners, Ellili and his wife, Warda, who were also assigned to be the caretakers of the new temple, once completed.

The temple would also contain a shrine for the martyr, Mayram, Guardian of the Virgins. The spot where the girl had been killed was being treated as a sacred space, with the dark bands of her blood on the floor kept undisturbed. The cloth and reed mats into which her blood had soaked were stored away, to be laid back in their original place and enclosed within a low fence once all the work was completed. Sections adjacent to that area were designated for the martyr's shrine and final resting place.

Allamu stood watching the demolition from the other side of the yard. Gloom clouded his face, just short of raining the tears down.

While the walls crumbled, he dwelled on all the arduous work he had put into the construction of this home, from the design plans, down to the supervision of the laborers to assure the even alignment of the bricks and the proper spread of bitumen between the joints for exceptionally solid, level walls.

Demolishing the walls of cities he had defeated gained him all that experience. On seeing a wall, his first thoughts focused on how best to tear it down. Thus started his fascination with the construction methods, and what factors made some walls more vulnerable than others.

"Temple of the Sanctified Bitch! Her Whoring Holiness!" Whispered curses flew freely from Allamu's mouth, directed at the goddess of love to whom the new temple would be dedicated.

Witnessing his house being dismantled before his very eyes, Allamu felt the walls of his own existence crumble. Only then could he fathom how the occupants of the cities he had raided must have felt when watching their protective walls grind to dust. The bitter taste of defeat and the horrid feeling of all hope lost was more than Allamu could bear. He turned around and went inside the servants' room, which had become his new residence after Sargon had *pardoned* and reinstated him to the rank of general, in command of some mysterious "special forces."

Two sentries stationed outside the room were to accompany him at all times, ostensibly for his own protection from angry people who deemed the traitor not worthy of a pardon. As promised by Sargon, Allamu's few close relatives in Uruk had been allowed safe passage out of the city.

All his house possessions had been carried away by looters who stormed the property on the day of Mayram's funeral. The only things left behind were two huge, winged bull statues. Yet no loss could've prepared Allamu for the ultimate humiliation when the ownership of his house was awarded to his servants. Both Ellili and his wife would occasionally walk past the room, giving him a disdainful glance as though he were an intruder on their property.

"You have a visitor," one of the sentries called from outside. "Gudea, the Phoenician merchant."

Gudea walked through a curtain of long hanging reeds where there used to be a door, which had also been looted.

"Greetings, Allamu."

"Greetings, Gudea. I deeply appreciate your visit."

Gudea nodded. "Those guards, and their security search; it felt so … shamelessly indecent."

"Forgive me for putting you in this situation, Gudea. Again, I'm sincerely grateful to you for taking the risk to come here. … It's funny how no one seems to know me anymore. Yet, I don't blame them; why associate with a man accused of treason?"

"To tell you the truth, Allamu, if I had family here, I wouldn't visit you either. But you were a good client, and I appreciate your help in providing me with good soldiers for the protection of my caravans during my trade trips. Still, I must confess to asking Sargon's permission to see you."

"*Sargon the Great!* I don't know how to repay his *generosity*," Allamu said, resentfully. "Anyway, did you see the winged bulls?"

"Yes, they're magnificent."

"Well, they're not up to the *high standards* of my servant—or should I say, the new house master, *Ellili*."

"How strange! I told him they look beautiful in that room. Still, he wants them out, or else he'll break them to tiny pebbles. But why?"

"I have no idea," Allamu lied; he knew very well why. The two bulls had been the only other witnesses the night when Warda was violated by Hadras. Ellili couldn't stand their cold stares.

"I hate to tell you this, Allamu, but those statues are too heavy. They must be broken down to pieces to remove. Still, any sculptor would love to have some of that stone."

"Without a doubt, Gudea, they do need to be cut down. I remember bringing the two rough stones into the house; I had my soldiers drag them in after we tore the door opening wider. The sculptors worked right there—right where the bulls are standing now."

"Is there anything else you need removed?" Gudea suspected that there was more to this invitation, but his host seemed reluctant to open up about it.

"Yes." Allamu hesitated, his unease evident. "Truth is … I don't care about the bulls. Ellili can throw them in the river or bury them in bull dung for all I care. Gudea, I called you to remove something heavier than those bulls … something that had been crushing my chest for ages."

The answer puzzled Gudea. He waited for Allamu to elaborate, but then the sentry outside announced:

"Another visitor … Ibrahem would like to see you."

Allamu was mouthing inaudible curses when Ibrahem walked inside through the curtain.

"By the grace of the gods," Ibrahem started. "Gudea! Greetings. Just the man I needed to see."

"And greetings to you, Ibrahem." Gudea nodded.

"Ibrahem!" Allamu scowled. "You honor me with your frequent visits. What brings you here today?"

"General, the honor is mine," Ibrahem replied. "I heard you need a buyer for some heavy statues you want to get rid of. Also, I came to express my joy for your receiving a pardon. Bless the gods for their intervention. Men like you, of such immense talent, are hard to replace."

"The gods work in mysterious ways, dear Ibrahem."

"Couldn't be more right, General. So mysterious is their work, I gave up on trying to understand them. The gods—I simply follow blindly."

"Don't we all!" Allamu feigned a smile. "Your visit the other day was truly … delightful. It also reminded me that I owe you for some work! So take one of the bull statues as payment. Gudea is here to take the other one, after he breaks it into smaller pieces."

"It's a shame they have to be sectioned," Ibrahem replied. "And the little sum you owe me does not justify a whole bull of fine stone for payment. I insist on paying a fair price for it."

"Ibrahem, consider it … a farewell gift."

"I sincerely appreciate your generosity. That's plenty of good stone to work with. In fact, I can't use all of it, and would gladly share it with other craftsmen, like this one gifted sculptor—Lubalanda, his name. He would surely love to work on such fine stone. But lately, I couldn't find him at his place. I learned from a neighbor that Lubalanda had sold his works; however, there was no mention of him moving. ... Gudea, you probably know him, or someone who knows him. Any idea where he could've gone?"

"I know Lubalanda," answered Gudea. "I delivered some stones for him after my last trade trip. But that was moons ago."

"I hope he didn't leave us." Ibrahem sighed. "He's one of the best sculptors in the city."

The best, not one of the best. Gudea wanted to correct him, but he just nodded in agreement.

"Well, if you find out his whereabouts, let me know," Ibrahem continued. "I'll come back tomorrow with some masons and laborers to section the winged bull and haul it away. ... Well, Allamu, if I don't see you, may the gods bless your mission to bring peace to our land."

"And peace to all of us—the pawns on their board game," Allamu replied sourly.

Ibrahem pondered that remark. "But then, the game will give them no thrill, and there won't be any further need for us humans. ... Anyway, noble sirs, it was good to see you, have a blessed day." Ibrahem nodded and stepped out.

Gudea felt the unhinged air of the last exchange.

"Allamu, what did you mean by 'pawns on their board game'?"

The general didn't answer but walked to the curtain and checked outside to assure that Ibrahem had indeed left the premises.

"How long have you known him?" Allamu asked while gazing out the reed curtain.

"Ibrahem! A long time. My son had a scuffle with Ibrahem's son in the tablet house. So, we met when they called us to discuss the matter. As a result, my son was expelled. Then, there were the chance encounters in the palace where Ibrahem started asking if I could get him certain types of stones through my trade trips. I wouldn't say we're friends—more like client and customer."

"Never trust that man!" Allamu could barely suppress his ire.

"What did he do to you?" Gudea was surprised at that sudden display of emotion.

"A lot. Look at me; I, the general who commanded armies that roamed free and conquered ... now a prisoner in a slave's room with two guards watching my every step. My house is being shredded, and my servants ... made masters of what's left of it. Cursed be the gods for their cruelty! I feel so pathetic, I can't even summon a true smile to my face." He sighed. "How brave of that girl to keep her smile till the end."

"What girl?" Gudea was intrigued.

Allamu looked at him, then turned his face away. "That's what I wanted to talk to you about."

"Then talk!"

"It's not easy; I tried to tell you before, but I couldn't summon the courage." Allamu rubbed his temples with both hands. "This could be my last opportunity, though. I don't trust Sargon; his pardon harbors a sinister plot, an ugly fate he has in store for me. Then again, at least I deserve it, and I'm given ample time to accept whatever my fate might be. But that girl didn't deserve what happened to her."

"Again, the girl!" Gudea frowned. "What girl? The Babylonian girl? The one you and Hadras—"

"No, not her. That Babylonian girl was sent to butcher me."

"Then which girl?"

Allamu looked so frail, he stepped to a chair and sank in it. "Forgive me, Gudea, I tried to help, but it was too late ... that was what they claimed."

"By the gods, what was too late?" Gudea asked, impatiently.

"They said she fit all the requirements," Allamu continued, not heeding Gudea's questions. "Young, beautiful, virgin, and best of all, an orphan. ... I swear by the gods I tried to get her out, but they argued that she had seen too much, and they would never allow her to leave."

Gudea's legs suddenly lost firmness. Realizing who Allamu was talking about, he fell back on the wall for support, shaking his head in anticipation of the painful truths about to be revealed.

"I've seen ... caused so much death and misery to people I defeated," Allamu sorrowed. "Guilt and compassion rarely touched me. I was immune to those sorts of sentiments ... until I was struck by her smile on that cursed day. She looked so innocent, beautiful, happy, as if it were her wedding day. My failure to save her awakened this torment of guilt, this … plague of shame within me. I felt so weak, could only gaze at her—sleeping, unaware of her dark destiny. That image has haunted me ever since, wakes up with me every morning, and it will stay with me until I depart this world. That unique, lovely smile—she kept to the end. It seemed like her last resort to ward off death."

"*Coward!* You were there, and you left her to die!" Gudea clenched his fists, craving to pummel Allamu to death. "Who led her there? Who were the bastards?"

"She must have carried that smile to the netherworld."

"Who were they? TELL ME!"

"Then I heard of your wife drowning in the river," Allamu continued, his distant stare traversing the wall.

Gudea squatted on the floor, hands cupping his head, resigned to listening.

"All because one son-of-a-bitch king wanted people to serve him in the next life. The bastard was utterly convinced that those to be doomed were lucky to be awarded this *privilege*, and their families should feel honored that their loved ones departed with him—*His Majesty*. Huh, that other pig, the high priest Ishullanu, had no shame in exhibiting extreme dismay at being denied this *great honor* of accompanying the former king. Obviously, our *Great King, Sargon*, had no objection to this horror happening. He must have plans for a larger entourage to accompany him when his time comes." Allamu paused to bury his anger.

"Reluctantly, I supplied the soldiers. The others were *invited* to their own *burial celebration* in that death chamber. Then, of all the girls in Uruk—as if it were a conspiracy by the wicked gods to add to my misery, your Amare had to be one of the virgins. Oh, the poor souls, how joyful they were—singing, dancing, thinking they were on their way to a royal banquet."

Stunned to stillness, Gudea resembled a statue crying real tears.

"She even met a boy who seemed to have fallen in love with her at first sight. They say love is blind, but what love could be so blind as to not see death looming over it?" Allamu's voice faded; pain soaked his eyes.

"I'm out of words that can express my sorrow for what you had to go through with the loss of Amare and your wife. I wanted to spare you the agony, but I had suffered to keep the secret. Forgive me for bringing back this cruel memory, but you need to know before the truth dies with me while those responsible are still rejoicing in this life with no lament over the calamity they brought on the victims and the grief to their families.

"Oh, Gudea—and to add to my torture, your Amare, after she drank the sleeping potion, she went into peaceful slumber, only to awake in a dream-like state. … Yes Gudea, she was alive … her face wore the same distinct smile that was sealed in my memory from a far earlier time when I saw her with you in the market. That joyful, lively smile … it was her words of farewell to us … before we closed and sealed the burial chamber."

DELUGE OF LIES

HOW UTTERLY FOOLISH—TO BE WISE ALL THE TIME!

It was the most popular proverb attributed to Nabu, the god of knowledge and wisdom.

On the last three days of every moon cycle, Nabu was in the habit of resting from the vexing litanies of tablet house students and their constant nagging to be granted more knowledge and skills. He was rumored to retreat to the big cities of the mortals. Pretending to be a human, Nabu would indulge himself in the reckless pleasures of foolish men.

Learning from one's own follies is the shortest path to attaining wisdom.

As a god, Nabu could afford to make the gravest blunders without having to worry about any repercussions.

Order is the first step on the long road to wisdom, was another shrewd proverb, and it survived long after the untimely demise of its mortal author, Ur-nammu. This wisest of all tablet house masters attempted to emulate Nabu in briefly abandoning wisdom by committing an extremely foolish act. Sadly, unlike Nabu, the great master lacked one main ingredient: being a god. His reckless deed—insulting a princess—resulted in his ghastly death.

Nabu was not to be disturbed in his wild, wisdom-free days. For that purpose, all tablet houses were closed. The day before Nabu's rest period, the students were assigned a comprehensive task of cleaning and tidying up the classrooms. The floors had to be left sparkling, and the stacks of tablets had to be hauled away to a storage room or dumped where the clay might be reused.

A few moons earlier, at one particular tablet house, a room had been repeatedly denied its allotted share of peace in Nabu's days off. A couple had exploited the opportunity to have that room exclusively for themselves as a retreat for an activity totally unrelated to reading or scribing.

Enheduanna and Isaa lay next to each other on a feather-stuffed cushion, resting over a reed mat on the floor. It was midafternoon, and the sunlight was just starting to penetrate through narrow openings in the west wall, where loose bricks could be wedged in or removed as needed to create openings for natural light and ventilation.

"How can you sleep here?" Enheduanna asked while she stared at the ceiling.

"I have no choice," Isaa replied. "It's for a sacred cause."

"Sleeping on the floor—a sacred cause!" she scoffed.

"Better said, it's a grand mission. I'll let you in on a secret … I've been chosen by the gods."

"For what?" She rolled on her side to face him.

"The gods came to me in a dream."

"Which gods?"

"The dream wasn't clear, but Nabu was one of them. They commanded, 'Isaa, build a mat of reeds, square in shape, so it can fit both you and one woman comfortably. Place it in the house of wisdom. We are going to send another flood, even greater than the previous deluge. It will wipe out all living things—except for you, the wisest amongst men, and a woman who is just as wise and endowed with the beauty of a goddess. When doomsday arrives, be close to your reed mat in that house of wisdom.'"

"Are you mocking the Great Deluge story?" Enheduanna laughed and sat up, exposing her firm breasts over the blanket. Isaa reached to touch her.

"No more." She slapped his hand. "I need to head back to the palace before my father sends the army to look for me. Just go on with this *Dream of Divine Revelation.*"

"But of course," he said haughtily. "So, single-handedly, I tackled the enormous, sacred task entrusted to me, down to the finest detail. And here you have it."

"Where?" She knit a brow.

"You're sitting on it; this great reed mat that will carry the only two surviving humans, who will bravely confront the mighty challenge of repopulating the Earth."

"So, tell me, O great favored one." She bowed and bit her lip to keep from laughing. "How is this *colossal* reed mat going to save the chosen *you* and the chosen woman, *hence* perpetuating mankind after the next deluge?"

"This is not just any reed mat." Isaa sat up and replied in a serious tone. "This one is equipped with divine powers; it's capable of flying. I tried it last night and, sure enough, it flew me to the four corners of the world in one trip."

"All in one night?" she laughed.

"You can laugh all you want. They all laughed at Zuisudra when he was building the great ark. But no one will be laughing when monster waves rush to swallow them, while they watch me fly to my sanctuary in the skies."

"I take it back. This story is even more absurd than Zuisudra's. But wait, you forgot about the animals!"

"No, I didn't. I told the gods: 'Why waste time in gathering a pair of every animal breed on Earth? It would be far more exciting to create newer kinds.' ... And with my skills as a scribe, I gave them tablets with drawings and descriptions of bizarre creatures: the ones for food, extremely luscious; others I sketched to look huge and mean, with a ferocity to make a lion appear like a kitten. The gods adored this idea to repopulate Earth with fresh, more fascinating creatures. Thus, we settled for a flying mat instead of a huge ark."

"And the woman," she teased, shaking her breasts. "Who is the lucky one?"

"Forgive me. At first, I thought it was you." He feigned sadness. "Very beautiful, smart, strong character. But the gods differed, for you lack one essential thing ... then again, it's not too hard to correct that."

"And what is this thing I lack that would disqualify me?"

Isaa cupped the palm of his right hand and moved it as if toying with a child's hair. "Remember? The most important task is repopulating the Earth—have children."

"Oh, foolish me!" She sprang to her feet, irritation obvious in her body language, and imitated his hand twists at the wrist. "Of course, the little ones." Furiously, she grabbed and slipped her raiment on, then waved a hand. "No, that's not going to happen."

"What's wrong?" He was baffled by her reaction.

"How could you bring up this subject?" she bickered. "Rebellion and mayhem are afflicting the land, and you want to talk about having a family! Only recently, I was with my father and *your* father in a secret tunnel, running underground like rats to escape a horde of traitors intent on butchering us. We had to sneak out of the city in the darkness to spend the night in a cold shack. You talk like none of that happened. I'd better go before I hear any more of this nonsense about bringing children into this world."

"Calm down." He stood and put on his clothing. "I was only fooling with you, just like this story about a flying reed mat. I didn't mean—"

Isaa stopped abruptly upon hearing the door open in the next room. Both went dead silent and listened attentively.

The sounds didn't announce much about the intruder. Footsteps could be heard in that room, stopping now and then, as if their owner were hesitant in pursuing whatever they came seeking.

Quietly, Isaa rolled the cover and cushion from over the mat and placed them out of sight behind a workbench. He had just bent down to silently roll up the reed mat when the door to the room opened.

Learned Brother Samian stood motionless, shocked by what he had always suspected but refused to believe. The two in front of him had stunned faces, realizing they had been exposed. All three remained still in awkward silence.

"Princess ... good day to you." Samian's tongue labored to expel the words.

"Good day to you, Samian." Her voice sounded loud with a false breeziness. "I was just ... in need of some material, to work on my own—to catch up with the others."

"Yes, she's behind in some tasks." Isaa came to her assistance, trying to sound normal, though he doubted that Samian would believe the lie. "What brings you here, Samian?"

"Same thing … picking up some items." Samian didn't volunteer any more reasons. He joined the act, reciting a script that told anything but the truth.

Seeking a much-needed diversion, Samian noticed the reed mat on the floor—a trace pointing to their love nest. Grudgingly, he walked over and rolled it up.

"Someone must have accidentally dropped this mat. Better put it away." He handed it to Isaa, then awkwardly moved toward the door. "I'll see you in a few days."

"Samian!" Enheduanna called after a moment of hesitation.

"Yes, Princess," he said in a subdued voice, looking down as he turned around.

"I know you wouldn't say anything, to anybody … about seeing us here," she said, a hint of an order in her voice. "Somebody might get the wrong idea and start spreading unpleasant rumors."

"You need not worry, Princess. I know how rumors grow; like innocent, puffy white clouds that build up to dark, ugly thunderstorms, then to floods, drowning everyone in their path."

Samian walked out and closed the door behind him, leaving Enheduanna and Isaa staring at each other, floating on a deluge of questions with no firm answers in sight.

BEATING FROM THE HEART

L AUGHTER FILLED THE AIR, BODIES UNDULATED IN DANCE, AND voices hummed in song to the lively melodies of the flute, drumbeats, and the swaying flames of oil lamps.

A bigger crowd packed the tavern that evening with a humble wedding party being celebrated there.

Shu-dagan slumped into a chair next to his two helpers, Tammuz and his eldest son.

"Could someone ask our god Marduk to stop shaking the earth," Shu-dagan joked. "I can't tell if I'm dancing or it's the ground rolling under me!"

"The ground under me is firm," Tammuz remarked. "The gods only shake your ground after you get cheerier than they do. Everyone knows gods are a jealous lot."

"Jealous of me! *I*, their humble servant! They should love me, not be jealous, after all those offerings I made. To Ishtar alone, I offered one whole goat."

"Is that all? After they blessed you with a boat and the two best boatmen in all of Babylon!"

"Huh—best two boatmen! My donkey, Ass-Tied-Outside, would make a better boatman than both of you put together."

And their laughter joined the merry music and singing.

Shu-dagan bought another round of beer for his two workers— his best friends. He felt great; life had given him another chance to reap its delights. After a long stretch of misery, the future was looking bright. He was the commander of his own destiny, determined not to allow fate to meddle with his plans, like it did before.

The merry sounds came to a conspicuous drop in intensity when all attention was drawn toward the entrance; two strong men in full military attire walked in. Their searching eyes made it obvious it was not a drink they sought. The tavern owner greeted them, and after a short exchange, he pointed in Shu-dagan's direction. Discreetly, the soldiers approached and stood over his table.

"Are you the boatman Shu-dagan?" the taller soldier asked.

"At your service," Shu-dagan answered with the levity that was his trademark. "Owner of the fastest boat on the Euphrates. I'll take you to the other side anytime, rain or shine, storm or calm," he said in a singsong tone.

The two soldiers didn't seem amused by this introduction. The shorter man, whose robust bulk seemed to give him the commanding rank, cleared his throat.

"We are messengers from Uruk, sent by His Majesty, King Sargon, the mightiest ruler on Earth from sunrise to sunset—"

"And we cross the river from sunrise to sunset," Shu-dagan interrupted. "Also, we offer the best deal for crossings from sunset to sunrise. And soon we will have a fleet of boats to reach anywhere within the four corners of Earth."

Tammuz and his son stared at their friend, wide-eyed, fighting the urge to laugh. The soldiers kept a stoic demeanor.

"Shu-dagan," the taller one spoke formally, "you are the father of a girl named Mayram?"

"Pardon me," Shu-dagan answered. "You forgot to say: the most beautiful girl on the face of Earth from sunrise to sunset. Yes, what's this all about?"

Shu-dagan was all smiles. Someone related to the king—possibly the prince himself—must have sent these two messengers with an invitation to her wedding.

The soldiers bowed, and the shorter one cleared his throat again.

"Honorable sir, it is with great sorrow I deliver this message. Your daughter Mayram was the innocent victim of some cowardly traitors. His Majesty, the king himself, sends his condolences to you and your family. His Majesty also wants you to know that you should be proud of your daughter, for she did not die in vain. Because of her sacrifice, a plot to assassinate His Majesty was foiled. Your daughter Mayram has been declared a martyr. A shrine is being dedicated to honor her in a newly built temple of our goddess Ishtar."

The flat words seeped through the tavern like poison, smothering the singers and paralyzing the dancers. Shu-dagan's smile vanished under a stiffened face and his head felt too heavy to keep raised. All revelers watched anxiously, smitten by an air of unnerving silence.

Long moments passed before Shu-dagan exhaled a denial. "I'm not the man you're seeking—can't be my Mayram. What nonsense! No, not my Mayram!"

He took a sip of beer with the cup trembling on his lips.

"When my girl visits us next moon … a surprise will be waiting for her. … I had a carver chisel her name on the boat."

With a forefinger, he started tracing imaginary symbols on the table.

"MAYRAM … the only word I know to write." His gaze rested on the ghostly name he sketched.

"What traitors? What plot? *King, assassins* … Mayram has nothing to do with any of that. Forgive me for being rude, I'm hungry—leave me to eat in peace. Go away!"

He took a bite of some crusty bread, but it felt too dry in his mouth, and he spat it out. He slammed the table and stood up, a crazed look on his face.

"My Mayram cannot die! There must be dozens of Shu-dagans out there … fathers of Mayram daughters!" He sat back in the chair. "Damn fools! They come here dressed like soldiers and spoil the fun. Forgive me, *O brave valiant soldiers*, but you're in the wrong place. There is no war raging here; the drumming you hear is not a call for battle. This, here, is *a wedding*. … What happened to the music? Why has everyone gone silent? Go on, sing—dance!"

No one moved. A somber air of a funeral mutilated the wedding party. All held their stares on the father of a girl named Mayram.

"Forgive me, sir," the shorter soldier spoke. "We were told to ask for the father of a certain beautiful girl—the very one who sacrificed animals outside the main temple of Ishtar."

From a leather bag he carried, the soldier pulled a dagger out and placed it on the table.

"This belonged to the martyred girl. Do you recognize it?"

Shu-dagan couldn't part his eyes from the dreadful handle—an animal's bone with a flared end. Whoever made the grip hadn't bothered much in trimming it around the grooves of the joint where it had once articulated to another bone.

Thoughtlessly, Shu-dagan's trembling hand reached and pushed the bone's flared end; the dagger spun around itself. Shu-dagan was entranced, his surroundings spiraled, and he lost awareness of space and time.

$$\text{𒀭 𒅆 𒈫}$$

The dagger stopped spinning, ending his deep gaze into the absurdities of life. Shu-dagan picked it up and turned the grip over a couple of times.

"This ugly dagger is hers?"

"Yes," came the assertive answer.

"She used this … to slaughter the animal!" Shu-dagan let out a drunken chuckle. "Where did … where did she get it from?"

"I bought it for her," Arbella answered. "Remember the gift you gave me that *miserable day* I agreed to marry you—that piece of lapis lazuli? I traded it for—"

"You wasted that precious stone on this—a blade attached to a rotten bone ripped from an animal. Why? Was the animal divine—like some bull of heaven?"

Angrily, Shu-dagan addressed a phantom crowd. "Babylonians, behold! Feast your eyes on this—this dagger with a *bone* grip! Not just any bone, but the blessed bone of a fucking holy cow, of a putrid sacred ass, of a stinking sanctified pig!"

"Anything is better than you stealing it," Arbella screamed back, "only to waste it in the tavern. I bought it for her protection—so *my daughter* could defend herself, since *her father* is too busy getting drunk!"

Shu-dagan threw the dagger to the floor, walked to Arbella, and slapped her with a force that made her fall to the side.

"You dare scream at me … call me a thief!" He crouched over her, slapped her again, when unexpectedly he felt a push on his shoulder.

"Leave Mother alone," Mayram cried. "I was the one who brought the sheep's head. Punish me, not her."

With his upper arm, he viciously shoved Mayram to the ground.

"And by the gods, punish you I will!" He left Arbella and went over to Mayram and began slapping her. "How dare you bring meat? You think I'm not capable of bringing meat? You little thief … where did you steal the sheep's head from?"

Suddenly he found himself thrown to the floor when something rammed into him like a bull. He was briefly stunned by the force, then watched Arbella grab the hand of their daughter and run out of the shack.

Shu-dagan stood up and shouted after them. "Run, you bitch, run—and don't worry, you can rely on your little bandit to provide for you."

He trudged back inside and dropped knees first on a cushioned mat. Slowly, his body started leaning to one side till his head hit the mat, and he fell asleep.

The morning arrived, and he got up as if nothing had happened. He needed to shave and thought of using Mayram's dagger but couldn't find it. Then, to his surprise, he felt the sharp blade of a dagger shaving his neck. He looked at his hands and, strangely, they weren't wielding anything. Then he felt the cut; he cursed the dagger but was dumbfounded when the dagger answered back.

"Did you have a good night's sleep, dear beloved?"

Blinking his eyes open, Shu-dagan departed the dream. He was lying on his stomach, an arm firmly locked around his neck. From the corner of his eye, he met the savage look on his wife's face that told him not to move, lest the dagger in her grip do more than shave his throat. Shu-dagan swallowed his fear; he knew his wife would not allow anyone to touch her daughter and get away with it. Not even her father.

"Now listen, you bastard." Her words singed with fury. "The girl was so impatient for you to come home, she wouldn't touch the meat unless you tasted it first. I told you what happened to her—how a shepherd boy tried to violate her, and how she more than handled him on her own. But instead of praising her or being happy for her safety, *you beat her*! The boy wanted to rape our girl! Which part didn't you understand? *Which? Was I speaking Phoenician?*

"Forgive me—I guess what happens to her doesn't matter. What matters is that your pride was hurt because *she* brought meat to feed *you*. By the gods, how dare she violate the pride of my drunk, shameless, child-beating husband? Now hear me well, you dog, son of dogs! Touch my Mayram again, and I swear by all the gods of Babylon, you will wake up with the face of a Galla demon staring you in the eyes as it drags your soul to the netherworld. I swear I will chop your body to pieces, rip your bones apart and use them to make grips for daggers—daggers I will trade in the bazaar claiming they have the divine bones of *a fucking holy cow, of a stinking blessed ass, of a rotten hallowed pig.*"

Shu-dagan closed his eyes and murmured in a penitent, conquered voice:

"Do it … I failed you and our daughter … end this pathetic life."

Arbella gripped harder on the dagger but knew she would never do it, and she flung the dagger to a corner.

"Fool, I leave you to indulge in that pleasure yourself." Arbella stood up over him. "Who are you? What happened to the loving, graceful man I married?" She wiped her wet eyes and left.

Shu-dagan rolled over to lie on his back, praying he would wake up from a sickening daydream. Hesitantly, his eyes traced the floor to the corner, only to find the blade's point staring at him. Overwhelmed by an unbearable guilt, he struggled to his feet, picked the dagger up, and stepped outside to where Arbella was standing.

"Where is she?" he asked, almost in a whisper.

Arbella pointed to a figure huddled under a palm tree.

Unhurriedly, he walked, thinking of what to say, feeling like a child about to ask an adult forgiveness for some folly he had committed.

Mayram sat against the tree, her knees tucked to her chest, when her father came to sit before her on the dirt. He looked in her eyes and was shocked by how their calm was overtaken by alarm. He turned his head slightly away to avoid the ugly image of himself that didn't deserve to be in her beautiful eyes.

"What happened … with the shepherd?" He was confused, not sure of where to start.

Mayram remained silent. She was present when he heard the details from Arbella; what more could she add? After all, she was a child, and relating such an incident to a man was mortifying. It was a task she entrusted to her mother.

Shu-dagan extended a hand holding her dagger. "Take it."

Mayram only tucked her knees in tighter.

"Take it," he repeated.

She shook her head, not wanting to touch the dagger at all.

"I'm …" He paused, almost saying, *the greatest fool in Babylon.* Instead, he continued, "I'm the proudest man in Babylon … for having the bravest daughter."

He placed the dagger at her side. She remained quiet.

"Beat me," he said.

She was taken aback as he closed in to within her arm's reach.

"I mean it. It's only fair. *Beat me.*"

She stared at him but didn't move a whisker.

"You must," he said firmly.

Mayram made a fist, hesitated, then tapped him on the chest.

He smiled. "Harder."

She put a little more force into the punch.

"That didn't hurt either. Much harder!"

Again and again he urged her to put in more effort, and she punched him until her eyes welled with tears.

"Father, I don't want to. Stop asking me to hurt you, I can't! I know you didn't mean to hurt me … I know. I know you love me."

Shu-dagan was speechless. He could only stare at her fist, still thinking of a way to make it inflict some real pain on him. But any hopes of that were dashed as he watched her fingers slowly break free of the punishing grip. Without thinking, he reached to tenderly touch the hand that denied him his just punishment, bringing it to his lips— and he kissed it. Nothing he could've said was enough to excuse his rage at the most precious thing in his life. He even felt ashamed of the way he had tried to apologize.

"I … have to go to work." He stood up and left.

The guilt never ebbed, even though he rowed the boat all day, harder than he ever had. Sunset arrived and he was still plagued with self-hatred. He vowed to go straight home, but at an intersection where the path to a tavern began, his legs moved in that direction involuntarily. He walked into the tavern and sat at a table. Struggling with his weakness, he knew he was going to lose, but resolved to lose in a winning way.

"What are you having?" the tavern owner asked.

"My friends should arrive shortly," answered Shu-dagan, "then we will decide."

The owner walked away. Shu-dagan surveyed the tavern and moved toward two men who were chatting and laughing. He picked a cup from their table, gulped some beer, and placed it back, then did the same with the companion's cup. The two men only stared in disbelief at the mad stranger who had just sampled their drinks.

"They say it tastes even better when you don't pay for it," Shu-dagan said, grinning. "Only now do I believe that."

One of the men, the strongest he could find in the tavern, stood up and punched him in the stomach. Shu-dagan hunched over, but the pain wasn't enough to free him from his self-loathing. He straightened up, a smile still firm on his face.

"Is that the best you can do?" he taunted the man, prompting him to follow with another punch.

"You punch like a temple priestess I didn't pay for her love service," Shu-dagan mocked.

"You want to fight, go outside—not in my tavern," hollered the owner.

"He's drunk," yelled a man from another table. "Just ignore him."

"Bless you, my friend, for understanding my condition." Shu-dagan nodded in gratitude, then grabbed both cups from the table and started walking away. The two men were briefly mesmerized by his audacity before they jumped on him, one grabbing him in a choke hold. The drinks spilled all over, followed by the cups shattering on the brick floor. The men dragged Shu-dagan outside, and more beating followed.

Shu-dagan offered little resistance, letting them knock him around. He needed to match the agony of a helpless child being beaten by a demented father.

Under a glamorous full moon, Shu-dagan dragged his aching body back home, but he was at peace with himself; the two men had done an excellent job in casting out his demons of guilt.

He arrived within sight of his shack. It was safely past the time when his wife and daughter went to sleep. He had to spare them the spectacle of his sorry condition. Cautiously he moved on, prepared to retreat, just in case the sleep spirits were late in visiting his shack.

All was quiet on his way to get some much-needed sleep, when suddenly, from a hailing distance away, a figure bolted in his direction. He cursed the sleep spirits, turned around to run, but his body protested; it was not going to take any more punishment for the night.

"Father, Father!" Mayram called out, all excited. "I went to pick some dates when this nice lady came to me and filled one whole basket with all kinds of fruits from her farm."

Shu-dagan stood still with his back to her.

"The nice lady gave me fresh pears, apricots, peaches, even pomegranates—all good ones, no worms inside. The basket was so heavy. She says I can go back tomorrow and ..." Mayram stopped, feeling something was wrong, and slowly went around him.

"Father, is that blood on your face? Oh, by the goddess, what happened to you?" She grabbed his hand and led him to the shack. Inside, she had him sit in a chair.

"Mother is very tired; she's sleeping. Don't worry, I'll take care of you. Wait here, Father, I'll be back."

She ran and came back with a jar of water and a rag; she started to wipe his face when, abruptly, she broke into heavy tears.

"Don't worry," he said in a tired voice. "It's just small cuts and bruises. Foolish of me, I fell in the dark ... right on my face."

"I don't believe you, Father ... I don't believe you." She kept crying and wiping her eyes. The blood staining her hand blended with the tears and slid down to her lips. The taste of his blood made her sob in torrents that flowed with the sweetest words he had ever heard:

"Forgive me, Father, I couldn't hurt you when you asked me to. But I swear by the goddess of love … by this beating heart of mine, next time I will beat you very hard—will truly hurt you … will not disappoint you, Father. Just, don't harm yourself like this—don't!"

With one fist she was tapping on his chest while the other hand worked on his wounds.

Shu-dagan ran a hand over her wet face and gently drew her to his aching body in a tight embrace.

"Don't worry, my sweet flower, don't cry. … There won't be a next time."

All eyes in the tavern were riveted on the bone-grip dagger that must have witnessed the tragic demise of its owner. As for Shu-dagan, it was the dagger that did the staring, defying him to take possession of it again. It was a reminder of his ugly side, yet it reflected the warm memory of the bittersweet turn of events that saved him from self-destruction and brought back the strong, proud man that he had thought was lost forever.

The two soldiers were patient for a reply from the silent father who appeared to be in a deep trance, when suddenly, his eyes welled with tears. No other answer could have been more convincing; beyond the slightest doubt, the martyr was the boatman's daughter.

A large pouch settled on the table, next to the dagger. It rang with a sound familiar to Shu-dagan—another distant memory from moons ago when Mayram gave him a pouch stuffed with the gold that made him a boat owner.

"This is a token of appreciation from His Majesty, King Sargon," the taller soldier said, "and on behalf of all the people, for your daughter's noble sacrifice in guarding the kingdom."

After a long gaze at the pouch, Shu-dagan hesitantly reached for it, untied the leather cord, and poured the contents out. Pieces of silver and gold scattered on the table. He held up one piece of silver.

"The ugliest thing I've ever seen." Furiously, he tossed it at the shorter soldier, before selecting a golden one.

"This is not my Mayram. It doesn't look anything like her beautiful face, her warm smile … nothing like her loving, innocent eyes … nothing like her, *nothing*! You can't change a precious goddess—*my girl*—into some worthless stones." He flung the nugget across the room; then with a sweep of his arm, his beer cup along with pieces of gold and silver went flying off the table. The two soldiers took a step back on seeing Shu-dagan erupt into a frenzy.

"I want my Mayram! You, lying bastards, what did you do to my Mayram?"

With anger flaring, Shu-dagan absently grabbed the dagger and lunged toward the tall messenger. But his vision, misted with beer and boiling with rage, failed to alert him to the silver and gold pieces on the floor. His ankle twisted, sending him staggering to one side. By the time he corrected his stance, the shorter soldier had one arm around his neck in a choke hold. Shu-dagan was frantically slicing the air around him with the dagger when a heavy fist landed in his stomach. This reversed the flow of beer back into his mouth, disrupting the airflow, and his thrashing halted. The soldier released his grip, and Shu-dagan fell to his knees, vomiting and smearing the floor with beer fermented in stomach acid. Despite that, there was no stopping the rage from driving him to pursue another assault, but he lacked the speed to surprise the two messengers. A kick to the chest flung him to the side. He managed to remain on hands and knees as he struggled for air, but there was no pain yet to stop him; his body was numb with sorrow for the loss of the one who was his reason to live.

"Stay down! We came here to honor, not hurt you," the heavy soldier shouted.

But words alone could not sway the crazed father from lashing out at the men who had dared declare his Mayram was gone. A leftover pulse of madness erupted, and he sprang up, but another kick, harder than the first, flung him onto his back and knocked the dagger out of his grip. It also knocked the numbness out of his body, awakening pain from a deep sleep.

The heavy soldier hunched over Shu-dagan and punched him twice in the face to make sure he stayed down. Shu-dagan tried to pick himself up but, like a turtle turned over onto its shell, he could only shake his limbs.

"Stay down!" the tall messenger shouted, pressing his boot on Shu-dagan's chest. "We understand your pain and anger, but don't blame us. We're only two messengers assigned this unfortunate task of informing you of the sad fate suffered by your honorable daughter Mayram."

"My Mayram is alive and well," Shu-dagan moaned. "She's immortal … more immortal than that Ark man, that Deluge fool, Zuisudra. She's forever … immortal."

The two messengers walked out of the tavern. Shortly, they were followed by the wedding party and all the clients except for Tammuz, who struggled to get his friend off the floor, not sure how to console him, while his son went around, collecting the scattered silver and gold pieces back into the leather pouch.

In the quiet tavern, Shu-dagan sat on a chair, casting an empty gaze that carried his battered body and soul back to the shack.

My Mayram will be there. … She will clean my wounds.

And he stared, watching her soothe his pain as she cried, only this time it was his tears that she let stream freely over his face, and it was with his fist she gently beat on his chest, while sweet words she kept chanting in his ears:

"Father, I will beat you much harder—will not disappoint you. Next time, I promise I will hurt you. Yes Father, hurt you I swear, by our sacred goddess of love … by this beating heart of mine."

The Grave Robber

He picked a rose from the heap of flowers. Only lifeless brown and crisp dryness greeted him. Gently, he rolled it over, seeking a clue as to what color it possessed, but there was none. He went peeling it to expose the intimate petals that were never given the chance to touch the light.

In that abode of the dead, Gudea was assailed by a need to find a residue of color or soft skin in those petals—a sign of life.

"Who did this to you?" he murmured, absently presuming the flower was asking for vengeance.

The heat—must be whipping me into madness.

Still, he kept stripping the dead petals until he reached the very heart. A trace of red on the bulb—the flower's last gasp of life—could be distinguished from the brown plaguing the outer petals. He stared at it, as though expecting it to divulge the name of the one who pruned its life.

Gudea was about to walk away from the grave when deep within he felt a haunting protest from the buried Babylonian girl for thieving one of her flowers.

"Forgive me, young lady; may I take this one rose?" He apologized, and the ghost floating over the dead flowers abandoned his thoughts. Somehow relieved from guilt, Gudea moved on.

The day was stifling, and as he expected, no one would be visiting the cemetery around noontime, unless they were grave robbers too.

Sizable sections of the graveyard had been stripped of trees; the residents who moved to the netherworld never made a single complaint about the lack of shaded areas caused by thieves harvesting the trees. As for Gudea, shade wouldn't have provided much comfort, for anger raged inside him hotter than the rays sent by the sun god Shamash.

On reaching his destination, he pulled a short, bronze spade from a leather sack he'd brought. He started digging at the grave when, unwillingly, his memories went digging in a past he hated to visit.

Both his wife, Tammara, and their adopted daughter, Amare, would've been alive had he persisted with his retirement plans. But those plans evaporated when the former king lured him into a trade trip that promised profits beyond compare. So instead of telling the king that his trading days were over, the lust for adventure coupled with greed took a hold of Gudea, and he dove head over heels, planning for that one last great endeavor.

If only I had declined that trip! Guilt haunted him again—a thing that had become part of Gudea's everyday life after Allamu had revealed the details of how Amare ended up joining an entourage of people who were intombed alive to please a departed king in the afterlife.

"His Putrid, Highly Stinking Majesty!" Gudea cursed the former king. "He should've been buried with nothing but dog dung to accompany him!"

Angrily, Gudea stabbed at the earth that only contained his wife's body.

Tammara's dismal end came shortly after Amare had vanished. She became an easy prey for death once denial had crazed her mind. The neighbors told Gudea how Tammara had never lost hope of finding Amare. She used to greet them every morning on the way out, saying she was going to find her girl. The servants gave up on trying to stop her after she threatened to replace them. Off she would go until the evening, when she would drag herself into the house, silent and defeated.

Gudea had talked to the last man to see Tammara alive: a boatman who had gotten to know her well after she began taking his boat regularly, across to the other side of the city in her search for Amare. He felt pity for Tammara and likened her to a stack of bones—a body baked thin and dry under the sun for long moons.

"On that sad day, she looked so happy," the boatman had recounted to Gudea, "I couldn't believe it was Tammara, for until then her face had never expressed anything but gloom. Also, for some reason, she came carrying a jar."

That revealed to Gudea the fate of the missing jar where Tammara guarded the remains of their own daughter who'd died in her infancy.

"How foolish of me," Tammara had told the boatman. "I should've known. Amare is with her mother and father. All that time I wasted, searching—and she was with them."

The boatman rowed briskly, delighted to see Tammara brimming with life. Halfway across the river, while rowing with his back to her, he heard her say:

"God bless you, dear friend, this is good; Amare is somewhere around here. At last, we will be together again—all of us."

Those were her last words. The boatman turned and saw Tammara firmly hugging the jar, smiling happily as she jumped into the water, confident she would finally find her girl, only to sink like a stone—down into the same river that had taken away Amare's parents.

Her body had washed up not far down the river. The boatman knew in which locality she lived, which helped in finding people to identify her.

Defying heat and the scorching sun, Gudea dug at the dry ground while his body drowned in sweat, until he reached the small vase that contained the gifts—two gifts that were supposed to shine alongside the bright smiles on his Tammara and Amare. But that was not to be; the gifts had ended up inside a clay vase, dressing a coffin, enshrined in the darkness of a grave.

Gudea reached down to pull the vase out. Upon touching it, he felt uneasy; the gifts weren't his for the taking.

"O Fate," he moaned, "you progeny of deceit and treachery. How cruel is your mockery, reducing me to a man who robs the grave of loved ones!"

And the man who didn't believe much in the gods had words of prayer pouring out of him. Then the man who didn't believe in ghosts began talking to the spirits of the ones dear to him.

Soon, those spirits consented to lend him the gifts, and Gudea effortlessly pulled the vase out, removed its lid, and turned it upside down. A necklace and a cylinder seal landed in his palm next to the dying heart of the rose he had picked from the other grave.

"Little flower," he said, slipping the rose into the vase, "welcome to your new home, where beautiful souls reside."

Gently, he lowered the vase back in place, and proceeded to shovel the dirt into the hole as he whispered soothing words to put the spirits he had disturbed back to rest.

"I will return these gifts soon, my beloved," he whispered, concluding his prayers and promises, when it occurred to him: he had just traded words in exchange for the treasure he had dug out.

"A Word Merchant I have become." He sighed, and his memory voyaged back to Phoenicia, to his young days when he had given away a belt studded with fine stones for a string of words coming from the mouth of an older merchant, thus forcing his destiny into a sharp turn that pointed him toward a life of adventure and wealth, filling him with a sense of power and security, only to later toss the ones he loved into the deep pits of tragedy.

Having obtained what he came for, along with the unforeseen designation of "Word Merchant," Gudea walked away from the burial grounds, leaving behind the peace of the ghosts to rejoin the struggle with the living.

Feast in Peace

HIS ROARS GREW LOUDER AS HE WATCHED THE SUN BREAK ITS bonds, step over the horizon, and climb free on its way to the heavens. Yet the brighter the disc glowed, the more it made the lion aware of his dark reality. Once again, his desperate screams were fully ignored by the treacherous sun.

It wasn't hunger that fed his desperation, nor was it the need for females that roused his anger; it was the yearning for his territory that had shrunk from the vast wide horizons to the meager four steps the cage offered.

Assaulting and scratching the wooden bars of the cage yielded no results. Cursing the gods with loud roars was all he could do. It was they who had reduced him from the king of all wild animals to the prisoner of those vicious, two-legged creatures who denied him the privilege of an honorable death in the heat of a fight. They showed absolute disregard for the laws of nature that bade a predator to kill the vanquished swiftly, prolonging not its suffering.

The lion enviously watched the birds wheeling between heaven and Earth. They had him yearn for the sanctuary offered by the darkness of night, which spared him the display of all the freedoms that now escaped him. Even his roar had suffered; normally, it would send all animals racing in terror before sighting him. Barred in the cage, his roar had a note of desperation that made it no more threatening than the purr of a cat. The flocks of livestock trailed behind and calmly followed in his path instead of running in the opposite direction.

Allamu stood with reins in hand, guiding a two-horse carriage. Attached behind was a flatbed on wheels where the lion's cage was secured. Not far ahead of him, Sargon rode on his royal chariot flanked by the chariots of his guards. To the rear came soldiers walking along with the so-called special forces, comprised of numerous drawn carriages with cages containing all sorts of fowl, pigs, wild boars, and countless jars of beer. Shepherds guiding sheep and goats followed the convoy all the way back.

What is Sargon scheming? Allamu brooded again over the same question that had baffled him throughout the march. Was Sargon really seeking peace with Ur by sending Allamu unharmed as a token of goodwill, along with an army of livestock to feed the starving city?

But the lion was the greater mystery. *What purpose would it serve?*

Knowing how unpredictable Sargon was, Allamu could only speculate that the fate chosen for him might be to satisfy a blood-thirsty Sargon; to have Allamu thrown in the lion's cage and eaten alive while Sargon and his men feasted in an open-air banquet. He could imagine the horror of the people of Ur, who would be watching helplessly from the parapets of the city walls.

Terrifying as it was, Allamu contemplated this glorious way of dying. He would even thank Sargon for granting him this death by the noblest of animals, no matter how gruesome it would be. To be spared a humiliating end at the hands of another human was what mattered to him most. He would face the lion bravely, unshaken by the beast's roar. He would endure the short moments of ruthless agony with the lion's crushing jaw locked on his neck—thus rendering him incapable of making the faintest sound even if the urge to scream managed to defeat his will to remain silent. He would prevail and not emit any sound, to the chagrin of those sadistic bastards who would be salivating to savor his shrieks of horror. Then finally—peace, and one he becomes with the king of beasts.

The walls of Ur shimmered in the distance, and before it, lines of soldiers waved like colonies of ants. The army ranks were coming alive with the heralded news of the king's arrival at the head of some special forces. The senior officers raced to greet the king and brief him on the latest developments. There weren't much of those to mention, for hardly anything had changed except for the troops' exacerbated frustration at the quality of food and drink, boredom, and the absence of women. There were always the quarrels over trivial things, like cheating at board games and accusations of theft of reed mats, palm fronds, and other petty materials used to build their tiny huts. This visit by the king would be a welcome change to the dull routine, with the added excitement and intense arguments it generated as to the nature of the elite special forces accompanying His Royal Highness.

Once it was revealed that the formidable special forces consisted of mere sheep, chicken, and their ilk, frowns of disbelief were the first exhibits on the faces, then gradually the sounds of laughter besieged the camp. The soldiers called out guesses about the plan of attack: perhaps ducks would covertly fly over the walls at night and open the gates. Then the brave boars and their pig cousins would lead the first wave to charge inside the city. Right behind, the elite fighting roosters would fly in the face of the enemies, pecking them blind, rendering them useless. Finally, the goats with their razor-sharpened horns would finish off the remaining fighters. Last to enter would be the sheep, to occupy the city and calm things down with their gentle bleats.

Sargon rode through the lines of soldiers assembled on the sides of the road leading to the city gates. He stopped at a distance deemed safely out of the enemy archers' range. The convoy that followed split to form a large semicircle behind him.

When the dust settled, Sargon walked to a sentry, grabbed his spear, and headed toward the lion's chariot.

Allamu braced himself, foreseeing Sargon's barbaric plan in using the spear to disable him before having him dragged to be fed to the lion alive. A fleeting thought occurred to him of whipping the horses and making a dash to the city gates, but he knew his cart was too heavy, and they would easily catch up to him.

This could be their plan—for me to flee for the gates; and if Kebboba were foolish enough to order the gates opened for me, then the archers on the pursuing chariots would aim their arrows to kill my horses upon reaching the gates, jamming them open for Sargon's army to penetrate the city.

Resigned to his unknown fate, Allamu stood still, casting a sad look at the walls of the imprisoned city, when Sargon's voice blared behind, addressing the lion.

"Such a handsome, noble creature. … Cursed be the cruel Destiny, to have dealt you a most atrocious treachery!"

The lion raved and sliced at the wooden bars with both paws in a hopeless attempt to break free and savage the one who dared approach him.

"No one understands your anger like I do, my fellow king. But such is your allotted fate. How horrible it must feel to be abandoned by the gods!"

The lion stopped roaring and fighting the cage, out of exhaustion and confusion at the sincerity in the voice of a fellow king giving him solace in this predicament.

"O Great King, I bow to you." Sargon went down on one knee to everyone's amazement. "I ask forgiveness for causing you this humiliation. But don't fret; yours will be an honorable death, by the hands of the King of all Kings."

Sargon stood up and gripped the spear with both hands.

The lion sensed that the end of his reign had arrived. He didn't cower but roared ferociously and stood up tall with both claws dug into the wooden bars. Sargon plunged the point of the spear deep into the lion's chest, planting the seed of death that sprouted savagely, chasing life out. The lion thundered in agony, loathing the treacherous gods in their heavens, while the demons within Earth's entrails trembled at the echoes of his last rage.

Sargon pulled the spear free, and the lion sank to his haunches. His last spasms of life quickened in a race with the streaming blood. He rested his head down and stared, eyes longing for one last taste of freedom. Vision blurring, he saw the skyline spread its wings and speed to his confinement; the bars it obliterated, and a sweet breeze of freedom embraced him. Deeply, he inhaled it in a last gasp then released the air of its duty, liberating his soul from both body and cage.

Sargon reached inside the cage and placed both hands on the lion's head in a solemn act of prayer, then turned to face the silence that enveloped the camp and shouted:

"Let the feast preparations begin!"

Everyone came back to life as if they had received an order to start breathing again.

Men rushed by with wood fashioned to be assembled into tables and benches. One huge table was set up and placed at the front for the best viewing from the city walls. Others carried firewood, jars of water, cooking pots, plates, and cups. The butchers pulled out their sharp knives, and the massacre of fowl and livestock commenced. Feathers were pulled off and flesh stripped of hide. The meat was prepared to be stewed, grilled, or roasted on fire.

The lion's body was carried out of the cage and placed on a large table where two butchers stood ready with their fine, hide-skinning tools.

Sargon walked to Allamu, who remained by his chariot, looking at the empty, bloodstained cage.

"Allamu!" Sargon called. "Why are you standing on your own, staring at the lion's ghost? Come, come. This feast is made in your honor—the man who will bring peace to our troubled land."

Allamu moved reluctantly, doubting every word uttered by Sargon's mouth. The slaughter of the lion only deepened his anguish.

"Your Majesty, I am overwhelmed by your generosity," he said, despite being convinced that the treacherous king had something sordid planned for him.

"Allamu, Allamu! Today, *you* are the center of attention. Forget about the honorifics, call me Sargon like all my friends do." Sargon wrapped an arm around the general's shoulder and led him to the table where the two butchers were working on the slaughtered lion.

"Are we ready?" Sargon asked them.

"Yes, Majesty. It's ready for extraction."

"Good." Sargon turned to the chief of guards, who was right behind him. "Hukura, let me have your dagger."

Sargon held the dagger by the blade and offered it to Allamu. "To you, my friend in battles and victories, I give the honor of extracting the heart of this brave lion."

Hukura was alarmed upon watching Sargon recklessly hand a weapon to a traitor; his hand tensed, ready to reach for the grip of his sword.

Cautiously, Allamu took hold of the dagger. He knew Hukura was prepared to cut him down at the sign of the slightest suspicious move that might endanger the king. He turned to the lion where it lay with the rib cage cracked open, exposing the heart that had gone silent in mourning for its departed king. Allamu cut out the heart, then handed it along with the dagger to Sargon. The butchers went back to their delicate task, neatly skinning the lion's hide.

"Now, my great general,"—Sargon patted Allamu on the shoulder—"you sit back and do as you please while we prepare the feast in your honor."

"I appreciate your kindness … Sargon."

Sargon handed the lion's heart to the man in charge of the cooks, who was waiting close by. Then, accompanied by Hukura, he took a leisurely stroll to observe the feast's preparations.

Chaos dominated the scene; it was like a battle zone where the only ones butchered belonged to the enemy's side. An enthralled Sargon walked among the crowd, joking with the cooks, discussing cooking recipes and suggesting some of his own. He couldn't resist participating—chopping meat, adding vegetables to the stew, turning the roasting spit. He even chased after an escaping chicken; many could have captured it, but they wisely chose to corner it for the king to easily grab. Grinning, Sargon held it upside down by the legs and announced:

"By royal decree, I pardon this chicken for her bravery and fighting spirit. Let no harm come upon her." He placed the chicken on the ground. It flapped its wings and scurried away, squawking amid the laughing men.

Sargon was in one of his best moods. Men ambled around him without feeling obligated to keep a respectful distance or bow. A walking band of musicians and singers added happy melodies to the festive scene.

The sun was just past its apex when Sargon walked to the large table at the front and sat on his chair—the only one shaded from the onslaught of sunrays by a lattice of palm fronds. The musicians followed him, their joyful tunes now spiced up by some scantily dressed women dancers; the small beads and transparent veils wound around their waists and over their breasts didn't leave much to the imagination.

Lured by the dancers, the high-ranking commanders hurriedly occupied all the seats, and the soldiers were quick to follow to the side lines. Starved for women after all those moons, ravenously they watched the girls sway to the music and show more of what little was hidden beneath their sparse veils.

But more than anything else, it was peace that everyone was starving for. The people of Ur needed to forget how the siege had made them resort to cannibalism. To the soldiers outside, peace meant returning to their own families instead of bringing death and destruction to the families of others.

Sargon had his hands full with the shaking buttocks of one dancer, when the head of cooks approached and spoke to him. Sargon whipped the dancer on her behind, and she walked away smiling.

"Rejoice, everyone—the food is ready to serve!" Sargon's announcement was met by heated applause. He invited Allamu to sit next to him.

Cups of wine and beer came first, then plates of food crammed the tables, but no one dared touch the food. They only gobbled down the aroma invading their noses from a wide assortment of dishes, while their stomachs screamed for the king to start eating. The feast seemed as if it had been prepared for the gods, bringing fears that the greedy gods might descend at any moment and not leave until their divine appetite had been fulfilled.

The head of cooks returned with a large pot. He placed it before Sargon and bowed.

"Majesty, King of all Kings, I will be honored if you start the feast with this special dish: the heart of the lion you slayed, prepared by me, your humble cook, uniquely to delight Your Majesty's fine taste."

"No, no, no." Sargon shook his head in disagreement. "How can a king eat food prepared by a humble cook? Everyone, raise your cups. A toast to our man here, the greatest—Master of all Cooks from sunrise to sunset!"

All happily obliged and rushed some wine to their pleading stomachs.

The cook was embarrassed by the attention and stammered words of appreciation.

Sargon wiped his mouth with a bare hand, then regarded the men seated at the table.

"By the gods, you look starved. … I can tell you're already plotting to overthrow me just to get to the food." Everyone laughed. "That I can understand, for it smells so good. But first, a few words in honor of our friend Allamu."

Sargon turned to the man to his right. "Even before I came to know him personally, we were fighting in the same battles. We probably saved each other without knowing it by finishing off the enemy swordsman who was about to deliver a treacherous stab in the back, or the spearman who was about to throw the lance, or the archer with his arrows of lightning speed. Only the gods know how close we fought next to each other. What matters is that we shared many glorious victories and some bitter defeats as we rose through the ranks. All—yes, all—in the service of our land and its people.

"Now, we do have our differences. Some bad decisions were made, but I don't want to go deep into that. The important thing is to put the good of the kingdom above all other trivial personal feelings.

"Allamu: You are our last hope for peace—to end the siege and bring the city of Ur back into the welcoming arms of the kingdom. But that can wait till after we have this feast. I don't want your sister Kebboba to say I didn't feed you well." Again, everyone laughed. "By the way, the wine is from her special vintage. … A toast to Allamu, to wish him success in his peace mission."

All drank to that, then watched Sargon use a knife to slice off a piece of the lion's heart, offering it to Allamu.

"Let's not keep our starving friends waiting. Allamu, do us the honor of starting the feast."

Allamu wondered for an instant whether poison was the choice platter that would consume his life. But such a killing method lacked the intense cruelty, suspense, and creativity that had lately characterized the king's punishments. Either way, poison or no poison, Allamu knew he had no choice. With the whole crowd looking at him, he took the chunk of heart from Sargon's hand. Without hesitation, he put it in his mouth and started chewing, expecting pain to tear his stomach apart at any moment.

"How is it?" Sargon asked.

"Very delicious." Allamu wasn't lying.

"Want another piece?"

"I would be very grateful," Allamu answered. If it was poisoned, then he might as well make it work faster.

Sargon sliced a larger piece, but as soon as Allamu reached for it, the piece disappeared into Sargon's mouth.

"Sorry, it's my turn." Sargon grinned as he chewed, and all the men roared with laughter.

With the suspicion of poison totally eradicated, even Allamu wore a smile on his face.

"It is delicious!" Sargon concurred, then noticed all the guests looking at him.

"What are you waiting for?" he shouted, tiny chunks of meat flying out of his mouth. "Charge! Attack the food!"

Never had an army followed a commander's order at a swifter speed. Instantly the table became a battleground with knives hacking meat and ripping bones apart. The table shook and wine spilled over the rims of cups, staining the wood red.

Allamu, now with an unshaken certainty that Sargon wasn't planning to kill him, had the appetite of the lion whose heart lay lodged in his stomach. He devoured more of the heart and tried many other dishes, eating voraciously like a silkworm that soon would transform into a butterfly—freed from the cocoon of fear that had incased him for the last few moons.

With bellies filling up and wine working its magic on the mood, humor and laughter took over the table and extended to the rest of the camp. The soldiers were also treated to a feast—but to a lesser degree than their commanders. The siege outside the city turned into a celebration—stomachs stretching out, music playing, and happy faces declaring victory over gloom.

"I'm praying to the gods," Sargon said to Allamu, "that your sister will not complain about how I treated you."

"It's useless. She'll still complain, for she was not invited," Allamu joked, surprising himself with the revival of his own humor.

Sargon laughed heartily. "Next feast, she'll be the first to be invited. Imagine if she stops sending me her wine—life will be unbearable. That's why I'm relying on you, my friend, to bring peace."

"I'll try my best." Allamu nodded.

Sargon waved to someone in the distance. Allamu, with some remnants of fear still resident in his heart, glanced over his shoulder. The two butchers who had worked on the lion approached, carrying something large, draped in cloth. They unfurled it; tucked inside was the lion's hide.

Sargon rose off his chair and, with the help of the butchers, shook the lion's skin loose. He told Allamu to stand up and placed the hide over his shoulders. Allamu appeared to have shrunk down with the lion swallowing him whole. He had to push the lion's head back to uncover his face.

"Remarkable! A perfect fit." Sargon beamed and announced for all to hear: "Allamu, you will wear this when you enter the city. Yes, that's how you will enter—like a lion, and people will listen to you."

"Oh Sargon, how generous of you—how extravagant! I'm not worthy of all of this."

"Nonsense, my friend." Sargon patted him on the shoulder. "A lot hangs on the success of your mission."

"I'm truly grateful, Sargon; I'm so overwhelmed. But what am I going to tell them? You still haven't detailed your terms for peace."

"My friend, we don't want to spoil the feast with boring talk of negotiations—that can wait. Anyway, the terms are few and reasonable, not much to memorize. For now, enjoy yourself; drink and eat to your heart's content."

"Sargon, I greatly appreciate this lavish treatment. But I swear by the gods, never in my life have I eaten so much." A smile traversed Allamu's wine-flushed face.

"Just a little bit more," Sargon insisted. "Even I took part in preparing this feast. Your sister must be standing up there, watching from the tower. I want her to know I come in good faith to feed all the people of Ur, just as I fed you. That's simply the major part of the message to deliver. So go on, eat, my friend—eat!"

"Sargon, I'm deeply gratified by all of this, but I ate like a savage lion." Allamu shook the beast's hide, and the men laughed. "Believe me when I say my stomach is screaming; it can't take any more food. There is not the tiniest space, not even for a single grain of wheat."

Smiling, Sargon nodded and proclaimed: "Allamu says, 'Enough of the food!' He's so full, his stomach ran out of space! I guess it's time he prepares for his peace mission."

Sargon removed the hide from Allamu's back, handing it to the butchers.

"Ooh, the lion looks very disappointed. I know he's still very hungry." And Sargon went into a chuckling fit, spreading contagious laughter that breezed away to the soldiers at the sidelines.

"Why are you laughing?" a soldier asked his friend. "What did I miss?"

"What do I know? When the king laughs, you laugh—it's the rule. Why laugh? Hopefully, we'll find out later."

A Wall of Eyes and Ears

"**S**ARGON GRABBED SOMETHING FROM THE TABLE ... I BELIEVE, a knife."

The herald shouted with his head angled sideways.

"Sargon appears to be slicing something ... he offered it to Allamu. I can tell that Allamu is chewing." The herald took a longer pause.

"Now Sargon is eating from that same plate ... the feast has started!"

A raucous cheer rebounded from the crowd gathered atop Ur's city wall.

It all started with the nobles who had bribed the soldiers to gain access to the foremost defensive points at the battlements, where they could watch all the preparations for the banquet. Wistfully they looked, nostalgic for the excesses they had missed because of the siege.

It didn't take long before word spread out, and the city's inhabitants invaded the parapets, defeating all attempts by the soldiers to force them down. Men clambered over each other's shoulders to catch a glimpse of the feast outside. All were excited by the prospect of peace that had arrived when Kebboba's half-brother, Allamu, and King Sargon crept over the horizon with the rising sun.

General Shulgi came out to assess the commotion at the top of the wall, but it was already too late. He chose not to spoil the thrill, which could give rise to a furious backlash or even a revolution by the bitter and hungry mob. The guards' duties he changed to keeping order and stopping scuffles that arose in the mayhem.

Those standing at the very front feasted their eyes on the delights prepared outside, happily welcoming the occasional aroma carried by the generous breeze. They gave something back to the public, volunteering their voices to relay what took place behind the enemy lines; how the lion was killed, the livestock butchered, the army of cooks, the stewing and roasting. The questions that flew back and forth were no longer about how many soldiers were amassed out there and what murderous weapons they possessed; instead the queries were about the livestock and the rough estimate of their numbers. Rumors spread fast that every family in Ur could get at least a sheep's weight in meat.

The prospect of the siege ending and life going back to normal framed smiles across the haggard faces. Men and women who could hardly walk before now found themselves dancing in the streets. Praises were showered on the hero Allamu, who was given the high honor of starting the feast by eating before King Sargon himself. Many interpreted the gesture as a good omen—that Sargon came in peace to negotiate a reasonable resolution to the conflict.

Kebboba stood next to Shulgi at the watchtower, the highest point on the wall no noble dared occupy. She kept squinting, having doubts that the man sitting to the king's right side was her half-brother.

"For sure, it is Allamu," Shulgi asserted. "Sargon has finally come to his senses. He's begging for peace and the return of that rotten, *pretty prince*—his only legitimate heir. All the others—bastards from concubines—don't count. He needs Naram-sin after all the time and effort spent on training him in the disciplines of war and ruling a kingdom. I tell you, Kebboba, it was a gift from the gods when that boy walked through the gates. Well, I must give you credit; the fool took commands from his hard shaft, and you were just the right bait for it." Shulgi laughed. "*The Great Sargon*, king of all dung from sunrise to sunset, will need a whole lot more than your half-brother for the exchange, and I'm not talking about sheep and chickens."

"You talk of success too early," Kebboba scoffed. "You see a white cloud in the desert and right away you start sowing seeds. So far, all you've done is close the gates and struggle to keep the enemy outside. Look at our people—starving, yet they are singing and dancing, happy simply with the thought there is food outside, waiting for them."

"Look who's talking!" Shulgi snapped. "How about you, Lady

Kebboba? A prince spills some seed inside you, and you think you'll grow to be a queen."

"Sometimes you have to make sacrifices for peace."

"And what did you sacrifice?" Shulgi countered scornfully. "Your vagina! Last time I checked, it was in perfect shape—firmly gripping, passionately flooding my rod."

Kebboba cast him a scorching look and turned her gaze back to the feast without saying a word.

"For heaven's sake, Kebboba." Shulgi adopted a soothing tone. "Let me handle things my way. Do you recall when you wanted me to send the troops out to fight after our scouts spied that a vast number of the siege army had departed in the night, following the road to Uruk?"

"I still think we should've attacked," Kebboba retorted. "The odds were more in our favor."

"Maybe I should address you as *General Kebboba*. But forgive me, you're totally ignorant about war devices. Their only hope for victory is luring us out into an ambush. Had we gone out, their entire army would've emerged out of hiding and crushed us."

"They weren't hiding," Kebboba persisted. "Our scouts followed them a long distance. And how about the Chaldean astrologers who foresaw the moon eclipse for the following night as a favorable sign. The eclipse came and went, and all you did was sit on the finely-combed hairy arse of yours, sipping wine with a golden straw."

"Chaldean astrologers! Lady, now you're talking horse-dung nonsense. Gungunum has Chaldean astrologers too, and I bet they foresaw the eclipse as favorable to their side. This General Gungunum is no fool, I know him. If he had any doubt that the troops left behind for the siege were to become vulnerable to our attack, he would've made sure none of our scouts made it back alive. Yet not a single scout got captured. I assure you, Gungunum was hoping the eclipse would encourage us to attack, but I'm not so easy to fool."

She was not convinced and gazed far in the distance.

"Please, Kebboba." Tenderly, Shulgi placed a hand over her shoulder. "I'm doing all this for you. I know the revolt didn't work out as I planned, and I know I'm not as handsome as that filth rotting in our dungeon, *Prince Naram-shit*. How could you trust him? Sooner than you know it, he will toss you out for a young whore, then toss *her* for another. His rod is always seeking a fresher hole to fill. You need someone faithful like me. Now that your husband is dead and the siege is about to end, we can be happy together. I forgive you for that night when you slept with our celebrated *prince of dung*. Filth like him won't change our destiny."

"Oh, how grateful I am to the *faithful you, forgiving me!*" She snickered. "Do I look like such a fool, or perhaps I'm blind! How often do you pick girls outside the temple for the *sacred vow fuck*?"

"I pray the goddess forgive you. I do it out of devotion, to honor Ishtar with this task."

"Honor Ishtar, my arse," Kebboba snapped. "This *Holy Fornication task* is nothing but the invention of some lustful nobles. And now they are so spoiled—no longer satisfied with just any girl—they want virgins. When this siege is over, we will have a new god—a male god of love; virgin boys will stand outside his temple and women will throw those silver pieces to help milk the virginity out of them. I can't wait to see how men would like that!"

"Now calm down, no need to talk heresy. Only gods can beget gods."

"Sure. That's why I will start praying for a god to bed and seed me with a divine son," countered Kebboba, before switching her attention to the feast outside the walls.

"What are they doing? Is that Sargon who stood up?"

Shulgi squinted. "Seems to be him. I see two men approaching the table, carrying something."

A sharp-eyed herald resumed announcing to the eager crowd. "They unfurled the wrapping. ... It's the lion's hide ... Sargon is dressing Allamu with the lion's hide."

"The lion's hide!" Shulgi exclaimed. "How nice; I wish I was in your brother's place. I would love to wear one of those."

"Nice? That's repulsive—*sickening*! They just killed it. All that oozing blood, now staining my brother through his garments."

"Still, it's a nice gesture, Kebboba. If Allamu doesn't like it, I will gladly take it."

The herald resumed. "Sargon has removed the lion coating from Allamu's back. It must be sweltering hot inside that hide."

"Bless the graceful gods," Kebboba sighed, "that appalling cover is off him. He will need a hot bath and clean clothing upon his release ... and one of my beautiful maids to soothe him through the night after his ordeal."

"I agree." Shulgi beamed. "We, too, need to soothe each other after this trying day."

She ignored him, eyeing the distant scene described by the heralds.

"Allamu is back in his seat. He's not touching the food anymore ... must've had enough to eat. I'm not surprised; in one sitting, he had gorged more than ten of us had eaten in ten days."

Smiles formed on many faces on imagining themselves the ones sitting at that table with a full stomach.

"They have set up another large table—in front of the banquet table ... two large soldiers are approaching Allamu ... they grab—" The herald went silent.

"What are they doing?" Kebboba called frantically. "Are they dragging him? I can see a struggle."

"Oh, mercy of the gods," another loud man hollered. "Now four men are carrying him to the other table."

Faint screams of distress could be heard over the wall, driving everyone to morbid silence. The foods they devoured in their imagination congealed to raw meat that revolted inside their empty stomachs.

Kebboba turned around, her heart drumming beats of terror that arrested her to the floor. She needed to hide from the shrieks of her brother, but the cruel walls screamed out all the details vividly, forcing images of sheer evil through the walls of her closed eyes.

"They have him pinned down on his back. Big men are holding his arms and legs. Oh, the pure evil, only the gods can help him! ... Two more men, carrying knives, are moving over him. ... They are going to stab poor Allamu!"

Kebboba was shaking her head to spin it clear from the screams of despair and the merciless howls of the wall. But nothing could stop the fear from seeping into her blood, pouring terror deep into her heart.

"No! They don't need all those men to stab him," another voice bellowed. "Oh, mercy of the gods! Those two—the butchers—the ones who skinned the lion on that same table. … In the name of the gods, spare him this cruelty. Not like this! Not skinned alive!"

LIONIZED

FOUR SOLDIERS CLAMPED DOWN ON HIS LIMBS WITH HANDS and knees, rendering Allamu motionless over the table. Still, he struggled with every fiber of his being. It was beyond doubt that his life was about to end, but how?

It didn't take long before the answer stared him coldly in the eyes; the same two butchers who had skinned the lion earlier, went up the table, equipped with their select knives for the delicate job. They stood still, eyes locked on the task below, exploring the most sadistic path to follow—a skill they must have acquired from patiently inflicting pain without rushing death to their victims. Torture seemed like the only talent they could exhibit and savor in the company of other fellow humans.

Allamu could hardly move a finger, yet kept on struggling. He abhorred being slaughtered in cold blood and hoped for his heart to cease before the torture started.

"Allamu, Allamu." Sargon's voice came from behind as he walked around the table to face him. "You've never appreciated anything I've done for you. I don't understand why. I allowed you to stay in Uruk, undisturbed, after your sister rebelled—still, you conspired to depose me. I forgave you and prepared this feast in your honor; even I participated in the cooking, and you—refuse to eat, which makes me feel awfully bad. You say you have no space for food! Well, that can be easily resolved."

Sargon announced: "Men, so much food was prepared for my friend Allamu, but he says he's full. I just hate throwing all this food away, so, let's help him recover his appetite by making space for more food. … Strip him of his clothes."

"I curse you, Sargon!" screamed Allamu.

"Ooh, it truly hurts to hear this from a dear friend. Sadly for you, the gods are deaf to your curses; they're busy, showering me with blessings. Well, Allamu, it's time to *fill you in* on the message to deliver to your sister. I pray you succeed in your *peace mission.*" He nodded to the two butchers.

"Sargon, you coward, dog son of—" Before finishing his words, a shriek issued out of Allamu as a sharp knife cut through the skin below his neck to a shallow depth, then sliced down slowly. His body needed to jolt with the pain, but the men arresting him to the table were hard to shake off.

All of his yearnings for a death befitting a brave warrior were thrown into total mockery; there were neither the chaotic sounds of screaming combatants with swords clashing in the heat of battle, nor the sharing of death with other fatally gored men on blood-soaked grounds. He was the only one dying, while an army on the ground and a traumatized city crowd on top of the wall stood in brutal silence, watching him being skinned with a cold knife on a cold table. They were even denying him a soldier's precious last moments to be cradled by the soothing earth—its parting gift in return for his warm blood. All he could do was scream up to the skies in the hope that the gods would heed his pleas for a swifter, less demeaning end.

Allamu was on his own, fully ignored by the gods. He wanted to heap curses on them for allotting him this cruel fate, but the only sound he could utter was his pain, carried on screams piercing the heavens.

The butchers stopped briefly upon hearing the air whizzing with a swarm of arrows landing in the distance. Allamu could only presume that his sister must have ordered the archers to shoot in his direction in the hope that one arrow would be guided inside him by a merciful god to end the torture. But the wind god was in no mood to waste his breath.

Allamu didn't place much hope on any divine help, but he felt the message that the city shared his agony, which boosted his spirits just enough to endure and stop reacting to the torture. That prompted the guards holding him to relax their grips slightly, thinking he was losing strength.

When the knife from one of the butchers resumed slicing the skin over his stomach, Allamu summoned all his willpower, and with a sudden jolt of his hips he had the knife sink deep, and he wriggled his body around it. The butcher pulled the blade out and cursed Allamu for ruining his delicate work.

While blood gushed out to rush his death, Allamu managed a brief, wheezing chuckle at this small victory over his tormentors, who in turn blamed each other for allowing this to happen.

The pain was excruciating but started to wane with the blood draining faster. Before long, Allamu found himself in another realm, facing a whole army of ghosts flaring with pale hues of light. They stood inert in place, and one by one Allamu slayed them, dowsing their glow. His screams of agony joined those of victory with every ghost he slaughtered until the whole army was snuffed out. And his life receded along with all remnants of light, into the silent darkness.

↗ ◇ 𐤃 𐤅 𐤊

From the distance it emerged—a scene that could only be conjured in a fairytale: A lion, standing in a cart, holding the reins that guided the donkey towing it.

It was a bumpy ride. The once evenly level terrain leading to the city gates was now disfigured by the blight of war that gored mortals and earth alike. Yet, the lion didn't appear to mind the rough ride. His head bobbed all around as if in jubilation at the miracle that restored his life back from the grisly fate he had suffered.

One wheel sank in a hole and sprang up violently. Now the lion appeared to throw up when his head folded on his back, revealing a hunched-down figure of a man, all naked save for the lion's hide.

The stuffing and stitching of Allamu's skin were done in haste. It wasn't a job done with the intention to impress. Soldiers had started with sticks of reed and palm fronds as an inner skeleton to hold the skin firmly in an upright position. Then, an assortment of all the foods from the feast was stuffed inside, along with chicken and duck feathers. The end result was a body completely out of proportion, bloated and horribly distorted, transforming Allamu into a creature that even nightmares would not dare conceive.

They had propped up their ghastly creation on the cart, with the head stuffed till it acquired a firm puffy shape. But with every step the donkey took toward the city wall, more of the stuffed food was disgorged through the loosely sutured mouth. The taut skin kept caving in, steadily morphing the head into more repulsive features.

The stitching done on the rest of the body didn't hold any better. It, too, slackened with the rocky ride. Food ingredients discharged through the gaps, gliding down the oozing saps, with feathers stubbornly sticking out. The upper half of what was Allamu slowly hunched over the cart's front edge while the lion's hide kept sliding down his back.

The donkey moved at a relaxed pace toward the gate. Somehow it sensed that the man pretending to be a lion was not in a hurry to get anywhere. It was going to be an easy day, but one thing bothered the donkey: the eerie silence. The creatures it left behind and the ones watching from the walls were acting strange; they were always loud when there was a group of them. The donkey stopped as if to figure out the reason behind their abnormal silence. After some wait, a mad holler was tossed down the wall.

"Open the cursed gates! How long do we have to suffer, watching this barbarity?"

More shouts followed; some angry, others pleading. This went on for a while before the gates opened just enough for a guard to step outside. Cautiously, he approached the donkey, grabbed its reins, then started walking it toward the gates that opened wider to allow the cart in. Upon entering the city, Allamu's grotesque upper body was dangling over the cart's front edge.

The gates closed behind the cart, and morbid silence plagued the place when death moved in. The only signs of life came from the braying donkey, heralding the delivery of a sack of food to the starving city.

King Humbaba

 WHIRL OF DUST RACED TOWARD THE CITY IN PURSUIT OF A chariot and its lone rider, who whipped the horse and sent it galloping to match the speed of his throbbing heart.

The fortified walls grew larger and higher, but they failed to intimidate Humbaba; his voice could conquer those walls. He was entrusted to deliver another formidable message from Sargon, and up till then Humbaba had never failed to deliver. Today, he was going to address the whole city of Ur, the only city on Earth that could rival Uruk in power. The fate of thousands of soldiers from both cities hung on the power of his words. On his shoulders rested a horrendous head with a message that could eerily bring the beauty of peace or reflect back the ugliness of death and destruction.

No matter how tiny he appeared next to the walls, Humbaba felt a divine energy flowing in his veins, confident as a god delivering a command to the lesser mortals. He was well within the archers' range with arrows pointing at him, yet he slowed the horse to a stroll, close to where his voice could be heard with clarity by the largest crowd.

Everyone in Ur had heard of Humbaba by then—the fearless one rumored to be the human reincarnation of the hideous monster from the cedar forests of Lebanon; the Messenger of Doom who'd ventured alone amidst the traitors in Sargon's palace and brought them to surrender. Rumors abounded that his horrendous appearance was the product of a body massively infested with demons, thus evolved the superstition that killing him would release all those demons, who would wreak havoc on the ones responsible for destroying their sanctuary.

As for the man himself, threats of death didn't scare him anymore. With every message he delivered, he faced the prospect of death. And why should he fear death? Every time he saw his own reflection, he envisaged Death riding on his shoulders.

Humbaba raised his head to meet the peering eyes from the wall's battlements. He prepared his voice to be brave and firm, and he thundered:

"People of the great city of Ur. A message from the mightiest king within the four corners of Earth, from sunrise to sunset, the magnanimous King Sargon. I will relay to you the exact message."

Humbaba took a deep breath to harness a king's authority, and with a strident voice he whipped the wall:

"I, Sargon—your king, and the gods' proxy on this Earth, chosen by them to faithfully carry out their bidding—with heavy heart, lament the death, suffering, and destruction afflicting our lands. I come here personally with the commitment and goodwill to put an end to this senseless calamity, to begin a new era of peace and prosperity throughout this blessed land.

"I, Sargon, am ready to forgive every single citizen—civilians and soldiers of the great Ur—knowing very well that all have been misled and forced to support this rebellion by a few rulers who used the meager new taxes as an excuse to revolt, when in fact it was greed for power and wealth that motivated them. Yes, you do pay more in taxes than other cities, but every tiny grain of it is used for your security. You have your taxes to thank for these walls that protected you so far; your taxes erected them and kept them strong. The pathetic walls of other cities would hardly stop the invasion of some desert nomads— and yet here you are, standing against the mightiest army on land.

"But don't go celebrating your successes yet, for I haven't shown you all the might of my armies. I am here in person to see to it that this standoff comes to an end. You, people of Ur, should have the final say. Don't let a few rulers, who have no interest in your well-being, decide your fate. Many among your families and friends, and many of ours too, have died or been injured. All this suffering—for what?"

A whizzing sound ripped through the air next to Humbaba's ear. He saw an arrow pierce the ground not far from the chariot. Moments later, his upper arm blazed in sharp pain when another arrow tore through it. He stiffened, gritting his teeth while he endured the urge to scream.

"Who shot the arrows?" an angry bark soared from the ramparts, followed by the faint sounds of a scuffle.

Humbaba couldn't suppress the agony for too long, and he roared the pain out in words.

"People of Ur! I, Sargon, have come for the common good—to unite and make our kingdom strong. Forgiveness is one of my virtues, but do refrain from trying my patience. You have two choices: Return to the fold of the kingdom, open the gates, let my son go free—and you will go back to your daily life just the same way it was before the rebellion. As a gift, all the livestock I brought will be yours to feed your families.

"Your other choice is to resume following the fools' path that your leaders chose—to be our enemies, to dissent and fight us. If you choose the latter, then I, Sargon, swear by all the gods who rule over this Earth to bring my entire wrath upon your city. I will dam the Euphrates with the corpses of your warriors. They will bloat in the river while your skin dries on your bones within the city walls. Piss will become a luxury you can't afford to waste. And may the gods have mercy on the ones who survive after I storm your city—and believe me I will, for I took an oath not to leave this camp before I do. I will peel your skins from your bones, stuff them with food, and throw the rest of you to the pigs, just as I did with Allamu.

"Having my son as hostage will not thwart me from making good on this promise. Naram-sin deserves the consequences of his folly. Go ahead, kill him, and doom yourselves and your loved ones to a most horrible of fates.

"These are your choices. Choose—to feed yourselves or have me feed you. Choose—to feed on pigs or have pigs feed on you. I need your answer by tomorrow when the sun nears its zenith—before it touches the feet of heaven. May the gods bless you with the wisdom to spare yourselves from death and destruction. I pray to mighty Anu to bring you back to reason—for peace and prosperity to be restored to this great city of Ur."

With that, Humbaba started turning the chariot to head back. Just then the gates screeched open, and a man fully stripped, save a cloth around his waist, was pushed out into the clearing.

"This is the man who struck you," a soldier shouted and disappeared inside, the gate closing behind him.

Humbaba didn't care to retaliate; just to remain on his feet was a struggle, so he continued the trajectory back to camp. On the way, he saw a chariot racing toward him. It was the chief of guards, Hukura, who stopped his chariot upon reaching Humbaba.

"How bad is your injury? Is that the man who cut you?"

"I doubt this would kill me." Humbaba nodded. "They say it was him."

Hukura raced away toward the abandoned enemy. The soldiers atop the walls of Ur were stricken with guilt as they watched one of their own dashing away in a desperate effort to evade death, driven by an absurd instinct to survive by outrunning the chariot. Perhaps he clung to a hope that by divine intervention one of the wheels would come off and stop the chariot in its tracks. But the wheels kept churning the dirt, coming closer and closer. Then, finally it happened: a strike to the back of his head, and he went tumbling down.

Stretched face down and gasping for air, the man waited for the demons who would carry him to the netherworld, but only a sound of mad laughter reached him. He sat up, dazed, feeling the back of his head, expecting blood to be pouring out. But there was no blood, nor any sharp pain. Totally baffled, he looked at the enemy on the chariot, who kept laughing over him with a hand pointing at something on the ground.

"For you, miserable bastard. A freshly cooked chicken," Hukura said, then he shouted to the crowd atop the wall:

"Lucky for him the gods intervened, and our messenger is not badly hurt. The magnanimous King Sargon forgives your man. Likewise, he will forgive all, but only if you accept his terms."

He turned back to the man he knocked down. "What are you waiting for? The chicken is for you, you son of dogs. Don't worry, I wouldn't need poison if I wanted to kill you." And Hukura turned the chariot around, heading back.

Right away, the man crawled, grabbed the chicken, and hastily brushed off the dirt. All eyes on the wall looked on; envy replaced their guilt when the man they had forsaken sank his teeth into his little feast.

Humbaba could hardly believe he'd made it back alive. He collapsed into the arms of two soldiers who rushed to assist him off the chariot. Behind them, Sargon came blaring:

"Humbaba, our most intrepid hero! Don't worry, my healer is right here to take care of you."

Sargon stood by his messenger's side as the healer told the soldiers to break the tip of the arrow that stuck out, then they pulled the arrow's shaft with Humbaba shrieking in agony.

"Is it bad?" Sargon asked his healer.

"I'm afraid so," said the healer. "There is not much you can do about it."

"Will he survive?" Gloom shrouded Sargon's face.

"Hard to tell. But I don't see why he wouldn't, after surviving to this age with this same face."

"I'm talking about his injury!" Sargon snapped. "Not his fucked-up face!"

"Oh, forgive me, Majesty, I misunderstood." Slyly, the healer chuckled. "Sure, this devil will survive a dozen injuries like this."

Sargon shook his head at the healer whose humor had caused him some moments of anxiety, then he turned to the injured man.

"Humbaba, you're the bravest—more feared than any warrior. I don't know which scares the people most, the messages you deliver or your face. But I tell you one thing, Humbaba, you scared the demons out of me when you kept screaming, 'I, Sargon' this, and 'I, Sargon' that. I was mortified, thinking, 'By the gods, how did I turn out to be this ugly?'" And Sargon went into one of his laughing fits.

Horror found a fleeting opportunity to physically manifest itself on Humbaba's haggard face when a smile twisted and deepened the folds of his skin, mangling his mutilated features even further, before he closed his eyes and surrendered to sleep.

Any Way Out

Though the city walls stood tall and defiant, the morale inside was shaky and ready to collapse. The winds of fear had swept hard against those walls along with Humbaba's words of merciless savagery. The starving people of Ur couldn't think of food anymore; it only brought the image of Allamu being butchered, then stuffed. Many walked in a state of shock after the wings on their newly risen hopes had been plucked of feathers, sending them crashing into pits of despair. The oasis of salvation that had peered from the distance morphed into an infernal pot, soon to cook them alive. They could only hunger for the torture to end.

A multitude confronted the guards stationed at the gates, demanding that the gates be thrown open to welcome peace and the army of food awaiting outside. Shulgi appeared and hollered at them to disperse.

A man driven by desperation and contempt for Shulgi pulled out a dagger and rushed him. But, within a mere step away from striking distance, the general's sword swiftly cut him down.

"Anyone else wants to play with a knife?" Shulgi challenged, while the man at his feet quivered in the throes of death.

Seeing the messy result of dissent, and being starved of the strength to fight the well-fed soldiers, the mob's fury lost its steam. The men went their separate ways, none daring to ask what Shulgi was planning—that was, if he had a plan at all.

After suffering through her half-brother's unbearable screams and his torturous demise, Kebboba had escaped the tower for her quarters. But a faint echo in her head refused to leave her alone. It was Allamu's ghost, blaming her for the rebellion that had brought unto him a most horrible and humiliating end. He demanded vengeance, or her thoughts he would haunt till her dying day. The voices dragged Kebboba to where she would find Shulgi.

"Sargon will never dare dam the river," Shulgi was screaming in the war room where the high-ranking commanders convened. "They would've done that a long time ago, before anything else. Obstructing the river flow to the cities further down would only invite more rebellion, and *that* is what worries Sargon the most. This foolish 'dam' threat proves he has no new plans at all. Climbing the walls like cockroaches is their only option. Now, to attack Sargon's army is out of the question. Preparing for their attacks is the only detail we should focus on."

Not a single new plan emerged. All options to strengthen the defense strategy had already been discussed and implemented. Three of the wisest Chaldean astrologers were present to be consulted about any omens from the heavens that might be taken advantage of to turn the city's fortunes for the better; but those mystics of the stars couldn't foresee much that promised a favorable outcome. Confusion prevailed with the added element of Sargon's pardon of the army, which didn't specify how far up the ranks he planned to forgive. Some of the commanders had already disappeared, and most likely others were planning to do the same. Soon, the gathering turned into a melee of shouting and cursing among men venting the desperation that had settled in like salt clogging the roots of a dying tree.

As the leader of the rebellion, Shulgi had already devised a plan to save his own skin, knowing that Sargon must have reserved for him a fate far more dreadful than Allamu's. Upon seeing Kebboba enter the room, Shulgi praised God for sending her and walked in her direction; he needed a respite from his squabbling men.

"Let's go outside." He took her arm and led her away.

Not wasting a moment, Kebboba's words sliced through her fury.

"I want to pay a visit to that son of dogs, *Prince Naram-sin*—stick a dagger in his heart with my own hands. I need your personal guards to gain me access to his cell."

"Kebboba, he could still be of some value to us."

"He's mine!" she snapped. "His value belongs to me alone, to avenge my brother! Like you said, peace or no peace, our heads will end up on spikes. I want his head to keep ours company."

Shulgi smiled and whispered to her, "Don't worry, we'll be fine. I can't leave the meeting with these pathetic commanders, so I'll have two guards escort you. Once you're done with the prince, the guards will lead you to meet me in a secret place. I have a plan for us."

Escorted by two guards, Kebboba walked the streets wearing a scarf, hoping it would conceal her identity. But with the guards trailing her, she attracted the attention of some people who soon identified her and began following and cussing her. The guards pulled out their swords and managed to keep the stalkers at bay, but not the biting comments.

"Bitch, you should've stuck to making wine," someone shouted.

"Whore, do you have any plans, aside from fucking Shulgi?" a woman screamed.

"Sure, they have a plan. Her and Shulgi would be somewhere beyond Phoenicia, sipping on wine while we get butchered by Sargon's swords."

By the time they reached the dungeon, Kebboba's head was spinning. With the siege dragging on and the prospect of bloodier confrontations growing more imminent, she was already getting hints of a fast brewing menace: the very people of Ur. And unlike the siege army, there was no wall to shield her from them, only thin air.

Following the two sentries, she descended the stairs to the dungeon. The guard unlatched a door at the order of her escort. The occupant at the end of the cell jumped off his cot and stood alert. The sentries went in first to stand between him and Kebboba.

Naram-sin looked like neither a prisoner nor a prince. The guards on duty in that holding cell knew it was to their benefit to take reasonable care of him in case things didn't work out as Shulgi planned. Still, the prince appeared frail, and a deep look of anxiety now dominated his face in contrast to the proud, buoyant image he had presented upon entering Ur.

"Your father … skinned my brother alive!" Kebboba's fist tightened on the dagger.

Naram-sin didn't show any reaction. All the grisly details about what had transpired outside had already found their way to the prince, just like the heavy air smothering the city.

"So, you think I am to blame?" a drained Naram-sin answered. "Would killing me make you feel better? Shulgi led you into this predicament. Shulgi killed your husband. Isn't he more to blame for the death of your brother and all who died on both sides?"

"Shulgi didn't skin people alive!"

"Yet, because of him, your people are eating human flesh. Is that any less barbaric?"

"They have no choice!" Kebboba erupted. "We ran out of dogs and cats. Now rats have become a luxury because of your siege."

"Lady Kebboba, I personally came in peace, seeking an end to this conflict. But your general—before hearing a single word from me—killed your husband and caged me in this hole."

Unexpectedly, a guard in her escort interrupted: "Noble lady, forgive me, but the prince keeps saying that General Shulgi killed the governor. Is that really what happened?"

Hesitantly, Kebboba nodded, and without wasting a moment, the guard went down on one knee, bowing to the prince.

"O honorable prince, do forgive us for we were told it was Your Highness who stabbed the governor."

His partner was quick to follow suit in kneeling, while Kebboba watched with unbelieving eyes.

None of the guards close to Shulgi had the least doubt that he was the one who butchered the governor. However, it was of no concern to them who had butchered whom. But now, with Shulgi facing doom, and the spread of strong rumors he would abandon the city, it became prudent to shift loyalty. The guards couldn't afford wasting this opportunity to extricate themselves from Shulgi's service and switch allegiance.

Naram-sin nodded in approval to the kneeling sentries. "Forgiven you are—you were simply following orders."

Winning the guards' loyalty restored his confidence, and he addressed Kebboba. "Noble lady, your people and army want this siege to end. Shulgi is finished; a horrible fate awaits him, and I hate to see you dragged into it. You have my word that my father will pardon you. However, you must act to end this."

Her surprise at the guards' betrayal didn't last long. Obviously, it was the wisest thing to do—the best escape path. She awoke from her confusion, aware that her brother's haunting voice had abandoned her; it was the fear of a gruesome fate that had tormented her all this time. In those assuring words from the prince, she saw a glimmer of hope.

"Just promise me one thing," she said to Naram-sin. "If your father decides to skin me alive … kill me."

⟨ ◊ ⅁ ⱽⱽ ⫪

The two soldiers dug a hole in the ground with their spears; it looked deep enough to serve the purpose. They walked away and stood at a distance. Shulgi came to inspect the hole.

"Next time make it deeper," he screamed at them, then lifted his garb and squatted over the hole.

Stress had his stomach churning the food and dispatching it hastily, in adherence to nature's genius design that kept a prey as light as possible to better escape an imminent danger. Being Sargon's main target, he had better be always prepared to flee as fast as a gazelle.

Shulgi squatted for quite a while, thinking of his plans. He often wondered if the arse was the seat of one's thoughts, and hence, clut-tered entrails were an obstacle for good thoughts to settle in. Lately, his fast-running entrails seemed as though screaming with a hint: Run—away from a grisly fate—away from Ur!

"Lady Kebboba is here to see you." A guard interrupted his entrail-rooted thoughts.

"Tell her to wait a little."

After a thorough purge, Shulgi started to stand up, but his legs betrayed him; the long squat had rendered them hopelessly numb. He fell backward, just missing the stinking hole.

"This must be a good omen," he murmured, shook his limbs free of numbness, and rose to his feet with thoughts sharp and assertive.

Kebboba approached her general, holding a dagger caked with dry blood. Farther back, one of her two escorts carried a round-shaped leather sack.

Shulgi let out a sigh of relief. "That's his head!"

"Yes—chopped by mine own hands."

"Oh, how I regret not being there to witness it, but those pestering generals and their vain war designs!" Shulgi hugged her and whispered in her ear. "I thought of a plan: We send Naram-sin's body to his father, just like he sent your brother—stuffed with food. Sargon will get mad and order a reckless attack. While they're busy fighting, we'll slip out through a secret tunnel. I have a donkey loaded with gold. It's no longer safe to stay here."

"I have a better plan," Kebboba whispered back. "Escape through a safer tunnel—*my vagina!*"

Shulgi squealed when sharp pain spiked his stomach. His two guards made a move toward Kebboba, but they were more than happy to halt their advance when her two escorts gestured for them not to interfere.

"Forgive me,"—Kebboba stabbed Shulgi again—"but I've been such a fool, listening to you for too long. You and your idiotic plans transformed us from proud people to cannibals. You, *the great expert in warfare*, saw through all their plans and traps; how sad you didn't see this trap coming your way."

Kebboba pushed the general away, dagger parting from his entrails. He collapsed to his knees in shock, pressing both hands to his belly.

"Still, one of your suspicions proved to be right," Kebboba went on. "Yes, I am fucking my way out! Rather than killing the prince, I decided to bed him. Like you mentioned, maybe with his princely seed I would grow to be ... a queen! One thing I do regret, though: not having bedded him right here, next to you—while you're dying!"

"Whore!" Shulgi labored to speak. "You only fucked your way ... out of your own skin. Sargon will skin you alive like he did your brother."

Right then, a hooded man approached, grabbed the leather sack from the escort, and stood over Shulgi.

"Greetings, General. I come to express my heartfelt gratitude for your *exceptional* hospitality. May the gods bless you with *an exceptional* long life."

"Why, it's Prince Naram-sin!" Kebboba feigned surprise. "Why are you holding a sack, Prince?"

"It's where I keep my head. Remember—the one you chopped!" Naram-sin quipped and proceeded to empty the contents. Dirt spilled out before a dead rat landed on top.

"Ooh no," Kebboba sighed. "Those dungeon jailers must be starving now. This was the rat they trapped—their dinner! Which reminds me, beloved Shulgi: the blood on the dagger, which blended with your blood just now, it came from this very rat.

"Oh dearest Shulgi, what were those great future plans you had in mind? Allow me to guess: to spend the rest of my life running, hiding—looking over my shoulder for assassins. Forgive me—not quite a plan to my liking; everything I love is here in Ur. I'd rather surrender and take the chance of a pardon over the life of a vagabond, running scared."

"Pardon!" Shulgi groaned, "for a filthy whore like you, Kebboba! ... Sure, a pardon ... once Sargon had stuffed a whole banquet up your arse."

Kebboba stepped over to Shulgi and slapped him hard. He fell to his side, shrieking in pain.

"Leave him to die on his own," she told the guards. "Then take his head and spike it over the wall. He will be the first to greet the new morning—to greet peace."

The Beauty in the Beast

EARTH LOOKED WITH ENVY AT THE MOON AND THE STARS after a long day cursing the sun. They all hung far away, blessed with a great distance from the unruly humans. Unlike the rest of God's creatures, those humans never followed any consistent pattern in their lives.

Long before the sun was scheduled for its daily assault on the night, the humans started preparing for another one of their mad affairs. Soon the air would be filled with the cries of the wounded, and the ground drenched with their sticky, red saps. Only after their frenzy of stabbing each other was spent would they stab the earth, dig out its entrails, and feed it with the bodies of those they had sacrificed, as if that were the agreed-upon compensation for the havoc they had brought to the firm ground.

The night promised a long day of gore, which roused many souls into abandoning sleep altogether. They stayed awake, uttering annoying sounds in a wide range of emotions. There were the fearful ones who worried about the battle brewing behind the walls, and the bold who couldn't wait to satiate a thirst for spilling blood. Some cried in yearning for their loved ones; others joked about a futile, treacherous existence. Songs filled the spirits of the living with hope, while poems bemoaned those who had died or in battle soon would fall. Commanders argued over tactics to harvest enemy lives more efficiently. And last were the sleepers who snored loudly, banishing all noise in their far-distant dreams of peace.

After a brief calm in the late night, and as the first ascending sunrays began to veil the stars, the cacophony came back with greater force. The camp was drowned in shouts, frantically calling the soldiers to prepare for the greatest savagery that only humans excelled at: War.

Sargon came out of his tent, and Chief General Gungunum joined him. They gazed at the figure peering down at them from the top of the wall.

"We don't know who that is," Gungunum said.

"Could it be Naram-sin?" asked a concerned Sargon.

"It's too far and too dark to tell."

"Three gold pieces for the one who finds out if that spiked head is my son's. I want the troops ready for combat … and get my chariot."

"Sargon, I don't think you should—"

"Just get my chariot ready. If that is my son's head, then it's more my battle than anyone's."

Gungunum didn't argue; to reason with a troubled Sargon was a daunting task. He mulled over finding the right man to verify whether Naram-sin's head was the one adorning the wall, then decided to go himself. He called his assistant to prepare the chariot for Sargon while he went to get his own.

The camp was in complete chaos, men running everywhere, but all heads appeared to orient in the same direction—to the lonesome head atop the wall.

Gungunum climbed in his chariot and tugged at the reins. The wheels rolled no more than a stone's throw away when the general pulled on the reins, bringing the chariot to a halt. Along with him, the camp's frenzy slowed to a standstill with eyes now fixated on the gates that creaked open.

Sargon came rushing out of his tent with a sentry helping him don thick leather armor over his military attire. Gungunum stepped off the chariot and met his king at the front of the troops.

The gates continued to open slowly as if reluctant to expose the secret that kept the city impenetrable. Outside, soldiers squinted to see what surprise those formidable gates were about to reveal. Would it be the army of a desperate city refusing to go down on its knees, or a messenger singing a sweet melody for peace?

"Where is my chariot?" Sargon shouted.

A soldier came running, guiding the chariot's two horses. Sargon climbed in, guided the horses to a safe point, and waited. A chariot emerged out of the gates, away from the safety of the walls.

Gungunum let his king move ahead without an escort. He recognized Naram-sin's chariot right away with its bright ornaments of precious stones and the two steeds pulling it. Soon enough he could discern the man holding the reins through the arrogant smile that was more telling than a birthmark. Next to the prince was a woman.

The charming Kebboba! Gungunum winced. *This will get ugly.*

Naram-sin brought his chariot to stop next to his father's, and bowed.

"Greetings, Father, I bring you good news," he said, brimming with pride. "The traitor Shulgi is dead. That's his head on the spike. He was the sole cause of the rebellion with his stronghold on the army. He killed Governor Elam for opposing him and threatened the honorable Lady Kebboba with the same fate if she did not submit to his orders. He was planning to kill me and thus force the people of Ur to fight to the death, while he cowardly schemed for himself and Lady Kebboba to escape with stacks of gold. But Lady Kebboba refused to betray her people and came to seek my help. I dispelled her fears and gave her the courage to face Shulgi, to spare her city and our soldiers the carnage that would follow."

Sargon was silent, nodding his head in assent to his son's account.

Gungunum arrived with a few soldiers. He smiled at the prince, showing joy at his safe return.

"Father, it took real bravery for Lady Kebboba to confront the tyrant, and she killed him with her own hands. We both risked our lives to foil his plans; this victory and the peace it would bring was worth all the risk. Lady Kebboba and I have convened with the city leaders. She has joined me here to personally relay their decision to accept your conditions and submit to your rule."

Sargon addressed Kebboba, who dared not raise her head.

"Lady Kebboba! Do you concur with everything the prince has detailed? Is Ur ready to desist from this act of rebellion and accept my rule as the undisputed king?"

"Your Majesty, King of all Kings." Kebboba bowed. "As the acting governor, and on behalf of all the citizens of Ur, I would like to express my sincere regret for all the bloodshed that was forced on us and your soldiers by the tyrant Shulgi. We solemnly agree to your terms. Our soldiers have disarmed. Ur awaits you and your brave men in peace. Ur welcomes you with open arms."

Sargon nodded to Kebboba's cordial answer, then reached over and patted his son on the shoulder.

"Son, I guess we owe this triumph to you." And Sargon turned around in his chariot and thundered to the eager men behind him:

"The rebellion ... is over!"

Without the need of messengers, the words took off to the air, stirring a thunder of hails from the army outside and the people within the walls. Waves of jubilation clashed ferociously, shaking the earth beneath.

Sargon turned his chariot around, steering the horses to stop next to his general's chariot.

"Gungunum, is the army ready to enter the city?"

"Yes. The army awaits your order."

"Did you make all the soldiers understand that I will not tolerate any pillaging or harm to the people?"

"They are well informed of this. But Sargon, you know there are always the defiant few who consider those acts as privileges they're entitled to after exposing themselves to the risk of a horrible death in battle. Even the dead are not spared their lust. Remember the slogan: 'For those who fight wars, where killing becomes an honorable duty, no other act of depravity should be frowned upon.'"

"Gungunum, my word to the people of Ur must be honored. Make an example of those who fall prey to their animal whims—have them publicly lashed, even executed for severe deeds. Now, you lead the way with some troops to make sure we're not walking into a trap. At your signal, I'll follow with the rest of the troops."

"Don't forget the *special forces*," Gungunum joked. "The hardest task will be to guard those delectable special forces from the assaults of the starving mob."

Sargon didn't seem to appreciate the general's humor.

"Brighten up, Sargon, the turbulent times are behind us. Ahead, we have a victory to celebrate. Why the serious face?"

"It is a victory, but where is the thrill of it?" came Sargon's answer, and he steered the horses back to his tent.

The crowds packed the vast square facing the grand ziggurat of Ur. A barrier of guards spanned its width, except for a gap of twenty paces at the center. Behind them they left a clearance of about thirty paces to the front wall of the towering temple. More soldiers stood to the sides to maintain order.

The haggard faces of the multitude managed to stretch into smiles and jovial talk, bringing to the city the soothing winds of lively noise that had been absent for many grim moons.

A gentle calm took over when the chief of guards, Hukura, stepped into the clear area and greeted the populace.

"Honorable citizens of Ur … today, you have a great reason to rejoice and celebrate. The darkness that veiled the city for those past horrible moons has been cast away. Before we start the distribution of the provisions, let us give thanks to the gods for sending the hero who spared us long battles that would've resulted in no winners. Hail the most intrepid, magnanimous ruler—God's surrogate on Earth—the Great King Sargon!"

Towering from the first level of the ziggurat, Sargon came into view, waving to the cheering crowd. Shortly, he proceeded down the stairs, to the front of the temple, where he kept saluting with raised hands until the hails faded.

"Noble and brave citizens of this proud, glorious city of Ur." His words of praise revived another gust of hails.

"People of Ur. You have gone through long moons of suffering where you were forced to fight your brothers from Uruk. Innocent blood was shed on both sides, and yes, savagery was committed by both sides. Such is the ugly specter of war. It could've grown tenfold uglier had it not been for the grace of the gods who had interfered to bring it to this peaceful conclusion. It is time to start healing. We are, and will always be, one family. The calamity we both endured is a lesson for future generations to avoid repeating.

"Infighting is a great evil that has never resulted in any good for family, tribe, city, or kingdom. Like a plague, it starts small then grows out of control. Its fertile breeding ground is the corrupt elites, who put their selfish interests before the good of the people they are supposed to serve. General Shulgi was a perfect example."

Sargon waved a hand, and four soldiers stepped over to join him; one guided a mule carrying two leather sacks on its back.

"These brave soldiers of Ur were personal guards to the traitor, Shulgi. Like everyone else in the city, they were misled by him. And just when the city was in its direst situation and in need of his *leadership*, our four heroes here witnessed what a coward General Shulgi was—his betrayal and selfishness. Bravely they foiled his plan to abandon you—the people he got embroiled in this bloody turmoil, bringing you abject pain and suffering as a consequence of his treachery."

Sargon turned to the four soldiers. "Empty the sacks."

The men grabbed the sacks off the mule, poured the contents, and the glitter of gold flooded the ground before the ziggurat.

"All this gold is the measure of Shulgi's loyalty—his reward for delivering death to your families and destruction to this great city while he prepared to flee—to save his own skin and live a life of luxury. Your people, your young soldiers, and ours, suffered the ravages of war and met horrible ends in battle. Yet, the only thing that died in Shulgi was his sense of guilt." Sargon waved for the soldiers to haul the gold away.

"There is a plague that sadly runs rampant in all classes of society. It corrupts not the body, but the soul. However, its lethal effects arise mostly from those in the higher ranks. Vanity and greed for power are a few of its symptoms. To stop this plague from spreading, those infected need to be identified and dealt with, one way or the other. And I, Sargon, promise you to make this a priority. I will not allow the shedding of innocent blood for the excesses of the few who would neglect their duties and sacrifice all, only to satisfy their selfish desires." Briefly, Sargon halted.

"People of Ur, let us salute two individuals who played a crucial role in the events prior to this peace. I would like to share the honors in asking for their vital assistance in combating this plague of greed and utter selfishness. ... Prince Naram-sin, Lady Kebboba, do join me!"

With the arrogance fully restored to his grin, Naram-sin stepped in with Kebboba, who wore a goddess-like smile. Sargon had his arms stretched wide with a grin to match when his son approached.

"Father." Naram-sin had his arms spread wide, ready for the hug.

The multitude cheered loudly in anticipation of the heartwarming, father-son royal embrace.

The grin on Sargon's face suddenly perished, betraying his pretense. Still, that wasn't enough for the prince to react to the fist aimed at his stomach with a speed that seemed to match a springing snake.

Before the prince could recover, another punch followed right above the left eye. Naram-sin swayed onto Kebboba, which helped him regain some balance.

"You address me as 'Your Majesty,' not 'Father'!" Sargon's roar was the next thing to smack the prince, burying his arrogance under the heavy punch mark on his face.

The surprise assault on Naram-sin forced Kebboba's head to bow as though in prayer that the furious king would not find her.

The stunned Naram-sin yearned for a sanctuary to hide his shame away from the crowd, who was equally dazed after witnessing His Majesty wage an impetuous attack on his own son, right after that passionate sermon against "infighting."

"Bring his chariot!" Sargon hollered.

Instantly, a group of soldiers came running while pulling two horses with Naram-sin's chariot in tow.

"Release the horses; he's not worthy of them."

The soldiers dashed to free the horses from their attachments to the chariot. Two more men were given a different task, and they left at once. Then Sargon returned to Naram-sin.

"The audacity ... to claim that you achieved victory! *You!*" Sargon bellowed for all to hear. "I sent you here so all your schooling in the military arts would be put into actual battles and war maneuvers.

And what do you do! Go to the enemy, showing off your chariot and bedding a whore who had our soldiers served on platters. What a genius—to think your charm will win wars for you!"

"Father, my plan would've worked if—"

"Your Majesty, not Father, you pile of dung!" Sargon shut him up. "You call that a plan! If you were a bastard son, I would've had you strapped by the balls to these horses and dragged across the desert. What did you expect for *your victory*? To be the governor of Ur—rule the city from your glittering chariot, or from your fucking bed next to her!" Sargon inhaled deeply, his furious stare shredding Naram-sin.

"From now on, I will treat you like a bastard son. You do as I tell you, go where I tell you to go. The chariots you ride in will be the poorest ones made. To bed a woman—you will need my permission. Spies will report to me on every one of your actions. Defy my rules, and I swear by the great Anu I will castrate you myself and throw your shaft and balls to the pigs. You are to abide by my rules until you prove your worth as a leader, deserving to be heir to this kingdom. Understood?"

"Yes, Fa—Your Majesty."

The soldiers who had left came back with other men, some carrying jars, others carrying a long pole of wood and ropes.

"Pour the contents of the jars on the chariot," Sargon ordered.

The men rushed to comply. They tilted the jars, and heavy oil slid lazily down, covering the chariot in a sticky black layer. Sargon went to a soldier holding a torch, grabbed it from him, and touched it all around the chariot. The flames sampled the oil with their tongues and swiftly burst into a ravenous conflagration, devouring the chariot.

Naram-sin's eyes welled with tears in a futile attempt to put out the grief burning inside him. The chariot was his pride and joy. Countless were the days he had spent with his craftsmen, making it the fastest thing on Earth; faster than the sandstorms and the birds of heaven. When he raced it on the plains, he could feel the gods watching with envy. The chariot was his child—his creation. Every detail—the meticulous carvings, paint, precious stones—all had been fashioned according to his instructions. Now, he stood powerless, watching all that elaborate work and charm go up in heavy, ugly smoke—soon to be nothing more than a charred skeleton.

A shriek of panic ripped his attention away from the fire to another challenge that would aggravate his torment.

Three soldiers had Kebboba in their clutches. Naram-sin rushed forward with the intention of freeing her.

"Do not interfere!" Sargon screamed at him.

"Your Majesty, I implore you. I promised her a pardon and assured her safety."

"You promised! I don't recall giving you the authority to make promises," Sargon hollered. "Strip her clothes off."

The soldiers joyfully complied, ripping Kebboba's clothes to pieces while she struggled in vain and shrieked in horror at the prospect of meeting a fate similar to her brother's—being skinned alive.

"Kill me now," she cried to Naram-sin. "You promised!"

"Don't waste your breath, Lady Kebboba," Sargon answered. "The prince has a bad habit of making promises he can't keep."

Naram-sin could have never dreamed that his pride and ego would be sunk to such a pathetic state. It wasn't that he cared about the woman; empathy for human or beast was not one of his virtues. He felt more kinship to the gods; suffering and disgrace were things that afflicted others. As reality struck, that vanity of the gods came crashing down. Even being imprisoned in Shulgi's dungeon hadn't made him feel this low, for at least the guards had shown him due respect. His father seemed intent on making him look like a foolish boy in front of the army and a city crowd of haggard men and women, who stood watching the flames engulf his chariot and his lover being groped and stripped by lowly soldiers. It was all too much to bear. He rushed the soldiers, pushing and kicking at them to restore some of his pride. The soldiers refrained from engaging him and backed away.

"What are you waiting for?" Sargon erupted. "Get the woman. If he interferes, beat him—hard, I want to see blood! I promised the people to fight the plagues of vanity, and where better to start than with an arrogant prince!"

Reluctantly, two of the soldiers moved to grab Kebboba, and the prince rushed to punch the closest one. The man dodged while simultaneously delivering a punch to Naram-sin's chest, and that was all the rest of the men needed. They piled up on the prince and beat him until his nose started bleeding. He was lying on his back when the circle over him opened.

"Majesty, the prince is bleeding," one soldier shouted.

"Good enough." Sargon nodded, then pointed to Kebboba. "Tie her to the pole."

The soldiers carried the naked Kebboba, who resisted to no avail. They forced her to hug the wooden pole and wound the rope around her. Confusion stopped her screams after it became clear she would not be skinned alive, yet her tears poured in torrents, faster than the dirt could absorb them.

Naram-sin was still stretched on the ground, throbbing with pain, when mad shrieks made him sit up and watch the soldiers carrying the pole toward the burning chariot with Kebboba strapped like a skinned goat, ready to be roasted.

"No, no! Not burned alive!" a panic-stricken Kebboba pleaded, hoping her people would stop this savagery. "By the gods, have mercy. I beg you!"

The crowd remained unmoved, silent as the towering ziggurat.

"Sadly, this is your allotted fate," came Sargon's answer as he walked along the pole bearers, probably with the intent of overseeing the process. "Your foolishness forced your people to develop a taste for men's flesh. I'm sure they'll appreciate my special gift: the more delicate taste of a woman, slowly cooked over the fire."

Naram-sin could only watch, impotent to take any action. Hate toward his father flared inside him with no lesser an intensity than the fire smoking his chariot and soon would consume his lover too.

Through her wails, Kebboba kept begging, unaware that Savagery is ignorant of human languages. When she felt the heat from the fire scorch her skin, shrieks erupted out of her in the language of absolute horror—words abandoned altogether.

The smoke shroud was about to acquire the smell of death, when a shrill voice surged over the square.

"Your Majesty!" the voice rang out sharp and clear, shifting the attention off the looming macabre scene, turning all faces like sun-chasing sunflowers. Sargon recognized the voice without looking back, and ordered the pole carriers to back up so he could assess the urgent matter prompting this interference.

"Speak up, Humbaba. … Guards, let him through!"

"O Great King, I beg your forgiveness," Humbaba shouted as he sluggishly moved with his injured arm bandaged and braced to his chest. He stopped within the wall of soldiers and bowed.

Seeing his face, the crowd marveled at how such a pleasant, harmonious voice could arise from the caverns of a demon's throat.

"Make it fast, Humbaba, the fire is dying down," Sargon said with a fury that went unnoticed as it blended with the flames behind him.

"Your Majesty, you have always shown great generosity to me for my humble service, and I greatly appreciate that. What's more, you extended your generosity with a promise that you would grant me a favor at any time. O Great King, may I have your permission to humbly ask for that favor, now?"

"Ask for it; and if it is within my grasp, it will be yours."

"O Great Sargon, it is very well within your grasp. It is tied to that pole."

"What is it, Humbaba?" Sargon smirked deviously. "Let me guess: Kebboba must have heaped curses on you after a shocking encounter, thinking of your face as a source of an evil capable of mutilating her beauty. Now you want to have the pleasure of roasting her face—make it like yours. … Humbaba, I grant you this wish. She's all yours to roast!"

"O Great King, forgive me, but that is not what I had in mind—far from it." Humbaba swallowed his trepidation. "I would like to … take her for a wife."

The proposal stunned Sargon, then hurled him into a laughing fit that instantly spread across the packed square.

Humbaba wasn't a stranger to such reactions. He kept his composure and resumed speaking. Everyone stopped laughing to listen to the maddest marriage proposal ever made.

"Your Majesty, I'm injured and not that young anymore. I need to settle down with a wife who cares for me. I would—"

"Humbaba!" Sargon interrupted, waving his hands. "Say no more. Your wish is granted. Of course, only if she consents—now *that* is out of my grasp. I tell you one thing, though, Humbaba, only so you won't be dismayed. If it were I in her place, it's the flames I would choose."

Everyone chuckled, not only for the joke but also for the truth of it.

Sargon walked to Kebboba, who was suspended from the pole with head dangling loose below her back.

"Kebboba," Sargon shouted, grinning, "I don't know who you prayed to—must be Ereshkigal—but your prayers have been answered. You heard the man. Well, he's not perfect, but believe me, he is human." Sargon couldn't help but laugh. "He's your only chance to save your skin. So, what do you say? Marry Humbaba, or marry the flames?"

Kebboba was sobbing so hard, she couldn't answer. Sargon gave his messenger a sad look, shaking his head.

"Humbaba, I'm afraid she prefers the flames."

Sargon waved, and the pole bearers started moving toward the chariot when Kebboba found her tongue; she screamed out the words higher than the raging fire that eagerly awaited to engulf her.

"Yes, Your Majesty! … I will take Humbaba for a husband! Will love and cherish him … for the rest of my life."

Like the silence after the storm, all went quiet, except for the flames that whined in anger at being denied a living reward.

"The gods work in mysterious ways!" Sargon howled, raising his hands to the heavens. Then he looked back at Humbaba, whose face had turned twice as ugly with joy.

"Humbaba, at last, someone agreed to marry you. And by god's grace, she's a beauty. Insane, I'd say, but I'm so happy for you."

Sargon walked to his messenger and hugged him lightly, when it came to his attention that his men were still carrying the pole.

"In the name of the gods, what are you doing to the bride?" he scolded them. "Is that how you treat Lady Humbaba! Cut her loose. She's not going to wear a pole and ropes for her wedding!"

Sargon turned to the audience and hollered:

"Citizens of Ur! Today, the gods have blessed you in so many ways. They spared you the wraths of death and ruin. Your great city is assured to return to its glory under the aegis of our great kingdom. And best of all, you will have a great man of valor—the greatest messenger of all times, Humbaba—to wed the best wine maker, Kebboba. And as a gift to the couple, I bestow on both the title of governor. Long live Governor Humbaba! Long live Governor Kebboba!" he shrieked to the cheers of the crowd.

"Now, I ask you to follow in an orderly fashion the instructions of my assigned men. The distribution of food and livestock will begin!"

The square erupted in frenzied screams of joy.

Sargon came back to Humbaba. "It's not too late to cook her face a little—make it look something like yours."

The messenger laughed. "I'm truly grateful, but you have already showered me with too many favors."

Sargon shrugged. "Well then, see you later at the wedding."

General Gungunum arrived with three soldiers and two of the dancers who accompanied the troops. They carried some clothing and jars of water to hastily wash Kebboba. She sat, dazed, allowing them to clean the ash and dirt off her naked body.

They dressed her to look more presentable for the short trip on a chariot, back to the palace where she would get groomed to look pretty for her wedding to the man with the nightmarish face.

𒆪 ◇ 𒑯 𒍝 𒌋𒌋

The newlyweds sat at the end of the long table to the right of the king. The main court in the governor's palace was chaotically crowded for this unforeseen happy occasion.

Sargon stood up with a cup of wine in hand and saluted.

"Today is a day surely to be remembered, when the fearsome, most dreadful messenger on Earth from sunrise to sunset, Humbaba, married a woman of grand beauty—none other than Kebboba, the best winemaker within the four corners of Earth. These two people, just as their birth cities, Ur and Uruk, are united in a perpetual bond— united in their history, heritage, pride, and dare I say ... beauty." Sargon chuckled, and everyone roared along with him. "Forgive me, Humbaba, but I couldn't resist the urge to say that.

"This marriage is a testimony to our strong bond. Any puny effort to divide us is doomed to fail. I, King Sargon, bless the union of a couple destined to be the greatest governors of Ur."

The whole court cheered, except for Naram-sin, who sat at the other end of the table with head down, laden with cuts and bruises.

"May the gods bless them with many children," Sargon howled, "and let us pray for those children to not follow in the *beauty* of their father. Forgive me, but one Humbaba is more than enough." Laughter stormed the table again. "Let's drink to the health of Kebboba and Humbaba—to the glory of both cities, Ur and Uruk."

All hailed and gulped down the wine.

"Also, I would like to share other good news," Sargon continued in a less enthusiastic voice. "To my son Naram-sin, who showed bravery and took a notable risk in an attempt to reach a peaceful end to the standoff. To him, I assign the proud task of leading the command to pacify other troubled regions of the kingdom … to General Naram-sin."

Again, cups went up and wine was gulped down. But the prince didn't feel like sharing a smile with the others. The title was more of a sentence to exile.

"Let the feast begin. Bring the food, more wine—the music, the dancers!"

Shortly, plates heaped the tables with delicacies from both cities.

The first dish placed before Kebboba had meat chunks on skewers. It triggered images of her hugging the pole. She felt dizzy and had to divert her eyes away.

"My dear Kebboba, you must try this dish." Sargon was watching her intently. "It's uniquely cooked—my own creation. Skewered pieces of meat, delectably spiced and cooked on a slow fire—deliciously succulent!"

Hesitantly, Kebboba pulled a piece, put it in her mouth, and chewed on the meat slowly. Sargon watched, enjoying every bite she took.

"How is it? Isn't this the best meat you've ever tasted?"

"Yes … it is," came her answer as she struggled to keep the food down. "It is … good."

"I'm glad you like it. I couldn't think of a name for this plate, but since you like it so much, I've decided to call it after you … Kebbob."

Laughter swamped Sargon again. Kebboba grasped her cup of wine and emptied it in one continuous gulp.

The feast, singing, and dancing went on. Humbaba hardly left his seat until he was forced by Sargon to dance with the bride. Humbaba, who had never danced in his life, nor ever dreamed of dancing, was so mortified that he wished he were delivering a message to some starving family of lions instead.

All eyes turned to watch the beast with a bandaged arm dance. After a few clumsy steps, his feet tangled and he almost tripped over, but Kebboba helped him regain his balance, drawing him closer to her. The whole place went hysterical with laughter, but the chuckles shortly faded when all were intrigued by something that seemed even stranger than the dancing Humbaba: a smile, planted on Kebboba's face while she looked at her husband.

After surviving the dance ordeal, which seemed to surpass in its peril the delivery of messages to the enemy, Humbaba leaned toward Sargon and whispered, "May I ask permission to retire for the night? Last couple of days have been rather rough."

Sargon gave him a long stare, then announced for all to hear, "Everyone, listen! Humbaba says he needs to retire, says he's exhausted. But am I right to assume he has something else in mind?"

"He's not fooling anyone," one shouted. "Look at his face, all twisted in a hideous lie."

"Tired! He looks more like a hungry lion, ready to devour his prey."

"Majesty, you should ask the hard thing between his legs to know the real answer."

Wild laughter stirred the air.

"All of you—you should be ashamed!" Sargon stood up, rebuking. "I trust him. If the man says he's tired, then he's truly tired. I, too, am tired. … Humbaba, Kebboba, let's go to bed."

Humbaba returned a look that clearly expressed unease despite his contorted face.

"What? What are you staring at?" Sargon asked irritably. "I am the king. I should go before you!"

Total silence crept over the table. Eyes focused on the ghastly face of Humbaba, whose mouth appeared to relish the idea of devouring kings.

"Yes, Majesty," the beast whispered with head bowed. "As you wish … Majesty."

Sargon's face hardened in anger, then exploded in laughter at his cruel humor.

"Go, Humbaba." Sargon sat back and waved. "Go get your rest, but—don't rest too much!"

"Bless you, Majesty." The messenger let out a subtle sigh of relief and his face twisted into a grotesque, happy form.

Many were still laughing when the couple walked away, but some had pity for Kebboba; to spend the rest of one's life with Humbaba—no punishment could get uglier. She probably would end her own life after the first night, if not before. No wonder she kept to herself; all quiet, except for the short answers she gave when spoken to.

Yet, that brief smile at the dance sent many wondering if there was a mystery hidden in that tiny seed of delight.

𒀭 ◇ � W 𝍣

She sat on her bed, sobbing. Her husband came to sit next to her.

"It's over, my love, you're safe with me now. No one will dare harm you."

Kebboba wiped the tears away and gently wrapped her arms around him.

"Oh my love, my Humbaba. I've dreamed of you countless nights since that one night. Praise the gods for their grace. Now you're all mine."

Careful not to hurt his injured arm, Kebboba eased her man onto the bed, just like she had once when her path had crossed with a fantasy she had never dreamed of.

It happened when her former husband, Elam, was away on a distant trip. She learned that the infamous, deformed messenger Humbaba was in the city. On the pretext that she needed to send a message to the king, she ordered that Humbaba be brought to her to see for herself the truth in the rumors about how his spoken words contrasted with his deformity.

When he showed up in her room, she got a little apprehensive, despite being prepared. Then, as he spoke, she was swiftly awestruck by words that veiled his horrible face behind a tolerable mask. Her daring spirit, along with an insatiable appetite for the wondrous and the abnormal, had Kebboba sit all evening, listening to his stories. They ranged from humorous tales about the plethora of people whom he had terrified out of their wits to nail-biting accounts of the risks he took when delivering ultimatums to the enemy. The time passed so fast for Kebboba, and just as quickly Humbaba morphed into a pleasant, entertaining man, and a man of more bravery, with words as his only weapon, than the toughest soldiers who wielded spears, arrows, or swords.

That was when the thought came to her: could it be possible that the gods had endowed him with a unique weapon for the love duel? Kebboba didn't waste time on fantasies; her lust was immense, and it didn't take much effort to get him naked. To her delight, the man had another charm hidden under his robes that had her struggle to keep her cries of joy from traveling outside the room. And with every man she bedded after that night, Humbaba's image she always invited.

Now Kebboba was sobbing with pleasure. Her cries of joy went out uninhibited for all to hear. She was the happiest woman in Ur—married to the very right monster to match her monstrous lust.

No Spitting!

T HE BOYS GATHERED AROUND THE MUD BOX, FILLING THEIR
tablet trays while fuming about the learned brother who, upon
entering the tablet house, lashed at them like a crazed tyrant.

Ranting about the quality of their works, Samian berated their
tablets as nothing more than lumps of mud trampled by a bull's hooves.
He ordered many to rewrite their assignments on fresh tablets.

They complained to Isaa, who announced loudly, making sure
Samian would hear, that their works were good, and they needed not
redo them. That left the boys at a loss, not sure of whose instructions
to ignore. But they all prayed for the day when a new master would
take charge of the classes so they wouldn't have to deal with two
learned brothers who had become bitter foes.

The rest period arrived with the sun perched at its zenith in the
clear skies. Enheduanna approached Isaa, looking serious, though
she was one of the lucky few to be spared the wrath of Samian.

"Isaa, we need to talk, now. Meet me by the palm trees." And she
walked away.

Isaa rushed to the storage room, picked a tablet, then dashed out
to meet her.

"What is wrong with you?" Enheduanna wasted no time snapping
at him. "Samian knows about our affair; instead of appeasing him,
you go off like some frantic bull of heaven, stomping on his judgment
of the boys' work—provoking him."

"Am I supposed to hide away and leave Samian's berating whims
unchallenged?"

"Who cares if the boys do the work again?" she argued. "It will only improve their skills."

"Fine, next time I'll ignore the fool. Though, truth is … something else is getting me agitated. I need to get it off my chest."

"Well, Isaa, better cast this demon out before it gets us in trouble."

"I … wrote a poem." Isaa produced the tablet.

"A poem has you agitated? How silly. So, what is the poem about?"

"Remember the day when we muddied each other?"

"How could I forget it?" She grinned. "And then, just when I thought I won the battle—molding your head with mud—I slid on the way to the gate under the rain and got all muddied." She knitted her eyebrows. "Is the poem making fun of me?"

"No, but it's based on all of that; the storm, and you running under the rain."

"Fine, let me hear it. But it had better be good, or I'll smash the tablet on your head!"

The tablet was given the prized treat of being baked in the kiln to give it a lasting life. Though Isaa knew the poem by heart, he kept staring at the tablet like he would a treasure.

"I called this poem 'Dancer Under the Thunder.'" And he began reciting:

She looked at the night through skies that cried and roared,
With a smile wild and bright, her spirit fluttered and soared.

Watching through the door, I said, "Well, enjoy the bath."
Inside I sipped on wine, safe, beyond heaven's wrath.

She leapt into the air, sending droplets to scatter.
Slid along shallow pools, as if walking on the water.

Lightning painted the dark, her image suddenly froze.
With beauty I was showered, stricken by love woes.

Raindrops flirted around her, joyful, sparking with light.
Some couldn't resist to touch and hold her tight.

A mermaid out of the sea, bathing in the air.
Goddess beneath weeping clouds, floating, no burden, no care.

Drums echoed through the void, she went swaying to the beat.
Assailed by passion tremors, 1 could only submit to defeat.

Then the storm faded; 1 deemed this just a dream.
Yet my heart pounded, shouting: *Silly, she's in your realm.*

"O Heaven, 1 pray you understand, try to feel my pain.
Go on, scream out loud, and please cry again.
Give this fool one more chance, 1 swear not to squander."
"Girl, may 1 take your hand, next dance under the thunder?"

Isaa looked at her to see her reaction. She took the tablet and ran a finger lightly over the cuneiform carvings.

"Oh, this is so sweet. I thought you were going to mock me. I love it."

"And … I love you, Enheduanna." He moved closer and reached for her hand. "May I take your hand—in marriage?"

"What are you doing?" She pulled her hand away, stepping back. "Someone might be watching."

"I don't care," he said defiantly. "Let them know. I don't want to keep hiding like a criminal. That bigmouth Samian has probably told everyone about us by now."

"I don't think so. He wouldn't dare."

"He's raging with jealousy. He can't keep it inside for too long—if he ever did keep it!"

"This is the wrong time and place to talk about marriage."

"Why? I didn't want to bring up the subject before with all the unrest in the land. Well, the rebellion is over, all is calm and peaceful. … You don't love me?"

"Love and marriage are different things." She turned her side to him. "Let's not talk about this."

"I understand; you—a royal princess, while I—some learned brother covered in mud splotches."

"Sadly, it's the reality we can't escape. The choice is never mine to decide. My father … he expects … you forgot how he planned to wed me to the pharaoh?"

"Why would your father object?" Isaa persisted. "After all, I'm a learned person, adept in the arts of writing and accounting … the son of a wealthy man—his personal sculptor. As for your wedding to the pharaoh, that's a thing of the past."

"That *thing of the past* has changed everything. My father never forgave me for ruining that wedding plan. I'm no longer his beautiful jasmine-scented flower but rather a bush of thorns. As for your father—aren't you forgetting he had disowned you?"

"A moment of anger. My mother visits me here and she believes he regrets it. I'm sure he will take me back if I am to marry you, just like I'm sure you will be able to convince your father now."

"Now?" she snapped at him. "And what makes you so sure he would be convinced *now*? Is it because *now* I am, like they say, *broken merchandise*?"

"No, no. Please, you know very well I didn't mean that."

"Forget it—this marriage thing." She shook her head.

"Why not?" Isaa demanded. "I thought you would be happy with my proposal. Yet here you are, putting obstacles in the way. Why? What's wrong with being a family and having children?" He waved his palm, stroking a phantom child's head with it.

"It seems like you have planned out the rest of my life." Enheduanna looked into the distance, wishing to be somewhere else.

"No, nothing like that. You go on with your life like always, no changes, except we will be family."

"By the gods, Isaa, wake up!" She became petulant. "You're dreaming! Oh, how absurd, come back to reason! You don't know my father. I, myself, don't know him anymore—nobody does. I care about you and don't want him to hurt you. Besides, I have my mind set on something … and it will not be to your liking."

"What is it? Try me."

"I was hoping you would figure it out by now. … I'm planning to be a priestess, dedicated to serve the goddess Ishtar."

Isaa thought he had been ready with all the answers, but this response took him by surprise.

"I know your faith in her is strong. I will not try to change that. But this dedication, this wish to spend your whole life serving her! … If it is true that the gods gave themselves eternal life whereas allotting mortality to us, why is it too much to ask that we enjoy some of this short life—just a small part, instead of spending it all worshipping them?"

"And what makes you think I don't enjoy serving my goddess? Before I loved you, there was, and will always be, my love for Ishtar. Nothing on this Earth could compare to the peace she provides me when I think of her."

"What nonsense … this obsession with Ishtar is driving me to madness!" Isaa labored to keep his temper from flaring. "To devote your life to her, it's insane."

"You don't seem to respect my goddess." Enheduanna was offended. "You ignore the fact that she was the one who made you follow to save me from the grips of the dirty bastard who profanely mocked the vow ritual and almost killed me. Ishtar made our love possible. Don't you appreciate any of that?"

"Forgive me, but she had no part in making me tail you. I followed on my own because I was worried sick about you, and I was—will always be—in love with you."

Isaa reached to her with pleading eyes. "I respect your beliefs, but think of our love. Where are we going with this affair?"

"I don't know. Ask the gods." She shrugged. "Oh, forgive me, ask your loner invisible god. He should give you an answer—an invisible answer."

"Who told you about that?" Isaa was surprised.

"So, it is true! Does it matter who told me? I thought they were jealous, starting up rumors to hurt you. But you never showed any devotion to any of our gods. Did you abandon our gods for the one who's always hiding?" Enheduanna's angry eyes searched him.

"He's not hiding. He is the Almighty One, mightier than all the other gods put together." Isaa spoke excitedly, unloading some of the weight of his massive belief. "My god is not a chiseled stone or some mold of mud. You can chisel a statue of Anu from the greatest mountain out there, and still my god will dwarf him. Most people don't see him because they are like ants with heads looking down, seeing only dirt and stones. That's why all those gods the people worship are made of dirt and stones."

"So, I'm just one insignificant ant in a colony of ants!" Enheduanna spoke with the calm that precedes the storm. "I'm but another narrow-sighted fool among the vast masses—worshippers of dirt and stone gods! While *you* are one of the gifted few with the sharp vision to perceive the real god. Well then, why do you want an ant for a wife? Go find yourself *a woman!*"

"Forgive me, I didn't mean it that way. I shouldn't have said that." Isaa was at a loss for words. "Can we keep the gods out of it? Our love should come first. The gods shouldn't be meddling in every detail of our lives."

"So, have I regressed from being an ant to a woman?" Her storm was gathering strength. "Now *you* forgive me, I still don't see your god ... do I revert to being an ant now?"

She turned away and her voice throbbed with the ferocity of a preaching priestess. "People of Sumer! Rejoice, for my beloved here has found the true god—one who cannot be seen, yet he's everywhere; he cannot be touched, yet he will squish you like a bug. His glory bests that of all other gods put together. My advice to all of you who depend on our antiquated gods for your livelihood—priests, priestesses, craftsmen, temple builders, traders of sacrificial animals— you had better find another way to make a living; join the bandits, beg in the streets, or simply drown yourselves in the river. And let's not forget to abolish all festivals that celebrate those obsolete gods. From here on, all kneel to the new god—the Mighty Loner, Invisible One!"

She turned back to Isaa, her words flying in a tirade. "Do you really believe any sane person will follow this god? He is but the creation of some beggars who roam the streets babbling madness. Those insane, wretched fools merged all our gods together to create this mighty entity of yours—god of war and peace, earth and water, health and sickness. He's merciful, loving, generous, yet to the same degree he's jealous, sadistic, and would erupt in a murderous fury at any given moment. Yes, those beggars, soaked in their own urine, muddled all our divine gods into this One Colossal Blasphemy!

"It was mighty Anu who created everything, long before the first man opened his eyes to the sunlight of Shamash. Now, all of a sudden, your *supreme* god reveals his *invisible* self, claiming to be the creator of all! Where was he hiding all that time? … Have you gone totally mad; have demons infested your mind? Tell me you're drunk or afflicted with some ailment that is driving you to believe this nonsense. Say it!"

"I can never believe in your stone gods again." Isaa shook his head, looking down. "They don't listen to me, nor say a thing. I only hear them scream in pain when they fall down and shatter."

He raised his head to meet her sharp gaze. "I beg of you, don't be angry. I could've continued lying, but I want to be honest, just as I am honest about my love for you. Follow your goddess, I will never interfere, but you don't need to be a priestess, chained with your devotion to her temple for the rest of your life."

"How about this god of yours?" Enheduanna had a remnant of the storm still raging. "I hear he's everywhere. So, I guess no matter where you go, you're in his temple, at all times—as you walk, sleep, eat, even when you squat to relieve yourself. He should be here right now, listening. Why not put an end to this argument, simply by him sending a proof of his existence—a sign?"

"A sign like what?" Isaa was getting agitated.

"Anything out of the ordinary."

"Who am I to test the Almighty and his powers?"

"Fine, then let me do it. Don't worry, I won't ask for much."

She placed the poem tablet on the ground, walked out of the tree shade, and blared with head raised high:

"O mighty god of Isaa, show me your powers. Wring a few drops of rain out of the blue sky, and I promise to take Isaa for a husband, so we, along with our future children, devote our lives to worshipping and honoring you."

Enheduanna stretched her arms out with palms open and sights reaching to heaven. She moved back and forth, then slowly circled around herself. Finally, she turned to Isaa and gave him a wicked smile.

"All he had to do was spit a few times. Such a disappointment, this *Mighty God* of yours."

Isaa returned a sad look and sighed. "For some time now, I anxiously and patiently waited for the right moment to ask the one I love to be my life partner. I didn't expect any of this. What a total fool I am." He let out a frustrated chuckle. "I wrote a poem to express my feelings. It sang of love, dancing, rain, music, heaven … I left the gods out. And what do I get for a response? You want my god to spit."

Isaa walked out of the shade, following the same path she had taken before him. He looked up and called to the skies.

"O Great Mighty Gods—Anu, Ishtar, Shamash; gods of Sumer, Babylon, Phoenicia; gods of the Nile and the far lands beyond, from sunrise to sunset—I beseech you: send me some rain, and I will never doubt your mighty powers. O divine gods, just a few raindrops, and I will worship you till my last, dying breath."

Isaa stretched his arms out, palms opened to the heavens to receive the rain. He walked back and forth, circled around, just like she had. Finally, he stopped and turned to her with sadness tearing him apart, as though he wished that rain had fallen to prove him wrong.

"If only … each one had spat once," he said, grief leading his voice.

Fire flashed in Enheduanna's eyes, and like lightning it went out, replaced by a cold, empty look that spelled the sudden demise of their love.

"My plan to join the temple priestesses … I delayed; I couldn't bear the thought of leaving you. Now, I have no reason to stay here any longer." She cast a glance at the poem tablet on the ground, then pointed a finger to the vast azure above.

"There, you have the answer to your proposal. Heaven is not screaming; heaven is not crying. My hand you cannot have … not for dancing, nor in marriage."

Enheduanna turned and walked away, not back to the classroom, but toward the gate where the guards waited. Isaa struggled to keep his mouth under control, but some invisible force set it loose.

"The gods don't spit!" His scream, riding on flying spittle, followed her. "You hear me? The gods—don't spit!"

She kept going as if he didn't exist anymore.

"Go to your Ishtar—kneel at Ishtar's feet! Pray to your statues for the rest of your life. And pray for Ishtar—to spit!"

The tempest of his shouts didn't sway her off her path. After she had disappeared, Isaa looked up to heaven, wanting to curse whoever resided there for their betrayal. The empty skies crowded his heart with a merciless void. He picked the poem tablet up from the ground and furiously hurled it upward to shatter the blue abyss above. It only managed to leave a tiny dent of clay color for a brief moment before plunging down. His heart sank then shattered upon watching the words of love he had poured into the tablet scatter to meaningless fragments, joining the dirt.

His soul screamed in pain, and he stood staring at the outside gate as if it led to a cell that had locked his love away forever.

He bemoaned not having asked forgiveness—of his father, who could have done him a great favor: slice his tongue shorter.

By the River of Babylon

"**T**HE BEST RED WINE IN BABYLON. ... DRINK, HAVE YOUR FILL. Invite everyone—family, friends, tribe to join you. One condition: finish the whole sack, or else you'll get a smack."

Slowly, she sucked with the straw to her mouth.

Shu-dagan watched impatiently; no one else had arrived after his generous invitation.

"Where are those friends of yours? You alone can't finish this river of wine."

He looked intently at her, awaiting an answer. However, she seemed to have had enough. With her stomach full, it was time to call it a day and go home.

"You are utterly useless." Shu-dagan slapped her hard, leaving a tiny streak of blood on his arm with traces of dark spots of what used to be a mosquito that had drained a drop of his blood.

There must be better ways to end one's own life. He rose off the chair and walked to the sleeping room in the shack. His wife was asleep, unaware of his attempted suicide by bug. He stared at the tiny flame from the oil lamp at the corner and mused:

Set the shack on fire with the two of us inside!

It was another thought of a suicide he had no intention to commit; he still had a few more things to attend to in this existence. Besides, this was no longer his shack.

"Wake up." He shook Arbella's shoulder. "It's time. Start getting ready. I'm leaving now—will meet you later by the river."

"I thought we were leaving together!"

"I need to take care of an urgent matter."

"What urgent matter?" she asked as she stood.

"Nourish the land with some shit." His answer came scolding. "Then to the temple—make an offering. Does that satisfy your curiosity? Just get ready, I'll meet you by the river."

Any other day, Arbella would've snapped back at him with an unpleasant response, but not today. Quietly, she retreated.

Shu-dagan followed her with his gaze and watched the ghost of his girl, giving her mother some comfort while not bothering to throw a single glance in his direction. Fraught with guilt, Shu-dagan rushed to Arbella and took her in his arms. Her tears were already flowing. He brushed a hand over her face and kissed her wet cheeks.

"Forgive me, I didn't mean to," he said softly. "Cry no more, Mayram wants us to be strong. I won't take long. Meet me by the river; Tammuz and his son should be waiting there."

As he turned to leave, he saw Mayram's ghost smiling at him.

Out of the shack, he stood looking at his most loyal helper, Ass-Tied-Outside. Hesitantly, he approached the donkey, patted it gently on the head, and combed his fingers through its short hair. Ass-Tied-Outside returned a soft bray to the master who treated him with the utmost care and never overworked him.

"Are you hungry, Ass-Tied-Outside?" Like always, Shu-dagan used the full name he had chosen for the donkey. It answered with a bray just a pitch higher than before. Shu-dagan picked some fodder and went on feeding it with his own hands.

The neighbor, Kuwari, came out yawning and greeted him.

"Shu. You're leaving too early."

"Yes, I thought I would get an early start—easier to row with the air still cool and fresh."

"True, and the river demons are in deep slumber at this time."

"Demons don't bother me." Shu-dagan grabbed more fodder. "Humans are capable of much graver evil than demons."

"True, very true." Kuwari paused briefly while Shu-dagan fed the donkey. "Are you sure you want to do this?"

"Very sure, my friend. There is nothing for us here anymore. As you know, my daughter Mayram is not coming back to Babylon, but we can go and be with her in Uruk."

Kuwari went quiet and watched the donkey chew, as if the animal's moving mouth would give him a hint of what to say to a man who kept his departed daughter alive in his chats.

"Don't forget your promise," Shu-dagan said. "Take good care of Ass-Tied-Outside, he's my gift to you. Treat my gift with care; don't overload him. Ass-Tied-Outside has a soul greater and nobler than the combined souls of dozens of the lowlifes, the so-called nobles."

"Don't worry, Shu, I'll treat Ass-Tied-Outside better than my wife." Kuwari let out a short laugh, and the donkey began braying.

"I don't know, my friend," Shu-dagan said, a soft smile on his face. "Ass-Tied-Outside doesn't seem to be happy with this answer."

The neighbor laughed some more.

"Well, Kuwari, it is time I leave. I need to make one last visit to the temple. I wish you happiness and the best of fortunes. You were a great neighbor and friend, one in a vast cluster of stars."

"It was a blessing from the gods to have you as a neighbor." Kuwari rested his hand on Shu-dagan's shoulder. "Shu, anytime you pass by Babylon, you have a place to stay here in my home. I mean it!"

After a warm embrace of farewell, Shu-dagan walked to a nearby shrub where he picked up a wicker basket wrapped in a rag, and he started away. After a handful of paces, the donkey let out a sad call. Shu-dagan hesitated, then walked back to the donkey.

"I will miss you, Ass-Tied-Outside." He hugged the donkey's neck. "Don't worry, I leave you in good hands."

He looked at his neighbor, who nodded to him. And Shu-dagan took off at a brisk walk with the loud braying of Ass-Tied-Outside chasing him, as if it knew this was farewell, begging to be taken along. It made Shu-dagan run to expand the buffer zone between him and the memories of his home. But the faint sound of Ass-Tied-Outside kept reverberating in his head as he took his last stroll in the quiet streets of Babylon, which was just waking up to the new morning.

Shu-dagan was overwhelmed by an eerie feeling of being a stranger—a man who didn't belong anymore to the city where he was born, where he had lived most of his life. He was free from belonging to any place, but that freedom carried the heavy chains of abandonment.

He arrived at the first Ishtar temple on his path. The doors had opened just a short while ago. Down the few stairs to the entrance, a middle-aged priestess received him with a smile.

"May the goddess bless your day with joy and love," she greeted.

Shu-dagan smiled back without saying a word. He was in a rush and had no time for joy and love with her.

"Making an offering?" the priestess asked, seeing the basket he carried. Shu-dagan simply nodded.

"May the gods shower blessings upon you for your devotion and generosity."

He went inside the temple, all the way to the front. There were only two women inside, kneeling to a life-sized statue placed on a waist-high brick platform. Shu-dagan went down to his knees, a handful of paces to their side. The women glanced at the faithful man who had joined them in this early-morning prayer.

Shu-dagan assumed that the elder was a mother who must have been teaching her daughter the sacred traditions of honoring the goddess.

The girl smiled at the good-looking man, dressed in a neat white tunic, tightened at the waist with a lapis lazuli-studded leather belt. She turned back to the goddess, but only briefly, and her face sneaked a warmer smile at the man, who smiled back. She blushed and her head snapped back to Ishtar in search of advice, and the goddess didn't keep her waiting.

The girl's face was glowing when she stared back at Shu-dagan. Her pupils moved up and down, telling him the goddess had fully approved of him. Shu-dagan became aware that he had been chosen for the love vows ritual. He gave the girl a sorry grin with a head shake, cordially declining the invitation.

The girl turned back to the altar, seeking further advice. The goddess seemed adamant in her choice of this believer, whom she had guided to this specific temple this early in the morning; he was the one, no mistake about it. There was only one thing for the girl to do. She turned to face the man sent by the goddess and switched from a kneeling to a sitting posture, spreading her robe to receive the silver piece.

The mother looked disapprovingly at her daughter's behavior, but she couldn't interfere—not in the temple; that would be sacrilegious, particularly if her daughter had somehow received some divine sign from the goddess. This could be one of those exceptions to the rules.

Pain and anger tore at Shu-dagan, for the girl was about his daughter's age. He frowned and shook his head, gesturing to be left alone, but that only made the girl more determined.

The goddess chose you for the task. Her gaze kept reaching for him. *You don't have to throw a silver piece—a bronze one will do, or even one of those lapis lazuli beads on your belt. Don't you find me desirable? Am I not young enough for you, or are you one of those boy-lovers?*

Stubborn, foolish girl. Shu-dagan's patience passed beyond its limits. *I need to be more convincing—can't wait any longer. Soon, more people will start arriving, and the plan will be ruined.*

Left with no choice, he stood up and braced his mind for the madness he had schemed: make an offering to the goddess.

The girl's heart skipped a beat, thinking he was going to volunteer for the sacred ritual. But instead of throwing something in her lap, he started to unwrap the cloth draping the basket, revealing another rag, which he also proceeded to remove.

The girl became alarmed when the first coating came off. After the second one flew off, she realized she had completely misunderstood her goddess. The ritual was forgotten, and she was on her feet, urging her mother to stand up. When Shu-dagan undid the final coating, the girl was racing toward the exit, leaving behind her mother, who was knocked off her knees and onto her side by a punch of foul odor that caught her unawares. She staggered to her feet in pursuit of her daughter with scarf pressed against her nose to fend off the rancid whiff that intensified with every passing moment.

Alone at last after evicting the mother and daughter, Shu-dagan picked up the basket with both hands, and after a long moment of hesitation, his arms catapulted in the direction of the statue, not letting the basket go. The contents flew, slamming the goddess with a blend of excrements, soggy and solid.

A loud scream shook the temple, and Shu-dagan's head spun in fear, thinking that the ferocious sound had issued from an invisible, wrathful goddess upon seeing her statue desecrated. But his fears retreated along with the reverberating echo when the scream's source became obvious.

The priestess had been at the back of the temple, lighting the oil lamps, when the girl and her mother came rushing out as if escaping a vile spirit. Then the foul smell invaded, obliterating the divine vapors of the burning myrrh incense. Oblivious to what was going on, the priestess thought that a worshipper had suffered an uncontrollable urge, letting loose of it right there in the heart of the temple. But after a closer look, she froze in a state of disbelief on seeing the man she greeted earlier aim his basket at the goddess, who stood helpless, with no choice but to receive the offering targeted at her.

"May mad dogs eat you alive!" the priestess cursed in a voice that seemed to magnify with the help of the residing goddess. "Ereshkigal will have you down to your waist shoveling demon shit in the netherworld!"

She threw the oil lamp she carried at him. The oil spilled and caught fire over the brick-paved floor, but the winding line of flames missed Shu-dagan by a few paces. Deprived of anything combustible, the fire started to consume itself.

With the first part of his mission accomplished, Shu-dagan turned to the priestess and took a few steps in her direction, which convinced her that it was far better to seek the gods' help from outside the temple, where her pleas to punish the heretic could be heard more clearly from heaven.

"Son of dogs—may you burn in boiling shit, forever!" she howled, and ran away while unleashing an uninterrupted litany of curses in some priestly tongue with the hope that those might achieve better results.

Miraculously unscathed by the barrage of malicious prayers aimed at him, Shu-dagan proceeded to finalize his sacrilegious task. Over the dying line of fire he hopped, then climbed the platform where the goddess stood.

A pile of solid dung slid to rest at the base of the statue. Shu-dagan pulled a small terracotta plate out of a side pocket in his tunic, scooped up a sizable amount of the waste, and started plastering the face of the goddess, praying:

"O revered goddess of love, do accept this offering, prepared by me personally with produce from the rear ends of this humble servant of yours and Ass-Tied-Outside, uniquely for your pleasure—*Holiness.*"

He kept smearing the statue's proud face until it was entirely masked with dung.

"O holy Ishtar, you took my Mayram away. Why? Were you jealous? Why would a goddess, or any god for that matter, be jealous? Now that you look like shit, what are you going to do—kill all the women?" He slapped the statue's face with the plate, where it remained pasted.

"You envious, whoring bitch, this is the last offering you'll get from me. Enjoy it!"

He leapt off the platform and walked out of the temple, not surprised when a small crowd of people, headed by the priestess, received him.

"That's him—the one who desecrated the temple!" the indignant priestess shrieked, and the belligerent crowd chanted angry curses that promised to follow with a severe punishment for the blasphemous one.

Shu-dagan walked down the stairs with a defiant, searing demeanor that would not tolerate the slightest assault on his person. The loud protest died down to whispers as the distance narrowed to better display the strong body that backed up the madman.

"Why all this hate?" Shu-dagan reacted. "This hostility to a devoted man who had just made a generous offering and chanted sincere prayers to the goddess of love?"

The crowd split as Shu-dagan walked in their midst. All went silent, with only glares of contempt to show for courage.

"Look—a guard over there!" someone announced, and the crowd found the mettle to scream again, lending one man enough courage to smack Shu-dagan on the shoulder from behind. Shu-dagan turned and snapped a fast punch to the man's face, knocking him to the ground.

The night guard was daydreaming of sleep. With his shift almost over, the last thing he needed was a disturbance. He saw the mob but wasn't sufficiently close to see the squabble.

Probably just some dispute between a drunk and a harlot who's demanding pay for her service, he prayed, but his curses soon followed when the priestess came out of the gaggle, barking, urging him to hurry.

He wasn't in the habit of running, unless ordered by someone higher in rank. As he approached, he could see two men on the ground and a strong man standing over them.

"Kill this heretic son of dogs, he's evil!" The priestess screamed the loudest among the throng, pointing at the one who violated her temple.

The guard locked eyes with the aggressor and saw a face confirming her claim. He reached for his sword, but Shu-dagan was already sprinting toward him, driven to even the score with someone, anyone, in a soldier's uniform. Before the guard's blade was halfway out of its leather sheath, a kick like the hoof of a horse found its way through the arch of his manly pride, bringing him down to his knees just when a fist took aim at his face, sending him flat to the ground.

The guard was clutching his punished crotch to soothe the screaming pain, when his sword hissed to tell him it was being separated from its sheath. Instantly, a rattle of sandals erupted with the crowd dispersing in a fear wave that spread out from where the crazed man stood, now armed with a sword pointing at the night guard.

Stunned by this quick turn of events, the guard could only curse his misfortune: the end of his work shift was about to become the end of his life.

"You wouldn't mind me borrowing your sword?" the madman asked, only to walk away without having the guard's consent.

Entranced by relief at his life being spared, the guard remained on the ground, content to see the menace retreat.

"Do you need a mat for a nap?" A scornful voice shredded his daze. It was the priestess, who had always given him tender loving in exchange for the security he offered. But now, with him lying in the dirt, she sounded as if she had gotten a bad deal for her services.

"Go after him! Kill that bastard!"

"With what? He took my sword." The guard stood and dusted

off his uniform. "I'm going to call for some help. You and the others chase him to see where he's heading."

✶ ◇ ⊐ ⩊ Ⅲ

"What's keeping him?" Arbella complained to the two boat helpers. "I should've listened to my mother; countless were her warnings about his type. She said I was marrying misfortune. If there were a god of misfortune, they should call him Shu-dagan. And she, my poor Mayram, followed in his recklessness. That's why she ended up—" The word choked her.

Tammuz patted her on the shoulder. "Don't worry, he'll be here. He must be saying farewell to some friends."

"Oh, look up there!" Tammuz's son exclaimed. "That man running, it's definitely him. He runs like a bull, ready to stampede all that gets in his way. But why is he running?"

They went silent, awaiting the answer.

"What took you so long?" Arbella shouted when he came within scolding range. "Got in trouble again!"

Shu-dagan stopped by the boat to catch his breath.

"Thank you, my friends." He embraced his two helpers. "Forgive me for I must leave right away. You, too, had better leave now for your own good. A mad mob is chasing me."

"I knew it," Arbella sighed.

They exchanged their speedy farewells, and Arbella went onto the boat as they released it from its mooring. Just then, a group of people showed up in the distance. Shu-dagan plodded in the water, pushed on the boat, and hopped aboard. He grasped the oar, thrusting with it to break free from the grip of the muddy bank and escape to clear water.

"Bless you, Shu, for leaving us the shack," Tammuz called out. "It was the best of times working with you. Forever, you will live in our memories."

Shu-dagan waved to them as the flow of the Euphrates River carried the boat south.

"You took your time back there," Arbella said. "Praying, I guess.

What did you offer to the gods?"

"It wasn't just any offering. The goddess loved it so much, she had me feed it to her, down to the last morsel."

Arbella studied him to figure out if he was joking, for since the death of Mayram his sense of humor had deserted him.

"I, too, had a mob chasing me, each time I made an offering!" she retorted, sarcastically.

"No, those people just wanted a ride to the other side of the river," he said calmly while rowing.

"I believe you, my beloved," she responded just as calmly. "And I believe … those two archers at the bank didn't appreciate that either, being left behind. Or could it be—the sword you came carrying is theirs and they want it back?"

Slowly, Shu-dagan turned around.

The bows were already pulled tight against the cords. The two archers adjusted the angle and released the arrows. Shu-dagan watched, unmoved, as one arrow hit the side of the boat and the other stuck to the oar. The two archers ran to keep the boat within range.

"Try again, my friends," Shu-dagan challenged, his arms stretched wide open while still holding the oar. "And pray the angry goddess will better guide your arrows."

One arrow whizzed over his head and the other landed inside the boat, close to where Arbella was sitting.

The two archers were already exhausted from running with their equipment to catch up to the heretic after the night guard had told them about the scuffle by the temple. Still, they pushed themselves to close in on the boat that drifted down with the current. Knowing this would be their last chance, they stopped to catch their breath, then nocked their arrows. As they took aim, they saw the woman step right before her man as though her marriage vows dictated that she share the deadly arrows with her husband. Her defiant pose seemed to taunt their archery skills. Fury blinded their accuracy and sent their blazing arrows to cool down in the Euphrates. They lowered their bows to their sides in defeat while the couple on the boat waved farewell to them.

Babylon faded behind in the distance. There was no jubilation from the boat's two occupants after their narrow escape. Somehow, they seemed disappointed that the arrows had missed, only to leave them with their hearts ripping apart at their desertion of the city where Mayram's memories lived. But Shu-dagan had already exhausted all his reserves of sadness, paving the way for anger to take control over him. He raised his head so the gods could get a better view of him, and hollered:

"O gods of Babylon, dwellers of heaven. I was a good servant and a believer. I prayed to you, made offerings—generous offerings, in good times and bad. I appreciated the little fortunes you bestowed upon me while I patiently endured the loads of suffering you stacked on my back. But you went too far with your cruelty—you savage beasts. How dare you? How dare you take my Mayram, my girl whom you clothed in beauty that brought smiles and hope, only to deliver her to the netherworld in the early spring of her life?

"Marduk, hear my next prayer: Die, you bastard, die! … Yes, from now on, that'll be my only prayer to you and all your filthy children, especially your whore of a daughter, Ishtar, mother of all harlots. Some fools say you test our faith from time to time! To the inferno with you and your tests, I'll be proud to fail them all! Now, it's my turn to test you—you supreme coward who hides in the cloud folds. This blasphemy surely merits your wrath, so kill me right here and now, strike me with lightning, send a sea monster to swallow me whole!"

Defiantly, Shu-dagan stood in wait for an agonizing death.

No flashing light tore down from the heavens. The skies remained calm except for the rippling of their reflection on the river, and no sea monster surfaced to guzzle the heretic boatman.

"Are you deaf? Coward—can't even face a mortal's challenge! Crush me like I crush a bug … crush me back to a lump of mud! How hard would it be, after all, you created us from mud? … What are you waiting for; LUMP ME BACK TO MUD! Do it, you worthless, impotent filth!

"I curse you, God! Moreover, I curse the grand fool who left you playing with mud! Utter fools are those who laud your creation—this miserable, murky world—this playground of yours."

Shu-dagan watched the last outlines of Babylon abandoning

them. A sudden wave of fear gripped him, and he turned to Arbella. She was staring at him, tears deserting her sorrowful eyes—tears that longed to join the jovial river only to be doomed to wither on the boat.

Shu-dagan stepped to Arbella and held her in a tight embrace. She was all he had left in this world after losing everything—his city, his home, his Mayram, and now, his gods.

Burning River

Streaming south, the Euphrates River snaked through the plains to join its brother, the Tigris, in their journey to the great sea. Countless were the stories told about the great sea, which was believed to stretch all the way to the outer rims of the world. Only fearless souls braved those distant oceans, where angry gods sent waves higher than ziggurats, and equipped sea monsters to gorge on human flesh with sharp obsidian teeth, longer than swords. Yet, there was no shortage of fools who dreamed of riches, believed in stories of fountains of youth, and sought fantasies of divine pleasures to be attained at the far beyond. Many of those journeys came to end with splintered ships and the broken bodies of men, along with their dreams, devoured by the deep, endless entrails of the sea.

The walls of Uruk greeted Shu-dagan, but his gaze was distant, dreamily chasing the river. He met all the requirements of a great fool who would venture out to the edges of Earth. Neither monsters nor high seas scared him; even the gods dared not answer his challenges.

Shu-dagan rowed the boat toward the riverbank, letting his dreams drift away with the Euphrates. Something was calling on him from within the great walls of Uruk that he could not fail to obey. He lived for one thing, and dreams had no part in it.

He pulled the boat by a grove of palm trees overlooking the river. A little boy was playing in the afternoon sun, wading and retreating in and out of the waves that brushed on the muddy bank while fooling around with him. A man and a woman peeled out of the tree shadows and walked toward the boat. The boy came running to join them.

"Greetings, my good man. May I ask you a favor?" the man said. "Can you cross us to the other side of the river? I only have a loaf of bread for your trouble. No boatman agreed to take us."

Shu-dagan stroked the scruffy beard he had grown during the journey.

"Though I'm tired ..." He glanced at the child, who wore a sad smile. "I'll take you, but only if this young man would help in the rowing."

"I'll help, I'll help!" The boy hopped in excitement.

"Very well, then. Just let me unload the boat, and my new boatman will take us across."

Arbella helped take out the few possessions they'd brought along, placing them under a tree where she would rest until her husband returned from this unexpected short trip.

"Onto the boat, young man!" Shu-dagan shouted, a smile shadowing his serious look. "Time to work. Move your lazy behind!"

The parents laughed as the boy rushed to the boat and struggled to climb over the edge. Finally, he triumphed, only to fall inside the boat, but instantly he stood up to cover for the mishap. With the parents aboard, Shu-dagan pushed the boat and climbed over once it cleared the bank.

"Let's row now," Shu-dagan said to the boy. "This oar is too heavy. You need two strong men to handle it. Are you strong enough?"

The boy hesitated for the oar was about twice his height. Nevertheless, he nodded yes.

"Good, help me, then." Shu-dagan pretended to have difficulty lifting the oar, but once the boy touched it, mysteriously, the oar became weightless, and Shu-dagan rowed with the boy right in front, giving his magic touch to make the oar easier to handle.

"Great work, young man; the hard part is over with. Get some rest, you've done way too much." The compliment came after a handful of strokes, for the boy was in the way, making the work twice as hard.

"How old are you, young man?"

The boy flashed one full hand, then went to sit by his mother, who smiled and wrapped an arm around him.

"He has made five winters," she confirmed.

"Bless you, sir, you're very warmhearted," the father said, handing over the loaf of bread.

Shu-dagan placed the bread in a wicker basket, fully aware that the boy had his eyes glued on it.

"People who work for me get to eat on the boat," he said to the boy. "Of course, only if they're hungry."

The boy jumped up. "I'm hungry, I'm hungry!"

"Now behave," his mother scolded, seating him down. "This man has been more than kind to us. It's his bread now."

"But today he's working for me," Shu-dagan said. "And it is his bread now." He offered the bread before they could reply, and the boy snatched it in a flash. The parents laughed and thanked the boatman again.

"You have children of your own?" the woman asked.

Shu-dagan hesitated. "Yes, a girl." He couldn't say more.

"She's blessed to have a father like you."

Shu-dagan nodded and kept rowing. To escape the sorrow, he found a refuge in the boy, who was chomping on the bread when he noticed the boatman staring at him.

"Better finish that loaf or I will toss you in the water," Shu-dagan threatened jokingly. He reminisced about the time his father had done that to him when he was about this boy's age. The parents laughed heartily as the child began to chew faster, glancing with anguish at the other side of the river, only to stop eating altogether upon nearing the bank. He gave Shu-dagan a defiant look while holding out the unfinished loaf with a sly smile on his face that said, *I'm not afraid. You can toss me in the water anytime.*

Once at the shore, the boy sensed the need to flee for defying the boatman, but he wasn't fast enough; within moments he was wiggling to free himself from the boatman's grip.

"Calm down, little rascal." Shu-dagan grinned and handed him a little bundle of cloth. "Here are your work wages: five pebbles; one for each of your winters. But be careful, don't unwrap the cloth just yet, for these are special pebbles—if they see me leave, they'll roll back to me. So, keep them in your pocket till I'm far out in the river; pebbles don't know how to swim."

The confused boy scratched his head but gave a nod of understanding.

"I don't know how to repay you, sir," the father said in thanks to Shu-dagan.

"To see a child happy and smiling is payment enough."

"You're very generous, sir. You can't be from Uruk!"

"Every place has its good and bad people. I'm from Babylon."

"I will start praying to the gods of Babylon for sending you to us."

"Gods of Babylon, Uruk, *all the same filth.*" Shu-dagan faintly murmured the last words. "May the future bring you good fortunes, my friend."

The man thanked him again, and Shu-dagan turned to board the boat when a shout came his way like an order to halt.

"Boatman! Boatman! Wait."

Five men walked toward him, all nicely dressed and richly adorned with chains and bracelets of precious stones. Excessive drinking soaked their demeanor with levity and inane humor.

"Are you crossing to the other side?" asked the most sober one among them. He had a golden cylinder seal hanging from a gold necklace.

"I am."

"Well, how about taking us there?"

"I can't," Shu-dagan answered impassively. "I need to rush back to my wife. With the five of you, it's a harder, longer crossing. Take that boat on its way here."

"That boat! It looks like it's falling apart. I don't feel like taking a dip in the water—too cold," the man said, making his companions laugh. "And these bastards here are no swimmers. Swim in wine, they do, but in water—they sink faster than the prized stones on them. Take us to the other side and there will be a nice piece of silver for your pocket."

Take that silver piece and stick it up your noble arse, Shu-dagan was tempted to scream back. "I can't. Wait for the next boat."

"Boatman, where are you from?" another noble asked. His body undulated and head swayed in tiny circles with the tides from the drinks he had consumed working on him. "I recognize this unique northern accent."

"Babylon," Shu-dagan replied, and stepped back to leave.

"Oh, Babylon!" The man turned to his friends, laughing. "Must have come on a pilgrimage to the shrine of that young whore. What was her name—Maura, Mariam?"

"Mayram, you fool," answered a corpulent one who had a jungle of hair sprouting out of his back and chest to his lower neck. "How could you forget her? I still remember when they brought her dead body to the court; a beauty I could've still fucked, lifeless as she was."

Shu-dagan froze in his place, whereas the group deemed that hilarious.

"You're one sick bastard," another man said jokingly.

"Look who's talking," the hairy man countered. "Had they passed her around, I bet you would've been the first one to mount her dead body." Fits of laughter followed.

Shu-dagan's teeth clenched so hard, he thought he would crack his jaw. Then he snapped; not into a fury, but with the strength to assume the calm of a dead man.

"Noble men," he addressed the group. "You got me curious. Show me that silver piece and tell me more about this Babylonian beauty while I cross you to the other side."

"Move, you fools," their sober leader rushed them, "before he changes his mind."

The family that Shu-dagan had just carried across the river were still there, watching from the side. After the nobles had boarded, the father came to help Shu-dagan, and together they pushed the boat away from the riverbank. Shu-dagan thanked him and jumped on the boat, took the oar, and pushed against the mud. The poor man kept pushing from below until he was up to his knees in the water. The boat floated away, the oar finding only water to batter on.

"Boatman! You've never heard of this Babylonian Mayram girl?" the leader asked. "You need to swim less with the fish and spend more time with humans. That bitch has become a demigoddess with her own shrine on Ishtar Walk, the most elegant street in Uruk."

"It must have been a divine experience to fuck her," another interjected. "Rumor is she was made for the enjoyment of the gods in heaven. Then, a jealous Ishtar planned to kill her. So Nabu, who used to give this Mayram wisdom in return for her sending him to Pleasure Kingdom, helped her escape to Earth. But it was only a matter of time before Ishtar found her and had her killed."

"They say, she was the best," another drunk added. "She would suck the juices out of your rod, then drain the body dry of blood. Yes sir, she was one thirsty bitch."

They raged in laughter while Shu-dagan raged in rowing.

"And how about the gods making her immortal?" the hairy man cut in. "Immortal—my arse! Let me show you something immortal." He turned around and raised his robe. "Yes! My arse—this is immortal!"

His companions turned their heads away, laughing raucously.

"Sure!" another shouted. "With all that hair, your arse will achieve immortality. *Alas*, immortality only for that lush bush, not the flesh that birthed it."

"*Alas!* Alas my arse!"

They became hysterical, folding over their aching stomachs, when a loud voice came hollering off the bank.

"Babylonian! Babylonian! May the gods bless you and your loved ones. Bless you!" The poor man was waving frantically while his boy kept jumping up and down, trying in vain to retrieve the pebbles, the hard-earned wages his father thieved from him.

"I will remember you in my prayers for the rest of my life. May the gods forever bless you, Babylonian."

Shu-dagan nodded, waved back to him, and resumed rowing.

"Boatman, what was that all about?" The leader was curious.

"I gave them a few gold pieces."

The casual answer from Shu-dagan took everyone by surprise.

"*You, a boatman*, gave him gold! Then … you don't need our silver piece," taunted the leader. And laughter ensued.

"Yes, boatman. Please, do extend your generosity to us," the hairy one humorously implored. "For we are awfully poor."

"Sir boatman!" Another pushed out his right palm, turned up like a beggar. "May you spare a gold piece for this wretched one? I have five mouths to feed; my five slaves are starving."

"Noble boatman!" His partner followed with the same act. "I

desperately need a silvery piece … to fuck a girl by the temple."

All were aching with laughter; two were down on their knees. Shu-dagan forced a smile on his face.

"You should reward us with a free ride," the leader said. "It's the least you should do for the good time you had in our company."

"We're almost halfway across," came Shu-dagan's answer, cold and firm. "I will take the silver now."

"Don't worry, boatman, we're only fooling with you." The leader threw the piece to him.

Shu-dagan caught it in midair, then stared at the others with knitted brows. "Come on, out with it. I'm short of four pieces of silver."

Bemused looks were all that he received.

"He's joking," one remarked. "Good one—you almost fooled us."

"I am dead serious, and you can bet your noble arses on that." Shu-dagan started rowing down the river instead of across. "A silver piece each, or I'll take you to the great sea and all the way to the precipice at the far edges of Earth."

"Are you mad?" Contempt eclipsed the leader's beaming face. "I said one piece for all of us!"

"Each! One piece each!" Shu-dagan was adamant. "The price has changed; you have to pay for the insults."

The nobles looked at each other and grumbled in disbelief.

"Insults! What insults?"

"The insults you heaped on the girl from my home city."

"The girl was a whore! Too bad she comes from your hometown!" shouted the incensed leader. "We're not paying you a date seed more. You're so full of shit, the worms in your arse must be eating at your senses. You know who you're speaking to? I'm Manishtusu, first cousin of King Sargon himself. So, better shut your stinking mouth and start rowing across, or else I will have the guards send you and this pathetic boat of yours to the riverbed." He turned to his friends, sniggering. "Bastard! Complaining about insults to a whore! Huh, says he gave gold to that miserable, wretched family. Any one of you fools believe this story?"

"I certainly believe him. He's not a boatman," another joked, bowing, "but a god pretending to be one. … O Graceful God, forgive me. Spare me your wrath, I regret my wrong deeds. Hand me the oar and I'll do the rowing for penance."

With that, some levity was restored after the tense exchange.

"Low-life scum!" Manishtusu went on and grasped the golden seal on his necklace. "For filth like him, I bet this is the closest he's ever been to a piece of gold."

Calmly, Shu-dagan responded. "King Sargon, *your cousin*, gave me a pouch full of gold and silver."

A laughing riot stormed the men.

"I like this man," the hairy one declared amid the laughter. "This is the best river-crossing story ever—a sidesplitting one. Boatman, we appreciate your humor ... now, for your own good, stop fooling around and row us across."

Shu-dagan held the oar to his chest and reached into his pocket. He came up with a closed fist, and slowly opened it. The nobles stared in disbelief as the gold and silver reflected the sunbeams with an intensity that seemed to thrust the air back into their lungs, choking the chuckles in their throats.

Satisfied with the silence he forced onto his rowdy passengers, Shu-dagan put the shining pebbles back into his pocket and kept the boat floating down the Euphrates.

"Now ask me,"—Shu-dagan moved his stare around the group—"why would a great king reward a lowly boatman with all of this?"

Anxious gazes were the response.

"ASK ME!" he snapped, propelling their behinds to bounce up.

"Sir boatman," timidly, the hairy one spoke; his humor he left behind, drowned in the river. "The boat is drifting downstream. Better start rowing across. You know if you drift too far, you'll need a bull to pull the boat back upstream."

"Why would I need a bull when I have—one, two, three ... five donkeys to do the job?" It was Shu-dagan's turn to chuckle. "Why the serious faces—you don't find that funny? Well then, let me tell you a story that will surely make you laugh."

With no prior warning, Manishtusu sprang up, dagger in hand. But Shu-dagan was alert for any surprise move, and he smacked the man's wrist with the oar, sending the dagger plunging into the water. He followed with a jab, using the oar to clobber the man's chest. Manishtusu screamed in pain and fell, defeated. He remained still in a ruse that lasted short moments; then, abruptly, he leapt in an attempt to go overboard, but another smack fell hard on his head, causing the flat end of the oar to break off. Dazed but still determined to escape, Sargon's cousin made another try, but the sharp point of the broken oar stabbed ferociously at his thigh, and he collapsed between the feet of his companions, only his screams of agony managing to escape.

"He's truly mad!" Manishtusu shrieked. "A thief who wants to rob us. Attack him! It's the five of us against him and the oar."

"He's right, it's only me and the oar." Shu-dagan dropped the broken oar hard on the man's shoulder to refresh his agony. "Why don't you listen to this wise man? *Attack me.* That might present him a better chance to abandon you."

Shu-dagan reached down and pulled the other oar he had in the boat before throwing the broken one to the river.

"Sargon will hand your head to me, you son of dogs," cried Manishtusu.

"Not before I have my way with you, *cousin!*" Shu-dagan sneered and returned to the others. "How rude of your friend to attack me with a dagger before I could tell my story! Now, I know all of you carry fancy daggers, just to show off, without the slightest skill in using them. One by one, I want all daggers out and thrown in the river. Do it, or I'll make you suffer."

No one hesitated. The river happily added to its treasures some of the finest-made daggers, studded with precious stones that had traveled from the far reaches of Earth.

"Boatman, take this." A noble who had acted as a beggar earlier held his hand out again, this time offering, not asking. "This bracelet is made from the purest silver. Just don't hurt us. Drop us on dry land anywhere you want."

Others followed suit. They rummaged through their pockets for silver and held out bracelets and necklaces.

"Oh, you embarrass me; such generosity, such true nobility! Please put these away, I'm not a brigand. All I want is to entertain you with my story. It's only fair after you amused me with your hilarious wit. I won't make it long, for surely noblemen like you have important things to attend to."

Shu-dagan paused to collect his thoughts, wondering where to begin the story. He listened to the river, his life partner.

Gently, the river caressed the sides of the boat with waves that whispered to Shu-dagan how to tell the story:

There once was a boy who accompanied his father on a boat he owned, ferrying people across the river. One day when they were alone, with no advance warning, the father grabbed the boy and tossed him off the boat. The boy, in a state of panic, frantically splashed in the water while the father urged him to swim back to the boat. The boy almost drowned before his father pulled him out.

The father then told his son the story of how Enkido and King Gilgamesh fought ferociously when they first met, only to become lifetime friends. Likewise, he told his son that he and the river were destined to become the best of friends. Sure enough, the boy grew up and became a boatman, working alongside his friend. Many were the days he took on the river when it was angry, but he wrestled it like a friend and never doubted its loyalty.

It was on a trip over the river when the man met his love. They got married and had a beautiful girl whom he loved more than life. Happiness showered the family until one ugly day when devious Fate arrived, and it convinced the ferryman to overload the boat; the river couldn't carry the extra weight and dropped the boat with all its occupants. People drowned and the boatman lost his boat; yet, he remained loyal to the river and kept working with it as a hired hand. The river god took note of this faithful friendship, and he arranged with other gods to reward the man with another boat through help from his daughter, who gave without being asked to give. And so, our boatman went back to his young, happy self, with his own boat and renewed hope. The river welcomed back the jovial smile that had been lost for eons from its friend's face, and their bond became stronger than ever.

But there are certain gods who, for mysterious reasons, hate seeing men in a joyful state for too long. The newly blessed boatman was soon surprised with a heavy pouch, filled with silver and gold, sent from the king as compensation for the sacrifice his daughter had made for the good of the kingdom. The messengers told the boatman—in brief, hollow words—that his treasured daughter had been killed by some greedy nobles who had ambitions for power. And just like Gilgamesh losing the plant of eternal youth, the boatman had lost his young, blossoming flower to some slithering, low-life, venomous snakes—snakes that always dressed in new clothes with scales of glittering silver and gold.

But unlike Gilgamesh, the boatman had no kingdom to return to. He had lost the will to live and could only seek solace from his longtime friend—the river. He rowed and rowed, pouring his sorrows into the waters, when he noticed the river changing color.

"Dear friend," the man asked, "your waters are turning red. Is it your heart, bleeding for my suffering?"

"Yes, it is a heart that is bleeding," answered the river, "though, it is not my heart; rather, it is the tender heart that made the sacrifice to get you this boat. Oh, my unfortunate friend, with every wave the boat splits, the blood will run thicker; and every slice of your oar weaves my waters deeper in red."

"He's truly insane!" one drunk noble grumbled.
Shu-dagan continued, undisturbed by the comment.

The boatman made up his mind to retire the boat with its bleeding heart close to where his daughter rested. On the way, he cursed all the gods he could think of. He felt vulnerable after having abandoned his own gods, when a newer god came to visit his troubled mind. Nobody had ever seen this one or shaped him in stone. Rumor is he's more powerful than Anu, Marduk, and all their children put together. The boatman had never given this invisible god a serious thought, but decided to ask a favor of him to make sure he wasn't just another disappointment.

"Sick, mad, and a heretic," Manishtusu groaned.
Shu-dagan ignored him too, and went on.

Rowing for days and resting through the nights, the boatman finally reached his destination—Uruk. Out of nowhere, when he least expected it, and as if sent by a god, five nobles walked up to him.

Fear seeped into the faces of his passengers when Shu-dagan's voice came to a halt, only to spike madly.

Five noblemen, who desecrated his daughter's name and violated her memory.

The oar suddenly arched up and fell on the nobles like lightning bolts, again and again. The men cowered in their tight space, each trying to get under the other to shield themselves from the furious strikes.

They joked and laughed about his daughter—his innocent flower. Even in death, they defiled her with their putrid, stinking mouths!

The beating stopped just as suddenly. None of the nobles dared raise his head, lest it might be targeted by the oar. Shu-dagan resumed his story as though all that madness was but a brief pause.

At last, the boatman found a god worthy of worship. Never in his whole life had his prayers been answered so fully and so quickly. His plan at first was to burn the boat down the river once he arrived at Uruk. But when this invisible god granted the boatman the opportunity for vengeance, the least the man could do was to thank this god with an offering.

Shu-dagan reached over to a wooden box he used for a seat and removed its cover. He picked up one of the jars stashed there, tossed the cap away, and frantically went on splashing the contents over the men.

"It's oil," a terrified voice screamed.

In that crowded space, the nobles slipped and stumbled in chaotic attempts to avoid being soaked.

Shu-dagan hurled the empty jar into the river, then immediately went wild with his oar again, striking harder than before, brutally targeting the limbs, rendering the nobles powerless, sobbing in pain.

"May you burn in the fire pits of the netherworld, forever," Manishtusu cursed, "along with that fucking whore daughter of yours."

Shu-dagan didn't bother to answer; instead, he picked up one oil jar after another from the box, emptying them all inside the boat. Much of the contents splashed on the living, who trembled at the oily touch of death. The crying of the same nobles who had been joking and laughing a short while ago was an eerie sound to Shu-dagan; he had never seen a noble cry before.

Imbued with an intoxicating sense of power, a euphoric Shu-dagan raised his head to the heavens and hollered:

"Gods of Babylon, Sumer, and the rest of you who dwell in the sky, land, water, and the netherworld—to hell with you all, you devious, savage murderers! What I'm offering here is not for any of you but solely to my new god, to whom I prayed for vengeance, and vengeance he delivered on this very boat that my Mayram paid for with her blood. My new god will bring us together soon in his paradise. He's not selfish like the rest of you who keep eternity for your own. He'll wipe you all out before you know what hit you, just like I'm going to wipe out these greedy, powerful, noble bastards—the closest thing to resemble you on this Earth."

The sobbing grew louder. Three of the men hung on to one last string of hope, holding out jewelry in trembling hands to buy some mercy from the heretic.

"Patience, dear friends. Not to worry, we're nearing the end." Shu-dagan regained his calm composure for the finale.

The gods that the boatman had just cursed didn't respond; they cowered away despite the insults. The sky remained clear, no lightning bolt hit the renegade, and no giant waves drowned him. So, the boatman made one more prayer, this time to his new deity:

"O mighty, invisible God, I pray you accept this humble sacrifice from the poor man whom you helped to exact vengeance on the wicked."

"Well, noble ones, I hope you enjoyed my story so far. *Alas*, I must leave. But I'm sure you'll figure out how the story ends as the boat takes you to your final destination."

Shu-dagan pulled out a rag and soaked it in oil from the floor. He uncovered a perforated pot of glazed clay where he kept red-hot smoldering wood and teased it with the rag. A tiny flame climbed the oiled cloth, consuming it with a voracious appetite. Shu-dagan tossed it on the deck, where it swelled in size and gave birth to a small fire that crawled; it grew bigger, and it walked, then it doubled and tripled in size, running wild in every direction, all in the space of few moments. Cries filled the air from those who didn't want to join the fiery monster that was quickly enveloping the boat.

The horror surpassed the pain in those broken bodies, driving them into desperate attempts to evade the advancing blaze, only to be stopped by Shu-dagan, who unleashed his rage with a fury that reduced his compassion to ashes. His vicious oar fell on them mercilessly, to reawaken their pain and convince them that the fire would be a better choice than trying to jump into the cool river.

Only when the oar broke did Shu-dagan notice his robe had caught fire. Satisfied with this vengeful feat, he dropped the oar, bid farewell to his boat, and jumped into the welcoming embrace of his friend, the Euphrates. He floated in the waters, reluctant to abandon the boat in its final journey to its resting place.

The cries had already died, leaving behind the sound of wood cracking under the weight of the blaze, when a movement on the side of the boat caught his attention. A figure embraced by flames crept over the edge and dropped into the river.

The man floated, encircled by a robe adorned with pale flames refusing to die out. Shu-dagan swam to his side and splashed water to douse the burning fabric.

The man's dark, disfigured face had lost all its human features, save for one eye that opened slowly, and it was like the moon had abruptly taken its place in the black night.

Shu-dagan stared deeply into the eye that survived. Vengeance had clouded his own eyes to the horror and death he had inflicted; even the river waters couldn't extinguish the embers of hate raging inside him. His stare challenged the eye to say something, but strangely the eye stared back, leaving the task of answering to the lips, which barely moved to let out a faint whisper. Shu-dagan strained to hear those sacred words that came with the last breaths of life, but most of the words drowned in the angry waves that slapped the boat when the river became furious at the mayhem storming its surface.

To his dismay, Shu-dagan failed to grasp the given message, except for the words, "Savage demon." He could only watch the dying man's lips go silent, and the lone eye was soon eclipsed by its dark lid as the body started to sink slowly. Shu-dagan held on to the man's pricy necklace and snapped off the golden cylinder seal hanging at its end.

Shu-dagan started swimming to the bank, glancing back with sadness at the boat that had replaced him with a new owner: the blazing fire that steered the boat downstream with reins of flames.

𒀭 � 𒐀

Three men stood by the river's edge where a vast field of freshly made clay bricks stretched behind them. They watched the burning boat as it drifted south, then rushed to the survivor who emerged from the water.

"Friend, are you all right?" the oldest of the brickmakers asked. "We saw the smoke and the fire. We would've helped, but none of us knows how to swim. What happened?"

"Demons," Shu-dagan murmured. "They assailed our boat, killed my five partners, then set it up in flames. I tried to fight them, but—"

"It's a miracle you're still alive, my friend," the older man nodded. "Without the intervention of the gods, no one can survive those savage demons."

"True. The gods … savage demons." Shu-dagan sighed but didn't care to say more. He started to walk away along the river, heading north.

"Where are you going? Rest a little, my friend," the older man called back at him.

Shu-dagan didn't hear him and kept walking. Echoing in his head were the last ghostly words from the dying noble who didn't mind gifting him the golden seal.

Savage demon. The words intrigued him. *Was that man referring to me ... or the invisible god?*

𐎡 ◇ 𐎂 ᗯ 𐎕

Arbella raced to the lonely, soaked figure that came walking along the bank. She hugged him and planted kisses all over his face, then fiercely pushed him away.

"You heartless bastard!" She shook her head, crying. "To disappear and leave me here—stranded with not a hint of what happened to you? How much more suffering do I have to endure? I was thinking of drowning myself in the river. Cursed be the day I met you!"

Drown myself in the river. Appalled by his savagery, Shu-dagan pondered the idea. *How could I commit such barbarity? Was that a nightmare?*

Eerie tremors of laughter drew his attention to where it had all started—across the river. And there they were—five ugly ghosts, laughing. He watched them violating his Mayram, his flower, viciously ripping the petals of her innocence.

And right then it returned to invade his body—the feral entity that he thought he had left behind on the burning boat. It had caught up to him and didn't waste time eradicating all the guilt inflicted on his conscience. He didn't resist its presence—that sweet taste of power he experienced made him hungry to savor more of it.

And I will give you more of the same—much more, promised the savage demon of vengeance.

"What's wrong with you?" A distant, familiar voice disrupted his reverie. "Look at me!"

"Are you sick?" Arbella was shaking his arm. "You were whispering to yourself. ... Here, change your wet clothes." She carried fresh, dry garb.

"Those men you picked up on the other side ...?" she asked while he disrobed.

"Not men! They were beasts—monsters. I sent them back where they belong."

She didn't seek more details for she firmly believed that this world was full of monsters shaped like humans, sent by angry gods. But she could never fathom any good reason to justify their anger.

Shouldn't the gods always be happy for having the gift of eternal life? Why this fury at the helpless, suffering mortals?

The sun had already sunk behind the western wall of Uruk. Shu-dagan looked south to where a smoke column hazed the distant sky.

"Is that … from the boat?" Arbella came to his side.

He nodded, closing his eyes. Within his blind refuge, the river came calling. To its edge Shu-dagan walked, and he immersed his sight in the waters.

"Look at the water. It's clear now."

Arbella looked at him as if he had lost his mind. "This murky water—clear?"

He knelt down and with a hand, he gently dabbled the water. "It is murky … but not a trace of blood. Clear, like it should be."

His hand kept dancing with the water. Something eerie left him reluctant to leave; the ripples from the river felt like his lifetime friend was bidding him farewell.

Arbella knew what he was going through, how he cherished those times with his boat and the river. She didn't rush him until it started getting dark, and tenderly, she patted his shoulder.

They picked up their meager belongings and headed toward the city.

The river poignantly flowed, sending sad ripples on the banks. Clearly, it was mourning the parting of a very dear companion, a treasured friend. It would deeply miss him, despite that chaotic, mad afternoon when he, in a crazed state, had tried to set it on fire.

PREDATOR OR PREY?

ROARING IN SHEER ANGER, THE LION LIMPED AND SCREAMED away the pain. If only he could've talked, he would've cursed the gods for allowing those two-legged creatures to cheat the laws of nature by using methods other than pure bodily strength and agility to win in the game of survival.

The lion put forth another brave effort to leap, but his left hind leg, pierced by an arrow in the thigh, collapsed again under him. Only a roar of agony rose out of him. Yet he was intent on getting revenge and dragged that leg until he reached the wheel and started gnawing on it.

"Foolish lion. It won't have any teeth left if it keeps chewing on the wheel," said the slim charioteer, only to regret it when two hands grabbed him by the shoulders and hurled him out of the chariot to land in the dirt. Before he could figure out what had just happened, he saw the lion let go of the wheel and crawl toward him.

"How dare you call the noblest king of all beasts foolish?" Sargon barked from the chariot. "Would you call me a fool if my enemies overpowered me while I tried to fight back with tooth and nail?"

"Forgive me, Majesty," screamed the charioteer in horror as his legs were clawed by the lion that dragged its body to straddle him. "Mercy, O Great Sargon, have mercy!"

Two other chariots that accompanied the king on the lion hunting trip were already on the scene. Their occupants stood by, not daring to help their pleading friend who had angered the king.

A piercing roar shredded the desperate shrieks, and the lion's mouth opened wide, ready to clamp on the throat of the one calling it foolish. But the jaw never closed, and its head collapsed, lifeless, on the face of the terror-stricken prey.

After twisting the spear in the back of the lion's neck, Sargon gripped the reins and rode toward the other two chariots, leaving his own charioteer under the dead lion, gasping for air sapped by fear.

"Help that fool of yours, and bring me the lion's hide," Sargon said to his chief of guards. "I'm heading back, on my own."

"Have you gone mad?" Hukura retorted, just short of yelling. "The sun must have hit you hard in the senses! It's too risky. Many out there harbor ill intents toward you and won't waste an opportunity to bring you harm."

"I'm going back—unaccompanied! Is that clear?"

"Yes, Majesty!" Hukura responded, gritting his teeth.

"O Great King," the charioteer's voice rose again after he slid out from beneath the lion, his face and clothing all stained with the beast's blood. "I beg forgiveness for my utterly foolish words. I am forever grateful for your kindness, Your Majesty."

Sargon guided the horses back to the man he had ejected off the chariot. "You're lucky the lion was dying, and your meat would've been wasted. I hope you learned a lesson. Show respect to the brave ones who are brought down by misfortune. Next time, I won't be so merciful, and I will personally deliver you to healthy beasts to feast on you."

Sargon snapped the reins, and the chariot took off, leaving in his wake the charioteer, screaming a litany of apologies and praises to him.

𒀭 𒁲 𒐊

Two vultures floated with wings fully extended. Effortlessly, they soared on the back of the hot air birthed by the dust devils that demons had belched out of the netherworld.

All creatures kept a distance from the racing chariot as it traversed the vast plains bordering the desert. The noise was exacerbated by the chariot's lone occupant—a king suffering a heated spat of self-rebuke.

"Foolish me—showing mercy! I should've let the lion shred his body, guzzle his blood—chew on his bones!"

Sargon's rants to the sky seemed to agitate the vultures.

"Mercy, huh! Of mercy they're not worthy. Like scavengers, they hover above, praying for you to die."

He kept watching the vultures that seemed to follow him. Soon, two more joined in the heavenly dance.

"O mighty Anu, why do they hate me? Is it because I'm both king and your surrogate? I can feel their murderous envy; patiently they're waiting for the opportune moment to stab me in the back and shred me to pieces—my reward for bringing them peace and uniting the kingdom into the most feared power on Earth. What better time to inherit all of that—to be a king with not much to do, after I risked my own life, doing all the hard work.

"Look at Ur—since I ended the rebellion, it's flourishing beyond any other city in trade and riches. My *loving* son keeps writing me letters that all cities under his assigned zone are peaceful, and he wants to come back! Surely he must think I'm a fool. The bastard will be the first to drive a dagger deep into my back while embracing me."

Sargon let out a sudden shriek, sending the horses into full gallop.

"Something is going on—it's oddly too peaceful. Behind their sly smiles, I can sense the plot to overthrow me. O Great Anu, send me a signal to warn me. I'm your reflection, don't abandon me to those vile traitors."

Sargon's paranoid conversation with his god went on until the city walls loomed in the distance. He slowed down while traversing the farmlands that supplied the city with produce.

Men and women laboring in the field stopped their work to look at the splendor of the passing chariot. They wondered about the fortunate owner who humbly brought such a luxury within view of their wretched, undeserving eyes.

Sargon fumed; no one seemed to know him. He was the king only when surrounded by an escort of soldiers or when sitting on a throne with scepter in hand and crown on head. None of the lowly farmers bowed to him or showed any gesture of respect. He could only discern faces full of hate and envy. Theirs was a ride on the cart of poverty that led only to one destination: Rebellion.

The unknown king whipped the two horses and sped away, not slowing until he entered the city. Again, none of the commoners bowed while his chariot passed through. Those who recognized his features believed he was a double, for a king would never risk riding alone among the crowds. They only stole glances at him and whispered.

At the main gate of the palace, the guards had no doubts about the chariot and its rider, and they rushed to open the gate. Once Sargon reached the palace steps, General Gungunum came out running.

"Why are you alone? Where are Hukura and the others?" Gungunum asked, anxiously.

"They're fine, I left them behind. Anything to report to me?"

"A dreadful thing happened, Sargon. We believe your cousin, Manishtusu … is dead."

"Manishtusu—dead?" Sargon snapped. "How, when?"

"Two days ago, the same day you left on your hunting trip. The families of your cousin and four of his friends were alarmed when the men didn't return that night. And yesterday we were informed of a boat, totally consumed by fire, sitting on the riverbank with four severely burned bodies. We identified two of them by distinct body marks known to their families, the other two by their leather boots. They were the men who left with your cousin. He's the only one missing … most likely somewhere in the river."

"But Manishtusu is a good swimmer."

"They were murdered; some of them had broken bones, pointing to a violent death. Three brickmakers witnessed a man swim out of the water; he told them the boat was raided by demons, but we believe it was he who killed the men. The boat settled farther down the river with the four bodies on board. All their jewelry, including their cylinder seals, were missing. Two were stripped of their boots. But I doubt the killer intended to rob them."

"Why is that?"

"Items those men wore—rings, chains, bracelets—must have fused to the burned skin, and the marks on the bodies make it clearly evident that those pieces were peeled off the bodies *after* the flames went out. The three brickmakers said the boat was still burning when the survivor came out of the water, so he couldn't have stolen those items. I don't believe he killed them for their jewelry."

"Did you arrest anyone?"

"I was told there was a crowd of men, women, even children who raided the boat when it ran aground. What am I supposed to do—arrest the whole village?"

"Five nobles were slain then robbed!" Fury flashed out of Sargon's narrowed eyes. "Their bones savagely broken, bodies burned, and my cousin is somewhere at the bottom of the river. Many will have to pay the ultimate price! Gungunum, I want you to go back and execute a dozen of the villagers, starting with their ruler."

"But there is a good chance the villagers are innocent," Gungunum protested. "Some men on another boat could've gone on board earlier while the boat was still drifting downstream, and removed—"

"Innocent, guilty—I don't care. Execute! No mercy, execute! And have the bodies impaled outside the city wall. You hear?"

Gungunum knew better than to argue with a frenzied Sargon.

"What else did those witnesses say about the one who escaped the fire?"

"Only a brief description of him: strong, well built, had a scruffy beard, and spoke in a dialect with a northern sound to it, more like a Babylonian. The boat, too, has construction details typical of the north. He must be some crazed man, possessed by demons. Only a madman would journey on a boat all the way from the north, kill five nobles in a brutal way, then burn his own boat."

"That should make finding him easier, shouldn't it, Gungunum? You are looking for a strong, mad boatman with a northern dialect. The beard he can always shave. Also, fetch those fools—the three brickmakers, and have them walk the city streets with soldiers, sunrise to sunset; their punishment for letting a savage escape after he fooled them with his demon story. They should remember his face and frame. I want him alive to find out who sent him here. There is a plot behind this—I can feel it. Gungunum, I'm relying on you; hunt him down, *alive*. Don't disappoint me."

"I will do everything—"

Sargon walked away, not the least interested in the general's response. He had sensed something was wrong when he asked God for advice. God had answered with a warning: Manishtusu, his own cousin, had been brutally burned alive and wiped off the face of Earth.

Paranoia assaulted Sargon again with visions of the most ugly ends that were always promised for leaders who lose their battles, when an echo reached him from afar.

Kings, too, could be hunted down. Roared a lion in agony. *You, Sargon, know firsthand how fate could easily turn a predator into prey.*

The Savage Demon of Vengeance

"Three. I swear by the gods, I will get you three."

"Good, I'll take three. Is he a gentle man?"

"He is gentle, if you're not lying."

"I don't lie."

"You look trustworthy. Come, I'll show you what to do."

The guard led her to a treed area, a good distance from where a row of girls sat.

"When you step out of the temple, wait for my signal by those two tall trees. Don't sit with the other girls until you see me wave to you. Only then are you to take your place at the end of the row to be ready."

The girl nodded and headed to the temple's entrance. The guard walked over to a noble standing on his own, away from the crowd.

"Warassa. You made sure she's a virgin?" the noble asked.

"And a beauty, sir, made by the gods just for your unique taste. Only the best for you, sir."

"Warassa! You didn't answer my question. Is she *a virgin*?"

"Sir, with all due respect, I'm not a midwife." Warassa laughed. "But I made it clear that if she was lying, she would have to deal with me personally."

"Well, she'd better not be like the last one you delivered. Not only was she not a virgin, but she fought me like a feral beast after I confronted her."

"I apologize for what happened, sir. I try my best to make sure you get what you desire. Things go wrong once in a while. So far, I've only failed you that once. Still, the girl you're talking about looked innocent enough. I would say she was *almost* a virgin."

"What utter nonsense! There is no such thing as *almost a virgin*! Girls are either virgins or nonvirgins."

"Sir, I hate to disagree with you. Just like there are gods, demigods, and mortals, there are virgins, semi-virgins, and the fucked-beyond-doubt." Warassa chuckled. "Sir, I assure you by the hairy crack on Marduk's arse, this one is untouched."

"Am I supposed to believe you when you swear by the god of the Babylonians? Try swearing by Anu."

"Trust me, sir. If I'm wrong this time, go to another guard. I'll even stop working as a guard by the temple. Now, let's go wait for her, sir, she'll be out soon; a beautiful virgin desperate for a man like you to fulfill her vows. We don't want her to slip into the hands of another man, do we?"

Soon, the girl walked out of the temple and proceeded to the agreed-upon area. Warassa timed the encounter and waved to the girl. She sat down when the noble was within paces of her. Three pieces of silver landed in her lap, and with the vow recited, she picked up the silver and reached for the noble's hand. On their way to perform the holy task, the noble moved toward Warassa and slipped something into his hand for his service.

"May the gods bless you with pleasure throughout the night, sir."

Warassa walked over to his companion, who was having some rest, chewing on a loaf of bread.

"Stinking noble," Warassa grumbled. "What a pig! Girls younger than his granddaughter are not good enough. *Has to be a virgin! ...* Who cares if that thin veil is missing?"

"To you and me, it's all the same," said the other. "But to those lazy pigs, it makes all the difference."

"Izdobar, why is that? I actually find virgins messy."

"This ritual and *virgin* thing were all started by the nobles," Izdobar explained. "The gods had no part in any of that. It goes back to when the king or the high lord of some regions demanded to be the first—before the husband—to sleep with the wife on the wedding day."

"Like in the Epic of Gilgamesh."

"Exactly. But sleeping with all the newlywed girls was too demanding—bound to shorten the ruler's life. So, his minions offered to assist in this *arduous* task. Gradually this *duty* spread to other ranks of society. Soon enough, the temples became involved and they created rituals and offerings to go along with this practice, while gradually expanding its application beyond the wedding event. Well, as you might know, the rituals that reap the most profits are the ones that exploit the believers' fears of the gods—drivel like, *honor this god to keep the demons away; exalt that goddess to protect your child*; or the best of them all—*a pilgrimage to some holy shrine is a must, at least once in a lifetime*. The nonsense is endless—all based on the same principle: bribing the priests so they mediate on our behalf to appease the gods, who for some mysterious reason are always *fucking angry*!

"So, here you have it, this once-in-a-lifetime ritual for women to sleep with a stranger to make the love goddess happy—better said, to make the priesthood wealthier. Luckily, *you and I* are blessed to be assisting in this *holy* mission."

"I've been here for a few moons," Warassa said, "but I never gave this 'virgin, no-virgin' thing much thought. What are the actual rules for this ritual?"

"There are many differing opinions. Some say virginity is not required, while others argue that the goddess is better served by a pure girl with virginity intact. Like with all the outlandish rules invented by the priests, there is no exact practice when it comes to applying them. I heard a story of a high priest from Phoenicia who became very sick after eating some pig meat when the moon was half-full. So, he came up with the rule that forbids eating pig's meat for five days around the half-moon period. For those who were not going to be denied their delectable pig, something miraculous happened—the moon started *skipping* its half-phase. Others ate the heart, liver, and other parts of the pig they did not consider to be meat, while the ardently devoted totally abstained from eating pigs.

"Yes, those priests have some brilliant ideas. No, no, forgive me; it's not that their ideas are great—it's the believers, those imbeciles who follow them blindly. Imagine, they are blessing livestock now, and hordes of fools would not eat the meat unless the animal was blessed by a priest. Soon they'll be blessing all sorts of food, including beer and wine." Izdobar waved the bread in his hand and took a bite of it. "One day, this bread would have to be blessed before you can eat it. … Hmm, I can't wait to taste a blessed piece of bread."

"You're out of your mind. That will never happen." Warassa let out a short chuckle. "Now, back to this ritual to honor the goddess; some of these girls are practically picking the man of their choice, and we're assisting to arrange for that."

Izdobar shrugged. "Still, there is the slight chance things don't go according to the plan, and the girl could end up with another man. I've seen it happen. Besides, if the goddess doesn't like what is taking place here, then I'm sure she would've intervened and demonstrated her anger. Did you ever feel her wrath, or hear of a girl you assisted who was punished for this *breach* of the rules?"

"No, not yet," Warassa answered hesitantly.

"One thing for sure, my friend," Izdobar went on. "Same with any other celebration, this ritual makes a lot of people happy, other than the lustful nobles: the girls get their silver, the guards get their wages and a generous something from the nobles, and the temple gets the offerings. Not to mention the traders who benefit from all those people; like the shameless, heretic baker who dared sell me this—this *blessless* bread." Izdobar laughed.

"Very true. But what puzzles me is this obsession among the nobles to have virgins."

"Ah, for them it's a triumph," Izdobar said as the last piece of bread disappeared into his mouth. "It's the blood quest; the rapture after the rupture."

"Blood quest, rapture!"

"Sure, Warassa! I'll explain. Soldiers like us have experienced the blood shedding in the battlefield. You must have felt the thrill of plunging your sword into an enemy then pulling it out with his blood staining the blade. True?"

"Izdobar, it's not exactly a thrill; more of a relief at surviving a deadly encounter."

"Same thing, Warassa. Now, for a noble who had never seen battle, who had only heard stories of blood drawn by heroic soldiers, this is his way to emulate that act—in bed. The virgin is the enemy, and his rod is the sword that will sink into her and draw the blood out, giving him the thrill of a triumphant soldier."

"Are you serious?" Warassa shook his head. "Just when I thought that finally some wise words were coming out of your mouth, you have to smear it with this biggest load of donkey dung I've ever heard. How absurd, to compare a sword with a man's rod, and a virgin's blood with that of a fallen foe?" He laughed. "I'm going to the tavern, and you should get me a beer for wasting my time, telling me this nonsense. Huh, warrior nobles stabbing virgins with their rods. *Rapture after the rupture!*"

ㅅ ◇ ㅍ ᴡ ⦀

"I will not be made a fool again."

The noble whined to the girl on the way to his home. "If I don't see virgin blood, then I will draw blood out of you from somewhere else. I'm serious, you had better be a virgin for your own sake. And I don't want to hear that load of dung the whores use, 'virgin by proxy, surrogate to a dead virgin.' Tell me that drivel, and I swear by the eternally wet vagina of Ishtar, I will—"

Before he could finish his rant, a blur of a ghost sprang out of the void and a fist landed on his face, knocking him down. He sat up dazed, but before he could lift his head to see what had hit him, a silver piece landed in his lap. Without thinking, he grabbed it, then looked up.

A strong-built man with a sad-looking face towered over him and started reciting:

> Goddess of wars, Mother of all whores,
> Cursed be your ritual. Bloody is my vow,
> The virgin flesh of this noble bastard, with this mine hand, I'll plow.

The noble stiffened with fear and looked at the girl as if expecting her to defend him. But the girl was stepping back in a slow retreat after she saw the dark intentions of the attacker reflected in the shiny blade he drew out of his robe. Panic robbed the noble of the strength to rise to his feet. He could only shift and slide back on his behind.

"I beg you, don't hurt me," he cried. "Take the girl … she's a virgin, she's all yours. By the gods I swear not to tell the guards. I have some silver. Here … take the silver and the virgin."

The girl felt her shaking legs gaining some firmness and took off running, glancing back at the vows she was leaving behind. The man who was to fulfill her vows was now a doomed subject bound to fulfill the murderous vows of an insane villain.

"There goes your virgin," came the answer to the pleading noble. "Shouldn't you follow her?"

The noble managed to stand up and turned on quivering legs. But before taking a step, an arm embraced him from behind, followed by a dagger, plunging in and out of his chest repeatedly.

"Vow fulfilled, my noble man. You're no longer a virgin."

The noble staggered in short strides, holding his chest in a futile attempt to stop the gushing blood, then collapsed to the ground. Out of his hand rolled a bloodstained piece of silver.

Shu-dagan wiped the blade clean on the noble's clothes and walked away at a fast pace through the streets of Uruk. He had studied those streets for several days and knew the alleys that best suited his lethal design. It wasn't long before he saw the next virgin. His hand went into his pocket for another piece of silver.

It's going to be a long evening. Plenty of vows to fulfill.

ᛚ ◊ ꒐ ∨∨ Ⅲ

"I vow … you are my witnesses. By Ishtar … I will cast the virgin out of you," the man slurred to the girl sitting outside the temple.

Like a boat on gentle waves, his body swayed by a breeze that went drunk upon passing a mouth reeking of beer. Next to him, two guards and a few nobles were holding their stomachs, laughing.

"Wrong! That's not the vow. Try again," a noble blurted to the drunk.

"For the love of Ishtar … with my help, virgin you'll no longer be." Once again, words scrambled out of Sakran while he held on to the shoulder of a guard for balance.

"Don't say it to me, say it to her." The chuckling guard oriented him to the sitting girl, who couldn't help but laugh.

Warassa came back from the tavern to join the spectacle, which attracted more onlookers.

"Like I said … Ishtar blessed me … to do away with your virgin … shroud. Now I bow … there, you have my vow." Sakran held his hand out for the girl, who struggled to contain the chuckles and wondered if her vows allowed her to laugh while she waited.

"You're hopeless," a noble mocked Sakran. "Be careful now! Recite the vow wrong again, and Ishtar will strike your rod with lightning. Besides, aren't you missing one major thing? I don't see the silver piece."

"Oh silly me—to forget that!" Sakran's hand went all over his gown looking for his pocket. Finally, he pulled a piece out and was about to throw it into the girl's lap.

"Wait, not so fast! Show me what you have." Warassa held the man's hand up to examine the piece. "Fool, do you expect to deceive anyone with this worthless, silver-plated scrap of some dull metal? Surely you are hopeless; no silver piece, you can't recite the vow. What else is missing? Do you have a rod—a working one, I should add? Make sure it's still there."

Overtly alarmed about the state of his manhood, Sakran's focus plummeted to his midsection, and the circle around him plunged into laughing fits, including the sitting girl, who could no longer control herself.

Amid the merry sound of laughter, the air shivered with a faint echo of fear. It kept rising until it dominated all the noise in the temple arena when a girl came racing with her shrieks, horror clinging to her face. She seemed to be heralding an imminent calamity, one greater than the Deluge. No one moved, as if in resignation to an inescapable doom.

The girl's piercing gaze traversed the shapes looming before her. Many had to rush out of the way as she sped through like a ghost undeterred by obstacles. Upon recognizing her, Warassa chased and grabbed her by the arm.

"He killed him!" she howled. "Stabbed him to death!"

"Calm down," Warassa said, holding her trembling arm. "Who stabbed whom?"

"The villain stabbed the man I left with!" she yelled frantically.

"I said calm down!" Warassa yelled back. He was upset, not out of affection for the noble but because the man was a frequent client. "Are you saying … the noble is dead?"

"Unless he's immortal!" She broke into sobs. "A madman plunged a knife in his chest, again and again … slaughtered him after reciting a vow—a vow just as mad as him."

"How do I know it wasn't you who killed him?" An angry Warassa shook her violently.

"What do you mean … why would I do that?" Her distress became terror; killing a noble meant certain execution.

"Maybe you aren't a virgin as you claimed—the noble got angry, he beat you up … and you stabbed him. It's not the first time a noble was killed by a girl for—" Warassa cut the details short. "Show me your hands."

The girl's first reaction was to back away, thinking it was a mistake to come to the guards, but it was too late by then. She displayed her open palms, turning them up and down.

"Look, no blood anywhere on me or my clothes. You believe me now?"

"I believe you." A voice came to her defense, and a hand gripped her shoulder. She turned and the taste of beer hit her nose.

"Oh, you are a beauty." Sakran waved his "silver" piece to her. "You come with me. I'll replace that noble … help with your vows."

"Stinking drunk fool!" a vexed Warassa shouted, pushing Sakran away. "Get out of here! Go to the other side of the road with this piece of dung before I shove it up your arse. We've had enough of your foolishness."

"We! Who are *we*?" Sakran protested. "Are you a virgin too?" It was Sakran's turn to laugh.

"You find that amusing?" Warassa rushed Sakran, but his partner Izdobar stopped him.

"Warassa, don't take this fool seriously. It's the drink talking through him." Izdobar grabbed Sakran and dragged him away.

"You are no better than this fool—all of you," the girl cried. "A noble is lying dead out there, and instead of chasing the criminal, you're standing here, arguing—accusing me of murder. By the gods, what evil has descended upon the land?"

"Well, there isn't much we can do for that dead noble now," Warassa retorted. "And the slayer is not going to hang around—wait for us to catch him."

The air around the temple became tense with fear masked by alert faces. Words were spoken with a hushed tone to elude the spying ears of the lurking evil, which soon announced itself again when shrill screams erupted from another road ending in the temple square.

Two girls emerged, racing next to each other. The guards didn't waste time and rushed to them.

"Mercy of the gods! He's a savage!" one girl wailed.

"He cut them down like sheep," the other cried. "A demon—he butchered them!"

"What happened?" Warassa felt like a fool for suspecting the first girl.

"We went with two nobles—two brothers. This brute leapt out of nowhere and beat them both to the ground. Then, just like in the holy ritual, he threw silver for both, recited some grim vow of his own, then stabbed them. We froze and could only watch in horror. When he was done slaying them, he walked away without touching us."

"We ran away," her companion continued. "I turned to see if he was following, when another noble with a girl showed up, and the savage rushed in their direction. We didn't stop to watch what happened, but I'm sure that one met the same fate as the two brothers."

"What does he look like?" Warassa asked, feeling uneasy. Had Ishtar finally decided to punish those who were making a mockery of the sacred ritual? Had she sent a demon?

"He didn't seem anything like the savage he is," one of the girls replied. "Quite the opposite; he's handsome looking."

"He's clean-shaven," added the other, "had a sad face, as though you should feel sorry for him. Stabbing the nobles seemed to bring him relief."

"He's taller than most men—strong. Probably has a job that involves heavy lifting."

"Or strong like a boatman." A voice of authority entered the mix.

"General Zambiya!" Warassa greeted the man.

"Ex-general. I retired recently. This villain must be the boat assassin they're looking for. I'm a friend of General Gungunum and the king. They told me about the one who burned the nobles on the boat. It must be him."

"Yes, sir, it must be him. He's only after the nobles," Warassa concurred.

The blood-soaked details splattered the crowded square, and faces turned ashen with dread. None of the nobles would dare pick a girl and walk the streets back home. Reigned by fear, the men dashed away from the girls to cluster around the guards.

"Useless, inept cowards!" An enraged voice tore out from the nobles' circle. "Guards standing idly while a murderer is out there hunting down nobles like trophies!"

The angry voice was the catalyst for a litany of curses from other terrified nobles, spewing forth their ire.

"If you don't move your lazy behinds and find this savage, Sargon is going to hear from us and have you transferred from this 'guards to the virgins' duty to the front lines of the next bloody battle."

"Everyone, calm down!" Zambiya shouted. "Threatening the guards and arguing won't help the situation. Here's the plan: we will send for more soldiers to help. In the meantime, all the guards will spread around the streets in pairs. Also, those men who are young, strong, and want to volunteer can be sent in groups of three or four; that should be enough, for it seems the madman has only a knife on him. I advise the other nobles to wait with me till the assassin is caught, or till we get soldiers to escort you home."

The wise words from the ex-general were met with approval by the anxious nobles. He took charge of organizing the guards and volunteers into search parties that were sent in different directions. The three girls were brought along against their will to help identify the one who dared slaughter the elites of society.

The modest new temple of Ishtar was a safe distance from the anguish infesting the arena by her grand temple. A handful of people knelt in silent prayer before an altar richly adorned with stone reliefs, portraying teams of girls standing with heads bowed to the goddess, who towered twice as tall with a seemingly frustrated look as if saying: *Why do I see only girls here? Are we out of men?*

A statue of Ishtar was erected behind the altar with inscribed incantations among a whole roster of attributes, glorifying her beauty and powers.

On the opposite end of the altar was a humble shrine with a large stone relief on the wall, showing Ishtar with a hand raised in a gesture of blessing a girl bowing in obeisance while drops trickled off her chest, depicting the girl's selfless devotion to her goddess which had led to her martyrdom.

Right below the relief, a rectangular area was enclosed within a low fence. It encompassed the original floor from the chilling murder scene, still marred with streaks of darkened blood stains that were left untouched. A reed mat and a bed cover, also stained in dark blotches, were laid there too. Next to the fenced area was a section of similar dimensions with glazed red bricks bordering a stone slab of alabaster. Engraved lines of inscription told a brief story about the buried martyr.

Arbella sat on the floor, next to the grave, caressing her daughter's soul with a hand that floated over the engraved characters which must have venerated her girl. Arbella didn't care to know what those symbols told; even the good sentiments from strangers could make a stranger of a loved one. She was not going to allow some cuts on a stone to change her memories of Mayram in any way. But she knew some of those cuts had the name Mayram, so she traced every single one with her finger.

Earlier that afternoon, Arbella and Shu-dagan had arrived at the temple. There were a few people making offerings for the goddess at the opposite end. Now and then, out of curiosity, someone would cross the room to take a brief look at the humble shrine to the girl who had been proclaimed "Guardian of the Virgins" by the goddess. Her coffin had been moved from the cemetery after that section of Allamu's residence was rebuilt into a temple to accommodate worshippers in that affluent neighborhood along Ishtar Walk.

Prior to starting his vengeful quest, Shu-dagan had visited Mayram's grave with his wife. Unlike Arbella, whose grief never tired from flooding her eyes, Shu-dagan remained quiet; the fires of his rage had dried out the tears.

Noticing their deep sorrow, a priestess couldn't help but ask if they knew the girl, but she was met with silence. Like two ghosts waiting for a third spirit, they totally ignored her fleshly presence.

"I knew her—an angel sent by the gods." The priestess consoled the couple despite not receiving any response. "She used to pray regularly at another temple I used to serve at. How sad that she had to leave us so soon to rejoin the gods."

She paused, still hoping for a response, when she became alarmed upon noticing the dagger's handle on the man's belt. It resembled the hideous bone grip she had once detected on the Babylonian girl during one of her visits.

Babylonian! The nobles' assassin they're looking for ... strong built, with a Babylonian tone of voice. That explains the silence of this couple—so their tongue won't get them exposed. Fool, it all fits. Beyond any doubt, the man is the girl's father, seeking vengeance, and the woman—her mother.

The priestess walked away and deliberated over alerting the guards about this "boat assassin." Within scant moments, she dismissed the thought.

She came from a poor family and wasn't fond of the nobles; rape was her earliest experience with a noble. She liked the Babylonian girl so much that she was not willing to bring any harm to her grieving parents. Besides, if those two were found out to be the parents, then Sargon might order the girl's shrine, and possibly the whole temple, ripped to pieces in revenge for his cousin. It would be foolish to imperil this new temple in this lush section of the city and risk being sent back to the gloomy one she had left.

Let him slay all of Uruk's nobles. The bastards more than deserve it. ... Did I see anything suspicious? No ... absolutely not. She put her mind to rest and walked out the temple to get something to eat.

Shortly after the priestess had left them alone, Shu-dagan took Arbella in his arms.

"I'm leaving," he whispered. "Be ready when I come back, or … if I don't come back."

She started sobbing.

"Weep no more." He wiped her tears. "Our mourning time is over; it's the nobles' turn to cry."

The night before, they had made passionate love. It wasn't like anything Arbella had ever experienced, but she had a disturbing intuition of what it was: the last passion to precede a farewell—and she was right. When the morning arrived, he'd revealed his vengeful intentions. Arbella didn't grieve, instead, she wanted to join him. Shu-dagan utterly rejected that idea, saying she would hamper his movements. She fiercely protested but to no avail.

"I will come back for you. … I … I promise."

His frail, hesitant assurance betrayed him. She slapped him on the face and walked away, losing the argument.

⟑ ◇ ⊐ ⋁ Ⅲ

"Where are you going with my virgin?"

While balancing himself on the steps of the temple, Sakran screamed at the departing guards. "Bring her back to me, thieves! May bulls ram their horns up your butts, … stinking bastards! May a horde of flies crash inside your throats and choke you—murderers! I hope cockroaches lay their young inside your ears and … and may lightning … strike down a palm tree to crush the ceiling over your arses while you shaft your wives."

"All this cursing and evil wishing! What did they do to you?"

The words caught Sakran by surprise. He turned to the stranger who seemed to sympathize with him.

"You look like an honest man, my friend." Sakran sat down on the stairs. "You see this in my hand? Tell those fools it's genuine silver, not some … fake, polished piece of metal."

"I'm not in the know about what you're holding," The man smiled and tossed something in Sakran's lap. "but I can assure you, *that* is pure silver."

Sakran picked up the piece and studied it thoroughly, confusion wrinkling his face. "Sir, you misunderstood. I'm not a beggar."

"I know. You're a friend; you just said so yourself. It's a gift, keep it."

"Thank you." Sakran nodded. "You must be wealthy—I can tell. All this red wine you have spilled." He pointed to stains on the lower section of the man's garment. "I've never seen such dark red wine. Must be the special Kebboba vintage I've heard of but never tasted."

"Indeed, you guessed it right. That's the absolute best … red wine."

"You are a lucky man, my friend," Sakran said, happy that someone valued his company. "You have wealth to throw around, good wine to spill, and I see you have the good looks and strength. But best of all, I feel the goodness in your heart." He paused, staring at the man.

"But there is sadness in those eyes … you're heartbroken. Must be some beauty who left you without saying farewell. I have seen this sorrow—this loneliness in another man's eyes. His love abandoned him too. In truth, I meet that man every time I look in a mirror." Sakran laughed. "Yes, my friend, you're looking at him, here, slouching on the stairs. I too was in love once and … lost her. I could only recover when I found a new love—beer and wine."

Shu-dagan smiled. "It's one way to recover from love."

"Keep that smile, my friend, it looks good on you. Life is too short; a smile will stretch it longer. Interesting, though, how you speak like there were other ways to recover from love."

"Mine are deep love wounds. Only the blood of the affluent can heal them." Shu-dagan sighed. "Does that make any sense to you?"

Sakran grinned and shook his head subtly.

"Do forgive my drivel. Well, it was pleasant talking to you." Shu-dagan started to walk away.

"Wait, wait! Before you go … could you tell me how to say the vow for Ishtar—the one to recite for the girls?"

Pensively, Shu-dagan replied. "I don't know that one. I know the one to recite for men. But if I tell it to you, I'll have to kill you."

"Yes, of course … the vow to recite for men," Sakran concurred, despite lacking the slightest idea of what the stranger meant. "My friend, are you sure about giving me the silver? At least let me get you a beer."

"I'm in a good mood." Shu-dagan shrugged. "I feel like having one intense, wild celebration. Like you said, life is too short, so I'll go spill some more of that rich, red wine."

"Where are you from? You can't be from Uruk."

"Babylon. I'm here on a short visit. I bid you farewell, my friend; there is much to do in this greatest of all cities." Briskly, Shu-dagan walked away before the man dragged him into more talk.

"Babylon! Of course, I should've figured that." Sakran examined the frog-shaped silver piece and rolled it in his hand. "This is fine silver."

He followed the stranger with his gaze. *A weird one! Throwing away fine silver. Dressed neatly, yet behaving nothing like an arrogant noble. Must be afflicted with insanity … to talk to me—a drunk screaming curses from the stairs of a temple!*

Sakran leaned back, resting his shoulders on the step behind, and started laughing. "Spilling vintage wine! A vow to recite for men. … Affluent blood to heal his wounds! What a load of nonsense? A mad Babylonian he is … hopelessly mad."

⟁ ◇ ⛩ ⩊ Ⅲ

Have you gone mad? Come back to your senses!

In the silence of the temple, her mother's voice echoed from the past through her head.

Arbella, what do you see in him? Handsome! You are beautiful and deserve better than a boatman. I know his type—marry him, and the day will come when you find yourself abandoned, on your own. Only then will you remember my words, but by then it will be too late.

He won't leave me. He is coming back, Arbella answered her mother's haunting advice, and patiently waited.

Shu, you promised. I will never forgive you if you leave me on my own.

She would remain next to her daughter until the temple shut its doors to the visitors.

I don't need you, Shu. I don't need anyone. The river will always be there, to welcome and take me in … to take me to my child.

Her hands started trembling. She pressed her palms on the grave's stone to steady them as whispers escaped her.

"Oh, my sweet flower, reach out to him, tell him to come back. He will listen to you. Tell him not to abandon me … like you did."

Her tears rushed down, soothing a few cuneiform wounds on the stone slab.

𒀭 𒁹 𒌋 𒉿 𒁹𒁹𒁹

The nobles tightened their circles at Ishtar Square in a hierarchy, with the least influential on the outside and the highest in rank standing the nearest to General Zambiya in the center. Many clutched whatever weapons they had or could get their hands on, whether a dagger, a thick tree branch, or a loose brick. Yet nothing could've proven to be a more reliable weapon against the mad butcher than their numbers. They put on brave faces and dressed their chats with a touch of humor to conceal their fears. Now and then, their bodies made lazy turns to survey the surrounds for a monster with a sad face, daggers in hand, charging like a crazed boar.

A red glow soaked the near setting sun while its body was being sliced by the remote western city wall. On a normal evening, the red hues of dusk were heartily welcomed; they offered a pulse of passion for lovers and a warm companion for the lonely souls. But today, they splattered the square with the menacing colors of carnage.

Zambiya, who always carried his sword as a symbol of rank and bravery, brandished it in a display of the art of swordsmanship. Ostensibly, he did this to calm anxieties and raise morale. The nobles watched as he repeatedly sliced the space surrounding him in a duel with an ominous enemy—the crimson sunrays that permeated the air. The sword cut through their red lucidity, but they eluded defeat and instantly regrouped for a fresh attack. Nevertheless, the rays grew weaker after every slice, with the wounded sun sinking lower and lower.

Zambiya attacked and retreated, swung and blocked, until finally the sun's body collapsed behind the city wall under the weight of its injuries, and Zambiya lunged forward with the sword in a decisive thrust, leaving no doubt the enemy was mortally wounded.

The nobles breathed a sigh of relief, for their protector was the victor in that duel of good against evil. Comments of admiration filled the air; all fears of vulnerability were erased. No man or beast, mad or sane, would dare approach a large crowd guided by an intrepid, fearsome general.

Flattering questions started to pour from the nobles about his war exploits.

"General, I heard you triumphed in all the battles you led."

"General, how many times did you confront death face-to-face?"

"General, what was the bloodiest conflict you were involved in?"

Zambiya answered the questions loudly for all to hear. A formidable face expressed the pride in his achievements.

"Noble general, how many were the unfortunate men doomed by your sword?"

"Too many," he replied with a wide grin. "I stopped counting after their numbers exceeded the count of my fingers and toes."

The nobles laughed joyously, and morale soared. The general had wit on top of bravery.

"Were they worthy opponents?" A voice rose above all the lively noise. "Or meek peasants, armed with wooden sticks? Or perhaps men so fatigued and starved, they could hardly carry a weapon!"

Silence reigned over the nobles, who tried to place those last words among the heaps of glorification that had dominated the exchange so far. But there was no way to interpret the phrase as praise; it bore nothing but ridicule and disdain. They watched the general, expecting a ruthless response that would bring the insolent inquirer to beg forgiveness.

Zambiya was stunned by this brazen attack, clearly aimed at degrading his tales of valor and smearing his reputation. Furiously, he blasted:

"All the men I slayed were formidable soldiers—well armed, vigorous, battle-ready! Who is this coward to speak such filth? Come to the front and show your face if you're a man."

The reply came right away when a section of the clustering crowd split open like a gaping mouth. The nobles pushed and shoved to clear the way for the man wielding a bloody dagger.

The inner circle, where the general had defeated the sunrays earlier, doubled in size once Shu-dagan stepped in it.

"I am the coward!" Shu-dagan declared. "And I learned how to be a coward when I was a soldier. Thanks to my commanding general—a general who would never step into the battlefield unless victory was secured—until the only enemies to kill were the injured and the ones who were too fatigued to carry their own weight. A general who was the first to flee, straight from his tent, when the battle plans went slightly wrong. Yes, I am a coward, for I was distraught with fear; not fear of the enemy, but fear of my obsessive thoughts of butchering that general and the likes of him—the real cowards, so-called *heroes*—for bringing death and misery to others. *Heroes*, for they show no fear of needlessly sacrificing legions of soldiers for their own glory ... so they and their *rotten* noble friends can indulge in the joys of life: wealth, power—deflowering virgins. All while their soldiers die!"

Silence reigned supreme over the circle for mere moments before it was disturbed by a sudden shuffle of feet. Shu-dagan made a fast turn, only to see a brick flying toward his face. He dodged, and it swiped his left ear. One noble at the front was heaving with excitement, which instantly turned into paralyzing panic when Shu-dagan, with not a moment wasted, reached to his side and brandished a hidden sword.

The noble's severe distress confessed to throwing the brick. Judgment and punishment came swiftly with the sword carving deep into his neck.

Death inhaled the air, and the inside circle swelled in size. Within were an ex-general, an ex-soldier, and an executed noble bleeding on the ground.

"You dog, son of dogs!" Zambiya shouted. "Killing defenseless men! Who's the coward, huh?"

"I already told you, I'm the murdering coward. Now shouldn't you do something about it, *brave general*?"

Zambiya went into a state of confusion. Unlike him, the man he was facing had no fear, and the ease with which he had cut the noble proved his prowess with the sword. But worst of all, this fiend didn't have a reputation to defend, nor did he seem to worry about something called honor, in stark contrast to the general, after all that bragging about his battle exploits.

To keep his hands from shaking, Zambiya kept a tight grip on his sword as he prayed to the gods that the nobles would attack. With their numbers and their knives and bricks, they should have no problem finishing the madman. But there was one major impediment: the ones to dare initiate the assault would most likely end up next to the one lying still on the ground.

"I guess I was right about your *bravery in battle*," Shu-dagan screamed in contempt. "If you don't have the courage to punish this *coward*, then give the sword to one of these *brave* nobles to do it."

Those words created a wave that pushed the nobles backward, and the circle stretched a few paces out. Clearly, none of the nobles was interested in the invitation.

It was the gods' answer to Zambiya's prayers. This was his fight; killing this commoner was the only way to restore his pride after being viciously slandered. Zambiya was aware that Sargon wanted this assassin alive, but it was the least of his concerns; this was a matter of kill or be killed. A thought flashed through his head that maybe, in their grace, the gods had planned all along for him to finish this notorious criminal, and a surge of courage tackled his fears.

Hollering a cry of war, Zambiya charged forward. He swung his sword in a diagonal cut that Shu-dagan blocked, pushing him back. Zambiya followed with more swings of his sword. His anxiety eased when the villain kept on the defensive, not offering any skills of attack of his own.

Shu-dagan restricted his movements closer to the center of the circle to direct more of his attention to the fight and away from the nobles who might find it more opportune to stone or stab him in the back while he countered the general's attacks. He was aware time was not on his side either; at any moment, soldiers would show up and that would be his doom. To make matters worse, his sword skills were not as good as they used to be when he was a soldier. All those factors told him this duel would not end in his favor, unless he employed skills from his street-fighting days. He had had more of those than his balding opponent had hairs on his head.

Zambiya was growing confident and envisioned victory, feeling his odds improving with every strike. The fiend kept on blocking, showing no offensive maneuvers whatsoever.

The general attacked feverishly and, just like Shu-dagan, he was concerned that soldiers might arrive. But in his case, he worried that they would rob him of the full credit for this kill. The criminal's blood was his to shed; the glory should be his alone.

Zambiya moved back, readying himself for the next assault when he saw Shu-dagan lean down and rest the tip of his sword on the ground; apparently, the duel had taken its toll on him.

While the villain hunched in a vulnerable pose, the general moved slowly toward him, then briskly lunged into full charge, employing every muscle in his legs. Zambiya could foresee the opponent's blood showering his face after a swift, mortal slice he would deliver before the villain could recover from those moments of weakness.

Shu-dagan was ready with his own gamble that employed the boatman's best skill—to swiftly row from one side of the boat to the other. Just as Zambiya was about to strike, Shu-dagan twisted and shifted his stance to one side in a flash. Zambiya's sword fell on empty air, and as his speed carried him forward, Shu-dagan was twisting back, his elbow slamming hard into the general's shoulder blade. Zambiya went into a dive and instinctively let go of his sword to protect his face, which still hit the ground hard while his right arm landed on the dropped sword.

The general raised his dirt-powdered, bruised face off the ground, a long thread of thick saliva stretching off his mouth.

The ghastly humiliation fueled an instant rage, yanking Zambiya up to his feet with sword back in hand, and he hurled himself in a charge that had no coordination or swordsmanship—only a mad scream and erratic swings of the sword, which sent blood spraying from his injured right arm onto the faces of his supporters. Once he neared the foe, his body was so teasingly exposed that Shu-dagan could not resist the temptation to strike with a diagonal slice, stretching from below the chest to the right ear.

The ex-general slowed to a halt and stared in shock, drool blending with his gushing blood. His legs buckled, and down to his knees he went, facing his stunned admirers as if asking forgiveness for lying about his heroic feats.

Zambiya's exploits ended with him collapsing on his face in a pool of blood.

𐤉 ◇ 𐎛 ᭪ 𐎟

Idling on the stairs of the temple, Sakran watched the human circle that formed in the middle of Ishtar Square. He saw its rings grow in size and diversity, starting with the nobles, then adding all sorts of curious onlookers.

At one point, Sakran could discern a section of the circle splitting, and as the gap moved inward, the circle healed, closing behind whatever sliced through it. Soon after, the hollow core stretched out twice before it started to subtly expand and retreat in a haphazard way, accompanied by the sounds of clashing metal. It took a while for the noise to stop, and the circle settled back for fleeting moments, when all of the sudden it exploded outward. Sakran looked in disbelief; people scattered as if a savage animal had been let loose in the center of the square.

The sight of the scampering nobles made his sides hurt from laughing. In his whole life he had never seen a noble run—and there they were, all running like a herd of gazelles.

"I must be losing my mind!" he muttered to himself. First, it was that madman giving him the silver, and now he was witnessing a mad run of the nobles.

Doubting his senses, he gazed intently. Only sheer madness could have explained the vivid scene that he would remember, drunk or sober, for the rest of his life. He saw four bodies lying still on the ground, and the man who had given him the silver cutting another before giving chase after the fleeing herd.

"Run for dear life, my poor nobles—RUN!" Sakran shouted. "May the gods help you. He's a mad butcher from Babylon, and it's your affluent blood he seeks to heal his wounds!"

Through her statue, standing at a porch outside the temple, the goddess of love and war coldly watched her love-inviting sacred grounds transform into a scene of a bloody massacre—a one-sided battle waged by one vicious invader who had chosen her arena to be his war zone.

All the life forms with legs—humans and livestock—knew one thing for sure: if a sizable flock is observed running away with fear shrouding the faces, then everyone nearby had better join the run. The pressing question of 'Why run?' could wait.

After Zambiya's body tumbled to the ground, Shu-dagan knew better than to offer the nobles any luxury of time to gang up on him. Their fear was his only ally, and he had to instill more of it in their hearts. Instantly, he leapt, slicing up the closest noble to him. The reaction was immediate; by the time he cut down two more of them, their circles had fully evaporated. On their tails he chased, hacking at those he could identify as nobles by the distinct way they dressed and the jewelry they flaunted. Moreover, the wealthiest, who occupied the inner circles, were the nearest and slowest to escape.

"Soldiers—the mercy of the gods—I see soldiers," someone shouted upon sighting uniformed, armed men at the end of a narrow street.

The words echoed to the fleeing hordes, and a large number of runners became aware of the road to salvation and converged on it. The first and fastest ones passed the soldiers, shouting something about a crazed butcher with a sword. The soldiers darted forward and soon realized their mistake as they ran head-on into bands of people that were getting denser and denser, only to become a solid wall, slowly trickling men. All the way behind, they could see a sword-wielding figure, dashing at the jam ahead. There was nothing the soldiers could do but helplessly watch the mad sword going up and down in a slaughter that nothing could escape save the screams of horror and the agony of death, piercing the air above.

Shu-dagan stepped back, his sword dripping virgin, noble blood. The corner of his eye caught sight of a noble hugging the wall in a desperate attempt to slip away undetected. Shu-dagan pounced on him and shoved him against the wall. He recognized the man by his distinct headdress, adorned with lapis lazuli beads; it was the one who'd asked General Zambiya about the count of men he'd killed.

"Answer an easy question and I'll let you go," Shu-dagan offered. "How many are the unfortunate ones, filth of your type, I have deflowered?"

With death staring him in the eyes, coupled with an absurd question, the only answer to come from the terrified noble was the quivering of his lips.

Disillusioned with the response, the inquisitor shook his head and volunteered the right answer:

"More than the count of my fingers and toes."

Ruthlessly, the blade lodged death deep within the noble's chest.

Shu-dagan turned back to the throng in search of the next quarry. Though he had never made it clear he was only after the wealthy nobles, some realized that, and they cautiously retreated around him before dashing away. One young man even dared to move over the dead nobles, ripping off their necklaces, bracelets, or anything of value, all in plain view of an indifferent Shu-dagan. Soon, the buffer of humans started thinning and the soldiers were passing through easily.

Seeing no more nobles within his reach, and satisfied with the results fulfilled by his savage quest, Shu-dagan retreated with two soldiers on his tail. He ran effortlessly, overwhelmed with a sense of calm, leaving behind that raging demon he had carried all those moons. He was but a free soul riding on a chariot of flesh and bones through the most elegant road in Uruk—the one where Ishtar strolls after she tires of her lovers. Today it was cleared just for him; even the goddess herself would not dare promenade down that road—down Ishtar Walk.

ᚲ ◊ ᛞ ᴡ ꘡꘡꘡

The stir from outside raided the new temple and made Arbella shiver. Shouting carried a tone of fear, which she could identify but not feel. What was there to fear? Fear of harm? Fear for life? … Losing Mayram had erased all her fears.

Shu must be out there. Hurry, my beloved, time to end the madness.

The doors burst wide open, and he stormed into the temple with the shouting getting louder behind him. Her eyes flooded with joy and excitement. She didn't see a man who was worn out, all disheveled with blood splattered on his clothes; instead, she saw a handsome lover who had kept his word to come back for her, to sweep her off her feet and carry her on the next journey.

He walked to her, looking tired, yet calm. She didn't ask about what he had done or who was chasing him, and she wasn't mad that he kept her waiting; time was too precious to waste on anger.

"Beloved, I prayed for your return … I'm ready."

He squeezed her tight, making her feel like a girl in the strong arms of her young lover. Those brief moments felt like a long, sweet dream, but sweet dreams are always destined for an abrupt end.

Heavy steps came pounding outside the entrance.

"It's time to be with her," Shu-dagan whispered, forcing his hand to draw the dagger. Arbella nodded and wiped her tears.

The dagger pressed against her chest and the tip tore through her robe, nicked her skin, then mercilessly stopped. Shu-dagan's hand was shaking in revolt; how could he stab his love and life partner like he did the nobles, with a dagger stained with their blood?

"Forgive me, I … I can't."

Arbella watched the tears well in his eyes as the trembling handle of the dagger slipped into her hand.

Shu-dagan kissed her, then turned around to face those who dared step inside his daughter's shrine and disturb her sleep. But he had no fight left in him, no demon, nor any resentment toward the two soldiers confronting him. He was a soldier once, and he knew the hardships they went through, with no choice but to follow orders. Nonetheless, he would not allow them to take him prisoner. He charged, swinging his sword.

Warassa studied the villain they faced. He looked human in every way; a man drained of energy. *Couldn't be a demon sent by Ishtar.* Still, Warassa had doubts; demons were a treacherous lot. Yet, demon or no demon, Sargon wanted him alive.

Warassa and his partner, Izdobar, halted briefly to evaluate the villain, who, after kissing a woman companion, initiated the attack with a feeble charge and labored swings, which they blocked easily. The assassin followed with another assault, which wasn't any more menacing, but this time Warassa delivered a light slash to the man's arm.

He bleeds! Can't be a demon. In no way was he sent by Ishtar.

Freed from worries about being the subject of the goddess's wrath, Warassa felt more at ease. Along with Izdobar, the two skillfully kept the duel going, careful not to mortally slash the butcher. But this was a madman determined to fight to the death, with nothing to lose except for an awaiting torture. Bringing him alive wouldn't be an easy task.

Shu-dagan was drained of strength and knew his two opponents were not going for the kill. Expecting more soldiers to close in on the temple, he had to end it right there—right where his daughter had fallen. Briskly he charged, swinging the sword as if ready to deliver a side cut to his foe, who prepared with a counter block. Shu-dagan's sword went for the strike, but it was only in a feigned short swing that didn't follow all the way across, all while he kept rushing in the travel path of the soldier's blade.

Paces away from his daughter's shrine, Shu-dagan fell to his knees, a deep gash across his chest screaming blood. The last light to touch his eyes blurred with the sight of his tearful wife clutching the dagger. The last sound to visit his ears was Arbella's scream of rage at his betrayal in leaving her behind. Gradually, the light and sound faded, and Shu-dagan was swept deep into a silent, serene void.

A stunned Warassa stood motionless over the fatally wounded assassin, after coming so close to capturing him alive. He prayed for a miracle to keep death away, while his partner, Izdobar, was on his knees, desperately trying to stop the outpouring of the villain's life.

Now Warassa would have to explain to his commander why a man drained of strength and facing two skilled guards had ended up being slaughtered by his sword. He was doomed to a severe punishment. For him, death would be the most lenient sentence, far better than being demoted and dragged back to one of those endless sieges or campaigns against barbarian tribes in desolate lands. But there remained a slim trace of hope: the assassin's companion. Whatever they needed to know from the villain, they could extract from his woman partner.

Before Warassa could exhale a sigh of relief, a cry of war erupted behind him. Quickly, he spun around, only to see his face contort with pain in the pupils of the woman's eyes as something sharp tore at his stomach. Her eyes also told him the gods had answered his wish to die, before she pulled the blade out.

Warassa gazed at her dagger in disbelief, checking if the red stain on it was his, as if his blood had a distinct color. Yet, brutal agony wouldn't allow him the time to fool himself. There was only one last thing he could do: deny rapture to the woman who had him ruptured.

"Warassa, don't!" yelled Izdobar.

But it was too late. The woman was already on her way down, her blood gushing out, mingling with her partner's blood, and reaching for the dark traces of their daughter's blood next to the shrine.

$$\text{𝘌 ◇ 𝗜 Ꮃ 𝗜𝗜𝗜}$$

Shu-dagan woke up and found himself standing by the river, swathed in fog, alone, but not for long. His friend, the river, sent him gentle rippling waves to welcome him with a surprise.

Out of the fog came a boat—the same boat his father had left him, the one that had toppled over and been lost. He hopped into the boat, which moved on its own, not needing him to row; inexplicably, the river flowed across to the other side instead of drifting south.

Shu-dagan sat in the boat, where nothing could be seen through the dense fog, when suddenly he felt a soft hand touch his own; gently he squeezed it. He didn't need to look to know that Arbella had just joined him on the journey.

Beams of light cut through the fog, clearing the view straight across. A ghost appeared on the other side of the river. Gradually the ghost took the shape of a girl—it was her. She was jumping with joy, waving and yelling for them to hurry up.

Swamped by happiness, Arbella could hardly wait to get to the other side. First thing she would do was hold her girl tight and shower her with kisses. She would follow that with a rebuke on a divine scale. But no, she knew she didn't have the heart to be very harsh with her Mayram. A mild scolding for not listening would do; just enough so her daughter would be more careful not to lose her best friend again. Only then would she hand the dagger back to Mayram.

LOVE LETTERS

THE MASTER SCRIBE ENTERED THE ROOM, FOLLOWED BY TWO slaves, each carrying a deep silver tray stacked to the rim with clay envelopes of varying sizes. They placed the trays on a table next to a lush armchair where the king leaned to one side, a leg folded over the seat while he sipped beer with a golden straw.

The scribe waved for the slaves to leave.

"The letters, Majesty." He handed Sargon a uniquely sealed clay envelope. "This one is from Prince Naram-sin, noted as urgent, for your immediate attention."

"Sure, it's urgent!" Sargon moaned. "Everything from my *beloved* son is urgent. The only thing that's not urgent for him is getting out of bed, especially with a woman in it."

Sargon studied the envelope fleetingly, then slammed it on the table, cracking the crust of clay containing the tablet. He split the pieces apart, took the clay tablet out, and commenced reading aloud.

"Huh. It says: 'From your loving son' … on and on with the usual warm, adoring dung … 'Father, all the tribes are abiding by the laws you dictated; there is not the slightest sign of revolt. I am just wasting my time in this no-man's-land. How am I supposed to learn the principles of ruling big cities and maintaining order in the kingdom when you have me exiled to this backward part of Earth? I beseech you, Father, to assign me to a major city, or at least a town where I can advance my experience in governing and my skills are better employed in serving your kingdom.'"

Sargon flung the tablet into the air, and on the floor it shattered.

"Chariot racing and whoring," Sargon snickered. "Those would be the skills he would exercise in the big city. ... He dares talk about serving me better. Sure, he'll serve my head on a platter after he stabs me in the back at the first opportunity. I know his type—so much in love with himself, there is no love left for others, not even family—the kind of heir who would rush his chariot at full speed over my body to inherit the kingdom."

Sargon turned to his scribe. "Write back to my son with orders to march farther north and camp by the outskirts east of the city of Nineveh. Some Assyrian tribes there have raided the trade convoys. That should keep him busy."

"I'll have the tablet ready for you to seal first thing in the morning."

The king picked another dry mud envelope. "From the *gluttonous* governor of Isin." In frustration, he put the envelope on the table and smashed it with his fist. The tablet inside broke in half.

"I bet you he wants more funds. By the rotten breath of Pazzuzu, I'm all fed up with their requests—*'Give me this. It's a matter of utmost importance. This can't wait.'* Even a god would fail to satisfy their demands. All of them think they have big problems that only I can solve. Meanwhile, I have an assassin out there and not the faintest idea who he is, who sent him, or what vicious plot they are brewing. I need to forget I'm the king. Where is Gaga? Bring me that useless whore of a jester!"

"Can't get any rest in this dung hole!" a voice hollered from outside. The door opened and Gaga walked in, face flaring with anger.

"Jester do this, jester do that! Working me like a slave. *Yes, Your Majesty!* What is it you desire, *Your Highness*?"

Sargon waved for the master scribe to leave and waited until the door closed behind him.

Gaga had become very blunt and daring since the day he knelt under Naplanam's sword, as if Sargon owed him a heavy debt for that terror. And Sargon found the new Gaga more entertaining, especially after having solidified his rule over the kingdom. Confident that his men feared him no matter what jokes the jester made at his expense, Sargon gave Gaga the reins to run almost free with his charades. But today, Sargon was somehow reticent in having others present when the master jester delivered his mocking wrath.

"How did you know I called for you?" Sargon frowned at Gaga. "Are you spying on me?"

"Of course, what else is there to do here? Did you just find out I'm a spy? How foolish! Any more questions?"

Sargon laughed. "Do you know the penalty for spying?"

"Another silly question! The most dreaded penalty of them all: life imprisonment and hard labor with your concubines, who would savagely milk me to death."

"Sure, keep on dreaming. You don't seem to be happy working here."

"No. I'm considering moving to Ur, to work for that ugly, scrambled-face governor, Humbaba."

"Not only a spy, but a traitor too. You forgot who brought you to the palace! If it weren't for me, you would still be a lowly scribe in the army—mud under your nails instead of this colorful manicure you're wearing."

"One thing I'll never forget: you almost had me lose my head."

"Oh, that! You know just as well as I do that Naplanam liked you. Also, the odd way your neck is attached to your hunched back would've made it a challenge to lop this head of yours with one strike. There was no way Naplanam could've hurt you, so get over it."

"And you know just as well that Naplanam, may Ereshkigal go easy on his soul in the netherworld, was just as unpredictable as you are. *Also*, Naplanam wasn't the type who would shy away from a challenge. The fear alone, kneeling under his sword, almost killed me. Humbaba would never do that to me, he was my friend in the army. And, unlike the *miserable you*, things are going well for him in Ur. People adore him; his shitty face attracts the crowd like flies. He and his bitch wife look like the happiest couple in the kingdom."

"I know ... how strange!" Sargon mused. "They came to brief me about the city's affairs, and Kebboba was smiling all the time. She even looked younger. It's as if his ugly face had some magic that brings the youth back to the one who sees more of it. Maybe I should bring him back to work for me here!"

"It's not his face, but his tongue," Gaga remarked. "That tongue delivers sweet ... alluring words. And when it comes to women, it works another kind of magic, one without words that sends the fountain of youth pouring freely inside them. Kebboba is the one brave woman who ventured past that horrible face of his to find the source of that fountain."

Sargon laughed. "Then he's of no use to me; not the fountain to my liking. Now, if you want to work for him, then by all means, go. Yet I must warn you—that face you see is the *pretty* side of him. May the gods help you when he laughs, for I've heard of men who were seized by convulsions at seeing him chuckle."

"You don't have to tell me." Gaga smiled. "I went through that experience once. I had to fight the urge to throw up the meal I had just consumed."

"Does that mean you will not leave me?"

"Well, not until I find a better jester job. You talked me out of working for Humbaba."

"Good, so do your job and read these dry dung letters for me."

"Read letters!" Gaga put on a lopsided face. "That's not in our job agreement. Only songs, poetry, and humor. Go learn how to read instead of ordering people to do it for you."

Sargon was laughing like mad. No one could change his mood like this man with a curved back. Gaga made him feel alive; if it weren't for him, he would've died of majestic misery. The hump on Gaga's back seemed like a storage container of endless humor and amusing tales.

"Then read the letters like you're telling a humorous event." Sargon slid the cracked tablet from the governor of Isin over the table toward Gaga.

"So where is this going to stop?" Gaga protested. "Next thing, you will ask me to recite a poem as I shave your hairy arse and while you shoot bursts of majestic gas in my delicate, poetic mouth."

"Shut up and read the tablet!"

"Shut up and read! I don't know this trick."

"*Read*, or I'll send you north to work with my son. You will love the tents, and I'm sure you will find the sunsets *very poetic*."

"Calm down, I don't need that. I'm too poetic as it is." Gaga grabbed the two pieces of the cracked tablet. He took his time, pretending to have difficulty putting them together. But he knew when to stop fooling around; he had become a master at guessing when the king's patience would run out.

"From the governor of Isin," Gaga recited. "To the Great Sargon, ruler of all that is between the tip of his wide flaring nose to the stinking ends of his toes. King over all the fleas that dwell within his hair to the worms that happily reside deep inside his fat rear."

Sargon sat laughing, not in the least bit offended by the jester.

"Majesty, I would like to inform you that the arduous project to construct the new temple of our god Anu is finished on schedule. It took a lot of sacrifices, expressly on my part; as governor, I had to sleep with every priestess to be assigned to that temple, which is an extremely strenuous task, for they are the hardest to satisfy.

"Now, a great undertaking like this one is bound to have some setbacks. The sculptor made a grievous mistake; he chiseled Anu's penis on the grand statue outside the temple to a similar proportion to ours, the mortal men. This resulted in a massive outcry, mainly from priests and farmers, for this was an insult to the god and would've brought disaster to the fertility of the land. Hence, we assembled an urgent meeting to resolve this problem, to grow Anu's penis both in length and girth. As you know, the expense to replace the colossal statue, not to mention the work, is immense. A decision was made, and the penis was enlarged by slipping a hollow rod of stone over it.

"Everyone seemed happy with the work … till the next day. A priestess went out early in the morning and came back wailing in horror after finding Anu's penis shattered to pieces on the temple's ground. The added extension must have been too heavy for the little penis to support, so the whole thing cracked and collapsed from the main body. Panic prevailed in anticipation of the calamity that would ensue if Anu noticed his mighty statue had no penis.

"We fully covered the statue and decided to make generous offerings of the sort the city of Isin had never witnessed, only to distract the mighty god till we found a solution to this quandary. There was no way to attach a penis to the main body. Then, the high priest came up with the brilliant idea of adding another statue—one of two girls kneeling by a penis of solid gold standing above them. We placed that statue next to the one of Anu's body in such a way that no one would notice it was a separate piece. Now, everyone is happy, including Anu; people swear the statue's face had grown a subtle smile.

"The only one left in misery is your humble governor. I am so depressed, my penis has stopped standing up. All the offerings that went on, days and nights at length, till the work was over, left Isin depleted of funds. Not to mention the golden penis; I had to melt down my own gold to help make it.

"Great King Sargon, I beseech you by the colossal, shimmering, gold penis of Anu to replenish the funds I exhausted on this great monument that will go down in history as another testament to your legacy."

Gaga placed the tablet back on the table. "Such a greedy whore, this governor of Isin. Wants more funds and gold that will end up on him. Gold rings, necklaces, wristbands—I bet you he'll make a golden hood to envelop his penis, too. It's amazing how this bastard, product of an unknown father, can still walk despite the mounds of gold and precious stones decorating him. If I were the king, I would goldplate his head and place it on a golden spike."

Sargon appeared to be appalled by the story. His worries had caught up to him.

"Sometimes I don't see the humor in your stories. No—not sometimes; rather, oftentimes you go too far mocking our great gods. Do you expect me to laugh at this outrageous drivel—the great Anu missing his penis!?"

"Who's mocking?" Gaga countered. "I'm exalting him with an enormous, hard, golden one, and two girls kneeling—"

"Enough!" Sargon slammed the table. "This has to stop. It must be your heresy that is inviting all the troublemakers who would soon bring doom to my kingdom and me!"

"Forgive me." Gaga feigned prudence. "For a moment, I thought I was in the presence of Sargon. Foolish of me to mistake the *high priest* for the king."

Sargon irritably reached and grabbed the two halves of the tablet. After reading the contents silently, he stared at Gaga.

"All this prick of a story, you created from a few lines; an invitation from the governor of Isin—for his daughter's wedding!"

"Everything I told you is in there, but sadly you don't see it," Gaga said with total conviction.

"How so?" Sargon frowned.

"When you attend the wedding, he'll give you a magnificent reception, second only to that of a mighty god; the best food, wine, music, dancing, charming girls. Soon after, he'll have you listen to the details I just mentioned."

"So, not only are you a jester but *a seer* of the future too."

"Absolutely!" Gaga bragged. "And best of all, I don't need putrid animal entrails to do it. Unlike those fools, your clairvoyants, who can't tell a mouth from an arse."

"And I am a seer too," Sargon declared. "I can tell what some men would've been if they were born girls. And you, Gaga, without the slightest doubt, would've been a whore. Not a temple priestess whore, but simply a plain, wretched street whore."

"And you, Your Majesty," Gaga said despite an effort to halt his tongue, "if you were born a girl, you would've become a queen—a queen whore for all the wretched, drifting street dwellers."

The daring words left Sargon speechless for long moments before he spoke with a tone dipped low yet full of rage.

"Sometimes you make me wish that Naplanam had sliced your head off and not the priest's. You don't show any due respect to anyone—mocking all: kings and gods, including our god Anu— Creator of the whole universe. Not even our divine beliefs are spared your ridicule. I'm sure the Epic of Creation is nothing more than a fairy tale to you."

"May the gods forgive you!" Gaga protested. "I'm an ardent believer in all the divine ones, the Epic of Creation, *and* the Epic Before Creation."

"Epic *Before Creation*! What nonsense are you uttering?"

"Nonsense it is not! Think of the eternal enigma of how our mighty god Anu came to be. ... Fatherless, no mother—not from beasts, demons, nor any matter! This epic clarifies this greatest of mysteries, though it is very brief—a few over a dozen words."

"It has to be an epic of *your* creation. Still, let me hear it, this brief *Epic Before Creation*."

Gaga inhaled deeply; he raised his arms, closed his eyes, and solemnly recited the sacred words:

"Then, out of nothing, absolutely nothing, he was birthed—God—the One, True, Absolute Bastard."

Gaga opened his eyes to meet a deep stare from Sargon, flashing with murder, while a hand slowly reached for his dagger and stayed there, debating whether God demanded the jester's blood for this unspeakable, sacrilegious statement.

A loud knock on the door brought a much-needed sigh of relief to Gaga, who had realized how imprudent it was of him to share those profane words with the king.

Gungunum came rushing in, escorted by a soldier.

"You're lucky." Sargon released his grip on the dagger. "These two arrived right on time to save your meaty, witty tongue from being served to me for dinner."

He turned to his general. "What bad news do you bring me now? Ereshkigal has let the dead go loose in our city?"

"On the contrary, Sargon, I bring good news. We got the bastard."

Before Gungunum could elaborate, Gaga interjected.

"You got the bastard! Which bastard? Legions of them are roaming out there."

Gungunum let out a tired sigh. He wasn't in the mood for joking with the jester.

"Don't pay attention to him," Sargon said irritably.

"He wouldn't pay attention to *you* if his head wouldn't end up on the chopping block," Gaga snapped back, again surprising himself. He started to wonder if his own tongue was conspiring to get him killed.

"Get out of here, whore!" Sargon's patience had reached its limits.

"I didn't finish reading my letters," Gaga answered back.

Sargon pulled his dagger and moved toward Gaga, who made a dash for the exit.

"Don't bother me for the rest of the day," Gaga shouted on the way out. "I'm too busy spying on the king."

"One day, I swear—" Sargon sliced at the air with his dagger after the door closed behind the jester. He turned back to Gungunum. "Did you get him alive?"

"Well, it all happened so fast. ... He was like a mad dog."

"You mean you killed him!" Sargon said, nostrils flaring.

"He killed dozens of people—all nobles. General Zambiya among them."

"Zambiya ... he killed Zambiya!"

"Sadly, yes. The guards who tackled him later tried to capture him alive, but that savage fought like a beast—to the death, then tricked a guard into killing him."

"I want that guard executed, right away!" Sargon hollered.

"He's already dead. There was a woman with the madman. She stabbed the guard in retaliation."

"Well then, did you interrogate the woman—about her partner? Who sent him? Why was he killing nobles?"

The questions sent Gungunum frowning at a side wall.

"Well?" Sargon had had enough of a wait for answers, though he knew his general's hesitation was preparing him for no answers.

"Sargon, there was nothing anyone could do. The same guard she stabbed cut her down too before he collapsed. A dying soldier would never waste a chance to stab back at the one who had given him the mortal wound. That should be of no surprise to you."

Sargon pounded on the table so hard with both fists that one leg splintered and another broke off. The whole table tilted sharply, causing the two trays with the clay letters to slide off, sending their contents crashing to the floor.

"*Surprise!* You talk of surprise!" Sargon fumed. "All this anarchy is happening outside the palace and I'm the last to know! Then, you come to tell me you got the bastard but have no idea who he was!"

"Well, like I said, all that mayhem happened so fast. First, he started stabbing nobles in remote alleys, off the main Ishtar temple. As soon as we learned about that, we didn't waste any time; soldiers were rushed out to help the guards find the madman, but he was tricky like a fox and moved where we least expected him to go—Ishtar Square. There, he killed Zambiya and created panic, which resulted in a stampede at one narrow street off the square. He was out to kill as many nobles as he could and was determined to die after that. The woman waited for him in another temple. Surely they had planned on dying together; no one could've stopped them. ... A drunk man said he had spoken to the savage before he went on the killing spree. According to the drunkard, the madman was a Babylonian."

"Are you certain he's the same man who burned my cousin, Manishtusu, on the boat?"

"Beyond any doubt, it is him. Your cousin's assassin is no longer among the living. The three brickmakers who saw him come out of the river are on their way to look at the body. He's clean-shaven, but that shouldn't confuse them."

"Then why are you here before finding all the facts?" Sargon snapped. "So far you don't know who he was—if he was acting alone or if others backed him—others who are scheming something bigger? The only information you bring comes from a drunk man. Maybe I should assign drunk men to do the investigation. Why do I have Babylonians here in Uruk killing our nobles? If that savage was the one who killed my cousin, where did he stay all these past days and nights?"

"Probably rented a room in a tavern. He had the means to afford it. He was throwing silver to the men before killing them. ... Sargon, stop worrying, calm down. I'm confident it was only one mad man and his mad woman, no one else is involved. Plotters with a plan never act in such a reckless way that would alarm the adversary. This beast must have been possessed by one of those ferocious Babylonian demons."

"This beast killed my cousin Manishtusu! Those foolish guards should've been able to take at least the woman alive."

"It was bad fortune for your cousin to be on that cursed boat," Gungunum reasoned. "Sargon, what's the matter? How long have we known each other? If at any time there were the slightest suspicion of a plot, I would be the first one to warn you. I assure you it was just those two. You know those Babylonians, no one can understand them. By the gods, they can't understand each other; they just babble nonsense. I heard rumors of them planning to build a tall ziggurat in Babylon—so tall, it would touch the heavens. Do they think the gods would be happy with mortals walking among them in heaven? There is good reason to believe the killer was mad, even by Babylonian standards; they must have chased him out of Babylon. The drunk man who talked to him at the square said the killer knew only a vow to recite for men before killing them. How insane—a vow to recite for *men*!"

"The drunk one—again!" Sargon scoffed.

"Though drunk, he is believable. The girls who accompanied the first murdered nobles gave a similar account of a vow uttered by the savage after he tossed a silver piece to his victims. ... Sargon, stop worrying. You're well-guarded, the madness is over."

"Sure, but soon another madness will follow. Huh, a mad Babylonian! I should raid Babylon just to piss on their god Marduk after all the trouble they've brought me."

"Not a good idea." Gungunum shook his head. "Let the kingdom settle for some peace. Insulting their father god would only bring rebellion."

"What if Marduk is scheming to replace Anu as the supreme father god?" Sargon argued. "Making of Anu nothing more than a shadow god. Then, what would become of me—I, the reflection of Anu? I would become the reflection of a shadow. ... Does a shadow have a reflection?"

"Sargon, you're torturing yourself with baseless fears." Gungunum sighed. "There is no plot against you, or the kingdom, or our gods. Go have some good wine, spend the night with your favorite concubine. Enjoy life, everything out there is just fine."

Gungunum turned to his escort. "Let's go, we have work to do." They walked away, leaving the king on his own.

Sargon paced the floor, mulling over all that had been reported by his most trusted man, when he noticed the trays that had fallen off the table. He stared at the strewn dry clay envelopes; some were slightly cracked, others split with the tablets inside exposed. The scene resembled something that his memory strived to recall, but to no avail. He refocused, examining the arrangement of the clutter, which might portray an omen from God, or some advice to put his mind at ease. Still, the chaotic scatter of fragmented dry clay didn't make any sense until his eyes fell on a piece he recognized very well: the tablet with the brief wedding invitation to Isin—the one that roused his anger after Gaga used it to conceive a tale where Anu's penis suffered an unfortunate incident. While trying to expel the blasphemous thought, he caught sight of a clay envelope with its top broken off and the tip of a cylindrical tablet sticking out of it.

That looks like …

Hard he struggled not to laugh, but his efforts only exacerbated the urge until it became uncontainable.

Forgive me, O Great Anu, he invoked as the outburst forced him down to his knees.

A priestess found Anu's prick, cracked and … Sargon prayed that Anu didn't hear his thoughts.

Firmly gripped by laughter, he collapsed on his back. Through the ceiling and all the way to the heavens, Sargon could envision the supreme god, mortified while staring from the firmaments at the floor where his penis had fallen and shattered to pieces.

Amid tears of laughter, Sargon appeased Anu to elude his wrath:

"You are fine, O mighty god. You still have it … it is still here in your reflection."

𒌋 𒆳 𒁹 𒍅 𒐉

Hukura walked in, leading Gaga, who had one arm stretched out, feeling the space around him.

"What's wrong with him?" Sargon asked.

"I don't know." Hukura shrugged, grinning. "He claims his vision is weak."

Gaga banged into the wall and almost tipped over a large vase despite being guided.

"The gods must have cursed me for my blasphemy!" Gaga wailed. "Did I hear the high priest just now? O high priest, do ask the gods to forgive me—I repent!"

"This is not the high priest." came Sargon's stern reply.

"Who is it, then?" Pleading, Gaga held firmly to his guide.

"Hukura, you promised not to take me to that demented king."

"Mortal!" Sargon blared like a judge. "You're no longer among the living. You're in the presence of the great soul tribunal, on trial for your extensive record of heresy and decadent acts."

"Blessed be the gods for their mercy." Gaga raised his hands. "My torture and suffering under Sargon is over. Peace at last!"

"Wait, there has been a mistake," Sargon quipped. "You shouldn't be dead. We'll have to send you back."

"No, no, there is no mistake! Better dead than go back."

"A mistake it is—must send you back."

"Then send me anywhere, but not to that lunatic—that wicked jester-abuser, malicious poet-torturer—"

"Welcome back, Gaga!" Sargon cut him off. "We missed you. Everyone thought you were dead."

"Cursed be the heavens." Gaga opened his eyes. "Why me, why? What do you want now, Your *Heinous*?"

"Stop clowning." Sargon frowned. "You didn't finish reading the letters. ... Hukura, you can leave."

"Are you sure?" Hukura feigned concern. "I sense boundless evil in this man. He could present a serious threat to Your Majesty."

"How witty!" Gaga smirked. "You would make a great jester. How about we swap places? I challenge you to take on the task of amusing the King of Misery."

Hukura walked out laughing while Gaga ambled to a new table stacked with clay envelopes.

"I thought you didn't like how I read your letters, *Majesty*."

"I never said that. As long as you leave the gods alone, I have no complaints."

"How can I leave them alone when they are all over the place? ... What happened here?" Gaga frowned once he saw the broken tablets. "All this clutter! Didn't I advise you to never, ever summon demons to read your letters!"

Sargon ignored the comment. "I've already read the broken ones. Pick one that is intact."

The jester did as he was told and handed the letter to Sargon.

"What?" Sargon scowled.

"Break the envelope. Don't expect me to do this job too."

Sargon smacked it on Gaga's head, shattering the letter's clay crust.

"I hope I cracked open this stubborn jester-head of yours. ... Now, don't get mad. Count your blessings—at least you still have a head."

"And you count your blessings," Gaga tossed back. "If I die, wave farewell to laughter, and prepare for the slowest of deaths: misery!"

The comment carried true merit. It was very lonely at the top for Sargon, and no one managed to bring him down safely like the jester did. He was surrounded by actors fawning over him; he could feel treachery masked by loyalty, mutiny dressed in obedience, and enmity shadowing a friendly smile. The jester was the only one who granted him relief from that guessing game. Behind the transparent veil of Gaga's humor, Sargon learned much about what his subjects thought of him—the matters that roused their anger and incited unsavory gossip about him, which no one dared bring to his attention. Gaga harbored no dirty schemes; his jests were either simply jests or candid advice to be taken seriously by the king after a good laugh.

Gaga went on reading the tablet.

"Great King Sargon ... blah blah blah, all the customary arse caressing. ... I built a house that sadly crumbled during the last rainstorm. The roof and walls collapsed over the occupants, and tragically the whole family was killed. The accident was blamed on the bricks, which were determined to be of poor quality, either because of the low-grade mud they were made of, or the inadequate quantity of reed fibers used to fortify them, resulting in their rapid deterioration. I was found guilty of negligence along with the brickmaker and sentenced to be buried alive. The brickmaker had already been executed by that horrible method. So far, I was spared this injustice with the help of many nobles who testified favorably to my workmanship. I was permitted to ask clemency from Your Majesty. My profession is to build, and my reputation is among the best. I should not be held responsible for the mistake made by the brickmaker, who used to make bricks of the highest quality; but for some fateful reason or an assortment of factors, the bricks deteriorated, causing this horrible tragedy. O Great King, you are my last recourse to reverse this unjust sentence. May the gods ... blah, blah, and blah."

Gaga threw the tablet on the table. "It's alarming; all these strange things happening—tablets cracking, buildings crashing, penises shatter—" Gaga stopped himself, expecting a rebuke from Sargon, but to his surprise, it was a grin that settled on the king's face.

"So, what do you think, Gaga? Should I grant the builder a pardon?"

Gaga kneaded the short beard on his chin in an act of seeking a wise answer.

"Every criminal has a good excuse for the wrong he commits. In fact, each one of us is complicit in every crime in a subtle way. But to follow this principle and allow all crimes to go unpunished would only bring chaos to society. So, we punish a few to make a deterring example. As for this case, if you let the builder go free, then the soul of the executed brickmaker will haunt your dreams for the injustice done to him—for, similarly, he should've been pardoned."

"Why is that?" The answer baffled Sargon.

"Because the brickmaker could've said: 'Why blame me? My workers are the ones who made the bricks with their own hands. They are the ones who should be punished for not mixing enough reed straws with the mud.'

"But the workers would protest: 'We *did* put enough reed fiber to mesh the bricks. The mud's quality is the culprit to blame for the crumbling of the bricks.'

"Then the Mud would soak in tears: 'I'm but a captive at the mercy of the brutal river that exiled me far from my home and tossed me aside on its bank.'

"Angry waves the River would rouse in an outburst: 'The mud I bring has always been of the finest quality till it gets mixed with all that shit—channeled from the big cities and dumped into my waters.'

"And Shit would stink back: 'How cruel of you to accuse me! Haven't I suffered enough—I, the victim of the humans who created me then viciously forced me out; instantly I was disavowed for no fault of mine.'

"Thus, and finally, the roots of this house-collapse tragedy would reach to lay the blame on all the city residents, who would simply shrug and say: 'Well, what can you do? Shit happens!'"

"That's one shrewd answer you have there." Sargon chuckled. "So impressive, I hereby promote you from Court Jester to Court Sage. Now, tell me, is this wisdom an ongoing thing for you, or is it one of those 'shit happens' things that only graces us once in a long while?"

"Your Majesty," Gaga answered in a serious tone to match his new, sage title. "Great King, while you are eating, drinking, fornicating, and sleeping from sunrise till the moon shows and from dusk till the rooster crows, I am out there exploring—gaining knowledge and wisdom."

"So, *Court Sage*, enlighten me—what judgment would you pass on the builder?"

"I would grant him the clemency of choosing his own means of death. Buried alive is too harsh since he didn't intend for this to happen."

"Excellent, Gaga. The scribe will write a letter to the judge; the man can choose a death by drowning, sword, arrows—"

"Or stoning with bricks!"

"Hmm, that too. Now, honorable sage of the kingdom,"—Sargon bowed mockingly—"pick another letter and enrich us with your never-ending flow of wisdom."

"Absolutely, my lord." Gaga went for another envelope about the size of his hands, which were huge in proportion to his body. The crust was already cracked, and it fell apart with a little bang on the table.

"Huh, a stone relief." Gaga held the rectangular tablet then started rotating it while his head tilted side to side.

"What does it say? Read it." Sargon became curious.

"There is no writing, yet it tells a story of profound love. … The sculpting is flawless—exceptional. Can I keep this one?"

"What is it about, tell me?"

"Now be patient!" Gaga scolded his king. "This work needs the proper passion and loving tenderness to be described. … It's about a girl telling her man, 'O sweet lover, don't stop, thrust and dig harder! For the treasures of joy lie deep between my thighs, where pleasures stream in rivers, through which my body delves in ecstatic quivers.'"

Gaga paused, but the stone kept orbiting between his fingers. "The detail is a marvel. This is one splendid arse—I mean art. The most refined cheeks—a beauty. I wish I could have a girl like her in my dreams."

"Let me see that which got you so excited." Sargon reached for the tablet, but Gaga didn't give it away. He simply turned it so Sargon could take a look from his seat. The relief showed a man embracing a girl from behind with his rod inserted up her buttocks.

"By the gods! Such a depraved, yet outstanding work. The one who carved this should be working for me."

"You keep the sculptor, and I keep the girl who posed for it. Agreed?" Gaga suggested.

"I keep the sculptor and we share the girl. That's the best deal you will get. Now hand the tablet over, let me take a closer look."

"Wait, I see something scribed on the back."

Squinting, Gaga studied the cuneiforms, only to shrink back in disbelief. Slowly, his stare abandoned the tablet, anxiety raiding his face.

"What's wrong? Is there a curse on the tablet?"

The court sage swallowed before answering, "Forgive my foolish words. I—I was only joking, had no idea … I won't say a thing to any soul."

"What curse is written on that tablet?" Sargon rose to his feet. "Give me that thing!"

Cautiously, Gaga sent the tablet sliding to him and stepped back. Sargon grabbed it, trained his eyes on the scribed cuneiforms, and flared in rage.

"Who dared make this—WHO? I will have their heads spiked high over the gates of heaven! … You!" he roared at Gaga. "Say a word of this, and I swear I will have you buried alive!"

"Never, my king. I swear I won't breathe a word of this."

Gaga stormed out the door accompanied by a savage scream from Sargon.

"GUARDS! BRING ME IBRAHEM!"

Reunion

IBRAHEM RESTED THE CHISEL OVER THE TIP OF THE NOSE AND tapped lightly on it with the hammer, but instead of a tiny shave in the stone, a sizable piece crumbled off.

He cursed the demons that had taken up residence in his right hand, bringing pain with every twist of the wrist. Nonetheless, he thanked the gods he wasn't working on a statue of Sargon. It was a statue of Anu, and the gods were known to change their physical appearance to match their moods. This one would have a flatter nose, making him look tougher and mightier than he would with the pointed, feminine nose that Ibrahem had initially aimed for.

"O Mighty Anu, I know you wouldn't mind this little change." Ibrahem started another one-sided chat. "You never showed any displeasure with my work. On the contrary, it is favors and protection you provided me throughout many a perilous situation. Moreover, I am grateful for the crafty imagination you bestowed on me to conceive the ideas of the army of livestock and the skinning of Allamu, which ended the rebellion in my birth city, Ur. Now, King Sargon holds me in high esteem for all the advice I offered, which fortified his control over the kingdom. I—*yes, I*—should get the full credit for his triumph in Ur, and its people should hail me as a hero for sparing them the atrocious wrath of the merciless—"

Abruptly, Ibrahem went quiet. Those self-praising monologues to Anu were happening more often.

Am I losing my mind?

With relative peace reigning over the land, his life had retreated to a tranquil setting—so excruciatingly tranquil, emptiness became a formidable enemy.

It started with his family; Saura treated him like an abhorred invader who forced Isaa into exile. Isma-el, his son from the concubine, lived on the far side of the city and rarely bothered to visit him. In the palace, he was shunned by most men, for the word was out that he could not be trusted.

The void was only filled by the frequent visits in his dreams from Mayram, the girl who brought him that most beautiful of emotions: Love. But the torture of guilt she brought along tore apart all the beauty in those dreams, leaving behind a carcass of ugliness, rendering him sleepless, drowned in tears of sorrow. He immersed himself in work at his stone statues, finding relief in their company. Those gods became his family and friends; humans brought nothing but suffering. He slept the nights on a modest cot he had brought to the palace workshop. Being surrounded by all that cold stone provided the warmth to help him sleep.

The door to the workroom burst open, and in rushed a cold wind. The sculpted gods seemed to tremble under the invading chill, and Ibrahem felt their warmth abandoning him.

Wearing grim faces, Hukura and another guard walked in like savage brigands on a raid, not showing the slightest intention to apologize for violating Ibrahem's sacred sanctuary.

"Drop whatever you're doing," Hukura yelled. "The king wants you in his presence right away."

Ibrahem placed the tools on a table. Only then did he notice his right hand was shaking. The chill that settled in the room was the harbinger of what awaited him. The two guards raced in front of him as he labored to keep up with them. Anguish, like a parasite, devoured much of the air he breathed.

Inside the court, Sargon was standing next to his throne with his side to them. Ibrahem sensed fury smoldering around the king. It was too intimidating to be met standing up, and he went down to his knees in obeisance. It was evident that Sargon hadn't called him to seek advice, nor to sculpt another statue to immortalize him.

"Leave us alone." Sargon waved. The guards walked out, closing the doors behind them.

The floor under Ibrahem felt as though it had suddenly frozen. He feared the skin on his hands would peel off if he tried to move them.

"Your Majesty." He had to talk to crack the ice crystals forming in his blood. "Is there a matter in which I can be of service to Your Highness?"

Sargon paced the floor like a swing being pushed back and forth by some furious wind. He came to a sudden halt and his gaze rolled down to hang over the kneeling man.

"Where is your son?"

Ibrahem's thoughts raced as if running for cover from an ominous storm about to bury him under a dune of fury.

"Your Majesty, my son from a concubine, Isma-el, lives in the outskirts of the city, I hardly see him. Why, Majesty—what did he do?"

"Do you take me for a fool?" Sargon hollered. "How dare you! Am I not talking about the one who goes to the tablet house—*Isaa, Son of Ibrahem*?"

"I beg you forgive me, Your Highness. I have but one son, Isma-el. As for Isaa, he is no longer a son of mine. He, I have disavowed and cast out of my house. I have never laid eyes on him since then. I do know he took residence in the tablet house, where he assists as a learned brother. May I know what folly he committed to cause so much unrest to Your Majesty?"

"*Folly!* He says 'folly'!" Sargon chuckled briefly. "Get on your feet and step to the table. Take a good look at the tablet placed there."

Ibrahem staggered to his feet and walked with head bowed. He picked the tablet up, studied the depraved relief at the front, then hesitantly flipped the tablet and read the few engraved cuneiforms. Under the gravity of the contents, his back hunched over slowly until what now felt like a large stone slab fell from his hands back onto the table.

"Oh, mercy of the gods!" were the only words he could voice.

"Yes, beg the gods for mercy, because you and your son won't get it from me."

"Majesty, I swear I knew nothing about this. I'm just as shocked as Your Highness. And may I say, this could be nothing more than a ploy by someone to hurt me."

"That is one thing *you* have to prove. All I have now is a stone relief with a man *fucking* a woman, and the inscribed names, Isaa Son of Ibrahem and Princess Enheduanna. *A ploy*, you say! I doubt that. With your son, *Learned Brother Isaa*, in the same tablet house she used to attend—it makes a lot of sense. And you, *Trusted Adviser,* you came to me showing absolute loyalty while your son was fucking up my plans to wed my daughter to the pharaoh!"

"Your Majesty." Ibrahem went back to his knees. "I must confess that Isaa had been possessed by some evil, which made him insult me—his own father. It was what prompted me to disavow him. I swear by all the divine gods, if I were in the know about any reckless or criminal act he could've committed, I would've been the first to report him, just like I would any traitor."

"Does throwing him out of your house release you of responsibility? A demon-possessed son—a creation of yours—that's what *you* thrust out onto the city, onto my daughter. ... Guards!"

Hukura walked back inside.

"Take this thing out of my sight for now. Gather ten more guards, then bring him along. We're going for a short trip."

The two guards plucked Ibrahem up by the elbows.

Feeling his head spinning around in chaotic circles, Ibrahem hardly managed to maintain balance. Only the gods could put his universe back in order, but none of them came to help—none missed him back in the workshop.

ᛁ ◊ ᴣ ᴡ Ⅲ

It was just another normal day for the boys in the tablet house. Normal as well for the two learned brothers, Samian and Isaa, whose conduct had become anything but normal.

After the many conflicts that had inverted their friendship into bitter enmity, they had entirely shunned each other, calculating their moves in time and space to keep a good distance and avoid the sight of each other. If there was a matter that could not be ignored and needed their collaboration, then they conversed indirectly through a classmate who relayed their suggestions as if he were a translator between two strangers from two faraway worlds.

Learned Brother Samian was outside, placing some freshly inscribed tablets on a bench to bake in the sun, when soldiers barged through the main gate, escorting a man who apparently was the one in charge, judging by his dress and the jewelry he donned. Samian squinted at one man he recognized, walking behind with head bowed like a slave despite being richly clothed. Not wasting a moment, Samian started back to the classroom.

All the boys became aware of the visitors. Isaa came out with heart pounding in excitement, thinking Enheduanna had returned. But this hope was short-lived when he spotted his estranged father in the group, walking with the posture of someone burdened like an animal, under a heavy weight on his back.

Isaa noticed Samian moving in his direction, which came as a surprise for that violated their tacit agreement in avoiding each other. And as if that was not enough of an offense, Samian gave him a long stare as he passed by. Isaa stared back, wondering what prompted those gestures. But his anguish over the beaten image of his father made him dismiss Samian's infractions. He went back into the classroom, which was shortly shaken by a loud announcement.

"The tablet house is closed!" Hukura bellowed upon entering with another guard. "No more playing with mud. Take all your belongings right away and leave—all of you, except for the one learned brother called Isaa. Which one is he?"

"I am Isaa." He raised his hand.

All the boys stared at him, wondering what trouble he had brought upon himself now. Only Samian kept busy gathering some items and was the first to leave.

"I said, move!" Hukura shouted. "Out of here, fools! You learned to scribe words, yet no longer understand what they mean. Out! Now!"

The boys scurried to the door, almost jamming the entrance. Once outside, they saw the rest of the entourage, which sent them running for the gate to escape the fearsome army storming the tablet house.

Sargon was next to enter the classroom, followed by Ibrahem and the rest of the guards. Isaa glanced at his father, who kept looking straight down at the floor.

"Is that him?" Sargon asked Hukura, staring at Isaa.

"Yes, Your Majesty."

Isaa's head snapped up at hearing "Majesty." Though he had been in the palace a few times, he had never gotten the chance to see Sargon.

"Your Majesty, I am very humbled to be in your presence." Isaa bowed, when, unexpectedly, a hard fist landed in his stomach. He hunched over in pain.

"You get down on your knees when you address our Great King Sargon." Viciously, Hukura pushed down on Isaa's shoulder.

"Ibrahem, is this your son?" Sargon asked without looking back at the man.

"He ... was my son, Your Majesty. Yes, this is Isaa." Ibrahem's gaze only departed the floor for a brief glance. That small floor space seemed to provide the only comfort in this treacherous world; venturing out of it threatened his sanity.

Hukura tightened his fists, knuckles turning white, ready to beat the mud boy to a pulp.

"Not yet, Hukura." Sargon knew the temptation was too great for his guard. "Is the chief of the tablet house here yet?"

Master Akiya was brought in. He collapsed to his knees, hugging the ground.

"Your Majesty, I am greatly honored to have Your Magnificence visit this house of learning. Please forgive me for the poor state—"

"Silence!" Sargon cut him off. "Are you renting rooms in this *house of learning*?"

"Never, Your Majesty. I would never dare do that in this celebrated establishment of wisdom."

"Well, I have witnesses who say this boy, Learned Brother Isaa, is using this place as his residence," Sargon said, knitting his brows.

"Forgive me, Your Majesty. I swear by the sacred god of this house, Nabu himself, I had no idea."

"Even if you had no idea, you're still guilty of negligence and failure to secure this house against intruders and improper use." Sargon waved to the guards behind Akiya. "Take him out and give him ten lashes. ... I'm being lenient here; next time I'll have your body *quartered* into ten pieces."

"May the gods bless you, Majesty," Akiya cried, while three guards dragged him out, "for your merciful and fair judgment. May you live forever, O Great King."

"Now … I want all rooms searched," Sargon instructed the other guards.

"Majesty, what are we searching for?" a frustrated Hukura asked, for he would rather be beating the boy.

"Anything hidden out of sight that doesn't belong to the tablet house, and all the sealed clay envelopes—every single one. Place them on this table for me to examine. There must be heaps of *wisdom* to be gained here."

"Majesty, what about this pile of tablets on the table?"

Sargon walked around the huge slab of limestone, which rested on a base of fire-glazed bricks, emblazoned with reliefs and cuneiform inscriptions. He passively appraised the tablets, picked up a small one, walked with it to the outside door, and sent it flying. It crashed to pieces on the brick-paved ground just when the sound of a whip cracked and Akiya's cry of agony tore out to the heavens, startling the god of wisdom, Nabu.

"Throw everything on this table out," Sargon ordered. "All of this— nothing but nonsense, inscribed on worthless mud."

The guards rushed to the task, and after a few short trips to the outside door, the tablets with their meticulously inscribed symbols and wisdom took a brief flight before returning to the warm embrace of Mother Earth, shattered and muddled in a heap of meaningless babble.

The adjacent rooms were searched, and whatever roused suspicion was brought to the table.

After a fleeting inspection of some shelves, Sargon went back to the table, and away he tossed the items he deemed insignificant.

Isaa was still kneeling on the floor, trying to keep himself numb to whatever fate had in store for him. Soon, fear caught up to him—not only for himself but for his father, who stood in a far corner, in his own isolated world that didn't extend beyond the tight space his eyes focused on. It was the first time Isaa had seen his father since their clash, but he had never felt so estranged and abandoned; with only a few steps separating them, his father didn't waste a genuine glance on him, entirely ignoring his existence.

Sargon picked a sealed envelope and slammed it on another over the stone table, shattering both envelopes and the tablets they contained. He examined the pieces, then irately swept them off the table.

"Have you nothing to say to your father?" Sargon's words strafed Isaa with a scent of fury.

"Your Majesty, I am not worthy to be called his son, and he was right to disown me." Isaa breathed again with those words, which broke through the siege of silence that was choking him. He was relieved to be given the opportunity to distance his father from whatever crime that undoubtedly was the result of his own folly—be it the affair with Enheduanna or the heresy of following the invisible god.

"Majesty!" Hukura came rushing in with a small wooden box. "This was hidden behind a stack of tablets, an arm deep under the lowest shelf. Only roaches would venture into that space."

Sargon took the box and flipped it upside down, emptying the contents onto the stone slab. All were cylinder seals made from an assortment of stones, with detailed engravings of gods, mythical creatures, legends, prayers, or quotes of wisdom. Sargon grabbed a few, walked to Isaa, and dropped the seals next to him on the floor.

"Nice collection!" Sargon taunted. "I thought making cylinder seals was learned by becoming an apprentice to a craftsman in this art. Did you make these, steal them—someone gave them to you?"

"Your Majesty, I swear I have no idea where those seals came from," Isaa said, terrified at what all of this was leading to.

"You came to live here after your father cast you out of his house. And as a trusted learned brother, you had access to all the rooms attached to this classroom."

"Your Majesty, these seals must have been there ... someone must have hidden them before I came to the tablet house. That is the truth, Your Majesty."

"Before you came, huh!" Sargon squatted down and opened a

closed fist next to Isaa's face. "How about this seal, was it also there before you came? Look at it."

Timidly, Isaa rolled his eyes up to meet a golden seal with intricate engravings. It could have only belonged to a wealthy man.

"Your Majesty, I have no idea. This … like the rest, it's the first time I've seen this seal, I swear."

Sargon's heavy hand went flying across Isaa's face with the seal still in his palm. Ibrahem snapped a glance out of his tight viewing confines to see his son falling to one side and a golden seal rolling on the floor. It was too ugly a sight, and his stare retreated to the comfort of the floor beneath him.

"You swear!" Sargon contained his fury in a whisper that only Isaa could hear. "Swear by what? By my daughter's virginity, you dog!"

Sargon stood up, now shouting. "This golden seal, engraved with Gilgamesh slaying the monster Humbaba, belonged to my cousin who vanished, leaving no trace, only days ago. Who … gave you … this seal?!"

Sargon delivered a kick to Isaa's ribs and was about to deliver another, when Hukura came racing again, jubilantly smiling.

"Majesty, look what we found. Is this what I think it is?" He handed the king a large seal.

Looking closely at it, Sargon went through a whole array of expressions: surprise, amusement, and finally triumph.

"By all the gods from pure heaven to the stinking demon world, it is! No doubt, it is!"

"Definitely," Hukura concurred. "It's not finished, though."

"Not even half done. They must have abandoned working on this fake after I gave the order to change the royal seal."

Sargon walked to Ibrahem.

"Here, my *trusted adviser*, look at this. Now we know who was behind the fake royal seal, or seals … your son. What we don't know is how involved he was with my cousin's killer. As for my daughter, that matter pales with the gravity of what we found here."

Ibrahem's fears were exacerbated by all the evidence. Life had thrown him to wander under the cold nights of its vast desert of treachery.

Lost in that same darkness was his son. Isaa would've laid his life down, right there, for him; but cruel fate only allowed the boy to cast glances in silent longing for an affectionate gesture or a hint of forgiveness from his father. Then abruptly, as if touched by Isaa's yearning, Ibrahem raised his head and targeted his son with a fleeting look. But contrary to what Isaa had anticipated, that glance from his father was heartlessly frigid, seeming to loathe having his vision stained by the son who brought him nothing but disgrace.

Resigned to his fate, Ibrahem sank to his knees. "Highness ... Your Majesty. I beg forgiveness, for I must be guilty ... if for anything, that would be for having him see the light of life."

No other words could've knocked anyone more senseless. The man who gave life to stone gods had just made a stone out of his own son. Isaa looked at his father with a stare to rival the emptiness of a cold statue.

"Hukura, I've seen more than enough here," Sargon concluded. "Keep a few guards to go through everything in these rooms. This tablet house is closed till a full search is completed. The rest of us, we're going back. Take these two in chains."

Sargon looked down at Ibrahem and calmly said, "*You* brought him to see the light of life, so, it is *your* burden to send him away— into the darkness of the netherworld."

BY THE GODS OF BABYLON

DARKNESS IN THAT DUNGEON HOLE WAS ABSOLUTE, MORE LIKE death incarnate, where even the ghosts of dreams would not dare visit the doomed. Light, too, never felt welcomed when it visited there; the eyes squinted and fluttered to ward off any bright glow, which was more like a herald for the condemned, announcing their release to their anticipated, horrid fate.

The tiny cell was about five paces deep, three paces wide. Whoever designed it must have had a lot of sympathy for those who would come to occupy its smothering space by offering a generous first taste of the netherworld—a transitional stage to prepare the condemned for the box that would house their body; that is, if they were fortunate enough to know someone who deemed them worthy of the wood to shelter their bones from the dirt.

Flickering colors began to seep into the cell, shaking awake the dormant life within. Ibrahem wondered if the intrusive light was real or the work of his imagination.

Since they had thrown him there, time had stopped moving. The gloomy pit acted like a tyrant with powers to annihilate the present and the future; yet, like a sadistic torturer, it granted the freedom to revisit the past. The good times that he had thought would last forever were now buried in the abyss of memories, leaving him haunted by regrets over mistakes he could've avoided. If only he had spent more time with Isaa, the boy would not have drifted away into this ruin, dragging him along into a sinkhole that reduced him from a man highly favored by the most powerful king to a doomed father of a traitor.

The door to the cell opened. Only the oil lamp came in, and the brute holding it spoke.

"God-Maker," the guard said mockingly, "you have a visitor. But don't rejoice; he's not godsent."

Amused by his own humor, he laughed and placed the oil lamp on the floor.

"Don't close the door," the guard warned a man behind him. "Demons in this room love to sniff the flame, and with that they suck all the air out; you will both suffocate, and our king would be horribly displeased with me. I'll leave you alone now."

The surge of light sent tears flushing out of Ibrahem's eyes. He wiped the tears away for a better look at the visitor, who had to bend down upon entering since the door opening was no higher than the stature of a boy in the early teens. Apparently, the carpenter who made the door must have run out of wood.

"Gudea!" A hint of delight surfaced on Ibrahem's haggard face. He stood up as though to offer hospitality to a welcomed guest. But it dawned on him that he had nothing to offer, not even a brick for his guest to sit on. As for food, even the cockroaches refused to spend any time there for the lack of it. A small jar of water was the only luxury. Food was not wasted on men condemned to die.

"Oh, Gudea, your presence brought a whiff of life to this tomb." Ibrahem put his arms around Gudea and began sobbing, overwhelmed by the flood of warmth from Gudea's body after the chill of the stone walls had settled in his core. Abruptly, he pulled away and faced the side wall to hide his shame.

"Tell me this is not happening, Gudea. Wake me up from this nightmare. You know how faithfully I served the king; I wouldn't do anything to bring him harm. Now, my whole family is cursed; me, my wife, even Isma-el—my son from the concubine—and his child, too. All because of that reckless boy whom I disowned. Oh, how he changed overnight from a docile, obeying son to a vicious rebel. I never believed in such things as spirits possessing men, but his madness has driven me to believe in that now.

"He went so far as to desecrate the gods we worshipped for countless generations, rejecting them for this new god—the lone outsider. He says his god is more powerful than Anu and all other gods combined. A one god who created all, who was before all and will endure after all. Cursed be my luck—to listen to such nonsense, coming from my own son! If this god created all, why declare his presence only now? Where was this recluse god hiding?

"Oh, Gudea, this is my reward for all I did for the king. Because of this boy's madness, the whole family is doomed—unless I slaughter him with my own hands. Isaa deserves to die, but I cannot ..." Ibrahem choked on the words.

Gudea hadn't uttered a word since he set foot in the cell. He kept a solemn expression while watching Ibrahem's shadow tremble on the wall behind.

"Gudea, dear friend, I plead to you: please go to the king and ask him not to force me to be ... the executioner."

"You know that my wife drowned in the river!" Gudea broke his silence.

"Gudea, I beg for your help. The gods must have sent you to save me. Sargon has probably calmed down by now and might listen to you."

"You didn't hear what I just said," Gudea rebuked him. "My wife *drowned in the river!*"

"I know ... and I deeply regret that," a baffled Ibrahem answered. "But ... that happened some time ago. Why talk about it now ... when I'm in this hole for the cursed?"

"Did you know she jumped in the river?" Gudea added resentfully.

Ibrahem was stunned by this diversion from his predicament to that of a woman who had long since departed.

"No, I didn't know that. Gudea ... can you consider the dire situation I'm in?"

"You speak of your son's madness," Gudea replied irritably. "Let me tell you about my wife's madness. ... Strange, how you never asked me about our adopted daughter, Amare. You saw her with me a few times in the streets. Remember her? Everyone does after seeing her once—a playful, spirited girl.

"Tammara, my wife, was the sister of Amare's mother. Amare was orphaned after her parents drowned; the boat they took on a river crossing sank. So, we adopted Amare. She filled the house with joy and laughter, easing the sorrow that dominated our days after our own child went to sleep one night and never woke up again. Tammara was so happy with Amare that she would often cry, laden with guilt and asking forgiveness of the souls of Amare's parents, for their death had brought her that happiness. In contrast, my son Nissan, born of my first wife, was nothing but trouble. After that school fight with your son, I ended up sending him to Babylon, to his mother."

Ibrahem kept silent, stunned at Gudea's indifference to his grim situation.

"Amare was like a gift from the gods, but those gods must have felt she was too good a gift for us. She disappeared like a sweet dream; you wake up, and no trace is left behind. And Amare, just like that, was gone. Taking her soul wasn't enough to satisfy the greedy gods, they had to snatch her body too."

Gudea paused briefly. Ibrahem was looking through him as if he were a ghost carrying a message from the dead.

"Amare was one among the multitude who disappeared the day of Sargon's coronation ceremony. I know, as surely you do too, they were all buried to keep the former king well cared for in his *next stinking life*! Huh, they claimed *Galla demons dragged the victims to the netherworld*; that was the best story they could come up with to fool the people. The absurdity in believing those fables! … The human ear is funny; you tell it a story and it shapes a ghost inside the head. Tell the same story some more, and people imagine the ghost growing flesh and bones. Tell it more often, and blood will flow in the veins. Keep recounting the story, and fools would swear to having seen the ghost walk and talk. Soon, before you know it, that entity becomes more real than all the things you can perceive; indestructible, everlasting— endowed of mystical powers to be feared. Huh, the nonsense, but it's everywhere.

"Now, Amare was real—flesh and blood, beauty, laughter, song and dance, love, joy, life—all were real in her, real as real can get. Do you think my wife could simply accept that Amare, her only reason for living, was gone—that Amare was … no longer real?

"So my wife found the only companion to console her in this loss:

Madness. Her all-merciful, compassionate Madness told her Amare was out there and for some reason couldn't find her way back home. So my wife went walking the streets, markets, temples, taverns, all over Uruk. Needless to say, all in vain—till the day when Madness, out of utter pity for Tammara, revealed to her where to find Amare. Tammara boarded a boat, and midway across the river she jumped—down into the depths of the same river that claimed Amare's parents. Madness had her convinced she would find Amare there—with her parents. Now *that* is what I call madness, sheer madness. Don't you agree, Ibrahem?"

Gudea swallowed to draw the tears away from his eyes.

"I arrived back from the trade trip to the welcoming embrace of misery—finding my wife and our adopted daughter gone. The two people I loved more than life—no longer real. Even our long-departed infant girl, whose remains rested inside a jar, was not spared; Tammara took her along, and the river robbed me of the only real thing about her.

"Most people believe that the souls of the departed visit us now and then. I'm not one of those lucky believers. Fate heaped wealth on me but condemned me to be lacking faith in the afterlife. I only experienced that luxury fleetingly, in times of total desperation.

"I found myself alone with only guilt to keep me company, till the day you saw me in Allamu's home, after his failed revolt." Gudea stared deep into Ibrahem's eyes. "He revealed something that replaced my torment and guilt with a raging quest for vengeance."

"What did Allamu tell you? … Why are you here, Gudea?"

"Allamu saw Amare in the burial chamber. He talked to the high priest, Ishullanu, and tried to have her released, but to no avail. The one thing he could get from the high priest was the name of the man who recommended Amare to be in the *stinking company of the dead king!*"

"Gudea!" Ibrahem protested. "Are you saying I had something to do with your girl's demise?"

"Not something, but everything! You are the demon who caused my loved ones to be taken away. Since my son and yours had that little school quarrel, I could sense the ill will you harbored toward me behind that friendly face of yours."

"Gudea, don't tell me you believed Allamu! He was lying. And Ishullanu was another liar if he ever mentioned me. They both hated me. Gudea, in the name of the gods, stop tormenting me on my last day among the living. Allamu fabricated this whole story to get back at me."

"Why would he do that, Ibrahem? Why would an army general want to cause you harm?"

"I don't have the slightest idea."

"Liar! How about the girl from Babylon? Just like Amare, your ploys and deceit caused her death."

"What girl?" Ibrahem said in a tired voice.

"The mantis assassin, Mayram. Another innocent girl, whom you turned into a vicious killer before you sacrificed her in one of your dirty schemes. You bastard—you enjoyed and used her, till she refused to comply with your orders, and she became nothing more than a lamb you delivered to the slaughterhouse."

"I don't know what you're talking about." Ibrahem whispered so the walls couldn't hear his lie.

"You mendacious dog!" Gudea struggled not to scream. "Why did you attempt to kill the sculptor Lubalanda? Surely he wasn't on the king's list of men to die. As for *your* list, he was the first. Mayram told Lubalanda everything about the killing of the nobles; another secret from the deep mines of your dark soul has come to light. Remember when you came to Allamu's house, when *by coincidence* I was there too, and you asked of Lubalanda's whereabouts. Lubalanda was hiding from you—guess where? Yes, *in my house.* He was going to run away with the same girl you sent to kill him. You were seething with envy of a young man who is a better sculptor than you ever dreamed to be. Without a doubt, you couldn't bear seeing him run away with Mayram, whom you must have considered to be your property—so, she had to die. Allamu, that other sick bastard, told me how you schemed for Mayram to end up in his home, totally oblivious that it was a death trap."

"Get out of here, Gudea! You came here to make me suffer as if I'm not suffering enough."

"No, Ibrahem, you haven't suffered enough. I'm not done with you yet. So many lives you have destroyed—and I'm not counting the noble scum. Aren't you eager to know how you ended up in this hole, after faithfully serving Sargon for so long?"

Ibrahem's curiosity wanted to know, but he kept quiet to preserve whatever pride he was left with.

"Well, Ibrahem," Gudea continued, generous with the intent of inflicting more humiliation, "after I learned about all those *exploits* of yours from Allamu and Lubalanda, I told one of my servants, who didn't have much to do in my empty house, to watch your movements. He detected a thing that baffled me: apparently, your son had made the tablet house his home, where his mother often visited. Another frequent visitor was a girl who dressed in normal street clothes. As for you, you were never on the list of visitors. You must have abandoned him, but why?"

Ibrahem remained silent.

"Poor Isaa, what did he do to deserve such wrath? Oh, forgive me, I forgot—he betrayed your gods."

"Enough, leave!" Ibrahem shouted. "Guard, get this dog out of here!"

"Don't waste your breath, dear Ibrahem, the man doesn't want to be disturbed. A silver piece goes a long way with those guards. They'll let me spend the whole night here if I choose to. … Now, back to your son. He was enjoying himself with that girl—royally." Gudea smirked. "It wasn't a quest for knowledge and wisdom that led our princess to those clandestine visits to the tablet house. Which answers another question: Why would the king suddenly abort the marriage of the princess to the pharaoh? … Virginity lost, what else!"

"Liar!" Ibrahem grumbled. "How could your spy know they were fornicating?"

"No, not my spy. Rather, someone blinded with envy—just like you: a learned brother in the same tablet house. He didn't know me, and I approached him pretending to be a concerned father who was thinking of sending his son to that tablet house. Who better to ask for advice than an accomplished learned brother? So, I invited Learned Brother to a tavern, and soon enough got him drunk. Now, as a trader, my first and most valuable tool is a convincing tongue. I had him spill his anger out with every gulp of beer he took in. His anger flowed and flowed till it ran dry. The poor boy was in love with the princess; who wouldn't be? But he had caught her with Isaa, inside the tablet house on a day when there were no classes. A reed mat on the floor instead of writing tablets on a table only confirmed his suspicions—and mine. I consoled this grievously devastated young man, took him to the best brothel in Uruk where a beauty ended his virgin days and calmed his obsession with the princess. Yet, his hatred toward Isaa never subsided. We became sort of friends after that."

Gudea paused to observe any reaction from the man he came to torment, but an absent stare of total indifference was all he could glean.

"Ibrahem, are you familiar with a board game from a faraway land in the east, where the sun first rises after its exit—"

"Stop your appalling game!" Ibrahem snapped. "You're only repeating what I said to Allamu when he was in a cell like this. You must've had a long talk with him."

A grin adorned Gudea's face; he had sabotaged Ibrahem's pretense, compelling him to reveal his pain in the bitter defeat.

"True, Ibrahem, very true. Allamu told me of how you brimmed with pride while detailing the ways you outsmarted him in your lethal game; how you lured him, with his friend Hadras, into waging an incursion to dethrone Sargon. They go for the kill, only to find themselves dug deep into a deadly trap.

"Excellent game, Ibrahem, except that the game of life does not abide by board game rules. The pieces you take out leave ghosts behind; not your typical ghosts—rather, real people who replace their departed loved ones only to seek vengeance.

"As for you, Ibrahem, with the opponent's big pieces annihilated, you sat back, feeling secure, favored by the king—another mistake, for this board game of the living differs greatly in that pieces on the same side can knock each other out. Someone like Sargon would not think twice about eliminating anyone, be it family or friend, who gives him the slightest discomfort—specifically, a shrewd one who might plot against him one day. All I had to do was gather and organize the vengeful small pieces to move the strongest piece, your own king, against you."

"Gudea! You plotted this entire scheme because of some lies Allamu had you believe. You hate me that much?"

"Ooh Ibrahem, only the god who created hate knows how much I abhor you."

"I was *not* involved in your girl's death."

"I'm not here to listen to your lies!" Gudea tore at him. "I used to worry about the barbarians and cutthroats we might encounter on the trade routes—the deserts and forests of foreign lands. We met many of those, yet I survived. Then, I return to the safety of the great walled city of Uruk, only to find my loved ones are dead. You are the brigand I should've prepared for over all others. Oh how often I prayed for a sandstorm to catch you by surprise and strip you of your skin to expose the demon inside."

Gudea pulled the necklace he wore out of his garment, exposing an attached cylinder seal of agate stone.

"See this seal? It was crafted by my son, meant to be a gift to my wife, Tammara. It shows the gods of Babylon, Marduk and Ishtar, standing over a boy, my son, who is kneeling, asking forgiveness for all the torment he caused her in his reckless youth. Tammara is shown standing behind him, bowing to the gods with a plea to accept his penance."

Gudea dug into his pocket and came up with another object. "For Amare, he made this lapis lazuli necklace, each bead engraved with the name of a Babylonian god. My son gave me these gifts on my way back from the last trip as I passed through Babylon to check on him. I couldn't wait to reach Uruk to watch the joy on their faces once they put these gifts on—but that was not to happen.

"I buried the gifts where my wife rested, and I lived my days steeped in sorrow, yet restless with doubts. I knew the former king very well and found it hard to believe that he was the one who had selected Amare to be delivered to his burial chamber. I agonized over who might be the culprit in arranging that *invitation*; the truth eluded me—all was mired in secrecy.

"I was also oblivious to the boundless extent of your evil, until the day Lubalanda came to hide in my house out of fear—and to my surprise, it was you whom Lubalanda feared, after that Mayram girl reneged on carrying out your orders to kill him. The night of her funeral, Lubalanda didn't show up. I thought you had him killed, but he came back the next morning looking like a dead man who had just walked out of a grave. He wanted to die, but I convinced him to keep on living, to avenge his love. Little did I know that *I* was the one who should seek vengeance.

"Allamu sought me on the pretext of disposing of the large, winged bulls in his home, where you *unexpectedly* showed up. Only then, after you left, did Allamu expose your role in weaving the horrible fate that awaited Amare in the burial chamber."

"I'm telling you, Allamu was lying!" Ibrahem shouted to the deaf ears of Gudea.

"That same night, Tammara and Amare visited my dreams. Both looked beautiful—cheerful, and along their bright smiles, my son's gifts sparkled on them. I found it absolutely strange, for not a word did they mention about their cruel fate, nor a rebuke for my absence. They appeared so real, so alive, I was convinced that their death was nothing but a nightmare I had ... until, in a flash, the scene changed. Tammara was floating in the river, holding on to a jar, scolding me for abandoning them; then abruptly, all light went out, and through the grim darkness of a sealed chamber, Amare's voice reached me, asking if I would avenge them. Words froze in my mouth, as if the darkness rendered me mute, and I started feeling my way in search of light—to find my tongue—when a faint glow flickered ... and I woke up in this cursed world.

"Around midday, I went to my wife's grave and dug out the gifts I had buried. There, I swore by the gods on these gifts, by the gods of Babylon, I would not rest until I make you suffer. Tammara's seal of forgiveness became my seal of vengeance."

Unexpectedly, Ibrahem lunged at the spiteful guest and clutched on his neck with both hands, but he was too weak for Gudea, who shoved him away. Ibrahem hit the wall; still, he dragged his feet for another try to punish his tormentor, but after a few short steps, strength abandoned him, and to his knees he folded.

"Forgive me, Ibrahem, I must be boring you with all the details, but for once I find it pleasurable talking to you." Gudea brushed the dust off his robe. "I devised a plan—asked Lubalanda to leave and stay with my son in Babylon, where they both worked on making a replica of the old royal seal, using a sealed letter I had from a previous trip. The seal didn't have to be finished; they just needed to show that somebody was working on a fake one. My son also provided some cylinder seals that had been exchanged for new ones by their owners; those came from where he worked as an apprentice to a seal maker in Babylon. As for the relief which depicted a mating couple, along with the names of Isaa and the princess, it was crafted by Lubalanda.

"While in Babylon, Lubalanda visited Mayram's parents to console them and ask forgiveness for failing to save her. The parents treated him like a son who equally shared their pain in her loss. After the fake royal seal had enough work done on it, the parents made the trip from Babylon to Uruk, bringing along the unfinished royal seal, the mating stone relief, and the cylinder seals that my son gave away.

"Mayram's father was the one who burned the boat with the nobles in it and grabbed the golden seal, which belonged to Sargon's cousin. I bet you didn't know this detail. This father, another one driven into madness, came on a quest for vengeance. And he satisfied it, butchering more nobles by Ishtar's temple before he was killed along with his wife—two more victims who found more mercy in death than the torture chamber you made of their lives. Now, let me tell you about your last victim … your son."

"Finish your story fast and get out of here—*Phoenician bastard!*" Ibrahem said defiantly as he found the energy to get back on his feet.

"Curse me all you want, Ibrahem, but you can't hurt me any worse than you already have. Patience, I'm almost done. … Shu-dagan's mission was to bring me the items from Babylon, nothing more. He and his wife stayed with me upon arrival and spent the next few days walking in the city and visiting their daughter's shrine. Shu-dagan did tell me how he snatched the golden seal from Sargon's cousin before the river took possession of the man's body. I thought that burning the boat with the nobles on it was enough to smother the fires of his wrath. I was entirely wrong; it was but the first ember before the inferno he unleashed on the nobles. I was just as shocked as everyone else by what he did later.

"Days before that bloodbath, I went to meet my new friend—Learned Brother from the tablet house—your son's good friend before love and murderous envy made them sworn enemies. I gave him all that was sent from Babylon. And Learned Brother took care of the final tasks: in the tablet house, he hid the unfinished fake royal seal, together with the golden seal grabbed from Sargon's missing cousin. Learned Brother also arranged for the delivery of the sensual, mating relief stone to the palace."

Gudea paused before triumphantly concluding the details of his plot.

"Isaa will be the last innocent soul sacrificed as a result of your evil deeds. The boy has no idea what's going on—well, apart from deflowering the princess without the king's approval. On its own, this infraction could have been resolved by wedding them. It's not something unheard of; after all, the princess had already lost the prized virginity, and Isaa—a learned son of a wealthy man.

"You should be proud of Isaa. The guard told me the boy has already confessed to making the fake royal seal, among other things. And admirably, he's doing all he could to clear you—the father who abandoned him—of any involvement.

"Poor Isaa, if only he didn't get entangled in that cursed school brawl; my son would've remained in Uruk with Tammara and Amare during my absence, and no harm would've come their way. Things would've taken a different path and none of this would've happened. Who knows what fate would've arranged? We probably would've been sitting now in a tavern, drinking like the best of friends. Sadly, all those 'would haves' were wiped out by a few foolish moments, and we are powerless to do anything but have 'would have' daydreams."

Ibrahem angrily rejoined, "That age-old, petty quarrel between our sons! You must have kept brooding over it ever since. Now you're using it to clear your guilty mind for being absent when tragedy struck your loved ones. You're desperate in trying to shift the blame onto someone else—onto me. I swear to having no part whatsoever in your family's demise."

"Sure! Just like you had no part in savaging the innocence of that Mayram girl, turning her into the beast she became."

"I curse you, Gudea. May Ereshkigal send her walking dead to rip your flesh from your bones, tiny piece by tiny piece. And may your soul boil in the fire pits of the netherworld, forever."

"Oh, dear Ibrahem." Gudea shook his head. "You disappoint me. I thought you were smarter than to believe in such nonsense. I've heard a lot of stories throughout my travels about demons, bloodsuckers, men changing into wolves; beasts that are half men, half animals; the walking dead. I've heard it all, but I've never witnessed any of that dung.

"Not to mention the gods. Throughout the far lands I traveled, I explored scores of religions. There are more gods out there than I know how to count. They come in all shapes and sizes: men, women, beasts, and, again, 'half this, half that.' You, Ibrahem—a god-maker— know that very well. The believers in those gods all claim the same things: their god is the *creator* of the universe; theirs is the most *powerful* god, the *greatest* this and the *supreme* that. This 'faith in the gods' is but a perpetual act most of us are forced to master out of fear of being shunned by family and friends should we abandon the tradition. So, we play the part to fool each other, and many excel in this act to the point where they succeed in deceiving their own selves.

"Amazing, how I was brought up to believe in the Phoenician gods, then I settled here and adopted the Sumerian gods, and now I'm swearing by the Babylonian gods. How about this latest god your son chose? Someone fused all the gods together into this invisible loner—the 'everywhere, anytime' god. One god to seek for all of one's needs. Makes life easy; no time wasted hopping between temples, praying to an assortment of gods. A brilliant concept, I must confess; still, it's just another addition to the nonsense they keep coming up with.

"Huh, God created the first man from mud! Or was it Man who created the first god from mud? That is the timeless ques- tion—a question no one would've ever asked had any—*any* of the gods—demonstrated their presence and boundless might in more obvious, convincing ways than those utterly absurd, storied myths—creations of mere mortals.

"Well, if it's true that a god created us *from mud*, then I can't help but heap curses on him for creating a world infested by the depraved likes of you, Ibrahem.

"How absurd! Now I'm the one hurling curses!" Gudea smirked. "Curses! Reminds me of a wealthy Egyptian I met once. He had me in tears, laughing at a mad account of his pathway to riches. Childhood—he spent as a beggar, then progressed to thief, and now he's a highly respected man, settled in my homeland, Phoenicia. He spoke of those elaborate curses the pharaohs of the Nile scribe at the entrance to their massive tombs, to scare thieves away. Despite all, the tomb raiders manage to enter and plunder all the treasures, leaving the pharaohs with nothing to enjoy for the next life but the fabric they were wrapped in. Well, this Egyptian tomb raider I met felt tinges of guilt at depriving the pharaohs of their possessions. So, in gratitude, the man made it a habit to leave something behind before abandoning a tomb: a generous pile of his shit.

"Curses, Ibrahem! Save your futile curses for the fools who believe in that dung. Sadly, it's a world swarming with their types—so intoxicated by blind faith and superstitions that facts and reason had become myths."

"Why have you told me all this? Are you not afraid I will expose this whole story to the king?"

"Afraid!" Gudea scoffed. "How afraid was Mayram's father when he went on a rampage, giving death to the nobles, knowing very well he would soon follow them to the grave? Not many are the selfish bastards—like you, Ibrahem—only seeking to reward themselves. Most would sacrifice all, even their own lives, for the ones they love; and if they lose those dear to them, life becomes worthless. Go ahead, Ibrahem, call the guard, tell him the whole story. Unfortunately, you're not in the palace anymore; you're nothing but a condemned prisoner uttering mad stories to clear yourself. Besides, those guards' miserable wages don't pay them enough to care. The only pleasure their job offers is watching wealthy pigs suffer while getting them ready for the netherworld. Anyway, like I just told you, your boy has already confessed his guilt. Now, suppose the guard would listen to you … see this."

Ibrahem jolted back when Gudea pulled out a sharp knife. In his head flashed the image of Mayram showing him her dagger in that first night with her.

"Don't worry, Ibrahem, it's not for you. I want your suffering to last. This is for me, to end my misery in the very unlikely chance I am to be arrested. As for my son, I sent a servant with a message for him to leave Babylon for Phoenicia, where I have relatives to help him. With his skills, he will prosper. Once I leave your pleasant company, I'll be on my way to Phoenicia too. You're right—I didn't have to tell you any of this. I could've been in bed enjoying the softness of a woman instead of the pleasure of your company in this stinking cell. But having this conversation with you feels more thrilling than bedding any beauty out there. I wouldn't miss it for the world; not after the long moons I endured, tormented in my dreams by the voices of my wife and Amare, asking for justice. So, when you and your son reach the netherworld, Tammara and Amare will get my message: Vengeance has been served.

"I swore by the gods of Babylon to get vengeance, and by the gods, what sweet vengeance I am granted! Who knows, maybe this is one step toward making me a believer in the gods."

Ibrahem was gazing at the floor, where a small bug stood still as if listening to all the details—a living witness to his innocence and his son's.

Gudea picked the oil lamp up from the floor. "It's payback time for all those victims you have wronged. Eye for an eye, Life for a life. I bid you farewell, Ibrahem; you need to gather some strength for your coming trip."

The bug began to dissolve into a blur, and Ibrahem went frantic upon noticing the light depart with the door closing behind Gudea. He sprang to follow, but the room went dark as if a flash of lightning had just gone out. He tripped, crashed on the door, and fell to the floor.

"Guard! Guard, arrest that man! Don't let him leave!" Ibrahem shouted as his fingers snaked over the floor, chasing the slivers of light that sneaked through the door gaps.

"He's a criminal! He's the one who should be in this cell. Guard, you must believe me!"

Before full darkness enveloped the cell, the light regrouped and intensified its push through the gaps. Ibrahem's heart pounded hard at hearing footsteps approach.

The guard would listen, and Sargon would know the truth. Soon, my nightmare would be over.

The door opened and the guard loomed in like a giant hope that would force justice back to the right path.

"You have something to tell me, God-Maker?" said the guard, calmly.

"The man who just left … hurry, chase him!" Ibrahem approached the guard, throbbing with excitement. "He's—he's a traitor. A friend of that other lying traitor, Allamu. The king needs to know I'm innocent—"

Without a warning, the heavy hand of the guard slammed across his face, crushing his words, knocking him down.

"Shut your mouth!" The guard's roar whipped the dust off the walls. "If you have a problem, you'll have eternity to complain about it when you meet Ereshkigal's demons tomorrow."

The guard stepped away and sighed. "God-Maker, I can't stomach anymore 'I'm innocent' stories. … I'm trying to sleep. Make another sound, and I swear by the Almighty Anu, I'll pummel you into silence."

The sound of the door latch snapping in the wall felt like a punch in Ibrahem's chest that knocked the air out of him. The guard's steps faded away, carrying the light along with them. Ibrahem gazed at the paling shadows that crept outside, almost begging them to have pity and keep him company. But the light was too self-absorbed to leave anything behind, abandoning another doomed man in the clutches of total darkness in the eternal night of that cell.

Ibrahem could hear faint echoes of laughter, which the dark void must have carried to him from the neighboring netherworld. One sound seemed familiar; it was Allamu, celebrating his triumph in a devastating move that evened the score with Ibrahem in the gods' deadly board game.

Blindly, Ibrahem felt his way along the wall, to a corner. He huddled, eyes open wide, searching the darkness for the ghosts he knew would soon arrive to rejoice in his misery.

52

No Pain, No Game

"Only one?"

"That's all they delivered to my tender care."

"But I heard there were a few of them."

"Like I said, only one was sent to my attention. Come, take a look."

All four went down the narrow stairs, which opened into a chamber. The first thing to greet a visitor was a sturdy table, standing in the middle, its surface all stained in dark blotches. Hooks and ropes dangled from a crossbeam below the ceiling.

They passed a room behind heavy bars. Locked away inside was a wide assortment of sharp tools, whips, and oddly shaped devices. Next to that room they arrived at a latched door.

"Anyone behind this door?" one of the visitors asked.

"No. Our last guest in this room wasn't happy with our hospitality. Like the ones before him, he was in a rush to depart. I could never understand why!" The guard laughed and walked to the next door, which was slightly ajar.

"This is it." The dungeon guard pushed the door wide open.

The figure in the far corner looked like a shadow missing its body—so fragile that a speck of light threatened to make it disintegrate.

"Very smart—where you have a prisoner, you keep the cell door open," one of the visitors quipped.

"Makes the job a little more exciting if they try to run away," the guard responded.

"Cat-and-mouse play. You must be really bored."

"Bored to death! Let me show you." The guard reached for his knife and slid it on the floor toward the prisoner. The figure remained glued to the wall, not even bothering to glance at the knife.

"We give them the toys, but they don't want to play with us." The guard snickered and walked over to retrieve his weapon.

"How much?" the slimmest of the three said.

"The highest bidder, what else? How much do you have to offer?"

"Well, just asking," the slim sentry replied. "I'm almost broke—spent plenty on a whore yesterday. Just wanted to know … for the future. For now, I'm just looking."

The prison guard stared, fighting the temptation to squeeze the life out of the man's slender neck.

"Just looking! Do I look like a fucking vendor in the market bazaar? O merciful gods, give me rivers of patience, or split the floor under my feet to swallow me—to spare me this idiocy."

The guard studied the other two men. "Are you 'just looking' too?"

"He looks spent. I would've liked a fresh one," a hefty sentry said.

"That's all I have to offer. Take it or leave it, no one is wringing your balls."

"Two bronze pieces. That's all I have on me."

"So be it. I'll take that."

The hefty sentry went into his pocket, but before handing the pieces over to the guard, the third man, a short sentry, stopped him.

"Wait, not so fast. I might give a silver piece for that." He grabbed the oil lamp from the guard and walked toward the huddled figure.

The shadow covered his face to shield it from the light. The sentry used his free hand to yank the prisoner's head up.

"By the blessed, hollowed vagina of Ishtar! It's him!" The short sentry brightened. "Tiny, you don't remember him? Come, take a closer look."

The hefty one, Tiny, stepped forward, took a fleeting look, and shrugged. "Am I supposed to know him?"

"You fool." The other slapped him on the back. "How could you forget? The tablet house! The board game!"

Tiny gripped the prisoner by the chin. After studying the face intently, he shouted, "By the wise arse of Nabu! You're right, Killer, it's him."

"He's mine." Killer handed a silver piece to the guard without hesitation.

"Yours he is, Killer." The guard pocketed the silver. "Now, whatever you do to him, he should be conscious and able to walk by tomorrow morning, or else you'll be in trouble."

"Don't worry, I know what shape you need them to be in. I'll be gentle."

Grinning wildly, Killer turned to his merchandise.

"We meet again, mud boy. Remember me—the guard by the tablet house, or did you forget like my foolish partner here? Let me show you what I got, thanks to you. ... Tiny, you too, show him."

The two sentries turned around and pulled their robes up. Carved on their backs were the squares resembling a game board.

Killer lowered his robe and went on. "That's why your face remains engraved in my memory. So, now we have till the morning to play games. And since you gave me hints for the board game, I'll return the favor and teach you some games of my own."

"Can I stay?" Tiny asked.

"Will cost you a bronze piece."

"You got it." Tiny dug the piece out and tossed it to Killer. "Let's carve a game board on his back, like ours."

"Tiny, you grew a robust frame at the expense of having a tiny imagination. No—this eye-for-an-eye dung doesn't work for me. I'm more of a head-for-an-eye type. Actually, I have a great idea. ... Tiny, it's time for us to learn the art of writing."

"What? Us, writing?"

"With our learned friend here to help, why waste the opportunity? We have a vast selection of sharpened *scribing* tools. The only thing missing is ... fresh mud tablets."

"Yes, Killer, the mud for tablets?" asked Tiny.

"Mud boy!" Killer addressed Isaa. "Any suggestions for something to carve on? ... No? No worries, I know someone who will provide."

Killer looked up and prayed: "God, we beseech You for some mud to learn the writing skills. ... Oh, silly me for asking; of course, You created man out of mud!"

Grinning sadistically, he eyed Isaa. "Tiny, here you have

it—enough fresh mud for an epic story."

"Can I stay too—just to watch?" the slim sentry asked eagerly.

"You have no bronze," Killer scoffed. "Nor a game board on your back. You've been 'just looking' for too long. You don't belong, be gone."

"All settled, then. I leave you with him." The dungeon guard handed a tool to Killer. "The key for our adorable toys room. Whatever you take out, make sure to put it back. Any filth you create is yours to clean; it's not my job to clean after you. Now, don't forget, he should be kept alive for the execution. And—what else? Oh yes, make sure that blade on your sword is well sharpened."

53

The Father, The Son, and the Holy Ones

DAWN ARRIVED WITH ITS ARMIES UNDER THE COMMAND OF THE god Shamash, who ordered the sun to send its troops to scale the walls of Uruk in another relentless attack on the city.

Most people within the walls were already battle-hardened; bravely, they fought the onslaught waged by the sunrays that pierced through their darkened skins in the battle that escalated to its fiercest when the sun dominated the highest point under the heavens.

The privileged few who ruled from the safety of their shaded command posts chose the early morning to get most of their assigned work done, or they simply remained out of the combat zone until the evening, when the blitz of the sun god finally weakened in ferocity.

It was the start of another normal day with the city preparing for the chaos soon to follow with the bustling crowds. Traders were busy raising their walls of merchandise, and scribes readied fresh clay tablets to draw up contracts and letters in cuneiform. Statues blessed by the gods, to act as gods, started to line up, ready to move to the abodes of believers, whose prayers the gods would choose to answer or ignore. A slave trader guided his merchandise of young boys and girls to the "Marriage" market. An ailing man with a woman helping him walk at the pace of a crawl was the first to reach the Healing Path. He sat there waiting, in the hope of getting some good advice from the mortals, after his prayers for recovery were fully ignored by the immortals.

Not far from that frenzy of life, in a secluded part of the city, peace and calm reigned. The early-morning rainbow lost its faint hues among the flamboyant colors of flowers and butterflies dancing in their midst. Tree limbs vibrated gently, beaming with pride at the fruits they bore while playing host to songbirds. Nature was undisturbed by the mayhem-loving humans, the only ones of god's creations who were never happy with their surrounds, always intent on changing nature's order to enjoy life with the least effort possible, as if mobility were a curse that should be eradicated. The trees wondered if their sedentary lives were the object of human envy, with their roots safely beneath the ground, tingling with pleasure while they sipped on the nutrients conveniently delivered by the earth god once dissolved in the waters sent by the rain and river gods.

The joy of the trees came to a sudden halt as the wind began to blow from a direction other than the four corners of the world. The peace was shattered by winds of fear, stirred by the shrill laughter of two humans. Together, they carried an executioner's block, about knee-high, which was butchered from a once vibrant, jovial tree. Away they flung it; on tender grass blades and dandelion flowers it landed, delivering them to an early grave.

It was another one of those occasions where sitting was deemed a luxury that the high functionaries of the court were not worthy of. Though they stood in the open garden, the air felt so thick that it could only be swallowed—a harbinger of another grisly event where a morbid stench could already be perceived despite the sweet fragrance from the adjacent flower field.

The gory memory of the failed attempt to depose Sargon had been resurrected from the depths of the buried past—a past that had developed an appetite for blood spilled on the palace grounds and always returned for another serving.

Sargon had the event moved outside the palace building. Even he knew that spilling any more blood inside the palace would've made it unbearable to live in. Not long after he had killed his loyal guard, Naplanam, he had started plans to build another palace a good distance from the guard's ghost.

Statues of the gods were brought outside to witness the tribunal from the second level of the brick-paved terrace overlooking the royal gardens. To everyone's surprise, Sargon's statue joined the gods, albeit rather modestly on the far-right side. No one dared question this promotion of the king to a godly status, not even the high priest. After all, being the reflection of the great Anu didn't leave much room for argument. Everyone assumed that if the gods had any objections, they should be the ones to show displeasure and punish the king for his insolence.

A column of guards arrived and spread out in a large semicircle to each side of the stairs, surrounding a clear area of short grasses with mingling varieties of tiny flowers, all humbled next to the chopping block that loomed like a god ready to crush them on a whim.

High anxiety engulfed the assembled men. Though the identities of the condemned were known, there was always the lingering fear that Sargon might get possessed by one of his impetuous furies. All faced the prospect of being implicated in the conspiracy and dragged right there and then to the execution block.

Silence prevailed, except for the rustling of leaves, trembling at the murmurs of death that invaded the feeble wind. The witnesses breathed cautiously, as if fearful of inhaling death by accident.

Soft footsteps came to dispel some of the macabre silence when the princess arrived with two of her maids, trailed by a guard. Enheduanna looked apprehensive with no idea why she had been thrown into this chilling scene. For the last few days, she had been locked in her quarters with strict orders that she was not to receive any outside visitors or messages.

Nearing the stairs, the guard held back the two maids. Another guard ushered Enheduanna up the stairs to a bare wicker armchair, placed at the side of the terrace's first level, below the one where her father's statue stood with the gods.

Enheduanna sat with her eyes avoiding the chopping block, wondering why she was among the invited. She had seen criminals executed in the city squares when she had covertly mingled with the crowds. But to be there as the one overseeing the execution was extremely unnerving.

The high priest Bilalama arrived, unaccompanied, walked up

the stairs, and stood a few paces away from her, not greeting her or saying a word.

"Bilalama, what is happening? Why am I here?" Enheduanna tried to keep her voice camouflaged in the breeze.

Bilalama responded by holding the palm of his hand to his mouth, which exacerbated her unease, for he was usually friendly to her. Undoubtedly, her father had ordered a fortress of silence built around her, and Bilalama was to be no exception. Her desire for an answer had to wait until Sargon arrived.

She endured in her chair, eyes studying the men below. None moved or made a sound. The guards, the high officials, Bilalama—all looked no more human than the statues of gods lined upstairs. She wondered what would happen if she went down and pushed one of the guards. Would he simply shatter upon hitting the floor?

Footsteps and the clanking of armor announced the arrival of the king, who came with an escort of four guards through the palace gate, which opened to the upper terrace. Sargon remained standing on that level, next to a throne-styled seat. The guards took their posts on both sides of the stair's landings.

A nerve-shattering silence reigned; even the air felt like it stopped exhaling the breeze. All prayed for the speedy start and finish of whatever blood-soaked event bound to be staged. The king was in no rush; he stood surveying the men assembled below him, his stare finally landing on his daughter.

"Father, why—" Enheduanna started with a faint voice, only to regret her haste.

"Majesty, not Father!" Sargon snapped with a shrill roar. "You're nothing more than one of my subjects. Another insolent word from you and you will be punished accordingly!"

"Yes … Your Majesty," she said, bowing. The man standing above sounded like a total stranger.

"Guards … bring them here!" Sargon hollered, then stepped to sit on his throne.

Shortly, guards came dragging what looked like a corpse, blood caked all over its face. Once they dropped the body next to the block, a moan of pain announced a trace of life left in it. Two more guards followed, escorting none other than the court sculptor, Ibrahem, and they had him kneel behind the first condemned. Next to be dragged were an older woman, a middle-aged man, and a boy of no more than nine springs of age.

Enheduanna's attention was fully drawn to the first man, who was striving to pick himself up to his knees. Red woven lines soaked through his white robe, following the paths of torture carved on his body. The face was distorted beyond recognition, behind blood lines and dark hues. Enheduanna had her suspicions as to who he was, but denial had stopped her from confirming what she feared until her eyes drifted to the man behind him, whom she knew very well—the father. It was beyond any doubt that the whole family was going to end up on the block. Dread had her heart pounding frantically, when a voice blared:

"Something troubling you, Princess?" the king asked, seemingly displeased.

"Your Majesty, I am not feeling well." She stood up, instinct urging her to escape. "I need to retire to my quarters and lie down."

"You can't leave. Your presence is essential." Sargon spoke with finality. "If you have to, lie down on the floor right here."

The commanding voice and the degrading answer told Enheduanna that only the gods' intervention could help her. Feeling helpless, she sat back and closed her eyes in the hope that when she opened them again, the nightmare would be over. But instead, the voice of the court speaker shook her back to the grim scene. He started heralding from the front of the same terrace where she sat.

"The court is convened to this urgent session in the presence of His Majesty, the Revered Great Sargon, King of all Kings within the four corners of Earth, from sunrise to sunset.

"The matter of concern is the crimes perpetrated by the criminal Isaa, son of the court sculptor, Ibrahem the Chaldean. The charges brought against the criminal cover a wide range: conspiracy to duplicate the royal seal, treason, assisting another criminal in the slaying of innocent citizens, the illegal production of cylinder seals, and—grand blasphemy against our gods through his worship of the greedy, solitary god.

"The criminal Isaa has confessed to all of these crimes—most are punishable by death. Due to the seriousness of the crimes, all the blood family related to the criminal Isaa should meet the same fate for their negligence to notice the perverted ways he had adopted, and for their failure to stop or report any of his suspicious activities, which would have helped in ending his crime spree. Their lack of action is tantamount to collaboration.

"Ibrahem the Chaldean: our great king placed so much trust in you, and yet this failure on your part subjected His Majesty to great peril. The gods are angry, and their judgement was for all of you to be sacrificed to calm their rage over the abominable acts your son Isaa has committed against all the people of the kingdom, and for your son's vile conspiracy against our great king—the gods' proxy and their generous gift to help bring peace and order to our lands.

"Yet, our magnanimous king, the all-merciful Sargon, intervened on your behalf. His Majesty pleaded with the gods to forgive your shortcomings and those of your family regarding the crimes of your son. The gods listened to their surrogate and agreed to grant a pardon for all of you, except for the criminal Isaa, on two conditions. First: *you* must sacrifice your son with your own hands to wash away with his blood the disgrace he has brought upon your family. Second: you must leave Uruk for exile to a land no nearer than ten days of travel by camel.

"These are your choices. May the gods bless our kind-hearted king for his intervention to secure clemency from the gods and save your worthless lives. May the gods grant Sargon the Great eternal life."

Once the court speaker finished delivering the verdict, Sargon stepped off his seat and walked to the front, carrying a sheathed sword—Naplanam's sword. He had made it his own, not for its beauty alone, but some odd feeling compelled him to keep possession of it. He told everyone that it was a gift from Naplanam before the man left on his "last mission." Now, it was becoming clear to Sargon why he had kept that sword despite the horrible memory it brought him. Through his dreams, his loyal guard's soul was crying to him from the netherworld, asking for vengeance. What better way to grant that wish than by having Ibrahem sacrifice his own son with Naplanam's own sword?

Sargon flung the leather-sheathed sword over the terrace. It landed, hitting the lower stairs before settling on the first step, a handful of paces from the chopping block. The clank breathed some life back into Isaa; it spoke a promise in rushing the comfort of eternal sleep to his tortured body.

Conversely, for Ibrahem, it was shock waves that issued out of Naplanam's sword upon hitting the stairs. Of all the swords in the world, he would always remember this one. The horned dragon engraved on its hilt appeared to awaken from deep sleep as its ruby-red eyes blazed with fury once the sunrays pierced them. Ibrahem was hurled back to those horrific moments from the past when the guard's eyes stared at him from the severed head.

Has Naplanam been given a permit out of the netherworld to revel in this vengeance to be carried out by his sword? The thought struck Ibrahem and made him lament that it was the loyal guard's head, and not his, that had been felled by Sargon's wrath.

What a fool I was … to think I had cheated Fate! O treacherous Fate, how you play a fool for amusement, only to come back for a good laugh at the ones who firmly believed in having deceived you.

Ibrahem cast a pleading glance at Sargon, who stood tall with a grandiose pose, matching those of the stone gods behind him. The statue of Sargon was one Ibrahem himself had sculpted. It portrayed the king in a divine state with a gaze out of reach, too busy to waste time on mortals as he conferred with the divine ones.

Doomed to failure, too, was Ibrahem's attempt to plea for mercy; sheer stress numbed his tongue. The memory of his slave Neti raided him. Had Neti also been given a permit to witness the disgrace and suffering of the master who had forced him to cook his own tongue?

Neti, are you cursing me with silence just when I needed to beg for clemency?

Fear paralyzed Ibrahem. He could never have foreseen such a morbid calamity coming his way. There was only one person to blame: himself—his ambitions for power. Death offered the only mercy to escape this humiliation—to be kneeling in front of all those nobles, nowhere to hide his face. He prayed for the execution to be carried out without delay. If he could only speak, he would beg the king to be the first in offering his head to the executioner.

Yet, within all this turmoil, there was no conflict in his resolve; he was not going to sacrifice his boy, who rightly rebelled against the tyranny of a selfish father. If Isaa was going to die, then the whole family should follow the same fate—himself, Saura, and Isaa's half-brother Isma-el, along with his child.

Ibrahem dwelled on the proximity of the end and the peace that would follow. But this hope of peace was ephemeral, shattered by throbs of pain from a heavily tortured body dragging itself over the ground.

"Stay still, you filthy criminal," blasted the voice of a man, his foot landing on flesh with a thud.

After a cry of agony and a brief pause, the crawling continued.

"I said stay still!" Another thud followed.

"Hukura! Leave him alone." Came the order from the top of the terrace.

"Yes, Your Majesty." Hukura bowed but remained attentive to Isaa, who continued to drag himself until he reached the sword by the stairs. With a trembling hand, he unsheathed it.

The two guards closest to the king clutched their weapons in alarm and ascended the stairs to shield him if needed.

"Do I need protection from someone who could hardly stand?" Sargon was incensed, and the guards traced their steps back to their posts.

Isaa began crawling back toward his father with Naplanam's sword.

Ibrahem couldn't look up. He knew what his son had in mind and was praying for someone to stop him, but the subtle sound of the grass blades, kneeling under the sword, kept encroaching closer until it stopped next to him. A trembling hand reached to touch his face.

"Father ..." The labored whisper sent violent tremors through Ibrahem's body.

"No, no!" Ibrahem was surprised at hearing his own words. Like a miracle, the word "Father" and the touch of the bloodied hand of his son, whom he had not touched since that cursed day, brought warmth to his frozen tongue. The quivering hand shook the words free of their confinement, along with the tears of guilt that burst through the rocky dam of his heart.

"Don't do this to me," Ibrahem begged, not daring to look at his son. "Don't ask me … don't call me Father. I'm not worthy of being your father."

"Father … you have to."

"No, never! We became separated in life, but fate has brought us together in death. Son, spare me the torture, we're all leaving this world with you."

"Then don't call me your son!" Isaa forced the grip of the sword under his father's clenched fist. "I disavow you, unless you do it; this I vow to my god. Sacrifice me to him."

"I am not sacrificing you to any god. We die together," whispered Ibrahem. "I wronged you. Forgive me, son, but don't ask me to make amends by slaughtering you."

Freed from his demons, Ibrahem became aware that the love he so desperately strived for could in no way have compensated for the love he had lost after renouncing his son. Now Isaa had returned with the gift of true love offered by the son who forgave and gave courage to the penitent father in admitting to his mistakes.

"Ibrahem! What is taking you so long?" the court speaker yelled after a subtle glance from Sargon. "You dare keep the divine gods waiting? Take the sword and do as you're told, or it is your head and those of your whole family that will be lopped off."

"Father, I beg you." Isaa glanced briefly at his mother, only to regret it when she let out a cry of pain on sighting his mutilated face.

"Do it, Father, save them—Mother, Isma-el, and his son—they had nothing to do with our mistakes."

"Executioner." The word came from Sargon himself, who had had enough of the drama. "Get ready."

"I am ready, Your Majesty." Killer wore a big smile as he walked from the periphery toward Isaa, who tightened his hand over his father's fist.

"Father, I beg you." Isaa's voice quivered with rage as the trembling in his hand extended to the rest of his body. "Don't let him … not him. Father, please, you must—" And he choked.

Ibrahem raised his head, only to be traumatized at the sight of a face ripped out of its humanity with craters dug deep in it as if chipped by a sculptor, except that they left the lumps of flesh hanging by strands of skin. Then, a wicked hand grabbed what must have been his son, dragging him to the block. Equally shocking to Ibrahem was the executioner, who flashed a grin like a plague that sprouted from inflicting dire misery on the living.

Killer positioned Isaa on the block and stood ready with his sword.

"Your Majesty!" Ibrahem was startled by his own booming voice. "I will … follow the gods' demands." He stared in disbelief at his hand, now tightly clutching Naplanam's sword.

The exhilaration on Killer's face vanished in an instant. He stood staring at Isaa as if someone were stealing his meal right from under his nose.

"Move aside." The order came from Hukura, who approached Killer. "Are you hard of hearing? The father is carrying out the execution."

"I paid a silver piece for him," Killer whispered, trying to control his temper.

"I said move, or you'll get a piece of my blade to fill your arse!" The chief of guards kept his voice down though he was incensed by Killer's reluctance to follow orders.

Killer dragged his feet, casting a murderous look at Ibrahem. But that only made Ibrahem more determined not to give that savage the satisfaction.

Ibrahem staggered to the execution block in short steps, as though hoping a delay of a few moments could bring Fate to reconsider its merciless ruling. His gaze fell on the standing nobles, and in them he detected lust for blood; a reflection of the monster he himself was. Stabs of humiliation pierced at him from men who appeared to be fighting the urge to bounce in song and dance to taunt the one who was behind the horrid ends of so many of their friends. Only a few men had a somber look; those saw further into the future with fears that a similar fate might befall them.

Standing next to his condemned son, Ibrahem yearned to caress his boy. He didn't see a disfigured being with chunks of flesh torn out of his body or a haggard prisoner hunched over the butcher's block; it was a handsome boy he saw, resting on a smooth pillow after a full day of play and laughter, feeling secure under the watchful eyes of a father who would put him to sleep. Those precious memories of worry-free days, filled with pure affection ... what madness had driven him to bury all of that, all for the sake of ambitions in scaling the hierarchy of power? Now, he was standing with sword in hand over his boy, who was begging to be put to eternal sleep, to escape this ghastly nightmare.

"High priest!" Sargon hollered. "Start reciting the sacrificial prayers."

Bilalama nodded, meditated in silence for long moments, then, with arms raised, his prayers soared.

"O great and mighty Anu, creator of all that exists,
From the highest heavens to Earth's endless pits.

O father of all gods, you who birthed the first dawn,
And forever you will remain when to oblivion all is gone."

"Wait!" Sargon shouted.

Bilalama stopped, hardly managing to conceal his anger at Sargon for daring interrupt the prayers to Anu. But Sargon was busy watching Enheduanna, like an eagle studying every subtle move of its prey from higher ground.

Through the unbearable torment, the princess sat rigidly, eyes closed in prayer, wishing she could shut her ears too. Thrown into the eye of a merciless storm, she found herself carried back to the time when fate had pushed her over the precipice into the tender arms of love. She had thought the winds of time would raze the carvings of love that Isaa had scribed in her heart. Only now she realized how wrong she was. Cruel fate was asking for payback in a most hideous way, forcing her to witness her love savagely mutilated, leaving on a journey of no return.

O Ishtar, why aren't you answering my prayers? You jealous bitch!

The thought flashed in her mind, only to be followed by supplications for pardon.

O Goddess, I beg you to forgive me, I didn't mean to curse you.

Oh yes I did, you mighty whore!

By the gods, what's happening to me? O gracious gods, spare me your anger, that can't be me. I must be possessed by an escaped evil spirit.

Possessed with hate for all of you. May you burn in the same hell where you boil humans!

Oh please, someone, rid my body of this heretic intruder.

You lifeless, cold stone bastards! From now on the only offering you will get is the spit I will shower on your dull faces to bring them some shine.

I must be losing my mind. Dear gods, it's not from me—this blasphemy.

The duel between her fury at the gods and her pleas for forgiveness was interrupted when Sargon called her name out loud.

"Princess Enheduanna will recite the prayers. She's a priestess—I want her to do it."

Awkwardly, Enheduanna rose off her seat and turned to face a heartless father. She felt his gaze reading her pain, dissecting her as though to expose deeply hidden secrets. He was an expert who saw those sentiments afflict the people to whom he brought death and destruction with his armies.

"Your Majesty." Hesitantly, Enheduanna spoke with head bowed. "I am but a humble new priestess in the service of our love goddess Ishtar. ... Prayers for our great god Anu should be done by the high priest ... given that he is present. Otherwise, the father of all gods will be angered."

She prayed in desperation that her answer would convince the king to leave her alone and not add to her agony.

Sargon looked at Bilalama, who nodded to confirm the truth behind that statement. He shifted back to her with a long stare before speaking again.

"Proud of you, Princess, a very smart answer. It appears your time was not wasted in the tablet house, or in the temple of our goddess.

I guess the high priest will have to recite the prayers after all … but not for this one." He pointed to Isaa. "Take him off the block. We will save him for later, for our love goddess. … Hukura, get another condemned prisoner for the sacrifice to our god Anu."

Hukura motioned to Killer, who irritably walked to Isaa, dragged him off the block, and flung him to the side. Isaa was so weak he couldn't move his hands up in time to cushion his face from hitting the ground. The wounds on his carved face opened, staining the dandelions beneath with blood.

Hukura went to have a word with a guard from the detention house, but that word grew to a heated discussion.

"What's the problem?" Sargon yelled impatiently. "Get another prisoner. Now!"

"Your Majesty, there are none left in the vicinity," Hukura replied. "They don't keep them too long. There might be a few in other cells in the city, but it will take time to fetch them. I suggest we use one of those already here."

"Hukura, weren't you here when the verdict was announced?" Sargon slammed the arms of the throne. "I will touch no one in his family if he complies with god's demands."

Irritably, Sargon sprang off his seat to face the gods behind him, seeking advice from the divine minds of heaven. Soon enough, he returned to Hukura, grinning.

"Take two guards and walk the crowded streets outside. It shouldn't take you long to find someone … a head out there that is not worthy of a body. Don't you agree?"

Sure, you need not ask. Hukura wanted to scream. *It's only a matter of going to the bazaar and picking a man from the "Primed for the Chopping Block" trader.*

"A very wise idea, Your Majesty." Hukura had to suppress his frustration; it wouldn't be smart to argue with the king in the presence of all those officials.

He picked two guards and left in a hurry. With the sound of their boots diminishing, silence crept in, gradually weighing so heavy on the air as to make breathing labored again.

Enheduanna was still standing, blasphemy about to depart her lips against the gods who only prolonged her suffering. She could feel the eyes of the nobles studying her as if she were the next item auctioned in the slave market—stripped of all dignity, being sold by her own father, and assaulted by the decadent thoughts of the onlookers. She felt alone; no one would come to her rescue now—definitely not the gods she cursed.

Only steps away was the one person who would've dashed to her aid had he not been crippled. Her glances skimmed over him in horror. The butchered face didn't look like it belonged to a human, let alone to the Isaa she knew. Yet despite this, her heart was yearning for him. There was so much she wanted to tell him, but to reach Isaa she would have to raise her voice, and her words would be snared by the whole congregation. Even then, Isaa might be the only one not to hear her, with the roars of his tortured body barring him from grasping her words. She endured, shivering inside the thin crust of calm she had cast over her skin.

Bilalama compassionately diverted the attention away from her when he walked to the back of the terrace and whispered to Sargon over the stairs separating them.

"I started my prayers and need to continue. Prayers should not be interrupted for too long; the gods don't like that. I need to go on until the sacrifice is ready to be performed." Bilalama spoke discreetly to avoid angering the king, being aware he needed his head to recite the prayers.

During that brief distraction, Enheduanna snuck back to her chair and sat down; she was about to collapse under the tension.

Bilalama started reciting the litanies to keep the gods amused. It didn't matter that many of the verses were repeated over and over, for it had been proven that the gods never tired of hearing the same prayers repeated by countless people every single day. Their appetite for having their names exalted could never be satiated. Surely if the prayers annoyed them, they would have not hesitated in showing their displeasure, and the heavens would've screamed: "Stop, enough of this babbling! We heard you, we're not deaf! Halt this torture—this whipping with your pestering prayers!"

Bilalama went on with his exaltations of Anu, to the consternation of the few who hoped the gods would vaporize him with lightning bolts. Most, by contrast, found his chants calming, offering a much-needed diversion considering the morbid event.

A sound in the distance started to distort the prayers. More fear came seeping into the yard, gradually gaining intensity. Prayers now came pouring from a man crying for mercy—not from the gods, but from the mortals who were dragging him toward what seemed inexplicably like a heavenly garden. His panicked eyes raked over the men dressed in clean garments and precious jewelry, standing firm like gods and looking at him with utter contempt.

"By the gods, I'm innocent," cried the man. He could only be a beggar, judging by his shredded clothes and a skeletal figure with skin baked by the sun throughout a life that forbade him human shelter.

"I never stole or harmed anyone. I beg you, let me go."

"Shut your mouth, you wretched thief!" Hukura scoffed at him. "You're in the presence of the Great King Sargon."

The guards dropped him next to the chopping block.

"This man is a criminal!" Sargon pressed a finger to his nose and tried to keep from laughing. "What is his crime, aside from his foul smell?"

"I never committed a crime, Your Majesty," the beggar cried, trembling with fear. "I swear by—aaah!"

A kick by one of the guards to his stomach scrambled his words to a mere shriek of agony. He coiled in pain, gasping for air.

"Have you lost your mind!" Hukura rebuked the guard and went down to check on the beggar. "If he dies, I swear by the gods you will replace him for sacrifice."

"Do forgive me, Chief." The guard went down to his knees. "I beg you, I just wanted him to show respect in His Majesty's presence."

"Enough!" Sargon shouted. "What is his crime?"

"Majesty," Hukura answered, relieved that the beggar would make it to the block still breathing. "This man walks the market with an accomplice. His part is to urinate next to a merchant's stand to start a loud scene while his partner gets away with stolen goods from distracted traders and shoppers. We arrived there just in time to snatch him before the crowd beat him to death; his partner ran away. Not to mention the fact that this man's stench is so menacing, the peril of a plague roams around him. He could wipe out the whole city single-handedly."

"I can smell the dreadful threat from up here." Sargon brushed the air by his nose with a palm. "There's a good chance he was sent by our enemies. In any case, the people outside passed their judgment; you said they were about to beat him to death?"

"Yes, Your Majesty." Hukura's eyes flickered rapidly to wipe the lie off his face. The story was true, except it was another beggar who was the perpetrator from a past incident in the market. Hukura didn't waste time, so he grabbed the first beggar they had encountered.

"Does anyone here want to dispute this judgment?" asked Sargon.

Palms shielding noses was the only reply.

"Very well, then," Sargon announced. "High Priest, finish your sacrificial prayers. Guards, ready him on the block before we suffocate."

As the guards came to grab him, the beggar sprang up off the ground with a vitality that took everyone by surprise. He himself was amazed by how fast he was running. He dashed past the guards toward the standing nobles, who opened a wide path to keep out of range of the invisible killer plague they thought he must certainly be hosting. But there was no escaping his fate. A guard threw a lance into his path, tripping the beggar. His body rolled, and before it came to rest, strong arms grabbed him. His wails filled the air, pleading directly to the gods above, who silently ignored him. His eyes became transfixed on the block which appeared to take the shape of a ravenous wild beast. The prayers of the priest became louder, calling for his blood to run free—to quench the thirst of the great Anu.

"Gently with him now. Don't kill him," were the last words he heard, spoken humorously by his would-be executioner—Killer. His body became limp with fear when his chest was eased onto the block, head sticking out. The last light to enter his eyes blinded him with terror. Then came the abrupt, sharp pain, followed by a peaceful dimming of light into a bottomless pit.

Hukura approached Killer and scolded him in a hushed voice.

"A real disgrace you are! Three strikes for a beggar with hardly any meat on his neck!"

"Forgive me, Chief," Killer said as he pulled the body off the block and flung it to the side. "I ran out of time to sharpen my sword."

"It's done!" Sargon announced. "Our god Anu is mightily happy with this sacrifice. Now, dear Princess—oh, forgive me, *Priestess*—it's your turn to sing to your goddess, to delight her with the sacrifice to be made in her honor—in appreciation for the divine gift of *Love* she has bestowed on the mortals."

Enheduanna was staring down at her dress, feeling too weak to stand.

"Detach your behind from the chair, *Priestess!*"

Sargon's piercing command forced Enheduanna to her feet, to display more of the shame heaped upon her by a father who appeared to have forsaken his daughter.

"Why is the beggar still here?" Sargon screamed again. "Haven't we had enough of his refreshing breeze? Take him and his stink away, and ready the boy."

After removing the beggar's remains, two guards dragged Isaa and placed him on the block. His face was slapped by the beggar's blood, which had collected in grooves carved by previous executions. Isaa tasted death on his lips but not the fear infused in it; he could no longer understand why anyone would fear for a life that only offered a few grains of joy under a tower of agony. Isaa embraced the trunk as if it were a boat that would float him away from the wickedness men were capable of—far from the brutality that fate had viciously rammed into his life.

"Executioner!" Sargon addressed Ibrahem. "Get ready."

Ibrahem couldn't move until his son turned his head to him from the block and gave him a subtle reassuring nod.

"Yes ... Your Majesty." Ibrahem was on the verge of tears. The sword shook in his grip as he stood over Isaa.

"Priestess—start your enchanting prayers. Let's not keep our love goddess waiting any longer."

Enheduanna didn't respond. Her attention was drawn to the

figure embracing the block. She could better recognize his face—the face she had kissed and once smoothly molded in mud. Now it looked grotesque, like some of that mud had cracked in deep lines, whole chunks of it falling off, leaving deep craters behind. Yet, that didn't stop the warm memories from racing back to her mind. The sheer madness that started the whole affair when Isaa dipped her face in the clay. She could still taste the sweetness of their first kiss with their mud-caked lips. She could still visualize the pure love she had seen then in his eyes when they opened through the mud that her fury had poured over their lids.

His eyes. She wondered why they were evading her. Did Isaa blame her for his misfortune? But then, he would've angrily stared at her. More likely, he was dwelling on his own guilt for pushing her into the affair. Or perhaps it was the awareness that his face was no longer a sight to be forced on people. Was he trying to spare her the pain that his eyes might betray to her?

With mere steps separating them, Enheduanna felt a powerful yearning for Isaa, yet a horrible death was much closer to him. Anger throbbed through her anguish as if death were another woman stealing her lover. She wanted to walk down, to hug and kiss him, but she was helpless against this brutal destiny. The only thing that could touch Isaa now was the sharp edge of a blade. Instead of her words of love and moans of pleasure, he was going to hear her prayers: *Her,* offering him as a sacrifice to a goddess. Despair had her pray.

Ishtar, if you want him, then take him. But why such cruelty? Why have my heart shatter in witnessing it? Why must I be the one calling for his blood to be spilled?

"Did you forget the prayers, Priestess?" Sargon announced his displeasure again.

Enheduanna came out of her daze. Her lips trembled for she had nothing to say, save begging this king to spare her lover, but that would be akin to asking the gods for immortality.

At the floor she gazed, when footsteps rushing down the stairs had Enheduanna brace herself for the oncoming assault. And sure enough, the heavy hand blasted across her face with a whipping sound that startled the men out of their inanimate state. The force of the slap sent her down to one knee with a hand on the floor for support. Being prepared helped her to not fully lose her balance.

While on her knee, she glanced down at the block and a glimmer of triumph lit up in her heart. Finally, it had happened: Isaa was looking at her.

A glassy line of tears floated over the drying blood on his face at the sight of his love being thus humiliated. The torment of the princess, kneeling before the whole court, felt more painful than his physical torture. Then, through the fog of his anguish, she surprised him with a faint, sad smile that only the ones who knew her best could perceive. She was staring at him with eyes begging to be read.

Enheduanna began to rise to her feet, and Isaa watched as her right hand moved across her stomach, over to her hip, cupping the palm that swiveled repeatedly around the wrist.

What is she doing? Did she sprain her wrist? At first, Isaa was baffled. *This hand movement …! Could it be …?*

They battered his body, but they couldn't touch his memory. It was the hand that ruffled a child's hair. Then the slight nod of her head confirmed it—the life inside her, the child she was carrying.

As if she had given birth to him, Isaa felt life gushing back throughout his brutalized body. A smile crossed his face that eluded the attention of everyone for his face had been mutilated into what appeared to be a fixed mask of pain. He daydreamed of running up the stairs, to hug and kiss her, but instead he could only watch help-lessly as Sargon stepped in, delivering another hard slap to her face, and Isaa winced in pain.

The second slap was more of a surprise, sending Enheduanna down to both knees. Her palms fell flat on the floor for support, and the mimed child was gone.

"Is he the one who deflowered you?" Sargon hollered. "Guard! Let her have a better look at his face."

The guard yanked up Isaa's head by the hair to exhibit more of the savage work done on it.

Nothing could've prepared Enheduanna for this, and her tears started pouring freely. She felt pathetic, powerless to offer Isaa any help or soothe any of his pain. Her thoughts raced back to the night when Isaa had come to her rescue from the stranger who was to fulfill her ritual vows—the one she slaughtered after he beat her.

Did that dog curse us while he was dying? The savage gods must have listened to his prayers. Her thoughts surged wildly in a litany of curses on the gods; no apologies interrupted their flow this time. Still, no divine wrath struck her in response to those blasphemous assaults.

Yes, my sanctified gods, take your horrid wraths and shove them up your stinking, hallowed Arses.

An ecstatic sense of liberation overwhelmed Enheduanna.

Furiously, Sargon erupted. "I don't need you to reveal who deflowered you! It's no longer a secret!" He ascended the stairs, back to his godly level. "Now stand up, *priestess*, and do your duties. Ishtar is getting impatient."

But silence was her answer. Enheduanna had become desensitized—freed from all those trivial feelings of fear and disgrace.

King, nobles, gods—may they all be swept by a deluge of shit.

None concerned her any longer. Even dear life lost its allure, making of death a welcomed guest. And memory struck again, inducing her to whisper a quote—the very quote she had used to mock Isaa after she had his head coated with clay.

God gave the gift of life—shaping dirt soaked in blood.
Yet many are the fools out there—yearning to go back to mud.

Silent trickles of laughter slipped out of her on realizing that she had joined the ranks of those fools.

"For the last time!" Sargon called, threatening. "Recite the prayers, or I will send you as a gift to the pharaoh of the Nile. Not as a princess, not even as a concubine, but as a slave."

Her thoughts screamed back. *Sure, send me there. This slave would chop up the pharaoh, and instead of his pyramid, it is the bellies of the Nile crocodiles to be his tomb.*

She rose to her feet, her face hardened by a fury that defied the men watching from below, forcing their stares to avoid her. She felt so powerful that she would've stared down the gods on the higher terrace had they dared to acquire moving eyeballs on their stone faces.

This trip to her new world of divine boldness was interrupted when her sight locked on Isaa and saw something that sent part of her back to the world of flesh and blood. On his face, disfigured as it was, she could see something that had been absent throughout his ordeal: Fear. Twice they had placed him on the chopping block, and he hadn't shown any signs of it. Yet now, his eyes welled with tears reflecting vivid fear. It wasn't about him and his grim fate, but fear coupled with a plea: to keep alive the memory of their love, the happy and sad times, the joy and heartbreak. Above all, it was the fear for the fruit of their love.

In his tears, Enheduanna saw an oasis that brought the quest for life back to her withered soul and a fountain thirsting to nourish the other soul she bore.

Surrendering to his plea, the lids closed on her defiant eyes.

"Guards!" Sargon waved for the two nearby. "Have this woman held in custody till the next trade voyage to the Nile. She will be sent as a slave gift to the pharaoh."

In his fury, Sargon's sights turned blind to his daughter's anguish. He could only discern a subject who disobeyed him.

Enheduanna gave Isaa one last look, immersed in tears of farewell, then she turned to face her father and the gods behind him. The guards were a few paces away when her prayer soared to the heavens in a strident voice fueled by her rage at the gods, the repulsive nobles, and the king.

"Goddess of love, giver of life, beloved of Anu and all who dwell in
the heavens.
Radiant light, ruler of all there is, from the highest zenith to the
far-stretching horizons."

The two guards halted, fearing that interrupting a priestess amid her prayers would bring the gods' wrath upon them. Their hesitant glances sought Sargon, who waved them back to their posts after he calmed down once his daughter submitted to his command.

Isaa relaxed his head on the block and listened to Enheduanna's sweet voice as if it were singing a melody to accompany him in his eternal sleep. It was the voice that would sing to his child and tell the story of two fools who had fallen in love, only to be separated by the gods until one of them paid the ultimate price. Still, his life was a worthwhile price for saving his love and their child.

"Father, I'm ready," Isaa said, calmly.

"Pray to your god to help me. I cannot do this alone," Ibrahem whispered. His tears trickled down, smearing his son's blood-stained face.

"I assure you, Father, he is with you right now." And Isaa closed his eyes to the soothing sound of his lover.

Where is this god? Ibrahem wanted to yell. *I don't see him, can't hear him; I can't feel him in any way.* Then the cries of his wife, Saura, came to his attention. He glanced back and saw her hugging the child of Isma-el.

Cursed is my destiny! The torment would have been over by now had I not been given this savage choice—to live a life plagued by the guilt of disowning Isaa and the insufferable horror of spilling his blood.

The relentless stress blurred his thoughts. *Why am I standing over my innocent boy with a sword?*

The love he felt for Isaa became so strong, Ibrahem grew desperate for a way to depart life along with him. Dark emptiness engulfed him, when the words of Gudea from that grim cell filled the void.

Bastard! Living this life only thinking of yourself.

Gudea proved to be right: choosing death offered Ibrahem the easiest path out of this ordeal.

Ibrahem loathed his selfishness, which only promised a ghastly end to his innocent family. To suffer the torture of a guilty mind for the rest of his life was a judgment he very well deserved.

The sword in his hands sliced up through the air with a sound that struck terror in his heart. It was as if Naplanam cheered from the netherworld through his vile sword, mocking Ibrahem as the moment of vengeance came within arm's reach.

Your god is not helping, Isaa. Without him forcing the sword down, I could never do it. Ibrahem's mind screamed as he looked down at Isaa, who amazingly appeared to be resting on the block in a state of total calm. Was it out of relief that his ordeal was about to end? Or was it faith in that god who would receive him in a promised paradise where believers dwelled?

It occurred to Ibrahem that he himself had never found peace, despite all the gods that surrounded him and despite all the wealth and power he had at his disposal. Why had the gods forsaken him? They must be busy, doing the only thing they were good at: collecting the dust of time until they tumbled and crashed to bits, bound to be trampled to dust.

The persistent assault waged by the joined forces of guilt, sorrow, disgrace, and helplessness mercilessly tore at Ibrahem's tortured mind. A spark of anger at the gods who had abandoned him flashed deep within his soul, causing it to erupt into a colossal storm that wreaked havoc on the temple of his beliefs, toppling and burying his gods under its ruins. Then, just as suddenly, the storm dissipated and calm settled within. An eerie silence sent him floating in a peaceful void that soon started whispering a melody sweeter than the song of the forest breeze, gentler than the ripples of the river waves, yet more powerful than the angry thunder. The sun of a new faith began to shower his soul with its glory. It flowed forth from an invisible source, purging his doubts, sending them to join the stone gods in their earthly grave.

Ibrahem tightened his grip on the sword and shook it in the air, dropping the ghost of Naplanam back to the netherworld, where he belonged. With a heart emboldened by a new faith, he whispered.

"Almighty One, here I am, ready to listen and obey."

While Enheduanna's strident prayers touched the heavens, another voice engaged Ibrahem's senses: a godly, foreboding voice—loud and clear, yet stealthily silent to the rest of the gathering.

The two voices flooded Ibrahem's universe, despite being Earth and heaven apart. And both realms shivered at the proximity of another of the eternal battles between the gods—this time to be fought on a sacrificial ground over a most cherished prize—the blood of the innocent. Their messages breached Ibrahem's head, and with shrill screams they clashed:

O hallowed Ishtar, ferocious dragon of war,
On our knees we tremble under your thunderous roar.
Ishtar, mother of whores, daughter of the devil's allure,
Your name I'll make a sound to abhor.

When mighty Anu thought of love, right then and there you were.
Before the moon was born, your face glowed—an awesome radiant sphere.
Ibrahem, I am the sole creator of all that is idle, and all that is aware.
No other should you worship, no other should cause you fear. Be strong, don't despair.

Love Goddess, you traversed the universe from the idyllic azure heavens—
To the caverns of death in the abysmal dwellings of demons.
Chaldee, in alleys of evil, blindly you followed in the steps of the heathen.
Open wide your eyes, behold the path of salvation to my blissful haven.

Rebels that defy you, you'll raze to absolute waste.
Those who invite heresy, torment is their only guest.
From the lands of sunrise and the realms of sunset,
Wars will visit the pagans in ghastly, ruthless conquests.

Those who defile your name, ruin shall be their sacrament.
Sprouting forests of flames will move hell to their firmament.
Their great rivers would ebb, leaving stranded ships of torment,
On parched withering shores, watered by tears of lament.

Plagues will plant their roots in the renegade's domain.
Death will be fruitful—harvest lives in swarms, like fields of grain.
O land between two rivers, fire and blades from the ether, upon you I will rain.
The blood of your young, the thirsty earth will drain, save for a pale red stain.

Swamped in a great deluge, with not a speck of dry ground,
Mud graves to become their abodes, only ghosts to roam their
lands.
Gods of the Nile, Sumer, and Babylon—to rubble I will pound.
Only place for them to hide, deep beneath the earth—under
desolate desert sands.

O Mother of mercy, for the sins of the few do not forsake our city.
But shower the venoms of wrath on the accursed with no pity.
Those who worship me will triumph over all adversity.
For I am the only victor, from times unknown, through everlasting
eternity.

The criminal on his knees, his blood pleads to be freed.
It seeks in earth a sanctuary, from a body where blasphemy breeds.
The martyr's blood will nourish the seeds of the one true creed.
Chaldee, grand is your offer, staunch is your belief. Among all the
faithful, it's you I choose to lead.

With the blood of renegade sons, fathers shall pay the price.
O glorious mighty Goddess, your blessings we beseech—accept
this sacrifice.
Among men, revered you'll be, for all to idolize.
Now hand Isaa to my angels—over their tender wings, to heaven
he will rise.

Time came to a sudden stop imposed by morbid silence. And
time patiently waited for a signal to move on from the man who
stood over his son with a sword. Those long moments extended their
cruelty to the men watching a father about to sacrifice his son. As
hard as they tried, many couldn't shake the image that carved horror
in their minds—their blurry figures in that arena, being forced to
butcher loved ones of their own.

The tormented father inhaled the toxic air that craved the scent
of blood, and the sword quivered with a hint of life as it prepared to
end one. Ibrahem breathed a prayer; it scorched with an offer of a

sacrifice and soothed with the promise of eternal life.

"O Merciful One, how I wish You had asked for my own demise. … To Your care I deliver Isaa—the innocent punished for my appalling vice.

"Isaa, no more will you suffer. Who tears in pain is I, from a well of sorrows that will never dry.

"Be on your way, beloved son—with a bleeding heart I pray:

Come near the day we meet in paradise."

EPILOGUE—THE SAGE'S SONG

HE SAT STRAIGHT IN HIS CHAIR, HUNCHED OVER THE TABLE. After a long pause, he pressed down with his reed pen to add the last line of cuneiforms to the fresh clay tablet.

"The gods won't like this. … Beyond any doubt, the gods will not like this." He babbled, smiling, for the gods were never a cause of worry for him. He only feared men who behaved like gods—men like Sargon.

The king had become more convinced than ever that he was destined to be a god—punishing like a god. In his hands, Naplanam's sword seemed to have awakened with an insatiable thirst for blood, akin to a drunk who could never have his fill.

After Sargon's delusions became unbearable, the court sage had made up his mind and left Uruk, following Enheduanna, who had moved to Ur moons earlier and settled to become a temple priestess.

When the sage visited her, she received him carrying an infant in her arm.

"I adopted this boy," she told him.

"Strange, he has your features!" remarked the sage, smiling as he lightly stroked the sleeping child's hair.

Enheduanna was entranced by the sage's hand as it caressed the boy's hair. Hesitantly, her free hand wanted to reach for what must have been the visiting ghost of Isaa, who was borrowing the sage's hand to ruffle his son's hair. But the child woke up and started crying at the sight of the hunchbacked stranger. To Enheduanna's dismay, the sage withdrew his hand.

"Don't cry, young man," the sage whispered to pacify the infant.

"There's nothing wrong with being adopted. I, too, was adopted."

"You were adopted? I didn't know that," said Enheduanna.

"Yes, just like this boy. Someone, somehow, managed to convince my mother to adopt me … right after she gave birth to me."

Enheduanna could only laugh, shaking her head at her feeble attempt to fool the court sage. But the long-forgotten taste of laughter proved too bitter, inducing her tears to accompany those of her child.

Gaga, with his curved back and the baby she was holding between them, clumsily embraced her, invoking ripples of laughter to float over her tears.

The door to his room opened. He didn't turn to the visitor; it was too early to be shocked by that face.

"Blessed be your morning, my wise friend," the smooth, articulate voice of Humbaba greeted him.

"It was blessed before you showed up. Now all the blessings are running scared."

"Well then, miserable be your morning." Humbaba shrugged. "Already busy with your writing! What's on the tablet?"

"Just a poem."

Humbaba leaned down and started reading the tablet while Gaga dared to study the distortions of the man's face in an attempt to decipher his reaction to the song. Soon he gave up after getting lost in the maze of deep, twisted lines where expressions ran amok.

Humbaba was shaking his head in a clear sign of disapproval as he silently read the tablet, when a voice from outside called.

"Beloved, are you with Gaga?" Shortly, Kebboba walked in and came to stand next to her husband. "I knew I would find you here. What are you doing?"

Gaga studied the impossibly happiest couple he had ever known. Kebboba seemed like a goddess who defied all the rules of attraction when she smiled at her husband. Gaga was certain the man was smiling back, but he couldn't tell from his features. Curiously, he stared to explore the valleys and hills that marked a smile on the map of Humbaba's horrid face.

"Wise man!" Humbaba grumbled. "What lunacy have you scribed

on this tablet? The gods will not like this." He used the exact words Gaga had uttered to himself earlier.

"The gods can't read," Gaga said mockingly while wondering if the man with the diabolic face could read minds.

"This poem is pure heresy!" Humbaba persisted.

"Heresy! Me—write heresy!" Gaga looked offended. "I'm a staunch believer in the gods … but only when I curse them."

"A staunch believer—but only when you curse the gods!"

"Absolutely! Why waste precious curses on characters I don't believe to exist? Only fools do that."

"Enough! I'll judge the poem," Kebboba intervened. "Sing it to me, beloved husband."

"And have the gods hear all the blasphemy! Are you mad?"

"The gods are too drunk to hear," came Gaga's ardent reply. "As drunk as the moment they piled mud to create me—or more aptly, *you*, Humbaba. So don't worry, read the poem for her."

"Gaga, I am the governor of the great city of Ur. I'm no longer a barking messenger."

"With a face like that, you can only rule over demons," Gaga taunted, only to marvel: *How could Kebboba love you? I'm sure she finds me more attractive.*

"Look who's talking," Humbaba countered as if he had heard that thought too. "This back of yours, *straighter than a palm tree*, oh how it kills me with envy! Now listen, Gaga, either you sing the poem for her or I'll have a dozen demons possess you."

"Doesn't scare me." Gaga shrugged. "Even if they dared, the space in my back can accommodate legions of demons."

Kebboba leaned down next to Gaga, hugging him, her cheek touching his as she rocked him gently side to side.

"Don't listen to him, Gaga. *I* am the factual governor of Ur." She assertively rebuffed her husband's claim. "Now, could you *please, please* read it. Better have your voice sing me your work."

"Only for you, Lady Governor. Not for your beloved *Lord of the Demons*."

Humbaba laughed. Kebboba planted a warm kiss on Gaga's cheek and sat next to him.

Gaga looked at her—a beauty, thrilled like a child about to hear a favorite story while sitting in the company of two hideously deformed men. And for a reason beyond him, the jester went into a fit, laughing so hard that the dune on his back seemed to press down on him until his forehead hit the table. A contagious force stripped the two governors of all powers, hurling them to sink next to Gaga into similar waves of uncontrollable laughter.

In the distance, Fate watched the three mortals, who by some miraculous intervention had not succumbed to its grim desires. And the supposedly undisputable Fate wondered resentfully if it were the subject of their frantic laughter.

Finally, after Gaga had poured out all the jesting demons, which Humbaba must have crammed inside him, he pushed back on the mound he carried, looked down at the tablet, and sang:

Above the turquoise shield that keeps the gods' affairs hidden,
Upheaval began to afflict the tranquil realm of heaven.

The gods always believed death would never dare come near.
Now they raved, all anxious, alert with morbid fear.
Once whispers from a heretic caught their attention—
A prayer to one unknown—a god beyond comprehension.

"How absurd—his promise, to those who win his favor!
What god is this—to share heaven with the mortals, have them
live forever?
The fool has lost his senses. Such lunacy! How utterly unwise.
He's a threat to all things holy. It's vital that he be vanquished,
along with his mad enterprise."

Heated gossip raged wild, a blasphemy of a new deity.
A burgeoning, conquering god, a One and Only Almighty.
People listened, some believed, with eternal hope they rejoiced.
Others wouldn't be fooled—mocking humor they voiced:
"To claim this One is forgiving, though grimmer is his wrath than
those of the Many!

Eternal, hellish damnation! A pervert's appalling fantasy.
Yet, behold the devout fools, brazenly singing praise to *His
gracious, boundless mercy!*"

But nothing could be more clever to induce the evil will,
With greed to reach God's heaven—what would better drive men
to kill?
Zealous in a quest for the promised immortality,
Gladly they would resort to the utmost brutality.
Savagery like no other would rip daughter from her mother,
Have father butcher son, urge brother to kill brother.

All the divine cowards—gods steeped in fabled pride,
Silent they remain, peeking through clouds that turn grim with
them inside.
Never a trace they leave behind—not a whisper of a sound nor a
wisp of them to sight.
Hide—it's how they abide, with only myths to provide for their
infinite might.

Wars: they'd assign the lead to proxies, bigots, and priests,
The ones best skilled in turning men into beasts.
Toxins they'd lace in slogans and chants of heavenly glory,
Render masses deaf to the truth, plagued with odious, vicious fury.
Their slithering tongues spit poison, blinding men to all reason.
Those who don't conform would be stricken down for treason.

Thus, carnage the gods would sculpt with their double-edged weapon,
Their favorite and most formidable—could only be forged in heaven.
One side the sanity it slashes, the other numbs the mind with venom.

Nothing would compare to the rivers of blood that'd be spilled,
For the bridge to heaven's glory they named *Kill and Be Killed.*

While the masters laze about, watch the endless atrocity.
Armies of the Earth's poor would clash in timeless ferocity.

Battle cries would reach beyond the ends of this wicked world.
Sending the braves to shiver—the timid, in dread they'd fold.
"Our deity promised us victory," again and again they're told,
"Your faith alone will shatter the mightiest enemy sword!"
United they'd march—a murderous savage horde,
Ready to swap death for the eternal reward.
Such is how the foolish mortals are driven to be gored.
On chariots of blazing prayers to their divine lords,
They ride, ignorance their guide—armed with the treacherous, mighty power of the word.

Notes from the Dirt of History

The following are some brief historic notes (relating to the novel) that reached us from excavations of ancient Mesopotamian sites. But before moving on, I have a few points to mention: since I'm out of the realm of the novel, I'm opting to go freestyle, breaking some language protocols. So, do forgive whatever anomalies you encounter.

Also, at certain points, I strayed from the topics and indulged in comments of my own—comments I excavated from the ruins of my sabotaged mind.

The Epic of Gilgamesh

Ages before *The Iliad* and *The Odyssey* were written, there was *The Epic of Gilgamesh*. According to historians, it's the oldest written full story to survive almost intact. Many versions of this epic were unearthed, written centuries apart, yet the main plot was basically the same in each. I used short sections of the epic in certain chapters, taking the liberty to make some modifications—my own version of the stories.

The Great Deluge story was part of *The Epic of Gilgamesh*. And just like the full epic, the original account of the Great Deluge evolved after giving birth to more versions over time. One of those, with a storyline remarkably similar to a Babylonian version, is the renowned bible story of Noah's Ark.

The ancestral legends that flooded the Mesopotamian cultures kept shifting to new narratives, along with the Sumerian gods, who changed names and relocated their residences to other lands. Time also unleashed its wrath on the cuneiform tablets that recorded the original stories, burying them underground, doomed to be forgotten. That wasn't the case for the much younger Noah's Ark story, which was written more than a thousand years after the original Sumerian account.

"Noah's Ark" survived as it sailed and set anchor in the Old Testament. It was kept afloat by believers who ardently repelled those intent on ridiculing the story as a mere work of fiction.

The forces attempting to sink the legend were greatly weakened when the Christians came to the rescue and boarded the Ark story, restoring it to its greatest shape and maintaining it through the millennia. Then Hollywood arrived and added a moving image to the story. And the Ark sailed again—this time into celebrity, with films giving credence to the account.

Next came the observations by some aviators of a shape resembling a buried ark atop a mountain in Turkey, which inspired organized expeditions to that location. Even though they all came back empty-handed, rumors had already been spread, with some churches telling their congregations that Noah's Ark had been found. Grainy videos of rotting wooden structures—more like some decrepit log cabins, lacking any close resemblance to an ark—acted as testimony to the "gigantic" discovery. Published literature was also commissioned to support the claim.

Somewhere in the land of ancient Mesopotamia lies the skeleton of the individual who inspired the story. He's praying to the gods to give him his arse back for just a few moments—so he can laugh it off over how the myth he had created led masses to embrace it as a reality.

The Epic(s) of Creation

Thousands of years before the biblical Genesis, several versions of creation stories were scribed on Mesopotamian tablets. They told of the earliest myths we know of, about how and why humans were created. One of those versions describes how the father of the Sumerian gods, Anu (or Marduk in the Babylonian version), had one of the lesser gods sacrificed and mixed his blood with clay to create man in his image. Other versions detail that the gods created the humans when they were drunk. All those versions agreed that while the gods could enjoy eternal life, they allotted certain death to the humans.

In the year 597 BC, the armies of the Chaldean king Nebuchadnezzar laid siege to the city of Jerusalem. The siege ended with the Chaldeans storming through the strong fortifications of the city, and a great number of the inhabitants were brought to exile in the city of Babylon. A decade later, the leaders in Jerusalem agreed to an alliance with Egypt, and a furious Nebuchadnezzar laid siege to that city again in the year 586 BC; this siege ended like the first one, with more of the city's population exiled to Babylon.

Most unbiased historians agree that the Old Testament, and much of the literature associated with it, was first written in the Babylonian exile. Much evidence points to great influence from the Mesopotamian cultures and myths in those writings, with many parallels. I will go briefly over some of those in the list below.

The Hebrew calendar uses month names similar to those of the Babylonians.

Genesis, according to many researchers, is essentially modified texts from select parts of creation stories originating from Mesopotamian myths. I already mentioned one example, that of man being created out of mud mixed with the blood of a sacrificed god.

Another similarity can be noted in the longevity of the earliest Sumerian kings before the Great Deluge. According to the deciphered tablets, those kings had lived and reigned for exaggerated periods, lasting thousands of years. Their counterparts in the early generations of the biblical Genesis also enjoyed unrealistic long lifespans. But, unlike the Sumerian kings, they showed modesty in their longevity, which merely lasted for several centuries.

Returning to Noah's Ark, it is a no-brainer for anyone with over 2.9 "open mind" brain cells to figure out the true origins of the Noah's Ark fable once they read the Deluge chapter in *The Epic of Gilgamesh*.

This same epic also contains a chapter where Gilgamesh loses the fruit of eternal youth to a snake—a close resemblance to the biblical account of the snake tempting Eve, which resulted in the loss of paradise.

The book of Esther: Scholars believe the names of the main protagonists in this story, Queen Esther and King Mordecai, were derived from the names of the love goddess, Ishtar, and the Babylonian father god, Marduk.

Certain mystical writings that branched from the Bible and delved into symbolism, hidden meanings, and "secret codes" (some supposedly foretell the future) descended from the Book of Numbers, originally authored by the pagan Chaldeans, who, in their pursuit of studying magic and astrology, became the earliest authority in mathematics and the sciences of the stars, both the factual and the mythical.

I don't want to dig extensively into the influence of the Mesopotamians on the Old Testament and the works associated with it. Those details can be explored in serious studies by experts in the subject. Suffice to say that many similarities in texts have been found among what little has been discovered *and* translated from cuneiform tablets. Archaeologists estimate that only an insignificant fraction of the likely sites of ancient Mesopotamia have been excavated. The turbulent events plaguing the region, with no end in sight, present a major obstacle for archaeologists trying to perform excavations there—not to mention the pillaging of artifacts, which end up buried, untranslated, in the chambers of private collectors. So, until more of the tablets are deciphered, and the dunes are dug out to bare the contents of their entrails for study, no one could make a guess as to the extent to which the pagan Mesopotamians influenced the Bible.

ANU

Many were the Mesopotamian gods who were given the title "Father of all gods," according to cuneiform tablets from different regions and eras. Anu was one of the earliest gods to be awarded this prestigious designation.

IBRAHEM (ABRAHAM) AND ISAA (ISAAC)

The Old Testament is the original source of reference to Abraham and his son Isaac. According to the scriptures, Abraham was a Chaldean, born in Ur to a father who was a sculptor of idols. Abraham assisted his father in this profession until he rebelled against his ancestral gods. Later, he passed the ultimate test administered by a new God when he showed true intentions of sacrificing his son, Isaac, before an angel stepped in to stop the butchery. Of course, that's not the script I followed in *this* work of fiction.

Interpreters of the Bible can only give rough estimates of the period when Abraham lived, and they differ by centuries. Some of the estimates revolve around the time when the Akkadian King Sargon reigned.

SARGON THE GREAT

Sargon, King of Akkad, ruled circa 2300 BC. He is believed to have been the first man in history to merit the title of emperor. He ruled an empire that combined the ancient regions of Mesopotamia and Phoenicia.

ENHEDUANNA

King Sargon's daughter. Researchers consider her as the first known author in history, based on clay tablets that survived 4,300 years on which the name Enheduanna was scribed as the author of works that included poetry, hymns of prayers to venerate her goddess Inanna (Ishtar), and correspondence related to her position as high priestess in the temple of Inanna at Ur.

NARAM-SIN

Naram-sin is actually King Sargon's grandson, not his son. He also became a great Akkadian king. In the novel, I made this name change simply because it is easier to pronounce, and it recurs more often with the larger role.

MANISHTUSU

The father of Naram-sin and Sargon's actual son, not his cousin. I found his name annoying, so I assigned it to Sargon's cousin for his brief role in the novel.

ISHTAR (INANNA)

Two names given to the same goddess of love and war in different regions of Mesopotamia. Enheduanna's hymns addressed Inanna, the name given to the goddess in Akkad. In the novel, I limited the use to her Babylonian name, Ishtar, which is more familiar as the origin of the name Esther, and also due to its association with the renowned Ishtar Gate, which was excavated in Babylon, Iraq. The gate now stands far from its original home, towering proudly for the admiration of visitors in a German museum, where it rejoices and thanks the gods more than ever for its new home while lamenting the grim fate of other structures and artifacts of its era—treasures that have been smashed to unrecognizable bits by some culturally defunct hordes—foreign and domestic—running rampant over its original home.

The following are notes related to events or characters found in the associated chapter heading.

IN THE COMPANY OF THE KING

In the early 1920s, archeologists digging at a site in southern Iraq unearthed thousands of tombs dating back to 3000 BC at what is now named the Royal Tombs of Ur. One particularly large chamber contained skeletal remains of men, women, and animals along with chariots and other worldly items—all were buried to accompany and serve the king in the next life. A section of that chamber contained the skeletal remains of a group of girls—judging by the headdresses, frontlets, and hair combs found on them. Some skulls carried residues of silver hair-ribbons. One of the girls, for some reason, didn't wear her ribbon; it was lying next to her, coiled and well preserved after thousands of years. Probably, she kept the ribbon clutched in her hand to the end, patiently waiting to wear it on a better occasion, which sadly never arrived. Now, 5,000 years after their sacrifice, I wholeheartedly dedicate this chapter to the memory of this girl and all her companions for being the inspiration behind this story.

TABLET HOUSE

Mud tablets from the Sumerian era presented the earliest evidence of the evolution of writing. A Tablet House was the name given to those first schools where the reading and writing skills were taught.

DOUBLES, DELUSIONS, AND REFLECTIONS

In ancient Sumer, the king was considered to be God's reflection, which led some kings to believe they were true gods. Sargon's grandson, Naram-sin, was one king who evidently promoted himself to a godly status.

KING OUT OF A REED BASKET

Tablets excavated from ancient Sumerian sites tell the story of Sargon the Great when he was an infant, and how his mother, a high priestess, placed him in a basket that floated down the river, to be rescued and later become a celebrated king.

A thousand years later—give or take a few centuries—the saga of another legend, Moses, started in a similar way. Moses was also set afloat by his mother in a basket on the crocodile-infested Nile River, then rescued by the pharaoh's daughter to become a prince, and later a great prophet.

One might wonder whether Moses' story was inspired by Sargon's, or was it a mere coincidence to have two infants, each starting his legendary journey from a basket over a treacherous river. Or could it have been some widespread ritual in those ages, placing infants in reed baskets as an offering to the river gods? Perhaps it was some sort of a popular river-racing contest where children *piloted* baskets over a river, with an unfortunate few drifting off course! Better leave the answer to the historians.

One word of caution before I move on, and I can't stress this enough, especially in this mad age when we are down to our last reserves of common sense, in an absurdly litigious society:

Parents! Please, NEVER EVER put your infant in some basket and leave him/her floating on some river in the hope of them attaining grandeur. *I BEG YOU, DON'T!* It only, *supposedly*, worked out twice among the billions of modern humans who walked this Earth. The chances of children surviving a similar basket ordeal, *and becoming legends*, are as slim as surviving the drop inside a barrel over Niagara Falls.

What? … You say it's a sport now, started by one Joe Barrella in Canada? Huh, I guess I should pick a better analogy. How about … as hopeless as surviving after being swallowed by a whale?

Sorry, say that again! … People *did* survive inside a whale for many days? Who? … Joe Noah! Noah had a son called Joe? … Ooh, Joe Nah, the guy who talked the Assyrian Ninevites into abandoning their evil ways. … Who else? … An Italian Joe! A Joe Petto, along with his son Pinocchio! Amazing—those whale-surviving Joes.

Let me try one last analogy: As hopeless as surviving the raging flames inside a furnace. … Go on, tell me some freaking Joe likes to take nap breaks inside a pizza oven—say it, and I'll punch you on the jaw!

What? Three men were condemned to be burned alive in Babylon, and they survived the inferno? No kidding! But none was a Joe, right? … That's better, *now* I believe you. … What? They were saved by *Joe Hova?*

Enough! I've had it with you and your Joes. Get out. OUT!

... Sorry, dear reader, but not to worry, I rarely experience these mild episodes of hearing voices, and it's nothing serious compared to individuals hearing commands from a god who has a fetish for son-sacrifice.

Let's move on. Forget about that analogy.

FROM HEAVEN TO THE NETHERWORLD

Some Sumerian tablets describe details of processions in which statues of gods were carried over platforms and marched between temples—a striking similarity to modern-day festivities in certain cultures where statues of saints are paraded.

The tablets also describe a performance in these festivities in which the king himself was humiliated in an act where he was stripped of all his insignia, then slapped by the high priest, who acted as God.

Other tablets describe mating rituals during the fertility celebrations of the Equinox. Historians are not clear on whether such ceremonial mating enactments took place in public or behind closed doors. But considering the convictions of a society where the promiscuous goddess of love was highly revered, and the practice by her priestesses of offering themselves for love in her honor, all of this points to a good probability that such ritualistic mating could have been performed theatrically in plain public view.

Personally, I would not find this as immoral, or even close in its depravity, as the public executions that were carried out throughout the ages (and still are) to satisfy the "moral" codes of the three Abrahamic faiths—the beheadings, burning at the stakes, hangings, and the Old Testament favored choice method—STD.

... No, you silly, not execution by Sexually Transmitted Disease; I'm talking about a speedy killer: Stoning To Death (though both STDs are possible side effects of having sex).

Yes, this classic STD, which still has its enthusiasts to this date, added to the *poetic spirituality* of the holy books and gained popularity through encouraging the believers to participate in a "moral" wild orgy of blood lust. What better way is there to demonstrate one's passionate love and devotion to the Almighty!

Holy Vow

In his book *The Histories*, Herodotus described how the girls of Babylon honored their love goddess Ishtar in a ritual performed once in a lifetime by sitting outside her temple and offering their love to the first man to throw a piece of silver into their lap.

This same ritual was also adopted by the Phoenicians to honor their goddess Estarte. Greek and Roman accounts described such sacred prostitution rites, practiced to revere this goddess in Phoenician settlements throughout Sicily, Cyprus, and Carthage.

This reminds us of biblical texts, except that the Bible called for the devout *men* to initiate the sexual act, urging them to "Spread your seed and multiply."

Bazaar

Again, in Herodotus' book *The Histories*, there is mention of a practice in Babylon in which the sick would go and lie in certain public squares to get advice from passersby that might help cure their ailments. (What a great idea for countries where health care is not affordable! How about a Healing Court next to the Food Court in every mall? … Just a suggestion.)

Some skulls dating to that ancient era were found with holes cut in a manner that indicates a crude surgical procedure was performed on them. The man in my story must've been one of the rare survivors of such an operation. (With my help, of course. He never thanked me though.)

When Myth Births Reality

The tablets of ancient Mesopotamia are rife with myths of soul snatchers, blood suckers, men turning into wolves, the walking dead, and other evil characters akin to many that are depicted in modern-day horror films and fiction.

… No, wise guy, there are no records of Sumerian chainsaw massacres—though archeologists digging at a site not far from

Babylon found an ancient artifact, dubbed "the Baghdad Battery," which they described as an actual battery. But they totally dismissed the idea that it was part of a portable chainsaw.

Now, if you are more into alien visitors from outer space, articles about the Sumerian Anunakis would greatly interest you.

The Sins of the Lamb

The idea for the "Butcher's Song" in this chapter originated in texts from the Holy Bible that I started to explore in my late teens, only to discover some horrendous, gory accounts that the churches never dare mention in their sermons. The first nightmarish story to snap me out of my hypnotic, religious state was about Moses. Yes, Moses, the supremely revered president of the multinational enterprise "Thou Shalt Not Kill, Inc." who, ironically, must have suffered a "Jekyll and Hyde" episode when he ordered his faithful followers to attack the Midianites and exterminate all men, women, and male children (Numbers 31:13-19). Yet to his credit, and for some *mysterious reason*, Moses *passionately* followed his "Thou Shalt Not Kill" rule in sparing the virgins, a whopping 32,000 girls (Numbers 31:32-36). Surely, God—the Almighty Misogynist—must have delivered him a fresh commandment, stating:

"Thou Shalt Grab Naught Save Virgin Pussies." (Potus 45:2).

What's more astounding, not a single man in Moses' army was killed (Numbers 31:49). I could only surmise that the Midianites were peace-loving and paragons of morality—contrary to how they were vilified. By failing to kill a single enemy soldier, those Midianites must have been fanatical adherents to the antiviolence teaching, "When slapped, turn the other cheek," ages before Jesus.

Being a Christian myself, brought up on the principles of respecting human life and forgiving one's enemy, I was shocked to the core and swamped by angry thoughts:

"This is pure savagery, mass rape—genocide beyond the slightest doubt. It should have no place anywhere within the boundaries of human morality. Yet there it is, sanctified in a 'Holy' book."

I continued reading the Bible, and the stories took a more

revolting tone, where even the virgins got butchered (undoubtedly after they were devirginized).

Then, to top it all, in another act of senseless extermination, God throws a bonus command into the bloody mix: "and kill all the livestock!" (1 Samuel 15:3).

"God damn it!" I fumed. "Just when the last straw was about to break my camel's back, they slaughtered it."

I was in a dilemma. So much for His "Thou Shalt Not Kill" clause, chiseled in stone. Talk about divine flip-flopping; perhaps God was a politician in a previous life! ... If only we could read His lips.

History had no shortage of marauding hordes that roamed the globe, wiping out whole populations. But why this absolute emphasis on the annihilation of livestock along with the people? Aside from mass butchering animals for food and hide, I never learned of a similar barbarity anywhere else—it is unique to the Holy Bible.

Repulsed by those divine demands of utter gore, my innocent, burgeoning mind wondered:

"Now what? How can I keep revering this God despite His bloodthirsty behavior? What is the moral message in such indiscriminate acts of carnage? Those deliberate massacres of animals next to humans seem to serve no other purpose than to dehumanize the victims through portraying them as equal to animals in death. ... I must be missing something."

So, I sought the wise ones who had thoroughly studied the holy books. They babbled answers too complex to heal the confusion in my simple mind. After failing to convince me, they resorted to the master answer, their key solution to all challenging questions—the Divine Mother of all Answers:

"GOD WORKS IN MYSTERIOUS WAYS!" they roared, triumphant.

Thus, I was steered away from eternal damnation by this phrase of wisdom. Better said, they had me protected by this one-size condom—a genuine "IGNORANT" brand that is easily slipped on to fit all skeptical dickheads (like mine) to stop the sperm of curiosity from wiggling their way to the abhorrent egg of doubt which could only lead to the birth of the abominable blasphemy. (Still, for some reason, I get this funny feeling that God had worked in mysterious ways—on my condom—pricked a bunch of holes in it).

It was many years later, after I had matured and developed better faculties of common sense, when one day I woke up to an inner voice that told me how I had made a big issue out of nothing. I felt so stupid, like an old man who keeps looking for his glasses while they rested over his head. Yes, the answer to my dilemma was so simple, and it was the inspiration for the "Butcher's Song": the livestock were justifiably butchered for the same reason that doomed their human counterparts. THEY SINNED!

The Father, The Son, and The Holy One

"Love Goddess, you traversed the universe from the idyllic azure heavens—
To the caverns of death in the abysmal dwellings of demons."

This line of Enheduanna's prayer in this chapter is based on a myth about Ishtar. When she visited the netherworld, her jealous sister Ereshkigal had her killed and hung on a hook for three days. Then the gods intervened, and Ishtar was resurrected in exchange for a lover who would take her place in the netherworld.

Makes me wonder! Hung on a hook ... resurrected after three days ... Ishtar ... Easter!

Nooo ... it can't be ... no way!

ALL BABBLINGS LEAD TO BABEL

When I had the idea to create this novel, one pressing question had to be addressed: what babbling tongue should I use? Well, the answer was very clear: I had to use the one I'm familiar with, modern English—otherwise, I would've quit at the first page. Still, I had misgivings about whether modern English would be the right choice for a story dated 4,300 years ago. Then I was struck by an *Aha* moment when a thought flashed and made me aware that even the most archaic English styles—whether the Victorian of Dickens, the Shakespearean approach, or the medieval tongue of Bloody Mary—all these fashions of the English language came after King Sargon's time by at least 3,500 years. So, relatively speaking, those styles could be considered just as modern as today's English, or that of the classical music rapper, Yo-Yo-Mai-Man, who will rise to celebrity sometime in the near future (a prophecy I hope will come true, so I can join the ranks of clairvoyants like Nostradamus).

Armed with this argument, I breathed a sigh of relief for having been awarded a pardon from the requirement of writing this novel in Shakespearean sonnet form. So, Dear Critic, please, don't make a big issue out of this, or else ... I swear by the gods of Babylon I will put a curse on you where you will be criticizing yourself, and no other but yourself, for the rest of your days.

Nevertheless, I did make an honest effort not to include any words that definitely have no place in that ancient period. For example: even though the Sumerians created the system of dividing time into 24 hours to a day, 60 minutes to an hour, etc., I avoided using those time units. After all, no one in that ancient period walked around with watches, and there were no clocks in the main squares to tell the time.

More examples, mostly from the first chapter, "The Jester's Song": I used the word "thwack" instead of "whack," as the latter is a very American Mafiosi term. Now, I'm not one of those people who claim, "There is no such thing as the Mafia," but I can safely say there *was* no such thing as the Mafia 4,300 years ago … well, unless they discover tablets with inscriptions translating to something like "Hammurabi— Whacked by Babylonian Mafia."

Another word I hesitated to employ was "screw," but I went ahead in using it after I learned that the Sumerians invented the concept of the screw, first used in a device that moved water up an incline.

I used the British word "arse" as the vulgar form for "behind," instead of the American "ass," to avoid any confusion with some donkey minor characters like "Ass-Tied-Outside."

There is no doubt that some of the language in this novel might seem out of place for the meticulous reader, but I do believe that all the terms I used would have corresponding expressions in Sumerian. Likewise, even in those ancient times, there must have been an assortment of words that convey the same meaning. After all, language has been the fastest thing to evolve throughout human history. … Sorry, I stand corrected; the second fastest to evolve, after the gods.

Only once, for a brief period, did language evolution come in first place; it was when God had the Babylonians speak in countless, differing tongues while they worked on the tower of Babel. The truth to this story is overwhelmingly evidenced to this day in the numerous churches where one can witness, firsthand, people speaking in tongues. All of them—no exceptions—have one thing in common: they held construction jobs in skyscrapers—just like in Babel.

As noted earlier, I had assigned easy-to-pronounce names to the novel characters. Many are Sumerian in origin. Kebboba, Allamu, Gaga are a few examples of Sumerian names that somehow, either through timelessness or sheer coincidence, are used in our time. Then there are the Sumerian names: "Gungunum," which perfectly fits an army general, and "Bilalama" for a priest. A few other names are closely modified from familiar ones, like Ibrahem for Abraham and Al-dem (Arabic for *blood*) for Adam. The name of the innkeeper, Shaku-shmakku, is from a local dialect which translates exactly as: "What is there and not there?" But practically it's a sort of greeting, like "What's up?" or "What's new?"

Lastly, the two brutes, Tiny and Killer—characters I assigned English nicknames for the sake of diversity.

The poems and songs were written in a simple style, for language at that early age of civilization was not as advanced as to contain today's sophistication or *abstracticity* (no, not a typo, just an abstract use of this word). If you walk into a cave with drawings dating back to the Stone Age, don't expect anything even close to a Dali, Da Vinci, or Van Gogh (Undoubtedly, some cave artists must have shared one similarity to the latter in his style of losing an ear—in their case, to a savage animal model).

This is not a poetry book, and I'm not a poet. But I didn't let that stop me from taking shots at *poeming* by dedicating extensive time and effort to it. Simply put, you don't need to be a Spaniard to shout "Olé!", neither need you be an Olympic sprinter, or a bull, to participate in Spain's Run of the Bulls festivities (but you absolutely need good butt protection; the Olé brand is highly recommended).

The Holy Mother of Plagiarism

The most complete and preserved version of *The Epic of Gilgamesh* reached us across the millennia on a set of tablets, authored by a Babylonian who lived around 1300 BC. His name was Sin Leqi Unninni.

I, the author of this novel, out of appreciation to this Babylonian's work, would like to add my voice to the few others, to give back what rightfully belongs to him, while those who fake history strive to keep his identity buried forever.

Believers in the Abrahamic faiths would undoubtedly consider this book a work of heresy. But true heresy lies in copying a story from a man who lived in ancient times, passing its credit to some Almighty, then continuing with the lies even when the undeniable truth comes to light after being unearthed from the dirt of history thousands of years later.

Imagine this author from Babylon, living in the present day, reading the brazen plagiarism of his own Deluge and Ark story in the Holy Bible, where the protagonist, the god maddened by the unruly humans, is switched to a non-Sumerian deity.

I would fully understand the reaction of this Babylonian writer when *he* goes raving mad at the audacity of those who stole his work. I can envision him darting to the courts with a clear case of copyright infringement against the Almighty God, who with all His infinite intelligence chose to resort to plagiarism.

But if I happened to be the lawyer for this Sin Leqi Unninni, I would advise him that despite all the evidence in his support, he would be facing a losing battle against a mightier opponent than God:

Ignorance. All the corroborating evidence of this Babylonian—the records from the earliest days of writing—would not get him too far in the case. *Definitely* no further than an institute for mental rehabilitation, where he would be held *indefinitely.*

One analogy that comes to mind, though a brief one, is the following quote:

"Ask not what your country can do for you; ask what *you* can do for your country."

Yes, that most memorable quote from the inaugural address by President John F. Kennedy. Alas, its real author, the Lebanese writer Gibran Khalil Gibran, rarely gets the credit for that quote, despite being a prodigy among writers. Thus, the plagiarism went unchallenged, and none of those who knew the truth dared tell the much-idolized president:

"John Kennedy, you are no Gibran Khalil Gibran."

I have to confess that I myself am marred by guilt for plagiarizing a handful of paragraphs from Sin Leqi Unninni's epic story.

Then again, Who Cares! Over 2,500 years have passed since God Almighty committed the first blatant act of plagiarism in history by replicating that Babylonian deluge story and shamelessly shoving it into the Holy Bible as his own.

Could anyone do a damn thing about it? NO—not those who translated the cuneiform tablets of Sin Leqi Unninni, nor any fair-minded person who had read this most ancient of all novels, *The Epic of Gilgamesh.* All thanks to the genius of God, who went out of his way in being mighty generous to certain humans, bestowing on them unmitigated talent in avoiding and denying the truth. Faithfully, they keep sweeping this thievery (along with the heaps of depraved and genocidal biblical accounts) under the boundless rug of ignorance.

Long Live Plagiarism

Lastly ... if you are a devout believer, may I ask a favor before we part ways: Please, pray for God to stop playing with mud.

Thank you and ... God bless.